Adept

CHAPTER 1

London after midnight – there are no stars; a lid of cloud like a damp old army blanket lies over the city. Sodium-vapour light from a hundred thousand street lamps leaks back from the sky, turning the corners of the world orange and making the night-time cloud glow faintly, like radioactive fog. The permanent false dawn nags birds from their sleep, punctuating the soundtrack of urban grind and rumble with sudden meadowland trills. On the edges of the old city a few foxes lope, a few late drinkers follow their homing instinct. In the warrens of the sooty Victorian warehouse district, things are still. One or two security guards drowse over magazines, killing time at their foyer reception desks.

Elsewhere the city never sleeps, but here the activity is commercial and, in a sense, solar-powered. At night the machines rest. All that moves through the folded streets are gusts of air with their freight of mist and pollution.

5

Robert Finn

Then there's a squeak of bouncing springs as a scuffed white Transit van pulls up outside a silent stretch of offices. The driver peers up and down the street, scanning every nook and doorway. There's a full minute's pause before the engine is turned off and the doors open. Cautiously, three figures emerge, like the last three members of some endangered species.

The driver is bulky and energetic; he's in his late forties but of the type to whom age is largely a cosmetic consideration.

The second figure is younger – late twenties – with a lanky, wiry build. Where his companion looks energised, he merely looks frightened. He wears a baseball cap, which he tugs at, pulling it down on his head.

In contrast to the other two, who are wearing overalls, the third man looks dressed for a mild day on the ski slopes – black, high-cut jacket zipped tight, black trousers in some highly-evolved descendant of nylon. His head is covered in a dark wool cap. His compact build and easy movements do nothing to dissipate the illusion that he is there to perfect his racing turns. He needs only sunglasses to complete the image. His neat, shaped beard is dark like the close-cropped hair visible at his side-burns and it gives a slightly Eastern air to features that might have originated anywhere from Oslo to Kabul. His composed, unreadable face suggests a forty-five-year-old in perfect health.

Alongside the van, a narrow path leads a little way down one side of the offices, giving access to various hatches and maintenance doors set into the side wall. The driver lugs a heavy tool-bag out of the van, and sets up in front of one of the hatches. His nervous companion fiddles with his baseball cap and mutters, "Our cleaners are all black," to the larger man.

Without looking up from his work inside the open hatch the driver says, "Maybe you're the supervisor." The sing-song tone he

6

6

uses makes it sound like he's talking to a child.

The younger man continues to tug at his baseball cap, his anxiety plain. Just above his pale forehead the badge on the cap reads 'T.J. Office Services'.

Meanwhile, the man in the ski clothes is at the main entrance of the building. Several steps up from the street, the unlit reception area is dimly visible behind the glass and metal double doors. The skier is working on the lock. He looks up, glances once to his left along the street, once to his right and then back towards the lock. Something in the door shatters with a sharp crack.

At the side of the building, the driver shoos his hovering companion back a couple of steps and, taking an involuntary deep breath, pulls on a handle inside the hatch. Nothing dramatic happens but an unnoticed background hiss is now silenced. Inside the building, the LEDs on the reception's switchboard wink out. The emergency exit lamp shines with lowered intensity. A red light begins to glow from a glass-fronted panel just inside the main doors.

"Count to one hundred and push this lever up," the driver says. "Give me your hand." He takes Baseball Cap's arm and guides his hand to the lever. "It won't bite you," he says, but the younger man doesn't look convinced.

"But it doesn't make sense," Baseball Cap says, a whine in his voice. He receives a sharp look but continues nonetheless, "Why don't we leave it off until we're done here?"

The older man is angry but keeps his voice down. "You leave that power off for five minutes and see what happens. We've turned off the lights and the fucking coffee machine; we've done nothing to the alarm system. It's got batteries to last a week."

"Then why bother…" The younger man doesn't get any further with his question. A hand clenches his overalls just below the throat and he stops talking. The larger man leans in, bringing them face to face.

"If you balls this up it'll be the last stupid thing you ever do. You understand me?" the larger man asks. He glances at his watch. "Count to seventy-five." Then he picks up his tool-bag and strides off towards the front doors.

Reaching the skier, the driver cocks his head towards the double doors, "They open?"

The skier nods. The driver pushes through the doors into the foyer and sets his tool-bag down in front of the glass-fronted alarm panel. The red 'Battery Power' light glows brightly. He sticks a steel rule in the gap between the edge of the glass door and the frame. Pushing upwards he presses in the catch and pops the door open. Dropping the rule into his bag he retrieves a pair of wire-cutters and hooks one handle into the pocket of his overalls. It hangs there like a cowboy's six-gun. Then he fishes out a cordless screwdriver and begins to undo the spring-loaded screws at the four corners of the panel. All the while, the flat of his left hand holds the panel in place.

Then he waits.

A minute goes by.

Beneath their feet, from somewhere in the basement comes a muffled thump, like the sound an anchor might make hitting the sea bottom. "There we go," mutters the driver. The red light winks out.

A green light marked 'Mains power' comes on. Beside it is another green light that begins to flash. It's marked 'Power On Self Test'.

"This is the clever bit," the driver whispers to the skier. Removing his hand from the panel he gets his fingernails under one edge and pulls the panel free. The back of the panel is festooned with criss-crossing loops of coloured wire. "Power cut? Might be trouble. Power back on? All's right with the world. Ideal moment for the system to run a quick diagnostic. Never occurred to the designer that someone would *restore* the power as part of a break-in." His fingers are teasing a bundle of wires apart. He selects two. Flipping the panel over he checks where they lead: a key-operated switch marked 'Offline'. He grabs the dangling cutters and snips the two wires, efficiently stripping the ends with his teeth and twisting the two sets of bared copper strands together. "And that's that," he says. He drops the cutters back into the bag and lets the panel rest against the wall, dangling from its connections. "Time for that little tosser to earn his keep," he says. He strides out the door leaving the skier on his own.

A minute later he's back, Baseball Cap preceding him. The skier speaks for the first time, "Treasury?" he asks in BBC English. Baseball Cap nods and sets off up the stairs. The other two follow him, the driver carrying his tool-bag.

On the first floor they move through a dark open-plan office, two rows of eight desks and computers, each decorated with stickers, pot plants and framed photographs. Stray light coming in through the windows partly illuminates their surroundings – sixteen little worlds – a pink crocheted cardigan stretched over a chair-back, a Weight Watchers diary, a lingering tendril of Opium.

At the end of this open space, they reach a locked door. The driver pulls a crow bar out of his bag and, with two fierce tugs, splinters the doorjamb around the lock sufficiently for the door to open. The noise sounds brutally loud in the silent office.

The private office within has a real wood desk by a large window. The chair is black leather, high-backed.

Baseball Cap opens a low cupboard underneath the window to reveal the front of a safe. The driver once again sets down his tool-bag and begins to size up the safe. Absent-mindedly he twists the dangling plastic pole of the Venetian blinds, gradually angling the slats to block out the view. The dark sky, the multi-storey car park opposite and the train tracks disappear.

Seeing the driver intent upon the safe, the skier turns to Baseball Cap and says, "The Chairman's office." They head back past the rows of desks, Baseball Cap leading the way.

They climb to the second floor. The décor is much more expensive, the carpet fitted, not tiled. "I only saw it the once," Baseball Cap is saying, "when I took him in the itinerary." He pronounces it *itinuary*. "I knew something was in there, but I thought it must be a drinks cabinet."

They arrive at the end of a corridor. There are no windows here; there's just enough light to sketch in the suggestion of a desk. The skier clicks on the desk's lamp, illuminating the triangle of deep red carpet on which the desk sits, angled across the corridor. Beyond are two doors of thick, polished beechwood. "It's that one," Baseball Cap says, taking his hand out of his trouser pocket long enough to gesture at the right-hand door.

The skier puts one of his gloved hands on the door handle and tests it. Locked. "I said they always lock it. I told you that," says Baseball Cap.

The skier runs his hand over the door lock, giving no sign that he's heard. "Look in the top drawer of the desk," he says in his newsreader's voice.

Baseball Cap moves round behind the desk, turning his back to the skier and tugs the drawer handle a couple of times. The drawer thunks against its lock. He pulls on the larger bottom drawer. "It's locked. They're both…" The rip of splitting wood interrupts him. His head snaps round, startled, frightened by the unexpected sound.

The right-hand door is now slightly ajar, the area around the lock and part of the frame are splintered. The skier has taken a step forwards. While Baseball Cap is still frozen, crouching behind the desk, the skier moves into the opened office. "Show me," he says without looking round.

The office within has no windows either. There's a set of three switches just inside the door and the skier turns on the bottom one. Halogen lights set in the tops of smoked-glass shelving illuminate a fitted wooden wall unit. It looks like something from the Presidential Suite in a modern American hotel. The six-metre glass and veneer unit contains everything: a small TV, glasses, a tiny black sink – all of it backed with mirrored glass.

A broad beechwood desk occupies another corner of the room. The remaining space contains a round table and two armchairs. There are several cupboards and free-standing sets of drawers.

Baseball Cap goes over to the far wall of the office and opens a full-height cupboard. A light comes on inside. Although the door suggests a place to hang coats, behind it is an alcove going back a couple of metres. It's less than a metre wide. There's a little vanity unit with a mirror at the end. On one side is a tiny bench, just wide enough to perch on. Shelves hold toiletries. Hanging from pegs opposite the bench are several suits and shirts on hangers. There's a faint smell of sandalwood.

"So that time, when I come in, the door's open and he's in here. It was just like this except you couldn't see the sink. This bit of wall was open," says Baseball Cap moving into the alcove. He pushes and prods among the hanging suits until he finds a catch. A section of the panelled wall opens in the middle, hinged like the doors of a cuckoo clock. From anywhere but between the doors it's difficult to see what's behind them. Because the hinged sections of wall include the two halves of the row of coat pegs, as the doors are

11

Robert Finn

opened the suits swing out with them.

"Now I didn't know what was in here. I thought maybe he kept the good stuff in here. But I got talking to one of the girls and she was in here once when the safe was open and she saw the door to it." And sure enough, behind the wooden panels is the grey steel door of a safe, complete with recessed dial and handle.

Baseball Cap has stepped back to allow the skier access to the alcove. He dips under the open panel, parting the suits, and regards the safe door. "Very good work, Peter. Find a window and make sure that all's well, then see if Alan needs you for anything. I'll join you when I'm done here," the skier says. Peter looks reluctant to leave. "Off you go," the skier says politely.

Peter heads back to the stairwell and finds a window that looks down onto the street. The road turns away sharply in both directions and the van is the only vehicle visible on their little stretch. It's all just as they left it: damp road, streetlights, night.

After twenty seconds, Peter's breath has fogged up too much of the window for him to see out properly so he makes his way downstairs. As he emerges from the stairwell on the first floor he can hear the distant sound of a drill. It gets louder as he moves through the open-plan area towards the private office.

Reaching the doorway, he can see the driver, Alan, over by the covered window. He's holding an industrial drill at waist height to the face of the safe. There's sweat visible through Alan's thinning hair. The drill has chewed its way through a couple of centimetres of door already. The noise, though considerable, is hardly deafening.

Peter raises his voice over the squeal of metal and calls, "All clear…" Alan starts violently, sending the drill bit skittering across the safe door. A wavy snake of bright metal is etched across the enamel finish. "…outside," Peter finishes weakly. The pitch of the drill drops as Alan's finger comes off the trigger.

12

"Christ Almighty. Did no one ever tell you, don't sneak up on people. Especially when they're busting into other people's safes," Alan says angrily, his voice rising towards the end of his rebuke. He puts the bit back in place and powers up the drill again, his gaze once again on the safe.

"Supposed to use goggles," mutters Peter under his breath. He watches for a minute, his face screwed up, unreadable. Then he wanders away towards the windows overlooking the street. He picks up a stapler from a desk by the window and looks around for something to staple. A movement catches his eye in the street outside. Four men in identical black clothing are moving quickly towards the front of the building. Two are carrying short rifles, the stocks tucked into their shoulders. Just at the bend in the road a high-end BMW, with the markings of a police car, is now visible.

As they near the front of the building, one of the armed policemen looks up at the window that Peter's watching from. Peter ducks down quickly.

Hunched over, under the window, he bites his lip. Panic is evident on his face. Then, still crouching to keep low, he sprints towards Alan, weaving between the desks. He collides with the last one, the corner catching him hard on the hip. The impact shunts the whole desk forward an inch, its feet eliciting a little yelp from the tortured nylon carpet. The collision scatters office supplies and knick-knacks from their nocturnal resting places.

"Shit," he gasps, clutching his hip. He rushes on, one leg held stiff, and bursts into the office, where Alan stands flexing his back, the hole finished, the drill silent.

"Police," yells Peter in the silence, one palm still rubbing his hip, "in the street outside, they're here."

At that moment, the skier comes racing up the stairs. He's moving very rapidly but his steps are almost silent. He stops in the open doorway that leads from their floor out into the stairwell. The door is made to open outwards towards the stairs; it was already open when they arrived, held in place by a fire extinguisher. The skier grabs the extinguisher. As he raises it, the door begins to swing closed and his foot comes down, trapping it. Lifting the bulky extinguisher to his shoulder he brings it down diagonally onto the outside handle of the door. Gold flashes at his wrist as he raises it high again. A second blow and the loop-shaped handle is bouncing across the stairwell carpet, the metal ringing like a bicycle bell.

Moving inside the office, the skier lets the door close behind him. Grabbing the middle of a nearby coat rack, he lifts the chrome centre-pole off its plastic base and inverts it, dumping the crown of hooks to the floor. Now he's left with a straight pole, which he spins once, expertly, and then feeds through the inside handle of the door at a forty-five degree angle. It won't pass all the way through; the end of the pole is gouging wood from the door when it's only a third of the way through.

With his hands spread wide, one on each end of the pole, he levers it round until it's level. With the pole wedged solidly, one end biting into the door, the other end hard against the wall, the door is now barred from the inside.

Although it only takes seconds to wedge the door closed, it's not a moment too soon. Already the police can be heard clattering up the stairs. They reach the sealed door at the same time the three intruders complete their retreat to the office at the other end of the floor.

The policeman in the lead paws at the door. With no handle to pull, only the frame of the little wired-glass window offers any purchase. It's not enough to allow a proper grip.

Alan is standing in the doorway of the small office watching the stairwell door. He turns his head to glance at the skier. "What were you doing downstairs?" he demands.

The skier makes no reply.

Peter, meanwhile, is panicking. "What do we do?" he says, repeating it several times under his breath. He yanks the cord on the blinds to reveal a ten metre drop down to glittering steel train tracks. His gaze flicks nervously from the tracks to the office door and back to the tracks again. He begins to scrabble at the frame of the window, trying to find a lock, but there isn't one. The window is a single sealed unit.

The skier steps past him, flexing his gloved hands. He bends over the tool-bag spread open in front of the safe, and grasps the handle of a screwdriver. He straightens up and runs the tip of the screwdriver firmly into Peter's chest.

Peter freezes. His stricken expression and seized limbs make him look as though he's just grabbed a live wire. For a moment, no one in the room moves.

Then Peter looks down, his twitchy frame still for the first time that evening. His chin drops and his gaze locks on the yellow plastic handle tacked to his ribcage. His eyes go wide like someone realising they have a scorpion pinned to their lapel. He raises one hand numbly and it's not clear if he intends to grasp the handle or swat at it. As his hand rises, his knees buckle and his terrified eyes roll back in their sockets. He crumples, to lay unmoving at the skier's feet.

Alan is paralysed for a second, then with a flinch the spell is broken and he's scrabbling frantically at the pocket of his overalls, a look of panic on his face.

The skier doesn't move.

A moment later Alan has located a revolver, tugged it free of his pocket and levelled it unsteadily at the skier who is standing framed against the window.

Their eyes lock and Alan takes an involuntary half-step back. Maintaining fierce eye contact the skier says, "I'm going to kill you next." Each word is clear, but the cut-glass accent is gone, the sounds no longer those of a native English speaker.

Alan's whole body is tensed, his muscles so tight that the gun trembles slightly in his sweaty hands. He is panting. His eyes, unblinking, are riveted on the skier who returns his gaze with feral intensity. Neither moves a hair.

Then the skier lunges violently towards Alan. Alan fires instinctively, but the skier's lunge is just a feint, he is moving sideways, not towards Alan. The bullet ricochets off something and shatters the sealed picture window. Glass tumbles onto the tracks below.

Coming out of his crouch, the skier asks, "Shall we try that again?" his crystal accent back in place.

* * *

Out in the stairwell, a police officer is working on the door with a crow bar. A black-clad figure with sergeant's stripes on his shoulder is resting on one knee, his MP5 semi-automatic braced against his shoulder and pointed towards the door. His trigger finger lays along the guard.

The policeman with the crow bar rips another chunk out of the door panel.

"What about a shotgun, Sarge?" asks one of the men.

The kneeling policeman shakes his head.

On the fourth attempt, the chisel end of the crow bar slips far enough under the edge of the door that the wood doesn't splinter. The policeman strains hard until suddenly the pole holding the door closed folds with a screech and drops noisily to the ground.

Released, the door springs open a few inches. But with nothing to hold it in place it bangs closed again a moment later.

At that moment, from the other side of the door, there's the unmistakable sound of a gun being fired.

The policeman with the crow bar jumps to one side, out of the firing line. The man with the semi-automatic crouches lower, rapidly sweeping the barrel backwards and forwards, looking for a target. There's nothing to see through the little glass window of the closed door.

After a couple of seconds, the sergeant speaks.

"Who fancies holding that door open for me?" he asks, still sighting through the wired window. A couple of the others snort. Seeing that no one volunteers he says, "Slap, there was a mop downstairs, run and fetch it would you? Chris, I want you to pull the door open a crack then push it the rest of the way with the mop. Slide it along the floor and put your foot on it when the door's open so we can get past you. Dean, over there to give a bit more cover."

The mop is fetched and passed to the policeman with the crow bar who does as instructed. As the door slides open there's a crash from beyond. A few seconds later there's a second shot. Both armed policemen tense, their fingers resting on their weapon's triggers. They can see nothing of what might be happening in the office.

"Dean, through to the right and cover," says the crouching sergeant.

"OK Sarge," Dean says and darts through the door and to one side. He drops one knee to the floor and aims his weapon at the far end of the room.

"Slap, weapon at the ready, through to the left and cover." Slap brings his semi-automatic to his shoulder, draws back the slide, flicks off the safety catch and moves through the door.

"Chris, when I'm through, weapon ready and cover these stairs, up and down. No surprises please." Chris nods. The sergeant steps through the doorway and the door closes behind him as Chris wedges himself in the corner of the stairwell.

Advancing in several quick stages, using desks as cover, the three armed policemen approach the silent office. The sergeant holds up a hand. He calls out, "Armed police. Surrender immediately. I repeat, armed police. Put down your weapons now. Do. You. Understand?"

Nothing.

They wait for thirty seconds. A few papers rattle as a gust of wind spills them from a desk.

With a hand signal, the sergeant fans the other two men out and has them advance on the office door. He stays still, his rifle trained on the open door.

"I can see a body," says Slap.

"I see two bodies – they're not moving," says Dean.

The sergeant motions Dean to move in closer. Dean shuffles forwards like a hesitant fencer, sliding his feet along the carpet until he is at the doorway. He crouches, takes a rapid look inside and ducks back. "They're down," he says.

Standing, the sergeant signs for the other two to remain still. He walks slowly towards the office. He sees two bodies, one inside the door, one lying beneath the broken window. He moves through the open door. His foot slips slightly as he steps in a pool of blood. The body by the window has a plastic handle sticking out of its chest. An outstretched hand holds a revolver.

The sergeant places the sole of his boot carefully over the wrist, pinning it, his gun trained on the unmoving body.

"Slap, secure the other one," he calls.

The sergeant bends down, his foot still trapping the gun hand, and feels for a pulse. "This one's dead."

"Same here," says Slap bending over the other body.

The sergeant leans out of the shattered window, peering down at the tracks. He looks left and right. There's nothing to see except sheer walls and hard track. Pulling his head in he looks at the two dead bodies.

"What the hell happened here then?" the sergeant asks no one in particular.

CHAPTER 2

Earlier that night

Monday 7th April

David Braun took a step back as his attacker flipped a fast right hand at his face. A second jab just missed the tip of his nose – a feature which, by the shape of it, hadn't always been so lucky.

His attacker, a beefy blond hulk with a fierce South African accent, was crowding him, throwing snap punches and keeping his guard high.

David took another step backwards. He was running out of room.

He dipped his left knee and twisted a little, pretending to stumble. He watched to see how his attacker would respond. The advancing South African pushed in quickly for the kill. Once his opponent had committed himself, David slapped away the next jab, pivoted on one heel and brought the other heel whirling round to crack the South African in the side of the head, knocking him down. His attacker sprawled on the mat.

David looked horrified.

"Jesus Tommy, I'm sorry," David said, instantly apologetic.

Tommy had risen to one knee, his head still down, one hand tentatively touching the site of the impact. He found a tender spot: "Eina! You kicked me in the head, man." Tommy sounded wounded – emotionally at any rate – rather than angry. He was carefully tracing the outline of his reddening ear, assessing the damage by feel. "You've disfigured me, brah. Now I doubt I'll pull that Vanessa bokkie."

David laughed. "I'm really sorry," he said. Hunching forward he looked from Tommy's red ear to its pale pink partner. "I think it's evened them up a bit, actually."

Both of them were panting a little as they talked and sweat covered them. Tommy said, "Lekker bliksem, man. I'm done for the day. Help me up."

David hauled Tommy to his feet and gave him a slap on the back. "What about a couple more goes? Really and truly no contact," David asked. "Scout's honour."

Tommy gave him a sidelong scornful look, but there was no real harm in it. "We've been at it for two hours, china. I'm finished."

Retying their gi they walked towards the changing rooms. A minute later they were both in the communal showers.

Tommy stood, back bowed, one hand against the wall, letting the water hit him in the face. David was showing a little more industry, scrubbing himself with shower gel.

Tommy turned so that his face was out of the water. When he spoke now, his accent sounded a little more English. "You train pretty hard, man. I mean really hard. What's your rush?"

David was rinsing now, almost finished with his shower.

"You train just as hard, Tommy," David said. He shut off the shower and flicked some of the water out of his hair. His breathing was steady while Tommy's was still a little laboured.

"Not like you, I don't. I've never seen anyone so serious about training, but I don't see you going in for competitions," Tommy said. "Is it true you don't even have any belts?"

David walked past Tommy on his way back towards the benches in the changing room. "Where did you hear that?" he asked, "I got to blue belt in Judo when I was nine. I've still got it somewhere," he said over his shoulder.

A few minutes later, David had said goodbye to Tommy and made his way outside into the dark, rain-slicked car park. He was dressed now in indigo jeans and a black sweater.

He ran a hand through his damp hair and looked around for his car. It was in the far corner of the car park, parked on its own under a lamppost; the sodium light made the blue paint look black.

Swinging his holdall over one shoulder, he crossed to his car. Micro-droplets of rain touched his face and clung to his eyelashes until he brushed them away.

Once inside the car, David passed his holdall over onto the back seat. He started the engine and then retrieved his mobile from the glove compartment, pushed the power button. As he pulled out onto the main road, his mobile beeped to announce that he'd got voicemail. He steered one-handed while holding the phone to his ear.

"First message," the automated recording said, followed by a girl's voice sounding weary: "David, it's Judy. Give me a call if you get this before nine." He glanced at the dashboard clock: 9:45.

There was a little intake of breath and then, "Actually, you know what? Don't bother!" this last with a certain vehemence. "You might as well... Look, I've had enough. It's like spending time with a... a zombie. You're easily the nicest guy I've been out with, in fact I almost can't fault you. Except that you wouldn't care if I dropped dead tomorrow. Do you know how that feels? It's insulting. Well, you know what? You can drop dead." Most of this was delivered in the voice of someone obviously unused to shouting. Her voice warbled with emotion. There were a couple of seconds in which she could be heard breathing heavily and then the message ended.

"Next message," the machine said, then there was the sound of choking. "Jesus, I think I've swallowed a wasp." More coughing, then the message ended.

The machine again: "Next message," and then, "It's Banjo, mate. Bastard peanuts, they're a fucking menace, if you ask me. Thought I was going to need a tracheotomy. I'm getting it looked at now."

A woman's voice in the background said, "Same again, dear?" then Banjo continued, "They want to keep me in over night. Come and visit your old mate if you've got a minute. I'll be in the intensive care unit at the Old Grey Goose getting mouth to mouth." The same woman's voice in the background commented, "Not likely," and then the call ended.

Smiling to himself, David drove towards Banjo's local. Ten minutes later he was parked and out of the car. As he walked into the brightly lit saloon bar, he saw Banjo at the bar, buttoning up his red lumberjack shirt. He'd clearly been showing the attractive, forty-something barmaid whatever lay beneath.

"I could come back," David said by way of greeting.

"Watcha, mate," Banjo said, looking up. "What are you having?"

David looked from Banjo to the barmaid, "I'm gasping. You couldn't get me a pint of water, could you?"

"And…" said Banjo.

"And a pint of Boddingtons, thanks."

"I'll have the same again, Helen love. And help yourself to anything that takes your fancy," Banjo said, pulling the neck of his shirt down to expose a freckly chest.

Helen pursed her lips in mild disgust. "Put it away. If that shark didn't want none of it, I'm hardly going to touch it, am I?" Helen said, pleasantly, and set about fetching the round. A moment later she returned and patted Banjo's hand. She whispered, "I'll have something after, pet." She pressed a button on the till which caused the display to register a sale of 50p.

Banjo indicated a quiet table by the window, David nodded, and they carried their drinks across.

Banjo looked David up and down. "Blimey, you look more like a bouncer every time I see you. You're probably saving up for one of them long leather coats, aren't you?" Banjo said. He poked curiously at one of David's biceps which bulged sufficiently to stretch the material of his sweater.

"If it was anyone but a ginger scarecrow saying that, I think I'd be hurt," David said. He took a long drink from his pint of water. When he set it back on the table the glass was nearly empty. He gave a little gasp of approval.

Banjo turned his attention to his pint. "So you been out scrapping this evening, then? Fighting sailors and wotnot? If you're going to exercise – and you know my views on the matter – why don't you go along to aerobics and spend an hour dancing around watching fit birds in Lycra waggle their arses at you?" Banjo said. "Common sense," he added.

"You've seen me dance. Imagine what I'd be like sober and wearing a leotard," David said. "Nobody wants that."

Banjo said, "Could have used you around earlier. My Uncle Jess dropped by. You remember Uncle Jess? From graduation?"

A look of pain crossed David's face, "The horror."

"Yeah, that's him. Anyway, you'll have to excuse the fact I'm a bit pissed. It's not easy persuading him to go while you've still got life left in you," Banjo said.

"I remember he likes to be the last man standing," David said.

Banjo took a swig of his pint. "So how's the world tour progressing? You're not letting all this stuff in the papers put you off, are you?"

"Nooo," David said. "Obviously I'm going to have to make some adjustments depending on, um, local developments."

"Like if they're actually bombing the place the week you want to stay, for instance?" Banjo asked.

"That would certainly be one factor, yes," David replied. "But I was thinking more about the air travel. Apparently flights are getting more and more unreliable and the airlines are cutting back their schedules."

"Well that might have something to do with them being war-torn, fucking combat zones," Banjo said, his voice rising. Helen glanced their way.

"It's really not as bad as all that," David replied. "Anyway, I might give the Middle East a miss. I haven't decided."

"Do you want to know what I think?" Banjo asked, leaning towards David and looking him in the eye. "I think you're so bored doing that pointless job of yours that you'd happily get yourself killed just to liven things up a little. Like all that martial arts business."

He went on, "When we were at college it was fair enough. Girls thought all that way of the warrior stuff sounded cool and there was a good crowd at the club. But you're still hard at it. I think you just do it now because kicking someone's head in, or getting yours kicked in, is the only way you can blow off steam and maybe feel a little bit alive at the same time."

David said nothing and Banjo continued, "All I know is there's tons of jobs you could be doing instead." He tapped a finger on his bottom lip, "Look, why not take the trip, but do something fun with it. Learn to surf, trek round Thailand, drive across Australia. I'll even come with you. But don't get yourself killed in some place I can't even pronounce. The Nine O'Clock News isn't bloody Wish You Were Here. They show all that stuff so you'll know to stay away."

Nothing was said for a few moments.

David began, "Look, Banjo…"

But Banjo butted in, "OK, OK. Sorry. I might just possibly be exaggerating. But there's a few things I want to get off my chest," he said, his voice quiet now. He took another sip.

Softly he said, "I think people are always doing idiotic things in their private lives to make up for all the damage they do when they're at work. Human beings weren't meant to spend their days in cubicles…" He was picking up a bit of speed again now.

David muttered, "I don't work in a cubicle."

"…preparing next quarter's sales budget for some bloke called Prenderghast," Banjo went on.

"You know there actually is someone called…" David tapered off as Banjo showed no sign of halting.

"The human soul is more plastic than elastic," Banjo stated emphatically, taking another big swig from his pint. His eyes were off somewhere in the distance now. "If you squeeze it hard and let go, it tries to go back to its old shape, but mainly it's got someone's dirty big handprint on it now. Every time you try to change yourself to fit in somewhere, it leaves an impression. Jobs, school, getting on with the snooty in-laws, all of that. You get a job by pretending to be an 'enthusiastic self-starter with dynamic potential' or whatever. Basically, you claim you've got a hearty appetite for whichever kind of horseshit they produce there.

"If you fool them and get invited into their world it's because you squeezed yourself into the right shape to pass through their particular eye of the needle." Banjo had a manic look in his eye. "Now you're in. But you can't relax, you can't just flop back to whatever shape you were before or they'll catch you. You've got that unsightly belly of individuality pulled in and you can't let your breath out. If you do, you're marked. You're not one of them. You get the speech about 'thing's aren't working out as we'd hoped'. But keep up the pretence and you can pass among them and gorge yourself at the corporate trough."

"Steady," David said quietly, but Banjo was unstoppable.

"Now you'd *like* to think if you took off the suit and let yourself relax you'd spring back into shape. That the real you is inside, working the levers, the master illusionist, fooling everyone, but it's not like that." He shook his head sadly. "No-one plays a part for years. If you do it for years, it's not pretend, it's really you."

Despite the fact that Banjo was ranting and well along in his evening's drinking, he still had David's attention. The points Banjo was making hadn't completely missed their marks.

"The worst thing, David, is those places you have to stoop to get in to. You could really be something if you wanted to be. But you hunch yourself over and hobble along pretending to be just the same as all the grey little management pygmies around you. You could tower over them whenever you chose to let the secret out."

He drew a deep breath. "Maybe. Or maybe you couldn't anymore. Maybe you'll spend the next forty years bent double believing that you've got the last laugh because you're only pretending."

Banjo's gaze fell to his drink. He seemed to be winding down now and he looked melancholy. "We mutilate ourselves everyday just to fit in; we hardly wait to be asked. We like to show willing. And if there's a GTI with a CD-player at the end of it, we'll reach into ourselves and rip our own fucking hearts out. Most of us will carve ourselves up with a smile, because at the end of the ordeal, when we're done, we're hoping whoever handed us the knife will smile and say 'welcome aboard, son'."

Out of breath, Banjo finished off his pint.

"Jesus Christ, Banjo. Now I won't sleep tonight. Not a wink," David said sounding a bit horrified.

There was a long pause. Banjo's face softened as the intensity he'd put into his words began to ebb.

After a minute he began to smile again.

He said, "You know what? Best cure for not sleeping is plenty of hard work. Get yourself up to that bar and get some drinks in. Do you the power of good. I've got to make a quick detour."

Banjo levered himself to his feet and headed off, roughly in the direction of the gents. He was muttering something under his breath as he went, the only word audible being 'insurance'.

David ordered Banjo another pint of the keg cider the pub was famous for. He glanced at his own pint and found he'd only drunk about a third of it. Helen, following his glance, said, "I could just put a bit of a head on that. For the look of the thing, eh ducks?"

"Thanks," said David. He added, "Did you really just call me 'ducks'?"

Helen winked at him. "I'm big on tradition," she said.

As David carried the drinks back, Banjo returned.

"Helen's a star, isn't she?" asked David.

"A priceless jewel. She used to be a schoolteacher before her husband died." Banjo glanced at the bar. "Don't bring it up though."

Drinks were sipped. "About what you said," David began,

holding his hand up to forestall Banjo's inevitable interruption. "I'm honestly not trying to get myself killed – but you're right, I am bored. And maybe I'm doing things I wouldn't do otherwise." He cleared his throat. "But if it helps, I'm not planning to stay in that job indefinitely. What you have to understand, though, is that I'm really pretty good at something that pays well. And a lot of the time I actually enjoy it. I know it's not 'me'. If I knew what was 'me' I can tell you I'd be off like a shot."

Banjo attempted to jump in again, but David again held up his hand, "No, let me get this out. I know what you're saying and I agree with a lot of it. And I appreciate the fact that you look out for me, even though god knows I'm ugly enough to look after myself." Banjo nodded seriously. "So how's this for an idea: I'll give you my word – right now – that I'll be doing something totally different a year from now. Even if it's not the right thing, I'll try something else." He sat back and looked at Banjo who was wearing a thoughtful expression. He added, "And while you're trying to talk me out of my current lucrative employment, I'd like to point out you don't seem bothered by the fact that I've paid for every curry we've eaten since 1995."

Banjo ignored the curry remark, just nodded slowly a couple of times and patted David's shoulder. "Yeah, OK. Good. And sorry if I went off on one."

After a minute, Banjo's expression lightened and he asked, "Anyway, how's the lovely Judy, then? God that girl's got legs that go on for weeks. Not to mention an arse that makes you want to take a bite out of it, if you'll pardon me talking about your future wife in those terms."

"Hmm. Things with Judy aren't too good," said David, rummaging in his pocket for his phone. "I think I've got the most recent update here." He pushed a couple of buttons and handed

Banjo the phone.

Banjo listened to the message play.

"Hoo hoo," piped Banjo when he'd finished listening. "You haven't lost the old magic, have you? Still able to screw up while doing everything right," he said. "Now let me ask you something veeerrrry important and you must tell me the truth: are you going to try and get back with her?"

"No," said David shaking his head. "I'm honestly a bit relieved."

"Good," said Banjo, "then I can tell you that I never thought you two were right for each other. Mark my words, next time you see her she'll have married an accountant, who she'll bully something chronic. She'll be as happy as Larry and no hard feelings."

David agreed. "Yeah, to be honest I've been trying to think of a way out that didn't leave either of us too traumatised. This is better than I'd expected. You remember when I split up with Hope, after that talking to she gave me? I was so shaken up I thought I was getting a stutter."

"Yeah, you were a state," snorted Banjo.

"But, I think that was just because I couldn't believe she could hate me so much with so little warning. Judy and I never got that far." David sighed, "I like her and everything, but what worried me was how easy it was to forget she existed when she wasn't around. That's not a good sign, is it?"

Banjo said nothing and David went on, "Anyway, what about you? How are things with that nurse, Melissa, you were drooling over?"

"Actually, there've been a few developments on that front, mate," Banjo said, clapping his hands and rubbing them together. "And what a front it is."

They were still talking about Banjo's romantic prospects,

and laughing, half an hour later when Helen called out, "Time gentlemen please. Hain't you got no 'omes to go to?" She winked at them both as she spoke.

David and Banjo brought their glasses back to the bar, Banjo draining the last of his, David handing over an almost full pint. "Night Helen," they both said and headed out into the night.

The smell of rain was still in the air, but a few gaps had opened in the clouds. Stars peeped through.

"I'll call you later in the week," David said.

"Right you are, matey," said Banjo, giving David a final clap on the shoulder and heading off on foot, leaving David to unlock his car.

* * *

David was home and fast asleep a few hours later when his pager began its piercing beep.

He clicked the bedside light on and swung his feet out of bed. He sat on the edge of the bed for a minute, rubbing his face and running both hands through his hair. Then he took a deep breath, shook his head a couple of times and reached over for his pager.

The pager display had a number to call. David stood, a little unsteadily, and pulled on a pair of shorts. Then he padded out into the living room and turned on the light. He picked up the cordless phone and the pad and pen that sat by it. He sat on his scuffed looking leather sofa, rested the pad on his knee and dialled the number from memory.

A voice answered after one ring, "David? Reg Cottrell." It was a very English voice and sounded like it belonged to an older man.

"Hi Reg. What's up?" David said.

"Apologies for the page. I think you'll need to get involved with this. I've just had a call from the alarm people. Interfinanzio's offices have been broken into. It sounds like a mess. Police are on site – armed police in fact. There's been some sort of incident, ambulances called. I don't know much more, except that the officer in charge is a DI Hammond of the Flying Squad; he's been told to expect you."

David had been jotting notes. "This is their offices in the East End? I think they've got another office somewhere."

"Errrm," Reg said, consulting his own notes, "Off Bow Road in Mile End. That's the one. Can you take it from here?"

"No problem, Reg. I'll get down there. Are you in tomorrow?" David said.

Reg muttered to himself, "Half three now," obviously thinking aloud. Then he said, "I might get a later train than usual, but I'll be in."

"OK, well I'll fill you in when I see you," David said.

"Good, good." Reg paused. "I mean I'm sure I don't have to say…"

"Absolutely. Have no fear. This is my top priority from this moment onwards," David said in reassuring tones.

"Splendid, splendid. Important clients. Well, tomorrow then," Reg said.

David was already on his feet as he replied, "Sure thing," and put the phone back in its cradle.

Ten minutes later he was shaved and dressed for work – dark blue suit, mid-blue shirt, dark-grey tie. He zipped the notepad into a leather portfolio, put his car keys and phone in his pocket and headed out the door.

CHAPTER 3

Susan Milton was getting angry. She sat looking over a table spread with papers. Her assistant, Kevin, was standing behind her chair.

"I just thought you looked a little tense," Kevin said, in his Midwest accent.

"I'm tense, Kevin, because you're bugging me. Stop screwing around and sit down," Susan said. She was also American but her accent was trickier to pin down.

"Look…" Kevin said, in a soothing voice, letting the word hang. He parted her shoulder length blonde hair and laid his hands on her shoulders. His thumbs started to massage the muscles of her back.

Susan's voice was icy, "Stop that now or you'll look back and decide this was the moment when it all started to go wrong for you."

Kevin lifted his hands from her shoulders and laughed, albeit a little nervously. He held his hands out, palms up. "OK. Jesus. See

33

what I mean, you're tense."

"Listen, genius, this is going to be difficult for you to grasp, but try. If I was Professor Shaw, would you be giving me a massage? You do that for everyone you work for? Seventy-year-old guys included?" Susan asked, sounding exasperated.

"No," Kevin said, peevishly, "But you're *not* my professor." Under his breath he muttered, "You're not even that much older than me," as though that clinched it.

"Right. And yet somehow the College thought you might learn something from assisting me – how to get your PhD finished, maybe." She twisted round to look at him, though he refused to meet her gaze. "Look, try to understand, I'm not your next big conquest, I'm someone you work for who thinks you're creepy. Is that reasonably clear?" Susan said.

Kevin snorted. He slumped down in his chair; his expression suggested he felt very harshly treated. He was sulking.

"We've got a lot to get through still," Susan said. Kevin gave no sign he'd heard. He was staring at one of his Cat desert boots, his leg stretched out in front of him.

Susan looked thoughtfully across at her pouting colleague. "Hey, I meant to say," she said brightly, "Jill said to tell you 'hi'."

Kevin's expression flickered for a second before he caught himself, erased the evidence of curiosity. "Yeah?" he said, sounding bored.

"Yeah, I bumped into her coming back from her dance class. Boy, that stuff really keeps you in good shape." Kevin was looking her way now. "God, I'd love to be that toned and flexible," she said to no one in particular. "Anyway, she says 'hi'." Kevin's expression was neutral, his mind elsewhere, as he considered Susan's words.

"Think I'll call it a day," she said in a whisper, standing up. She slipped her pale lavender denim jacket off the back of her chair and swung her courier bag over one shoulder. She headed out into the corridor and down towards the senior common room. She left Kevin sitting in her office.

It was early evening and the college was largely deserted. All the students had gone home and, this evening, so had most of the staff. As she crossed the hall and neared the common room door, she saw Professor Shaw himself approaching.

"Hey, Professor," she said, smiling. She held the door wedged open with her foot waiting for him to catch her up.

"Well here's a nice surprise. Are you coming in for a drink?" the Professor inquired.

"Just a cup of coffee. Want to join me?" she asked, warmth in her voice.

"What have I done to deserve this?" he asked, amused. "Never mind. If you've nothing better to do with your time, that's my good fortune."

The common room was a large, square, wood-panelled room filled with wooden tables and chairs, darkly varnished. High, latticed windows looked out onto a college courtyard and a Cambridge sky nearing sunset. On the opposite side of the room ran an oak bar.

Two coffee jugs sat on hot-plates beside the bar and Susan poured herself a mug from the fuller of the two. Professor Shaw exchanged quiet words with the waist-coated man behind the bar and received a schooner of sherry and a courteous nod.

They made their way over to a couple of elderly leather armchairs. Besides them, the room was almost deserted.

Susan's tan hipster cords and loose, white t-shirt – Polo written across the front in red letters – looked a little too style-conscious to be standard academic issue. The Professor, on the other hand, looked every inch the elderly academic: flannel shirt in some pale, buff tartan, sage green cardigan and trousers in a worn russet corduroy.

"The young men of today are obviously a less assiduous lot than I'd realised if you have nothing more tempting to do with your evenings," the Professor said, toasting her with his sherry. "My gain, however."

"Oh no, they're a pretty assiduous bunch if you ask me, and not just in the evenings. Kevin Hartman being a prime example," Susan said.

"Oh dear, is he making a nuisance of himself?" Professor Shaw asked.

"That was an off-the-record remark, Professor," she said softly, "it's not a problem. It's just a bit like working with an untrained puppy. He's got plenty of energy but not much focus," she said, examining the design on her mug.

He replied, "Well, I suspect notions of propriety have migrated so far since I was young that my opinions would only be of interest to a fellow historian. In my day, it was quite unthinkable to court a female member of staff, but perfectly proper to marry her. It makes you wonder how those things ever got started, doesn't it?" said the Professor.

"Well it's a minefield these days, I can tell you that." She stared at her mug, her fingers absently tracing the raised college emblem. She mused, almost to herself, "I wanted this top in a six, but then I'd never have got any peace."

Focussing again, she said, "You know if a guy did me the courtesy of focussing on work, I might actually be so impressed that I'd want to go out with him. That's a modern irony for you."

She went on, "It's probably best if we all get used to separating our social life from what goes on at work. Just a shame I only know people from work."

"Oh, I doubt that will be the case for very long. You're still settling in. I know you're a long way from home, but there are splendid people all around you; just allow some of the newness to rub off and you'll soon find yourself desperate for a little solitude. And what about that club of yours? Do they not have a social secretary? Or are they all terribly business-like and to the point?" He chuckled as though he'd said something funny, "Oh, I say, that's rather good."

Susan smiled wanly.

He said, "At any rate, let me know if Mr Hartman begins to make you uncomfortable. We have a veritable firebrand in Human Relations or Resources or whatever it's called this week, and I'm sure he'd enjoy nothing more than lecturing Mr Hartman in the latest fashionable thinking on appropriate workplace behaviour."

He smiled. "Or I could rough him up a little," he said. "That was very big in my day, too."

"Did the BBC show a Jimmy Cagney gangster movie recently?" Susan asked.

"It was Humphrey Bogart, actually. Rousing stuff," he said. "So tell me," he went on, "how's the paper progressing?"

Susan blew air through pursed lips. "Kevin's unwanted contributions aside, it's going slowly. To be honest, I'm not even sure I've got enough material. It looked a lot more solid before I got into it."

Professor Shaw suddenly raised his eyebrows and said, "Do you know what? I've just had a marvellous idea. In fact, I should have thought of it this morning."

He put his sherry down and pressed his palms to his thighs, leaning forwards slightly, "The most fascinating thing has turned up, down in London. I would have thought of you instantly except I knew you were up to your neck with that paper. But this way it works out perfectly."

She was smiling but with a little puzzlement in her expression.

He went on, "I should really tell you what I'm talking about, shouldn't I? The School of Antiquities in London have just come into possession of a totally unknown collection of documents after their last owner passed away. From what I've been told, most of them concern magical practices and beliefs and they originate from a number of different centuries. The school wondered if we wanted to send someone. They're more used to, well I suppose you might call it non-fiction: histories, letters and various sort of records. I was going to go down myself, although it's a bit of a bind. I'd much rather send you. Besides, it's all right up your street. You'd get first look at a collection of material that sounds absolutely fascinating. You might even find something useful for the paper and you'll give Mr Hartman a chance to cool off. Or better still to set his sights on whoever that woman is who wanders round in her underwear."

"Jill Jenkins," Susan enunciated slowly. "Great minds think alike. So tell me more. What do you know about this find?"

The Professor told her what he knew, which was really only enough to excite her curiosity. After a few minutes he enquired, "You have nowhere to stay in London, I suppose?"

"I thought I'd get the train down each day," she replied.

"I have a better idea," the Professor said, "although you can make up your own mind of course. But you're more than welcome to stay at my late sister's house. I've been meaning to let it out, but it's just so convenient whenever I have business in town – which I suppose is not that often these days. At any rate, if there's any justification for retaining it, this would be it: so that I can make the occasional *beau geste*."

"Well, that's very kind of you…" Susan said, unsure whether to accept.

"Terribly awkward these things, aren't they? Excess is just as off-putting as meanness. Well, I'll leave it up to you. Take the keys with you and if you do nothing more than pop round to make sure the place is still standing I'd be grateful. Doctor Williams has stayed there a couple of times, but he always leaves the place in such a muddle for the lady who comes in to dust that I'm afraid I've allowed him to believe it's no longer available," he said.

Susan's expression suggested her mind was now made up, "I'm quite sure I can be a better houseguest than The Walrus. Thank you Professor. First you find me a proper office and now this. You're a sweetie." Then she raised an eyebrow, "Hmm, I wonder if college policy allows me to say that?"

"I'll see that it does next time I'm forced to sit in on one of their incomprehensible meetings," he said. "And let's be clear, my dear. I'm sure we'd get along splendidly anyway, but it's the quality of your work that puts you at the top of the list. The last time I let charm or a well-turned ankle influence me on a matter of college business, George VI was still on the throne."

They carried on chatting and in the end Susan stayed for a glass of white wine. The Professor had a glass of college red and a ham sandwich while they discussed Susan's London expedition. While he had little more to offer regarding the collection, he knew a considerable amount about the School of Antiquities and its staff. Eventually, the conversation turned back to the house.

"You know Lizzy never could discuss her work and I never enquired. I do know that when she passed away, even though she'd been retired for several years, some gentlemen from the government came to take away all her papers. I suggested on several occasions that she settle somewhere like Hampstead, but her work kept her close to the City. By the time she was free to move I don't think she wanted to. I imagine you and she would have got on well. Both sharp as tacks."

A few minutes later, the barman came over to ask whether they wanted anything else before he closed the bar. It was just after nine, but they were the only two left in the common room. Both agreed it was time to be on their way.

Susan expressed her enthusiasm for the Professor's idea one last time and said she would head down to London the following afternoon, once she'd attended to a couple of loose ends in college. She left the common room wearing an expression that was far less troubled than when she'd entered it.

CHAPTER 4

Threading the pre-dawn London maze, driving southwards from Islington towards the old City, David followed the forgotten course of the River Fleet, sleeping these last hundred years sealed beneath the streets.

He neared his destination. Up ahead a silver, fluorescent-striped BMW blocked the road – executive police for executive victims.

David pulled his blue Saab into an empty, metered parking place a dozen metres short of the police car. His dashboard clock read 4.35am.

In the street beyond, partly concealed by a bend in the road, a three-storey office block had apparently made the switch to twenty-four-hour operation. While elsewhere in the street windows were dark and doors were closed, this building had all its lights on. Uniformed figures stood near the open doors and several official vehicles were parked at various angles in the street outside.

David walked towards the activity, his little leather portfolio case under his arm. The night air was still damp and the temperature had dropped while he'd slept. Tiny pieces of rain-misted gravel crunched under his leather soles. He was fifteen metres from a group of three uniformed policemen when they looked up from their conversation.

"Good morning, I'm here to see Detective Inspector Hammond. Can I go in?" David asked.

Radios squawked in the background. "Name please, sir?" asked the police officer closest to him. His expression was stern.

"I'm David Braun, I'm from the insurance company Marshall and Liberty." He held up a business card that identified him as an Account Manager.

"Is he expecting you, sir?" the policeman asked, without looking at the card.

"Yes," David said, simply offering the policeman a polite smile.

The constable nodded and eased up on the stern look. "Yeah, go on up," he said, sounding almost friendly. "And don't touch anything."

David nodded and moved past the little gathering, up the steps and through open doors into the glass-fronted lobby: lots of textured concrete, smart but not quite stylish. An alarm panel was open just inside the door; wires were spread out in all directions. A flight case sat beneath the panel, its open lid revealing several jars and plastic bottles. No one was around.

David climbed the steps to the first floor and met another uniformed policeman standing at the fire door leading off from the staircase.

The door itself was propped open with a fire extinguisher. The door and door-frame were dented, splintered and chipped. One of the door handles lay on the concrete floor nearby.

"I'm looking for DI Hammond," David said.

"Won't be a minute, guv," the constable said. "Would you wait here?"

"I'm not on the force. I'm from the insurance," David said.

"You just looked… Just wait here, sir," the constable said. No 'guv' this time. The officer headed into the open-plan office beyond.

David could hear voices from the other side of the brightly lit space. A breath of wind brushed his face and stirred papers on nearby desks.

A moment later the constable returned with a stocky man in his late forties. He was wearing dark suit trousers, a white shirt and a blue tie decorated with tiny penguins. He looked blankly at David and pushed his fingers through his few long strands of brown hair.

"I'm with the insurance company. Actually, we've met before, Inspector. I'm David Braun." David held out his hand.

And for a moment, Hammond just stared at it. Then he lifted his chin suddenly, as though something had occurred to him and pumped David's hand a couple of times.

"Yes, yes. Jewellers on Bond Street. That's right." Hammond didn't smile, but his body language suggested that David had ceased to be a stranger. "I remember that case. You helped us along with that one. All went a lot quicker once the owner was, er, forthcoming."

Hammond turned his back on David and walked into the office. He left one hand stuck out behind him, a single finger flicking, almost as though he expected David to take it and said, "Come. Come," without looking round. David followed.

"Want some fucking horrible coffee?" Hammond asked, pointing off to the right as they passed a little kitchen area.

"Maybe not," David said, following in Hammond's wake.

"Probably wise," Hammond said without turning round.

When they neared the door of the corner office, where most activity seemed to be concentrated, Hammond stopped and David came to stand beside him.

"You want me to tell you what we know?" he glanced sharply at David.

"Thank you," said David, unzipping his portfolio case to uncover the notepad inside. He took a pen from his suit pocket.

"Alarm was triggered just after one. Alarm company passed the call along. There've been several armed robberies in this area so an armed response vehicle was sent, a four-man team in this case.

"Main doors downstairs were open. They came in and found the door to this floor barred. They heard two shots fired while they were opening this door. Once through, they approached this office," he indicated the corner office they were standing outside. "Found two dead bodies. One was stabbed with a screwdriver, his partner was shot. The one with the screwdriver in his chest was holding a revolver – two chambers fired – but only one bullet hole in his victim. The window was busted, so maybe that's where the second shot went. The one who was shot also had half his rib-cage crushed, we're not sure how that happened.

"The safe over there's been drilled, but it doesn't seem to have been opened. It looks like they might have been disturbed by the ARV boys at the last minute.

"Also looks like they broke into the chairman's office upstairs. No obvious signs of theft.

"I'll let you know about the post mortems and forensic reports. Perhaps you could coordinate with your client to double-check nothing's missing. I'd be a bit surprised if you come back with anything though, because there was nothing on either of the dead men." Hammond concluded, "Questions?"

"I've got three, if you wouldn't mind," David said. Hammond

nodded once. "Well, I'm wondering about the alarm system. Pardon me for asking this, but if the intruders set it off when they broke in, how did they have time to drill the safe before being interrupted?" David asked.

Hammond replied, "We're working on that. The alarm was disabled at the time of the break-in. Don't know exactly how yet, although the panel's obviously been tampered with. About a quarter of an hour later the alarm was somehow triggered. Sloppy job on the bypass maybe. I'll let you know what we turn up. Our response time, by the way, was just under five minutes, including the alarm company's handover. Next."

David said, "Have you ever heard of something like this? Two intruders dead, killed by each other?"

"No. Not as such. I've found bodies before where a gang has, er, made someone redundant right in the middle of a job. This is the first one I've heard of where no one's left alive. Did you want to make a point, Mr Braun?" Hammond asked.

"No. I only wondered how unusual something like this is," David said.

"Well they're all unusual. Usual is being at home in bed, not breaking into someone's office. But, I'll grant you, this is more like that telly programme America's Thickest Villains. I might have to write a monograph for the Detective's Gazette," Hammond said completely deadpan.

It took David a few moments to realise that Hammond had made a joke. He snorted.

"What's your last question?" Hammond asked.

David said, "Can I look out that window?" indicating the office door from which the night-time breeze was blowing.

For the first time Hammond's face registered something emotional; his brows scrunched together. Perhaps it was irritation.

He said nothing for a moment. Then he strode into the office. "Don't touch anything, either with your hands or your feet. There's a lot of clutter in here."

The floor was covered in markers, tape and various damp marks. A large stain was obviously blood. It was alarmingly large – the red appearing black on the dark grey, nylon carpet. They both stepped round the stain, keeping to the edge of the room.

David joined Hammond at the glassless window. Only a few jagged pieces of the double-glazing remained in the corners of the frame. David peered out and down into the damp night.

Beneath the window, maybe ten metres below, ran railway lines. There were two sets of tracks, the bright steel of their polished top surfaces reflected the faint ambient light. In between the tracks, broken glass twinkled. Some of the pieces were jagged shards as big as a fist; elsewhere a dusting of tiny fragments glittered like distant stars.

The train-tracks seemed to be lower than street level. Steep walls enclosed that section of railway for many metres in either direction. The tracks ran through an artificial canyon formed by the basement walls of the buildings on both sides.

On the opposite side of the tracks from where David looked out, a sheer wall rose ten metres. Above that, the featureless wall gave way to big rectangular windows in the plain concrete, but the holes were filled with chain-link not glass. The other side of the mesh, faint fluorescent burned. The building appeared to be a multi-storey car park.

Hammond said, "Nobody jumps – what? thirty-five feet? – onto broken glass and steel. At least not without putting themselves in the hospital. And it's a hell of a climb back out. We're shutting off the track for an hour to check it out, but only because there might be evidence down there. We're not expecting to find Spiderman's footprint."

David bent down and studied the bottom of the window frame.

Now Hammond's voice was clearly registering irritation at David's interest, "Braun, I want you to liaise with your clients, get me the information I want, keep them sweet. Don't start investigating this case. For a start, there's no theft."

David stood up, turned away from the window frame to face Hammond.

"Right. Thanks Inspector. I'm going to make some phone calls and some notes. Would you remind me of your phone number?" David said.

Hammond left his potent stare trained on David for a couple of moments before pulling a business card from his top pocket and handing it over. David offered one of his in exchange. "Call me if there's anything I can do to help," David said.

David made his way back through the office. Papers were beginning to blow around as the breeze stiffened a little.

Downstairs, there was now a technician dusting the alarm panel for fingerprints. David stopped and said, "Hi, DI Hammond was just telling me you haven't worked out yet why the alarm went off."

The technician glanced up quickly from his brushing, took in David's suit, his short hair and chunky frame. He said, "Well, yes sir, I suppose we haven't officially. But if you're in a rush, I can tell you what the report's going to say. These wires," he indicated a couple of bare-ended strands with one latex-clad finger, "were pulled apart. You can even see where they were gripped."

Two wires emerged from the panel in an arc, then they each

went through a little zigzag. From the zigzags to the naked copper ends they ran straight.

The technician explained, "The kinks are where someone gripped each wire. As the wire comes off a drum in the factory, it's got a little curve to it. Outside of the kinks, the curve's still there. Inside the kinks – where the wires took the tension of being pulled apart – they got straightened out.

"Somebody disabled the alarm and then they either thought better of it or someone else came along to break this circuit."

"Thanks," said David and left the technician to his work. He went through the main doors and out into the damp darkness.

For a moment, David stood in the street outside the lit office block. He looked at the buildings on either side, then he began to walk back to his car, peering at the gaps between the buildings as he went.

When he reached the car he got in and started the engine. He didn't move off right away, but instead pulled a street atlas from the glove box. He found the street he was currently parked in and ran his finger down the adjacent railway line. His fingertip came to rest on a road which crossed the tracks.

Putting the car into reverse, he turned it round and then set off, following the route he'd scouted on the map.

A few hundred metres from the office block, the level of the tracks was nearly four metres below street level. A road bridge need only rise half a metre or so in order to cross the line. Sure enough, David found the little humpback bridge, crossed over, and then set about trying to find the multi-storey car park that had been facing him when he'd stood at the broken office window.

With a little trial and error he located it. Leaving his Saab in the street outside, he ducked under the entry barrier to the car park and peered into the little security hut. No sign of life. He walked up the ramp, through several levels without windows, until he reached a floor with openings and found himself looking out towards the Interfinanzio building.

No cars remained in the multi-storey and only two of the six fluorescent strip lights on his level were working.

David walked to the window and peered out through the chain-link, over the railway lines, and into the glassless window of the lit office opposite. The room was empty, but he could see activity in the large open-plan office beyond.

Taking a handkerchief from his pocket he grasped the bottom of the chain-link and pushed. It was solidly anchored to the concrete wall. He moved further down, passing the first of two pillars which divided up the aperture. Every metre or so he tested the barrier. None of the chain-link could be lifted, nor was it cut.

Putting his hands in his pockets he stood and stared at the chain-link, his lips pursed. After nearly a minute of deliberating and scrutinising, his eyes suddenly narrowed.

He walked to the particular section of chain-link that had caught his eye. Using his handkerchief to touch it, he stretched up high and pushed at the top of the barrier. It came away from the concrete. If a person were somehow suspended outside, they could pull the top of the mesh away from the wall and find enough of a gap to squeeze through into the fourth floor of the car park.

Now David turned his attention to the car park floor. He dropped down into a press-up position and peered sideways along the ground. He moved to a different spot and repeated his inspection. Five times he moved and dropped down low enough that the front of his suit was almost brushing the ground. He found nothing of interest.

He stood up, and gazed around the car park, slapping his hands together to dislodge the dust and grit. His face wore the same expression of thoughtfulness as when he'd studied the mesh covering.

His eyes roamed the concrete floor, then took in the walls – searching in every direction.

Then something occurred to him. Turning his back on that level, he strode down the nearest ramp onto a level with windows that overlooked the street where he'd just parked. The illumination was a little better; only one fluorescent fitting was dark.

This time he only needed to drop into his press-up position once before he sprang back to his feet, a smile on his face. He walked over to where a single splinter of glass twinkled in the dim fluorescent gloom.

There were four broad tyre marks in the parking bay, black rectangles half a metre long, the rear set wider than the front. One of them went right over the splinter.

Bending down, David took his pen out of his pocket and crouched down. He gently nudged the glass fragment a millimetre or two to one side. In the dim light, it was difficult to tell whether the concrete beneath the chip had rubber on it or not. He nudged the chip back to its original position.

He pulled his mobile phone out of its belt clip and retrieved Hammond's card. He dialled the first number on the card.

It rang once and was answered, "Hammond."

"It's David Braun. Listen, there's something I think you should know. My route home took me past that multi-storey car park the other side of the railway tracks from your crime scene. I thought I'd have a quick look round and I noticed a bit of broken glass in one of the parking bays. It isn't one of those little cubes you get if you break a car window; it looks like window glass. You might want to send someone to have a look over here," David said.

Hammond's response was angry, "Braun, did I not make myself

plain? You don't investigate, you don't interfere, you keep the owner happy like it says in your job description. If you've screwed up a crime scene, lad, I'll have you charged with interference."

He might have continued but David butted in, "Hold on Hammond," David's voice had a hard edge to it. "You told me there were two people involved in this break-in and they're both in your morgue. If you're right, then this isn't a crime scene. And if I'm right, how does correcting your mistake constitute interference? This car park opens in an hour and a half, so decide whether you want to inspect the third man's tyre tracks before or after a couple of hundred early commuters have driven through here. I'll wait fifteen minutes then I'm going home." He pushed the red button on his phone ending the call.

Just under ten minutes later, a van pulled up beside David's car. He had gone out to stand by it and waved at the van as it approached.

A fifty-ish, barrel-shaped woman with bright, gingery hair got out of the driver's side door, immediately followed by the passenger, a thin, sad-looking man in his mid-twenties.

"You found something interesting?" she said, her voice energetic and horsy.

"I think so. Let me show you," said David, leading them into the multi-storey.

First he took them to the detached chain-link.

"Don't ask me how he got up there, but if he did, he could have slipped through here," he said, pointing to a section of the mesh. The younger technician pushed at the barrier with a latex-covered hand and peered up through the resulting gap.

Then David led them down one floor.

"On this side of the building you look out over the street and from here down there are no windows on the other side. So if he parked here he could drive down without being seen from the crime scene, even if he had his lights on," David said.

He approached the glass chip. "There," he said, "is a bit of glass I think came from the office window they broke."

"You could have tracked it in yourself," the woman said, brusquely.

"Well, firstly I didn't – I saw it before I reached this part of the car park. But look," he raised one foot and showed them the sole, "hard leather. There's almost no glass in that office, it all went out onto the tracks, and I had to walk about four hundred metres to get here. Very unlikely I could bring something this far. Compare that with a suspect who jumped down onto glass about forty metres from here, who – if he had any sense – was wearing rubber soles and who would have twisted his foot against the ground exactly here," he pointed at the chip, "if he were getting into the car that made these marks."

"Marvellous," the woman boomed, clapping her hands once. She turned to her assistant and said, "Now why can't you be more like that?" The assistant shrugged half-heartedly. She went on, brightly, "It'll probably turn out to be the wrong sort of glass, but it's a lovely story. We'll give this place a good going over."

She added, "You might want to be running along. Whatever you said to George Hammond, I think he's had enough of you for one day." She smiled at him.

Then she turned to her assistant and said, "Right then, mopey drawers, you can get the evidence case and the camera bag, while I measure up here."

David left them to it. He made his way back to his car and drove home. He just had time to freshen himself up before it was time to go to start his normal work day.

CHAPTER 5

Mahogany map drawers, parquet floors, high windows and indestructible iron radiators: all the trappings of nineteenth century science. Susan stood in the Assyrian room at the London School of Antiquities gazing out of the first floor window.

She'd been wearing a knee-length white raincoat which was now draped over her arm. Over the other shoulder was her courier bag. Her simple outfit of dark jeans and a white lambswool sweater, plus her carmine boots, still somehow made her look dressier than the people she'd passed on the way in.

From the window she could see the oppressive tower of the Senate House Library rising to her left – Orwell's inspiration for the Ministry of Truth. More books than one person could count: a mountain of learning too high for any scholar to climb.

In the street outside a tourist couple paused to look at the building and started fussing with a camera.

"Ms Milton," a voice behind her said. She turned to see a soft-featured, plump man addressing her from the doorway, an uncertain smile on his face, his hands clasped behind his back. He wore a faded blood-orange shirt and washed-out black jeans. He looked to be in his late thirties.

"Yes, but Susan is fine," she said. Now that they had made eye contact, he seemed to be blushing a little.

"Oh well, I'm delighted to meet you. I'm Bernard, Bernie Lampwick." He gave a little laugh as he said it. "I'm mostly called Bernie. To my face at least." Another little laugh. He rocked a little on his heels, looking uneasy. "I'm supervising the Teracus collection."

Susan frowned a little, puzzled. Bernie explained, "Oh that's what we're calling the collection you're here to look at. Anyway, welcome." He began to put out his hand for her to shake. With her coat and bag, Susan wasn't going to be able to reciprocate. His arm dropped back to his side and he smiled nervously. "OK. Listen, put your stuff down, it'll be fine here. I'll give you the lightning tour and then perhaps we'll go to tea. Or coffee if you prefer. That's a bit more American, isn't it?" he said.

"Coffee would be good," Susan said. She laid her coat over the back of the nearest chair and placed her bag by it. "Here?" she asked.

"Oh yes, that will be fine there," Bernie said. "If anyone were going to pinch something from this room it would most likely be one of the priceless antiques." Susan laughed.

Bernie turned towards the door and indicated that she should precede him through it. They walked back to the reception area and through some double doors, chatting as they went.

Out of the corner of her eye Susan could see Bernie checking her out. She turned her head a little towards him and he rapidly transferred his gaze to the corridor ahead. His blush returned.

"So do you get many visitors like me?" she asked, catching his eye and holding it. "You know…" she left a pause, allowed it to lengthen. Bernie licked his lips nervously as he waited for her to continue. His face showed his discomfort. She finished, "…Americans?"

He laughed loudly, relief evident. "Indeed, no. No it's something of the monastic life here. Not a lot of contact with the outside world." He laughed again. "Apologies if the old social skills are a bit rusty."

This time when she looked away his gaze remained fixed forwards.

"So why Teracus?" Susan asked.

Bernie said, "It was the pen name of the owner of the collection. His real name was probably Terry Cousins – although there does seem to be some doubt about that. For whatever reason, he used more than one name when he was acquiring new documents. But most of the correspondence we've got is signed Teracus.

"He was quite a character, or a man of mystery I should say. He died in Greece in a car crash, but it took a while for the local police to work out who he was and track down some paperwork on him. They notified the British police, who sent someone to his house.

"He had no family, only a landlady who rented out her upstairs flat to him. He'd already been dead two months when they gave her the bad news, so the question arose of what to do with his collection. She knew he'd flown all over the world assembling it and she felt he'd have wanted it to be appreciated, so she donated the lot to the University. Apparently her husband had been a beadle here." He missed Susan's confused look at this last. "We sent someone over to have a quick look just in case there was anything to it." He explained conspiratorially, "We get back editions of Picture Post or

Victorian copies of the Bible being left to us as priceless treasures the whole time. Anyway, the assistant we sent along phoned us almost beside himself at what he'd found.

"We're keeping it all downstairs in the Alexandrian room. There are over four hundred documents in all, ranging in ages from Teracus's recent notes to some leaves from a book written in the mid-seventeenth century, assuming they authenticate. Of course what's much more interesting is that a number of them are recent copies of much older documents. There's even one fragment where the ink is Biro but the words are in Hieratic. We've translated just enough to satisfy ourselves it's not gibberish or obviously part of a known work."

They arrived at a busy refectory. Bernie spoke a little more loudly to compete with the din of voices and the scrape and squeak of chairs being moved on vinyl flooring. He took a tray, and laid it on the guides that ran along the front of the food counter. He loaded the tray up with a mug of tea, a cup of coffee and a couple of doughnuts for himself. Susan chose a little pack of ginger biscuits.

When Bernie had paid, they found a quiet table away from most of the bustle and resumed their conversation.

"I'm most of the way through a first draft of a catalogue," Bernie said. "I've recorded what I think each document is, along with a few particulars of its style and appearance. It's obviously been important to draw a distinction between the age of the words compared with the age of the paper and the ink."

Bernie drank some of his tea. He said, "I'm thinking the catalogue would be a good place for you to start. Have a look through my classifications, maybe start checking them. If you think I've got something wrong, then sing out. I'm not precious about these things. The more mistakes you uncover, the better, I think."

Susan asked, "Have you scanned any of it?"

"No. Obviously we keep a digital archive of our documents, but we tend to get the classification sorted before we put them in the archive," Bernie said, slightly officiously.

"I'd *really* like to get some of them scanned," Susan said. "It will help me work if I can start annotating digital copies as soon as possible."

Bernie looked a little ruffled. "Well there is a process to follow," he said, not very reassuringly.

"Whose permission do we need? I can take care of that," Susan said, energetically.

Now Bernie looked alarmed, "Ah, now, hold on a minute. I didn't say we couldn't do it. Why don't you leave it with me?"

She looked him straight in the eye, "I was hoping we could get the scanning underway today, Bernie." She volunteered, "I'll work on documents you've already classified. That way I won't be holding you up. And vice versa." Her tone was very direct, but the effect was softened a little with a smile.

Bernie's slight huffiness had become resignation. "I'm sure we'll work something out if it's that important, I mean if it helps."

"Thanks, Bernie," she said, responding to his slightly beaten expression with a cheerful smile. "I'm fascinated by this man Teracus. Do you have any idea why he assembled this collection? Was he a dealer or a scholar?"

Bernie brightened, "Well, it's curious. Since the whole collection was locked away in his digs, it was obviously about as much of a private collection as you can get. And looking at his correspondence, he only seems to have acquired; I haven't seen a single record of a sale. So he wasn't a dealer. But on the other hand, he wasn't with any academic institution that I've been able to see. He seems to have spent the last thirty years building the collection purely for his own enjoyment. What he did for money, we have no idea. Like I say, a man of mystery."

"Really," Susan said, appreciatively. "That's so interesting. And does the whole collection relate to myths and magic?"

"There's a great deal about magic – legends of great sorcerers, manuals of instruction, spells, even some philosophy. Most of it is in Medieval Latin – I mean the language it's written in; the materials aren't medieval. Since it's mainly recent copies, it's not going to be easy to work out when the original sources were written unless we find references elsewhere. I'm reasonably sure they are copies, by the way, not fakes, but you should be aware of the possibility.

"It hasn't been easy figuring out what's what. I would have said some of his recent notes dated from the Middle Ages except he put last year's date on them. It looks like Teracus's Latin was pretty good," Bernie said.

He went on, "There are also some bits and bobs about mystical relics. The first document I looked at was absolutely fascinating. It looks to be the newest addition to the collection. It purports to be a Latin translation of a classical Tibetan text about something called the signs or sigils of the healer. Supposedly, the gods find certain patterns interesting. By marking the body of a sick person with one of these patterns, it will attract the interest of a god who may choose to heal them. Really very interesting.

"Then there's another text, supposedly 16th century Florentine, discussing ways around the rule banning sorcerers from attacking each other with spells. I find myself wondering who wrote that. Who was supposed to read it? Did they believe what they were saying? Whichever document you choose, they all seem to cry out for further investigation."

Susan nodded. "I can't wait to get started," she agreed.

Bernie replied, "Well, I'm done here." Somehow, as he'd been speaking he'd found time to eat a couple of doughnuts and drain his mug of tea. "Let's go below. You know, there's as much of this building below ground as there is above. We'll be in basement two, right at the bottom. Wonderful environment for storing documents, providing you keep the moisture level right down. You're not claustrophobic, are you? Anyway, you'll get used to it pretty quickly."

Bernie led Susan back to the main hall and around to an old, cage-style lift big enough to hold a grand piano. To enter the building Susan had come up a flight of steps, which meant that the ground floor she stood on was nearly two metres above street level. As the lift descended, it passed a lower-ground floor, set a little below the street outside. Beneath that were two more floors, where sunlight was replaced by fluorescent light. Above the lift controls, a row of indicators lit up in sequence, tracking their descent. As they reached the bottom of the building, the leftmost light was illuminated. The label above it read '-2'.

Bernie took Susan to a large room opposite the lift entrance. Overall it was dimly lit, but bright task lighting illuminated the tables or workstations that were in use. Bernie spent a couple of minutes showing Susan where everything was, how to open the document store and how to log on to a workstation. He left her looking through documents and went off to get her an ID card.

Susan inspected several documents in the store and removed one. She placed it on the stand which sat next to her chosen workstation and turned on its little halogen light. Then she pulled a yellow pad and a draughtsman's pen from her bag and began to make notes. She hardly looked up when Bernie returned.

Two hours passed before Susan paused. She put down her pen and turned to Bernie, reminding him about the document scanning.

Bernie showed her how to use their new planetary camera as well as the flatbed scanner. Susan got straight to work, spending an hour efficiently scanning papers before Bernie announced that he was going home.

"Thanks for all your help, Bernie," Susan said. "We'll catch up in the morning, OK? Make a plan for my time here."

Bernie agreed and said, "Don't work too late. They'll ask you to leave at nine, anyway."

"Hey, Bernie, is it possible to make a phone call? I want to call my Professor in Cambridge," Susan asked.

"Ah yes, the famous Professor Shaw. Our Dean here was one of his old students – possibly during the crusades. Oh, no offence intended," Bernie said.

There was a code for making long distance calls and Bernie wrote it on a Post-it note. Then with a little wave he was gone.

A couple of other researchers had wandered in and out during the course of the afternoon, but Susan now had the room to herself. Most of it was in darkness.

She moved to the next desk, which had a phone on it, punched in Bernie's code and then a number from memory. It was answered promptly.

"Professor, it's Susan Milton."

"Susan, my dear, how are you getting on?"

"Professor, it's fabulous. I have to thank you for sending me down here. They're going to have to throw me out or I'm never going to leave. This collection is amazing."

"There now, that's just as I hoped."

"Listen, Professor, are you OK to talk? I don't want to interrupt anything."

"I've just received a brochure offering holidays in Tuscany. Some of them look rather inviting, but I don't mind putting off a detailed review of their merits for a few minutes since you've been kind enough to call."

Susan said, "I'm sure you're right in the middle of something important, but it's really sweet of you to deny it. Can I tell you what I've been working on this afternoon?"

They chatted happily for a few minutes, with the Professor making occasional suggestions or asking for more information when a particular detail caught his interest.

After a little while, the Professor said, "And everyone is behaving themselves and treating you well, I hope."

"Oh god, what did you do?" Susan asked, suddenly aghast, "I heard the Dean was an old student of yours. Did you threaten to call his parents, or something, if he didn't treat me like royalty?"

He chided her, "You really do have such an undisciplined imagination for an otherwise sensible young woman. I might perhaps, in passing, have expressed an interest in your well-being. I certainly don't recall any explicit threats."

"Well, my thanks to you and Humphrey Bogart. This guy, Bernie Lampwick, has been taking great care of me. He was a little jumpy at first, which at the time I put down to my arresting presence. Fear for his life might have played a part in it, I can see now. Although it doesn't help matters that these guys don't talk to a woman from one year to the next. Anyhow, we're getting on fine now."

"Splendid. So long as it's all plain sailing, I'll leave well alone. Now have you had a chance to visit the house yet?"

"No, I came straight to the School. If it's OK, I'd like to stay there tonight." She glanced at the clock on the wall, "I don't have time to make any other arrangements."

"And neither should you. Unless you really can't abide the place, it seems obvious to me that you should stay there." Then, as though he were thinking carefully, he added, "Though I suppose I could talk to the Dean about finding you somewhere else?"

Susan snorted, "Yeah, I'd probably end up with the keys to his place while he slept in his office. No, I can take a hint. If it's really OK with you, then I'd be honoured to stay there. I've got one more call to make and then I'm going to head over there, see it in the light."

"Maybe you'll let me know how you find it."

"Sure thing. I'll phone around this time tomorrow, if that's OK."

"I shall look forward to it. Now don't let me keep you."

"Yup, thanks again, Professor."

"Goodbye Susan."

Susan set the phone down slowly. She was looking off into an imaginary distance with a fond smile on her face. She didn't move for a few moments. Then, coming back to life, she rooted around in her bag and pulled out an address book. She flipped to 'D' and glanced at her watch. She paused and tapped one of her bottom teeth with a thumbnail. Then, resolved, she pulled out an international phone card, pinned the phone between her shoulder and her neck and once again punched in Bernie's code. Then she entered a long string of digits, three at a time, reading from the card and then her address book.

It rang a couple of times – the single, long hum of an American exchange, not the double trill of the U.K.

"Dee," a woman's voice said.

"Hey, Dee, it's Susan," she said, not sounding too sure.

"Wo, Sis," the tone effervescent and confident, "where you been? I've been leaving messages for a week."

"Sorry, Dee, I've been travelling with work," she said, sounding a little down-trodden. She volunteered, "I'm in London at the moment. Gonna be here a couple of weeks at least."

"That's perfect, Susie. I wanna come over. You've been there god knows how long, I never see you except at Christmas and I've never been to England. I've got a conference over there coming up and I thought I'd see my big sis and check out all those British guys you've got hanging round you. See if any of them look good enough to steal."

"Dee, that's not even funny. And what do you mean you're coming over? I thought you hated anywhere that wasn't New York."

"Listen, you can't say no, you're family, it's like a legal contract or something. *Sue casa, me casa*, remember? I've got it here in black and white. So have you got somewhere for me to stay in London or am I going to have to find some Fawlty Towers motel?"

"I don't know. I'm going to be staying in this place my Professor owns, but I haven't been along to see what it's like yet. Could you call me in a couple of days once I know more? You're really serious about coming?"

"Don't sound so horrified, Susie. I won't ruin your life or anything. Just tell your friends that I'm adopted or something, they need never know you've got a low-brow sibling."

"Dee, don't. It wouldn't make any difference to me if you'd never finished the eighth grade. I'm not embarrassed about you; I'm just busy. God, you make more money in a month than I make in a year. You're ridiculously successful."

"This is new. Flattery. Well, I could get to like it. So listen, I'll call you with the details in a day or two. Meantime, you want me to get you anything? I'm going shopping this weekend. Unless you've piled on the pounds you should still look pretty good in anything that fits me. How about that Betsey Johnson top I told you about?"

"That's really generous, Dee, but I don't wear anything with a neck line below my navel. The floral one was more my thing."

"God it's no wonder you ended up surrounded by books. I'll get you the little virginal embroidered one. So, um, you called Mom recently?"

"Have you?"

"I called her about a week ago. Well, maybe a couple of weeks. We should go and see them. Come over during your summer break."

"Nah, that's just a student thing. I don't get a summer break anymore, but I'll call her. I will."

"Good. OK, Susie, gotta hustle. We sure appreciate your call and y'all have a good day."

"Bye Dee."

Susan hung up. She flipped through her address book to 'M' and sat thinking for a while. Then she snapped the little book shut and began to gather up her things.

CHAPTER 6

TWO DAYS LATER
THURSDAY 10TH APRIL

David was back at the scene of the break-in. He'd parked a few streets away and walked, briefcase in hand, towards the office block. There was no sign that the building had been the centre of so much activity earlier in the week.

Climbing the front steps, he glanced at the lock on the front doors. The plate around the keyhole had a mirror finish – brand new. He pulled open the door and stepped into the reception area.

Glancing to his left, he could see, behind the smoked-glass cover, a new alarm panel. An LCD display featured prominently on the new model. Instead of black, the replacement panel was pale cream, matching the walls.

David approached the reception desk where an over-made-up girl in her late teens sat talking into a headset. "Gotta go, yeah?" she whispered into the mike and pressed a button on the console in front of her.

She activated a smile wide enough to display her back teeth.

"Hell-oo!" she said, in the sing-song speech of switchboard operators, and tilted her head to one side.

"Hi, I'm David Braun from Marshall and Liberty. I'm here to see Alessandro Dass," David said. As he spoke the Chairman's name, the receptionist's smile lost a little power.

"Was he expecting you?" she asked. David nodded, "Nine thirty appointment." He checked his wristwatch: 09.25.

"I'll just…" she said and glanced up towards the ceiling. She tapped a number into her console.

"Mrs Billings, it's Stephanie. I've got a young man here," she glanced at David and pursed her lips, "to see Mr Dass."

David fished a business card out of his top pocket and handed it to her just as she asked, "What was your name again?"

Stephanie read the name, listened for a moment and said, "Right." She punched a button and looked back to David. "Someone is coming for you. If you'd like to take a seat." She indicated two orange banquettes set against the wall between a shrub and a low table. The table held newspapers.

David sat himself down and began to flick through the sports section of the Telegraph. He didn't get very far. A stern, stick-like woman dressed in a dark-brown sleeveless sack-dress appeared at his side with a tinkle of bracelets. She had the leathery skin of the perma-tanned and it suited her expression well.

"The Chairman was expecting you at eleven," she said flatly. David's jaw tightened a little. Then it relaxed.

Getting up he said pleasantly, "Whatever's most convenient for Mr Dass." He set down the newspaper. "Why don't I come back at eleven?"

There was an impatient sigh. "I'll see if Mr Dass is prepared to see you now anyway," she said, though her tone suggested it was asking a great deal.

"Please, Mrs Billings, don't put Mr Dass to any trouble. If he's expecting me at eleven, why disappoint him?" he asked amiably, spreading his hands, palms up.

Mrs Billings narrowed her eyes suspiciously at David. The slitted gaze made her leathery face resemble a baby Cayman's.

"There's no point now you're here," she said testily. "You might as well come up." She turned and walked to the stairs. David followed.

As David passed Stephanie at the reception desk she caught his eye, flicked her gaze to the departing back of the Chairman's secretary and, opening her mouth expressively wide, mouthed the word 'Bitch'.

David laughed despite himself, but not loud enough for Mrs Billings to hear. He followed her upstairs.

She took him to the second floor, down a long carpeted corridor. A desk set at an angle narrowed the corridor, creating a secretarial checkpoint which any visitors would need to pass. A sign on the desk read 'M. Billings'.

Beyond the desk were two doors.

Mrs Billings held up a hand, indicating 'stop' and tapped on the right-hand door. She opened the door a little and put her head round it. When she pulled back, the last traces of what must have been a sunny smile were giving way to hard frost. Winter had once more set in when she turned to David and said, "The Chairman will see you."

David squeezed past her into an expensively, if tastelessly, decorated office. Behind a broad and nearly empty beechwood desk sat an immaculately dressed man in a cream suit – the cut of which, and the way it blended perfectly with the pale silk tie and off-white shirt, made him look almost like a fashion plate. His skin, tanned and lined, but with the distinguished ruggedness cultivated by mature movie stars, glowed with health. His silver hair was thick and impeccably neat. He smiled – his teeth too were perfect – and the contrast with his dark, expressionless eyes was unsettling.

David approached the desk and held out his hand, saying, "Mr Dass."

Dass stood and gripped David's hand for a tiny fraction of a second. Mrs Billings was still hovering at the door. Dass said, "Thank you, Maureen." She closed the door behind her.

"What can I do to help, Mr Dass?" David asked. They were both standing now. Dass had tilted his head back and was staring at a point some distance beyond the ceiling. He pursed his lips, thoughtfully.

Dass's voice was rich, the accent Italian and cultured. "Marshall and Liberty – we have done business with them for a number of years. Just over one hundred if my history serves me."

He went on, "We have always found them to be attentive. They don't go in for this modern marketing." He said the word with great distaste. "Special offers or the like." His tone became firmer, "A company doing something well for their customers has no need of those things, all the clamouring and pleading for business. Do not beg for your customers' trust; earn it. Well, Marshall and Liberty have earned *our* trust."

Dass was still gazing at the ceiling, not at David, so David made no reply; he simply waited.

Dass said, "You – oh now what is that expression? – put the policeman's nose out of joint with your detective work the other night. The third man. That was you?" He glanced at David.

"Yes," David said.

Dass smiled and looked around him. He said softly, almost to himself, "My god, but this is a hideous office. Why does a country that could command an empire allow its greatness to slip away?

Weak governments, lazy civil servants, corrupt policemen – the newspapers talk of little else," he pivoted his hand so that his pointing finger took in the room, "and designers who don't design." He swished his hand, waving the thought away.

"Yes, this third man intrigues us. One man on the inside who worked here, *yes*, a second who understands alarm systems and security, *certainly*, but a third man who has the brains," Dass tapped the middle of his forehead, "to conceive of the idea. Someone who thinks, someone who plans – perhaps someone who first observes."

Dass walked over to the far corner of his office and pulled open a door. Inside a light came on revealing an alcove. A moment later Dass pushed the door closed again. "Interfinanzio is an old company. In a sense it is a family company. Like any family it has its heirlooms, its little treasures."

Dass suddenly dropped down into one of the room's two armchairs. His movements were lithe, much younger than his grey hair and lined face would have suggested. "Forgive the unpleasant topic, but I once met a man, an American, who collected famous racehorses. Not, you understand while they were still with us, as it were. Dead creatures. What fascination does something like that hold? He had made for himself a private room, like a museum." Dass again made a dismissive gesture, a swipe of his hand. "No, it is unfathomable," he sneered.

He continued, "At any rate, I suspect he saw not the dead flesh but the former glory. The symbolism comes not from the thing itself; it originates in the mind of those regarding it. And how could it be any different? So it is with the matter that brings you here. You have come to discuss those things which to my people are powerful symbols, things which resonate with past glories."

Dass was still not looking directly at David; he was staring at a painting above his desk. It was a dark, abstract impressionist piece suggestive of too many paint colours mixed together. He looked slightly troubled by it, or by whatever he was thinking as his gaze rested there. David still stood in the centre of the room, his briefcase held in both hands in front of him.

Dass pointed to the door that he had opened a moment before. "There is a safe within. It has been opened."

David stirred.

Dass gestured towards the other armchair, "Sit. Make notes." David sat down, his briefcase on his lap. He opened the case, slipped out a pad and laid it on top of the case. He pulled a fountain pen from his inside jacket pocket and began writing.

Dass said, "I think somehow our third man learned that I was to be in England for a time. Perhaps he knew that there are one or two of our family treasures that we like to have with us. I am speaking of this because we have faith in Marshall and Liberty, in their seriousness, in their discretion.

"There are other institutions which inspire in us considerably less faith. Your detective work the other night revealed the error I would make if I placed myself entirely in the hands of the police. The police whom I read of everyday in my newspaper, the police who cannot count as high as three without assistance from a professional," he indicated David, "a competent and thorough mind dedicated to his company."

Dass looked directly at David now. He turned his dark eyes to David's with such sudden intensity that David flinched. For a moment David couldn't meet his stare. An expression which might have been fear rippled across David's face. But a second later, he had brought his gaze up to connect with Dass's. As eye contact was made, David blinked once, involuntarily, but did not look away.

Dass stood and looked down at David. His voice was light,

almost airy, but the intensity of his expression was startling. "I may call you David? Listen to me David. I want you to investigate this theft. I wish you to undertake this task. I wish for the police to keep you informed of their progress so that you can add what they know to whatever you learn. I have not lived this long without making some friends, so this will not be a problem. But I must have someone in whom I can place my faith at the centre of this matter."

David began to speak, struggled to get the words out, but Dass held up a hand. His eyes still drilled into David's.

"Let us understand, I am not asking anything improper. I wish you to establish a liaison with the police, to acquaint yourself with this incident and to push forward independently whenever you discern that their efforts are falling short. I am aware that facts are checked whenever a client is suspected of misleading his insurer. Details are verified and investigators are hired in secrecy. Well, on this occasion it is to be done with the client's approval – and if it is successful – with their grateful appreciation.

"We would like to recover what we have lost, without publicity, without noise or untidiness." Dass paused and turned over one hand. "I could of course content myself with making an insurance claim." He waved his hands lightly to indicate that this was the easiest thing in the world. "I could satisfy myself with a sum of money in place of a treasure that has been held dear by our family since Alexander VI was Pope. Although I fear that Marshall and Liberty would find that a costly decision. One is hardly aware of the monetary value which something possesses until one comes to pay for its loss. No, I doubt Marshall and Liberty would survive such a decision and it is almost unthinkable to me that we would follow that course when it may still be that we can recover what we have lost." As he finished speaking, Dass disengaged his piercing gaze and once more let his eyes roam upwards towards the ceiling. His focus returned to whatever it was that he perceived beyond the walls of the office.

David found that he had been holding his breath and let it out quietly. He looked back down at his notes and readied his pen. A gleam of perspiration had appeared at his hairline.

Dass said, "I regret that I cannot give you photographs. We have always felt that invisibility to the world at large was the best protection for our treasures." He frowned and spread his hands a little, allowing that he may have been mistaken. "But we are speaking of something of great antiquity. A box of unusual construction, covered in leather, the structure made from bone."

He explained, "The building materials of the time." Then he went on, "Inside is an ornament, a filigree of intricate design. The metal is platinum, beloved of the Incas and the Ancient Egyptians, though we do not believe this piece originated in either of those two empires. It is from the East, from China and the only one of its kind."

Dass stood, crossed to his desk and opened a drawer. He took out a single sheet of paper and a pencil and began to sketch. "There was an attempt made to steal the piece some years ago. Very powerful criminals. Since then we have allowed no explicit reports of its existence to circulate. Your company's records, for instance, do list the item (though I trust they will not have volunteered that information to you until now) but they do so in a roundabout way. A precise weight, a length and width, the total distance the interlocking design would reach if it were stretched out. No pictures, no drawings.

"In effect, we have given them a riddle to which the lost item is the answer – enough to recognise it, but not enough to describe it." He was nearly finished drawing. "But you may require a little more information."

"The man who took this," Dass indicated the drawing, "must have reasoned that we would not wish the police – and moments later the world – to know of its existence and thus we could not report its loss. That in turn would mean the investigation would be closed – because there would be no reason for the police to suspect the involvement of a third man. Not only did you establish the third man's existence independently, but you also provided us with a way to report a theft without revealing our secret. The police have a misleading description of what has been taken; you will work alongside them, entrusted with the truth."

Dass stopped sketching and held up the results. A weaving, intertwining web of lines criss-crossed the page, forming an intricate Mandala. Overall, the pattern looked a little like a feather, but broad like a palm leaf and symmetrical about its centre line. "It was once revered for its mystical properties, in more primitive times, as I suppose is any item of exceptional antiquity. I'm told if one travels sufficiently widely in China and talks to enough people, one can still hear stories that link it with various fables and folk tales, despite the fact that it was removed from China centuries ago."

From the pocket of his immaculate suit, Dass retrieved a slim Dunhill lighter. With a tiny pop it produced a flame which Dass waved under the lower edge of the paper. "I have no wish for melodrama, but it will not be through me that a description of our lost treasure reaches the avid collectors of the world. I hope, likewise, it will not be through you," Dass said, giving David another dose of his direct, penetrating gaze. He maintained eye contact with David as the drawing burned brightly and little scraps of ash began to move around the room. When the paper had burned down to Dass's fingers he allowed the black, ash-ghost of the paper to drop into the bin by his desk. He appeared untroubled by the flames touching his fingers. "I love to cook," he volunteered, "It teaches one not to be afraid of a little heat."

He bent and stirred the perfect tissue of ash, breaking it up. With his other hand he produced a handkerchief in lemon silk and cleaned his fingers.

"Call my secretary if I can help with your quest. Perhaps you will be good enough to keep me informed of your progress," Dass said.

The interview was evidently over; David returned the notepad to his case with unsteady hands, stood and moved towards the door. Dass was still dabbing at his fingers. "Forgive me if I don't shake your hand," he said.

David nodded, numbly, and twisted the door handle with a damp palm. He stepped out into the corridor beyond and pushed the door closed, leaning back against it for a moment.

He made a fist with his hand, which was trembling. He was visibly shaken. He closed his eyes for a moment. Then, shakily echoing Dass's actions, he fumbled for a handkerchief, wiping at the perspiration on his forehead.

He opened his eyes to see Mrs Billings seated behind her desk, scrutinising him like a cat regards a mouse. She had an almost sensual grin on her face. "Is something wrong?" she asked, sounding delighted at his lack of composure.

He didn't reply. Gathering himself, David strode rapidly past her, with a curt 'goodbye' as he did so, and made his way briskly down to reception. He walked past Stephanie, without heeding her attempts to attract his attention, and out into the street. He headed towards his car.

On the corner before the car park stood a pub. Outside on the pavement a sign read, "Morning coffees, cappuccinos, open for breakfast." David went in. Two dusty looking builders were standing at one end of the bar drinking pints. Around them, several tables were occupied by people eating cooked breakfasts. David ordered a pint of Guinness, glancing at his watch as he did so. The time was 10.04.

Once he had been served, he made his way to the table furthest from the door and sat, sipping at his drink for some minutes. He placed one hand on the table in front of him. It was almost steady, though a slight tremor could still be detected.

He took out his mobile phone and retrieved a number from its memory. He held the phone to his ear.

"Kieran, it's David." He listened to the reply.

Then he said, "Fine, thank you. Listen, are you free for lunch? I want to pick your brains, so choose anywhere you like and the company will pay."

He listened and then said, "I'll tell you when I see you, but you're free then?"

Another pause and he said, "Yes, who'd have thought it? I'm sure I was never quite that critical about history, but I take your point. Let's hope all that expertise is what I need for this project."

Pause. "No, early is good. I'll meet you there then. Call me if you're held up."

Pause. "Great. See you at twelve."

David hung up and put the phone back in his pocket. He took out the notepad. He continued to sip from his pint and make occasional notes as they occurred to him, until his glass was empty.

He took the glass up to the bar and noticed that they sold mints. He bought a pack and put one in his mouth. Then he headed back to his car.

* * *

Two hours later he was seated opposite Kieran in a smart, West End brasserie. Many of the diners wore suits, most of the rest were dressed with an eye to fashion; Kieran was the only one wearing an open-collared polo shirt.

"I wish you'd given me more notice, I feel I'm letting the side down coming here in my civvies," Kieran said.

David smiled pleasantly, looking past him to the street outside the restaurant. He took a sip of his water.

Kieran asked, "Are you alright David? You seem a bit not-altogether-with-us. Tough morning in the salt mines?"

"Sorry Kieran. I met the most... Have you ever met anyone who just frightens the life out of you and you don't know why?" David said.

Kieran looked at him for a moment and said, "All the time. I'm a librarian. But the thought that there are people in the world who scare you is an unsettling one. Who is this Neanderthal?"

"A client. A businessman. He must be in his sixties, not big, not hostile – quite polite actually – but I almost couldn't look him in the eye." David was still gazing out at the street.

"God almighty. Well whoever he is, he must have something about him. Didn't he realise you could have killed him with your little finger?" Kieran asked.

David snorted and looked at Kieran, "Evidently not. Anyway, forget all that. How are you, how's things?"

"Things? You mean Hope? You know she's in Hollywood now? She's making some film about an escaped wolf that's the product of a CIA genetic engineering program. Sounds awful; will probably do well. We haven't really seen that much of her since you two split up. She calls home occasionally, talking nineteen to the dozen, all insider speak that's wasted on us and then has to dash. I think she's happy for once, though," Kieran said.

"I'm glad she's happy. It's always been important to Hope to feel appreciated. Ideally by several million people at once," David said, smiling.

"Really, I won't have you speak that way about my sister. That's *my* job," Kieran said.

They fell to studying their menus for a minute and then the waiter appeared. Once they had ordered, Kieran said, "Drinking at lunchtime? I thought you were very strict with yourself about that sort of thing. Not part of the warrior monk lifestyle."

David said, "I don't think your sister dates monks, Kieran. And I have a glass of wine every now and then," David sounded a little defensive.

Kieran held up his hands in surrender, "Sorry, didn't mean to get at you."

Just then the drinks arrived and David took a sip of his. "To tell you the truth, I'm still a bit jumpy from my meeting with the Demon Client this morning."

Kieran said, "Is it this client that brings you begging for my help?"

"Buying you an expensive lunch and asking politely for your help, yes. He's lost something and I need to find it. I need to find out who'd want this thing, where someone might try to sell it, who to talk to," David said.

"Sounds like you need an expert. Tell me about this missing bauble. What's he lost?" Kieran said.

"Well, The Count was reluctant to give me too much information, but I know it's old, valuable, some sort of intricate piece of Eastern jewellery. If you made a doily from platinum, it might look like that. He said it was from somewhere in China where they still have legends about its magical powers," David said.

Their hors d'oeuvres arrived and they each took a mouthful. Kieran, chewing, held up a fork and gestured towards David with it, "You know what? If it's got some superstitious significance the boys at the School of Antiquities might be able to help you. They've just set up a team to look at all things mythic and venerable. I know the fellow who runs the team, Bernie Lampwick – he was in my house at school."

David nodded, unsurprised. "If he wasn't in your house at school he would have been a friend of the family's or his dad would have been one of your father's indentured servants or something."

"Don't let my father hear you talking like that. He hasn't been allowed to put the rent up in any of the estate's cottages since 1981. He says they live better than he does," Kieran said.

David let that pass and said, "Anyway, can you talk to this Bernie guy? See if he might be prepared to do a couple of day's consultancy for us. The company are fairly generous with this sort of thing; he should get a new set of tweeds out of it."

"I think Bernie's more grunge than county, but I'll call him. Do I get a cut?" Kieran asked.

"You get smoked salmon, followed by *boeuf en croute*, followed by *tarte tatin*, two glasses of wine and a coffee. Not bad for ten seconds work," David said.

"Ten seconds to tell you and a lifetime to build up the contacts and the encyclopaedic knowledge that goes with them. You're getting all that, you know," Kieran said.

"Fair enough. I'll throw in a brandy," David said. "Is Bernie any use at legwork? Would he be prepared to talk to a few dealers, assuming they exist for this sort of item?"

Kieran considered. "Mmm. Bernie's not what you'd call a people person. He gets ulcers if they make him give a lecture.

Anyway, leave it with me, I'll find someone capable, with a bit of nous – who's desperate for the cash."

The conversation turned back to Hope, and Kieran's attempt to explain the plot of her current film. He suggested that David come to dinner when Hope returned in the autumn. David wondered aloud whether that was such a good idea. The matter was left unsettled, but they agreed to meet again in a few weeks to catch up properly. No more was said about David's encounter with Dass.

CHAPTER 7

THE NEXT DAY
THURSDAY 10TH APRIL

Susan showed her new badge to the security guard, who nodded and pushed a foot pedal allowing her through the hip-height turnstile. She crossed the foyer, glancing up once to catch a glimpse of the ornamental ceiling. To the right of the main staircase stood the wide cage-door of the lift. The lift car was waiting for her. She rode down to the lower basement.

A minute later she was entering the subterranean Alexandrian room. Bernie was already in and he waved from his corner as he saw her.

Susan put down her bag and her coffee, hung her white rain-coat on the coat-stand by the door. Bernie sidled over.

"Good morning, Susan. How are you today?" Bernie asked.

"Peachy. You OK?" Susan said cheerfully.

"Oh, yes. Marvellous. Um. I wanted to talk to you about

something," Bernie said, his tendency towards nervousness evident once again.

Susan, who was now sitting down, thrust out one of her legs and pulled a nearby chair out from under its desk with her foot. "Sure. Sit down," she said, rotating her chair towards Bernie's and reaching back over her shoulder to retrieve her Starbucks cup.

Bernie sat down, leaning back. He looked uncomfortable like that and leaned forwards instead. "I had a call from an old friend of mine last night. It seems he knows someone who works in insurance. They've got a client who's lost a rare antique and they want some expert guidance on where it might turn up. The piece they're looking for seemed like the sort of thing you might know about."

Susan said nothing and Bernie hastily added, "I didn't say you'd definitely do it. Certainly not." Bernie was smiling nervously as though there was more to his tale than what he'd said.

"But…" Susan said, inquiringly.

"Mmm. But I said you'd talk to the man from the insurance company," Bernie said, raising his eyes to Susan, gauging her reaction.

Susan showed no sign that she was displeased. "They pay for that sort of help, don't they?" she asked, intrigued.

Bernie nodded. "Good money, I believe. My friend suggested they were looking for a few days assistance, probably not all at once, but spread out over a couple of weeks. Research the lost item, write a little memo pointing their investigator in the right direction, maybe accompany him to a couple of dealers or auctions. He wasn't sure of the specifics, but you get the idea."

Susan said, "Well, you know, that actually sounds kind of fun. I'm not up for taking much time out, though. How did you leave it with him?"

"Well, I said I'd ask if you'd meet the insurance chappie this afternoon. I've got his number here," Bernie said, attempting to hand Susan a Post-it note, which remained attached to his fingers. He tried again, but it was still stuck to his hand.

"Bernie!" she said firmly, to attract his attention. As he looked up, she darted out a hand to pluck the note from his grasp so swiftly he didn't have time to move. She turned it around so that it was readable and looked at the number.

"Thanks for setting this up, Bernie. I might get kind of a kick out of it. And god knows I could do with a few extra bucks," she said.

"Oh well then," Bernie said, looking happier, "that's good." He got up to return to his workstation.

"Oh, hey, Bernie," Susan said. "I'm going out in a little while. I'm going to drop in on the woman who donated this collection, Teracus's landlady. If I meet this guy this afternoon, that might be it for the day. I thought someone should know where I am. You might think I'm playing hooky or something."

Bernie didn't look sure what to do with this information. "Don't think me... I hope you don't mind me asking, but why do you want to see her?"

"Lots of reasons. I want to know more about where all this stuff came from. I want to know if there could be any more. I'm also pretty curious to know who this Teracus guy really was." She concluded, "I'll tell you what I discover tomorrow."

Bernie smiled appreciatively and nodded a couple of times, returning to his side of the room.

Susan took another sip of her latte and stuck Bernie's Post-it to her phone. She hooked the handset under her shoulder and started pushing numbers.

"David Braun," a voice said after the second ring.

"David, hi, I'm Susan Milton. Bernie Lampwick gave me your number," Susan said.

"Ms Milton, hi. So do you think you might be interested?" David asked.

"Could be. Bernie said you wanted to meet with me this afternoon. Have you got a plan?" she said.

"For this afternoon? Not really. Let's make one. When are you free?" David asked.

"If it's Central London, I can be anywhere by four. We could do earlier, but I'm taking a little trip and I don't know how long it will take," Susan said.

"Then let's say four. How about the Natural History Museum by the big dinosaur in the entrance hall?" David said.

Susan laughed. "You're for real, right? This is about insurance."

"I swear on my actuarial tables. You can come to the office if you'd be more comfortable there. I just thought…"

"No, no. The dinosaur's fine. I've been meaning to visit that place since I came to England," Susan said.

"That's easy then. Save any travel receipts and I'll reimburse you," David said.

"Not a problem. So, er, what do you look like?" Susan asked.

"According to most of my friends, a security guard. Anyway, I'll be the one visiting a museum in a suit. Call my mobile if you can't see me," David said.

"Great. Listen, I gotta run. I'll be there at four," Susan said.

"Bye."

Susan hung up. She fished her address book out of her bag and wrote David's name and number into it.

Then she flipped to 'H' and dialled again.

The phone was answered with, "Hello?" It was the brittle voice of an older woman.

"Mrs Harris, it's Susan from the University," Susan said.

"Oh, call me Hilda, pet," Mrs Harris said.

"Thank you. Is it still OK if I drop in to talk to you a little later?" Susan asked.

"Of course, dear. You come when you like. I've made some scones. There's too many for me anyway."

"I hope you haven't gone to a lot of trouble... Hilda. If I come over at midday, is that OK?" Susan said.

"It's no bother. I'll be here all day. 'Cept I might pop to the shops for a bit of fish later. I love a bit of fish for my tea and so does Herbert. You'll meet my little boy later. You're not allergic are you?" Hilda said.

"To cats," Susan guessed.

"To the fur."

"No. I like cats. I'll look forward to meeting you, and Herbert, at twelve," Susan said.

"Won't that be nice for us," Hilda said, though apparently not to Susan.

"See you later Hilda," Susan said.

"Righto, dear."

Susan hung up.

She had nearly completed the scanning of the collection. After making her calls, she finished running the last few documents through the planetary camera. Then she burned a CD-ROM with the entire collection on it. She slotted it into the optical drive of her iBook, before slipping the laptop into her courier bag.

Then it was time for her to leave. She caught the lift up to the surface, emerged into the bright April sunshine, and strode towards Russell Square tube station.

An hour later she was in the far west of London, walking

through Brentford, an A-to-Z in her hand.

The residential street she was walking along had a kink near its halfway point, almost as though building work had started from both ends but hadn't quite met in the middle. Susan's destination was set in the crook of the first twist.

When she found herself outside the right address, she took a moment to look up at the house. It was a large, but shabby, detached house, circa 1920s. Set in the centre of the crazy-paved front garden was a tiny oval of flowerbed. It contained healthy-looking roses with huge, floppy, pale-pink blossoms already in bloom.

Susan opened the wrought iron gate and stepped up to the front door. She pushed the buzzer and heard a distant, electronic rendition of *Green Sleeves*. A moment later a woman in her late sixties, her lacquered hair a vibrant blonde, opened the door. She wore beige slacks and a white, long-sleeved top with a tiger embroidered in sparkly gold thread on the front. Underneath the tiger was the word 'Nepal'.

"Hi, I'm Susan," Susan said.

"Oh hello dear. Did you find us alright? Come on in," Hilda said. Inside the main door, a tiny vestibule contained two more front doors. The one to the left was open, revealing walls decorated with red textured wallpaper and a room dominated by a three-piece suite in light pink.

Hilda led Susan through. "I'll pop the kettle on. Tea or instant?" Hilda asked.

"Tea please," Susan said.

Hilda had Susan sit on the large sofa by the window. Behind her, ruched, fuchsia curtains framed the view of the street. Once Susan was seated, Hilda went off to fuss in the kitchen, occasionally calling back partly audible snippets concerning the weather and the amount of litter in the street.

In a little while, the tea was made and brought through, a plate of bourbon biscuits had been placed on the teak-veneer and glass occasional-table by Susan's knee and Hilda had taken her seat by the door. A red square of cloth lay over the right arm of Hilda's chair and the reason for this soon became apparent when a chubby black cat wandered in, from the direction of the kitchen, whined once towards Susan and jumped onto the cloth. He folded himself up neatly so that his legs were tucked beneath him and then he looked towards Susan.

Hilda seemed to take this as a signal to begin and said, "Terry was a lovely man. Very quiet. Always very wrapped up in his collections but never a bit of bother to me. I shed a little tear when I heard he'd passed on. He had my upstairs room ever since Herbert, that's my husband as was and not his little namesake here, kitted it out, which must have been 1977, because the tea-towels were all silver jubilee ones," she whispered, "from the market." Then continued, "Don't you think all her pictures since then are a fright? If I was the one took that picture of her that's on the money now, I'd be waiting for my trip to The Tower. I can't see why she puts up with it," Hilda said.

Susan was about to speak when Hilda picked up the teapot, swirled it a couple of times and poured out two steaming cups of tea. Even with milk added, there was a red tinge to the brew that suggested considerable strength.

"Thanks," Susan said when she was handed her cup and saucer. The crockery was bone china with pastoral scenes in pastel colours adorning its white surfaces – mainly maids with streamers.

"Do you know what else Terry did, besides work on his collection?" Susan asked.

"I never saw him take much of an interest in anything else. I think he did other work, but not for long. He was away a great deal.

A lot of his little scraps he collected were foreign, and I don't mean nearby foreign. Proper foreign, like Africa or Nepal." She glanced down at her top. "He brought this back for me. I was always teasing him that he never got himself any sort of colour while he was away. How can you spend a month in Africa and come home pale as a bed sheet? But I don't suppose he stirred from his hotel. Somehow I can't picture him outdoors," Hilda said, looking thoughtful for a moment.

"Do you know why he kept the collection? He doesn't seem to have sold anything, so it wasn't really a business. Was it just for him?" Susan asked.

"I've never really thought about it, but he never had anyone round. So it wasn't exactly a lending library, if you know what I mean. No, it was his hobby, was what it was. There's lots worse things to collect than old paper and I reckon there's probably some valuable bits of history in there." She caught Susan's eye. "Have your lot gone over it yet?" she asked.

"Well, there's a great deal more to do, but, yes, we've spent a lot of time looking through it. It's extraordinary and we're all very grateful that you passed it on to us," Susan said.

"Well, even though Terry wouldn't be happy with a lot of strangers going through his things, I had a long think about it, and I reckon he'd have liked it even less if the whole lot went in the bin. No, it came to me that I needed to find a home for it. If it had to be strangers who got their hands on it, I like to think Terry would have preferred it to be someone who'd take good care of it and get pleasure from it like he did," Hilda said.

"So where did he keep the collection?" Susan asked. At that moment there was a thump from the room above.

Hilda heard it too and looked up towards the ceiling. She answered Susan's question absent-mindedly, while cocking her ear towards the door. "He had a big tin footlocker bolted into the wall up there. The key was with his things when the police returned his effects. All his collection was in there except…" There was another sound from upstairs, like a rusty hinge and the sound of weight being shifted. Hilda looked up at the ceiling.

"Is everything alright?" Susan asked.

"I wonder if Herbert's got himself shut in… Bless me, what am I saying, you're right here aren't you darling? I must have left a window ajar or something. I better have a look-see in case the wind's whistling through the place."

Hilda set her tea down and went in to the kitchen. She came back a moment later with a brass key on a loop of postman's string.

"I won't be a minute, dear. Help yourself to more tea," she said and opened the front door. She slipped the key into the lock of the other door in the vestibule and then Susan could hear the hollow thump, thump of footsteps as Hilda climbed stairs that must have lay just the other side of her front room wall.

Susan sipped her tea, barely wetting her tongue. She made a face and set the cup down. She could hear Hilda moving around upstairs.

Then there was a heavy thump and a sound like a gasp or a cry. Susan stood up. She called in the general direction of the door, "Is everything alright, Mrs Harris?" while her eyes roved the room.

In the brick fireplace stood an electric, flame-effect fire and by it a set of ornamental irons. Susan took the short poker, gripping it firmly in her right fist and went out the open front door.

She stepped in through the door of the other flat and began climbing the stairs, the poker held out in front of her. "Mrs Harris, do you want one of us to come up?" she called, loudly.

She heard a yelp and climbed the rest of the uncarpeted stairs quickly.

At the top of the staircase was a large room. One side held a bed, the other a writing desk and a filing cabinet. The far wall was mainly windows. On the floor in the middle of the room lay Mrs Harris struggling to get up. A figure, a man all in black, was standing just outside the window.

The figure looked towards Susan once and then ran along whatever he was standing on and dropped from sight. Before he did so, his right side was visible. He was wearing a long-sleeved black top from which most of the right sleeve was ripped. Susan could see his muscular upper arm. A large, dark blotch was spread across the olive skin of his bicep. Two smaller patches marked his forearm.

Holding the poker high, Susan rushed to the window. The house had been extended on the ground floor, but not upstairs, which left a flat roof, like a terrace, stretching five metres beyond the upstairs window.

Susan looked out, but the man had gone.

She quickly latched the window closed and ran back to where Hilda lay.

Hilda was struggling to rise and to speak, her mouth working soundlessly and a look of wild-eyed panic on her face. She didn't seem to register Susan's presence.

"Mrs Harris," Susan repeated several times, but Hilda didn't focus on her. For a moment, Susan tried to help her up, but the older woman's legs weren't solid and she tumbled back to the floor, nearly dragging Susan with her.

"Don't worry Hilda, I'll be right back," Susan said. She ran back downstairs and into the front room. A white, cordless phone sat on the table by the armchair (which Herbert had vacated). Susan grabbed it and pushed the green button to get a dialling tone. She dialled 999 and asked for an ambulance. She gave as many details as she could, guessing Hilda's age at a little short of seventy. She had no idea what her injuries might be. As she talked, she made her way upstairs again, extending the aerial of the cordless phone to maintain reception.

When she was finished with the call she hung up and laid the phone down at the top of the stairs. Taking a pillow from the bed in the corner, she put it under Hilda's head and tried to persuade her to lie back and to stop her struggling. Susan held her hand, patting it gently.

A few moments later, she released Hilda's hand and picked up the phone again. She dialled 999 once more, pushing the numbers with her thumb, and asked for the police.

It was the police who arrived first, about three minutes after her call. When she heard the doorbell, Susan released Hilda's hand and took up the poker again. She went downstairs to the outer door where she could clearly see, through the frosted glass window, two figures in uniform. She opened the door, letting the policemen in.

She led them straight upstairs.

"What happened, Miss?" asked the policeman who was crouching next to Hilda.

"We were downstairs. She came up here to investigate a noise and someone was here. I thought I heard – well I don't know what exactly – but she sounded like she was in trouble. I called out and came up. There was a man on the roof, but he disappeared a moment later," she said.

The other policeman had been examining the metal footlocker by the bed; its lid was torn nearly off its hinges. He moved over to the window, opened it and stepped out onto the roof. He began talking into his lapel mike as he peered over the edge of the gravelled, asphalt surface.

The first policeman talked soothingly to Hilda, "Don't you

worry, love. You're alright now. Don't you worry." Then to Susan he said softly, "You can probably put that poker down now." Susan was still holding it in her left hand and she let out a little sigh, almost a laugh.

"I think I hear the ambulance," she said a moment later. She went downstairs, detoured quickly to return the poker and the phone, and went out to greet the two ambulance men who were moving quickly towards the front door. She led them to Hilda and told them what little she knew.

With the upstairs room getting a little crowded, Susan returned again to Hilda's front room and retrieved the cordless phone. It had four speed-dial buttons, each with a name next to it. The first button was labelled 'Daisy'.

Susan pushed the button.

When a woman answered, Susan asked, "Excuse me, you're a friend of Hilda Harris's?"

"I'm her sister," the woman replied.

Susan told her what had happened.

Daisy's reaction was shock. She began asking Susan questions, not waiting for the answers, beginning to panic. Susan interrupted in a firm, calm voice, explaining to her what needed doing, reassuring her, and then she began to help Daisy get organised.

Susan gave Daisy her mobile number and had her write it down. Susan would travel with Hilda to the hospital, Daisy could find out what was happening by calling Susan's mobile.

Then Susan asked whether Daisy had a key to Hilda's house. She did. That meant Susan could leave the police to close up and Daisy could let herself in later, if the need arose.

Susan suggested that Daisy take a couple of minutes to calm herself and then travel to the hospital in her own time. Susan would meet her there.

Asking Daisy to hold for a second, Susan checked with the ambulance men which hospital Hilda would be taken to.

When that call was completed, Susan went through the kitchen into the bedroom, found a little valise and packed a few essentials for Hilda. She had just finished when the ambulance men started carrying Hilda down on a stretcher.

Susan took a piece of notepaper from her bag and wrote her contact details on it. Then she gathered up her coat and bag. Once the stretcher had passed the door, the policemen came down. Susan explained to them that she was going with Hilda, gave them the piece of paper listing her details and asked them to pull the door closed once they were done.

Then she flatly refused when the ambulance men told her she should get a taxi. Reluctantly, they let her ride in the front of the ambulance with the driver, while Hilda and the other ambulance man rode in the back.

"Herbert," Susan said, suddenly, remembering. She pulled out a pen and wrote the name on her hand.

CHAPTER 8

Susan Milton was late. David looked at his wristwatch again – 16.49. He paced very slowly round the Diplodocus.

"David Braun?" a soft, female American voice said. There was a little Southern in it and a little East Coast.

David turned to see a pretty girl in dark jeans and a white cotton blouse, clutching a bag and a raincoat and wearing a worried expression.

"Ms Milton?" David said. "Actually, it's Doctor Milton, isn't it?"

Susan didn't answer him directly. She dragged the strap of her bag further up her shoulder and stuck out her hand. They shook and Susan said, "OK. In no special order: I'm really sorry I kept you waiting. Two: call me Susan. And three: I've had an unbelievable bitch of a day, excuse me for saying it, so you might have to go easy on me."

David ticked the points off on his fingers, "No problem. Hi,

93

Susan. And I'm sorry to hear that." He smiled. "Let's get to the café before it closes so at least you can sit down," David said. He led the way and Susan followed.

They entered the cafeteria, which was mostly deserted. David put his folio case down on a chair and gestured for Susan to sit.

"Normally people get dinner for agreeing to talk to me about work. Let me at least fetch you some coffee while you catch your breath," David said. Susan nodded with a weak smile on her face.

As he turned to go she called, "Can you get me a sandwich? I'm famished."

"Absolutely," he said and walked over to pick up a tray and join the queue.

David was the last person in the line. He paid for coffee and several packs of sandwiches and brought them back to the table.

While he'd been queuing, David had glanced over at Susan a couple of times and seen her hunched over, running her fingers through her hair, her head low. As he finished paying, he saw her take a deep breath, and compose herself. She pulled her shoulders back and her chin came up.

He returned to the table and set the tray down. "I don't know what you like so I got tuna, cheese and pickle or ham salad. Help yourself and I'll eat whatever you don't fancy." He passed her over a cup of coffee and spread the sandwiches out in front of her. She immediately went for the coffee.

He said, "Listen, I must apologise; I'm a bit slow on the uptake sometimes. You told me you've had a disastrous day; would you like to do this another time?" Susan was just peeling back the plastic on the tuna sandwich and she looked up. David laughed, "You can have the sandwich either way."

"Just try taking it back," she said, biting a big chunk out of it. She chewed for a minute. "No, I'm OK. I'm a bit wrung out, but that's all. Let's just say today could have been a lot worse for me."

David held her gaze for a moment, gauging her sincerity about continuing, and then nodded. "Well let me tell you what I need help with and perhaps you can tell me whether it's in your area of expertise and if you might be interested."

Susan was busy munching but she nodded enthusiastically, twirling one finger, signalling for David to keep going.

"OK," he said. "I work for what you might call an up-market insurance company. Most of our clients tend to be wealthy individuals or families. It's my job to make sure everything goes smoothly whenever they want something or they need to make a claim. I do all the running around and the form-filling and even things like talking to the police, a lot of the time.

"Earlier this week, one of our clients had a break-in at their offices. It was quite elaborately planned. Whoever was in charge made it look like they were after money in the main safe, but what they really wanted was something rare and valuable in the Chairman's personal safe.

"That's where you come in. If someone stole some eighteenth century silver I'd have a fair idea which dealers to talk to because I've had a little experience with that sort of thing. I know something about the way these things get passed on and sold. With this piece, I don't know where to start, so I need some help."

Susan swallowed her last mouthful of tuna sandwich and reached for the cheese and pickle while saying, "I thought that was police work, not insurance work."

"Well, if we're lucky, it's both. The police investigate, we poke about a bit, everything gets shared and hopefully something good happens. Obviously an investigation like that goes a lot faster if the policemen involved are experts on, say, eighteenth century silver

– but there aren't many of those. But, yes, a lot of times we'll just leave it to them. In this case, there are several reasons why we want to do all we can, not least of which is that the client has asked us to. His firm have been paying for our services for over a century; it would be good if it wasn't me who let the side down." David smiled.

"So what's been *pinched*?" she asked, playfully.

He gave her a sarcastic smile and said, "Oh yes, the Dick Van Dyke school of Cockney English. Very good." She nodded as though taking a bow and got stuck into another sandwich.

"Well I don't have very much. It's a leather and bone box containing a piece of ancient platinum jewellery. Like a piece of filigree. I can draw you a rough sketch based on a fairly rough sketch I was shown," he said, pulling his notepad out of his folio case and starting to draw.

"I thought platinum was a modern thing, like aloom…" she paused. "Alum*in*ium," she said carefully.

"Well, not so, apparently. According to my client, the Egyptians and the Aztecs both made platinum jewellery. Or it may have been Mayans," he said, unsure.

"I'm guessing Incas, actually," Susan suggested. "Point is, people who lived a long time ago. So is this Egyptian or South American?" she asked.

David had finished sketching. "Apparently Chinese, although I don't know from where exactly." He turned the pad round and slid it towards Susan. "Not exactly Michelangelo, but…" He broke off when he saw Susan's expression. "What is it?" he asked.

Susan was trying to open her bag and in her haste failing to unclip the catch. "Hold on," she said, getting the bag open, pulling out her iBook and flipping up the screen. She turned on the power. "When you say Chinese, might you maybe mean Tibetan?" she asked. The iBook was coming to life.

"Well, all I have is China and the fact that there are supposedly legends told about it there. You being an expert in legends and mythology…" he trailed off.

She was clicking on things. "Sorry, won't be a minute," she said. And then said triumphantly, "Yeah, there *are* legends about it and here's one of them." She rotated the laptop around so that David could see the screen. The image displayed was a piece of paper containing a lot of hand-written text, in the roman alphabet, and a sketch that looked not unlike the one on David's notepad.

"Damn, you're good," said David. "So what is it?"

"You don't understand," Susan said, "I was reading *this*," she tapped the screen, "this morning. And then this afternoon you ask me to identify it. How spooky is that?"

David didn't say anything for a moment, just raised his eyebrows. Susan on the other hand had a very curious expression on her face. She suddenly leaned forwards and looked David in the eye.

"Let me tell you what was so awful about my day," she said earnestly.

"OK," David said, stretching the word out in his uncertainty.

"I'm based in Cambridge, normally, but I've come down to London because of a big find. The School of Antiquities inherited a private collection of documents when its owner died a few months ago. It's full of the most remarkable documents, so I went to have a chat with the woman who donated it: the landlady of the collection's owner."

She continued, "The owner was always going off on trips to acquire new documents, only one time he didn't come back. I visited his landlady this morning to see what she knew about the collection or its owner. While I was there," her voice gained emphasis, "someone broke in and attacked her. I've just come from the hospital where they took her. She's in pretty bad shape, internal bruising like she was beaten with something. The guy who attacked her had broken open the box where the collection used to be kept." She tapped the screen again, "Where this document used to be. The one that describes your stolen antique. How's that for a coincidence? Whoever was after the antique might also be after the paperwork about it."

They both thought for a moment. "How did the owner of the collection die?" David asked meaningfully.

"I think the word the police used was 'unexplained'." She too had a question. "Was there any violence in your break-in?" she asked.

"Plenty," David said. "What's the opposite of pacifist? Two people dead apparently just to help misdirect the police."

They paused again, both thinking.

"So where's the collection now?" David asked.

"Safely locked up at the School of Antiquities," Susan said, though the sentence tapered off in its confidence level towards the end.

David lifted an eyebrow, "Well, I think you should have a talk to DI Hammond of the Serious Crime Squad and tell him what you've told me." David began looking for Hammond's details. "I think it would make a lot of sense if that collection had some extra security." He took a moment to copy the details out and then tore the page from his pad.

He said, "I'll call him too, to let him know what's going on." Then his features fell and he said, "My god, I'm sorry. I've just realised, you mean you were right there when it happened?"

Susan said, "Yeah, pretty much. The old lady went upstairs to see what the noise was and I heard something and got worried.

I called up and said something about there being a bunch of us. When I got to the top of the stairs someone was climbing out the window."

"Are *you* OK, though?" David asked.

"Listen, I did volunteer work in New York City for a year. I've seen a lot worse than the back end of a mugger. It's just sitting with that poor old lady… It took about twenty seconds for her to go from someone who was on top of the world, to a frail old woman who they were saying… who the doctors think might not recover." She sounded quite choked up as she said this last. But then it slid away and Susan was collected once again.

David asked, "Why didn't you just call me and cancel? In fact, just not turn up. I could hardly have blamed you."

"That's not really how I work," she said. "God, if I fold up when I don't have a scratch on me, how would I cope with a real emergency?" she asked. David looked impressed.

"Pardon the cliché, but let's hope you don't have to find out the answer to that question," David said. His eyes wandered, in search of something to gaze at besides the distress on Susan's face. He found himself looking at the screen of her laptop. He stared more carefully at the image it showed.

He said, "Listen, let's swap roles. I'll be in charge of close shaves and you can handle the research. Like this for instance," he indicated the text on the screen, "can you read it?"

"Sure," Susan said, "it's in Latin and supposedly a translation from Tibetan. That's what it says at the bottom, anyway."

Susan's voice was back to normal now.

She said, "It's a story about a Magic Marker." She gave a little laugh, as though realising what she was saying as she said it. David looked blank. "Sorry, American humour. A Magic Marker is a big, thick kind of pen in the States. It's like you guys say Biro or

Sellotape. Anyway, this Marker, in the story, is magic in that it attracts the attention of the gods. They get fascinated by the pattern. The idea is that you place it on a sick person and if a god happens to notice the Marker he might heal them."

"It's like a divine medic alert bracelet?" David said, a little flippantly.

"Well, it's not a bracelet, but yes, basically," Susan said. She got a far-off look in her eyes which David noticed.

"What?" he asked, gently.

"You just made me think of something. It's really crazy, but it's just such a weird coincidence. No, forget it," she said.

"What?" David asked again, encouragingly.

"When I told you about doing volunteer work it got me thinking about some of the homeless people we'd see. Listen, I'm not saying this is true, it's just a thought, but this guy who attacked the little old lady, I got a look at him. She tore his sleeve and I saw these funny marks on his arm," she said.

"Like tattoos?" David asked.

Susan shook her head. "Not tattoos. They reminded me of something a couple of the addicts at our shelter had. Do you know what Kaposi's Sarcoma is?" she said.

David said, "That's something to do with AIDS, isn't it?"

"Yeah, it's a kind of skin cancer that used to be pretty rare before AIDS came along. You generally only get it if your immune system is shot."

After a pause she went on, "I mean it just occurred to me reading this." She nodded towards the laptop. "You said this guy is really violent. Well I watched him jump off a roof. One of the quickest ways to get AIDS is to be a serious drug-user. It fits with violent, it fits with reckless behaviour like jumping off a roof. He might even be on something that makes him aggressive and stops him feeling pain, like PCP."

David added, "It looks like he jumped out of a thirty-foot high window to escape after the break-in."

"Right. So that fits," she said.

"So he's a drug-user," David concluded.

"Maybe. But I was getting at something else. What if he's a violent junkie and he's pretty sick? If he's on something powerful enough to make him imagine he's Batman he might be thinking some pretty strange things," she said. She seemed reluctant to go on.

"And..." David said, gently coaxing.

"What if he doesn't want this thing in order to sell it? What if he actually believes it will cure him?" she asked.

They both considered that question for a few moments. David didn't look convinced, but neither of them said anything.

The conversation then turned to more practical matters. It was obvious that Susan should be involved in David's investigation; they didn't even bother to debate it. David explained the sorts of things he needed and what his company would pay.

Susan agreed to put her work on the Medic Marker (as they called it) at the top of her list – which it pretty much had been anyway, even before the day's events.

"When can we get together again?" David asked.

"Well, I need a couple of days. How about Tuesday?" she said.

"Fine by me. What's a good time?" David said.

"Well I tend to finish work around six..." Susan said thoughtfully.

David looked slightly surprised, "Oh. OK, we can meet in the evening if that's easier."

"No, I just meant... I was just thinking out loud. I mean unless...

It would probably be easier, actually. But maybe you don't usually work in the evenings?" she said.

"If only. Listen, my pal Kieran got a three-course meal out of me and all he did was spend two minutes calling your friend Bernie. On that scale you certainly deserve more than a sandwich." He glanced down at the empty wrappers. "A measly three sandwiches."

"I hadn't eaten all day," she said, coyly.

"OK. How about," he thought for a minute, "Villandry on Great Portland Street, seven thirty on Tuesday. Paid for by the company, of course. Including taxis." He jotted himself a note about reservations.

"Sure," Susan said, perhaps a little uncertain.

"And do call Hammond. Lots of people must know where that collection is by now. If someone's looking for it…" David said, seriously.

Susan nodded. "Don't worry, I'm not likely to forget."

They packed up their things and began wandering towards the exit. It was just a few minutes before closing time.

"Next time I'm going to have a look round," Susan said as they left.

They walked out of the main entrance towards the tube station, David asking about Susan's research work and how she was finding London.

Still chatting, they made their way down into the tube station and through the barriers. It turned out they were getting on different lines.

"Tuesday evening," Susan called stepping onto her escalator.

David waved, "See you then," he said. He stood for a moment watching her back before turning and heading towards the other set of escalators.

CHAPTER 9

Four days later
Monday 14th April

David sat in Reg Cottrell's office discussing the Interfinanzio account.

Reg said, "So you've met their Chairman." It had the tenor of a leading question.

David looked at Reg's face, gauging his meaning, and said, "He's got quite a presence, hasn't he?"

"Presence, quite so. Presence is a good way of putting it. Perhaps I should have said something beforehand," Reg considered this for a moment. "How did the interview go?"

David said, "Well I won't pretend I wasn't rattled by him, but we seemed to get on well enough. He was very keen for us to get involved. He wants us to investigate, to supplement what the police are doing. Actually, to be honest, he seemed to be saying he wanted us to retrieve the missing item and bugger the police."

Reg looked a little taken aback.

David said, "Perhaps I could have phrased it better, but that's the gist of it. That and implying that Marshall & Liberty would be bankrupted if it came to making a claim."

Reg nodded seriously, "There's a very real chance of that, unless we could work something out on the valuation. Times are a little tougher for our sector than when that policy was drafted." Reg went on, "At any rate, the ball's in your court. How do you think you'll play it?"

"Well, I was hoping for some guidance from the partners," David said cautiously. "If I do too little, I'm jeopardising not only one of our best accounts, it seems like I'm risking financial ruin for the company. If I push as hard as Mr Dass wants me to, I'd say I run a good chance of getting on the wrong side of the police, which won't do us any good. We rely on a good relationship with the police and we don't want the bad PR – both of which could be a problem depending on how much trouble I get myself into."

Reg looked rather uncomfortable as he considered his words. "As I say, it's your decision, and it's a tricky one. But bear in mind that Alessandro Dass is quite a heavyweight – he's been known to pull quite a few strings in his time. He's certainly not a fellow you would want to let down. And by the same token, whatever meets with his approval will go over pretty well in other quarters too – he'll see to that. I doubt the police would get their knickers in a twist over something that suited Dass and his associates, not unless some gross impropriety were involved."

David considered this, "Reg, perhaps I'm being a little slow to get the message, so I hope you'll forgive me for being dogged, but why isn't one of the partners handling this?"

Reg looked even more awkward. "I don't know, er, how much more there is to discuss here. Let's just say that the partners believe you show a great deal of promise. This is really your chance to show us what you're capable of, without someone looking over your shoulder. You're being given a free hand and I'm sure you can imagine how grateful the firm will be if you're able to bring matters to a satisfactory conclusion."

David nodded slowly, an expression of weary comprehension on his face, "That's what I thought: a chance to shine and no one looking over my shoulder. So I'll get all the credit if it goes well. And if it all goes pear-shaped…"

Reg said briskly, "Well let's not dwell on that. I think you've got a good grasp of what we're dealing with here."

"I think so," David said, and added significantly, "Thanks for putting me in the picture."

Reg didn't meet his eye, but busied himself flicking through some papers on his desk, making a show of looking for something.

"Well that's marvellous then," Reg said. "Let me know if I can help with anything else."

David stood and made his way to the door. Reg was still avoiding his gaze, scrutinising a page in his desk diary. "See you later," David said.

"Cheerio," Reg replied. "All the best."

* * *

"Hi, I've got an appointment with DI Hammond," David told the constable on the desk.

"Won't be a minute, sir," the constable said, picking up a phone. He consulted a tatty, photocopied phone directory and dialled a number. There was a brief conversation that David couldn't hear.

"Come through please," the constable said, pointing to a door in the corner of the reception area. He pushed a button beneath the counter and held it down. The door lock buzzed loudly, indicating that the lock was disengaged. Once David had passed through, the constable released the button and the buzzing stopped.

The policeman peered around a nearby doorway, "I'd take you up, but I'm on my own here. Just go to the second floor and turn left. The DI's office is the first one you reach."

"Thanks," David said and started up the stairs. He found Hammond's office easily enough and knocked on the cheap, veneered-plywood door.

"Come," a voice called.

David opened the door and stepped into a small office. Directly ahead was a single desk, behind which George Hammond sat. The room also contained a filing cabinet and a small table. Opposite the door was a dusty window through which David could see a lime-scaled drainpipe and a section of brick wall. Scattered about the office were lots of papers, some loose, others in folders.

"Mr Braun," Hammond said, by way of greeting.

"Detective Inspector," David replied.

Hammond wore his default half-scowl. He nodded towards the room's one empty chair. David sat.

Hammond spoke first, "So, your client has connections."

David said, "He told me he was going to make some calls. Is that what you mean?"

"Yes, that's what I mean," Hammond said, rather nastily. David was unfazed.

"So do you want to go first or shall I?" David asked.

Hammond merely frowned.

Seeing that he wasn't going to get a proper reply, David said pleasantly, "OK I'll go first, but before I do, can you tell me if it's me you're pissed off with or my client?"

Hammond continued to scowl.

David said nothing.

"Alright, get on with it then," Hammond said in a tone that might have been his gruff version of conciliatory.

Adept

"Fair enough. You got my message about Susan Milton, I hope. Has she called you?" David asked.

Hammond nodded.

"She's an academic historian. She's tracked down some copies of old documents describing the piece that was stolen from the Chairman's safe by the third member of the gang. If you've spoken to her then you know that someone has come looking for those documents."

Hammond still volunteered nothing.

David continued, "Dr Milton is going to be finding out what she can about the piece and, if we're lucky, a little about dealers we should talk to. I'm happy to let you have whatever we find out before taking any action." He added, "I'd also be happy to talk to a few people myself."

"You'll do no such thing," snapped Hammond.

David's temper flared, "Oh grow up, Hammond. I just said it was your choice."

Hammond looked furious and leaned angrily forwards, planting his fists on the desk, ready to lever himself to his feet.

David didn't blink. He said, a little more calmly but with equal force, "I'm sorry if someone's put pressure on you to involve me in your investigation. It wasn't my idea and I didn't want it. But don't go in the opposite direction just to be stubborn. When I speak to Mr Dass, I won't pretend you're being helpful if you're not. He could get me fired with one phone call. If he asks me how it's going, I'll tell him the truth. If you choose to make an enemy out of Dass, you're on your own."

Hammond glared at David for a few more seconds, his weight still on his hands as though he were about to jump to his feet. David didn't waver.

After a pause, Hammond asked, all irritation having vanished from his voice, "You ever think of joining the force?"

David surreptitiously let his breath out. He shook his head in answer to Hammond's question, "There's exams and so forth. Plus I'm not that good with people."

Hammond laughed loudly, tipping his head back. "Cocky little shit," he said agreeably.

Hammond was clearly amused, though there was no smile, just a little scrunching of the skin around his eyes. It faded and he said, "Don't do anything else like you did the other night or we really will fall out. Clear?"

"Yes," David said levelly. "I won't get in your way."

"Then we'll get along fine."

Hammond turned his attention to the piles of paperwork on his desk. He rummaged around until he found a particular file. He took a moment to gather and stack several dozen others that littered his desk. Then he moved them to one side and laid the first one open in the space he'd cleared.

"We had a result with forensics," Hammond said, scanning the top page in the folder.

While Hammond's eyes were focused on the report, David stole a quick glance too, reading upside-down. He looked back up again before Hammond noticed.

"The glass in the car park *does* match the office window. Which means the tyre tracks were very likely our suspect's – given that they were fresh and they went over the splinter of window glass. You want to guess what the getaway car was?" he asked David.

"A big old Jag?" David offered.

Hammond snorted. "A…" he looked down again at the report and read aloud, "new Porsche 911 Turbo. That's a ninety grand car, so even in London there aren't that many of them. We're still working through the list of owners, but we've already found one registered to someone who died in 1996. Our guess is that a car like that gets stopped all the time, so unless the real owner wants our lot following him everywhere he most likely keeps it properly insured. Which means even if the name's a dud, the address is probably something to do with him – he needs to be able to get his post. Anyway, there's no one at home, so we've got it staked out in case he comes back. That do you?"

"That's all good news. What about the two men who died in the break-in?" David asked.

"Right. One worked in that office. He's the one who would have known where the safe was and what was in it. The other was an old lag. Been inside twice for taking what didn't belong to him. He's the safe-cracker – though it looks like they didn't need him for the Chairman's safe. The insider must have had the combination," Hammond said.

"But they didn't really kill each other, surely?" David said.

Hammond shook his head. "It was nicely staged. There's a couple of little hiccups, though. First I'll tell you what we were *supposed* to think, OK?" Hammond pulled his sleeves up a bit. "There's a falling out – maybe because the Bizzies have turned up – and the safe-cracker stabs the inside-man with his screwdriver. The insider pulls a gun and fires two shots – one goes out the window and the safe-cracker bangs himself up getting out of the way of it. But the second shot gets him through the heart. Then the inside-man expires a few moments afterwards.

"Now, what we think *really* happened is that the third man stabbed the insider with the safe-cracker's screwdriver – he's got gloves, so only the safe-cracker's fingerprints are on it. The cracker pulls a gun, realising he's next, but misses the third man and hits the window. The third man clobbers the cracker with something, doing enough damage that he's incapacitated. Then he puts the gun in the dead man's hand and pulls the trigger for him, killing the cracker. Then he's off out the window," Hammond concluded.

"Any idea why he didn't break his neck jumping that far?" David asked.

"We're still working on it. In fact we've got a little sweepstake going within the department. We've had all sorts of suggestions." He glanced at a list, "That car park opposite is five floors high with a hand-rail at the top; hook a rope over that rail and you could swing across. Someone else thought maybe he was a pole-vaulter. Don't know about that one. Someone else thought he chucked an inflatable mattress down there, jumped onto it, then slit it open and took it with him. They're all a bit barmy, but most of them might actually work. We reckon he got lucky with that first bullet missing him, but chances are he was wearing some Kevlar."

Hammond closed the folder and stood up. "That's going to have to do you. I've got to be somewhere else."

David said, "I appreciate it. I'll get out of your way."

Hammond asked, "So are we square? You're happy? Not going to tell your boss on me?"

"There's nothing to tell him, except what a good job you're doing. Speak to you soon," David said, politely.

Hammond just waved a hand in a gesture that could be interpreted either as dismissal or a wave. David left.

He hurried downstairs, out through the security door and back out into the street. As soon as he was clear of the police station he pulled out a pad and wrote down an address. It was the address that had been visible, albeit upside-down, on the top-most piece of paper in Hammond's file.

* * *

That evening, David was heading home after training. He'd hung around afterwards for a quick drink in the nearby pub. It looked like everyone else was going to be there until closing time, but David excused himself just after ten and began the drive homeward.

Behind the passenger seat of his car, tucked out of sight, sat his folio case. As he drove, he reached over, steering one-handed, and retrieved it. He laid it on the passenger seat.

His gaze kept returning to it.

At the next red light he reached over, unzipped the case, and pulled out his notepad. Nearby streetlamps gave just enough light to read by. Several pages in he found the address he'd copied from Hammond's report. It was an address in Notting Hill.

He tapped the steering wheel, waiting for the light to change, glancing occasionally at the pad.

As the lights turned green, he glanced both ways – the street was clear – and made a u-turn. He headed west.

Traffic was light. He dropped down to the Euston Road, was swept along with the flow westward. Dropping a little further south, he reached the Westway.

Once he was roughly in the right area he turned off the main road, pulled in and fetched a map from the glove box. One finger wedged into the map book, marking his destination, he wound his way towards it, driving slowly.

The house he was looking for sat on the corner where a quiet side road joined a slightly larger residential street.

He approached the property, driving along the larger road, his eyes scanning ahead, looking for the corner.

He caught sight of it and began to indicate left. Just before he reached the turn he noticed a dark blue Mondeo with two men sitting in the front seats. Two pairs of eyes in synchrony tracked his approach. "Subtle," he muttered to himself.

He avoided looking directly at his observers and turned smoothly into the side street. Cars lined both sides of the road and there were few opportunities to pull in. Twenty metres from the corner, one or two parking places remained unoccupied. He ignored the first couple, only pulling in when he was a hundred metres from the corner.

He turned off the engine and the lights and sat there unmoving. He adjusted his mirror so that he could see the street behind him. All was quiet. It was getting on for eleven in a very smart residential area and there seemed to be little activity – certainly nothing untoward.

For a couple of minutes David sat waiting. Occasionally he glanced in the mirror, though there was nothing to see.

After a little over five minutes he shook his head, as though disappointed with his own foolishness, and started the engine. He tapped the wheel thoughtfully for another few seconds as the engine silently idled and then he reached to turn the headlights on.

He paused before completing the motion; a car was coming towards him down the little side street, heading towards the corner and its lights were off.

Instinctively he ducked down, laying flat on the passenger seat. A powerful engine burbled slowly past his door, moving almost at a walking pace.

He could hear the deep chuckle of the engine grow quieter, more distant. Moving just his fingers, he pushed the button to lower his window a few centimetres and strained to hear. The engine sound was still there. It sounded like it was idling.

He slowly raised himself to an upright position. The headrests on his front seats helped to hide him from view. He looked in the mirror.

A low, black Porsche was pulling into a double parking space twenty metres behind him. He turned off his car's engine.

Very slowly he lowered his head again, leaning over the passenger seat. The left-hand wing mirror was adjustable and he moved it until he could see back along the pavement from his ducked-down position.

A man, dressed all in black, appeared a moment later from behind the Porsche. He crossed the pavement swiftly and flattened himself against the wall. Overhanging branches created little pockets of gloom into which his dark shape blended. He was only visible if one knew where to look.

The figure raised a hand, pointed towards the car, and a set of keys momentarily caught the light. But the indicators on the Porsche didn't flash; there was no chirp from the alarm system.

The figure lowered the hand again and the keys went into a jacket pocket and were zipped up.

"Changed your mind," David whispered to himself.

Moving stealthily, the figure crept towards the corner, getting further away from David. His dark outline became even more indistinct as he moved deeper into the shadows.

The front door of the corner property lay in the next road, where the policemen waited. From David's vantage point, all that could be seen was the side of the house and a high garden wall.

The figure drew level with the far end of the garden wall. The corner property was sufficiently large that he was still thirty metres from the corner and comfortably out of sight of the policemen.

The man took two quick steps and jumped the wall, placing one hand on the top of it as he vaulted over. He made it look simple and fluid enough but it was a strange motion nonetheless because the wall stood a metre taller than he did.

David continued to watch. A full minute went by. Then he

reached up and changed the setting on the interior light of his car so that it wouldn't come on when he opened the door. He also pulled a cleaning cloth out of the driver's side door compartment.

He opened his car door and got out slowly. He pushed the door closed gently with the palm of his hand. It didn't shut completely, but he left it that way.

Keeping to a crouch, he made his way to the side of the Porsche and peered in. The passenger seat contained a briefcase. With the cloth covering his hand, David gripped the door handle. He looked up and down the street and then, seeing no one around, tried the door.

It was unlocked.

David leaned in and, still using the cloth, flicked the catches on the briefcase. He raised the lid and looked inside. It was full of loose papers.

Grabbing a handful, David began to rapidly flick through them. It was difficult to make out what they were in the dim light. As with David's car, the interior light in the Porsche had been turned off.

Several papers were bills. Another was written in some language other than English. He found a piece of paper printed on headed notepaper and held it up, angling the paper to catch the light from the streetlamp.

It was from a letting agency. It appeared to be a rental agreement for an apartment. David read the address.

A dog barked and elsewhere a door slammed, almost simultaneously. It sounded like it came from the direction of the corner property. Quickly David pulled his head out of the car and scanned the street. Nothing.

He dropped the documents back in the case, closed the lid and snapped the catches down. Then he pushed the door closed, quietly, but firmly, using the flat of his hand still wrapped in the cloth.

He walked, half-crouched, back to his car. Moving around to the driver's side, he opened the door, but didn't get in. He gave the ignition key a single twist and the warm engine caught immediately, making hardly a sound.

He left the driver's door wide open, sticking out into the street and walked to the car behind him. He placed his cloth-covered hand on the wing of the Mercedes and pushed down hard. The car bounced on its springs. He did it again even harder and this time the alarm shrieked into life, destroying the silence. Lights flashed.

David ran back to his car, jumped in and, as quickly as he could, pulled out of his parking space. He sounded his horn and kept it blaring as he drove rapidly up the street.

A light came on in a nearby house.

He drove rapidly, horn still sounding, until he reached a bend in the road fifty metres on. Releasing the horn, he turned on his headlights and dropped down to the speed limit.

From there he headed home. He found he was driving like someone over the limit – too cautious, geriatrically legal.

CHAPTER 10

This time Susan was early.

The restaurant was also a delicatessen and Susan wandered among the bottles, tins and boxes, peering at anything which caught her interest.

Her navy suit gave her a business-like appearance, without seeming severe. The faded-pink silk blouse she wore underneath was sleeveless with a deep v-neck, giving her the option of a much softer look if she chose at some later point to shed the jacket.

Her straight blonde hair was down and it had picked up a slight wave since the previous week. Her skin had the healthy bloom of someone with no use for cosmetics – an effect that had taken her quite a while to create.

She happened to glance up as David entered the restaurant. He was wearing a charcoal suit with a midnight-blue shirt and tie. His short, dark hair was spiked a little and he looked freshly scrubbed and shaved.

"Hi," said Susan smiling.

"Hi," said David. "You look…" he paused as though remembering something, "very well. How are you?"

"I'm great." She looked around. "This is a lovely place."

"Well, the food's usually good, although I'm not exactly a restaurant expert. I don't really eat out that much," David said.

"Me neither, unless you count a muffin in Starbucks," Susan said.

David glanced towards the restaurant area.

"Let's see if they've lost my reservation," he said conspiratorially, leading the way.

The restaurant area was invitingly dim. Glowing lamps set on pillars throughout the room gave the impression of candlelight. The outside wall was floor-to-ceiling glass, looking out onto the smart town houses opposite and the night beyond.

A waitress seated them right in the centre of the room.

After a quick discussion, they agreed to share a bottle of Chablis. They both contemplated their menus for a moment.

Susan was the first to mention work. "I spoke to Mr Hammond. I don't get the impression he's going to do much, though. He apparently called security at the School and made some suggestions to them. There's now some sixty-year-old guy in what looked to me like a UPS uniform sitting by the elevator. What that's supposed to do if our evil junkie mastermind turns up I don't know. Fortunately, we're all the way down in the lowest basement. He'd have to get past the front desk and then find his way down a couple of floors before he'd reach the Senior Citizen on Patrol, so we should be OK." She gave an ironic smile.

A waiter brought the wine, which David nodded at rather than tasted. Their glasses were being filled as David said, "I'm sorry Hammond wasn't much help. I think he might be my old maths teacher reincarnated. He seems to be either miserable or angry depending on what sort of day he's having."

He added, "Hammond and I nearly had a falling out when I went to see him yesterday. My client had pulled some strings and done the worst possible thing in Hammond's eyes: put him in a position where he has to be helpful. I can see it's causing him real pain. I should say though, that he's probably a pretty good copper, aside from his personality."

They sipped their wine.

"Listen I was thinking about my junkie theory," Susan said, but just then the waiter returned to take their order.

They chose, Susan having soup then fish and David opting for bruschetta followed by a steak.

"Junkies," David said, prompting Susan, when the waiter had gone.

"Yeah. I don't like the idea any more," Susan said.

"Because?" David asked.

She narrowed her eyes at him. "I think you already know," she said suspiciously.

David offered, "Because he's organised, disciplined and a meticulous planner. It doesn't sound like an intravenous drug user losing touch with reality. Plus, physically he's the most amazing gymnast I've ever seen."

"You've seen him?" Susan said, surprised.

"Well, I…" For a moment David seemed about to backtrack, but he didn't. He looked awkward, sucked air through his teeth and admitted, "Yeah, I saw him last night."

Susan's mood, which had been warming as they talked, now chilled by several degrees. "What did you do?" she asked, scrutinising him.

"It was just coincidence," he said. "I drove past the address

Hammond thinks he lives at. The Old Bill have a couple of men outside waiting for him. I just thought I'd drive by; I don't know why."

"And you saw him? He was there?" she said. She didn't sound impressed.

"Well, someone was there. The car matches the one Hammond's looking for. I saw him sneak into the garden of the house. The coppers at the front wouldn't have been any the wiser so I made a bit of a racket and set off a car alarm. If they came to investigate they would have seen his Porsche. If they didn't... well what else could I do? I couldn't go and tap on their window. At least this way they would have stood a chance of catching him," he said, somewhat on the defensive.

"Why on earth would you..." Susan began, incredulous.

Then an angry look of comprehension crossed her face. She pointed at David. "Your client didn't ask you to investigate this theft at all, did he? This is some sort of macho fantasy you're acting out," she said, accusingly. Her voice was getting louder.

"Hey, calm down," he said, in hushed tones. "I am acting on the express wishes of my client and with the approval of my company. If it hadn't been for the most incredible coincidence, our villain would have had a chance to pick up his things, the police would have been none the wiser and my evening would have involved a quick look at the outside of his house, nothing more. What did I do that was so wrong?" he asked.

"Nothing that Rambo would have considered over the top," she said a little more calmly, but she was only half-joking.

"I might be wrong," David said, "but I don't have the impression you always do what you're told. When the old lady was attacked you went upstairs unarmed, didn't you?"

"I had a poker," Susan said quietly. David laughed, humourlessly, and nodded.

Susan spoke softly, but her intensity hadn't lessened when she said, "I was trying to help someone I thought was in trouble. I wasn't barging into the middle of a police investigation just because there was nothing to watch on TV."

They were both getting a little heated. David looked like he was going to make some piqued response when a beaming waiter asked in generic Mediterranean, "Oo is 'aving ze bruschetta?" This last was pronounced with an indulgent flourish.

"Thanks," David said.

Susan was served with her soup a minute later.

Neither touched their food for a moment, then they both reached for their wine simultaneously.

David took a breath and let it out. "You're right – it wasn't my job to get involved, but for some reason I did."

He went on, before she could say anything, "Did I tell you that the police thought there were two men involved in the break-in? That's how it would have stayed except I poked around and proved there were three. It was wrong of me; I'm a bad person. But everyone is better off because of the evidence I found. We wouldn't have even known about the Porsche and the house in Notting Hill otherwise. We'd have nothing.

"And last night, he would have come and gone – picked up his things and vanished without a trace. Again, because I broke the rules and poked my nose in, I have a pretty good idea where he's going next." His voice was level but with a hint of urgency that suggested he really wanted Susan to understand. "And I'm not saying this to be antagonistic, but it's not your job to tell me off about this, is it? But you're getting involved too, you're taking it personally."

Susan said nothing but looked somewhat mollified. They began to eat their food.

After several seconds, the beginnings of a twinkle returned to Susan's eyes. "So you know where he's going, Sherlock?" she asked.

"I thought I was Rambo," he reminded her.

"The jury's still out." She paused and then said, "I'm sorry if I got high and mighty with you. You're right, it's not my job to tell you off."

David gave a smile of relief, his shoulders relaxing, "If you hate apologising as much as I hate asking for someone else's approval then I think we're even."

"So you wanted to tell me to butt out just now?" she asked, teasingly.

"You didn't deserve it, but that's what I'd normally do. I'm not good at teams," he said. "So do you want to know what I know?"

"I'm not going to beg," she said, pretending to be angry.

"OK. While he was inside I had a look in his car," David said. Susan's eyes went wide.

David held up a hand, "Don't crucify me until you've learned all my secrets; your curiosity will never forgive you." He took a sip of wine to wet his lips. "He left his car unlocked and I found a briefcase full of papers. One of them was about renting an apartment near the City."

Susan looked troubled, "Our mastermind can't remember to lock his car?"

"I think he thought about it. I reckon he's got one of those irritating alarm systems that gives a little *bip bip* to let you know it's armed. When you've paid ninety grand for a car, it's important everyone looks round when you get out of it. One of the many reasons rare sports cars make bad getaway vehicles," David said.

"So you found an address?" Susan asked.

"Yes, it's just off the Great Eastern Road, down from Old Street," David said.

"What are you going to do with it? The address?" Susan asked. It was clearly a leading question. She wasn't giving him a hard time, but neither had she let him off the hook yet.

"Well, I think it will depend on whether they caught him last night. If we're lucky, it might all be done and dusted by now. He might be behind bars," David said.

"You don't sound convinced," Susan said.

"You should have seen this guy. He hopped over a wall that must have been nine foot high. I've never seen anything like it and I've seen a lot of amazing things," David said.

"Maybe he's some sort of martial arts guru," Susan suggested.

"Believe me, I know a few people who fit that description and none of them can do what he did," David said.

"Really? You've got an interesting circle of friends," Susan said, raising an eyebrow.

David shrugged.

Susan reached over and took David's arm, holding his wrist through his jacket. He didn't resist. She turned his hand over and inspected his knuckles. The first two had a glossy callous, almost like wax, covering them.

"You must train pretty hard to get knuckles like that," she said, releasing his arm.

He shrugged again, "Some people do crosswords." He looked down at her hands.

"What do you do to keep in shape?" he asked.

"Guess," she said, turning over her hands which had no calluses on their backs, but looked a little more resilient on the palm side.

"You row?" David said.

"Nope," she said, but didn't elaborate.

The waiter returned, clearing away their empty plates, re-filling their wine glasses. The bottle ran out as he was topping up David's glass.

"So who can jump a wall like that?" Susan asked.

"That's a good question," David said, "and there's also the riddle of how he escaped from the office break-in. It's a thirty foot drop onto railway lines. Then somehow he climbed a sheer wall the other side. One of Hammond's lot suggested he was a pole-vaulter. This might sound stupid, but instead of a pole, imagine you had a ladder. You could step onto it and then push off behind you."

"Like Buster Keaton? So this guy's a field and track athlete using his pole-vaulting and high-jumping skills to pull off daring raids. Please." Susan said.

"What? Professional athletes never go bad? What about O.J.?" David asked.

Susan laughed.

David said, "I don't know. But he managed this stuff somehow. For someone we think is terminally ill, he's in extraordinary shape."

Their main courses arrived.

"This is good," Susan said, after her first mouthful.

David asked, "Have you learned any more about the Medic Marker?"

"A lot," she said, "but nothing that will help us get it back. I have no idea yet where someone would go to sell a thing like that, and I'm less convinced than ever that the thief intends to sell it."

She continued, "If you just wanted to raise some money, there are lots of better things to steal – cash, for one. You said there was a safe full of money they could have had instead."

David said, "Well, he might have been planning to take that too, but ran out of time. Except Hammond did say the main safe was actually open when they arrived. So there's a good chance he passed up the cash in favour of the Medic Marker."

"Of course it could be worth a lot more than the cash was," said Susan. "I've found what might be a reference to the Marker from the reign of Emperor Shi Huangdi. He offered a prize to anyone who would bring it to him. It could be irrelevant, or on the other hand this could be a Chinese cultural treasure from the third century B.C."

"Huangdi?" David said.

"First Emperor of all China. Qin dynasty. Built the wall," Susan said.

"So this thing would be like the crown jewels. It would be priceless," David said.

"If it's the same thing. But how would anyone ever prove it? You can't date metal and there are no pictures of it that I could find. The Huangdi reference is about a piece of jewellery made from a metal more precious than gold that conferred immortality. I found it because I was looking for references to jewellery with amazing healing powers. But the idea that it's got healing powers comes from a document found in someone's attic in Brentford. There's nothing to tie the stolen jewellery to the Huangdi story except that passage I showed you," Susan said.

"So you couldn't really sell it?" David said.

"Well, it's still a fabulous platinum filigree, so it's certainly worth thousands, and you could probably prove that the platinum came from China. But, all in all, I don't think you could ever demonstrate it was the Huangdi piece. So, I think you'd still be better off with a bag full of money," Susan said.

"Unless your AIDS theory is right," David said.

"You don't believe it," she said.

"I wouldn't say that. I just think there might be several possible explanations for what you saw. I'm beginning to think this guy is some sort of Special Forces character – maybe someone left over from the Cold War – trained to do some government's dirty work, who's now out of a job. We know he's a patient planner as well as being hands-on. Maybe he used to be a spy? And it's bound to be a pretty rough lifestyle; could be what you saw were burns or injuries. Or perhaps he really does have AIDS and the legends about the Marker are just a coincidence."

He went on, "If he thinks the legends are nonsense he'd be better off with the cash, so maybe he believes in them. But then I just can't quite square the black-ops stuff we know he's capable of with the idea that he believes in fairy tales," David winced at his own words and said, "myths and legends, I mean. Sorry."

Susan flicked her hand in a 'don't worry about it' gesture. "Me neither. We're not just talking superstitious – like, no thirteens or something – he'd have to really be into the occult." She added, "The only other thing I can think is that it's stealing-to-order. If someone knew your client had this thing and arranged for it to be stolen, then authentication wouldn't be a problem."

David looked interested, "That makes a lot of sense, you know. If you wanted something stolen, our mystery man is just the sort of person you'd try to hire."

He noticed her look of unease and said, "It fits the facts better than anything else we've come up with. What am I missing?"

"Just one thing," she said. "Say he's a mercenary and he's stealing the Marker for a collector somewhere; why did he come after the collection too? Those documents aren't valuable except to an academic. They're nearly all recent copies of older works. The one you saw the other day is written in ballpoint pen. It's worthless except for the information it contains."

"Well maybe he's after that information. What exactly does it say?" David asked.

"There's a little bit of background about a mad monk who made it, but mainly it's just the same as you'd get with a food processor or a stereo," she said.

David looked puzzled and said, "Which is?"

"Directions for use," she said. "He came back for the instructions. Whichever way you slice it, someone – either mercenary guy or his boss – believes in the legend."

They were both quietly considering this when a waiter asked them, "Is everything OK?"

David said, "Great thanks. Do you think you could get me a glass of the house red?" He glanced at Susan.

"Yeah, the white for me. Thanks," Susan said.

Then, turning to David, she said, "You didn't really answer my question about the address you found. What if mercenary guy isn't in custody? You have information the police need and the clock is ticking."

David looked uncomfortable again, "Well, there's no way I can tell Hammond directly. He was pretty pissed off about the third man thing. You'd think I'd got in the way of the investigation instead of helped it along."

Susan said, patiently, "He does kind of have a point. You see that, don't you?"

David said, "It's the old vigilante dilemma, isn't it. When the authorities let you down, are you supposed to shrug and say, 'oh well', or are you allowed to lend a hand?"

Susan asked, "Are you sure you're giving them a chance to fail before you jump in?"

"Well I definitely did with the third man's getaway car. They had no plans to search the car park that night. Their crime scene would literally have had a thousand vehicles driven through it by the following evening."

Susan shrugged, "OK. Well we might disagree on whether you've got your testosterone set a little high, but I think we're both clear that it's not my job to smack your wrists. But I really think you could get yourself into a lot of trouble, even danger, if you do much more of this lone ranger stuff. I'm just saying that as a friend."

David, who had been examining his plate, looked up at her. She looked away and added, "or a paid employee, at any rate."

"Oh well, in that case..." he said, laughing.

Susan said, "Listen, can't you just phone this address in as, you know, an anonymous tip-off?"

David didn't look convinced, "I don't know. I don't want the police spending too much time thinking about who the informant might be. Before you know where we are, they'll have a theory that it's two guys behind it all. On the other hand, I wouldn't be surprised if Hammond ignored a tip-off completely."

Susan touched a finger to her lips, thoughtfully, "Well, you've done this sort of thing before. Why don't you say it's your tip-off? Call Hammond and say you can't explain but you think he should check it out."

David was considering it. "I like that idea better. Hammond won't be happy, but equally he'd be risking his job if he ignored it."

"Cool," Susan said. "Just do it soon, OK? The police need that address."

"That reminds me, I must phone my mum." David said, sarcastically.

Susan made a face, "Don't start getting me confused with your mother," she said, slipping off her jacket.

As she twisted to put the jacket on the back of her chair the tailored waist of her blouse rose to reveal her trim midriff. David's eyes wandered a little. "I don't think that's going to be a problem," he said.

The waiter arrived with their glasses of wine.

Impulsively, David picked up his wine glass and held it forwards, making a toast, "Here's to our little team!"

"Here's to Rambo and his mother," Susan said, clinking glasses with him.

Work matters were left behind for a while and the conversation moved on to their personal histories. Susan talked a little about her work and David followed on by explaining more about what he did. Both of them were jokey and self-deprecating in their accounts.

Instead of desserts, they opted for Irish coffees.

David took a couple of sips of his, getting cream on his nose. They both laughed and he dabbed at his nose with a napkin.

"You know that's not actually funny," he said. "We're drunk."

"I might be," Susan said, "but you're twice my size. It must take more than three glasses of wine to get you drunk."

He held up four fingers, frowned and then folded one of them over, "Three and a half and they were large." He asked, "Have you ever done one of those magazine questionnaires where you work out how many units of alcohol you drink a week?"

"Might have," she said playfully.

"Mine was easy – two units a week – a pint with my mate Banjo. Never could hold my drink. And I train a lot; believe me, you never want to turn up for a training session with a hangover – it's torture."

"I know," said Susan, holding up her toughened palms to remind him that she trained too.

"Bell ringing," he said, decisively.

"Uh uh," she said, wagging a finger to indicate an incorrect answer. Then she said, "No, my parents were pretty strict Methodists. The churching seems to have worn off, but not the attitude to the devil's tipple."

"Except this evening," David pointed out.

She looked confused, "Yeah, I don't know what happened there. This won't go on my personnel record will it?" she said, gravely.

"Don't be silly. I might have to call your parents though," he said.

They talked a little about London as they drank their coffees. It felt as though the evening was winding down and when the glasses were empty David called for the bill.

"Let's talk in a couple of days. I should be sober again by then," David said.

"OK. Let me know what happens with Hammond, won't you. And call me if it turns out our guy's in jail." She wrote out her mobile number on David's copy of the bill.

"Remind me to scribble that out before I pass it on to accounts," he said. She laughed.

"You know," she said, "this is the most fun I've had in a business meeting."

"Yup, you'd hardly know we were working, would you?" David agreed.

They stood, Susan put her jacket back on, and then they made their way out of the restaurant. It was a mild night and they walked along the street for a hundred yards or so, hardly speaking, until David spotted a taxi. He hailed it, saying to Susan, "Get a receipt."

The taxi pulled in. Susan told the driver her address and then she opened the back door. Before getting in, she turned to David and said, "I've had a really nice evening."

"Me too," David said and for a moment things were awkward.

It didn't seem right to shake hands, but it wasn't clear what they should do instead.

"Get home safely," David said, his arms hanging stiffly at his sides.

Susan nodded, smiling, and hopped into the cab. He closed the door behind her and watched it drive away.

CHAPTER 11

THE NEXT DAY
WEDNESDAY 16TH APRIL

David was in DI Hammond's office again. Hammond was being reasonably civil today, but then he'd been on the phone for most of the ten minutes David had been sitting there, so his opportunities for hostility had been limited.

Much of Hammond's phone dialogue consisted of little grunts. At last he said, "I'll hold you to that. Must get on." He hung up.

He turned to look at David who sat the other side of his desk. "So you heard what happened with our stake-out?" Hammond said, adding a stream of swear words under his breath.

"No I didn't," David said.

Hammond's face twitched into a humourless smile and relaxed again. "Your third man beat the tar out of two officers and disappeared. It seems he'd returned to the house to pick up some of his things. The officers came upon him as he was returning to his car. They drew their weapons and cautioned him. When they

131

attempted to handcuff him, he went for them. Somehow – and believe me I *will* get to the bottom of this – he managed to disarm them and then gave them a good battering as well. I've got a list somewhere – broken this, punctured that. They're not going to die and neither will they win any beauty competitions for a bit. He made quite a mess of them."

Hammond, who had been glancing through papers on his desk as he spoke, looked up and caught David's eye. "Satisfied?" he said. David's jaw muscles tightened a little.

"I'm very sorry to hear that – I mean that your men were hurt." David paused a moment and said, "There's something I've learned that I think you should know. On the other hand, you might consider it interference."

"What have you done, Braun?" growled Hammond.

"Me? Nothing. But as you know, my company has recovered hundreds of stolen items over the years; they've got quite a lot of contacts. One of them passed some information on to us," David said.

Hammond's hands started to twitch in agitation. "Come on, spit it out," he said aggressively.

David leaned forwards and spoke softly, "Calm down, Hammond, you're starting to give me a headache."

"If you're winding me up…" Hammond said, his voice rising. He didn't finish the sentence.

David said nothing for a few seconds either, just breathed evenly. Hammond sat glaring at him. David pulled a piece of paper out of his pocket and laid it on the table. He said, "A Porsche Turbo, black, with this registration," he tapped the paper, "has been spending a lot of time parked outside this address," he tapped a bit further down the same sheet, "and our informant thought it looked suspicious."

"You leaked details of the car we were looking for?" Hammond asked, still belligerent.

"I don't like the word *leaked*. Your people made several hundred phone calls identifying themselves as police officers on each occasion; I asked a few very discreet contacts to keep an eye out. It's hardly the same thing," David said, his voice level.

"And what do you want me to do with this?" Hammond asked.

"Well, if it's the right registration, I'd like you to arrest the owner and put him in prison. If not, then accept my apologies for wasting your time," David said.

Hammond drew the paper towards him and pivoted it round so that he could read it. His head began bobbing as he read. He stuck out his lower lip.

He continued making little nodding motions and said in a monotone, "Leave this with me."

When David didn't respond, Hammond asked, in the same monotone, "Anything else?"

David shook his head and got up to go. "Goodbye," he said. Hammond gave no sign that he had heard.

* * *

Through some unknown process, the smell of stale beer and cigarette smoke had mixed and matured in the walls of the pub to become the scent of home from home, a comforting yeasty tang as instinctively familiar as the house you grew up in.

Breathing pub air, at a table within reaching distance of the bar, Banjo was giving David what he called his 'media briefing'. David watched almost no TV and Banjo took it upon himself to give David the executive summary of what he was missing.

"So what's special about these people?" asked David, confused.

"Nothing. They're whiney, mindless drones," said Banjo.

"I thought they were celebrities," David said, not getting it.

"Well there was one done with celebrities and then there was another thing in the jungle called 'Get me back on telly, I used to be a celebrity'. And of course, they're all celebrities afterwards because the entire nation has watched them pick their nose and loaf around looking bored for weeks," Banjo said.

"So that's what they're talking about constantly in the office – half a dozen ordinary people doing more or less nothing and never going anywhere?" David said.

"That's it," Banjo said, brightly. "It's like watching monkeys at the zoo."

"Why do they volunteer for it?" David asked.

"Well there's a prize, but I think most of them do it because it's a way to stop being a talentless, vacuous nobody for a little while…"

"And become a talentless, vacuous somebody," David interjected.

"And it's a lot easier than doing something with your life," Banjo finished.

"So you're not a fan. Certainly sounds like they've got your back up," David said.

"I've nothing against any of them, if I met them in the street. They're like my postman, in a way – he's a nice enough fella, always seems very cheerful. Brings my post, which is nice. But he wouldn't half start to get on my nerves if he got his own chat show. Or imagine if I went to the Tate and all they'd got was my niece Siobhan's crayon pictures of her dog, Pokey," Banjo said. "Pointing a camera at someone doesn't make them more interesting or more special. To believe the nation will want to watch you eat breakfast and sit on the sofa you'd need an ego the size of a water buffalo. You can't help but dislike someone who believes the fact of their existence constitutes prime-time entertainment."

David said, "Watch the eloquence, Banjo. Someone from the snooker club might wander in and hear you talking like that. Better tell me an offensive joke to make up for it."

"Blimey mate, you're such a snob," said Banjo, with listless scorn.

David said, "I don't mean to be. But that's not what I'm getting at when I'm, you know, getting at you. I just find it funny that you're overeducated. I thought that sort of thing died out with Queen Victoria. But the truth is, you'd probably be happier if you didn't know so much."

He went on, "If you'd never moved away from Bromley, you'd have the same outlook as everyone else in that mob you grew up with. And you wouldn't know that there was anything wrong with that. I just think it's ironic that something that's such a power for good, like education, can be such a thorn in someone's side."

Banjo seemed lost for words. It was difficult to tell from his expression whether he was hurt, but he was certainly off balance.

David looked concerned and said, "I meant funny peculiar, by the way, not funny ha ha. I'm not taking the piss, I'm just saying that I think sometimes you feel a bit of a traitor to your gang back home. Even though you didn't mean to, you've outgrown them."

He continued, "Everybody does it, though. You have to decide which world you fancy living in. And it's not easy. The biggest crime in a group like that is to think you're better than everyone else, but it's difficult not to feel like that when you can see that they're being a bit simpleminded about a lot of things."

Banjo blew out his breath noisily, his eyebrows raised, his eyes staring into the imaginary depths of his pint glass. "This is private stuff. It's not really pub chat," Banjo said, avoiding David's gaze.

David looked worried. "I'm sorry if I just dumped this on you, but I'm allowed to be wise and insightful occasionally." He said very gently, "It's not your job exclusively."

Banjo gave David a glum smile and showed some signs of rallying, "You're right, you know. I can dish it out, but I can't take it. It's what you're talking about, really. I like to pretend I take the world at face value but I also like to show off by telling someone their fortune. Maybe I can't have it both ways."

David nodded, encouragingly, "That's sort of what I'm saying. You're deep, but you try not to look it because you're actually a bit embarrassed about it. You'd rather keep it as a party trick."

David continued, "Remember your speech about fitting in? The more I think about it, the more I think you're right – but I think it applies to you too. Not that I think any less of you for not being perfect."

Banjo gave a sort of comic sneer, "You smug bastard. So is that it or have you got any more turn-the-tables-on-Banjo penetrating insights?"

David replied, "I don't know what the answer is, if that's what you're asking. If you succeed in bettering yourself – whatever that means – it can drive a wedge between you and the people around you and if you don't… Well I don't suppose wasting your potential feels that wonderful either. Look at me and my parents – I have nothing in common with them now. We live in different worlds. I thought they'd be proud of me if I got a good degree and all that, but all it did was make me a mystery to them and make them seem a bit small to me."

Banjo said, "And you think I'm suffering from a bit of the same?"

David nodded.

Banjo acquiesced, "I think you're right mate. So should I button my lip when I'm with the gang or should I show them what a clever old stick I am? It's a pretty crappy choice, isn't it? Lie to your friends about who you are or risk losing them instead?"

David shrugged, "Well, I went with the second one. You tell me how it's working out."

"Well, since we're being all truthful and soul-searching," Banjo said, lowering his voice, "I sometimes think you're a bit lonely and maybe a bit frustrated with your lot."

"You might not be a million miles from the truth there," said David, awkwardly. Now it was his turn to avoid the other's gaze. "You know I hate to talk about this stuff, but it almost feels like I made a deal – don't ask me with who – and they haven't come through. That choice we're talking about: whether to try and lift yourself up and reach your potential, or sort of hang back with the rest of the pack – well I knew there'd be a price to pay if I pushed myself. I knew I'd risk cutting myself off from people, but... I dunno, I just thought there'd be a few more compensations, a bit more of a payoff."

"Like what?" Banjo asked, fascinated.

"It sounds a bit simple, now I'm saying it out loud, but I just thought if I pushed myself, you know, trained and worked hard and studied, I just thought something would come along that was bigger and better than if I hadn't bothered."

"Build it and they will come?" Banjo asked. "Like a sort of karmic communism. To each according to their needs, from each according to their abilities."

"I suppose. In a way, I'm still waiting for my life to start – the real one in which all the really big stuff happens. I suppose somewhere deep down I thought the more capable I made myself as a person, the more impressive my destiny would be when it finally arrived." David threw up his hands, "It sounds demented."

Banjo's face said the opposite, "Everyone believes in destiny, David, everyone. Listen to birds talking about their blokes and going on about 'is he the one?' If life was random there'd be no right person for you, there'd be no correct choices. No one could say, 'is this what I'm meant to do, is this the right thing?' because it wouldn't mean anything. There'd just be one random day after another. Even people who don't believe in god, or superstition or heaven or anything, believe that there's a link between today and tomorrow and the future. No matter how faint it is, everyone believes they have some sort of destiny."

David said, "Right. And to tell you the truth, I'm feeling a bit gypped by mine. I feel like I put my name down for something, I kept my end of the bargain and then nothing happened. God, I sound so ungrateful."

"I don't think it's about being grateful," Banjo said, frowning. "You've probably got it a lot easier this way than if your big, bad destiny turned up. After all, it's about being challenged, isn't it? Finding out what you're really made of? Like going off to war. Lots of blokes wonder how they'd cope. It's not supposed to be a picnic."

David said, "You're not making it sound any less stupid, but at least put that way I can see I'm not the only idiot who thinks like this."

"Human beings are storytellers; we can't help it if we want our lives to make a good story." Banjo said. "Maybe even a legend," he added, melodramatically.

"I should talk to Susan about that. She's the expert on legends," David said.

"Ahh, yes. The woman ever-so-briefly known as Ms Milton.

How is Susan?" Banjo asked.

"Don't get carried away. She's an interesting girl, but we're just working together," David said.

"Oh, make it a bit more difficult for me, mate. This is too easy. I like a challenge too, you know." Banjo closed his eyes, put his fingers to his temples and said haltingly, "I'm sensing something. I'm getting a message from beyond. It says... It says..." His voice became tremulous and moaning, "'David likes this girl.'"

David laughed.

Banjo continued hamming, "Wait there's more." The moaning voice again, "'David wants to ask this girl out but he's too much of a pink girl's skipping rope to risk it.' And what's that the voices are saying? 'David...'"

David interrupted, "Maybe now's a good moment to show you this move I learned at training. If I do it right, I should be able to crush your larynx without anyone noticing."

"At your own peril, mate" Banjo said haughtily. "As a master of Dimac, I have access to the legendary Count Dante's full array of crippling, maiming and mutilating techniques."

David did his cockney pensioner voice, "Alright Banjo, I was only joshing with you. You wouldn't hurt a man whose round it is, would you?"

"Now that's more like it. I've got to turn me bike round; I'll expect a pint of Old Nasty to be waiting for me when I get back, unless you want a taste of the quivering palm," Banjo said, warily holding up a trembling hand as though even he was afraid of its power. He sauntered off towards the toilet as David turned to the bar.

When Banjo returned there was a fresh pint of cider waiting for him. David too had a full pint.

Banjo commented, "Not switched to the elderflower cordial?

You've become a drinking machine, man. Three pints? Whatever next."

David said, "Susan and I ended up hoovering back quite a lot of wine last night. There's nothing like drinking too much to give you a thirst." He looked down at his drink and puffed, "Actually, you're right. I don't even want this and I've got to speak to this hard man from the Flying Squad again tomorrow. Best done without a hangover."

"That's more like it," Banjo said as David put aside his untouched pint. "Wuss," he whispered, not that quietly.

David ordered a coke. "This is going spare then?" Banjo asked, indicating David's beer. David nodded.

Banjo hopped up, taking the full pint with him, and wandered over to the other side of the pub. There was an elderly man sitting at a table on his own, hands folded over the top of a walking stick, the tip of which rested between his boots. A broadsheet newspaper lay folded on the table, exposing a partially completed crossword. The man wore a species of old black suit which somehow looked as comfy and informal as Banjo's tatty jeans, and about as expensive.

David couldn't hear the conversation but Banjo came back without the pint. The old man lifted his chin and tipped his stick at David in neighbourly acknowledgement.

When Banjo sat back down, David said, "Listen, I want to ask you something."

Banjo said, "I'm all ears."

"This bit of stolen jewellery I was telling you about..." David said. Banjo nodded. "Well, it's from China and apparently in the old days they used to believe it had healing powers. What's weird is that the thug who's stolen it seems to believe the stories. Susan thinks he's dying and that he wants this thing – the Marker we've been calling it – he wants it to cure him."

"Sounds pretty weird. What did you want to ask me about?" Banjo said.

"I'm wondering if it's completely out of the question," David said, closing one eye and glancing up at Banjo.

"What's out of the question?" Banjo asked, not following.

"I reckon I've said enough stupid things this evening that one more won't hurt. I'm wondering if there might be something to the idea of being healed by a two-thousand-year-old piece of metal," David said.

"You mean, as opposed to being healed by a twentieth century piece of metal like a radiotherapy machine," Banjo said.

David didn't respond, but instead went on with his account, "You remember I said I had this client who frightened the life out of me? Well, the guy who stole the Marker from him isn't much better. In fact, considering he's killed several people he should be a lot scarier. There's just something about both of them. It's like they're aliens or something. They look like people but there's something about them that just makes your hair stand up," David said. He glanced thoughtfully at Banjo's heavily spiked red hair.

Banjo puckered his lips thoughtfully. "I don't think I've ever seen you scared. You remember when we went to Rebecca Stevenson's twenty-first and her brother's townie mates wanted to kick the crap out of us. You remember? You should have been scared then, they were huge."

David smiled, "That's the best thing about training – once you've been beaten up a few times by experts, you don't get so worked up about the amateurs having a bash."

Banjo shook his head. "Well maybe you ought to think about that, then. You said this guy frightened the life out of you. If you're not afraid of getting hurt, what are you afraid of?"

They sat quietly for a moment and then Banjo returned to the question, "Just thinking about bizarre cures. I reckon I believe in faith-healing – some of it anyway – and maybe hypnotherapy. And I think most people are prepared to believe that some of the Chinese remedies for things, like cures they've been using for thousands of years, might have something to them. Maybe this Marker is like, I don't know, like acupuncture. Have you seen those pictures of people having operations while they're awake and the only thing stopping them feeling it are a couple of needles?"

"That's true," said David. "I'm sure if people could debunk acupuncture, it would have been done by now. And that's just sticking little bits of metal in someone."

"In the right place," Banjo pointed out helpfully.

Banjo thought of something. "Didn't you say one of your senseis used to be paralysed?"

"Yeah, they had the x-rays pinned up in his dojo – a fracture of the spine. I forget which vertebra, but he couldn't move his legs for a year. It's supposedly an incurable condition, but he got better. He claimed he did it with meditation and breathing techniques," David said.

"And you believe that?" Banjo asked.

"I suppose I do," said David, considering. "It's a lot of trouble to fake. If he was going to falsify a story he should have claimed he knocked out Bruce Lee's front teeth or at least whomped a bar full of bikers. If you were going to bribe half a dozen people to back your story, you'd pick something a bit more macho and hands-on, I reckon."

Banjo said, "So it's not that difficult to see how your man could talk himself into believing in miracles."

Then he looked at David's expression and asked, "Are you saying you believe it too?"

David paused for a moment, made a face, "Naah. He might be as fit as Captain America's stunt double, but that doesn't mean he knows what he's talking about."

"What, is he a bit tasty then?" Banjo asked.

"Like you wouldn't believe. He's either popping something or he's got a training routine that makes me look like your old Uncle Jess," David said.

"Well you'd best keep out his way then, hadn't you?" Banjo said.

CHAPTER 12

THE NEXT DAY
THURSDAY 17TH APRIL

Seven in the evening and outside it was still light. Two floors below ground, in the School of Antiquities' vaults, Susan was finishing up her notes.

Her fingers rested on the keys of her pearl iBook, the pad of her right index finger tapping gently on the 'H' key without pressing it – a metronome to her thoughts.

Then her fingers sprang to life. "Reference to hydrargum," she wrote, "exception to the Aristotelian elements?"

She had set the laptop a little to her left; a document from the collection was clipped to a stand on her right. By twisting her head a little she could type at the same time as she scrutinised the yellowed paper with its precise, tiny script. She had been sitting like this for a number of hours.

She lifted her hands from the keyboard and hunched up her right shoulder, rotating it in its socket. With her left hand, she squeezed and released the side of her neck several times.

She made a decision. "M'out of here," she said, saving and

closing the on-screen document she was working on. She began shutting the laptop down, then carefully removed the piece of paper from its stand and slid it back into its transparent plastic envelope. While her computer still whirred away, preparing for sleep, she took the sticker-covered envelope with her out into the hallway.

There was now a second document store in a separate room to the researchers' workstations. Fishing a key-ring from the pocket of her sea-green jeans, she opened the heavy fire door and snapped on the light.

Cabinets and racking lined the walls and were stacked in the centre of the room. Though apparently spotless, the room smelled of dust – dust that began to singe if the bare light bulbs were left on for any length of time.

In the corner opposite the door, the document store had been set on a wooden pallet. In appearance, it was halfway between a safe and a filing cabinet. It had no combination dial, just a covered key-hole and a large chromed handle.

Undoing the lock, Susan levered the handle upright (it made a metallic swallowing noise) and pulled open the door. On three shelves, plastic envelopes and yellow-tagged folders were arranged, their code numbers and hand-lettered labels facing outwards.

Sliding the envelope she carried back into its assigned slot, she closed the door. On top of the store lay a clipboard. Half a splintered Biro was attached to its metal clip by a length of frayed, white-plastic twine. Glancing first at her watch, Susan filled in a couple of boxes on the form – its ghostly outlines and titles faded by endless serial photocopying.

She walked out of the room, turning out the light and locking the door behind her. To make room for the document store, a pallet of ancient odds and ends had been removed from the storage room and now lay stranded in the hallway near the door. Susan noticed an ancient green filing cabinet, swathed in polythene. It lay on its side – a sure sign that its end was near. Enamelled card index drawers and an aging roller blind, backed in perished black rubber, shared the cabinet's bier.

Stopping at the drinks dispenser by the silent lift she selected tomato soup and started slightly as the machine snapped a plastic cup into its dispenser with a gunshot rapidity that made its front panel rattle. The machine's explosive 'chunk', followed by a rising gurgle, was the only sound on the quiet floor.

Susan was the last person working on her level. The occasional daytime noises had ceased. A sound like a ball-bearing being repeatedly dropped onto marble flooring would sometimes filter down to her, but in the evening everything was peaceful. Even the new guard was nowhere to be seen.

Taking her soup back into the Alexandrian room, Susan dropped down into her chair. The dim overhead strips, and her single bright, halogen task-light, were the only illumination.

She slurped a few atoms of piping hot soup into her mouth and then began rooting in her bag for her address book. Wedged into its spine was her phone card, which she placed on the table.

Flicking through the addresses, she found the page she was looking for and pinned the address book flat with the palm of her hand. Tucking the phone under her ear she punched the long sequence of numbers and waited for it to start ringing.

"Shoot," Dee's voice said.

"Dee, it's Susan."

"Hold on Susie." Then Dee's voice, slightly muffled, could be heard yelling, "Get it out of my office before I kill it, Jack. Scram. And get the door behind you."

The muffled quality vanished and Dee's voice, quiet and calm, said, "Sorry about that. And sorry for calling you Susie. How are you Sis?"

Dee's sudden warmth caught Susan by surprise. She said, "Err, great. I'm great; how are you Dee?"

"Like gangbusters." Then Dee hesitated momentarily, "Have you thought any more about my visit?" Hardly giving Susan time to respond she continued, "I could maybe cancel if you don't think..."

Susan butted in softly, "Dee, I just meant I was pretty busy. I'd love to see you. I feel bad because I've got a lot to do at the moment. I won't be able to spend anywhere near as much time with you as I'd like. That's what was giving me reservations."

Dee considered for a second. "Well, what if I'm self-sufficient? I'll get a guidebook, show myself around. Maybe I can get a hotel downtown."

Susan brightened, "Oh that place I'm staying in, the one that belongs to my Professor, it's priceless," she said enthusiastically. "You have to stay with me – even if I'm not around that much. Imagine Miss Marple bought a townhouse. Décor's all Edwardian. Everything's an antique – so no TV. You'll love it."

"Sounds great. So you're OK with this?" Dee asked.

"Yeah, Dee," Susan said with sincerity in her voice, "I'm looking forward to it."

"Well, I'm getting in on Tuesday. Is that too soon?" Dee said.

"This Tuesday? Like five days from now Tuesday?" Susan said, sounding a little taken aback.

"Yup," Dee said, in a small voice.

"I just thought... Never mind. That's fine. Great I mean," Susan said.

Dee cleared her throat and then said brightly, "So what's keeping you so busy? Would I understand it if you told me?"

"You know what paper is, right?" Susan said, teasing. "Well,

I'm going through a ton of it. Lots of old paper that needs reading and analysing and alphabetizing. Only a nerd could love it. Fortunately…"

Dee asked, "So you're not party-towning it every night then?"

"Cocoa, and in bed by eleven," Susan assured her sister. "Although, one cool thing I'm doing is help investigate a robbery. This insurance company is paying me to do some background research on a stolen antique. Real cops and robbers."

"Nancy Drew. So not just librarians, you're hanging around with insurance types too. Good job," Dee said, amused.

"He's not your stereotypical insurance guy," Susan said, snipping off the last word as though regretting she'd said anything.

"Who guy? Which guy?" Dee demanded.

"From the insurance company," Susan said breezily. She added, "His name's David."

"If he were a celebrity impersonator he'd be…" she asked.

"God, I don't know. A young Clancy Brown, darker though," Susan said.

"The Kurgan? Selling insurance? My mind refuses to form an image," Dee said, slightly incredulous.

"Bad choice. He's not scary looking, just solid. Anyway, the point of the story was the interesting work I'm doing, not the guy I'm doing it for," Susan said.

"Sure, sure," Dee said dismissively. "He single?"

"I guess," Susan said nonchalantly. "Stop quizzing me about him. He's just something on the side." She corrected herself, "It's some work on the side, and it's one of the reasons I thought I might not have enough time to see you." She added emphatically, "He's not my type anyway."

Dee said, "OK. I get the message. He's kind of a hunk, he's available and you're not interested in him. I get it. Say no more."

Dee sounded conspiratorial, like she'd just figured out what was going on. "So can I give you my flight details? See if you can meet me. No sweat either way; I can get into the city by myself."

Susan blinked. She seemed surprised that Dee was dropping the inquisition about David so readily. "Ah yeah. Let me get a pen. OK, shoot."

Dee was getting into London Heathrow on Tuesday evening. Susan would have enough time to get to the airport without cutting into her working day.

"So do you look any different? Taller? Tattoos?" Dee asked.

"Don't worry. I'll hold up a sign," Susan said. "I'll see you Tuesday, Dee."

"Yeah, see you then, Sis," Dee said, hanging up.

Susan held the phone in her hand for a moment, her elbow resting on the desk. As she returned the receiver to its cradle, the small click of plastic on plastic happened to coincide with a distant thump, as though she were hanging up a phone weighing tons.

Idly flicking through her address book, she found herself looking at the page that contained David's number. She stuck out her lower lip for a moment, considering the entry. Then she spent a minute entering the number into the memory of her mobile. She accidentally erased it all and had to input the details a second time before she had it successfully stored. Still holding the phone in her hand, her thoughts wandered.

A sound cut suddenly through her daydream, a sound like two fist-sized flints being slammed together. It came from the other side of the wall – the storage room.

Susan cocked her head, straining to hear more, holding herself completely still. A faint, drawn-out squeak reached her ears, like the sound of something being slid over lino, or perhaps the shriek of distant metal being twisted and deformed.

She looked around the room, alarmed, her eyes searching. Whatever she was looking for, she didn't find it.

She picked up the phone and hit zero. It rang several times, but no one answered. She hung up.

On silent feet she moved to the door, pushed down the handle with infinite slowness, one hand covering the other. When the handle was fully depressed, she pulled it open a fraction. She could make out the storage room door ajar, the light on.

Just as slowly as she'd pushed it down, she cautiously released the handle. She pulled the door open far enough for her to squeeze through.

Before moving through the gap, she studied the pallet of oddments that lay between her vantage point and the opened door. Her eyes alighted on an old, oak window pole – a metre-long oak shaft capped with a tilde of black iron, designed to hook the looped catches of high Victorian windows. She crept towards it, weight on her back leg, sliding her front foot forwards in stealthy increments.

Her hands closed around the window pole and slid it carefully from its tangled nest. The pallet was in the corner of the hallway between the two rooms. She was out of sight of anyone who might be in the storage room, but neither could she see in.

A snap, like a steel cable parting under tension, echoed from the unseen room.

Placing her hands shoulder-width apart on the pole, she gripped it like a shortened quarterstaff, and advanced – in her silent, sliding gait – closing the distance to the open doorway.

Reaching it, she looked in and saw a man, dressed in black and grey, sitting on one heel in front of the opened door of the document store. A scatter of folders lay fanned around his feet. In his hands he held a piece of paper on which an intricate design was evident – it was the same document she had shown David on her laptop.

The intruder was holding the paper up, inclined to catch the light, and was apparently captivated by what he saw.

He wore a tight-fitting, black wool cap which, seen from behind at an angle, was shielding his face from Susan. But in partly obscuring his features, it also blocked some of his peripheral vision, helping to hide Susan's presence from him.

Susan took a step towards him. She froze as he turned suddenly (but in the direction of the document store) and snatched another folder from the rack.

He hadn't spotted her yet, but she could see that it was the same man she had glimpsed as she rushed to help Mrs Harris. He was clean-shaven now, but there was no mistaking his face.

She stepped forwards again. And again. She was almost there.

One more step and she twisted the pole up over her right shoulder before bringing it down hard, the wood and metal whacking him across the side of his head, sending his cap flying, knocking him sprawling.

The impact made a curious sound, sharp and inorganic. A flash of glittering metal caught Susan's eye. The displaced woollen cap lay at her feet and visible within it was a gilt band. The intruder had been wearing a circle of metal around his temples.

A blow of such force on an unprotected head might have been fatal; as it was, although blood streamed from a raw groove in his short, dark hair, and his eyes seemed momentarily unable to focus on anything, he was very much alive. The metal band had deflected part of the blow's momentum.

He was now lying on his side, one elbow beneath him, his other hand held with its palm in front of his face as though he were struggling to see it clearly.

Advancing on him, Susan raised the pole for another blow.

The intruder sprang back, with a scrabbling of feet. He collided with the sharp edge of a tall, grey cabinet, but was standing upright a moment later.

He was unsteady on his feet, and his eyes seemed to track a point that wandered, like a heat-dazed fly, in an orbit around Susan's head. Nonetheless he took a step towards Susan, his hands held up in a boxer's guard, but with the hands unclenched and twisted edge-on to her.

Without diverting an ounce of her attention from her adversary Susan screamed at the top of her lungs. In the confined space it stopped the intruder dead.

A moment later he sprang at her.

As soon as he moved, Susan brought the butt end of the pole whipping across in front of her. It connected with his jaw. Susan's grunt of exertion covered the noise of heavy wood on bone.

He dropped, felled, to one knee and then immediately came bounding back up, like something springing from a trapdoor, to slam the pole from Susan's hands and twist her off balance. She put a foot back to steady herself and stepped forward straight into a punch, a fast left jab that caught her high cheekbone, instantly buckling her knees and sending her toppling backwards. Her head caught the corner of the document store's open, twisted door on the way down. She fell onto her back, the intruder's metal band painful beneath her.

A clattering sound came from the hallway.

The left side of the intruder's face, where Susan had first struck, was painted with blood, droplets of which fell, one a second, from his chin. His right jaw-line was marked with a purple channel of wounded skin, the imprint of the makeshift staff. His mouth was hanging open.

He took a step towards Susan who was struggling to get a hand beneath her, momentarily unable to rise.

Two figures in uniform pelted into the room and stopped short. The intruder twisted his head to see them, his neck turning stiffly and with an unnatural motion of his shoulders. The two newcomers wore the patches of security guards.

"The police will be here in seconds," the young, black guard yelled at the intruder who stood, wounded and panting, glaring at them. "Come away from her," the guard ordered advancing towards them. The guard's hand came to rest on a collapsed metal tripod which lay atop a packing case, its telescoped limbs bunched and stubby enough to make it a possible weapon.

"Come on," the guard said, firmly but with a coaxing tone, his hand neither raising nor releasing the metal stand. The other guard, pale and nervous-looking, remained by the door.

The intruder took two hesitant steps towards the guards, his back bowed, his head lowered, blood running down his cheekbone and dripping from his down-turned nose. He walked like a man crippled.

It was a feint and suddenly the intruder scooped a handful of documents from the ground and ran, shoulder first towards the door. The first guard was knocked sideways as he attempted to tackle the intruder. His colleague, who merely grabbed at the intruder's sleeve, found the cloth torn from his grip as the man forced past him. Something on the intruder's wrist glittered in the light before the sleeve was released.

"Ernie, see to the girl," the black man barked, scrambling to his feet and running after the fleeing intruder who had already banged through the echoing fire door adjacent to the lift and was taking the stairs three at a time.

The remaining guard looked anxiously at Susan and then at his receding partner.

Susan held out her hand to him and quickly he came over and helped her to her feet.

She was quite unsteady and was forced to throw an arm over the guard's dandruff-sprinkled shoulders to keep herself upright.

"Help me into the other room, quickly," she said to the guard. He steadied her as she made her precarious way back towards her desk. Several drips of bright blood fell from a strand of her blonde hair and stitched a scarlet ellipsis across her white cotton t-shirt.

She tripped and almost fell into her chair. The address book still lay open, her mobile phone sitting in its centre, an outsized bookmark.

She snatched up the phone and dialled as quickly as she could. She winced as it touched her cheek.

It rang – once, twice and was answered.

"David," she said.

CHAPTER 13

"I'll call them, but I'm only minutes from there myself," David said, phone to his ear, other hand on the steering wheel.

He listened to Susan's voice on the line. "My god, are you OK? Jesus."

He listened some more. "Jesus. Listen, you're right near University College Hospital. I'll call you there on your mobile. Are you OK?"

He listened. "Yeah, yeah. I'm calling them now." He paused a moment to concentrate on swerving around a bus which was slowing him down. "Get to the hospital, I'll call you really soon." He hung up and dialled 999.

It took a little explaining, but he managed to make it clear to the woman on the police switchboard that a man who had just committed a violent crime in one part of London might be heading to a second location. He mentioned DI Hammond's name and gave his own details. After a few minutes he received assurance that a car was on its way and hung up.

He was momentarily stuck in traffic, waiting for the lights to change, on the road from Islington down to Old Street. He searched the memory of his mobile phone, found Hammond's mobile number and dialled it.

"Hammond," a voice barked on the first ring.

"It's David Braun," and without giving Hammond a chance to speak went on, "our third man just attacked Susan Milton at the University and stole those papers she told you about. Have you got anyone at that address I gave you?"

"Not right now," Hammond said.

"Well I've called 999, but I thought you should know. Maybe you've got an ARV in the area," David said. Holding the wheel steady with his knee, he pulled at his tie, sawing the knot down until it slipped free. His jacket was already off, laying on the passenger seat at his side.

Hammond said, "I need to take care of this. Goodbye Braun." He added curtly, almost under his breath, "Thanks."

The address David was racing towards lay on a side road off the Great Eastern Road, the thoroughfare which ran from Old Street down towards the City and the Tower. The area was a warren of red-brick, three-storey studios and workshops – many still with hayloft doors on their upper storeys and old iron pulleys anchored beneath their roofs – remnants of their hard-working, pre-gentrified past.

Somewhere, the sun was dipping down beneath the unseen horizon. The gathering gloom made the switchback streets seem narrower. Hidden in the warren of lanes, David was now driving over cobbles.

He turned a final corner into the beam of headlights. A black

Porsche sat idling, tucked into the kerb, just short of a recessed entranceway. Tall, blue-painted, wooden double doors barred access to the ground floor of a workshop. A dark-dressed figure had one of the doors open and was tugging at the lower bolt of the second door.

Once David had rounded the corner and the halide-purple sparkle of the Porsche's headlamps no longer dazzled him, he could recognise the man from their encounter earlier in the week. The man he had seen vault a three-metre wall stood in front of him, tugging at the doors' left-hand bolt, unable to pull it out of the ground. The figure's dipped right shoulder and the way his left hand held on to the heavy iron door handle suggested that his legs were doing less than the door was to hold him upright.

The high wooden doors, when opened, would be wide enough to admit the Porsche. A bare concrete floor just visible within had the look of a garage space.

David didn't begin to slow until he was level with the open door, giving no advance warning that he might have reached his destination. As he passed the struggling figure, he braked hard and put the nose of his Saab across the street, stopping inches from the Porsche's front end and blocking the street.

David burst out of the car, but the other man didn't run, he merely raised himself from his stooped position and squared his shoulders.

One side of his face was now black, a skin of drying blood covered it from forehead to chin. On the other side, his jaw line bulged horribly, the swarthy skin tight across his distorted cheek. The record of an impact was imprinted in the flesh.

He spoke through tight-clenched teeth, his lips drawn back from his blood-soaked gums; the effect was of a talking skull. "Only one hound and him without tribute. I'm insulted," he sucked blood through his teeth. "Perhaps mortally," he said with a little hiss, possibly intended as a laugh.

David had stopped a few paces short of his quarry, who stood unmoving in the doorway.

The battered figure studied him. "How clever of your master to send a loyal child. A hundred years from now you'll wish you'd kept it for yourself."

David said nothing.

"Well, let's see how well you've learned your lessons," the figure said, the final liquid sibilant forcing a pink bubble of blood to catch in the corner of his mouth. He took a step forwards and bringing his left hand out from behind his back revealed a knife clutched in his sticky fist.

David took an involuntary half step backwards, instinctively reacting to the sight of a weapon by creating more space. He shifted more weight to his back foot, the added danger of a knife making a kick preferable to a punch. He lifted his guard higher, making it more defensive, his hands now in front of his face, the bony points of his elbows presented to his enemy.

The wounded man transferred his knife to his right hand, holding it out as though he were about to hand it to David. Its tip made little circular patterns as its owner stirred the air in front of him. He took a small step towards David and another, forcing David to retreat. He began to back David towards the parked cars.

The knife suddenly flashed out towards David's guard, aimed high, at the level of eyes and fingers, but the attacking arm was not fully extended which left David room to dip back from its glittering point.

Twice more the knife arced out, forcing David back. He was almost against the flank of his slewed car, wedged in the vee between side panel and open door. He was trapped.

He glanced quickly to one side as though gauging his retreat, his eyes left his opponent's. The instant eye contact was broken the knife was swinging towards his face. Just as he dipped his gaze, David took his weight off his right foot. As his attacker swung, he brought his right heel straight up into the kneecap of his adversary's front leg. He allowed his upper body to fall back, out of the path of the knife, dropping him against the side of the car.

David's opponent stumbled backwards, his damaged knee buckling, his hands going up and out to steady him.

David pushed off from the car, thrusting forwards and driving his left foot flat into the centre of his opponent's chest. His adversary was thrown backwards, knocked off his feet, his head glancing off the glassy granite of the kerbstone, his hands thrown high. He lay sprawled on his back.

David stepped forwards and grabbed the man's out-flung wrist with one hand, covered it with a second, and pulled, meanwhile placing his right foot on his fallen attacker's shoulder. The arm was wrenched straight, the elbow holding, but the captured hand could barely retain its grip on the knife. The injured man gasped.

David wrapped one palm around the other's fist, grasped the base of the thumb and rotated his attacker's hand until the fingers opened like a flower and spilled the knife out onto the cobbles. Twisting further he stopped pulling and allowed the other's straight arm to bend at the elbow. The arm folded until the knifeless hand was up by its owner's ear. The downed man's shoulder came off the ground in an attempt to lessen the painful tension in his twisted arm.

Still holding the thumb and twisted wrist, David continued to rotate the arm until he had forced his opponent to turn completely over. As the injured man lay face down in the street, David dropped a knee into the centre of his back. Pinned, wrist-locked and battered, the fallen man had ceased to struggle.

Neither spoke nor moved for several minutes until sirens, high revving engines and finally the sound of running feet announced the arrival of the police.

Two officers approached while a third and fourth fanned out to either side. David said, "There's a knife to my left. I won't move if one of you wants to retrieve it. My name is David Braun. DI Hammond of the Flying Squad can vouch for me. This is the man Hammond's looking for." An officer was approaching David from behind, just visible in David's peripheral vision. A kick and a clatter and the knife was skittering away across the cobbles.

"Tell me when you're ready for me to let him up," David said.

"Just stay there, sir," an officer said. Then he spoke into his lapel mike. "Let's ascertain who's who before anyone starts moving around."

A couple more minutes passed with David and his captive locked together and immobile while the policeman conducted a radio conversation. Eventually the officer addressed him again, "I think it's pretty clear that you're Mr Braun, sir. If you'd let me put a handcuff on that wrist you've got there, you can let him go."

David held up one and then the other of his captive's wrists so that the officer could fasten them together. Then he stood up and moved aside, brushing dirt from his trousers and inspecting himself for injuries. He was still breathing fast despite the fact he had hardly moved for five minutes.

David produced a business card and said, "DI Hammond has all my details, but here they are again anyway. I assume there'll be some paperwork…"

The officer nodded and muttered, "Ohhh yes."

"…just get in touch when you want me."

The captive, who was now in a sitting position in the middle of the road, spoke to David. "Were your orders not to kill me?"

"I don't know what you mean," David said, as much to the policemen as to their prisoner.

"You might want to get yourself checked out," the officer said. "It's very easy to hurt yourself and not notice when the adrenaline's flowing." Turning to his colleagues he said, "You two take a quick look inside, check there's no one in there. Watch yourselves. We'll take the prisoner in. And get that towed," he said, nodding towards the Porsche.

Once the prisoner was folded into the back of one of the police cars, it set off, reversing up the street.

"I'd better move this," David said, indicating his car and received a nod from one of the two remaining officers.

David walked over to his car and got in. The keys were still in the ignition. He held up his hands which shook a little. He turned the key, started the engine and reversed until the car was straight again. Then he drove forwards, past the Porsche and pulled in.

He got out and wandered back to the open garage door, but the policemen had gone inside. David took a couple of steps through the open door, seeing only a bare patch of oil-stained concrete and a wooden staircase leading to an unseen upper floor. Businesslike voices drifted down the stairs.

He turned around to go and something caught his eye. His attacker had never managed to open the second of the double doors. In the deep shadows between the bolted door and the wall rested a bag.

David took a closer look. A smart black holdall, almost brand new and still spotless, sat on the filthy concrete floor. It plainly hadn't been there long. It sat just where someone who momentarily needed both hands might place it.

David looked up the stairs. No sign of the policemen. He looked back at the bag. It was almost invisible in the gloom.

He grabbed it and walked rapidly and stiffly back to his car. As quickly as possible he got the vehicle moving. There was still no sign of the policemen as the street vanished from his rear-view mirror.

CHAPTER 14

An hour later
Thursday 17th April

Susan sat with her head in her hands. A few of the hard orange chairs around her were occupied, but the majority remained empty. Most would not be required until the pubs began emptying out. She had, a droll British-Asian doctor told her, picked a good time to drop in.

She had only waited half an hour to be seen. The presence of a police constable taking her details and asking the nurses how long she would have to wait helped ensure that she was given prompt attention. The constable left when she went behind a curtain to have her wounds cleaned and stitched.

The cut to her scalp, where she'd banged her head, had received five stitches. The blood had dried, matting her hair and plastering it to her head. The blow to her cheek had split the skin and would bruise spectacularly, she was assured. The doctor had closed the wound with a steristrip. They concluded her treatment with a tetanus jab.

Not yet ready to make the trip home, she returned to the waiting area. In the warm, bright room, surrounded by alert and watchful staff, she had found her eyelids beginning to droop, though it was only just after nine in the evening.

The doctor who had treated her emerged from behind a curtain and wandered over to her.

"You look pretty tired," he said and gave her a professional smile.

"It's been quite a day," she said, looking up.

"You remember what you were doing just before all this happened?" he asked.

"Sure. I called my sister," she said.

"And you didn't black-out," he asked.

"Like I said, I don't remember it if I did. I don't think there was time," she said.

He looked troubled and placed his fingertips on her head, tilted her head down, peered at her skull again.

"Is there anyone at home to keep an eye on you tonight?" he asked.

At that moment, a voice said, "Susan," and she looked round to see David standing there in a creased and dirty, grey business shirt.

"Have you come to collect the patient?" the doctor asked David.

"Yes. Is she OK?" he asked, a frown of deep concern on his face.

"There's no reason to think otherwise, but a bang on the head is always unpredictable. Can you do me a favour? Can you keep an eye on your girlfriend tonight?" He looked towards Susan. "You're probably just worn out, but if you find yourself getting groggy, confused," he looked back to David, "or if you can't wake her up, call an ambulance. There's only the very smallest risk, but we might as well be safe," he said.

Susan began to say, "He's not..." but David interrupted, saying to Susan, "You're welcome to stay. I feel responsible."

The doctor looked from one of them to the other. "So you're not quite at the 'staying over' stage yet. Well, guess what? You are now. Think of it as fate."

He turned to go and paused, "Those stitches can probably come out in a week. Drop in here, or get your GP to do it." He strode away, calling out, "Good luck."

David sat down beside Susan. He put his hand on her shoulder and said, "I'm so sorry. What's... What kind of shape are you in?"

Susan gave him a weak smile. "I'm alright. Did they get him?"

"Yup," David said, grimly triumphant. "He's in custody. Somebody really knocked him around before I got to him."

"You tackled him?" she asked, glancing up sharply.

"And you did too?" asked David, looking at her eye.

Susan gave a tired little laugh, "I hit him with a window pole," she said. "Twice."

David returned the smile, raising his eyebrows. "He looked like he'd been hit by a bus." His smile receded. "What did he do to you?"

"Just what you can see," she said indicating her swollen and patched cheek, "plus I hit my head on something."

"I'm so sorry for getting you involved in this," he said.

She shrugged, "I think I got myself involved. I want to be mad at you for going off on a one-man crusade again, but I don't suppose anyone forced me to take a swing at him instead of running like hell. Anyway, I'm too tired to think about it. He's behind bars and we're both in one piece."

She stood up, stiffly, and he helped her. "I meant what I said," he assured her, "you're welcome to stay with me or we can go to your place if you'd prefer."

"Are you trying to pick me up?" she said narrowing her eyes at him.

"No, I just meant…" he began, stumbling over the words.

She leant on him and said, "I'm kidding. Relax. If it's all the same to you, let's head to your place. A big, old Victorian house is not what I feel like at the moment. I want somewhere cosy. Is your place cosy?" She was talking more and more slowly, holding his arm to steady herself.

"I'm straight, male and under fifty, so no, it's not cosy. But it's comfortable enough and, thank god, pretty tidy at the moment," he said.

David found himself steering Susan towards the doors; she could walk, but she didn't seem too good at navigation. She was almost asleep on her feet. "Boy, that adrenaline really takes it out of you. Or maybe it's the local," she said.

David had parked on a meter a few minutes walk from the hospital. The cool evening air seemed to wake Susan up a little, though she still held on to David.

"You know what I think?" she said. "I think it's a miracle we're both still alive."

David said nothing.

She went on, "I was going over this while I was waiting back there. He's killed two people – maybe took a gun off one of them to do it. He's put two police officers and a security guard in the hospital, as well as one little old lady. And he can force open a locked door and then wrench the front off something that's basically a safe, apparently with his bare hands – god knows how. And you saw him jump a nine-foot wall. We were unbelievably lucky not to get ourselves killed. Everyone else who's encountered him has met some sort of monster; for some reason we only had to deal with a man."

David nodded gravely.

He said, "I got to his place before the police did. I should have left him alone. I was just… I didn't know what he'd done to you and I didn't want him to get away."

"You weren't afraid?" she asked.

"At one point. Not beforehand though. I just didn't think about it. I didn't get scared until I saw he'd got a knife."

Susan squeezed his arm, "Oh my god."

"He could have had a gun. He could have had half a dozen friends. In fact, if you hadn't given him such a hiding, I don't think he'd have needed anything, maybe not even the knife. And I knew that; I'd seen him move. Somehow it didn't matter. I was such an idiot, but I didn't care. I wanted to stop him."

"So what were you thinking about when you tackled him?" she asked.

"I was thinking, 'I can beat him'," David answered. "I think maybe all the training's warped my mind. Somehow it just seemed like a test, something I had to get through." He threw up his hands. He looked at her, "So, what's your excuse?"

They had arrived at David's car. He unlocked it, separated himself from Susan's arm and opened the passenger door for her. Once she was in, he closed the door and went round to his side, got in.

She was thoughtful as he started the car, waited for a break in the traffic.

"I caught him by surprise," she said. "He'd found the document describing the Marker and he just *had* to have a peek. I knew for a couple of seconds he was off guard. After that, maybe he'd go back to being pretty much unstoppable. Obviously, I wish someone else had caught him with his guard down, but there was just me. So I took my shot."

David reached over and squeezed her hand. "Like you say: we were pretty lucky."

They drove in silence for a few minutes. Susan turned to look out of the passenger window, let her forehead rest against the glass.

Suddenly she asked, "Did the police recover the documents? The ones he stole?"

"Not exactly," David said, mysteriously.

She waited for him to speak.

"I picked up his bag," he said. He didn't explain for a moment. Then he said, "He had a bag with him. It's got the papers in it. And something else in a box. I think it's the Marker." He glanced over at Susan, taking his eyes off the road for a second, trying to gauge her reaction.

For a moment she said nothing. Then she began to laugh. "Oh well, why not?" she said, almost recklessly, in between laughs, a wild tone in her voice.

David found himself smiling, her good humour contagious, despite the fact she sounded a little manic. After a minute or so she got herself under control and said, "Why aren't I surprised?"

David couldn't think of a reply.

"Have you got a plan?" she said.

"I'll hand it over tomorrow, make up some story," he said. "But I wanted to see this thing." He sounded emphatic.

He glanced at her. She was watching him, waiting for him to go on. He said, "You've seen him now. You know there's something weird, bizarre, whatever you want to call it, about him. Well the owner of the Marker is the same. There's something strange about him too. And both of them are obsessed with the Marker," he said.

She was still listening, patiently.

He went on, "He thought I'd come to kill him." He shook his head in disbelief. "He called me a child and said that in a hundred years I'd wish I'd kept it for myself. I didn't know what to make of it. And he said something about tribute," he paused. "Whatever's going on here, I want to figure it out. I want to know who the hell these people are and what he was talking about," David said, his voice loud with exasperation.

"He said 'tribute'?" Susan asked, curiously.

"Yeah, he said I had no tribute. Does that mean something to you?" he asked.

"It's in one of the documents in the collection. It talks about tribute. It's… It's like a badge of office, something you wear. I think the derivation is sort of a pun. Tribute means, literally, an offering from the tribe, but it also means three of something. Whatever tribute is, I think it's in three parts. The scroll mentions tribute on someone's brow; one part is obviously a headpiece."

She was quiet for a moment.

"We're not totally different, you and me," she said. She gave a crooked smile, "You're worse, no question about it. But I'm guilty too."

"What do you mean?" David asked. "What are you talking about?"

"I kept something from the police," she said, quietly.

"What?" David asked, his voice quiet and level.

"He was wearing something on his head, a metal band. I think it might be gold. When I hit him with the pole, what I really hit was the band. I think maybe I might have killed him otherwise." She stopped talking for a minute. She was very quiet, her hand over her mouth. She made a tiny sound, a single sob. Then she lifted her head again and her voice was stronger, "I kept the band. It's in my desk."

David asked, "Are you saying that's what he meant by 'tribute', the gold band he was wearing?"

Susan shrugged.

"What does it mean?" David said passionately. "Is this some sort of secret society? Like, I dunno, the Templars or the Illuminati or something?" he said, sounding incredulous.

"You know about that stuff?" Susan asked.

"I don't know anything about them except that they're popular with conspiracy theorists," David said.

"Or you could have said the Masons or maybe the Priory of Sion. There's a ton of them," she said.

"You don't believe any of it?" he asked.

"Not at face value, no. I don't think every last detail is made up, I just think most conspiracies are bits of disconnected things linked together when they shouldn't be," she said.

"So how do we link this together properly so that it makes sense instead of looking like a paranoid delusion?"

Susan sighed. "Maybe we can't. We'll look at the Marker. You'll give it back to its owners. The bad guy will go to jail, or maybe a lunatic asylum. Maybe we never get to work it out. Maybe we don't have enough of the pieces. Maybe that's how conspiracy theories get started, by taking half the picture and pretending it tells the whole story."

David drove in silence, brooding.

Susan put a hand on his shoulder and said softly, "It might not be such a bad thing. We had our brush with danger and we found out that neither of us are cowards – or maybe that both of us need our heads looking at. This is a good point to get off the ride. I don't think I'd care to go round a second time."

"You might be right," David said. "I'll have a happy client, you'll get to look at your collection in peace. We're both still alive. That's not a bad outcome, is it?"

"Definitely not," she said, reassuringly. "We might even end up as friends," she said, smiling.

While they had been talking, they had reached David's flat. He found a parking space right outside.

David's flat was the upper floor of a converted, turn of the century terrace. It had a large main bedroom and a second much smaller one, with a single bed in it, currently piled up with boxes.

David offered Susan his room, but she insisted that she'd be a lot happier in a small bed than he would.

Susan, whose white top was gruesomely bloodstained and whose matted hair hung stiffly, asked if she could take a shower.

While she was doing that, David searched around for clean clothes, finding a comfortable old rugby shirt, tracksuit trousers, a pair of towelling socks and some white cotton boxer shorts – all laundry-fresh. He laid them out on the single bed once he'd moved the boxes and put fresh bedclothes on. Susan was still in the shower.

She emerged, after nearly twenty minutes, wrapped in various towels and scuttled into her new room.

David tapped at the closed door. "Hot chocolate?" he called. "Everyone needs hot chocolate when they're feeling a bit banged up."

She opened the door a little and peeked round the edge, displaying wet hair and a bare shoulder covered in droplets of water. "Got any of that almond stuff? The liqueur?"

"Amaretto?" asked David.

"Yeah, that," she said.

"I might have, if my pal Banjo hasn't hoovered it. He tends to assume if I don't drink something within a month I need help with it. You want it in the hot chocolate or on its own?" he asked.

"In the chocolate. To start with," she said.

"You don't look like you're dressed yet. Have I got time for a shower?" he asked.

"Hey, it's your place. Help yourself. I don't suppose there's any hot water left in the whole street though. Sorry about that," she said.

David put some milk on to heat, on a low setting, and headed for the bathroom. When he returned, he was wearing similar clothes to Susan's, who sat on his black leather couch, legs tucked under her.

"The underwear was a nice touch," she said.

David looked a little awkward, "I didn't know if you wanted... If you'd wear..."

"Easy. I'll have to stop teasing you; it's no challenge. Actually, I used to wear men's boxers when I was in high school. Sort of undercover rebellion," she said.

"Don't tell me that," he said, shaking his head, "there's no way I should know what you used to wear under your school uniform. In fact I'm probably guilty of some sort of crime now."

"Oh, now you're worried about committing crimes," she said. And then pointed to the pan of milk. "Be a good boy and find that Amaretto," she said, and then in a throaty Southern drawl, "Momma needs her medicine."

David laughed. "Hold on," he said, wandering into the kitchen area, which was just an extension of the living room. He began looking in cupboards. "Are you even allowed alcohol?" he asked. "I don't remember the doctor mentioning that."

"Gimme," she said. "I get cranky otherwise."

He chuckled again. "OK." Pulling a dusty bottle from the back of a cupboard he said, "Here we are. Banjo is obviously slipping."

He made two mugs of hot chocolate, topped hers up with liqueur. He put a splash of Irish Whiskey in his and then grimaced as he tasted it. He brought the drinks over to the sofa. Susan took her mug and pulled her feet in enough so that he could sit next to her. She sighed and let her head loll back against the sofa for a minute. "I need a holiday," she said.

"Where would you go?" he asked softly, sipping from his mug.

"An island somewhere," she said dreamily. "Maybe a Greek island. One bar, one hotel, a restaurant and a post office. Maybe a goat."

"Sounds nice. What would you do there?" he said, his voice even lower.

Susan, when she spoke, sounded almost asleep, "Sit under a tree with my books. Look for olives. Talk to the goat."

The mug in her hand started to tip and David leaned across to catch it, cupping his hands round hers. She opened her eyes and lifted her head in surprise. She sat up a bit, which brought them very close. Their fingers were tangled up and it took David a moment to disengage.

"You got it?" he asked.

"I've got it," she replied.

He let go of her hand and they moved apart. Neither of them spoke for a moment.

After a few seconds they realised they were staring at each other and Susan looked away. "I'd better get to bed," she said. "What's your plan for the morning?"

"The doctor said I should keep an eye on you. I know it's a pain, but I want to check in on you every couple of hours," he said.

She made a face but conceded, "Oh yeah, he said that, didn't he?"

"I'll tap on your door, that's all, just let me know you're still functioning. I'll probably get up around six, so when I check on you then, we can make a plan," he said.

She took a few more sips of her chocolate and set down the half-finished mug. "Can I borrow a toothbrush?" she said standing up and shuffling towards the bathroom, dragging her feet in their oversized socks and baggy trousers.

"I left one out," he said.

When she had pulled the bathroom door closed behind her, he went into her room and scooped up her clothes. Her jeans and underwear went into the washing machine on a cool wash, the bloody top he left to soak in a bowl of cold water. While he was doing that, he heard the toilet flush and sock-muffled feet padding about.

"Night," she called and then he heard her door close.

When he tapped on her closed door at one, he called, "How many fingers am I holding up?"

"Better be more than one," a drowsy voice said.

At three he called, "Who's President?"

"Al Gore," she said.

He put her clothes in the dryer while he was up and set his alarm for six.

CHAPTER 15

The car contained three people: driver, passenger and prisoner.

"Name?" repeated the officer from the front passenger seat, this time more harshly.

The prisoner was on his own in the back, head down, his breathing audible even over the engine noise of the rapidly moving police car. There was a harsh catch and rasp to each breath which, when considered alongside David's shoe print plainly visible on his chest, didn't paint a picture of perfect health. The bleeding from his head wound had stopped, but it was unclear from his appearance whether the police station or the hospital should be his first stop.

His hands lay in his lap, his wrists linked by handcuffs. Instead of fastening his hands with the palms together, his arresting officer had folded his arms – each hand reaching for the opposite elbow – before the cuffs had been attached.

His head was down, his gaze lost in infinity. His posture was

175

hunched, his focus turned inward. There was no sign that he was aware of his surroundings or registering the questions occasionally directed at him.

Having received no reply or reaction, the officer in the passenger seat turned away from the prisoner. As he did so, the battered figure croaked, "Jan."

"Jan or Chan," the officer asked, but there was no response.

A few seconds later, Jan began a quiet bout of coughing, his fastened arms pressed against his chest as though to hold his ribs together. His face was taut with discomfort.

After a minute or so, the silent fit subsided and he was still. He sank down to lie on the back seat, his eyes closed.

The officer in the passenger seat said to his colleague, "Get the duty doctor to check him out as soon as he's locked up. And get some pictures of those injuries. I don't want anyone thinking they happened in the cells."

The driver glanced quickly over his shoulder, took in the inert form. "He doesn't look too good," he said quietly. "Should we wake him up?"

"No, leave him," said the first. "Be good if they were all this easy."

With both officers facing forwards, the figure on the back seat began to stir. Using his teeth, he began to inch one sleeve up his arm. He'd pinch the cloth just below his shoulder and pull, angling his head back. The dark grey cloth gradually receded from his right wrist exposing a wide metal bracelet.

"What are we booking him with?" the driver asked, eyes intent on the road.

"The Sweeney are handling that. You might want to make sure someone's been down to start the paperwork before you go off tonight," the passenger replied.

The underside of the prisoner's bracelet had two raised pellets of metal set in grooves. Jan began to tug at one of them, manipulating it with his front teeth, trying to unhook it from the slot in which it sat.

Once he had succeeded in releasing one of the pellets, it became clear that a cord ran through the hollow interior of the bracelet, winding round and round. The pellets capping each end of the cord were secured by hooking them into the channels cut into the bracelet's shell.

The back part of the bracelet was open, allowing the cord, made of braided metal, to be withdrawn from the hollow interior. Jan slowly extracted the glittering strand, concealing it in his fist until he had it all.

Moving stealthily and greatly hampered by his handcuffed wrists, he began to wrap the cord – which extended perhaps a metre when unravelled – around his head, wincing each time the metal encountered the edges of his clotted wound.

He fastened the cord by knotting the ends in front. Then, methodically, he began to repeat the process with the other bracelet.

"I might as well get the doc on his way," the passenger said, unhooking the microphone on the side of the police radio. The driver's attention was fully occupied dealing with traffic as the police car moved briskly through the twilight London streets.

Less than a minute later, Jan had fastened the gold cord from his other bracelet around his temples, knotting it tightly in place. Now he held his handcuffed wrists in front of his face.

The passenger carried on a radio conversation with a remote voice, the squawked replies unintelligible to the untrained ear. When he'd finished, he said to his colleague, "So have you met Saunders yet, the transfer?"

"Bumped into him in court. Didn't get much out of him. What's his story?" the driver said.

"I don't know how reliable this is but I heard…" he paused. "Is something burning?" he asked, leaning forwards and sniffing in the direction of the radio.

The driver tilted his head and sniffed too. "It's outside," he said, dismissively.

At that moment, they were driving past massive Edwardian town houses set back from a wide boulevard. There was nothing visible along the magnificent sweep of expensive homes to suggest a fire.

The passenger continued sniffing the air and after a moment turned his head and caught sight of the prisoner, still laying flat, his linked wrists held in front of him.

The handcuffs he wore were of the one-piece kind, with no chain; the two loops and the wide, metal centrepiece that joined them were a single solid unit. But now there was something strange about the middle section of the prisoner's handcuffs. It was damaged. As the officer looked round, a curl of smoke rose from the black, disintegrating metal.

"What are you doing?" the passenger commanded, noticing the yellow metal which wrapped the prisoner's forehead. "Stop that," he said sharply, sounding alarmed.

With a grunt, the prisoner strained to pull his hands apart. The cuffs' centre bar separated like unmoistened clay, opening a vee-shaped gap along its middle, until only a narrow twist of metal secured the two halves.

Straining hard, the prisoner rotated his forearms in opposite directions, putting pressure on the join. With a sound like a pebble dropped onto stone the final strand broke. The prisoner's wrists were no longer fastened.

"Stop the car," the passenger called out, turning in his seat to grab one of the prisoner's arms and attempting to immobilise it.

The driver was at that second overtaking a slow-moving vehicle – a driver under instruction. He accelerated hard, the quicker to complete the manoeuvre. He attempted a rapid glance over his shoulder, but could see little before snatching his eyes back to the road. The engine roared as he floored the right-hand pedal.

The officer in the passenger seat, having gripped the prisoner's right arm just below the elbow, was attempting to capture the man's other hand. It was pulled back out of reach, but the prisoner himself was not fighting back. He was immobile. Instead of struggling, he was holding himself completely rigid. For a moment the prisoner's eyes flickered up into his head and his eyelids dipped.

With a bang and screech of torn steel, the rear left-hand door of the car exploded from its frame and blew out into the street.

The police car had barely pulled ahead of the vehicle it was overtaking. The jettisoned door whipped across in front of the startled learner-driver to collide with one of the huge iron lamp-posts spaced along the pavement. The door rebounded, disappearing under the wheels of the driving-school car, which swerved violently, mounting the curb.

The police car too slammed on its brakes. The wheels locked, throwing the car into a slide, the back end threatening to slew round. The driver twisted the steering wheel in the opposite direction, attempting to maintain control.

The animal squeal of shredding rubber was deafening for the two seconds it took the police car to slither to a halt. In those moments the officer in the passenger seat, twisted half round as he was, lost his grip on Jan's arm. He was thrown sideways, his shoulder and the back of his head striking the side window. The smack of skull against glass was drowned in the mechanical din, but the officer's eyes went wide and he doubled instinctively over, pulling his face down into his chest, arms wrapping his head, lips pursed for an uncompleted curse, as the pain incapacitated him.

Almost before the police car stopped sliding, the prisoner was boosting himself upright, scrambling out of the hole where the door had been.

The driver, a second slower off the mark, wrenched at his door handle and flung the door wide. He pushed up from the steering wheel, attempting to propel himself from the car only to be gripped fast by his seatbelt. Another fraction of a second was lost before his brain registered the problem. His hand clawed at the belt release, finding it on the second try, popping the metal tongue free from its slot.

The prisoner was sprinting along the pavement in the direction the police car had been heading (and was now almost at right angles to). Fifteen metres away he halted.

He turned to regard the vehicle from which he had just escaped, taking in the two occupants, one stunned, the other fighting to free himself.

His neck muscles tightened and his eyelids drooped, as though a heavy current was being drawn elsewhere in his body, leaving his eyes momentarily without the strength to open. His hands rose in front of him, turning, the fingers folding, until he looked as though he were pleading for something. He touched his clenched fists to each other and drew his face down almost to meet them.

The driver, finally freed, planted one foot on the tarmac of the roadway and rose rapidly from the vehicle. At once, he saw that his prisoner had not disappeared, but instead was standing facing him some metres down the street. He checked his impulse to rush towards him and raised one hand, saying in a firm and level tone, "Stop there. Don't move." One hand crept down to his holster and unbuttoned his side-arm.

And the prisoner didn't move – for a moment. He simply drew a breath in deeply and lowered his head to his touching fists, his eyes unseeing, his shoulders high and hunched.

The explosion threw the driver sideways and onto the other side of the road as the police car's petrol tank ignited. The occupants of the crashed driving-school car – which had struck a garden wall – were the only other witnesses.

The majority of the burning fuel which erupted from the burst tank flew out and up, issuing from the shattered filler cap like steam from a ruptured boiler. Flame instantly transformed the cloud to blinding orange-white, erasing all detail.

The sound of exploding gas punching out of its container sounded like a shotgun blast and was instantly followed by the monstrous 'whump' of ignition which boomed and rattled for several seconds, just like thunder, as it shook window-frames and rolled in echoes around the neighbourhood. Burning droplets showered from the cloud, spraying the ground with incendiary rain.

The massive surge of heat was such that hair on the sprawled policeman's head shrivelled. The blast had knocked him down, face first, leaving only the back of his head and his hands exposed to the wash of scorching air.

Stunned for several seconds, he turned over, pressing several burning spots on his uniform into the tarmac. With one hand over his eyes, he struggled to move back from the flames, the fire billowing above him, preventing him from rising.

Scrambling backwards to the opposite curb, he hauled himself to his feet, clutching a litter bin for support. His grilled hand shielding his eyes, he took in the scene: his whole vehicle was wrapped in flames, its interior so crammed with fire nothing else could be discerned. There was no sign of its other occupant, but the front passenger door was still closed.

Only after ten seconds had passed, having taken one sudden, lurching, abortive step towards the burning wreck, did he look round. There was no sign of his prisoner.

CHAPTER 16

"Coffee," David called softly, tapping on the bedroom door.

"Hnnggh," Susan said faintly from within.

"Suuusan?" he enquired gently, holding his ear close to the door.

"Adyawant?" a husky voice responded, torpor running the words together.

"Do you want some coffee?" he said.

"Got to sleep," the dreamy voice replied.

David sighed and knocked again. "Can I come in?" he said.

There was no answer. He opened the door and peered into the dimly lit room. Outside, the sun was rising and light was just creeping in around the edges of the curtains. There was just enough illumination to reveal the bed and something of its occupant. A mop of blonde hair and one arm poked out of the top of the duvet.

No other features were visible, beyond a covered, person-sized hump in the centre, the lair of some hibernating creature.

"I'll put this over here," David said, tiptoeing over to place the mug of coffee he held on top of the bedside cabinet.

A moan coincided with some motion beneath the covers. The outstretched arm withdrew.

"Susan," David said again, laying one hand on the quilt-covered form and gently shaking. He stopped suddenly halfway through the motion.

"Take your hand off that," a clear voice said from beneath the covers, the muzziness of sleep completely dispelled.

His hand quickly withdrew.

From within the cocoon, fingers emerged and folded down a flap of duvet. Blue eyes were revealed. They regarded David, blinking once.

Susan drew the duvet back a little more, uncovering her cotton-covered shoulders. She had been lying contorted, back arched, one shoulder buried in the pillow, the other one raised, pulled up towards her ear – which would have placed David's hand somewhere around her left breast.

"It's like being back in my undergrad dorm," she said.

"I thought it was your shoulder," David said, humbly.

"Uhhuh," she agreed, without conviction.

David stepped away from the bed, backing towards the door. "I'll leave you to wake up," he said and nodded towards the coffee. He was already dressed; he had on a cream-coloured shirt with dark trousers and no tie.

"What time is it?" Susan asked, reaching for the mug.

"Just after six," he replied. "I'm not going to go into the office until later. I've got some thinking to do and I'd appreciate your input," he looked momentarily irritated at his phrasing, "I mean

I'd like your help, if you're up to it. How are you feeling, by the way?"

Susan propped herself up on one elbow and took a sip of the coffee. Setting it down, she touched her bruised cheek gently.

"I feel fine," she said. "Just give me a few minutes and I'll be with you. The bathroom free?" she asked.

"It's all yours. Your clothes should be dry by now," he said. He made to go.

She raised her voice a little to halt him, "I'm starved. Got any food?" she asked.

"Get dressed and we'll go to the café on the corner," he glanced at his watch, "they open early."

While Susan was in the shower, David took her clothes out of the dryer. The top was still bloodstained. Although the blood had faded, it was still conspicuous.

He sneaked into the vacated spare room and began to rummage through the cheap pine wardrobe at the foot of the bed. Clothes of varying vintage and ancestry had been relegated there. He found a silk blouse in dark blue and held it up, attempting to judge the size. It was still draped in clear plastic from the dry-cleaners. He made the bed and left Susan's other clothes – along with the blouse – spread out on top of it.

Susan's head wound had left several spots of blood on the pillow. He caught sight of them and turned the pillow over.

He was sitting in the living room a few minutes later when Susan, her hair still damp, appeared. She was dressed and wearing the blouse. It was a good fit.

"So whose is this?" Susan asked. "Mom? Sister? *Girl*friend?"

He said, "Ex-girlfriend. She never came back to collect it, and since she already owns 4% of the world's supply of clothes..."

Susan shrugged. "Anyway it fits. I'll get it back to you. Thanks for the thought. I guess my top…"

David shook his head with melodramatic sadness. "It didn't make it," he said with a sniff, indicating where it lay on the arm of the chair. Susan examined it, inspecting the spots and putting it down again.

David watched her move around the room. "You look tired," David said.

"You just haven't seen me without make-up before," Susan said with a thin smile. "It's not easy looking glamorous twenty-four seven. But I guess you're out of eyeliner."

David said softly, "I didn't mean that. I wasn't complaining."

She shrugged, gave him a smile that was weak, but more sincere. "And another twelve hours sleep would be good too," she added.

"Yeah, I'm in the same boat," David said, emphatically. He continued, "The sleep I mean; I don't really care about the eyeliner." Her smile was genuine this time.

Susan picked up the empty coffee cup she had brought through from the bedroom. She raised it with a little jiggling motion. "Got any more before we head out?" she asked.

"Yeah," David said. "Same as before?" he asked, getting up from the sofa.

"No milk, thanks," she said, distractedly, her eyes alighting on a black, leather holdall which lay on the sofa.

"Is that," she nodded in the direction of the bag, "what I think it is?" Her voice had acquired a little tension.

David moved past her, poured coffee. "It is," he said over his shoulder.

Susan looked nervous, as though she were drawn to the bag but at the same time didn't want to approach it. "I want to see it," she said.

David returned to the sofa and handed her the replenished mug. He sat down next to the bag and twisted round so that he could reach it properly. Unzipping the top, he lifted out a heavy wooden box.

Susan stood and moved round to sit behind him, on one arm of the sofa. The box had her full attention. She placed a hand on David's shoulder, leaning over him to get a better look.

The box looked like a very beautiful, old-fashioned cigar humidor, though it was a little on the large side for that role – about the same dimensions as a stack of a dozen or so magazines. It was constructed from rosewood so dark, smooth and close-grained it seemed more like black chrome until the light caught it.

David moved the bag to the floor and placed the box on the sofa. It stood about 10cm high – featureless polished wood, except for a little button on the front for releasing the catch.

He pushed in the button and lifted the lid.

There was a box within the box.

The rosewood case was even more beautiful when seen this way. An interior space had been smoothly excised from what must have been a single piece of lustrous, glassy heartwood. The centre had been scooped out until the outer box was no more than a thumb's width thick at any point. Into the cavity had been placed something greatly at odds with the perfect sheen of its ruby-grained enclosure.

The inner box was a strange, ragged-looking thing. The top was made of sagging grey leather, its texture like unfinished paper. At the edges, the skeleton of the box was visible. Scrolled ivory-coloured rods, yellow with age, formed a frame over which the mottled skin was stretched to form the sides of the box. Some species of translucent thread secured membrane to bone. The needlework was fine and accurate, but the stitching had long since begun to disintegrate. The wrinkled top covering, with its blotchy colouration, seemed to have been water-damaged.

"It looks like the wing of some dead thing," David said, sounding uneasy as he looked at the inner box.

"Like a bat maybe. A big, mangy, mildew-eaten bat," Susan agreed.

A smell of rich, creeping damp rose from the box. It was an unhealthy smell that tickled the back of the throat with each breath taken, making it easy to imagine bright yellow spores taking root in soft pink lung tissue.

"Are you going to open it?" Susan asked, almost whispering.

"I don't even want to touch it," David said. "It looks like it died from the plague."

Susan hopped off the arm of the sofa, stepped to the table and picked up a pencil. She handed it to David, offering him the end with the eraser.

"I'd call you a wimp, but then you might make me open it," she said, looking at the box with disgust.

David took the pencil, holding it by the sharpened end, placing the little rubber pad in contact with the front strut of the box.

Susan said, "You really haven't opened it yet?"

David shook his head, pausing a moment and withdrawing the pencil. "I just opened the outer box to see what I'd got," he said.

Without detaching her eyes from the box, she said, "Thanks for waiting."

David put the rubber end of the pencil back in contact with the lid of the inner box.

"What kind of bone is that?" he asked unhappily, as he began to raise the lid.

"I don't know much about bones. It looks like a radius. Some part of a front leg. Don't know what critter it came off." She held up her hand, gauging the length of her own forearm. "The ones at the sides would need to have come from something much smaller than a man."

"Like a child, maybe," David said blackly, lifting the lid the rest of the way.

Both of them drew in their breath as they saw the Marker. It lay on a folded pad of black velvet, pinned in place with numerous, tiny, ivory hoops. The intricate lace of interlocking platinum had all the minute, ordered complexity of something organic – the veins of a leaf or the delicate, branching barbules of a down feather.

The Marker was about the same width and height as one of David's large hands when fully outstretched.

"It's beautiful," David said.

They both stared at the Marker – Susan moving round to lean against David's leg, so that she could peer into the box. She took the pencil from him, folded the lid of the wretched inner box back and put her hands on the rosewood outer case. She tilted the whole thing to catch the light. The platinum had a buttery lustre like silver as it begins to oxidise. Holding her breath, one hand over her mouth, Susan leaned right in to scrutinise the tracery.

It was made from slender platinum wire which tapered as the pattern wound further from the centre. It was unclear what held it together. The metal branched and met, crossed and joined, as though it had been cast as a single piece. And yet if it were moulded, molten metal would have needed to somehow fill the metres and metres of whisker-fine capillary – with no breaks or bubbles – in order to create the filigreed pattern. No tool marks were evident either.

David went to his bookshelf and took down an encyclopaedia. After a minute he said, "One thousand, seven hundred and sixty-eight degrees Celsius. That's over three thousand Fahrenheit."

Susan looked up at him questioningly.

He said, "The temperature platinum melts at. I just wondered how someone makes a thing like that." He carried on reading. "Hey, listen to this, 'Platinum is unique in that it corrupts metal tools used to work it. By combining with the edge of the tool, platinum weakens even tungsten carbide cutters.' I didn't know that."

"Me neither. No wonder McDonalds use plastic for their cutlery," she said.

He didn't hear her; he was pondering. He said, "I don't see how this could be anything but recent. The only way to make those joints is to weld them, but that makes no sense."

Susan said, "Huh? What's the problem?"

David said, "I studied engineering at university – so I know a certain amount about metalworking. Good steel is a new thing, relatively speaking, because you need exceptionally hot fires to make it and to work it. Welding is even newer, because it involves getting your very high temperatures confined to one precise spot. If you could make this filigree, then working steel would be child's play. That's modern technology. There's no way this could be more than a couple of hundred years old. I think we're having our legs pulled."

Susan said, "It could be a one-off. Look at the Phaistos disk – writing made with metal type three thousand years before Gutenberg was born."

David said, "Yeah, I'd forgotten about the Phaistos disk," a look of total incomprehension on his face.

She gave him a pretend pitying look, "Next you're going to tell me you haven't been to the Herakleion museum."

Susan tried a different tack. "Well, take the library at Alexandria then. A city-state with free speech, a passion for learning built around a vast, ever-expanding reference library. But it didn't last.

The industrial revolution might have been underway before the end of the first millennium, but it takes more than just a single concentration of knowledge." She passed a hand over her forehead. "Listen, can we talk about this over breakfast? I'm about to pass out with hunger."

He said, "Oh god, of course." He closed the lid of the inner then the outer box and returned it to the holdall. He looked around for somewhere to put it. "Stand back a minute," he said to Susan who was still kneeling by the sofa. She got to her feet and moved to the doorway.

With one hand he lifted up the back of the sofa, pivoting it forwards onto its front legs. The webbing on the underside was ripped, revealing the hollow interior. David placed the holdall on the floor and carefully lowered the sofa on top of it, aligning the bag with the tear in the webbing. The bag disappeared up inside the couch.

Susan said, "Not the first time you've used that trick."

David smiled. "It is actually. But I remembered we ripped the webbing open carrying it up here when I moved in." He stood back and examined his handiwork. "Somehow I couldn't just leave that thing sitting on display."

Susan nodded. "I know what you mean," she said.

As they left the house, David found himself looking around, checking the activity in the street. A postman was delivering letters. A middle-aged woman was walking her dog. Nothing seemed out of place.

They cut through an alleyway that divided the terrace opposite, emerging onto a small parade of shops. Between a post office and a cab company, a greasy spoon café was open for business. Three of its tables were occupied by young, fit-looking men. By their clothing and paraphernalia – a toolbox near one table, a spirit-level resting on a chair – they probably all worked in the building trade.

David suggested Susan take a seat by the door while he went up to the counter. They had discussed food on the way over so David was able to order for both of them. He returned to the table with two mugs of tea.

Waiting for their breakfasts to be cooked, they sipped from their mugs. Susan spoke first. "Do you have any idea what's going on here?" she asked.

David looked uncertain of her meaning. He smiled, about to make a quip. She jumped in with, "I mean the robbery, the third man, the impossibility of most of it."

David shook his head. "No, I don't really have any idea what's going on."

Susan said, "Because I don't see how the thief pulled off that break-in." She was starting to look distinctly irritated. "I don't see how he got in and out of the old lady's house. I don't see how he opened that footlocker or the document store at the college." Her voice was rising, "I don't understand how he could jump that wall. I don't see how he could overpower two armed policemen. And I don't know what that thing is," she lowered her voice, "you've got in a bag back home."

She went on, "Not only do I not understand any of it, I'm starting to add up how many people have been hurt or even killed so far. And what I see is us, blundering about in the middle of something dangerous – suicidally dangerous, if you ask me. And I want to get the hell out of it before I get myself killed."

David looked at her, taking in the whispered anger with which she spoke. "You blame me for this, don't you?" he said, the beginnings of an edge in his voice.

"Of course I don't blame you for it. You're not the madman behind all this." She paused and it was clear there was a 'but' coming. "But you don't have a clue what's going on and still you're determined to get into the middle of it."

David said, "It's my job to be…" but she didn't let him finish.

"It's not your job," she said dismissively, almost contemptuously. "All you had to do last night was leave that bag for the police. Hammond could finish tidying this up. But you found a way to keep yourself involved, to keep me involved. Don't you get it; it's not your job? That's what the police are there for, that's what they do."

Susan had been keeping her voice down, despite the emotion in her voice. David sounded worked up when he spoke, but he too managed not to raise his voice. He said, "Do you honestly think Hammond knows more than you do, that he's brighter than you are? If I had left this to the police, I'd be out of a job and my firm would be bankrupt."

He counted off points on his fingers, "First off, they wouldn't have had a lead on the third man, in fact they wouldn't have even known there *was* a third man. Second, they wouldn't have known where to look for him – they even let him clear his things out of a house they were supposed to be watching. Thirdly, if they did know where to look, they wouldn't have caught him. They didn't catch him the last time they had the chance – a chance I created for them."

He leaned forwards and lowered his voice a little more, "It was made very clear to me that if the client put in a claim for that piece," he gestured over his shoulder, meaning the Marker, "I'd be out of work even if the business survived – which was doubtful."

He went on, "Dass wants his property back and he's got contacts at high levels. If I told Dass that Hammond was a nuisance, I'd bet you it wouldn't take twenty-four hours for Hammond to be reassigned. The police aren't some ultimate authority in this, they're just civil servants.

"I've managed to get Dass his prize back, I've seen to it that the thief is behind bars, I've stopped my employers from going out of business and I've kept my job. Not one of those things would have happened if I'd left it to the police. So how exactly do you work out that I'm not doing my job?"

He sat back, silent. Susan too was quiet. A woman in a bright apron bustled up with their food and still neither of them spoke.

They ate for a while.

After several minutes had passed, both of them had calmed their breathing. They were once again taking in their surroundings, instead of staring at one another or into space.

Holding up her knife, pointing it towards the ceiling, Susan said in a level voice, "I don't want to fall out with you. I know you're trying to do what you've been told to do and you're right: you've achieved it against all the odds. But don't forget that there's a lot more to this than a job. We've got every reason to think we're standing between a professional killer and the thing he wants most in the world. He knows who you are, he knows who I am and – for reasons I *think* I understand – we've put ourselves in his way again." She took a breath. "Have you considered what happens if it's not just him? All he'd need was one accomplice still on the loose and we'd be in huge trouble. Somehow, last night both of us got away with just a few knocks. Do you think we'd be so lucky a second time? No one else has been."

David didn't reply and Susan went on, speaking slowly, calmly, "I've been known to struggle with the idea of trusting people." She said it with a little, self-mocking smile – like it was a private joke. "I want to trust that you're thinking about more than keeping your job when you pull these stunts of yours. I want to believe that you're aware that people might die – have already died. I want to believe you'll think twice before you do something that could get one of us killed. I *want* to trust you, but you're not making it easy for me."

She put out one hand and laid it for a moment on top of David's. She squeezed it once and let go. They looked into each other's eyes. Neither of their expressions were easy to read, the mixture of emotions and the residue of their recent tense words clouded their features.

Someone's phone started ringing.

After a moment, David realised it was his. "Who the hell's this?" he wondered aloud as he reached into his back pocket.

Having retrieved the phone, he looked at the display. "It's Hammond," he said.

"Take it," Susan said.

David answered the call, "David Braun."

Susan watched intently as David listened to a monologue she couldn't hear. It went on for twenty seconds before David said, "What happened?"

David's face had become taut. He was listening to something that was making him very uncomfortable, but he didn't interrupt. The voice on the other end continued talking. A minute went by and David was still listening.

He asked, "What do you suggest? I'm talking to Susan Milton right now. What should we do?"

He listened again for another minute.

"Oh, believe me I'll call," David reassured Hammond. "Please let me know if anything changes," he said. "OK. Goodbye." He slipped the phone back in his pocket.

Turning his eyes to Susan, a mixture of discomfort and disbelief on his face, he said, "Their prisoner escaped. They couldn't stop him. They don't know where he is now."

Susan took a moment to absorb that information. Her only response was a single sarcastic comment, "Great."

A moment later she said firmly, "Let's get out of here."

CHAPTER 17

FRIDAY 18TH APRIL

David was stuffing clothes into a bag. "Let's just start driving and figure out what we're going to do next, OK?" he said.

"I agree," Susan said. "But tell me what Hammond said while you're getting ready." She stood in David's living room watching him rush around.

"Give me two minutes and I'll tell you everything I know." David hurried into the other room, taking his bag with him. When he came back he was zipping it up.

He said, "Right. Anything else we might need we stop and buy." He lifted the side of the sofa with one hand, slid the holdall out. "Can you take this?" he said, handing it to Susan.

Holding a bag each, they left David's flat and made their way downstairs towards the front door. Susan held up her hand suddenly and David, who was following her, halted.

Through the frosted glass of the front door a figure could be seen. The outline was stationary. Then there was a rattle as the figure did something to the door.

A moment later a beige envelope dropped to the mat and the figure began to recede. They both relaxed. "Now I remember why I'm not a spy," Susan said, laughing nervously.

When they got outside, the postman was two doors along. He waved to David.

Quickly they got the two bags into the boot of the Saab and got themselves buckled in. Moments later they were pulling away. David put a little bit of distance between them and his flat before he started speaking.

He said, "OK. Sorry to keep you in suspense. Right, what did Hammond tell me?" he said, as though trying to think how to phrase it. "I'll tell you his exact words as best as I can remember them and you can interpret them yourself.

"OK, something like, *You should know that fucking madman is on the loose. Your third man* – Hammond always likes to call him my third man. Like, if I hadn't pointed him out, he wouldn't have ever bothered anyone. Anyway, he said, *Your third man never made it to a cell. He incinerated a police car with an officer still inside it and made a run for it.*"

Susan said, "My god!"

"So I asked him what happened," David said. "He said, *The driver's still not sure which way's up, but in his story he claims the prisoner told them his name was Jan and then promptly passed out from his wounds. Sure you never thought of being a copper?*"

Susan said, "What does that mean?"

"It's police humour. I beat the prisoner up – you're supposed to leave that to the authorities. So then he said, *The next thing the driver saw was this Jan with the handcuffs off. He'd somehow burnt through them, like with a cutting torch, the driver said. Then the door came off its hinges and the prisoner jumped out. He ran a few feet down the street, turned and looked at them. Then the car blew up. Driver's in the hospital, his sergeant's in the mortuary.*"

Susan was staring straight ahead as she quietly took this in. David went on, "Let me think, what comes next? Yeah, he said, *I'm always telling them to search their prisoners. This bloke must have been loaded up with more gadgets than James Bond's Christmas stocking. How can you miss a grenade? The driver also claims the prisoner had wrapped a load of gold wire round his head. That'll be to stop us reading his thoughts, no doubt.*"

"Tribute," Susan said. "I knocked the gold band off his head and he replaced it. It's got to be more than just a fashion statement," she said forcefully. She looked over at David. "What else? You asked him what we should do?"

David said, "Yeah, that was next. He told me he thought Jan would be going back to retrieve the jewellery he stole – which is what he thinks the Marker is – or maybe to get some of the papers he missed at the School of Antiquities. Hammond said they'd got four men waiting for him there. Of course, what he didn't know – and I didn't tell him – was that Jan doesn't have the Marker; we do. He said we probably weren't in any danger, but we should take a few precautions nonetheless. Oh and to call him if we should happen to run into his escaped prisoner."

Susan said, "Well we can have a good game of I-told-you-so some other time. What do you think we should do?"

David said, "Well, Jan doesn't know where the Marker is. He'd have to assume the police would find it, so if he's going after it, he'd be going after them not us. In the meantime, we get the Marker back to Dass. Dass can make up some story about how his people got it back. If Jan doesn't know what's going on, then he'll think the police have what he wants and if by some chance he's got a contact in the police he'll learn the Marker's back with Dass. Either way we're off the hook."

Susan said, "Unless his contacts are *really* good, in which case he knows that right this moment, the Marker's unaccounted for."

David said, "Yeah, so we have to be cautious for a few hours until we meet with Dass."

Susan asked, "What does Jan know about you?"

"Not that much," David said, then winced. "Unless he was paying attention when I told the police my name and who I work for."

There was silence for a little while and then Susan asked, "Where are we?"

It was 7.15 a.m. and they were heading west on the Marylebone Road. Traffic was heavy but it was still early enough that they were making progress.

David said, "I'm vaguely heading for the motorway. I want to get out of London. Pick somewhere you've never been and we'll drive there."

Susan said, "OK. But listen, let's not phone Dass until we've thought this through. A few hours won't make any difference provided we make sure we're good and lost before we stop anywhere."

David said, "Alright. Where do you want to go?"

"Brighton," Susan said, decisively. "Can we do that?"

"It's perfect," David said.

* * *

It took another hour and a half before they were flying down the M23 towards the coast. The sun was out and they'd been listening to the radio for much of the trip. By unspoken agreement, either of them could turn the music down if they wanted to say something.

They were just passing Gatwick airport when David cut the

Sugababes off in mid-refrain. "He didn't have a grenade," David said.

"What do you mean?" Susan asked, intrigued.

"You saw what he was wearing. Where would you keep a grenade, just supposing you thought it was a good idea to carry one with you," David said.

"Well, I guess I'd try to find a little clutch bag that went with these shoes. If I were Jan, though… I don't know. Pocket? Clipped to my belt?"

David said, "That's about all I could come up with. I sat with my knee in the small of his back for about five minutes and I can tell you he didn't have anything bulky on him. Do they make miniature grenades? Likewise that cutting torch he was supposed to have. I've seen them small, but small like this," he spread his fingers, "not small like a lighter or something. Plus there's whatever he used to rip the car door off."

Susan said, "What about your black ops theory, that he used to be some sort of spy? If those miniature James Bond gadgets exist, it's spies who'd use them. When a secret agent wants a cutting torch they probably don't go to B&Q."

They were out in the country now. Fields and trees flanked the motorway.

David glanced over at Susan. He said, "That's another thing. Did you ever think it was funny that at the start of each film, James Bond would be given two or three gadgets that turned out to be just the ones he needed later on? He never got issued with a super-powered magnet and it later turned out that he needed the watch with the laser in it."

Susan smiled. "Right. Or found himself tackling a shark armed only with a miniature camera. I think I saw a comedy sketch along those lines."

David nodded and went on, "So even if Jan did somehow have two lots of explosives and a cutting torch on him, how did he know that's what he'd need? He didn't expect to be caught or he wouldn't have returned to that address."

Susan said, "What, you mean in real life, you'd have to carry two dozen little gadgets just to guarantee you'd got the three you actually needed?"

David said, "That's sort of what I'm saying, yes."

Susan considered. She said thoughtfully, "They *are* the things I'd take along if I was going to break in somewhere and open a safe. In fact, that's exactly what I'd take."

David made a face. He said, "You're right. Forget the James Bond stuff." He looked a bit sheepish. "I was just thinking out loud."

Susan said, "Hold on there. Don't give up yet. I said that's exactly what *I'd* take – that and maybe a gun. But I'm not Jan."

David looked puzzled, "Clearly. Are you saying he'd take something different?"

Susan said, "Who knows? He might have had pockets stuffed with explosives and tiny cutting torches and he might not. But if he did, they weren't there to help with the break-in, because he didn't use them. He cracked a door-lock and then peeled the steel front off a document store without blowing anything up or burning a hole in it. Did you happen to notice whether he was concealing a sledgehammer and a hydraulic jack while you were sitting on him? That's what it looked like he'd used."

David looked astounded, "You don't think he can... How can he do that stuff?"

Susan said, "What do you want me to say? Do normal rules even apply here? One thing's for sure, I'm going to read up on this deal with wrapping gold round your head. I wish I had my laptop

– the whole collection's on there."

David said, "The papers he stole are in the holdall with the Marker. There's only a handful of them – literally – but you can start with them today if you want."

They drove in silence for another five minutes. Susan only spoke once. She pressed her index finger suddenly against the passenger window and said, "Baby sheep." She sounded excited. David glanced out at the field and then smiled at Susan. She noticed his amused attention and shrugged.

David said, "You know Brighton, traditionally, is where bosses take their secretaries for a dirty weekend."

Susan said, "I think I can guess what that quaint little phrase means. This would be in the days when 'boss' automatically meant a guy, right?"

David said, "Yeah, it's funny. Plenty of bosses are women these days, but none of the secretaries are men. Where's the equality in that?"

Susan gave him a mildly scornful look, "Gee, what a mystery. Just doesn't seem to be as much competition to get to the bottom of a company."

Susan looked at fields for a few seconds more and then said, "So is that why you were keen on Brighton? Take your little employee there?" Her words were full of sarcasm.

David looked outraged. "What? You picked Brighton!" he spluttered.

Susan replied haughtily, "And you said 'Perfect'. I just wondered why you thought it was so perfect. The only comment you've made about it is bosses screwing their female workers."

David was obviously insulted. He said forcefully, "OK. One, it's about the right distance from London. Two, it's an easy drive. Three, it's awash with tourists and visitors who we can blend in with. And four, it's a place where people go to have fun, so it's the last place you'd expect people in danger to think of."

Susan didn't say anything. David was still pretty worked up. "Why do you do that?" he demanded. "We'll be having a nice conversation and you'll say something to get me totally on the defensive."

Susan spread her hands and lifted her eyebrows. She said acidly, "Hey, how was I to know you didn't have a sense of humour?"

David shook his head, not accepting that. He said, "No, when you want to be funny, you're funny. This is something else. It's almost like it bothers you if we go too long without a few tense words."

Susan was the one on the defensive now. She said, "What, our argument over breakfast about you recklessly endangering the lives around you doesn't count as a few tense words? Wouldn't that keep me going for the rest of the day?"

David said, "That was for real. Despite the fact you feel strongly about it, you were fair with me. Just now though, you didn't believe for a moment I'd set this up to seduce you but you accused me of it anyway, knowing you'd get a reaction."

Susan was facing away from him now, staring fixedly out of her window. "I don't know what you mean," she said coldly. Her gaze was directed sideways, out of the car, towards the woodland they were passing, but her eyes weren't focussing on it.

David kept his eyes fixed on the road. He looked like he was fuming. They drove on in silence.

Motorway turned to fast A-road. Five minutes passed.

Eventually Susan said, "So are you saying you find me unattractive?" her voice hard and accusing.

David's nostrils flared and he glanced sharply at Susan. She was smiling sweetly back at him. He burst out laughing, relieved.

She laughed too.

When they'd stopped laughing they were still smiling. After a minute David asked, "Is there a boyfriend somewhere who gets tortured like this?"

She pretended to be offended, saying, "You think I'm torturing you now?"

"Not really," he conceded.

After a little pause she growled, "No, I've driven them all away." Then she asked, "So where's the owner of this blouse?"

David said, "Hollywood. Seeking her fortune."

Susan chuckled, "Oh nice work. I've never driven anyone *that* far away before. Is five thousand miles your record?"

David looked pleased with himself, "It was nothing really. A little emotional neglect, a few hints about cheap airfares."

Susan asked, with a little less levity, "What happened?"

David considered for a moment and said, "Can you ever really summarise a relationship? She's just a very hungry person – hungry for more attention, more excitement. We couldn't find a compromise between what I wanted and what she wanted."

Susan asked, "So are you friends now?"

David replied, "Probably we are. Now. I would think Hope would have forgiven me and I was never that annoyed with her."

Susan said, "Maybe that was the problem?"

David gave her a questioning look.

She explained, "She's an actress, right? Maybe she wanted the full range of passion, not just the good stuff. A leading man in the movies is a lot more than just someone who's nice to you."

David said with resignation, "That's as good an explanation as I've heard. Anyway, she'll be in her element where she is and I'm happy to let her get on with it."

"*Lasciate speranza*," Susan said, without explanation and

David didn't ask.

David said, "So anyway, you're American, you must be on about your fourth husband by now."

Susan smiled. "I see you know your stereotypes. Just between you and me, that's why I had to leave. I wasn't getting married enough and it was dragging the average down. Elizabeth Taylor was on double shifts trying to balance things out."

David asked, "So not even one husband?"

Susan shrugged, "Nope. A few lucky escapes. One false alarm. My sister is the expert at telling that story. She's flying over next week, maybe she can fill you in." A look of concern crossed Susan's face. "Jesus, I nearly forgot all about her visit. It's amazing how a brush with death will distract you. I hope all this is sorted out by then."

David said authoritatively, "Once Dass has the Marker the excitement's over. Whatever happens after that, it's not my problem. And you'll be left in peace to do whatever it is you do when I'm not trying to get you killed."

Susan nodded.

They carried on talking about relationships for a while. Whatever had surfaced to make them angry at one another had disappeared. They talked naturally and with light-hearted ease.

Soon they were driving past manicured municipal lawns on the outskirts of Brighton. It was only half past ten in the morning and yet both of them found themselves yawning uncontrollably.

David said, "Can I trust you not to go berserk if I suggest a change of plan?"

Susan said, "I don't know that I like 'berserk'. But I'll do my best. What's your suggestion?"

David seemed hesitant. "Listen, this is nothing more than what I'm saying, whatever it might sound like…"

Susan interrupted. "Spit it out, for god's sake, or I will get pissed," she said, but without conviction.

David got to the point, "You know we're both tired and we've got some important thinking to do and some calls to make. I was thinking we need a base here. So why don't we get a hotel room?"

Susan gave David an appraising look and as she did so she yawned widely. David said, "See? Let's get two hours sleep and some lunch and then work out how we're going to play things with Dass."

Susan said, "And I suppose it should be one room instead of two because…"

David said, "Because the last thing we should do is split up if we're going to get some sleep."

Susan said, after a moment's pause, "That's actually an excellent idea."

David added, "It doesn't have to be the Bridal Suite or anything, just so long as the Jacuzzi's big enough for two."

She gave him a sarcastic smile.

David said, "I've only stayed here once – on business. We can use the same hotel; it's right on the sea-front."

Susan yawned again while trying to say, "Fine."

* * *

They got a twin room at The Grand, looking out over a sea that had turned grey. The early morning sun had retreated behind midday cloud and a stiffening breeze was raking spray onto the promenade.

They had both made phone calls to say they wouldn't be at work that day. Susan had set the alarm on her watch for half three. Now David pulled the curtains. They were thick and lined, but they still let in a certain amount of light. The room was dim, but not dark.

Neither of them were happy with the idea of laying, fully clothed, on top of the covers. On the other hand, neither of them was about to undress in front of the other.

"Wow, I feel self-conscious," David said. "I think people usually do this for the first time drunk."

Susan volunteered to change into a robe in the bathroom. When she had closed the door behind her, David undressed rapidly so as to be in bed when she returned.

"This is very weird," she said when she emerged.

"It can't be any weirder than hiding from a thief with super powers," David said.

"Different weird," Susan replied. "This feels like the time I played Doctors and Nurses with Arty Hickson." She slipped into her bed and wriggled out of her robe.

David asked innocently, "He's someone you work with?"

Susan looked for something to throw. "He lived next door when I was six. I still believed in hell in those days, was sure I was going there," she said. "You know what's funny? He actually *is* a doctor now."

A few moments later, she asked "Are you actually sleepy? I'm suddenly wide awake."

There was no reply – just steady breathing.

Somewhere in the hotel the distant sound of a Hoover waxed and waned. It blended with the faint sound of the sea. Through the thick walls, the occasional far-off bump as the Hoover struck a chair leg was muffled into quiet timpani and the distant screams of gulls were robbed of their melodrama.

They both slept.

CHAPTER 18

It was the end of the afternoon and the temperature was dropping. David and Susan had wandered aimlessly through the town, talking and occasionally stopping to look in shop windows, until the sharp breeze began to make their eyes water.

They ducked into the first restaurant that looked warm and inviting. Now they were eating a very late lunch gazing out at the grey world.

Susan was eating spicy tomato soup, breaking off chunks of crusty bread to go with it. She said, "I feel worse than if I'd never slept."

David said, "I know it seems like that, but you were looking pretty pale before. I think the sleep's done you some good."

A waitress arrived with David's dish of baked ravioli. Despite its volcanic heat he made rapid inroads into it.

While they'd been walking they'd talked about Dass and the handover of the Marker. David now picked up the thread again. "So why did you think we should be cautious about calling him?"

Susan replied, "I started thinking over the things you said about him – how you felt when you first met him. You said you got a bad vibe from him – and from Jan – but it was worse with Dass. Well, Jan's the ruthless killer; what does that make Dass?"

David said, "Yeah, but that wasn't really based on anything. It was just a feeling. With Jan I was all revved up on adrenaline and able to take some action. It's different when you're in a social setting, in someone's office, when you're constrained. Like I bet you'd find there were soldiers who were much more intimidated by the thought of getting a medal from the Queen than by whatever they did to earn it."

Susan said, "I think you're rationalising it. The first time you told me about Dass, you said he'd really got to you. I think you're talking it down now. A couple more renditions and you'll remember it as mild unease. Remember, I keep telling you to show a little caution, to keep in mind the danger, so I'm the last person to accuse you of being a coward. You had what sounded like a really visceral reaction to this guy. I just think we should bear that in mind before we trust him."

Susan suggested a few precautions they might take in dealing with Dass. David was still not convinced there was any need. He said, "I'm doing what he told me and he's getting what he wants; I don't see that I've got anything to worry about. If I crossed him, then I think all bets would be off, but I reckon I can trust him as long as I'm being a loyal foot-soldier."

Susan shook her head. "Woodward and Bernstein, man – trust no one."

"Except you, right?" he said.

"Oh, absolutely. Trust no one – except Susan," she said.

"Does that mean you've decided to trust *me*?" he asked.

She nodded with genuine seriousness a couple of times. "I'm

really working on it," she said sincerely.

They carried on talking through another course and through coffee, Susan suggesting possibilities, David for the most part sceptical about the need for them – but nonetheless he allowed himself to be swayed. Susan managed to persuade him not to rush back to London for an evening handover.

After thirty minutes they had a plan which didn't strike Susan as reckless or David as unbearably paranoid.

David glanced at his watch. It was a little before five. "I want to call before anyone goes home for the weekend," David said.

They hurried back to the hotel so that David could make the call from the quiet of their room. He used his mobile and called the switchboard of Interfinanzio, asking for Alessandro Dass. He was put through to Mrs Billings, Dass's secretary, who told him it was impossible for him to talk to the Chairman.

David said politely, but with evident concern, "Mrs Billings, it will probably cost us both our jobs if this message isn't delivered at once. I assure you, this is information Mr Dass is extremely eager to hear. Please do your very best to get me in touch with him."

"Let me have the message and I'll see that it's passed on," she conceded snippily.

"I would need Mr Dass's express permission before I could do that. He made himself very clear on this point," David said.

Mrs Billings was silent, obviously considering her next move. When she spoke again it was with a much more agreeable quality to her voice. "Let me have your number and I'll see what I can do," she said.

David gave it to her and hung up. "Dass is going to call me back," he said to Susan.

David sat at the room's reproduction desk, his back to the window. Susan was sitting on her bed, facing him, her feet tucked under her. She was gently chewing her bottom lip. Neither of them spoke.

Less than two minutes after the end of his conversation with Mrs Billings, David's phone started ringing.

"Mr Dass?" David said, answering it.

The elegant voice said, "Mr Braun, do you have good news for me?"

David said, "I do. I've recovered the box that was taken from your safe, with its contents intact."

Dass breathed a sigh and said, "*Mirabile!* It is gratifying to have one's confidence rewarded. Tell me where you are and one of my people will be with you shortly."

David said, "I'm afraid we'll have to make a slightly different plan Mr Dass. You might have heard: the thief is no longer in custody and nobody knows where he is. My first priority was to get the box somewhere safe, so I took it out of London. I can get it to you tomorrow morning, but any sooner will be difficult." He paused a moment. "Would you like me to come to the office?"

Dass replied, "Initiative, such a rare quality. The office would not be ideal, no. By the time any interested parties learn of the item's return I would like it already to be on its way elsewhere. This would be considerably more difficult if you must make your way through a workplace full of eager eyes in order to meet with me. It will be too busy, even on a Saturday. Perhaps you would be so kind as to come to my house?"

"No problem," David said and wrote 'at his house' on the pad in front of him. He held it up so that Susan could see. She nodded when she saw it and gave a grim little smile.

"Let me give you the details," Dass said and dictated an address.

"I don't want to spend too much time in stationary traffic,"

David said. "It's too vulnerable a situation. So I'd like to travel after the rush hour. How would eleven o'clock suit you, Mr Dass?"

Dass said, "That's quite acceptable. There is a reserved parking space immediately outside; I'll see that it's free. I'd rather you didn't linger on the street."

David said, "Don't have any worries on that score. I'll see you tomorrow at eleven."

David hung up and set the phone down on the table. He let his breath out. "It's arranged," he said.

Susan asked, "What do you think the chances are that someone could trace that call back to a physical location?"

David replied, "Well, the mobile phone company could do it, no question." He let his gaze travel around the room as he thought about it. "But I think you'd need either a warrant or exactly the right man on the inside in order to arrange for the trace to be done. Same with tracking my credit card usage. Be tough to do quickly, no matter how much clout you had – if you didn't want questions asked later. I think you'd only do it as a rush job if you didn't mind jeopardising your connections. Maybe if Dass thought we were planning to keep the Marker – but then why would we have just volunteered to bring it to him? And I can't see how any other interested party would know we've got it."

Susan looked impressed. "You've been using that brain of yours, haven't you? I'm glad it's not just me who's decided that paranoia is the better part of valour."

David nodded. "I don't think there's anything more we can do to make ourselves safe for now. Maybe the police could track us down if they wanted to, but the thief doesn't have access to police info. He didn't know the cops had the address of his own hideout, so I don't see him using police resources to learn about ours."

Susan nodded in agreement and flopped back onto her bed. Her hands stretched up to touch the headboard. "What do you want to do now?" she asked.

He shrugged, "Can't eat any more, can't sleep any more. I don't know. I want to take my mind off all this for a little while." He moved to the window and looked out over the sea, leaning down to rest his elbows on the windowsill, one hand holding the net curtain aside.

"There's a cinema nearby, we could see what's on," he said. He didn't look round to see her reaction, but continued to stare out of the window. "It seems trivial with all that's going on, but I can't think of anything we need to be doing except giving ourselves a rest."

While he'd been speaking, Susan had hauled herself wearily off the bed and came to stand behind him. She looked over his shoulder, out through the window at a pencilled world of greys, devoid of colour.

"It looks how I feel out there," she said, resting a hand on David's shoulder and leaning closer to the glass. After a moment, David stood and turned to look at her – which brought them very close.

They were standing almost facing each other. Susan's gaze was still directed outside. She was watching the distant grey-green rollers filing through the dense sea.

David looked at Susan. He held up one hand to her cheek, not quite touching it. "Are your cuts bothering you?" he asked. She didn't retreat from his hand. He laid it gently along her jaw, tilted her head very carefully to one side and leaned forwards to look at her bruised cheek.

Rather than pull her head back to allow her to speak normally, she left David's hand cupping her jaw and spoke, hardly moving her mouth. Her voice was quiet and muffled-sounding as she said,

"It just aches a little."

With a tired sigh a little energy seemed to go out of her and she allowed her head to drop forwards and rest against the upper slope of David's chest.

She said, "I'm exhausted, but I know I wouldn't be able to sleep."

He wrapped his arms around her, completely enfolding her. "I know. I know," he said, with no apparent meaning beyond the soothing sound of the words.

Susan relaxed in the circle of his arms, allowing her body to slump a little, letting him hold her up.

David brought one hand up to her head and eased his parted fingers slowly through her soft blonde hair, allowing it to divide around his fingertips. She stood without moving, leaning against him, breathing into his chest.

He laid his palm against the bare skin of her neck and began to delicately knead the muscles. She gave a quiet murmur of approval.

He turned his head a little and placed a soft kiss on her forehead. His fingers continued to gently explore the stiffness in her neck. He tilted his head a little further and placed a second kiss on her unblemished cheekbone.

She stiffened and a moment later pushed slowly away from him, his arms coming unwrapped and falling to his sides. "No," she said quietly and shook her head sadly. "This isn't right. I don't want this." Her voice was hardly audible.

David stepped slowly back so as not to crowd her. "I'm sorry," he said, the words quiet, the tone sincere.

Susan's eyes were downcast; she wasn't moving, just looking at her feet. She was wrapped now in her own arms, hugging herself, seemingly unaware of how the gesture mirrored David's attentions a moment before.

"There's nothing to be sorry for," she said. Her voice was laden with sadness as she said, "But this isn't what I want from you."

They separated further, Susan gradually retreating to sit on the edge of her bed, David moving to the other side of the room and occupying himself listlessly flipping the pages of the hotel directory, which lay on top of the room's tiny TV. Their faces showed that they had both withdrawn into their own inner worlds. They were immersed in their own thoughts.

David turned another page in the hotel directory, not really taking it in. His gaze wandered.

Next to the TV was a chest of drawers on top of which sat a tray. There was a kettle, with a neatly knotted cord, along with cups and saucers and various sachets and packets.

His eyes settled on the kettle. He picked it up and took it into the bathroom, where he half-filled it with cold water. Bringing it back to the tray, he plugged it in and flicked its switch.

After what seemed like many minutes, the kettle began to make the distant-traffic sound of heating water.

Five minutes had passed since their abandoned embrace and David said, "I don't want to be a cliché or anything, but do you fancy a cup of tea?"

Susan smiled. "Sure," she said, with an effort at brightness. "What do you suppose is on at the movies?"

David had returned to flicking through the transparent pockets of the hotel directory. "There's a flyer somewhere here," he said. Eventually he found it, just as the kettle finished boiling and turned itself off.

"So have you got *any* interest in watching Spiderman?" he asked, sounding unsure.

She said enthusiastically, "Modern mythology. It's practically my duty to see it. It'll be fun."

David looked at his watch and said, "OK. I'm game. We've got about an hour before the next showing." He looked at his watch again, calculating, "Then we can eat fish and chips – can't come to the seaside without doing that."

Susan said, "Fish and chips. Of course," as though she'd been foolish not to mention it earlier. "I've been meaning to get my order in before the North Sea is completely empty. Maybe we can grab the last two cod."

David said, "That's the spirit," slightly sarcastically. "We'll ask for whatever's most endangered." As he spoke he was pouring hot water, making tea. "I was thinking we could also get you a change of clothes. We've just got time to pick something up if you're not too fussy about being fashionable."

Susan nodded. "Now that's a good idea. Can we hit The Gap or something? I'm starting to feel a bit scuzzy wearing the same outfit. Even though you did a great job on the laundry."

They drank their tea quickly and then headed out. From the hotel, they walked up the hill towards the shopping centre. Susan, who had been shivering as she walked, made her first stop at an outdoors shop and headed straight for the sale rack. David offered her the services of his company credit card. She found a shiny black puffer jacket reduced to half price and asked David if she could have it. Two minutes later she was wearing it as they left the store to continue their shopping.

* * *

After the film and the fish and chips, David and Susan sat in the hotel bar. It was ten thirty. David had a glass of Jameson's Whiskey in front of him, Susan a glass of Canadian Club.

Susan said, "The movie was fun, huh? In a mindless sort of way."

David said, "I liked everything except the action sequences. As soon as he put his mask on it was like a cartoon. Like watching a rubber ball bounce round the scenery. How worked up can you get watching a piece of elastic in danger?"

Susan took a sip of her whisky and gave a little shudder. "Just at the moment, I don't see that as a weakness. I don't know if I could have stomached anything too realistic. Tom and Jerry action sequences suited me fine."

When their drinks were gone they ordered replacements. It wasn't many minutes before the conversation dwindled and the silences grew longer. They were both feeling drained. By eleven it was clear they should turn in. Little was said as they returned to the room and got ready for bed.

Susan was in the bathroom for nearly fifteen minutes. When she finally emerged, her bedside lamp was the only illumination. David was in bed, facing away from her, his breathing quiet and even.

She didn't enquire whether he was asleep but got quietly into her own bed and turned out the light. In moments she was asleep.

CHAPTER 19

David was in the heart of Belgravia, driving slowly along Dass's street. He passed a house with a flag fixed to its ornate portico and a policeman stationed outside. A few metres later, the road turned to the left and the embassy disappeared from view.

David was alone in the car, driving slowly – his eyes roving constantly, peering in through the windows of the elegant townhouses, scrutinising parked cars, exploring doorways.

It was almost eleven and he was nearing his destination.

His speed had now slowed almost to a walking pace. Beside him, on the passenger seat, sat the holdall he had taken from Jan.

He continued to search the quiet street for anything out of the ordinary.

Up ahead he could now see the empty parking place waiting for him, the word 'Reserved' in white paint across its centre. The parking bay was directly outside a gleaming black front door set into an otherwise featureless brick wall. The residence within appeared to have no windows on the ground floor, at least none which overlooked the street.

It was a curious building. It seemed to have been built facing onto a road that no longer existed. Instead, the street ran along what appeared to be the blank right side of the house. From the pavement, all that one could see was unadorned brick rising three storeys until it met the edge of the roof. Just below the roofline was set a single broad window; it was an ideal vantage point from which to monitor the neighbourhood. And anyone gazing up from the street, hoping to look inside, would find themselves defeated by the steep angle – all they'd see would be reflections of the sky.

Almost at the reserved bay, David took a final look around before it was too late for him to change his mind about pulling in.

Fifty metres further down the street a half-seen figure flitted between two parked cars. At that distance it was difficult to make out details; the figure was now stationary, partly concealed by a plane tree. From David's point of view, all that could be seen was a glimpse of black clothing and a few hesitant movements that suggested someone hanging back from view, trying to avoid detection. His hands tensed on the steering wheel.

Then the figure moved and he could see a female outline, an orange shopping bag in her hand. It wasn't Jan. He relaxed.

He was now at his destination. Seeing no one else around he pulled quickly into the designated parking space and turned off the engine. He got swiftly out of the car, taking the holdall with him. With three rapid steps he was at the glossy black door.

No one rushed out at him from concealment, the street remained deserted.

To the right of the door was an intercom. He pressed the button set below its speaker. Despite the mildness of the bright spring morning he was wearing a heavy leather jacket. He shrugged his shoulders within it now as though he was cold.

Only a second or two passed before the door was opened by a pale young man wearing a dark-blue tracksuit with the hood pulled up. "Inside," the man said.

David stepped into the hallway and the door was closed swiftly behind him. The man in the tracksuit dropped a metal bar across the door once it was closed.

A second man appeared. His features were East Asian. He was wearing jeans, a grey t-shirt and a baseball cap. The t-shirt was tight over the flat blocks of muscle visible in his arms.

The man in the tracksuit began to pat David down for weapons. "Is that really necessary?" David asked. The Tracksuit didn't answer him; he simply continued his inspection. As his hands slapped and prodded he encountered something in the pocket of David's jacket. His gaze met David's meaningfully. The other man noticed and took a step towards them, close enough that David was within easy reach.

David lifted his hands slowly until they were level with his head, palms forward, allowing access to his jacket. Tracksuit leaned in, sliding a hand into David's pocket.

He withdrew a cell phone.

David shrugged. Tracksuit replaced the phone and continued frisking. When he was finished checking David's person he examined the bag, finding only a polished wooden box within it, which he avoided touching. Tracksuit nodded to the Oriental man who said, "Come with me."

The Oriental in front, Tracksuit behind, they led David up two flights of panelled staircase and out onto a landing heavy with antiques. A sea of carpet in toned-down burgundy lay between walls twining with William Morris flowers on pale paper.

A dozen tiny, hand-carved picture frames were scattered about the walls, but none of them contained pictures. Instead, each held a scrap of paper or parchment. On some a dark brushstroke or penned inscription was visible. Others appeared to be blank, simply corners torn from some antique document.

They stepped through double doors into a windowless sitting room artfully lit to seem filled with sunlight. Everything within was deep red, gold or ivory. It was a heavy colour scheme somewhat relieved by the magnificent proportions of the room, which occupied nearly the entire storey. Various cabinets and tables in red cedar and dark-stained cherrywood were spaced around the walls. Ox-blood Chesterfield sofas and armchairs formed a cluster in the centre of the room.

Fresh tulips in buttery yellows and natural scarlets were arranged in half a dozen vases scattered about, their scent a bright note amidst the background of beeswax and old leather.

There was no one else in the room. The Oriental pointed to an armchair facing the door and commanded, "Sit," then he turned around and left. Tracksuit took up a position to the side of the door, like a bouncer, hands crossed in front of him, his eyes on David.

Instead of sitting in the armchair, David found a high-backed chair tucked under a writing desk and moved it to the centre of the room. He sat down on it, setting the holdall beside the chair, and slipped his hands into his pockets.

A minute passed and the Oriental returned, followed by Alessandro Dass a few steps behind. Dass was wearing a suit of similar cut to the one David had seen him in previously – this one, though, was a pale misty grey. His tie was a vibrant, robin's-breast of red, engorged with colour, against a shirt the colour of ash.

As Dass crossed the room it became clear that a mark he bore across his forehead, which from a distance looked like a deep wrinkle or an old scar, was in fact a slim metal band. Its finish blended with Dass's skin tone, so that from any distance it was invisible.

Dass said, "You made it here without incident. Good." His cultured voice was full of charm. He took the armchair facing David and sank down into the leather. "Where did you disappear to when you left London? Don't feel you have to tell me, of course. I wonder, was there anyone you trusted with the secret of your hiding place?"

David replied, "I thought it was best if I just disappeared. I couldn't see why anyone needed to know where I was going. It would just have multiplied the risks unnecessarily." His voice was inflexionless, like a wary suspect giving a statement.

Dass parted his clasped hands in a little 'just so' gesture. "But I suppose your employers will have been curious. You will undoubtedly have told them of your plans to leave London..." he said with a solicitous interest in his eyes. His gaze met David's as he continued, "your plans to come here?"

As he had been speaking, the Oriental had moved stealthily round until he was standing almost behind David. Now David became aware of the Oriental's presence close by his right shoulder. He made to rise from the chair. The Oriental reached forward to press him back into his seat.

David broke the Oriental's hold on his shoulder before it was properly established and sprang to his feet. His high-backed chair pitched to one side, colliding with a glass-topped table. At the same time the Oriental closed on David who skipped back, hands held high, ready to defend himself, his shoulders side-on to his potential opponent.

The toppled chair bounced off the edge of the table, making a great deal of noise and spoiling the smooth finish of the wood, but leaving the glass intact.

Again, the Oriental took an aggressive step towards David who shifted his weight a little in preparation for rapid movement.

Dass barked something exceedingly curt in a language other than English. The Oriental stepped back so quickly it looked almost as though the words had stung him.

"Please," said Dass more calmly. "Do let us retain our composure." He addressed the Oriental, saying, "Kim, I don't think you're helping to put our guest at his ease. Why don't you take a seat?" He gestured with a couple of flicking fingers to the furthest armchair.

Kim kept his eyes on David but sat down as he was commanded. He looked awkward now that he had been forced to sit.

Dass said, "Now where were we? I believe I was going to invite you to stay for lunch if you have time." He leaned forwards and enquired earnestly, "Tell me, when exactly is your office expecting you?"

David was able to meet Dass's gaze without apparent effort now. He looked appraisingly at the older man and it was several seconds before he spoke. "People know I am here," he said deliberately.

Dass raised an eyebrow. "I'm sure they do," he said reassuringly, leaning back again. "I must commend you on your precautions this morning. You've evidently been at pains not to draw unwanted attention to your visit here. In fact, I'm sure no one at all saw you arrive. Very impressive." Dass paused as though giving David time to absorb the implications of what he was saying. Then he went on, "And I must also say how relieved I am that you were able to join us. If you had failed to appear today, if you had not returned from wherever it was you disappeared to overnight, how would anyone learn what had become of you? How would we have come to your aid? It would be as though you had vanished." Dass's voice was conversational, carrying no menace except what was implied in the subtext of his words.

David sat listening. His face looked grim. He said pointedly,

"Let's imagine you denied ever having seen me today; what would you gain from my disappearance?"

Dass made a display of somewhat astonished innocence. He looked for support from his two henchmen, both of whom remained alert but impassive, staring at David but giving no sign that they were listening to the conversation.

Then it seemed a thought occurred to Dass. "Oh, I see; you are being hypothetical. We are exercising our imaginations." He looked around to see if his colleagues had also come to this conclusion. They remained stony-faced.

Dass said, "Well if we were playing a game, I might say that the return of our lost treasure brings with it the return of unwelcome scrutiny from those who covet it. For the world to think it lost and for us alone to know it was safe might be the ideal outcome," he nodded at David and waved a hand airily, "assuming it could be accomplished without anything underhand taking place, of course." He shifted a little in his seat and then continued, "Who knows, there are also those in the world who might want to eat their cake and have it still. Perhaps you are familiar with those breathlessly venal American game shows where the victorious contestant must choose between a sum of money and the contents of a mysterious box. Even the Americans would consider it unacceptably greedy to reach for both. But hypothetically it would be possible. A truly avaricious person might allow an insurance claim to go ahead even now," he indicated the holdall by David's side, "as a means of throwing others off the scent." He stretched out his left hand, "It would protect our assets," then he stretched out his right, "even while it paid our bills."

Dass leaned forwards in his seat. "But before we spend any more time exploring the hypothetical, shall we just make sure of the facts of our situation. Would you be so kind as to return to me what is rightfully mine," he said, extending an arm towards the bag.

David considered for a moment and then reached for the holdall. He lifted it onto his lap and unzipped it. He took out the rosewood box, laid the holdall back on the floor and rested the box across his knees.

He made as if to open the box and then paused and leaned back. He blew out his breath and pushed his hands into his coat pockets; he seemed to be wrestling with a dilemma. "What worries me Mr Dass," he said, "is that you have no intention of letting me leave here."

Dass said nothing and David continued, "Which is why I decided to call the police before I came to your house." For the first time since David had met him Dass smiled with a look of genuine amusement.

David went on, "I told them that one of your people had recovered the box and that you had invited me over to be present as it was returned to you."

Dass smiled benevolently as though delighted by the story. David said, "I told them that I was worried that the thief might try again. In fact I mentioned that I *might* have spotted him lurking nearby."

Dass was nodding thoughtfully as though he were getting ready to speak. David pressed on, "And I asked them to call for me here," he said. He shrugged inside his coat, as though there was little point in saying more.

Dass stretched out a hand in the direction of the box. He said, "A very entertaining tale, if a little lacking in originality. Kim, fetch me the box."

As he said these words, David slipped his right hand quickly inside the box and withdrew something. As soon as he had done so, he jumped out of his seat, the box clutched in his left hand, and sprang to the far corner of the room. With a sharp downward flick of his right wrist the device in his hand extended into a metal baton. He held it out in front of him ready to meet any attack.

Kim and Tracksuit both advanced instinctively on David's position. "Wait," Dass snapped at them. They paused, like dogs straining at their leads, waiting to be released.

Dass stood and took a casual step towards David. "When I heard you had bested our little stray I did wonder how you could possibly have achieved such a victory. Jan, while no match for me, should have trampled you underfoot."

Dass reached out a hand towards the box and David brought the metal baton crashing down on his wrist. But Dass didn't react, except to pause momentarily as the blow fell. The heavy shaft of the baton encountered an invisible obstacle before it reached Dass's arm. The impact made a sound like a hammer hitting a cement floor.

They remained frozen in position, Dass reaching for the box, David's baton resting a few centimetres above the outstretched arm. David seemed to be pinned to the corner of the room, as Dass said, "I began to suspect that you possessed some special quality which allowed you to overcome one of us – even an exile."

David was struggling to move. There was no sign of any impediment, no apparent reason why he shouldn't burst past Dass, shoving the older man aside – but David was twisting and tensing as though he was encased in something solid or perhaps pressed against the wall by something massive.

The expression on Dass's face wavered for a moment as though a bad memory had flitted through his mind. Simultaneously, the baton was wrenched from David's hand and flew across the room – pulled by an unseen force.

Dass leaned close to David until their faces were a hand's width apart. Dass said, "I think I've realised what that quality was."

A line of perspiration ran down David's forehead as he continued to strain – totally without success.

"You were lucky," Dass said, turning his back and allowing David to topple forwards, the invisible barrier suddenly gone. Dass strode back to his chair as David pitched forwards, almost falling. "Simply lucky."

Dass dropped into his armchair, bringing David once more into his field of view. He looked at David who had regained his feet and was now glancing nervously around the room. Dass wore an expression which combined interest with disgust as he regarded his prisoner.

"I think I've learned all I'm going to," Dass said. Then his voice hardened, "Kim, take it from him," he said. Kim smiled.

As he took his first step towards David, a buzzer sounded elsewhere in the house.

Now it was David's turn to smile, albeit a little weakly. "Speaking of luck – that will be the police," he said.

Dass looked sharply at David, but his words were evidently aimed at Tracksuit, as he said, "See who that is, without answering it." Tracksuit darted out of the room.

Dass seemed to be sizing David up. He was clearly calculating his next move. David helped him along in his analysis. "My car's sitting right outside," he said pleasantly.

A moment later Tracksuit put his head back round the door and said, "There are police cars in the street outside." He added, "Karst is nearby. I could..." but a look from Dass silenced him.

David said, "I was particularly concerned that the thief might overpower you and lock the police out. I hope they remembered to bring their battering ram. But I don't suppose you'll wait for them to break down the door, will you." It wasn't a question.

Dass looked angry now. His eyes bored into David, who chose that moment to get to his feet.

Everyone tensed.

But David simply leaned towards Dass and offered him the box. "On behalf of Marshall & Liberty, I'm pleased to be able to return this to you, Mr Dass. I would say that we look forward to serving your insurance needs for years to come, but regrettably I'm going to have to recommend a full review of your account. We will of course continue to respect your privacy."

The buzzer sounded again and this time the button was held in for a number of seconds.

A look of sullen resignation came over Dass's face as he took the box. He said, "Let's all go down to meet our visitors shall we?" He lifted the lid of the box and peered inside the inner compartment. Then he snapped it shut again and, handing it to Tracksuit, said, "William, perhaps you would take care of this."

Dass led the way downstairs. After a few moments he seemed to recover some of his characteristic composure. "Where are my manners? Thank you for your help Mr Braun. I shall have nothing but good words to say about you to your superiors. Under other circumstances I might be tempted to recruit you..." Dass said. He looked back at the Oriental and said, "You can't greet the police wearing a baseball cap, Kim; what would they think?" He darted his eyes to one of the doors they were passing and Kim, taking it as an instruction, ducked in there. A second later he emerged without the hat, smoothing his short hair into place.

David peered at Dass, craning his head slightly as they descended the stairs, surreptitiously trying to get a good look at him. As they passed a tiny window which let a little daylight into the dim stairway, he could see that Dass had already removed the metal band from his forehead. Wherever he had stashed it, it wasn't in evidence now.

When they reached the door, Kim unbarred it and opened it wide. David and Dass stood back to let him do so. On the step outside stood two police officers; behind them was DI Hammond and beyond him were several men in body armour.

A second group of policemen stood over by one of the three official vehicles parked in the street. With them was a woman wearing a black jacket and carrying a bright orange shopping bag – it was Susan.

She caught David's eye for a split second and then turned away, her back to the door. Dass was already focussed on Hammond, thanking him profusely for his interest. Hammond and the first two uniforms stepped inside at Dass's invitation. Once they were in the hallway, David slipped past them into the street; no one was paying him very much attention.

Dass and Hammond were talking and the police officers were peering around, looking for something to fasten their interest upon. They eyed the muscular Oriental suspiciously and he returned the favour.

Once outside, David called back through the open door, "Inspector Hammond, you don't need me for anything do you?" He held up his car keys, indicating that he was about to depart. Hammond grunted. David said, "Congratulations again Mr Dass. I'll get the paperwork started," he said, offering a cheery wave.

He got into his car without anything more being said.

Susan was standing some distance from the open front door, out of line of sight of Dass and his people. She was talking to a policeman who was glancing periodically at his notebook. She looked up as David's car pulled away and they locked eyes for the briefest moment. Then he was gone and she continued smoothly with what she had been saying to the officer at her side.

CHAPTER 20

A few hours later, David's mobile rang.

He was at his desk, in the Marshall & Liberty offices, trying to organise an emergency partners' meeting. Despite the fact that it was Saturday, several of the partners were currently in the office. The rest he was phoning at home.

He glanced down at his mobile's display; it was Susan calling.

His desk was largely screened from the open plan area where the assistants sat, but still he turned in his seat and brought his shoulder up to block the sound of his words. He said gently, "Hey," as he answered the phone.

Susan's voice was anxious as she said, "David? Are you OK?"

He replied, "I'm fine – absolutely fine." He paused a moment and said quietly, "You were right. He was going to kill me."

She said, "God, I'm so glad you're alright. I mean you looked fine, but I didn't know… I would have called earlier but they kept me talking for ages."

David's forehead wrinkled. He said, "Have they been grilling you all this time?" He looked at his watch. It was after three.

"No," she replied, "but I didn't want to call you from the street; I'm home now. The police ran me back to the station with them and I signed my statement about the break-in last week. Have they called you yet? Because they will."

"No, they haven't been in touch yet," he said. "What did you tell them in the end?"

She said, "Just what we agreed. We were getting together for lunch after your meeting with Dass. I was early and I thought I saw Jan. I ducked behind a bush and called them – didn't move 'til I saw a police car coming down the street. Dass obviously didn't mention *your* version of the story to the police because they seemed quite happy with what I'd told them."

David asked, "So are you in trouble for phoning in a false report?"

Susan replied, "They don't think it was false. Now they know that Dass was getting his treasure back, they think I really did see Jan, but he bolted when the cops showed up. They think they saved the day." A moment later she said, "You know you could have just told Dass you had an accomplice. If he'd compared notes with Hammond we could have been in trouble."

David said, "I think it was worth the risk. I'm even more glad now that we didn't let Dass know you were involved. Why have him carrying a grudge against both of us? He's angry with me for refusing to be bumped off; he might as well blame me for calling the cops too."

Susan said, "They took so long to arrive. That was me pushing the buzzer the first time; I couldn't wait any longer. God knows what I'd have done if someone had actually answered the door. But then the first police car arrived a few seconds later. While I was waiting I was going crazy imagining what Dass might be doing to you."

Shaking his head in recollection and disbelief, David said, "Well, whatever scenario you imagined, I somehow doubt it was 100% accurate." Then he said with seriousness, "You know, you talked me into having a plan, then you did exactly what you said you'd do and you got the police there just in the nick of time. It's down to you that I'm still breathing." He considered his own words for a moment and asked, "How many times did I call you in the end? I was just hitting redial and cancel over and over. I kept thinking Dass would ask me to take my hands out of my pockets."

Susan said, "While I was talking to the police there were nine missed calls from your mobile – plus there was the one that made me phone them in the first place. It was almost a relief in a funny way. I kept thinking, what if they take your phone off you and I'm sitting outside while they... you know, while something terrible happens. As long as you were calling I knew there was still a little bit more time. But you'd only been in there about two minutes before the first call."

David said, "Yeah, well it was pretty obvious from the first question that Dass was up to something. He was sounding me out, asking who knew my whereabouts. By the time the Old Bill turned up, Dass had worked out that he could get rid of me and I wouldn't be missed."

"Well, I'd have missed you," Susan said. "You're quite sure killing you was what he'd got in mind?"

David said with black humour, "Ohhh yes. He was even good enough to explain why my permanent disappearance would be such a good thing for him. Things were getting a bit physical by the time the doorbell went. He'd brought in a couple of blokes who can't have had any other use besides hurting people – not that he needed any help in that department."

Susan sounded puzzled, "What do you mean? Dass wouldn't

stand a chance against you by himself, would he?"

David struggled to explain, "I don't... Listen, there's no easy way to explain this. Well, there is I suppose, but you're not..."

"David?" Susan said, cutting into his preamble.

David said, "Sorry. I can't tell you this over the phone. I need to say it face to face."

Susan said, "Come on, that's for the movies. Tell me now."

David was firm. "You're going to want to look me in the eye when I tell you the story. Believe me." He looked down at the list of partners, counted the un-ticked names. "I'll be done in another hour; can you meet me?"

Susan was obviously not happy, but she said patiently, "Sure. Tell me where you're going to be."

David glanced at his watch and pursed his lips for a moment. "I'm starved," he said, "can you come to Islington? There's a place called S & M on Essex Road just off Upper Street."

"S & M?" Susan said, unsure.

David laughed, "Don't worry; it stands for sausage and mash. Can you be there for 4.30?"

"I'll be there," she said.

"OK. See you then," David said, hanging up.

* * *

Susan was already sitting at one of the little blue Formica tables when David arrived. The restaurant was a tiny, low-key fifties diner – black and white colour scheme, lots of chrome. David gave Susan a quick kiss on the cheek before sitting down. She squeezed his arm and gave him a concerned smile.

David said, "Before we get into this, let's get the food on its way, OK?"

Susan pursed her lips and narrowed her eyes as if to say he was pushing his luck, but she agreed and turned her attention to her menu. "Sausage and mash," she said thoughtfully, "or sausage and mash."

A minute later they ordered from a friendly American waitress. As soon as she had gone, Susan pounced. "What?" she asked dramatically, "You can tell me that someone tried to kill you," she lowered her voice to say the word, "but you can't tell me the rest of it over the phone. What's bigger news than attempted murder?" she demanded.

David made as if to speak but nothing came out. His shoulders dropped as though he were giving up on whatever he'd been planning to say. He tried again while Susan watched him, a look of borderline exasperation on her face.

Finally, he began to speak firmly, and the words just tumbled out, "I know how Jan can open a safe and jump thirty feet out of a window and let himself get shot at and burn his way out of a set of handcuffs – I know how he does it. Well, I don't know how he does it, but I know what he does... I mean..."

"David!" Susan said in an angry whisper, determined that he should stay on track. Her expression said that she might scream if he didn't get to the point soon. "What happened?" she pleaded.

David took a deep breath. "OK," he said. He let the breath out and then he began, "Dass pinned me to a wall and tore that asp, that baton thing, out of my hand and he did it without moving. I hit him with it before he took it off me and it just bounced off him – or rather it bounced off something before it reached him. It was like I'd tried to hit him and hadn't noticed there was a wall in the way – except there wasn't a wall. Do you know what I'm talking about?"

Susan looked stunned. "Are you saying he did it with his mind?

Like a scene out of *Carrie*?" she said, incredulous.

"What's Carrie?" David asked, confused.

Susan waved it away, "Never mind." She looked him in the eye, "But you're saying psychic powers, that sort of thing? There's no way it could have been something else? You sure he wasn't actually wearing some sort of body armour?"

David said quietly but fervently, "Something ripped that asp out of my hand and pinned me to the wall and Dass wasn't touching me. He didn't even move."

Susan stared into David's eyes for a moment, looking for confirmation. Then she flopped back in her chair. "Jesus," she said. And a moment later, "Jesus!"

Then she leaned forwards again. "You're absolutely..." she began.

"I'm sure," he said with finality, before she could finish. "I promise you, that's what happened. And Dass referred to Jan, he knew who he was. He said Jan was a stray and an exile, which means he's the same as Dass. They can both do this stuff. Whatever the two of them are, I don't think they're human."

Their food and drinks arrived a moment later and neither of them moved or acknowledged the waitress, who went away with a puzzled look on her face.

David picked up his cutlery and began to eat mechanically, as though he wasn't fully aware of what he was doing. Susan continued to stare, unfocussed, past his shoulder. Her blank expression indicated total absorption in whatever her mind was working on.

When she focussed again she said, "Was he wearing tribute?" She rephrased, "Was he wearing a gold band?"

David said, "I don't know if it was gold, but yes, he was wearing a metal band around his head when I arrived. He took it off before he met the police." Susan absorbed this information without saying anything.

Robert Finn

David added, "Actually, the two henchmen had their heads covered, so they might have been wearing them too."

Susan picked up her fork and began to eat. After a few moments her expression changed, as though something had occurred to her, as though a weight had been lifted.

"What are you thinking?" asked David, having noticed the change in her expression.

"That this is really good," she explained playfully, gesturing towards her plate with the fork she was holding.

"Any thoughts not related to food?" David asked witheringly.

Susan's expression was almost jubilant now. She was looking confident. She said, "Don't get irritated with me, but I want to tell you a silly little story." He didn't look convinced so she added, "Seeing as how you made me wait an hour after your cliff-hanger phone call."

He nodded, acknowledging her point and she began, "I read in the newspaper a long time ago about this guy who taught people to swim. He had a talent for it – frightened kids, nervous adults – he could help anyone. The reporter from the newspaper finished up the story by asking the instructor how often he himself liked to go swimming. And the answer was, 'I teach it, I don't know how to do it.'"

She looked at David expectantly. He looked back just as expectantly and said, "And? You'll have to give me more than that."

Susan was getting enthusiastic now. She said, "Don't you see? They're not aliens, they're just people, humans."

David still showed no sign that he knew what she was talking about.

She continued, "What an idiot I've been. I spend all day going through page after page of documents describing people able to

238

do all the things we're talking about here. Then I put the papers back in the safe and come out and tell you that I have no idea what's going on. That's like…" she searched for an example, "a map-maker who can't find his way home from work. Or," she was grinning now, "an ornithologist who can't figure out why his milk bottle tops have little holes in them."

A hint of comprehension appeared on David's face. "Are you saying that all we need to do is treat the Teracus collection…" Susan couldn't wait for him to finish his sentence and did it for him, "as fact not fiction."

She threw up her hands in triumph. "Maybe this is what it feels like when you finally lose touch with reality. But let's just forget about sanity for a minute. Why don't we stop looking for the *real* reason behind all this madness and take it at face value? Jan, Dass and his merry men can do the stuff in the documents. And the Marker really can heal people, which is why they both want it. It's so simple."

She was eating quickly now, taking small bites and then talking around them. "God, I wonder if the longevity document is true. Jesus, that would explain why alchemy was so popular for hundreds of years." She wasn't really addressing David, just thinking aloud. "I must talk to Professor Shaw about this," she said. And then a frown appeared on her face, "Oh no, I can't."

David inquired, "Because he'll have you locked up?"

Susan nodded, "Right, exactly," she agreed, looking disappointed now. "Oh well," she shrugged. Then another thought occurred to her. "Shit," she said.

David asked, "What's up?"

Susan said, "You've just wrecked my post-doc. I can't pretend the collection's allegorical, knowing what I know. But I can hardly start writing about how magic really works. I'm screwed."

David had been watching her as she had her revelation and then thought her way through the implications. Now that she was looking dejected, he took it as his cue to take a turn at grumbling, "Yeah, and what am I supposed to do? Do I forget about it all? We agreed that whatever Dass was up to, we'd let him have the Marker back – and we'd let *him* handle Jan. But I can't just let him try to kill me and then forget about it." A moment later he said, "Only what other choices are there? Particularly given that he's probably capable of killing me with a wave of his hand." He brooded on that for a moment. "What else do you suppose he can do? Fly? Turn into a bat? Saw a woman in half?"

Susan wasn't sure. "Well," she said, "for the time being, I'm going to assume that Teracus knew what he was talking about. So I'm only going to trust documents in the collection – forget about all the other things I've read about magic. In which case I've got some work to do to answer that question. Believe it or not, I wasn't thinking along those lines when I first went through the collection."

She ate another couple of forkfuls of food while she considered. "You say Dass put some sort of shield around himself and then moved something without touching it. Jan seemed to be able to burn things as well. I've also read a document which refers to healing. I think these guys heal very quickly and they don't get sick."

David looked puzzled by that. "Well, if we're assuming this stuff is all true – and I have to say Dass hasn't left me much leeway there – then why would anyone care about the Marker? If they can heal themselves using a bit of ordinary gold wire then why fight each other for the Marker?"

Susan corrected David, "Tribute includes gold on each wrist as well as a band around the head. But you've got a good point. I think we've still got some mysteries to solve. Maybe I'm wrong and only the Marker can heal." Another thought occurred to her. "Imagine if you'd tackled Jan when he was wearing his headpiece. Or if I hadn't managed to knock it loose the first time I hit him."

David nodded, "I think it's safe to say we wouldn't be having this conversation. How could you ever stop someone like that? I think Jan let someone fire a gun at him, knowing they couldn't hurt him." Something else occurred to him. "God, imagine if they fought each other."

Susan waggled her knife and said, "Apparently there's a law against it. There's this whole scroll about how you can't attack magic with magic." She looked thoughtful, "Not that you'd imagine these guys would pay attention to the rules. Maybe something terrible happens if they try." She sighed. "You know, I'm going to have to reread every single word of those documents. I just wasn't thinking in the right way the first time around." She paused a moment and blew out her breath, then she said, "So what do you want to do about Dass?"

David shrugged, "Even setting aside the fact that he's rich, powerful and probably indestructible – and I'm none of those things – I don't see what I *can* do. Even if he was a normal man, it would be difficult to get him arrested. Given that he isn't a normal man, it would just result in a few policemen getting killed even if I could persuade them to try it. I'm going to think about it, but I don't see any way forward."

Susan asked, "And what about Jan? Do you think he'll want to hush us up? It's a no-brainer that these guys rely on secrecy to survive. Obviously, if enough people knew what they were capable of, someone would find a way to take them down. You'd send a hundred guys and a tank or something. Their power is vastly more effective if no one knows they have it until it's too late. And – lucky for us – we're in on the secret. But if they're really serious about their privacy, won't they want to get rid of us?"

David thought about it. "Dass only knows about me, we reckon. He can imagine I'll cause trouble for him at work. I might even tell people he was going to bump me off. But he can guess what would happen if I accused him of having demonic powers without so much as a Polaroid of him shaking hands with Satan to back it up. Alive I'll spread some rumours that he's a crook, but won't be able to prove them. If I suddenly up and died, that would be my proof that he was out to get me – much good it would do me. He'd be better off leaving me alive and sounding like a looney."

Susan said, "And Jan?"

David said, "Wouldn't you think killing us would be low on his list of priorities? Not only is he on the run from the police, we can also be pretty sure Dass will have dispatched someone to find him. Dass knows the police won't be able to stop him, after all. In fact, there could be a small army of Dass's people after Jan – we don't really have any idea what Dass's resources are. It's only Jan we've got reason to think is a loner. He had surprise on his side when he stole the Marker, but now everyone's after him and he's on his own. I don't think he can afford grudges at the moment."

Susan didn't look totally convinced. "Hmmm," she said. "That's a lot of supposition. I can buy the idea that Dass is better off ignoring you – I doubt he has too much to worry about from 'some insurance guy', as my sister would call you." She reflected a moment and said, "But I haven't forgotten that five minutes ago you were telling me I was better off if Dass didn't know I was involved, and now you reckon there's nothing to worry about anyway." David gave her a weak grin. She concluded, "At any rate, it's Jan I'm not sure about. We really messed up his week."

David said, "We could always ask Dass for help."

Susan looked appalled, "Are you kidding?"

David shook his head. "Think about it," he said. "If he gave us a bodyguard he'd stand a better chance of finding Jan than if he just combs the streets – let Jan come to us and then grab him. It would definitely be in Dass's interest to keep us alive as bait."

"I understand all that," Susan said. "I just can't believe you'd go back to the guy who tried to kill you this morning and ask him for protection!" she said with some passion.

"Dessert?" a voice at Susan's shoulder enquired.

"Apple crumble and custard, please," said David, who'd seen the waitress approaching and checked the specials board while Susan was berating him.

Susan had been surprised by the interruption but recovered quickly. "Me too, but can I have ice cream instead of custard?"

The waitress smiled, "Sure. That's no problem," she said and left, taking their empty plates with her.

"Still not quite up to speed on the custard thing," Susan said uneasily. "Anyway, as regards our life expectancies, I have no idea where all that leaves us. Should we be running for our lives or is it all over? For that matter, have you just fired me?"

David said, "Well, I suppose this is the logical point to stop paying you. But I think this has gone beyond a job, don't you think? I'm hoping you'll keep talking to me even if you're not on the payroll. You're going to be burrowing into that collection regardless, so maybe you could keep me up to speed with whatever you find out? If you can learn a little bit more about these guys, maybe that'll set our minds at rest or perhaps it'll tell us how to protect ourselves. I stand by what I said, though. I think the way things are, Dass doesn't care about us and Jan's best bet is to move to Uruguay as quickly as possible and change his name."

Shortly after that, their desserts arrived and both of them tucked in.

Susan said, "Well give me a few days. You know what they say about paradigm shifts – they sort of invalidate all the things you thought you knew. I've got about seven years of thinking to re-evaluate." She finished another mouthful of crumble and said, "Obviously we should talk if anything happens, but otherwise I'll give you a call…" she petered out. She had one eye half closed as though either the ice cream was too cold or she was recalling something painful. "Of all the weeks for my sister to visit."

David said, "Listen, there's no rush. I don't think either of us is prepared to just let this go, but it's not as though there's anything we can actually do – apart from you re-evaluating the collection. Why don't you enjoy your sister's visit? Take advantage of the distraction and have a break from this do-or-die stuff. I'll still be waiting by the phone, full of curiosity, even if it takes you a month instead of a week to call." He looked her in the eye, "Though I'd rather see you sooner than that." He put his hand on her forearm, gave it a little squeeze.

"Yeah, I can't imagine going a month and not talking to you," she said. "Plus you're the only one I could talk to about all this." She was wrestling with her thoughts, conflicting emotions showing on her face. She took his hand. "About the hotel room, when I…" she said haltingly.

"Yeah, I'm sorry about that," David said, rushing in. "I misread… Well I don't know what I thought."

Susan said, "I want you to understand… I mean I don't think I did a very good job of explaining…"

David jumped in again, "Really, don't worry about it. You don't have to explain. If anything, after what we argued about…" He didn't go on.

Susan nodded. "Well, the main thing, I guess, is that we're still speaking to each other. Some time," she looked around at the diner, "not here, but sometime, we need to have a talk." She squeezed his hand and then let it go.

David's expression showed he really didn't think any more needed to be said, but he dipped his head solemnly and said, "OK."

She brightened, saying, "In the meantime, if you really don't want to go too long without seeing me you could come round to dinner, say this Friday, and meet my sister."

David smiled mischievously, "Why do I get the feeling that's not the generous offer the casual observer might think it was?"

Susan said, "You've got nothing to worry about. Dee's a charmer. You'll love her; everyone does. The vibe you're picking up is my lack of altruism in asking you. We just tend to get on each other's nerves after a few days and a little moral support and a change of pace would give me something to look forward to. Help a gal out and come?"

David smiled and said, "I'd love to."

CHAPTER 21

The sun was low, but not yet setting, as David stood in front of the same lifeless townhouse where he'd been standing two minutes earlier. "This must be it," he muttered to himself.

He was in a tiny street in the City of London – not much more than two little terraces facing each other.

The street began as an unpromising single-lane cut-through between the headquarters of a bank and a shipping company. Thirty metres back and round a corner, the narrow lane opened out and there were the houses, three on either side, hidden from the world. There was just enough room to accommodate a fenced-off Electricity Board transformer before the road ended with the back wall of a seventeenth-century church.

Outside the first house on the left, David climbed the six steps up to a tall, windowless front door and pushed the doorbell. In the distance an electric bell rang. He waited.

He was wearing a navy jacket and trousers, and an open-necked shirt in dark red cotton. He was carrying a neat little package wrapped in gold paper, the ribbon inscribed with the name of a company renowned for its hand-made chocolates.

To the right of the front door was a bay window – its wooden shutters closed – behind very elegant wrought-iron bars. Beneath the window, the pavement stopped at the railing and he could see down into the one tiny window set into the basement wall.

He looked up again as the door opened. Standing on the top step, appraising him, was a slim woman dressed all in black, holding a crystal wine glass. She wore a short woollen wrap-skirt over long, darkly-stockinged legs; a merino sweater with a deep v-neck was tight around her trim waist. Her face, a paler, more delicate version of Susan's, had the same blue eyes, but her silky black hair was longer and fell almost straight to her collar-bone. She smiled at David with her dark-red lips and took a sip of red wine.

"Hi," David said, "Dee?"

Dee smiled down at him for a moment from the threshold, without replying. Her arms were twined together holding the wineglass near her mouth and she let the rim tap against her very white teeth a couple of times as though she were working something out. The light caught a tiny fleck of sky-blue sapphire above her right nostril.

A moment later, after David had begun to blush, her eyebrows flicked up for a split-second and she held out a hand. "Oh I'm sorry. You must be David," she said.

Her accent was polished New York City – melodious and a little husky at the same time.

They shook hands and Dee said, "Come in. Susan's in the kitchen." She glanced over her shoulder. "Let's get you a drink," she said, enunciating each word separately.

They stepped into a dim hallway, lots of dark wood on the walls and floors, and too few lights. The house smelled a little musty, but it wasn't unpleasant – a smell of age, but not neglect. To their left was a staircase and running to the right of it was a passageway leading to the back of the house and an open door, from which light and the sound of reggae were coming.

They followed the music.

Susan was cooking. As they came through the door, she was checking the contents of several big, old, aluminium saucepans that were bubbling away on a spotless cream-coloured cooker that looked like the latest in Fifties labour-saving appliances. Susan's face was pinker than usual and the steam had fixed a few strands of hair to her forehead. Her white silk blouse was sticking to her back.

Susan looked up as David came into the kitchen. She gave him a hassled smile which was abruptly terminated by an urgent hiss from the gas stove. A gulp of water had bubbled out of the front saucepan and dropped onto the flames of the gas ring with a crash of steam.

"Behold, the housewife of the future," Dee said in corny voiceover tones. David laughed. Dee went on, "With the latest space-age gadgets at her disposal, hubby's dinner is ready in a flash, leaving more time to gossip with the girls."

Dee held up a bottle of red wine for David to see. "Merlot?" she asked, continuing in a whisper, "Susan's got the keys to the cellar. In booze terms, we're millionaires."

David said, "Thanks," to Dee's offer and to Susan he said, "Can I do anything to help?"

Susan said, "I don't think…" but a loud crack from the oven interrupted her. Susan's face looked stricken as she hunted around for a cloth.

Dee winced, "Well. Now we know whether the dish is oven-proof or not."

Susan was swearing as she opened the oven door and peered inside.

Once more using her stage whisper, Dee said, "Why don't I show you round?" To Susan she called, "We'll leave you to it, Champ."

Dee handed David a glass of wine and took his arm. "You wanna see the wine vaults?" she asked.

* * *

Twenty minutes later, Susan yelled for them to come downstairs to eat. Dee had been showing David the bedrooms and the attic study from which it was possible to see a sliver of the dome of St Paul's Cathedral. Most of the time she had been telling David funny stories about her and Susan's childhood. They were still laughing as they came down the stairs.

Susan ushered them into the old-fashioned dining room at the back of the house. Two tiny chandeliers spread a listless mellow glow over the linen-covered table as though the electricity itself was from an earlier time. Candles were arranged between the place settings. The overall impression was an island of illumination twinkling at the centre of a room full of shadows.

David said, "It feels Christmasy," as he took his seat.

Dee and David sat, as Susan made a couple of quick runs to the kitchen fetching plates of food – chicken breasts in a red pepper sauce, green beans, carrots and cauliflower. Steam rose from the plates.

"I'm pretty sure I got all the china out of it," she said as she served the food.

David said, "This looks fabulous," as Susan dropped into her seat and motioned for them to start eating.

Dee said, amazed, "Wow, I haven't had cauliflower since Mom used to make it."

"I only gave you a tiny bit," Susan said reassuringly, "I know you don't like it that much."

David said, "This is excellent," after his first mouthful and Susan smiled appreciatively.

"You deserve a glass of wine, Sis. Jolly good show," Dee said, reaching for the bottle. She hesitated, "Hmm, are we allowed to have red wine with chicken? Isn't that a shocking *faux pas*?" She looked to David to provide the answer.

"Let's be peasants," he said raising his glass and toasting the ladies.

"I'm sorry the beans are a bit underdone. Just leave them," Susan said.

"Nonsense," David said warmly, "It's all lovely."

Dee looked up. "Remember when you cooked Thanksgiving Dinner?" she asked Susan, with a glance towards David.

Susan shrank a bit, looking embarrassed, "I was only twelve, Dee," she said quietly.

Dee quipped, "Nearly didn't make it to thirteen." She spread her hands dramatically, indicating newspaper headlines, and announced, "Family of Four in Salmonella Suicide Pact. Come to think of it, that was chicken too," Dee said, like a whodunit detective spotting an important clue. David laughed.

"Come on, Dee," Susan said, sounding a little bit tired.

Dee held up her hands in surrender. "Sorry. Never tease the cook; it's too easy for them to take their revenge. We'll talk about something else." She looked over at David, set her chin in her hands, and said breathlessly, "So, David, you're in insurance. That must be fascinating." Her eyes twinkled playfully as she said it.

David was amused and pretended to be puffed up with flattery as he said, "Oh, absolutely. It's glamorous, often dangerous work, but at least you feel truly alive. I'm so glad now that I decided not to go into space." He raised an eyebrow and said, "What about you? Didn't Susan say you deliver newspapers? That must be interesting work." Then he sat back, beaming, to see how she'd respond.

Now it was Dee's turn to smile and there was more than a little mischief in her expression. She said sarcastically, "Well, I'm stuck on the writing side at the moment, unfortunately. And, worse still, it's magazines, not newspapers. But I don't let it get me down. In a few years I'll be able to make the jump from fashion and entertainment into sports journalism, and then I'm hoping to get onto a declining local paper somewhere. From there it's just a matter of getting my name down for one of those little newsstands outside a subway station. Of course they prefer it if you drive a cab for a few years before they give you your own stand, but I sent the Commissioner of Outdoor Vending a box of fingerless gloves on his birthday and let's just say I'm quietly confident." Dee gave David a rather self-satisfied little pout, amused by her own wit.

David was grinning at Dee. He said, "Really? That's marvellous! Have you decided what you're going to hold the papers down with yet?" He made a flattening gesture, "A lot of people seem to think it has to be a lump of rock or half a roof tile maybe, but I've always leaned in favour of a good chunk of metal. You know, a bit off an old car, something like that."

Dee nodded seriously, but held up a finger, saying, "Don't forget New York winters; metal can get very cold to the touch until the cheap whisky kicks in. It's kind of premature to make a final decision, but lately I'm hearing some good things about composites." David laughed.

From her end of the table, Susan said, "There's more chicken if anyone wants it? David?"

David broke eye contact with Dee, and focussed on Susan for a moment, "Oh yes. That would be great, thanks," he said. Then he turned back to Dee and said, "Maybe that's OK in the States, but I don't think we're ready for anything too new-fangled over here. There's a lot of tradition. For instance, no London paper-seller worth his salt would shout anything in modern English. It might be the Evening Standard to you or me, but it's always going to be the..." he raised his voice, "'hipnee stannaaar' to a professional."

Dee said, "I guess you're right. There's sure a lot to learn. You want to know what's worrying me most, right now?" her face looking anxious, "getting the moustache right." She rested a finger just below her nose. "I've been letting this one grow for about eight months now and I'm nowhere with it." She held out her upper lip, the way a horse reaches for a sugar-lump, trying to show it to David.

He leaned across the table, squinting, and Dee stood up. Tilting her head back she tried to hold her lip forwards and at the same time talk, saying, "Shee? Shee?"

Susan came back in with David's replenished plate, set it down in front of him.

David shook his head, "I wouldn't worry. That's OK. Give it another couple of weeks."

Dee gave David a narrow-eyed look and then said to Susan, "He's feisty. I like that."

Dee and David were laughing with each other as Susan sat down. She glanced at both of them, looking a little left out.

After a moment, David noticed Susan's expression and put on a more serious face. Turning to Susan he said, "So what have you shown Dee while she's been here? The usual sights?"

Dee answered for her, saying, "We went shopping, which was cool, but we haven't done much sightseeing yet."

Susan sounded guilty as she explained, "Well, I've been pretty busy this week…"

Dee said, "Plus, Susie's not much more English than I am. We need a native guide."

David said, "Well, maybe I can help. I've lived in London for most of my life and while I haven't actually *been* to any of the famous sights, I think I've absorbed a fair amount of info. Maybe we could go to St Nelson's Square tomorrow, the three of us, and Buckingham Cathedral on Sunday? How does that sound?"

"See," Dee said sarcastically to Susan, "I told you you'd got the names all wrong. Listen to the expert," she said, pointing at David.

Susan looked awkward and said with reluctance, "I really need to work tomorrow. I've got to go into college."

David pointed out, "Susan, it's Saturday."

A flicker of annoyance crossed Susan's face as she said, "Well, there's some important stuff I'm working on at the moment." Her eyes were on David's as she said it.

Dee, undimmed in her enthusiasm, said to Susan, "Well *we* could go," indicating herself and David, "couldn't we?"

Susan looked at David who was keeping his expression neutral, obviously waiting for Susan to make the decision for him.

Dee nagged, "Can we, huh, can we?" She started to bounce a little and pout, "I'll do all my stupid chores first."

David shook his head slowly and, glancing sidelong at Susan, said, "Well, maybe we should wait until Susan has a bit more…"

But Susan interrupted, insisting, "You guys go. Maybe I'll join you later, when I get done."

Their plates were empty and Susan set about clearing the table. Dee got up to help.

David asked Susan, "Err, wouldn't you rather we made it

another day?"

Dee complained, "She said go; let's go. It's no big deal. It's not like we're leaving Susie home alone. She's busy."

David continued to look at Susan, studying her expression for signs of disapproval. "What?" she said, exasperated, noticing his look, "Go. Have fun." Then more quietly, "I'll let you know what I find out."

David didn't look happy, but Dee was on to the next topic. As she took the used plates from Susan she said, "Dessert I bought myself. I even set it out to defrost without any help. Susan, you sit, I'll get this." And she bustled off towards the kitchen.

Susan sat back down. With the two of them left on their own, a silence welled up.

David broke it. "So how's the research going?" he asked, his voice neutral.

Susan replied, "Good. Well, kind of good. There's still a million questions, but I think I'm getting somewhere," a pause, "We should really have a talk before long."

David nodded and said, "Well, maybe I should tell Dee that I'm busy tomorrow." He sounded tentative.

"Jesus," Susan snapped, "give it a break, will you. I'm not your mother; you don't need my permission to do things. I thought we'd covered that."

David looked awkward, "I'm sorry, I just meant…"

Dee breezed back into the room. "You like cheesecake, right? What am I saying? Everyone likes cheesecake." She was oblivious to any tension between David and Susan. She asked Susan, "Big bit? Small bit?" An impressive cheesecake sat in front of her and she was waving a cake slice over it, demonstrating the range of sizes available.

Susan tore her gaze away from David. "I'm not really hungry, thanks," she said to Dee, with a shrug.

Dee frowned. "Impossible. Well, we'll come back to you. David?"

Dee's relentless good cheer gradually dispelled the concealed awkwardness of the other two. David was soon bantering with Dee again, though not quite as enthusiastically as before. Susan was still quiet, but she accepted a piece of cheesecake and then allowed herself to be gently teased by Dee when she asked for a second helping a few minutes later.

After that, Susan made coffee while Dee opened the doors of the sideboard to reveal an astonishing array of antique spirits and arcane liqueurs. They puzzled over the label of a large orange bottle with a twist in its neck. When Susan returned with a cafetière and cups, she was carrying David's chocolates under her arm. She held them up and said, "I found these."

David said, "Oh yeah, I thought I'd left them on the tube. I took a chance that you girls like chocolate." Susan and Dee gave him identical pitying looks.

Susan took a look at the bottle with the twisted neck and translated the key ingredient as violets. The bottle was returned to the cupboard promptly, as was a hexagonal green one with oriental script on the label. One whiff of the contents was enough to satisfy everyone it would be difficult, and perhaps dangerous, to swallow any.

David said, "See, it's probably intended for *cleaning* drinks cabinets with. That's why it's in there. It's an understandable mistake to make."

Dee said, "My guess is you wave a capful under the nose of anyone who's had a bit too much of the regular stuff."

Susan said, "And if that doesn't work you could probably embalm them with it – it's dual-action."

David chuckled and Dee said, "Susie, you made a funny. Does that mean you've forgiven me for bringing up Thanksgiving Dinner?" She realised what she'd said and corrected herself, "I mean for mentioning it. Obviously, we brought it up at the time."

David laughed loudly. Susan rolled her eyes, but looked amused. Dee said, "I'll take that as a yes."

The mood remained light as they pushed their chairs back from the table and continued to experiment with the contents of the sideboard.

Around eleven, David said he should get going, which triggered a discussion with Dee about plans for meeting up the following day.

David made another attempt to include Susan by suggesting that Dee should meet him late in the afternoon, which would give Susan most of the day to finish her work and perhaps join them. He arranged to meet Dee at the London Eye at 4pm and to take it from there.

As David walked back along the street, waving over his shoulder, Dee stood at the open door waving back, while Susan retreated inside. As David strolled towards the tube his expression was happy but thoughtful.

CHAPTER 22

A hundred metres from Alessandro Dass's front door stood a late Georgian house large enough to be called a mansion. It sat behind a high brick wall, which rose to flank broad, scrolled-iron gates and then dipped down again towards the far side of the property. The double gates (complete with intercom and closed-circuit camera) allowed those walking by to catch a quick glimpse of how the other half lived.

Currently, the lowest of the house's three magnificent storeys was caged in scaffolding. Thick polythene sheeting covered several windows, which were missing their frames.

In front of the house, on the sand and gravel drive, sat a skip. Two lines of duck-boards ran out from the front of the house, allowing workmen and their wheelbarrows to cross the lawn and reach the skip without damaging the grass.

The house itself was empty. The ground floor had been stripped down to plaster and floorboards – and in some places even the boards had been removed. The upper two storeys were still carpeted and papered, but no furniture remained. The doors leading to the upstairs parts of the house were sealed.

The roofline, which originally had run straight, in parallel with the road, had become more complex as the house had been added to. Now it included a number of geometric planes and angles where extensions met the original construction. In the dip between two of the roof's peaks, a man lay stretched out flat on his stomach looking down onto the street from complete concealment.

He was wearing lightweight Gore-Tex clothing and high-topped training shoes, all in dark colours. To his right lay an open backpack. A mobile phone, a pair of binoculars and a bottle of water rested on top of the pack. The handle of some long implement protruded from the bag's open top.

The mobile phone began to vibrate and the man snatched it up, swiftly inspecting the display before answering it. He said, amiably, "Good afternoon, Edward."

A voice – old but full of nervous agitation – said, "Yeah, yeah. Jan? Got something for you."

Jan said calmly, "Well done, Edward. What is it?"

Edward replied in his hurried, almost stuttering way, "Put that watch on exit points, like you asked. Got a flag on some airline tickets. Looks like your party. First class to Rome-Fiumicino on British Airways. Flight's tomorrow at 19:35. It's AZ209 on the boards." Edward paused a moment before asking, "Watcha gonna do with that? That info? Anything I need to know about?"

Jan replied in his measured tones, "Let's just say you'll probably want to clear away any signs of your interest in the man and his dealings. A lot of people will be asking questions about Mr Dass by the end of Saturday. It might be best if you had concealed your current interest by then."

Edward said, "Christ! What are you up to? Are you dropping

me in it? Am I burned?" He was agitated, but still somewhat deferential.

Jan turned over onto his back, looked up at the sky and said warmly, "If there's any problem, Edward, I'm sure I've got enough time to pop round there and crush the life out of you. Just let me know if being well paid and continuing to breathe is distressing to you."

Edward was unable to speak for a few seconds. "No need. No need for that," he managed to say eventually. "It's just preparations. The more I know about what's going on, the more I can smooth the way at this end. Continue to be useful to you. If I'm in the know, that is. You can see that?"

Jan said soothingly, "Calm down, Edward. I'm sorry I said anything to upset you. After all," he chuckled jovially, "if I keep threatening your life, you'll probably conclude that I'm going to kill you whatever happens and then things really will get strained."

Edward was completely speechless now.

Jan said, reflectively, into the silence on the line, "No. It's probably best that you continue struggling to be useful to me. It helps both of us stay focussed."

Edward still made no response. The only sound from his end of the line was staccato breathing.

Something occurred to Jan and he asked, "Oh, you wouldn't happen to know which terminal that flight leaves from, would you?"

Edward sputtered "tuh" a few times.

Jan made a suggestion, "If you don't think you can get past the first syllable, can I ask you to skip over the word 'terminal' – ironic though it is – and try for the number itself?"

Edward remained silent. Then he managed to say "tuh" again.

Jan was full of patience as he enquired, "Or perhaps you were saying 'two'. *Do* B.A. fly out of terminal two these days?"

Edward gasped out, "Yes. Two. It's terminal two."

Jan was languidly surprised, "Well, well. It's a good job I asked, isn't it? There could have been a mix-up."

The line was still open. Jan said, "I think that's all for now, Edward. I'll call you if I want anything else. Take it easy, old man." He hung up.

Jan made another call. "Al, it's Jan."

Al was pleasantly surprised, "Jan? Good god, it's been a while – a long while. You after something?"

"Yes, and it's very short notice," Jan said.

"Well," Al said in a friendly way, "you tell me what you want and I'll see what I can do."

They chatted for a couple of minutes and Al read the list he'd been making back to Jan, "Stock M16, one off, under-slung with an M203 launcher, two 40 mil rounds supplied, plus a clip of 20 times M995 AP rounds."

Jan said, "That sounds like it. I need it tomorrow morning. Is that a problem?"

Al laughed, "It's just a shame you don't want five hundred of them. Technically it's all obsolete stuff – though it'll kill you just as dead. There's tons of it kicking around. Will any of it come under direct scrutiny?"

Jan replied, "Well, casings and slugs, of course. Is it a problem if the rifle *is* picked up?"

Al chuckled again, "Shouldn't be. You can get them mail-order in the States." Al paused a moment, "Listen, why isn't whatsisname calling this through for you? The kid? You haven't had a falling out with Mr Dass, have you?"

Jan sounded casual as he answered, "It's just quicker to do it myself. By the time I'd explained what I want... You know how it is."

Al said, "Fair enough. Aren't you getting a bit old for this lark, eh Jan? I know I am. My two lads handle most of it now. You know I'll be sixty next month?"

Jan sounded just a little impatient as he said, "No? Well, we'll have a proper natter once I've taken care of this bit of business."

Al said, "Right. I'm gassing on, aren't I? You sure you don't need a scope? Maybe a side-arm or a blade for this outing? You still got that gimmicky Jap thing?"

Jan considered a moment. "You know the way things have been going lately, you're probably right." He added a few more items to his shopping list and Al assured him that they'd be ready in the morning.

* * *

Hours later, after dark, a car pulled up in front of Dass's house. It was a huge, glossy black Mercedes 500SEL sitting low on its suspension.

The driver remained behind the wheel, with the car in gear, as a second man stepped out onto the street. He put his back to the wall of the house and slowly turned his head through one hundred and eighty degrees, taking in every detail of his surroundings. When he had completed his reconnaissance, he hammered twice on the front door, before resuming his vigilance. The front door was opened part way a moment later.

Dass stepped out of the rear of the car and crossed the pavement into the house, the heavy door opening at the last moment for him to enter. Only once Dass was inside did the driver turn off the engine and get out of the car. He locked the vehicle, pocketing the keys and he, and the man watching the street, disappeared into the house.

There was no movement outside for fifteen minutes.

Then, a man wearing dark trousers and boots and a light, ill-fitting sports jacket approached the house, preceded by a scruffy terrier on a lead. The dog leaned against its lead to sniff at the tyres of the Mercedes. The man paused and took a puff of his cigarette.

After a moment, he muttered, "Come on," to the dog and gave a half-hearted tug on the lead. The dog continued to investigate the back wheel of the limousine.

The man stepped across to the car, dropping to one knee and said to the dog, "That's enough, come on now." He reached out for the dog's collar (and swiftly attached something to the inside lip of the rear wheel-arch) before grasping the dog's collar and pulling it away from the car.

Having got the dog's attention, he set off back the way he'd come, the dog following without protest. After a few metres, he dropped the lit cigarette, half smoked, and ground it out with his toe.

He led the dog back up the darkened street and down a side turning. Fifty metres further along he dipped behind a hedge. Between the hedge and a sprawling hydrangea bush, a man lay motionless on his back. He was in his shirtsleeves, spread-eagled in the grass. The dog-walker slipped the loop of the dog's lead over the man's outstretched foot, lifting the leg a little to slide the leather strap beneath his calf. The foot twitched as he lifted it.

Laying on the ground beside the unconscious man was a black ski jacket. Slipping out of the sports jacket and dropping it over the supine figure's face, the dog-walker pulled on the ski jacket. Then he bent down to extract the wallet from the man's back pocket.

The man in the ski jacket emerged from behind the hedge and continued walking along the street, moving further away from Dass's house. A hundred metres later, he passed a rubbish bin, into which he dropped a nearly full packet of Dunhill cigarettes, a disposable lighter and the wallet.

* * *

THE NEXT DAY

At the very end of the afternoon, while it was still light, a filthy white Transit van, with a jagged and rusty rip in one of its side panels, broke down on a road bridge near Heathrow. The bridge spanned one of the main approaches to the airport and on the roadway ten metres below, traffic in three lanes continued to zip past, oblivious to the van's presence.

As the engine cut out, the van steered into the side of the road, coming to a halt halfway across the bridge. A moment later its hazard flashers came on.

The driver of the van, who was wearing heavy motorcycle leathers, got out and opened the bonnet. He stood and peered listlessly at the engine for a few moments, holding the hinged cover open with one latex-gloved hand. Then he secured the bonnet in its open position before climbing back behind the wheel and closing the door.

Lifting a copy of The Sun newspaper that lay on the passenger seat, he revealed a black box inlaid with various switches and dials. A gauge in the centre of the device was calibrated from 1 to 100%. The needle lay just below the 50% mark. The driver dropped the newspaper back in place.

Getting out of the van, he went round to the side door and, with a little bit of effort, managed to pull it open. Inside, a motorbike was anchored to the floor by thick straps which attached to loops in the corners of the grimy metal floorpan. He pulled the door most of the way closed behind him as he got in.

Immediately behind the front seats, a battered tool chest had been crudely welded into place. The driver fished a key from the pocket of his reinforced bikers jacket and unfastened the padlock which held the chest closed. He lifted the lid for a second and dropped the padlock inside.

He glanced at his watch and leaned over the passenger seat to check the hidden dial. The needle had climbed to 70%.

Next he unfastened the straps holding the motorbike in place, moved it up until the front wheel was almost against the rear doors of the van and setting it on its kickstand. He put the keys in the bike's ignition. Then he unfastened the rear doors of the van, but didn't push them open.

With the side door slightly ajar, there was a 5cm gap through which the traffic passing below could be seen. He peered out for a moment at the cars below, closing one eye and then the other, before sliding the door open another few centimetres.

He checked the device on the front seat again.

When the needle had climbed to 80%, the driver flipped open the top of the metal chest and took out a small metal canister and laid it on the floor just inside the door of the van. Next he removed a gold headband from its custom-made box and laid it next to the canister.

A long, slim, black tube, with a grip at one end, followed the headband. He slung it across his back, grip uppermost, using its integral strap.

Finally, he lifted out the rifle. He wrapped the sling around his left wrist and forearm and braced the butt against his shoulder. He flipped off both safety catches and sighted out through the gap in the door, keeping the tip of the muzzle just within the van.

He waited.

Several minutes passed and the traffic continued to flow. The sniper maintained his aim.

Finally, in the distance, a black Mercedes appeared. It was in the outside lane, moving swiftly towards the bridge.

The sniper reached behind him and turned the ignition key on the bike. The electric starter gave its rapid chirp as the engine skipped into life. The engine settled into a steady burble. The sniper returned his gaze to the road below. He took several deep breaths of fresh air through the gap in the side door and blew them out forcefully. Then he settled the rifle more comfortably into his shoulder and took aim at the approaching Mercedes.

The muzzle of the rifle gradually angled down as it followed the approach of the bulky limousine. He kept the weapon trained on the vehicle, until the driver's outline was visible behind the thick windscreen.

The car was now a hundred metres away as the sniper pulled the trigger. In the confines of the van, the sound was ear-splitting. The rifle cracked three times in rapid succession.

The first shot cratered the thick polycarbonate windscreen of the Mercedes without penetrating it. The second and third shots punched through, piercing the driver and slamming into the bodywork at the rear of the vehicle.

As soon as he had fired, the sniper slung the rifle over his shoulder and heaved the side door of the van open – the rusty runners on the door shrieked.

He jumped out onto the pavement and whipped the rifle up to his shoulder again, pointing it over the handrail and down into the traffic.

With a dead man at the wheel, the Mercedes swung across into the middle lane, shunting a Fiat Uno out of its way. The Fiat, in turn, was forced into the inside lane, where it narrowly avoided a black cab. The Fiat driver braked hard causing those behind him to do the same.

The sniper aimed his weapon at the swerving Mercedes and moved his hand to the grenade launcher slung beneath the rifle's barrel. He pulled the launcher's trigger.

A 40mm grenade leapt from the weapon and streaked down towards the driverless car. It struck the front bumper and exploded, lifting the front of the vehicle a metre in the air. The blast destroyed part of the engine and cancelled a considerable fraction of the vehicle's forward momentum.

The sniper pulled forwards on the grip of the grenade launcher, opening the barrel, and raised the muzzle. The remains of the spent round dropped to the concrete. Grabbing the metal canister from the floor of the van, he loaded it into the barrel of the launcher and pulled the grip back into place. Then he snatched up the gold band and jammed it onto his head. His eyelids flickered for a moment in concentration.

He took two rapid steps forwards and jumped over the handrail of the road bridge.

CHAPTER 23

THE NEXT DAY
SATURDAY 26TH APRIL

"So what are your parents like?" David asked.

They'd been talking about this and that – random subjects. He and Dee were standing in the queue for the London Eye, gradually shuffling forwards as each car descended and scooped away another party of tourists.

Dee put her head on one side and said, "Conventional, I guess. And kind of old-fashioned. Mom's always had her plans for both of us and Dad's always let her get on with it."

David said, "I suppose you and Susan don't see much of them these days?"

Dee had her hands in the pockets of her knee-length black wool coat. The late-afternoon breeze coming off the river was cool and she had pulled up her collar to keep her neck warm.

"Well, I'm in Manhattan, Susie's over here and they're in New Mexico," Dee said, then looked contrite and continued, "I shouldn't call her Susie, she hates it."

David said, "So it's just 'Susan' then? No nicknames or abbreviations allowed?"

Dee smiled at David and confessed, "Susan and I had a big fight about names once. She hates being called Susan and I hate being called Dorothy."

David began to react and caught the warning in Dee's raised eyebrow. He still sounded surprised when he asked, "You're Dorothy?"

Dee nodded and said, "Mmhmm. But no one calls me that. I don't know who came up with 'Dee', but it stuck – much to my relief. Somehow Susan stayed Susan."

David considered, "Sue? Susie? Ess? It's a tricky one."

Dee nodded, "But Susan being Susan, she likes to take it on the chin. She hates the name, but she doesn't let anyone try to dress it up or disguise it."

David said, "I quite like 'Susan'. The name."

Dee shrugged, "It's a good-girl's name and Susan was always a good girl. Mom was determined that..." she stopped, "You don't really want to know about this stuff," she said shaking her head.

David was nodding. "Really, I do," he assured her.

She gauged his sincerity for a moment and said, "OK. Background. Mom and Dad met in college. Dad was a geographer, still works for the U.S. Geological Survey. Mom was a journalist, worked on the college newspaper, got a job on a growed-up newspaper once she graduated. But then Dad asked her to marry him, she got pregnant and she hasn't worked full-time since. Susan was her chance to do all the things she was itching to do before marriage and kids happened. So Susan's had tutoring and extra classes and her pick of schools." Dee's voice held a note of frustration, which she now appeared to become aware of. Her voice softened as she said reflectively, "It can't have been very much fun for her, I guess. Lots of pressure."

David asked, "So what were you doing while Susan was being hot-housed?"

Dee bugged her eyes and held a shrug for a moment, "I dunno – watching TV? I was always hanging around with the neighbourhood kids, I think. Honing my people skills. We moved around too much for that to work out really well though."

David said cautiously, "Susan said – and I'm not making fun – Susan said you had an amazing job in New York. You managed that even though you didn't have all the pushing that Susan got."

Dee's introspective gloominess dispersed at the mention of New York and her voice filled with energy again as she said, "Well, what you have to understand is that at age eighteen, I'd had enough of life in the Midwest to last me until six weeks after the end of time. I took off. You could say I ran away from home, but I was eighteen, so really I just *left* home – though it felt more like a jailbreak. I went to Chicago, waitressed, temped, worked in clubs, met a guy. Met a *few* guys actually," she gave David a sly grin.

"One of those guys ran a club. He was, like, the King of New Stuff in Chicago. I don't mean the establishment things; I mean the underground – music, fashion – and art if it was subversive enough.

"I used to tag along, take some notes and then write it up in a newsletter – just a flyer really – telling the world what was hot, clueing the folks in. It started almost as a joke. I wrote it pretty ironically, like kind of a street-twist on a swanky society column.

"We'd give a few copies away at the club and they were always running out of them. It just kind of took off and we ended up distributing it all over. I got myself a cheap Mac and a ratty little office. I bumped up the page count and sold a little sub-culture adspace. Long story short, after six months it got picked up and really did become a column in a city newspaper. Part of some youth-credibility makeover dreamed up by their PR wonks, no doubt, but no one else was doing anything real. It got me some exposure and I was offered an editorial job on a magazine in New York. I moved there about four years ago – where I lived happily ever after."

While Dee had been talking, they'd advanced almost to the head of the queue.

David said, "Wow. So your mum's pleased, I imagine? You're a journalist like she wanted to be. Given what you were saying about her living vicariously through you girls."

Dee gave David a 'yeah right' look. "Well even if I was the heir apparent, which I'm not, Mom was writing about foreign policy; I'm writing about how jeans are the new little black dress." She let the thought hang for a moment and then added, "But then they say parody is a form of flattery."

The next capsule was level with the walkway and people were disembarking. Once it was empty, Dee and David were moved up with a group of a dozen or so others and ushered into the pod.

Dee took David's arm, and said, "Listen, I forbid you to ask me any more questions about myself. You're stepping on my feminine mystique. Now hold on to me, heights scare the crap out of me."

"Why didn't you say?" David asked, following her into the car as it began to lift clear of the ground. It would gradually climb 130 metres into the air, laying London out around them.

Dee sat in the middle of the capsule, on the bench, while those around her pressed their noses to the full-height windows. Even from the bench, they had a great view and David pointed out various landmarks, freely mixing fact with fiction. "That's Battersea Power Station, where they used to generate the electricity for the Pink Floyd albums. And beyond," he pointed to the Crystal Palace radio mast, "you can just see the Eiffel Tower. Looks like the tide's out in the channel at the moment."

Dee hit him on the arm and said brightly, "I'm so lucky you're here. My flaky guide book has nothing like this level of, um, local colour." She smiled at him and he grinned back.

With gentle coaxing, David managed to get Dee to come to one of the windows. She gripped his solid forearm tightly throughout. She was frightened, but exhilarated, until an almost imperceptible movement of the capsule sent her scuttling back to the bench.

"This must be what Godzilla feels like," Dee said, as their part of the wheel reached the top of its rotation. "Help me pick out what I'm going to squash first."

Nearly half an hour passed before their capsule was once again level with the walkway. Susan still hadn't phoned, so when they were both back on the ground they talked about where to go next.

At Dee's insistence, they caught an open-topped bus which gave them a live commentary of London sights as it wound its way through the capital. Their guide had a tough-sounding cockney accent – like someone from a British gangster movie – and it made Dee laugh whenever he made an announcement. David imitated him, making additions to the commentary, but quietly so that only Dee could hear.

The guide said, "An' on yer left is the National Gallery where you can see many of the nation's favourite paintings."

"Some of which are worth a few bob," David said, sniffing, "if you can get 'em out without the bloke on the door seeing you."

The guide said, "An' this is Oxford Street, world-famous for its shopping. Oo knows, you might be able to pick up a bargain."

David added, "Speaking of which, if anyone wants a cheap camcorder, no questions asked, see me at the back of the bus."

As the bus finished its tour, Dee was giggling and shivering in equal parts. "Is it possible that this place is colder than Chicago?" she asked.

David said, "London can get as cold as it wants, from what I can tell. Two degrees in London beats minus fifteen in the Alps, I can vouch for that. Mind you, us locals tend to make sure a bus has got a roof on it before they get aboard."

They were strolling away from the bus stop now. Dee said through chattering teeth, "I've learned my lesson. Find me somewhere I can thaw out my icy tourist butt?"

David gave Dee an exaggerated wink and said, "Watch this." He stuck two fingers in his mouth and whistled loudly enough that people on the other side of the street looked round in surprise. At the same time he threw his other hand in the air. A black cab, which had just driven past, u-turned smartly in the middle of the street and came to a stop in front of them.

David said something to the driver and held the door for Dee. She was laughing as she said, "Impressive. You've just passed the practical section of the New York citizenship exam right there."

David hopped into the warm cab after Dee and slammed the door. She slid across the shiny and ancient black leather to make room for him. He tucked in next to her and confessed, "That must be, ooh, the ninth time I've done that. I've never had a taxi stop before."

Dee said, "So my nine predecessors were left on the sidewalk calling you an idiot, instead of snuggling up in the warm," she hugged his arm, "and sighing 'my hero'?"

"Pretty much," he said, cockily, then conceded, "I think it helps that it's not closing time and that you're not three drunk blokes holding up a fourth."

"That's one of my most endearing features," she said.

The cab was off and moving now, somehow threading its way

through the slow-moving traffic.

David said, "So, let me ask you something. How come neither you or Susan seem to have boyfriends? Gipsy curse?"

Dee turned to him with a sharp look. "Who says I don't have a boyfriend?" she said haughtily, as though he were implying that she was unattractive.

"Of course you do," David said smoothly, "what was I thinking? So where is he at the moment?"

Dee looked at him curiously. David asked, "What did I say?"

"Nothing," Dee said. "I'll tell you later."

David looked intrigued but didn't pursue it. "Let me guess," he said, "you're seeing your boss who's ten years older than you. He's brilliant, but married."

Dee spluttered, "That witch! Blood is thicker than water, my ass. Susan's a dead woman."

David looked amazed, "You mean I'm right," he said, scratching his head.

Dee wasn't buying it; she gave him the evil eye and said, "You saying she didn't squeal?"

David assured her, "Susan tells me nothing." He made a zipping motion across his lips.

Dee looked grumpy but amused, "Well, score one for the psychic hotline. He's actually twenty years older than me, he's separated, in a complicated sort of way and he's my boss's boss. But he is brilliant. I mean it's ten parts doomed to one part future fairytale wedding, but it keeps me out of trouble for the time being." She wrinkled her forehead, "Depending on how you define trouble." She gave David another suspicious look and asked, "Susan said nothing?"

David shook his head emphatically.

Dee seemed to accept his denial and grumbled, "Oh shit, I'm

a stereotype."

"Noo," David assured her, "I'm just good at that sort of thing. What else would a young, ambitious, hot-blooded women with high standards and no free time do?"

Dee asked, "A cliché?"

"Call it a tradition," he suggested. "So you're spoken for?" he asked, "It's just Susan who's the confirmed spinster?"

Dee gave him that curious look again as the cabby slid back the glass partition and called, "Here we are guv'nor," out of the corner of his mouth.

David caught Dee's strange expression and looked questioningly at her. She whispered, "I'll tell you inside."

They got out of the cab, David closing the door behind them and asking the cabby through the side-window, "How much is it?"

"Five pounds sixty, chief," the cabby said. David gave him a ten-pound note and told him to keep it.

The cabby said, "Much obliged." He lowered his voice, "This is for the smart pull-up isn't it? Reckon that might of cracked it for you," he said, nodding towards Dee.

David said nothing, just smiled sheepishly and glanced quickly over at Dee to see if she was listening. She seemed oblivious.

They descended into the sophisticated subterranean cosiness of Café des Amis du Vin. David ordered a bottle of Montepulciano and had them take the chill off it.

He said to Dee, "Call me a philistine, but we can't go drinking cold wine – it might give you chilblains. Gotta watch out for those Victorian ailments now you're in London."

They found a quiet table in the corner farthest from the door and David poured two large glasses of warm wine.

David looked like he was about to speak but Dee got there first, "So Susan was pretty mysterious about what you guys have been up to? She said she'd got that chunk taken out of her cheek when someone broke into her college. What's up with that?"

David said, "Yeah. Things got a bit hairy for a while. It's a long story and not a very believable one. I'm embarrassed to have dragged Susan into it all. I just didn't realise that she was in any danger until too late. Though, god knows, she doesn't exactly shy away from trouble."

He continued, "Anyway it all revolved around this stolen antique which is now back with its owner, so that should be that. There's just a few loose ends to tie up."

Dee said, "Sounds like you two had some close scrapes together."

"What's the American expression? Things were pretty *intense*." He nodded at his own words and said, "Susan's an amazing person. I hope we'll find a way to be friends once there's no, umm, work reason for us to see each other."

Dee agreed, almost sarcastically, "Yeah, friends. Let's hope, huh?"

David didn't get it. "What's up?" he said, quizzically, "I keep getting this feeling that I'm saying something that I shouldn't, but I don't know what it is."

Dee sighed slowly and let her shoulders drop. She didn't speak for a few moments and David waited patiently. Finally, she said, "You know, you're kind of attractive, David."

"Er, thanks," David said awkwardly.

"And I'm getting a bad feeling about us spending time together," Dee said.

David looked at her blankly.

Dee lifted her chin and asked him directly, "What exactly are we doing here?"

David was at a loss for an answer. He began to say something, but nothing coherent came out. Dee said, "OK. Try this. Have you got something going with Susan?"

David looked defensive. He shook his head. "No," he said defiantly, and then when Dee continued to say nothing, he added, "She isn't interested."

Dee raised one eyebrow and said, "So you thought you'd try me?"

David was flustered and a little bit annoyed. "Woah! Hang on a minute. I thought we were having a nice afternoon out. If something else has happened here, then I'm sorry, but I missed it," he said.

Dee continued to give David a challenging look for a moment longer and then let it dissipate. She began to look conciliatory. "Let's try this another way. When I asked Susan about you she got weird. All she'd say was that you were sweet. She told me how whenever she pretended to take offence at something, you'd practically fall over yourself to apologise. It made her laugh."

She checked that he was still following her and continued, "I tried a couple of times to tease you but you refused to be rattled. I was just wondering why Susan makes you nervous but I don't."

David still made no comment. Dee sipped her wine and said, "And you keep asking me about her. Maybe you're just being polite, right?"

David sat forwards. He said, "I don't see what you're getting at. OK, yes I think Susan's kind of fabulous. You're right. But she's pretty much let the air out of my tyres, if you know what I mean. There's nothing happening between her and me, and I'm trying to respect her wishes. She's busy today and her completely charming sister needs a tour guide. It's true, it feels more like she's doing me a favour, instead of the other way round, but it's what she wanted. I can't help it if I'm having the nicest day I've had for ages and maybe forgetting to hide the fact."

Dee looked at him impassively for a few seconds and then she gave him a very sexy smile. "It really is too bad you know. I could just about eat you up. But I think we're playing with fire here, whether you've realised it or not." She leant forward now and rested her elbows on the table. "So here's what you need to know, Sport. She's got a major thing for you. I'd put big bucks on it."

David's eyebrows went up and he leaned back. "I don't think so," he said cautiously.

Dee made a click with her tongue and said, "Yup. As soon as I realised how much you liked her, it suddenly gelled." Something else occurred to her then and she butted herself gently on the forehead with the palm of her hand. "God. I should have known something was up when I asked her about spending some time with you. If she'd shrugged and said 'whatever', that would have meant go ahead. But she practically insisted I hang out with you." She shook her head.

David said nothing. Dee went on, "Why this should be I don't know, but Susan doesn't trust a soul. Not me, not Mom and Dad, especially not guys. But for some reason I think she trusts *you*. Maybe it's something to do with all the cops and robbers stuff you two have been through together, but there's something different in the way she talks about you."

Dee gave a cynical laugh. "Knowing her, it'll be another ten years before she's sure about it, but I think deep-down she's already there. She told me you weren't her type and I took it at face value. Because, you know, it's her choice. She's a big girl. If you've seen her in any of her competitions you know she can take care of herself just fine. So why would she say she didn't like you if she did?"

David was enthralled and at the same time profoundly uneasy as he listened to Dee talk. He made no move to interrupt her.

She had a little more wine and continued, "Do you want to hear my theory? If she trusts you, that means she might actually find herself opening up to you. Now, there's never been any danger of that in her past relationships. It's like me and my married man, I guess – despite what we tell each other, there's no real risk of intimacy. But I think with you, maybe Susan's realised she's kind of vulnerable. I think she was pushing me towards you because she's a little bit scared."

David asked, "Scared of getting on too well with me?"

Dee nodded, "Scared that she's met someone who'll figure her out. Isn't everyone scared of that?"

"What's she got to hide?" David asked.

"Nothing," Dee replied, "as far as I know. But she's always been very private. This would be unknown territory for her."

David was trying to follow Dee's argument, "So if she's nervous about her and me, why would she be encouraging you to spend time with me?"

Dee drained her glass and poured herself some more wine. "My guess is that I'm supposed to steal you. Like I did to her once before," she said.

"That makes no sense," David said, confused.

"Sure it does," Dee replied. "People are always pushing others away just to see if they come back. It's a way of reassuring yourself that they care."

"So she's testing me?" David asked. "It's not that she doesn't like me?" He sounded as though he was doing his best to believe it but not having much success.

The wine had brought a bit of a flush to Dee's cheeks. She said, passionately, "Think about it. It adds up. She's nervous so she pushes you and me together. She tells herself it's so she can be sure of you, but it's really fear talking. If I steal you she has someone else to blame for the relationship going wrong, plus she's off the hook – her secrets are safe."

David had folded his arms. "Hmm," he said, noncommittally, "Well, it's one theory. How long have you known all this?"

Dee said, "I've just been putting it together since the taxi ride. I knew something was going on, but I didn't see what it was until I realised you had a thing for her."

David continued to be far from convinced by Dee's theory, but as they carried on talking, both of them would keep mentioning things that Susan had said or done which leant weight to Dee's interpretation of events.

The more David was swayed, the more he began to worry. Eventually he voiced his concern, "Do you think she sees this as a date?"

Dee shrugged.

David blew his breath out and looked dejected. He said, "It's been a while since I had such a fun day, Dee. You're really easy to spend time with and I was enjoying not thinking about where it might be leading. I suppose I should have known there'd be some terrible price to pay for giving my conscience the day off. I promised Susan that I wouldn't let her down. Do you think that's what I've just done?"

Dee thought about it. "I think you being here is how she gets out of the fix she's in. She might be pushing you away, but I'm sure that behind it all she's hoping that you'll come straight back again."

David was looking genuinely worried as he said, "Dee, I really don't want to disappoint her. I know this is putting you in the middle of something, and I know that's unfair on you, but I need your advice. Do you think by just being here I've blown it?"

Dee smiled sadly. "Well, I guess it depends on how today went.

If I tell her you were polite but kind of frosty, then maybe you pass the test."

David looked hopeful. "Would you... Could you do that?" Then he said, "Wait, I don't want you to lie to her. There must be... What else could you say?"

Dee looked David in the eye. "How's this then?" she said with a sigh, "I tell her I had a great time and that you're a wonderful guy, but it's obvious to me that you're crazy about her."

* * *

Dee had continued to make light work of the wine. David had taken some time over his first glass and when he went to pour some more, there was only enough for half a refill. As David pointed out when he returned from the bar with a second bottle, it was starting to feel like they were old friends.

Neither of them were flirting, but that seemed to make the conversation somehow more intimate, in a platonic kind of way. Both of them seemed better able to relax now that there was no pressure to sparkle.

It was getting on for nine o'clock when Dee checked her phone. "I thought Susan might have called by now," she said. She'd had a good part of the second bottle by this stage and was beginning to speak with deliberate precision as the wine strengthened its hold. "I'm wondering if this thing's busted. I swiped Susan's charger but I don't know if it's working," she said, showing him the display on her phone. It was blank apart from a battery-level indicator with four of its five bars showing. There was no signal or network name.

David suddenly looked awkward. "Dee, we're underground. I completely forgot," he said.

Dee looked embarrassed, "Oops," she said, "Ahh, I don't suppose we'd have heard the ringing, even if she did prise herself out of a book to call us. We should she if see's... see if she's been trying to reach us."

David nodded and said, "We should probably call it a night anyway. We're not supposed to be having too much fun, remember?"

David left his wine and stood up to pull on his heavy leather jacket. Dee began to get her coat on as well. She leaned over and drained her glass before smacking her lips and announcing she was ready to go.

It had turned into a frosty night above ground. Dee shivered as soon as the chill air touched her skin.

David turned to her as they stood on the pavement outside the bar and said, "Dee, I really have had a lovely day. And thank you so much for helping rescue things with Susan. I just hope I haven't screwed it up already."

Dee smiled and said, "Fingers crossed. You can repay me by convincing Susan that I pick my own bridesmaid's dress." She muttered under her breath, "Sisters always get the cerise puff-sleeve bullshit."

David's and Dee's phones simultaneously began beeping and they grinned sheepishly at each other.

Dee was first to connect to her answerphone. It was a brief message. Dee looked puzzled. "And the prize for Girl of Mystery goes to Susan Milton. I wonder where she's planning on staying tonight." Dee was going to say more, but then she caught sight of David's face. A look of horror was spreading across his features as he listened to his own messages.

Dee's voice was filled with concern as she said, "What is it?"

David made a curt gesture for her to be quiet. He continued

listening for a moment, his face becoming even more grave.

When it was finished he announced, "I've got to go." His voice was clipped, his throat tight with tension.

Dee demanded, "What is it?"

But all David would say, sounding distracted, was, "Dee, I have got to go. Right now."

"Tell me," she said angrily, grabbing his sleeve. It was clear that David was going to have to wrench her hand free or else explain.

"I think something's happened to Susan," he said.

CHAPTER 24

EARLIER THE SAME DAY
SATURDAY 26TH APRIL

Susan stood once again in the foyer of the London School of
Antiquities. Above her, on a stepladder, was a man in blue overalls
peering into a trapdoor in the ornate plaster ceiling. His assistant
stood by and held the ladder with bovine patience. The only other
person in the heavily marbled atrium was the security guard
behind the main desk from whom she'd just signed out the keys
to the Alexandrian room. According to the guard, no one else was
working down there today.

As she waited for the lift, Susan was playing an answer-phone
message on her mobile. "Hi Susan, it's David," the message began.
"I just wanted to say thanks for last night and I hope you can make
it later today. Anyway, it was lovely to…" she pushed a button
on her phone cutting the recording off. "Message deleted. End of
messages," an automated voice confirmed. She disconnected the
call and dropped the phone back into her bag.

The ancient cage of the lift slowly descended a moment later. She wrestled the cantilevered doors open, then shut them behind her, riding down three floors in quiet contemplation, the occasional flicker of an unidentified emotion troubling her features.

When she got out of the lift, the basement was silent and deserted. The fluorescents in the hallway blazed, but the doors of the various rooms leading off it were closed. She unlocked the Alexandrian room and turned a couple of the lights on.

At her usual workstation, she got her iBook out of her bag and pushed the power switch, attaching cables for power and network access while it went through its start-up routine. Then she wandered over to her locker. Even though the room was silent and empty, she glanced over her shoulder before putting the key in the padlock.

Once the louvred grey metal door was open, she lifted out a Tesco's shopping bag, tightly wrapped around an object about the size and heft of half a dozen sleeveless vinyl LPs.

Taking the bundle back to her workstation she unwrapped the bag, revealing a second bag underneath and a swaddling of bubble-wrap under that. Pausing a moment, she got up and went to the door. She peered out into the silent hallway.

According to the indicator above the lift doors, the cage was idling on the ground floor. Around her, the building was silent.

Closing the door, Susan locked it from the inside and went back to her desk. She finished unwrapping the bundle.

Inside was a plain gold band. A furrow was visible on one side of the band where she had struck it with the iron end of a window pole. She set it almost reverentially on the desk in front of her.

Then she took a jewellery case from her courier bag and laid it next to the circlet. The box was made from the same curious, hard, fuzzy, black material favoured by jewellers the world over. Prising open the snap-shut lid with its awkward spring, she revealed two gold bracelets pressed into the depression meant for one.

She removed them from their ruffled, white-silk nest and placed them on the desk. Inscribed around the inside circumference of one bracelet were the words, "To Susan, from Mom and Dad. We're so proud."

The inscription on the second read, "To Dorothy, with all our love, Mom and Dad."

Susan sat and stared for a while at the headband and the two bracelets. Her face was unreadable. Some powerful emotion was compressing her mouth and pulling her jaw muscles tight. The tip of her tongue emerged for a second, swiping moisture rapidly onto her dry lips. She absent-mindedly tried to hook her bottom lip with one of her canines, her eyes fixed all the while on the glittering haul in front of her.

Emerging suddenly from her reverie, she grabbed papers from her bag and began to spread them out on the desk. Then, she pulled the iBook towards her and opened Acrobat. A few moments later, an image of a document, handwritten in Latin, appeared on the display.

She flipped the top sheet of her legal pad over and began to make notes.

After a quarter of an hour she fetched a bulky Latin dictionary from her open locker.

For another hour, Susan shuffled and scrutinised the documents, periodically scribbling with rapid industry. Soon, sheets of paper had obscured the gold jewellery on her desktop. She kept returning her attention to one page in particular.

She created a new text document and, over the course of the next hour, she typed the following:

Lift your head out of the water and see the lay of the land correctly for the first time. Touch is the first of the senses to awaken. Touch and then feeling and seeing and hearing and the spirit of temperature and the permanence of air and the violent motions of things barely out of reach. Healthiness is one day a sense but comes first as an invisible companion/ friend.

In some there is a greater knowledge but it is [occlusive?]. Lesser knowledge is to have one foot in two countries/lands; greater knowledge is to lift the back foot and to be an exile/wanderer from the country of one's birth. Greater knowledge is without effective power because it has not [got] the intention to use it any longer. It turns inward, but that is another matter.

Begin here with this [song?] and consider very well this drawing and think for a long time about what you wish to lay your unseen hand upon. It has been asserted by a lot of people that a knife [for eating?] is the most suitable object with which to start but perhaps what comes to mind first is simply what comes to hand first [correct idiom?].

Susan saved the file and pushed her laptop aside. She gathered her documents into a pile and transferred them to the next desk. Two pieces of laser-printed paper remained in front of her; they were reproductions of handwritten documents. One was decorated with a complex swirling pattern, roughly circular in shape. Parts of the pattern looked like details from Moorish tiles, other areas like Celtic knots. The ten-point-Arial title read 'Pattern 3 Ter-119G'.

The second paper had the title 'Nonsense rhyme? Ter-016L' printed on the top. Below the title were strings of handwritten letters in groups, certain sequences of syllables appearing repeatedly in different arrangements.

Susan fastened one bracelet on each of her wrists. Then she placed the gold band on her head. It fitted almost perfectly. Finally, from her bag she took a letter-opener. It was a slim bar of silver, without a guard or a covering over the handle – a gleaming metal pin, double-edged at one end and squared at the other. She laid it in the centre of the drawing and took several deep breaths. Then she began to read the poetry aloud. When she finished the page, she began again at the top.

She read it without pause, twenty times. Her voice was beginning to get a little croaky, but she continued.

After she had read it thirty-five times she hardly needed to glance at the paper and instead focussed on the knife and the pattern beneath it. She continued to repeat the poem, sounding the syllables quietly with her dry throat.

She had been speaking continually for one hour and fifty minutes when the knife rocked slightly, the tip bouncing once on the paper. "Shit," she said and stopped dead.

She stared at the knife for a while, her lips still. She had just pronounced the word 'pervolo' when the knife had stirred. She leaned in now and repeated it forcefully, "Pervolo, pervolo."

She dropped her head and sounded the 'per' syllable sharply several times, bringing her mouth close to the knife, allowing her breath to mist its surface. It didn't move. She blew directly on it, without trying to shape any particular syllable. Still no movement. She blew harder and the knife rocked slightly, as it had done before. The other sheet of paper slipped to the floor, disturbed by her breath. She retrieved it.

"Damn," she said wonderingly. She stood up and put her hands on her hips. She looked at the knife again and muttered, "Oh boy."

Then she removed the jewellery she was wearing and laid it on the desk. She placed a few sheets of paper on top of it.

She went to the door and unlocked it, peering cautiously out into the corridor before opening it wide. No one was around.

Crossing to the coffee machine, she pressed the buttons for cold water. She drank two shiny beige plastic cups of icy water before entering the code for black coffee. She took the coffee back into the Alexandrian room, locking the door behind her.

She sat down at her desk, sipping the hot liquid. Setting the cup down, she winced a little and rubbed the back of her head. "Man," she said, as though she was in pain. She rotated one of her shoulders, then the other, and kneaded the back of her neck with one hand.

She sat, looking contemplative and taking delicate sips of coffee, one carmine-booted foot propped on the edge of her desk. When the cup was empty, she threw it in the bin. Then she gathered the bracelets and put them back in their box. The headband she once again double-wrapped and returned to her locker.

Then she spread out her papers and began reading and taking notes again.

An hour later, she took another break, this time making her way upstairs and outside into the daylight. She returned through the late afternoon chill with sandwiches, a Starbucks latte and a slice of carrot cake.

She ate while studying.

On the wall, behind her, hung an electric clock. The hands showed six o'clock by the time she had typed the following:

To begin is to take up the reins of a responsive beast of burden. Others have their hands resting on the reins also. They cannot contradict/silence your commands nor can they know what is said, but they will hear your voice if they listen. When you both walk dressed/adorned in [the clothes/covering of power?] it is as though you are walking nearby to your enemies but separated by a third of a third of a third of a parasang [5.6km/27=~200m] on a windless day.

Susan stopped writing for a moment and ran her fingers through her hair. Then she began to look concerned. She continued to scrutinise the document she was working on, periodically looking up to tap a phrase into her computer. Finally, she had written:

It is in this as in everything else that men undertake. There is a small amount of treasure/riches and it is guarded jealously. There is never love between those who have been awakened because the world is not big enough for everyone. In truth, to discover a neighbour is to discover a deadly enemy. The approach of a stranger is equivalent to a challenge. To overhear another is to listen to the voice of your conqueror. You will make him instead your prey if you think wisely. Contention without diplomacy is the natural order of things. For these reasons, do not sleep and never lie down comfortably. Be alert always and be ready to fight hard even in the quietest part of each night.

Susan was now frowning. She got up and went to her locker. From inside she took a second, smaller dictionary, bound in worn black leather, and returned to her seat with it. She began to fine-tune her translation. At the end of another hour she had made very few changes, but she had added the following lines to her document:

Fledglings are not found to be alive for long away from the nest. Only those with the protection of an ancient [school for kings?] survive. The first utterance of the tiny bird is very likely to bring the hawks towards it without fail. It is the best moment to do away with one's future enemies. Vigilance and quick action in this matter is the most important thing. Listen always for new voices and then cut across them angrily as quickly as you can.

Susan was chewing her lip again. She had wrapped one hand around the other in front of her and was bouncing them up and down, repetitively, subconsciously. As she stared at the document, she was rocking her head a little in nervousness. "I don't like this," she muttered, "I don't like this."

She fired up Eudora on her laptop and scrolled through several e-mails until she found the one she was looking for. It was from Bernie Lampwick. She paged down through the text until she reached the following:

> ...albeit a rapid one, it seems to me to bear a resemblance to passages from Il Principe. Political treatises being all the rage at the time, I wonder if this might not be an allegorical piece in the same vein. Perhaps it leans a little more towards Savonarola than Machiavelli and the language is far more obscure (perhaps the author was out of favour at the time and masking his true meaning?), but nevertheless I wonder if we might not have here the work of a previously unknown 'Prophet of Force'. As I noted

in my doctoral thesis…

The sudden muffled sound of a drill, conveyed to her through the bones of the building, made Susan jump. The workmen in the foyer had been carrying a heavy, three-phase drill into the building as she had returned with her lunch, but still the distant rattling grind of the masonry bit chewing its way into a wall took her by surprise.

She forced her attention back to the e-mail and muttered, "What were you thinking, Bernie? It's not about governing Florence; it's about magic."

She sat thinking for a little longer, nodding to herself. "It's a warning," she said softly, but decisively.

She flinched a second time, moments later, when the lift doors clattered open out in the hallway. For a moment she held her breath. Slow footsteps could be heard on the heavy vinyl floor outside the door – a gentle thump and squeak as each foot was placed then lifted. The door handle rattled as someone tried to open the door. Then a knock and a deep, serious voice saying, "Dr Milton. Hello?"

She sounded reasonably nonchalant as she called, "I won't be a minute. Who's that?" but her eyes were riveted on the door throughout.

"It is Oswald Olabayo, Dr Milton. I work for the security company employed by the college. I am making my rounds," a cultured voice said from the other side of the door.

Susan smiled and muttered to herself with relief, "Too goofy to fake." She unlocked the door to see a tall, elegant man with jet-black skin, wearing a baggy RAF-surplus blue jumper.

"Sorry," said Susan, "I'm a bit paranoid about security at the moment."

The guard smiled widely and said, "Of course Madam. We

have to be vigilant. Is everything in order?"

"Yes. Thank you," she said, "Um, how often do you patrol down here?"

"Every hour I make my rounds, Doctor, as instructed," he said.

Susan didn't mention that whoever had the shift before him obviously operated according to a different set of instructions. She said, "Oh, OK then. See you in an hour."

"Yes, Madam," the guard said and turned his attention to the storeroom door.

Susan was still smiling as she returned to her chair. She took a couple of slow breaths. Her grin dropped away as her attention returned to her e-mail. A new message had appeared in her Inbox. The title read:

```
CustomNews.biz - Requested news alert
```

She opened the e-mail and read:

```
Susan Milton,

One of your pre-defined NewsAlert keywords
- "Dass" - occurs in at least one current
news story. Click on the link below to
read the news item(s).

www.CustomNews.biz/storyid=1447916
```

Susan clicked on the link and read the following:

```
Possible terrorist attack near Heathrow
Airport.

In the last hour...

A broad daylight attack on a chauffeured
limousine as it entered London's Heathrow
```

```
airport left three dead and motorists
stunned. Gunfire and an explosion disabled
the limousine while spectators looked
on. A CustomNews reporter investigating
the incident uncovered the fact that
Alexandero Dass, a respected Italian
businessman, was the target of the attack
when he and his two associates failed to
arrive for a flight to Rome's Fiorentino
airport.
```

Susan read on, though there was little more to learn from the story – beyond the author's lack of attention to detail. The article had no information about the assailant, except to say that it appeared to be a man acting alone. She tried several other online news services without turning up any new facts.

Lifting the phone on her desk, she punched in her access code followed by Dee's mobile number. It went straight through to her answer-phone. "Dee," she said, "Susan. Listen, I might not make it back there tonight. I'll call you in the morning to let you know what's going on." She hung up.

Glancing at her address book she punched another number. The tip of her index finger was resting on David's name as her other hand pressed the buttons. Again, she got an answerphone message.

She began to leave a message. "David," she said, "it's Susan. Listen, I need to talk to you – right away. Dass is dead and I think it was Jan who did it. Which means he could have the Marker again. That'd mean Teracus's collection is his next priority. He blew Dass's car up in broad daylight, so I don't think he'd have any reservations about busting in here and wrecking the place to get what he wants. I think he's past caring about the mess he makes. You know there's no way security here would stop him and I can't even tell them what they're up against – they'd think I'd flipped. I'm thinking… what I think I might do… I think I need to move the collection. Now. Jan'll come here either way, but I don't want him to get this stuff. Whatever he's up to, it's nothing good."

She paused a minute and then said, "There's something else. I think I've miscalculated. I tried something… an experiment. I think I shouldn't have. I think maybe I've called attention to myself. There's a possibility Jan might come after me now. I'm going to…"

The door handle rattled. Susan froze. There had been no sound of anyone approaching but someone was right outside the door. It was forty minutes before the next security patrol was due.

There was a crash from above. Something heavy had struck the building. The impact rattled small objects all round the room.

"There's somebody here," Susan whispered, almost absentmindedly, into the phone – her attention focussed on the door handle. Without glancing down, she ended the call. Someone was trying the door.

CHAPTER 25

Dee was furious. And though her anger didn't seem to be intended for anyone in particular, David was getting the brunt of it, being the only available target.

They braked hard before taking a sharp corner and Dee snapped, "Should you even be driving? We had two bottles of wine, remember?" Her tone was openly hostile.

David was in nearly as bad a mood. "Right," he said, "and you drank them. I had two glasses in two hours. I've never felt more sober." He shot through a newly-red light and around a bus as it tried to pull out. Dee was bracing herself against the dashboard to avoid being thrown around.

"Well could you at least slow down please," she said, in some icy Manhattan dialect intended for rebuking the help. It didn't sound like a request.

"No I fucking well couldn't," David growled through gritted teeth.

That shut Dee up temporarily.

Outside the bar, she'd made it clear that she was sticking with David until they found out what was going on with her sister. So together they'd caught a cab to David's car. When they'd reached it, he'd bundled her in and before she even had her seatbelt done up they were racing through back streets constricted with parked cars, rocketing through gaps with only millimetres to spare. David had cut around any vehicle that slowed him down, intimidating oncoming drivers into giving way.

It was a couple of minutes after David's angry words to her that Dee ventured to speak again. They were now crossing the Euston Road heading south. Dee still sounded just as angry as she said, "I can't help it, OK? I don't deal well with this kind of situation. It makes me crazy." Her voice was thick from the wine she'd drunk earlier.

Even though her tone was far from conciliatory, her words seemed to affect David. His face softened and he reached across to squeeze Dee's hand without taking his eyes off the road. "I'm sorry I swore at you," he said. After a moment, he added, "When I panic I focus. It's not good for my manners."

Dee said nothing. David had slowed for a moment while he was speaking to Dee but he picked up the pace again now.

Another minute passed, the sudden pitch changes of the high-revving engine filling the car. David glanced over and saw a mascara-laden tear rolling down Dee's cheek.

He sounded both surprised and awkward as he said, "I really am sorry, Dee."

"I live in New York, remember? It's not the yelling," she sniffed, "I'm crying because I'm worried. I can't..." The last word was drawn out into the beginnings of a wail, cut short as she clamped her jaws together. Her shoulders bobbed in time to the puffing sound of her sobs – barely discernible over the straining engine.

Dee groaned loudly, a sound full of sorrow, and then slapped herself hard on the cheek a moment later. David looked shocked, "Hey, hey," he said soothingly, somewhat alarmed.

Dee sniffed viciously and said, "I'm OK, I'm OK," then added unhappily, "I can't believe I'm crying." She sniffed again and began hunting in her bag, eventually producing a pack of tissues. She blew her nose.

A moment later, they arrived at the School of Antiquities. David pulled up on the double yellow lines right outside, threw open the car door and ran in. Dee followed, scooping tears back up her face with her index finger as she bustled after him.

When she caught up with him, David was already in conversation with the guard behind the security desk. It took five minutes of talking at cross-purposes, before David managed to ascertain that there'd been no break-in – not this week at any rate – and to satisfactorily explain his interest. His initial demands for information had put the guard on the defensive. Only by starting again from the beginning, and forcing himself to be patient, had he made progress.

It turned out that the most excitement the School had seen that day was the accident which had shattered an area of the lustrous marble floor in the centre of the ornate entrance hall. The evidence was still there for David to see. A heavy, industrial drill lay at the heart of a web of cracked Italian marble, its cord like the slack tail of a crushed animal. A tall stepladder straddled its corpse.

The guard told them how he'd checked on Susan soon after he'd come on duty. Then, shortly after the workmen had dropped the drill, he had seen her hasten out of the building, seemingly late for a pressing appointment. She was heavily burdened with paperwork, and had flung her keys at him, in too much of a rush for even the most basic of pleasantries. "Besides..." he said, shaking his head sadly and indicating the cracked floor, which apparently occupied most of his thoughts at present.

A second guard had appeared in the foyer and heard the end of the conversation. He spoke now, "Dr Milton? I went to tell her the power was going off. She was a bundle of nerves – wouldn't open the door to start with. She usually like that, then?"

"No, she's not," David said.

He turned back to the first guard and said, "Thank you." And then added, "Excuse me," as he extracted his mobile phone and turned away to make the call. Dee had tried Susan's number twice since leaving the bar, but David made a third attempt. All he got was her answerphone.

Dee had left frantic messages at the end of both her calls and David evidently couldn't think of anything new to add; he hung up before Susan's recorded voice finished speaking.

The security guard offered to call David and Dee if he received any news or if he saw Susan. They both left their numbers with him, thanking him for his trouble.

They made their way slowly back to the car which was as yet undiscovered by late-shift traffic wardens or roving wheel-clampers.

"Dee," David said, once they were inside, "it sounds like she panicked for some reason and went to ground. If *we* don't know where she is, then no one else will either. If she thinks she might be in trouble, she'll be hiding somewhere. All we can do is wait to hear from her. She's probably cleverer than both of us put together; I'm sure she'll be alright."

Dee said nothing for a while. She looked awful. The worry, the inky tears and the dregs of alcohol in her system made her look years older than she had at the start of the evening.

"I think you should stop in a hotel tonight," David said, once they were both back in the car. "We'll go back to the Professor's place in the City and I'll run in and grab a few of your things and then we'll find you somewhere to stay."

Dee offered no resistance. The fight seemed to have gone out of her and she looked exhausted. She nodded, sadly, and sat quietly while David drove, hardly moving and saying nothing.

It took fifteen minutes to reach the house. David asked Dee for the keys and told her to sit in the driver's seat with the engine running. "If anything happens, just drive away. I'll sort myself out."

"I can't drive stick," she said, her voice tiny and hoarse.

David considered this for a second, and then offered, "Well, lock the doors while I'm in there and sound the horn if you need me. I'll come running," he said.

Getting out, he went round to the boot and opened it for a moment in order to retrieve the telescopic baton he'd carried with him when he'd visited Dass. He slipped it into his sleeve and slammed the boot, signalling to Dee to lock the doors.

Approaching the house, he looked for signs of life. It seemed as deserted as ever. The windows on the ground floor were still shuttered and no lights showed through the cracks.

He made his way up the steps and took a good look at the front door. The heavy-duty door lock seemed intact, its dull patina unmarked – no signs of uninvited entry.

Slipping the key in the door he pushed it open and stepped into the dark hallway. With the front door open, there was just enough light shining in from the street for him to make out the foot of the stairs. Quietly, he moved a potted fern so that it prevented the door from closing and then he made his way stealthily up the stairs.

The upper-storey windows weren't shuttered and the night, like all London nights, was far from pitch-black. Twice, distant noises caused him to stop abruptly, straining to hear more, but it was impossible to tell whether the sounds came from outside or not – or what might be making them.

He moved into the rear bedroom. The floor-length curtains lay open and through the sash window the branches of a plane tree were revealed, black in the faint orange light. The leaves were fidgeting sleepily in the evening breeze, stirring the shadows in the bedroom.

David grabbed Dee's toiletry bag, her cosmetics case and the partially unpacked cabin case which sat on the ottoman at the end of the bed. Thus laden, he retraced his steps, emerging from the house to find everything just as he had left it. Dee was sitting watching him from the car.

He put what he was carrying in the boot and had Dee wind the window down. "While we're here, I might as well grab everything. What else is there?" he asked.

"Two garment bags and whatever's scattered around the room," she said, after a moment's thought.

He nodded, had her wind the window back up, and headed once more into the darkened house.

He appeared two minutes later holding the two bags and a bulging duty-free carrier bag. With the edge of his foot, he pushed the plant pot aside and allowed the heavy door to swing closed.

David laid the bags on the back seat and hopped into the front, slipping in behind the wheel. He activated the central locking and moved away. He drove for a couple of minutes before speaking. "So have you got any ideas for where you could stay?"

"I've got a corporate account with Hilton," she said.

"Well, let's start with Park Lane then," David said with forced cheeriness.

* * *

A second ring on the bell was accompanied by a knock this time.

Banjo flung open the door ready to take aim. He was wearing a paisley silk dressing gown in a rich scarlet base tone and carrying a pump-action water pistol – the kind that looked like Disney's attempt at an assault rifle.

"What did I tell you?" he yelled, as the door opened. Then he stopped short as he caught sight of David standing on his bottom step.

"Did those kids put you up to this?" he asked David suspiciously. "Just tell me the truth and I won't be cross." The water-gun was no longer being aimed, but it was still held in casual readiness.

Banjo took a proper look at David, who appeared to have slept in his clothes. He hadn't shaved and his expression suggested a tired sort of pain.

Banjo said, "You look like my sister Doreen just after she had the twins." Shouldering the weapon, and with a single, darting glance down the street, Banjo retreated back inside, beckoning David to follow. "And what I said to her seems equally appropriate here: I'll stick the kettle on."

He led David through to the draughty Thirties-era kitchen, with its rickety, handmade cupboards and dark lino, now pimpled like the surface of a poppadom.

David slumped into a squeaky kitchen chair, while Banjo put a battered aluminium kettle on the gas hob. "You look all in, mate. You want some brekky?"

David shook his head, so Banjo concentrated on the tea. He bustled about, humming and occasionally stealing surreptitious glances at David. His piped scarlet slippers kept snagging rips in the lino, forcing him to shuffle like a geisha to keep them on.

A couple of minutes later, two mugs of tea were placed on the kitchen table. David's sat on a white patch the size of a soup plate, where the Formica's gingham pattern had worn away, leaving not even a ghost.

As Banjo sat, he suddenly looked alarmed. "Oh god, it's not the Pope is it? Has something happened to him?"

David's slow smile brought to mind someone with a fish-hook in their upper lip, but it contained a tired twinkle of amusement too.

Seeing the smile, Banjo said, "I don't know the meaning of the phrase 'inappropriate humour', do I?"

They sat and smiled at each other for a moment, the smile of old friends. The morning sunlight creeping down the far wall glowed suddenly bright as a gap in the clouds opened up. For a second, the air was yellow and filled with floating dust like microcosmic snowflakes in a tiny tabletop world. The break in the cloud passed a few moments later, leaching away the colour, and Banjo shivered slightly in his dressing gown as the room dimmed.

"So, is it Susan?" he asked softly.

David nodded slowly and took a sip of his tea. He looked up from under a lowered brow. "Can I tell you what's been going on?" he asked, sounding suddenly hopeless.

"Course, mate," Banjo murmured warmly, "You can tell me anything."

"You might not believe me," David said, giving fair warning.

"You know me better than that," Banjo said. "This sounds like a good 'un."

They were on their third mug of tea by the time David had reached the events of that evening. Banjo appeared to be taking it all in his stride.

"What you told Dee," Banjo said, "that sounds right. Susan's done a bunk to be on the safe side. She's probably doing what you're doing; she's nipped round to see some old mate of hers until she gets over the collywobbles."

David rubbed the back of his neck and nodded slowly.

Banjo asked, "Where have you been since midnight then?"

David shrugged. "Here and there. I stopped in at Susan's work again, I sat in the car for a while, keeping an eye on the house she's staying in. And I, er, went round to both of that bloke Jan's addresses looking for signs of life. Oh yeah, and I stopped in at the Nick to see if they could tell me anything."

Banjo blew his breath out expressively. "I'd say that pretty much exhausts all the possibilities. You should probably just keep the mobile switched on and lay low yourself. That's about all you can do." He added, "Although a bath probably wouldn't be a bad idea sometime before you two lovebirds are reunited. Why don't you use my bathwater – and before you say anything it's still in the tank, I haven't used it yet – and then get a couple of hours kip. I won't let the phone out of my sight – guide's honour."

David nodded his thanks and then said, "You don't sound very surprised about the... more unlikely bits of my story."

Banjo arranged his sticky-up hair into a floppy Mohican, saying, "Any sufficiently advanced technology is indistinguishable from magic, as the man said. Granted, it's a bit too pat to expect the laws of physics to respond to human willpower. On the other hand, my mum phoned me last week from an aeroplane four miles above America. Seemed like science fiction to me." He shrugged. "People are always finding ways to make the universe do what they want. Where's technology heading if it's not working towards exactly the sorts of amazing things you've seen? What you're talking about, it sounds sort of like the ultimate Swiss Army knife." He flattened his hair back down and said, "Anyway, it's all ready for you up there. Towels are all fresh. I'll get the Presidential Suite sorted while you're soaking."

David made his way upstairs while Banjo went to hunt for fresh bed linen. Just as he reached the door of the bathroom it opened and out came a plump girl with perfect skin wearing only a pair of peach-coloured knickers. Her long red hair was flopped down over her heart-shaped face and she was forced to tip her head sideways to see who was standing in front of her.

"Hi," she said shyly and padded past David into one of the bedrooms. Before she disappeared, she yelled pleasantly, "Banjo, you big stud, where's my tea?" over her shoulder.

"Coming, Princess," came a distant reply from below.

With a look of surprise on his face David stepped into the bathroom and locked the door. With both taps full on, the old cast-iron bath began to fill rapidly, steam rising from the piping water into the cool air of the room.

David was up to his neck in hot water – and fast asleep – when Banjo knocked on the door and said, "I'm keeping an eye on your phone. The room's all ready. I'll call you in a couple of hours."

David managed to stay awake long enough to emerge from the bath, dry himself off, and scamper naked, carrying his clothes, into a bedroom with a fake American licence plate on the door which really did say 'The Presidential Suite' on it.

CHAPTER 26

"Tell me, dear girl, is there anything I might say or do that would persuade you that your embarrassment is quite unnecessary?" said Professor Shaw.

Susan continued to look ill at ease, saying, "I just couldn't think of anywhere else…"

The Professor broke in, "As you keep saying. And as I keep saying, you are very welcome here. These days, Saturday night feels much the way I remember wet Sunday afternoons as a small boy." His voice took on a gentle, patronising quality as he said, "I steel myself to wait until after the BBC's midnight news before I make myself a cup of camomile tea. It's a routine that just clamours to be interrupted, wouldn't you say?"

He left Susan sitting on the huge, sagging sofa and disappeared into the kitchen. His voice carried from there. "I'm also experiencing a long-forgotten sensation that might well prove to be chivalry.

Give me a moment to work out where my housekeeper puts the cups for visitors and then let's get to the bottom of whatever's bothering you."

A few minutes later, they were sitting at opposite ends of the sofa sipping herbal tea which was still too hot to drink.

Susan launched into it. "Well," she began, "I've made the single biggest discovery in the history of our field. That's what we'll call the good news. The bad news is that I've just finished robbing the School of Antiquities, I'm probably going to need a new career – assuming I don't get arrested – I think someone is trying to kill me and if I tell you the story behind it all you'll think I've lost my mind and probably arrange to have me locked up for my own good. That's what I'm thinking of as the not-so-good news." This all came out in a rush. When she'd finished speaking, she looked up at the Professor to gauge his reaction.

"Do tell me if that tea's too hot," he said, "I can put a drop of cold in it. It's no bother."

Susan stared at him, waiting for him to say more.

"I'm terribly sorry," he said, "I suppose aplomb has become rather an indulgence of mine. Showing off really, but I like to think I can take an announcement such as yours at least as coolly as the next man." He took another tiny sip from his delicate china teacup and then set it back in its saucer. "I'm actually rather pleased that it's not a romantic setback that brings you here. I'd have done my best to sound sympathetic, I hope, but it's been the same old story since Adam was a lad. I was preparing myself to be a little disappointed in you." He slapped his thighs with both hands. "But instead you tell me that you're ruined, pursued, driven to crime and in possession of a tale you claim will defeat my best efforts to encompass it. I find my faith in you once again amply rewarded.

And, in case it needs to be said, I will help in whatever way I can."

And so Susan told the Professor a similar story to the one David had told Banjo. Susan made more of the role played by the Teracus collection and rather less of the various violent encounters. The sequence in which the events were related was somewhat altered too, but when she had finished speaking she had covered approximately the same ground as David: a criminal with impossible abilities was intent on taking a mysterious artefact from another of his kind.

"Good god," the Professor said, rather sharply, at several points during Susan's narrative. When she finally sat back and picked up her cold tea, he said to her, "I'm very thankful you weren't killed while all that was taking place. Miraculously, you don't seem to have a scratch on you."

"I wouldn't say that, Professor. Thank god for concealer, is all I can say. I've got five stitches in the…" She stopped short. She'd run her hands over the back of her head, parting the hair with her fingertips as she spoke. Now she looked confused, continuing to probe.

"Indulge me a minute, Professor," she said, twisting round in her seat, "Will you tell me what you see here?" She held the end of her finger to a section of exposed scalp, the hair pulled to either side. "This is where I got hit."

Obligingly, the Professor came to stand over her and investigated. He said, "A little pinkness, the residual rubor of a wound perhaps. When did you say you were attacked?" the Professor asked as he retook his seat. Susan let her hair fall back.

She lifted her gaze vaguely skywards for a second while she calculated. "Ten days today. Actually I think I was supposed to have the stitches out a few days ago."

Professor Shaw nodded and said, "That's one of the problems with a blow to the head; it's a most inopportune moment to impart important medical advice. I worked in a London hospital during the last world war. I saw a lot of pretty young women too silly to wear their tin hats." He brought himself back to the present and said, "Perhaps you can tell me what it means, but I'd say that injury has been healing for at least four, more probably six weeks and there are no stitches in evidence."

Susan's face went blank and she confessed, almost blurting it out, "I used the headband my attacker left behind." She repeated, "This afternoon I tried to use it." She flared her nostrils and tipped her chin up as though the words were being pulled painfully from her. "I'm not sure, but I think," it seemed to be an effort to continue, but she managed it, "I think I made a letter-opener move just by concentrating on it. No, ignore that: I did; I'm positive about it."

"Can you…" the Professor hesitated. He wet his lips with the tip of his tongue. "Can you show me?"

Susan looked very uncomfortable, "I can't," she said, almost pleading. "I know how this sounds, but I don't dare show you. I re-read one of my colleague's précis and realised he'd botched the translation. From what I can tell, it's a standing order amongst… amongst whoever these people are, to bump off any newcomers. It's a sort of reverse apprenticeship, whereby the old hands make sure there's no new talent coming through. They neutralise any potential challenges before they can find their feet."

"Adepts, my dear. You wondered what to call them. That's what I'd suggest. Those proficient in the *ars obscura*," he said. He added, sotto voce, and to himself, "Not the Latin for underpants as a pupil of mine once suggested."

Susan ignored his aside and said, "Well if I practice any of those concealed arts I'm apparently broadcasting the fact. Not my identity, from what I can tell, but my presence. I have no idea what range we're talking about or how close they have to be to sense me. But, having done the equivalent of lighting a beacon last night, I wanted to get the hell out of Dodge for the time being." She shivered, "It's a pretty creepy thought. Ears pricking up and heads turning, adepts everywhere suddenly tuned in to what I'm doing." She looked genuinely horrified.

Professor Shaw said swiftly, "Ahh, perhaps I should have encouraged you to venture out in your smalls, like that Jenkins woman in her dance attire. You might have got used to the universal attention by now." He pushed on, trying to distract her, "And incidentally, I believe our scheming has borne fruit. Your Mr Hartman has been seen in Ms Jenkins' company on a number of occasions since you decamped for the Big Smoke."

The Professor's attempts to change the subject seemed to have successfully derailed Susan's macabre train of thought. Her face had relaxed and she was shaking her head in disbelief, "That seems like a hundred years ago and another life. Remember when all I had to worry about was having a downmarket Don Juan for an assistant?"

The Professor cleared his throat and said, "You certainly do seem to have packed quite a bit into your time away, there's no denying it. But to return to our present predicament, what is it you thought I might do to help?"

"Well," Susan said, "receiving stolen goods, harbouring a fugitive and helping me unravel the secret of the ages were the top items on my list."

She reached across and squeezed his hand, receiving a raised eyebrow in response. She said, "I feel so much better than I did two hours ago, I can't tell you. Just talking to you makes me feel that maybe I haven't gone mad after all."

"You mean relative to present company?" he asked and Susan laughed. He eyed the bulging courier bag and the enormous flight case that Susan had arrived with and asked, mischievously, "So are you going to let me have a look at the swag then?"

"If you're ready for a life of crime," she said, nodding.

The Professor's living room included what must have once been a separate dining room – though now it was all one room. They cleared a heavy green cloth from the monumental mahogany dining table and began to spread Susan's stolen documents out. The originals were in plastic wallets, the reproductions paper-clipped to the outside.

Unable to resist, the Professor started exploring one of the document packs nearest him, becoming so absorbed that seconds later he seemed oblivious to Susan's presence.

Susan buried herself in another of the documents and the two of them sat quietly, the only sound the loud, wooden ticking of the mantle clock.

Some time later, Susan slipped into the kitchen and made them more tea – this time English Breakfast. The Professor received his cup and then a moment later seemed to remember himself and said, "Have I been away long? I really must beg your pardon; my manners are a disgrace. It's just that these documents, especially in light of what you've told me, make for the most extraordinary reading."

Having turned away from the collection to look at Susan, something seemed to occur to the Professor. He said, "I know you like to tease me over my fondness for gangster movies, but I should ask whether you think we are in any danger here. I can't seem to get very worked up at the thought for myself, but I really couldn't allow any harm to come to you. I could make a telephone call if you think we might need a, um, couple of heavies."

He went on to explain, "I tutored the son of a local policeman. A most unfortunate lad in respect of his medical difficulties, but scarcely a burden. Nonetheless, I'm assured that I have favours to call in if ever I need them."

Susan assured him that it was unnecessary. She came and sat down beside him. "Oh you would have been proud of my getaway, Professor," Susan said, "I got on a tube train and then got off again just before the doors closed. Then I travelled one stop down the line, got off and stood by the exit barriers pretending to look for my ticket until everyone who came up the stairs had passed me. Then I ran back down and jumped on a train heading the other way. Unless I'm bugged somehow then I'm sure no one knows where I am."

The Professor commented, "I really have no idea what's possible in that regard, although surely being underground must help. In my day the fugitive generally left a matchbook behind, often with an important phone number written on it. You were careful not to make that mistake, I trust."

Susan nodded. The Professor asked, "You've read nothing in these papers," he indicated the piles covering the table, "to suggest an arcane method of locating missing persons?"

Susan shrugged, "Some of these documents seem to suggest that anything's possible, but there's a consensus that abilities fall into two categories: a kind of working-set that David and I have seen evidence of and then the premium package – a kind of mystical guru version that's out of reach except to a few mad old hermits. The way it works seems very Zen: it looks like you can only have these extra powers if you're so disconnected from the world that you'd never use them in pursuit of a practical goal. I don't know if a mystic could track me, but there's no mention that the regular foot-soldiers have any way of doing so."

She added, "Originally I thought the higher-level abilities were just empty boasting, but given what I've already come to accept, it's probably best to keep an open mind."

After a moment of reflection, she went on to say, "Anyway, to answer your original question, I don't think I'm in any immediate danger. I came here with two problems. First, I alerted the locals back in London that there was a stranger in town – although I think I got away with that. I wasn't followed, so they can't know I'm here.

"My second problem is the collection. I think this guy Jan will be coming for it, but I don't believe he's got any way of knowing that I've moved it. I realise I'm totally dropping this in your lap, and it's a hell of a thing to ask, but I'm hoping you can help me figure my way out of this."

The Professor had just stood, as though he was about to head into the kitchen. He paused and acquired rather a calculating look, asking, "You don't think this vigorous young man, David, would be of more help?"

Susan looked down at the table. "It's complicated," she said. "And anyway, I couldn't get hold of him when I needed him, when I thought this madman was breathing down my neck. I need someone a little more trustworthy," she said.

"Ahh," the Professor said knowingly. Then he patted her affectionately on the shoulder and said, "A romantic setback after all, and no time to straighten it out. Your plate is certainly rather full." He nodded wisely and said, "But still, trying times can cement as easily as they divide."

Susan said nothing, lost as she was in her own thoughts. In the midst of her reverie she yawned and covered her mouth with her hand. After a couple of seconds she was still yawning and flapping her other hand to indicate that she was trying, unsuccessfully, to bring the yawn to an end.

The Professor chuckled at her display.

She said, "Boy, excuse me. Wow," having finally regained control of her mouth.

The Professor set off for the kitchen and the stairs beyond, saying, "I'd better turn down the covers in the guest bedroom. There's hot water and all the trappings of civilisation. You remember your way round?"

Susan made to reply and found herself yawning again. She shook her head, "You'd think I'd be used to adrenaline by now. I think I'm going to have to crash out pretty soon. I'll worry about all this in the morning." She gestured at the table.

Susan followed the Professor through the kitchen and up the stairs. She ducked into the bathroom while he attended to the guest room. When she emerged he was halfway down the stairs. He stopped and said to her, "Why don't I leave you to sleep in a little – unless you'd rather not?"

Susan's watch showed a quarter to one in the morning. "Could you call me at nine if I'm not up?" she said.

"Of course. Mrs Potter comes in at about eight to straighten things up. I'll see if I can't persuade her to lay on some breakfast. Sleep well, dear girl," he said.

"Thanks Professor," Susan said and wandered into her room. The bedside lamp was on, the bedspread was turned back from the pillow and a red light down near the valence indicated that an electric blanket was warming the bed's interior.

Susan undressed quickly, switched the blanket off and slid under the covers with a sigh. Her eyelids dipped for a second before lifting again just long enough for her to turn out the light.

CHAPTER 27

Susan sat eating bacon, scrambled eggs, sausage, fried bread, fried tomato and mushrooms. The Professor sat opposite her at the little kitchen table doing the same.

"My doctor estimates," the Professor said, holding up a section of sausage skewered on a fork, "that I can have one of these every two or three years with almost no ill effects. Although he suggests waiting six months before going swimming."

Susan took a swig of tea from a golden jubilee mug and asked, "Did you sleep at all last night Professor?"

"You know," he said, "you're quite welcome to call me Joseph or Joe. I don't suppose you will, but it seems to me that after tipping our entire profession on its ear you really shouldn't defer to me as though I'm the expert."

Susan said nothing. The Professor went on, "Well, whatever's most comfortable for you. But to answer your question, I might

314

have nodded off in my chair for a couple of minutes, but most likely not. What sort of scholar would I be if I could receive those papers into my house, knowing what they contain, and then toddle off to bed? Besides which, sleeping these days is no more of a necessity than cleaning my spectacles – simply an aid to seeing things more clearly."

"So did you turn up anything earth-shattering?" Susan asked, "I mean besides the massive bombshells we already knew about, er, Joseph? Joe. Professor."

"I found a code," the Professor said nonchalantly, plainly rather pleased with himself, but attempting to conceal his excitement.

Susan was instantly avid. "Spill," she said, refusing to be teased.

The Professor said, "Your Dr Lampwick is falling down on the job. One of the documents in the collection makes use of an old merchant's cipher, one I happen to have come across before. I might have expected that the content of the document would have aroused some suspicion – being, as it is, a letter discussing chiefly the weather, the state of the roads and the health of an extended family with improbable names."

Susan looked slightly sheepish and said, "If it's the one I'm thinking of, Bernie had it classified as part of the personal correspondence of an earlier owner of the collection. I've been focussing on the documents that discuss magic directly and leaving the contextual pieces to him."

"Hmm," the Professor said, "well Dr Lampwick overlooked rather an interesting hidden message. The artefact you've been referring to as the Marker is discussed within. I believe I now know its function. But before I tell you, will you remind me of your working hypothesis?"

Susan looked dubious. "I'm not sure why you want to know,

given that you've uncovered the truth, but I'll trust that you've got something nobler in mind than rubbing my nose in it." She collected her thoughts for a moment and said, "We know the Marker has something to do with healing and for a while I was convinced that this guy Jan was seriously sick."

The Professor broke in, "Excuse me, but why did you think that?"

Susan frowned, "Maybe I didn't mention it, but I saw these marks on him. They looked just like Kaposi's Sarcoma. I saw it when I did some volunteer work – working with addicts and homeless people. It's something you get if…"

The Professor interrupted again, "If AIDS has weakened your immune system. Of course," he said, as though it fitted perfectly. "No you didn't mention that, but you did mention you thought he was suffering from some terminal affliction. Given his extraordinary physical prowess, I wondered why."

They had finished eating and now they pushed their plates aside. On cue, Mrs Potter bustled into the room, collected the plates, refilled their mugs from a huge teapot covered in a crocheted cosy and bustled out again humming vibrantly all the while.

"Thank you Mrs Potter. A delicious breakfast," the Professor said to her departing back and then returned his attention to Susan. "And you are of course correct that Kaposi's is well-known for its tendency to follow in the wake of AIDS. Did you know also that it is also an affliction of the elderly? Old age weakens the immune system just as AIDS or certain medicines can. There is also a form common to equatorial Africa, if memory serves, which I assume is not germane here."

Susan looked surprised. "How do you know all this?" she asked.

The Professor smiled. "Consider that I've spent some part of each day for very nearly eighty years now reading and, for the most part, committing to memory. I was part way through training to be a doctor at the end of World War II. And though I realised it wasn't for me, I've never lost my interest in medicine."

Susan said, "Wow, I didn't know that. Your training would have been post-leeches, right?"

The Professor gave her a tart smile and she sniggered for a moment and then looked more serious, saying, "I'll shut up now. Don't let me distract you any more until you've told me what was in that code."

The Professor said, "Quite. According to the plain-text I extracted, it is alleged that the Marker does no less than restore the youth of those who know its secret. The passage describes passing into some sort of death-like trance, of what duration I'm unsure – but when it has run its course, the recipient is once more in their physical prime. The description makes it sound almost as though they emerge from a cocoon, but it's difficult to distinguish the figurative from the literal elements of the description."

Susan said, "Well I've got some direct experience that the practice of magic has immediate health benefits," then muttered, "even if it lowers your life expectancy in other ways." She went on, "I just couldn't figure out where the Marker came in." She stuck out her bottom lip as she put it all together in her mind, "So adepts get old, though maybe not as quickly as the rest of us, and when they do, they need the Marker to extend their life. So we're saying that Jan is actually an old man?"

"I believe he may be a few years my senior," the Professor said, "and I'll be eighty-three this June."

Both of them sat and considered this for a moment. Susan spoke first, "We should be having this discussion at midnight, in the flickering firelight. I can't sit here looking out the window at sparrows eating bacon-rind from the bird table and talk about immortality and ninety-year-olds who could sweep the board at the Olympics. I almost wish I still had my scars to remind me that this is real."

The Professor said, "I admit that while I believe what you've told me and what I've read since last night, it almost seems like a dream. It's like descriptions of the Big Bang – doubtless accurate, but difficult to reconcile with the view from a Clapham Omnibus."

Something else occurred to Susan. "Unless Jan's already used the Marker some time in the past, then he's a product of the twentieth century – which is certainly my impression – though I don't really know why I think that. Anyway, how old do you suppose Dass was?"

The Professor spread his hands, "We could speculate. In theory, I suppose he could be as old as the Marker, but you didn't describe him as Oriental in appearance and I doubt there were many Europeans in Qin dynasty China. The cipher I discovered dates from late sixteenth century Italy." He paused a moment, "Whoever wrote the message possessed the Marker at the time and I don't believe that person was Dass; I believe he was an Arab by birth. If we put the pieces together: Dass had yet to acquire the Marker when the message was written, and the message uses a code first invented around 1580." He summed up, "So, we could say that Dass probably didn't get the Marker until, let's pick a date, 1600 at the earliest. In order for him to make use of it immediately, he would have to have been born early in the previous century. I think we can tentatively assume that he was no more than five hundred years old."

Susan dropped back in her chair, obviously reeling with the idea. "No more than five hundred years old. Man, no wonder David found him imposing."

Susan considered for a moment longer and said, "And somehow, you're accepting all this?"

The Professor pursed his lips thoughtfully. "It is a fundamental shift in the order of things, I'll grant you. Perhaps I'm simply deluding myself that I believe it. But in a curious way, this makes much more sense than the world I've been living in all these years." He extended a hand, palm up, and said, "Take the persistence of alchemy as an illustration: how could it be so popular for so many hundreds of years without a single success?"

Susan looked excited, "Oh, alchemy, I've got a theory about that." She was almost wriggling in her seat. Seeing as how the Professor didn't object, she explained, "You know that the language alchemists use is always intentionally ambiguous, like using the same symbol for man, Mars and iron or for woman, Venus and copper, so that you can't tell whether you're reading astrology or chemistry?" She looked foolish for a second. "I'm being rhetorical, of course you know all that. Anyway, I was thinking about the way most alchemists seemed to believe you had to purify the body and the mind before you could move on to purifying base metal into gold – they felt those three things were linked. Well what if scholars have been confusing cause and effect? What if you have to purify the mind and the base metal before you can purify the body? Pure gold – in the form of tribute – plus certain mental exercises give you…" She pointed to the back of her head, "…a superhuman constitution. Look at Jan; he's ninety years old and he could hand Bruce Lee his ass." The Professor's eyebrows tipped back. Susan didn't pause for breath, "If that's what alchemy offered, that would explain a few things. It never made sense to me that alchemy was supposedly about making gold – because it was expensive and it never worked. What kind of ever-popular get-rich-quick scheme requires you to start off wealthy and then get poorer?"

The Professor had an approving look on his face. "Intriguing," he said, "You're thinking of the fabled Comte St Germain."

"And others," Susan said.

The Professor continued, "You see why it's surprisingly easy to accept what you've told me and the papers you've brought me? When a new idea re-opens so many previously exhausted avenues of enquiry, one can't help but feel that it's correct – how else could it be so fruitful?"

Susan was bubbling over with suggestions now. "Exactly. Think of the healing powers of The King's Touch – powerful men who wore gold bands around their heads for a living. For that matter, how do you suppose the idea of haloes became associated with people able to do the impossible?"

They were each occupied with their own ruminations for a moment and then the Professor composed his face, signalling a change of topic. "But tell me, my dear, what are your plans for the collection?" Susan immediately began to look tense. The Professor continued smoothly, saying, "Shall I take it off your hands?"

Susan's expression suggested she was experiencing two contradictory emotions. The Professor's offer plainly delighted and horrified her in equal parts. The inner conflict showed on her face for a few seconds before she said, "I need to do something with it. But it could be a death sentence for whoever looks after it. And it needs to be someone who understands the true risks Jan poses. If I'd left it at the School, they would have put it under lock and key, perhaps with a couple of guards, and Jan would have strolled in there and taken it. I could keep it, but I don't know where I'd go." She was starting to look panicked now, speaking more quickly, "I suppose I could go back to the States, try to get lost somewhere."

The Professor made a wafting gesture with his hands, meaning 'slow down'. He said, "My apologies for raising a subject that is both indelicately morbid and rather personal, but I assure you I have a relevant point: I wonder how long you imagine I might live."

Susan was taken by surprise. She appeared to have no answer.

The Professor said, "During my time at Princeton I had a friend, a fellow quite a bit older than myself, who was then in his eighty-fifth year. He used to say that he was living in 'bonus time'. One couldn't reasonably expect to live as long as he had, one could only hope. So it would hardly be a crime if one failed to make sensible, dutiful plans for how to spend those years. If one were lucky enough to reach such an age and find oneself in reasonable fettle, then it should be treated as a gift to do with as one pleased."

He looked up to see whether Susan was following him. Then the shadow of something crossed his face and he dropped his gaze from hers.

He said nothing for a few moments and some instinct prevented Susan from interrupting the silence. A weight now seemed to press upon the Professor and when he spoke at last, the heaviness had invaded his words too, "Despite my early interest in medicine, I don't relish my annual check-ups. My last such conversation with my physician was a particularly cheerless occasion."

He gave Susan a rather bleak smile and said, "He had one or two pieces of disappointing news for me, and precious little in the way of encouragement." He paused to see that she understood what he was implying.

He said, "It is not a matter of 'whether'; it is a matter of 'how soon'."

Susan's face had drained of colour as she listened to these words.

The Professor continued, his voice a little strained as though his throat were sore. "Perhaps you can see what I'm trying to say, but the essence of it is that I'd relish the prospect of spending more time with this collection. And should you-know-who come calling for it, I'm confident I can keep it out of his clutches whatever inducements he may offer. It seems, if my physician is to be trusted, that there is little he can threaten to deprive me of at this point. Whereas you, my dear, do have a future, a very promising one ahead of you, and we must do what we can to secure it."

A sudden tear rolled down Susan's face. Her lower lip refused to stay quite still and she stared at the Professor as though she had already lost him.

He did his best to seem untroubled as he said, "Think of it this way: in those documents are answers to questions I have wondered about since your grandmother was a girl. I can bring those answers tantalisingly close and at the same time help a friend in her hour of need – or I can opt for a few more months of the quiet life." He looked at her apologetically. "If you'll excuse my abominable self-flattery, I rather fancy ending a life of scholarship with something dimly reminiscent of heroism."

The old man's eyes were beginning to look red-rimmed and watery as he finished speaking. Susan was simply letting the teardrops roll down her cheeks.

The Professor stood, pushing his chair back, and crossed to the kettle. "I think that pot's a little stewed. What say we make some fresh?"

With her sixth sense for these things, Mrs Potter appeared in the room at that moment, saying, "I'll do that Professor, you sit yourself down with your guest." She spoke loudly, as though the Professor was a little hard of hearing, though he appeared to have no difficulty understanding Susan's softer tones.

Mrs Potter appeared not to notice Susan's distress. But as the Professor retook his seat, Mrs Potter placed a glass cake-stand

– apparently produced from thin air – in front of Susan. It was layered with shortbread biscuits. "Try one. I make them myself. Lovely, if I do say so." Next to the cake stand was a tissue, which Susan quickly used to dry her face.

The Professor said to Susan, "We'll talk again later."

She nodded and then looked around her for something to occupy her attention, to distract her from her distress. "I should really phone my sister," she said, her voice a little thicker than usual. "And David is probably panicking. I told him I needed to see him urgently." She wandered into the living room to where her courier bag was hooked over the back of a dining chair. She pulled out her mobile phone and said, "Shit."

The Professor turned to his housekeeper and said, "I never hear language like that from you Mrs Potter. You're not repressing I hope."

"And neither shall you hear it," Mrs Potter said, her lips pursed. "My mum would never have tolerated it."

"A formidable woman by all accounts," the Professor agreed, offering a dubious smile. "Problem?" he asked Susan.

She said, "My battery is dead. I always keep it charged but my sister borrowed my charger. May I use your phone Professor?" She began to rummage in her bag for her address book.

"Of course. There's one in the hall," he said airily. Then moving close to where she was standing, he said, his voice low, "And remind me to tell you what I learned about combat between adepts."

Susan raised an eyebrow, as if to say 'go on', but didn't stop hunting in her bag.

"I rather think it's significant," he said, "though I have no idea of what. But apparently," he dropped his voice even lower, "one cannot use magic to attack a fellow adept."

Susan had her head almost inside her bag. Her muffled voice said, "Some sort of golden rule, right?"

"No, my dear, not a rule," he said, "It simply will not operate. No more, the text says, than if they attempted to use magic without their gold adornment."

Susan at last discovered her phone book and stepped out into the hall. The Professor had the look of someone about to deliver an amusing punch-line. "So you'll never guess how they resolve their disputes," he said expectantly.

Susan had the phone to her ear and was waiting for the call to connect. She was only giving his remarks half her attention. "Hmm?" she said absent-mindedly, "Does the defensive stuff still work?"

"It does," the Professor confirmed, still delighted with what he was going to impart.

"Well in that case, I suppose if they want to attack each other they must…" Susan only got that far. Her call was answered and she said, "David?"

CHAPTER 28

David and Banjo were drinking coffee, sitting in Banjo's workshop.

The room would originally have been a conservatory or a greenhouse in some previous chapter of the house's history. Whatever pale sunlight the day offered streamed unimpeded through the sloping glass roof. Scattered about the room were several pieces of furniture in various stages of repair. There were also large chunks of iron and glass, which might have been art or simply fire-damaged machinery, and there was a separate bench area for some sort of delicate metalworking.

The two of them sat on high stools, the kind intended for working at a bench, the tops of which had been reupholstered with layers of carpet. A convection heater blew warm air towards their feet.

Banjo said, "This has been a new lease of life for your job, I'll bet."

David nodded. "Well it's certainly been a bit more interesting lately," he said, wearing a poker face and restraining his smile, "what with one thing and another. A bit different from a couple of months ago."

"Yeah," Banjo acknowledged, "who'd have thought a month ago that you'd be prepared to risk your life for your company." There was an odd note in his voice.

David looked up. He took a moment to scrutinise Banjo's face before he said, cautiously, "Are you referring to my so-called death-wish?"

Banjo held up his hands. "I never said death-wish. I just thought you were getting what you might call dangerously bored. Remember, you were planning to bicycle through Cambodia and then hitchhike round Syria blindfold or something. Only now you can get your near-death kicks at work."

David looked as though he was becoming irritated. "Do we have to have this talk again, Banjo?"

Banjo held up a finger for a minute, as though he was about to speak. He held them both to silence for a few seconds and then said, in a very reasonable voice, "Tell me you haven't risked your life more than, ooh, say once a week since we last talked and I'll let it drop."

"You know I have," David said, sounding tired.

"Right. And I just want to know why. Surely there's no harm in telling me that," Banjo said, his voice still meticulously reasonable.

David went to speak, but found himself at a loss for words. Banjo didn't push him or appear impatient; he waited quietly for David to collect his thoughts.

When David finally spoke, he said, "Well, for want of a word that doesn't sound stupid when I say it, I'd say it was about destiny." He sounded a little defiant as he said the word, as though he almost expected to be challenged or laughed at. Banjo, however, was simply attentive.

David went on, "Like you said to me, we all believe in destiny. I'm sure most of us believe that the lives we lead will somehow match up with the sort of people we are. I don't suppose it's anything most people dwell on because it's not causing them a problem. They're nice quiet people living nice quiet lives. Their insides and their outsides match, if you know what I mean." He looked up. "Well mine don't," he said firmly.

"I don't think I'm meant to have a quiet life," he said, glancing at Banjo again, gauging his expression, "Of course I don't want to get myself killed, but when all this nonsense started I had a choice – I could see where it all led and take whatever risks came up or I could do the sensible thing and, basically, run away." He shrugged. "I knew I had to jump in." Then he nodded. "And you know what? It's the first time in I don't know how long that I've really felt like I was me." He pointed at his own chest.

He seemed to have finished, but Banjo said, "Go on."

David found he had more to say. "I think you know it was starting to get to me, the last year or so. So many things around me that I didn't care about and nothing for me to do that felt like it really mattered one way or the other." He nodded to Banjo, "And you were right that I was prepared to start taking risks – maybe even some stupid risks, I suppose – just to see if I could make something happen. But this is different." He emphasised the words, "This found me."

He went on, "I don't know if there's any such thing as destiny – maybe it's just that 'character is fate' thing and it's all in my head – but I'm telling you that this feels like what I'm supposed to be doing. Getting to the bottom of this thing, stopping this Jan bloke, doing whatever I have to do." He drew in a breath, "I don't want to sound like I've lost my marbles, but I'd rather come a cropper doing this than have fifty years living in suburbia and playing golf at the weekend."

David had been focussing inward as he spoke, and once the passion with which he'd spoken started to leave him he became more aware that Banjo had been watching him closely. He added, plainly looking for a laugh, "To summarise: frankly, I'm wasted on insurance."

Banjo didn't laugh. He ruminated on David's speech for a bit before finally announcing, "Yup, I can believe all that." He brightened as though David had passed some test or been forgiven some past offence.

Banjo said, "You know, within the bounds of following your destiny, and all that, do you think maybe you could try not to get yourself killed?" Another thought occurred to him, "And if you'd got any sense you'd start letting that Susan bird do some of your thinking for you." David appeared to be weighing the idea. Banjo continued, "I mean face it, she's a lot more clever than you are, isn't she?" As he said this, Banjo smiled as though he'd paid David a compliment.

A few moments later, David changed the subject, "So how are things with you and Melissa? Assuming that was Melissa whose boobs I was staring at."

"Oy," said Banjo, playfully, "get your own. No, she's fantastic, mate. I'm in that stage where you can't tell whether it's love or something a bit more shallow but equally as nice. I suppose I'll just have to see if it wears off. Be, um, really good if it didn't though."

Their chat seemed to have reached a natural conclusion. David was standing, ready to move back into the main body of the house. He'd picked up his mobile from the bench and was holding it, checking the display for the hundredth time.

Banjo stood too, saying, "Listen, is there anything you want me to do about all this cops and robbers stuff? I mean, just for the sake of argument, if Susan doesn't call in the next couple of hours, can I help you look for her? Or did you want to do something about the bad guy? I don't know what use I could be, but if anything occurs to you, the offer's there." Banjo managed to come extremely close to sounding nonchalant and unconcerned about the risks.

David shook his head appreciatively, saying, "It's handy for me if you're not involved; makes this sort of a secret bolt-hole. But thanks."

Then he put his arm round Banjo's shoulders and gave him a squeeze. "You're a good friend," David said, grinning.

"Get off," Banjo said, pretending to be uncomfortable with the contact. "Turning me all gay when I've got a bird upstairs."

David was smiling, about to say something, when a sound stopped him. His mobile was ringing. He glanced at the display. "Don't know the number," he said aloud.

Banjo gave a little flick of his head and point of his fingers, meaning, 'I'll leave you to it' and ducked out of the workshop into the hallway, pulling the door most of the way closed behind him.

Alone in the workshop, David answered the call, "Hello?"

"David, it's Susan," she sounded relieved to be speaking with him.

"Are you OK? Where are you?" he said, anxiously.

"I'm with my Professor in Cambridge. I'm fine," she said airily.

David frowned, uncertain. "That's great," he said, not sounding like he was too sure. "Why, um, why didn't you call?"

"I am calling," she said, her voice no longer quite so friendly.

David's concern had turned into something else. It seemed

as though her breezy attitude had offended him. "I meant before now. I spent all of last night looking for you, because I thought you needed my help." It started as an explanation, but it was beginning to sound accusatory. "I've been frantic, waiting for you to call. I even staked out Jan's place in case he took you back there..."

"You did what?" she exploded.

He tried to be patient, "You left me a message saying that he was right outside your door."

"I did no such thing," she said, but a moment's doubt took some of the boldness from the statement. "After all we've been through, you still went to confront him?"

He sounded defensive as he said, "You tell me Jan's outside your door, then I hear nothing. What was I supposed to do? Have an early night?" This last was rather louder than the rest of the conversation. He got himself under slightly better control and said, "Listen, I don't want us to have an argument."

"I don't know that you get to decide that all by yourself," Susan said coldly. "But it doesn't surprise me that you'd think you could."

David had placed one hand on the bench beside him. He leaned on it heavily now, his mouth open, his cheeks flushed. "I..." was all he could manage.

Susan spoke. "This isn't..." She too was having trouble finishing her sentences. A moment later her voice seemed milder but it wasn't clear whether she was backing down or merely refusing to be drawn. "Come to Cambridge," she said, at last.

"Fine," David said, his voice full of some indeterminate emotion.

"I'll text you with the exact address," Susan said; her tone was definitely softer.

David's voice was merely stiff now, his sudden anger replaced with some sort of strained composure. "So I'll see you in a bit, then," he said, attempting to sound upbeat and missing by a mile.

They both hung up.

Banjo, who had in fact been listening at the door, which he'd held an inch ajar throughout the call, now pushed it open, apparently unconcerned about disguising his eavesdropping.

David didn't react. He looked as though he'd been hit in the stomach. Banjo put on an over-the-top American accent and blared, "What was *her* problem?" evidently not taking the spat seriously.

David's head was still dipped. He blew air through his fringe. He sounded lost as he said, "She obviously changed her mind about needing my help last night and didn't think it was worth a phone call." His tone was both hurt and slightly incredulous.

"Yeah, well, birds, eh?" Banjo said, not sounding as though he shared David's despair. "Why don't you chew on this," he waited until he had David's attention and then said, "What if she asked for your help, then you find out she doesn't want you to save her after all, but she hasn't changed her mind either? You with me?"

David looked up at Banjo. "I don't get it," he said vaguely, having only given it half his attention, the other half being reserved for brooding.

Banjo intoned slowly, "I said: what if she asked for your help, then you find out she doesn't want you to save her after all, but she hasn't changed her mind either?"

David was trying to make sense of what Banjo was saying.

While he stood there looking confused, Banjo added, "I may not be able to cast out my own planks..." With which cryptic comment he wandered out, muttering, "Woman like that, stands to reason."

* * *

David was already halfway up the M11, twenty minutes from Cambridge when his phoned beeped. The text message, from Susan's mobile, started with the words, "Had to buy new charger," followed by an address and instructions for finding it.

Once in the outskirts of the city, he had to pull over for a couple of minutes to scrutinise a road atlas, but locating the Professor's beautiful cottage just outside the town centre wasn't difficult. What *was* difficult was parking. Eventually, David drove into one of the large multi-storey car parks intended for shoppers and hiked back out to the Professor's street.

When he arrived, it was Susan who opened the door. She was wearing a trim, white, fleecy v-neck, with a pair of jeans and her red boots. She looked worried, her lower lip twisting uncertainly. He gazed at her guardedly as she stood on the top step. But before he could speak she came forwards and hugged him. He put his arms around her and returned the squeeze.

"David," she said, sounding relieved, her face pressed into his coat.

"Hi," he said, laughing uncertainly, the tension suddenly gone from his throat.

They separated and she said, "I'm sorry I gave you a hard time on the phone." She obviously had a couple of things to say before they moved from the doorstep to the cosy-looking interior.

He tipped his head on one side. "I think I started this one," he said, "I think I was doing that parental thing. I was so worried about you that the first thing I did when I realised you were safe was try to bite your head off." He looked her in the eye, "I really was worried. Your voicemail sounded pretty bad."

"And...?" she said, as though he'd forgotten to say 'please'.

He looked awkward as he realised what she meant. He smiled, almost shyly, and said, "And I'm sorry too."

She gave him another hug and led him into the living room.

"Ah," the Professor said exuberantly, "you've finished letting the last of the heat out. Good, good."

David smiled, but Susan looked concerned and said, "Let me get you a sweater, Professor."

The Professor waved his hand, gently dismissive, "It was sarcasm not hypothermia talking." He looked at David standing there, his bulk exaggerated in his chunky leather jacket. The Professor's expression was amiable but appraising.

David smiled politely, taking a couple of steps forwards and holding out his hand. "Hi, I'm David Braun."

They shook. The Professor said with a chuckle, "A weak handshake, I like that in a man."

David seemed unsure how to take the remark and the Professor explained, "Preserving my bones rather than demonstrating the doubtless formidable strength of your grip."

Then he said, "I'm Joseph Shaw, but most people call me by my nickname, 'Professor'," he glanced significantly at Susan. "Either are perfectly fine."

"Pleased to meet you, Joseph," David said, earning another delighted smile from the Professor.

"Susan?" the Professor asked, "Would you consider making us some tea if I give you my word that rheumatic knees, and not outdated views on gender roles, prompt my request?"

"Of course," Susan said sweetly, heading for the kitchen.

"I'll, um…" David said, pointing his finger, indicating that he intended to assist.

He joined Susan in the kitchen, leaving the Professor to sit in his customary armchair, apparently comfortably absorbed in his own thoughts.

Once out of the Professor's earshot, David said, "So have you spoken to Dee today?"

Susan gave him a look that was both indulgent and unimpressed. "You'd suck at poker," she said. She began to arrange the tea things on a tray.

David appeared confused, though it wasn't clear whether that appearance was genuine. "I meant whether she's OK," he said.

"*Oh,*" Susan with exaggerated realisation, opening her mouth wide to make the sound. In other words she understood him, but didn't necessarily believe that's what he'd meant by his question.

"She's not happy," Susan said, "but she's not sure who to be pissed off with. She's going to stay put in that rather swanky hotel you took her to for the time being. She's got London to entertain her if she gets bored."

The kettle was close to boiling, the water rumbling.

"Good," David said and then realised that it wasn't necessarily good news, "I mean it's good that she's not more unhappy."

Susan seemed amused at his discomfiture. Sidelong, she gave him a fond look. She said, "She told me about your date." She turned to the kettle which had just clicked off.

David instantly registered concern. "Susan, you should know…" he began, sounding agitated. As he said it, he made some negating gesture with his hands to indicate that she might have got the wrong end of the stick. His hand bumped the edge of the tray as it overhung the worktop, rattling the cups and knocking one of them off the counter.

Susan saw David dislodge the cup. She turned and snatched it out of the air before it could shatter on the tiled floor. "David," she almost wailed, "for the millionth time, I'm teasing you. Dee told me what you guys talked about. She made you sound noble and chivalrous far beyond the bounds of credibility. But I get the message."

David was still staring in amazement at Susan's unbelievable swiftness and dexterity in rescuing the cup. He pulled himself back to the moment and realised what she was saying. A smile crept across his face. He said, "I know it's not what you want, but I can't help..." He got no further because Susan had placed one cool finger against his lips, silencing him. "Another time," she said.

They didn't speak again until they'd rejoined the Professor in the living room. Susan had found Mrs Potter's cache of shortbread biscuits, which she'd placed on a plate near David.

When each of them had their tea, the Professor spoke, "A colleague of mine told me about a wonderful new species of manager known as a facilitator." He looked from Susan to David. "Just savour the ugly newness of that word," he said with relish, addressing them both. "Seemingly, one is secretly still in charge, but without the need to take responsibility for any unpleasant outcomes and neither is one expected to actually do any of the work." He beamed at them, gauging their reaction. "In fact it's positively discouraged."

David looked confused, Susan was amused but patient, confident that the Professor was going somewhere with his remarks.

He continued, "It sounds just the thing for me. I thought I'd try it now, if you two are agreeable."

Taking their complete immobility as assent he became more serious, saying, "So what I'm thinking we need to do, before many more hours elapse, is the following: first, put the documents concerning the Marker somewhere safe. I know it goes against the spirit of facilitation, but I'd like to nominate myself for that job."

He checked for signs of dissent and then continued, "We'll also need to do something about the fact that the collection is now missing from the School of Antiquities. Before very long, someone is likely to point the finger at Susan – if for no other reason than that she's the one responsible." David glanced at Susan with alarm, but didn't speak.

The Professor went on, "Now, I'd like to volunteer to sort that one out as well; I have some influence there." He looked mildly troubled, "Oh dear, I seem to be making a hash of this facilitation business. No matter. Onward," he urged, holding a finger on high as though flourishing a standard. "Thirdly, we need to learn more about the predicament in which we are currently entangled. Many of the answers lie in the collection I believe. This being its new temporary home, I'd like to volunteer to handle that too," he looked positively disappointed as he continued, "though I suspect it rather puts the kibosh on my facilitating career."

He addressed them both as he said, "Finally, and perhaps most importantly, we need to do something about this fellow Jan and the fact that he will soon be vigorously casting about for the collection. We clearly cannot turn matters over to the usual temporal authorities, for the same reason one would not seek help from the Cats Protection League if one had cornered a wounded leopard. I think it's that last little matter that needs to occupy us now."

David cleared his throat. "I have some catching up to do," he said. "But I have to ask: Joseph, are you sure you want to get dragged into this? It's difficult enough to work out why I'm still involved and I was at least being paid to take an interest."

The Professor said, "Would it seem as if I were eluding the question if I asked Susan to set your mind at rest on that score once we're finished here? For the meantime, would you be prepared to take it on trust that I have my reasons and that I'm comfortable both that I can accept the risks and contribute to the endeavour?"

David didn't look as though he had any immediate objection. The Professor glanced at Susan and said, "Perhaps you would tell David whichever parts of our discussion you think he would benefit from hearing."

Accepting this, David said, "OK, then." He looked from the Professor to Susan and said, "Now we are three." Then he asked, "Is there anything you two book-savvy types have learned that I need to know before I wade in with my suggestions?"

Susan and the Professor exchanged a glance. As though by telepathic consensus she began to explain the Professor's discovery of the Marker's true function and the light which it shed on Jan's motivations. She briefly touched on her own abortive foray into magic use, acknowledging that the full story was one of a list of things to tell him later. As she summarised a few of the other discussions she'd had with the Professor, the conversation began to broaden into a debate.

David cut into the amiable banter with a note of concern. He asked the other two, "Do you think Dass is really dead? Do these people die like normal folk or is he going to be coming back to haunt us?"

Susan tackled that question. "I think we've got a fairly good idea of what they're capable of. We don't know all the little nuances, but I'm pretty sure we've got the basics. And there's no coming back from the dead. The police found Dass's body. He even had a passport with him to help the identification along. I think he's gone."

That seemed to relieve some of David's concern. He moved onto his next worry. "I think it's probably difficult to feel in much danger in a place like this," he said looking up and gesturing around him at the sunny living room. "And it clearly doesn't help us if we panic. But on the other hand," he said, his voice taking on a note of urgency, "Jan could tear that door off its hinges at any second." Involuntarily, Susan glanced at the front door. "So here's another management notion." He paused. "Let's tackle the urgent stuff right now and get onto the other important things later." No one stirred. "So first: is the collection safe?"

The Professor nodded. "Would you like to know where it is?"

David said, "I don't think I need to. Not unless…" he faltered.

The Professor stepped in, diplomatically, to complete the sentence, "Unless something happens to me."

The Professor lowered his voice. "Should you be, um, suddenly deprived of my involvement, you might wish to take a look at the particular copy of my doctoral thesis presently residing in the University Library. The last time I checked, it had not been requested since 1973. Starting on page 411 are some pencil notes – you'd be able to read the language, Susan. They hint at where I keep one or two items of value – which now includes the collection. Without that guidance, one would need to take this house down stone by stone to discover their hiding place."

David seemed about to speak, but doubt was evidently restraining him. The Professor gave him a wan smile of tissue-thin heartiness. "And I will keep my mouth shut whatever happens," he said simply – which seemed to answer David's unspoken question.

"Are there any other copies?" David asked.

"I trashed the network copy at the School, as well as their backups," Susan said, "and I brought the hard copies and the originals with me."

She went on, "There's also a digital copy on a CD," she pointed towards her bag. "I'm pretty sure I can make an encrypted copy of it, then I'll stick the unencrypted CD in the microwave."

David said, "Better write 'Dave's party mix' on it and keep it in a Discman, to be on the safe side." He sounded as though he approved of Susan's organisation.

The Professor muttered, "Just what I was going to say," evidently having no idea what David was talking about.

David glanced at him, explaining "My generation's way of hiding microfilm in with the holiday negatives."

Susan got up and fished the CD from her bag. Then she went into the kitchen and put it into the little portable stereo that sat on the window sill.

"Just for now," she said when she came back.

"OK," David said, "now how is Jan going to find us?"

There was a short pause and Susan said, "Through me. It'll be through me. He just has to figure out that the collection is missing and a bit about the circumstances and he'll know who took it." Susan added, "By the way, David, we don't think he has any special powers to help him find me, he'll have to do it the old-fashioned way."

David nodded, "So I think we need to vanish – Susan and me."

Susan said, "What, go on the run?"

"I think we had the right instinct when we headed for Brighton," he said. "We'll make for some destination that right now even we couldn't predict. Like you said, unless he's got us bugged, I don't see how he can find us."

"And then what?" Susan said.

David said, "And then, once you're safe, we take our time and make a proper plan."

CHAPTER 29

THAT SAME DAY
SUNDAY 27TH APRIL

An hour after they'd decided to vanish, David and Susan were in David's car, driving. They'd agreed that one of them would come up with an initial plan and the other would modify it slightly – that way their next move would be unguessable – even to someone who knew a lot about both of them.

They acknowledged that it was a paranoid and faintly ridiculous idea, but neither of them wanted to veto it.

"OK. I've got family I never see who live south of Dublin," David said. "We get the ferry across from Holyhead, which gets us out of the country; it's the closest thing Britain's got to a back-door. The harbour and the boat are enclosed spaces with crowds, but before we get there we'll have plenty of time to double-check no one is following us." Then he added, "Sorry," as he realised how morbidly cloak-and-dagger he was sounding. Susan shrugged.

"OK," she said, "I like the ferry idea, but what's the one that goes to the southern tip of Ireland?"

"Fishguard to Rosslare," David said after a moment's thought.

"Right," Susan said, "We go that way and drive up from the South. Plus we only contact your relatives if we need something. It'll be like having local reserves we can call up if there's a problem – and in the meantime there's no risk they'll give our position away." She smiled glumly, "Now who's talking like a spy?"

"That's settled then," David said.

Susan let a couple of minutes pass and then asked him, "Why haven't you tried to talk me out of this little escapade? You made an attempt with the Professor. I mean I wouldn't listen, but you could always try."

"At this point," David said seriously, "I can't think of any way to prove to Jan that you're not involved. He'll still think you're part of this even if you and me agree you're not. If you go back to your old routine, I think he'll just, you know..." He couldn't think of a good way of finishing the sentence. "It won't get you off the hook with him," he said instead.

"Yeah," Susan said, sounding dejected, "I figured it was something like that."

"We could just give him the collection," David said suddenly, "that would probably do it."

The suggestion hung in the air, but neither of them seemed to want to comment on it.

A minute passed and Susan said, "I'll see about encrypting that CD. I downloaded some software that says it'll encode every block of data on a disk, I'm just not sure how to use it yet."

She hauled her bag over from the back seat and set her iBook up on her lap. For the next hour, she muttered to herself until, at last, she announced success.

"Wanna know what the secret password is?" she asked.

"OK," David said.

"It's Fuzzbundle Milton, all one word, with the zees as sevens and the 'o' as a zero," she said.

"Any particular reason?" David asked.

"Oh, it was my cat's name," Susan explained, "Though Mom refused to pay for all the letters to be engraved on her name tag, so she was just Fuzz to strangers." Susan looked off into the distance.

David turned to smile softly at Susan, saying nothing.

A moment later, Susan said, "What shall we do with this?" She held up the old, unencrypted CD.

"Have you got a plastic bag?" David asked.

Susan fished out the bag from the office-supplies shop where she'd bought blank disks and a phone charger. Stealing glances away from the motorway traffic, David took the CD from her, stuck his hand in the bag and folded the disk in two. It shattered with a snap into half a dozen jagged pieces and lots of smaller fragments.

"I don't know why," Susan said, "but I thought a CD-ROM would fold up."

"Maybe you're thinking of credit cards," David said.

Susan looked at the pieces in the bag. "You really would need to be very dedicated to put that back together." She held up one of the tiniest pieces, like a speck of glitter on her fingertip and waved it under David's nose. "Fiddly," she said, relishing the word.

She pulled some of the metallic backing away from the larger fragments, leaving clear plastic. Then she slapped her hands together to brush off the scraps of foil.

"And check this out," she said, showing him the new, encrypted disk. With a permanent marker, she'd written 'Rap compilation' on it and drawn some stars. "I figure if there's one thing a ninety-year-old guy won't be able to handle it's rap."

"Nice," said David, amused, "Good thinking." Then he said,

"And it'll work even better if you encrypt a load of old rubbish and write 'Teracus Collection' on it, nice and neatly. In films, people always stop searching the instant they find something promising. So unless Hollywood have got so desperate for plot lines that they've started making things up, we'll be fine."

They both smiled. Once again a silence opened up, David concentrating on driving, Susan pondering.

Susan said after a while, "You know why I like the idea of a ferry crossing?"

"Because sorcerers can't cross open water?" David joked.

"Oh, hey, you know I think I get that now. I bet they don't like to."

She obviously wanted to share her theory, so David said, "Yeah?" encouragingly.

She launched into it, saying, "So, we know they can make this shield around them that will stop almost anything, even bullets I'm pretty sure. But what if you caught them on a boat and just sank it? There's nothing they could do. They'd drown just like anyone else. On land, an army might not be enough to stop them; at sea, one flaming arrow might be all you need."

David looked impressed.

"Anyway," Susan said, "that wasn't the reason I had in mind." She kept her voice neutral as she said, "I want to use the headband again."

Then she told David about her attempt to move the silver letter opener and her panic when she realised it might act like a beacon bringing her to the attention of Jan – and whoever else was out there. She said, "A few hours at sea is perfect. I mean what are the chances that the magical master race travel by car ferry? Same way I don't figure Dass owned a caravan." She grinned.

David looked over at her, taking in the grin. "You seem almost perky about this trip," David said, curious.

Susan grunted. "Well, I don't much like the alternatives. And I'm going through one of those dream-like periods where imminent death by supernatural means just doesn't seem like something I can get very worked up about. Real life doesn't feel very real at the moment. Maybe I'm just hungry." She looked sideways at the passing countryside, "You know what was really weird? I had a great time staying at the Professor's – in spite of everything. Having too many worries is almost like having none at all."

David said nothing for a while and then picked up an earlier thread. He said, "You know sorcery is still one of the so-called sins of the flesh according to the Catholic Church. Funny that they'd still include that in with licentiousness and gluttony."

For the next few hours, they chatted on and off. Sometimes Susan would tell David about something she'd read in the collection or discussed with the Professor; at other times they'd talk about inconsequential things, like wondering about the species of the birds they saw fanning their wings, hovering over the motorway's grass verges, ready to plunge down on whatever was scurrying below.

As they talked about birds of prey, David's attention drifted away. Seeing that she was losing his interest, Susan abandoned what she was saying and asked, "What's up?"

David returned to the moment, looking self-conscious and asking sheepishly, "How did Jan get down from that office window? It's not... He couldn't fly could he?"

Susan gave a polite smile, not laughing at him, acknowledging that it might *sound* ridiculous but it wasn't. She said, "I don't think so. There's no mention of any flying. Adepts can generate a sort of cushioning force that will hold part of their weight. So they can jump higher than normal people and a big drop will seem like a small one to them – but the force doesn't seem to be strong enough to lift them all by itself. They do seem to be able to generate something more powerful, but it's not a push, it's more like hitting something with a hammer. It's not the sort of thing you'd try to use on yourself."

David nodded, apparently relieved, "My friend Banjo said their powers sounded like the ultimate Swiss Army knife."

Susan considered this, finding that she agreed, "I guess they do. Or maybe like a set of outdoor gear that you don't have to lug around." She counted points off on her fingers, "There's a shield, there's something that seems to heat or cool, there's a means of getting down from a height, there's a first aid kit and there's a hammer." She looked suddenly thoughtful, "God, where do you think it comes from? Do you suppose anyone has ever tried to find out the source of these powers? There's nothing in the collection. And there's no way it's just a natural part of physics." She looked up at David to check, "Is there?" she asked.

David looked uncertain, "I don't see how. It's not the abilities themselves; they're exactly the sorts of things we used to do in physics class, but I don't believe the human brain would just happen to evolve as a remote control for the forces of nature." He shrugged, his train of thought losing momentum, "But can you even apply logic to something like this? I mean ordinary logic would tell you that the whole thing is impossible."

"Anyway," he said after a moment, "that list of powers is *it* you reckon? No unpleasant surprises?"

Susan said, "Too many of the documents agree – plus they fit with what we've seen. I think we've got the full list. Only the crazy mystics can do more and it sounds like no one's ever had any luck involving one of those guys in anything worldly – like chasing us, for instance."

David nodded, but made no reply, and once again they separated into their own private inner worlds, leaving the conversation to pass through another of its dry spells, dormant until some new idea occurred to one of them.

At one point, in the midst of a long silent stretch, David glanced over and saw tears running down Susan's face. She showed no other signs of distress and he said nothing. Ten minutes later, the tears were gone and she seemed in as good a mood as ever, volunteering her views about US freeways and how much better the diners were.

They stopped for petrol and sandwiches and then Susan settled down to doze through most of their trip across Wales. She finally woke up just as they arrived at the harbour. David was pulling in to buy tickets. A wide, low, glass-and-concrete building was directly in front of them as David edged into one of a long line of angled parking bays.

"Won't be long," he said. "Honk if you want me," he said cheerfully, indicating the horn control. Then he slipped off his seat belt and jumped out of the car.

From the passenger seat, Susan looked around her as David ran into the nearby building. It was early evening. The sun had already set and the wind had picked up. A few gulls were up late, fooling around in the unpredictable gusts.

A vast concrete apron extended behind them. Arcane paint marks, lighting poles, buried rails and snaking lines of cars decorated the immense expanse. Seemingly incongruous, the monstrous bulk of a ship lay behind it all, as though someone had built the vessel on the edge of a car park as some sort of tourist attraction. There was no sense of being near the sea.

When David came back, he jumped into the car quickly, the chill air buffeting the interior for the second or two that the door was open. He sniffed, the cold air having made his nose run. Susan had been sitting with her coat pulled over her, legs curled sideways in her seat. She sat up now to listen to him.

"Well," David said, "Our timing's spot on. The boats are running spectacularly late. The afternoon sailing hasn't left yet because the sea was too rough. They're loading it up now, though, and I got us one of the last three cabins."

He started the engine and pulled out of the parking bay to join the end of one of the enormous queues. Marshals, swaddled against the weather, waved and gestured, like some Eskimo dance troupe, lining the cars up as they approached the ship, acting according to some plan not obvious to the casual observer.

It took nearly an hour before David and Susan had left the Saab behind them among the tightly packed array of vehicles filling the cramped, permanent twilight of the car deck. They joined the throng, all climbing narrow metal staircases towards the well-lit passenger decks.

A few minutes later they'd left the mob behind them and found their cramped but cosy cabin. David shut the door behind them and then crossed the room to slump down on one of the two narrow beds. He rose again, momentarily, to pull off his boots and then stretched out once more, fully clothed, on the right-hand bunk.

Distant sounds and a vague sensation of shifting weight suggested that they'd got underway.

"You look beat," Susan said, turning out the main overhead light and switching on a small vanity light above a mirror. The tiny bulb was now the room's only illumination.

"I just need to close my eyes for a few minutes," he said in the gloom, his eyes already shut.

"Move over," she told him, before slipping onto the narrow bunk next to him, her shoulders pressing back against his chest until they were both arranged comfortably. He draped the flap of his heavy jacket over her, letting his arm rest along her side, his palm on her hip. After a minute she took his left hand, drew it under the coat and placed it tightly over her breast, her hand on top of his. "Sleep," she said.

* * *

When David woke up, he was alone on the bunk. Susan was sitting cross-legged on the floor, her back to him. Her head was dipped and in the dim light he couldn't quite see what she was doing. She still wore her jeans, but she had shed her fleecy top, stripping down to a white camisole and sports bra.

David turned around on the bunk, wriggling closer, moving around so that the light from the mirror's tiny lamp struck the gold headband Susan was wearing and picked out the drops of perspiration creeping down her face.

Looking at her uncovered shoulders, he could see the flare and tuck of compact muscles at the tops of each arm, the grooved bunching beneath the skin, as her posture shifted slightly. If Dee had the willowy proportions of a dancer, it was Susan who had a dancer's extraordinary muscle tone. And while her neat, delineated muscles hardly made her bulky, she would never look vulnerable or slight as Dee sometimes did.

He slid a little further down the bed until he could see over her shoulder.

She had set a little plastic disk on the floor just in front of her – a red, patterned circle a few finger-widths across, covered with a hard, transparent lid.

He looked closer. It was a cheap travel game, a little covered maze through which a tiny metal ball could be made to advance – if the disc were held in a steady hand and tilted skilfully enough.

As he watched, a bead of perspiration detached itself from Susan's hairline and ran down between her shoulder blades, following the smooth channel of her spine.

Pulling his eyes away from her damp skin, he looked back over her shoulder towards the plastic game.

The silver ball was making its way through the maze.

Susan's hands were folded in her lap and the game sat level on the cabin's motionless floor, in its own little circle of space, untouched. Nevertheless, the ball continued to make its way through the red plastic labyrinth of the puzzle.

He could hear Susan breathing – deeply and with effort.

Susan caught sight of David out of the corner of her eye and simultaneously the ball stopped moving. "Takes a lot of concentration," she said, through clamped teeth. Now the ball was stuck, despite her obvious effort. "Nah, I've lost it," she gasped, letting out her breath. She looked away from the puzzle and up at him.

"That's incredible," he said, looking at her with wonder.

"Yeah, I'm hoping to challenge Jan to a game of pinball in a couple of years time," she said, sarcastically.

She unfastened the top of a water bottle and took a long drink. When she'd finished gulping, she said, "Want some?" holding the bottle out to David.

"Thanks," he said, sitting back on the bunk and drinking.

"Man, it's sweaty work," she said, wiping her wet forehead with her hand. She looked up and caught David glancing at the shape her damp camisole made as it clung to her.

"You like?" she said playfully, in some mock-Eastern

accent, striking a little pose with her hands. She raised an eyebrow suggestively, the corners of her mouth twitching up in amusement.

David laughed and nearly choked on the water he was trying to swallow. He coughed a couple of times, still amused. Susan rose gracefully to her feet.

Without warning, she moved to the bed and placed a hand on his shoulder. Before David realised what she was doing, she leaned down and pressed her mouth, still wet from the spring water, against his. She kissed him passionately for a couple of seconds, opening her lips and brushing the back of his neck lightly with her fingers. Then she broke away, looking fiercely elated and a little out of breath.

"That feels better, doesn't it?" she said, challengingly, looking him in the eye.

David seemed slightly stunned. "Did I miss something? Is magic some sort of aphrodisiac?" he asked, then added, "Not that I'm complaining. You can do that whenever you want." He stressed the last three words.

Susan smiled and considered her answer. "You know it might even be kind of a turn-on, I'll see how I feel next time," she replied.

Then she looked at him and said, "That," meaning the kiss, "was about something else, though." Then she said dreamily, "After all, we might be dead tomorrow." She spoke absent-mindedly as though she were reminiscing.

"Oh," David said, sounding deflated. "I can see how that thought would make you frisky," he said, meaning the opposite.

"You know what I mean," Susan said, focussing on him. "Why worry about the long-term stuff? It all seems a bit academic, right now. Why not take a few chances?"

"I suppose," David said, not sure whether to feel slightly insulted or not.

He sat up and swung his feet onto the floor. Then he reached for one of his boots.

It slid out of his reach.

He glanced sharply at Susan. A look of painful concentration had tightened her features and pulled her mouth open. The intensity slid away swiftly as she relaxed and she said, a little apologetically, "I just wanted to see if I could."

"You're starting to scare me," he said, half joking.

He pulled on his boots as she stretched. She was also working her jaw as though realising her teeth had been clenched together for too long.

There was a change in the sense of the boat's motion. "I think we're coming in to dock," Susan said, taking off the headband. She gave him a flirty peck on the cheek and ducked into the room's tiny bathroom, turning on the shower. "I'll just be a minute," she told him.

He rummaged in his pockets, pulling out various papers as she thumped about on the other side of the thin bulkhead. The muted patter of the shower sounded like heavy rain on a metal roof.

When she emerged, Susan was wearing the same clothes, but her drying hair was kinked and full and rather wild. "We're going to need to go clothes shopping again soon," she said, "else anyone with a sense of smell will know where I am."

She sat on the unused bunk opposite David, who was studying a free map he'd picked up when he bought the tickets. "Be quite a nice drive, if it wasn't the middle of the night," he said.

A beeping noise caught their attention. It took Susan a moment to realise it was her phone. She retrieved it from her bag and saw the voicemail symbol. "Hmm," she said thoughtfully and set about playing the message.

She had only listened to a couple of seconds of it when she snatched the phone from her ear, hit the button to play the recording from the beginning and plonked down beside David. She held the phone between them, their heads together, the tinny speaker loud enough that they could both hear the message.

The phone company's virtual-woman finished her preamble about the timing of the recording, then a man's voice spoke, his accent like an RAF captain from an old war film troubled by the turn the fighting was taking.

"I should think you can guess who this is," the voice began, pleasantly, but without enthusiasm.

Then, as though continuing a previous conversation, he said, "People talk about violence as though it were all much of a muchness. But surely, that makes a mockery of life. Of course there's opposition – given that we all want different things – and naturally that opposition can turn nasty. But it seems to me that there's a world of difference between honest combat and the idea of simply inflicting damage on a helpless prisoner."

A queasy charm warmed his voice now – charm of the kind found in chummy voice-overs for commercials selling funeral insurance. "Whereas torture," the voice announced, "is simply the province of anyone with a strong stomach and access to a toolbox." He sounded slightly put out, "No, it's a horrible thought, it really is – I can't see any satisfaction in something like that." He sighed and then the sigh turned to a drawn-out chuckle, "Listen to me go on – as though I hadn't butchered my way across half a continent." He sighed again, amused, and then cleared his throat, reluctantly getting down to business, "Anyway, what I called for was this: if you don't want your sister back one charred strip at a time, the thing to do is bring me the documents I want."

He finished amiably, "Call me on her portable phone at any time. I'm looking after it for her," he added.

Neither David nor Susan moved or spoke as the automated voice reeled off the various options for storing or deleting the message. The system was listing a second set of options it evidently reserved for those not tempted by the standard menu when Susan emerged from her clouded reverie to end the call.

CHAPTER 30

The answerphone message shattered Susan's fey good humour. With her own life in danger, she had settled into some strategy for coping that allowed her to function almost normally. She had seemed to register the danger she was in without being paralysed by it. But the news of Dee's kidnapping pierced her composure, coming at her from a direction she was defenceless against.

Though she avoided many of the signs of panic – she wasn't shouting or crying – still, her focus had somehow been dislodged from the present, shifting away from her immediate surroundings to some inner purgatory. When David spoke to her, it was as though he were attempting, unsuccessfully, to break into another conversation, one that only she was hearing.

Her replies to his questions were sluggish and vague. She didn't look him in the eye or take note of his movements as he fidgeted around their tiny cabin.

At last, David stood and picked up his jacket, saying to her, "Stay here." She was sitting, hands in her lap, eyes distant, turned away from him on the opposite bunk. Had she heard him?

He came to stand above her and said, "I'm going to go and arrange for us to head straight back to England. It might take a while and I'll have to move the car." Her attitude didn't alter. He tried to get some sense that he had her attention by crouching in front of her, touching her hand, "So stay here," he said again with gentle emphasis. Her eyes wandered over him, not settling. She made some move of her head that might have been a nod or an indication that he should go. She didn't say anything, but it appeared that she was at least registering his words.

Leaving her caught up in the knot of her own thoughts, David left the cabin and fought his way down through the crush of passengers who were readying themselves to disembark. More than once he had to duck under a carelessly out-flung arm or ease his way sideways through a family absorbed in a corridor-wide squabble. The lights of the Irish harbour were sliding glacially past the dark, rain-beaten windows as he found the information desk.

The desk's harassed-looking steward was attempting to pacify a fierce woman passenger with flaming cheeks who was berating him in some shrill, contemptuous register. She stormed away as David arrived, leaving the steward twitching with defensiveness and unspent adrenaline.

Taking in the scene, and sizing up the steward's mood, David allowed his hurried stride to evaporate into a troubled hesitancy as he approached the desk. He composed his features in an approximation of Susan's distressed blankness.

When he stood in front of the fuming steward, he said in a halting monotone of helplessness, "I don't know what to do. Something awful has happened. I've just had a phone call. We need to get back to England." He looked down at his hands, never meeting the steward's eyes, copying Susan's attitude of shock.

The combination of David's tough-looking bulk and his unguarded, abject demeanour left a vacuum of authority into which the steward gladly stepped. He mustered a grave little smile and said calmly, authoritatively, "Tell me what's happened, sir. I'm sure we'll be able to work something out."

David made a struggle of telling his story, being scrupulously economical with the details, leaving Dee's predicament unspecified but open to interpretation as some sort of medical emergency. Having gleaned what he could, the steward took him to see the captain.

The conversation with the captain seemed to go more smoothly if David said little, limiting his contribution to one or two wild looks, and allowed the steward to intercede for him. The captain was as sure-handed and helpful when confronted with David's frayed nerves as the steward had been.

Having ascertained that David was at least composed enough to drive a car, the captain arranged that when David drove out of the hold he would be diverted from the normal exit route. He would instead wait in a reserved area adjacent to the ramp for a few minutes and then be allowed back onto the boat, the first car aboard for the return journey.

It took nearly an hour before everything was arranged for their trip back to Britain, the car had been moved and David could return to the cabin.

When he opened the door he saw that Susan seemed to have emerged from her morbid daydream. She appeared once again connected to her surroundings, looking up instantly, her face unreadable, as he entered the cabin.

He told her with an embarrassed look, "Well, I've just finished doing my 'Lassie with a bad paw' imitation. Thank god it seems to have worked. The Captain's trying to get back on schedule, so we should be underway in another hour. No way to get us back faster than that."

Susan nodded. She was wedged into the corner, on the bunk they'd shared, a pillow propped behind her, a pad and pen in her hands.

She returned her gaze to the pad and scribbled something, her concentration absorbed by the notes she was making.

David came to crouch next to her, kneeling by the bunk. He reached out and took her hand, lifting it gently away from the pad, wrapping his fingers around hers. She looked up slowly, her clear, blank eyes meeting his serious, examining gaze.

He told her, "I don't know what to say." He continued to hold her hand, her cool eyes resting on his as he searched her face, trying to read her.

He spoke again, his tone suddenly passionate as though some emotion had bubbled up inside him that he couldn't contain, "Don't worry, Susan. Please don't worry. I'll find a way to get Dee back safely, I promise you I will. I don't care what I have to do. Just trust me; I'll find a way."

Susan's calmness, serene and almost eerie as it was, continued for a second or two after he finished speaking and then it began to come apart. A flush crept into her cheeks and the evenness of her smooth brow tightened into a lost-looking frown. As her expressionless poise disintegrated, her shoulders began to sag.

She took her hand out from within his grasp and laid her palm on top of his hand. She seemed choked with emotion.

"What?" he asked, sensing something, "What did I say?"

She reached up to stroke the back of her hand gently down his cheek. Her touch was delicate, full of care and somehow tragic. She said, "I know you would, David. I know you'd do your very best to save Dee and to save me – but I can't agree to that. I know you only want what's best for us, but do you see, I'll never forgive myself if I let you take over? I can't let go of this. I know what to do and you have to help me do it." Now she searched his eyes, which were beginning to cloud with confusion as he processed her words.

She said, "I've got a plan."

* * *

Ten minutes later they were sipping bitter coffee from white polystyrene cups. David had found someone to give them coffee and doughnuts from the staff restaurant. He had used the interruption to conceal the uncomfortable surprise and the sting of rejection written on his face at the way Susan had responded to his offer of help. She could see that he wanted to justify himself, to explain that he wasn't trying to take over, that she was doing him an injustice. But he didn't.

Susan watched him stifle the impulse to pull away from her, to withdraw. As he realised that Susan considered his guidance a luxury they couldn't afford, his hurt was evident in his face. And Susan's fond gaze almost gave way to tears as she saw him suppress his wounded pride. He had looked taken aback, almost affronted, as she spoke, as he felt their relationship shift, but she could see him willing that away, replacing it with the determined, receptive look she could see now in his eyes. It was obvious that he'd pushed past his instinctive, irritated reaction and accepted her lead.

He had come to sit on the edge of the bunk next to her, handing over one of the coffee cups, and asked, "So what's the plan?" his voice genuine, supportive.

She reached out, a trembling smile on her lips and touched his lower lip with the side of her thumb, gently. He looked bemused, but didn't question. She said, "One day I'll tell you why those words mean more to me than anything."

Then she nodded, as though settling something she had been inwardly debating, and addressed herself to his question.

"A flag of truce," she said. "I was trying to think of somewhere neutral we could meet – somewhere safe for an exchange. I was wracking my brains for something, anything, that an adept would respect enough to stop him double-crossing us."

He asked, "What did you come up with?"

"Nothing," she replied, "Nothing short of open warfare seems to deter them – the prospect of a fight big enough that the world would notice. So I decided to use that." She took a sip of her coffee and said, "I decided we needed an environment where Jan would have to deal with hundreds of people if he tried anything."

She tapped her pad, "I made a list of our requirements. We need somewhere very controlled, somewhere with crowds of people, somewhere with an escape route for us, a really good one – if possible, somewhere with dozens of heavily armed guards. Granted, that wouldn't stop him, but it would make life pretty difficult and hopefully give us a chance to get away. And ideally we want somewhere he couldn't bring tribute to, somewhere with metal detectors. You following me? This giving you any ideas?"

He shrugged. "A prison?" he suggested, unsure.

"An airport," she said, stressing the word. "Sure, Jan could fight his way past the armed police, but imagine the chaos. He'd never be able to control an environment like that. And he'll have to come through the metal detectors. We tell him no luggage and then we loiter near the entrance to see if he sets off the alarms as he comes through."

David said, "And what if he does? We can't go anywhere. They won't stop him carrying a gold band and a couple of bracelets with him; they won't think anything of it. Then he's free to come and find us."

Susan said, "Not if we figure out some way of destroying the collection before he can get to us, and we make sure he knows about it."

She looked down at her pad. At some point, while David had been out of the cabin, a single tear must have struck the paper. Now there was a dried wrinkle in the smooth paper where the droplet had obliterated part of a line of writing.

Susan's expression showed that some misplaced detail was still pricking her. "What's it called?" she said to herself, pressing a knuckle under the point of her chin. She looked up at David and explained, "A lot of the work I do is with archives. Storing documents properly and knowing a bit about the various kinds of paper is part of the job. I had a presentation from some guys once about some indestructible, acid-free paper they'd invented for use in archives. While they were there, I remember them telling me that they also sold some other stuff," she suddenly looked elated, "MDP, that was it! It dissolves in water very quickly – instantly, according to the brochure. It's kind of a novelty thing, like you could wrap bath salts in it and just throw a packet of it into your tub, no need to open it first."

David was wondering if he was following her, "So we'd print a copy of the collection on that stuff? Threaten to get it wet if anyone rushes us?"

Susan nodded, "Exactly. We can't very well set light to anything in the middle of a departure lounge and if we could it wouldn't be quick enough. But imagine we put the papers in a clear carrier bag, so he can see them, and hold an open bottle of Evian ready. It doesn't really look suspicious, but we only need a fraction of a second to destroy everything."

David was gradually getting up to speed. "So where do we get this paper?" he asked.

She gave him a pitying look and said, "We don't. All we do is tell Jan about it. He can easily verify it exists. I'll just print off some Pliny, or something, on regular paper, nice small print and maybe book-end it with some irrelevant bits of the real collection. It'll look fine until he gets a chance to study it, and thinking it's water-soluble should keep him honest."

David looked slightly shocked. "You're not going to give him the collection then? I just thought you'd... that you wouldn't want to risk..." he didn't finish that thought.

Susan said patiently, "The thing about this is that if we set it up right, so we can get away safely and he can't touch us, it works equally well whether we cheat him or not."

David didn't look convinced. Susan explained, "Let me put it another way. If we're honest with him, it doesn't guarantee he won't just kill us. And if we set it up so he *can't* just kill us, we might as well double-cross him." A fierce light twinkled in her eye as she declared, "There's no way I'm handing that bastard another century of life."

David was beginning to look horrified, "And what then, once we've double-crossed him? He's just going to come tearing after us as soon as he discovers he's been tricked."

Susan refused to be rattled. She said, "Well, I'm just thinking this through, I guess it's not set in stone, but I was assuming we'd make a run for it. The beauty of doing this in a departure lounge is that we book ourselves on one flight, he books himself on another – neither of us know where the other one's going – and assuming we don't accidentally pick the same destination, the next time we're out in the open again we could be anywhere. He won't know whether we got on a flight to China, Iceland or Ghana. I've already got somewhere in mind to stash Dee for a little while. I just have to persuade my dad to take my mom on one of his wilderness camping trips. You'd need to do the same for your family, of course."

She looked up expectantly at him and saw doubt written across his face. "Maybe it's easier for me," she said, "I'm not likely to be continuing my post-doc knowing what I know and I'm just a visitor to England – I don't have roots here. But there can't be too many people who could be used as leverage against you, can there?"

While she'd been speaking, David had been looking at her with growing impatience; now he threw up his hands, "Susan, this is insane. We can't go on the run, hide up a mountain somewhere. We can't just flee to the other side of the world. There must be another way."

She let him consider it himself for a little while and then said, "Either we give him what he wants, or we kill him or we run. You tell me what our other options are?" She looked him in the eye and said, "You think we should help him? Is that what you think?"

He looked awkward, far from convinced, but unable to think of an objection. She continued, "Think what he'd do with another hundred years. Trust me, he's not about to start doing charity work. We're the only thing standing in his way. If we help him, how are you going to feel, going back to your job, thinking about this for the next fifty years, knowing he's out there? That's even assuming he doesn't come after us. Face it: our old lives are over however this ends up." Her passion shifted to something like rage as she said, "God knows what he's done to Dee. He's not getting any help from me."

They sat in silence for a few seconds. Susan was breathing hard. She'd stirred up her adrenaline giving that speech and it had brought an angry flush to her neck and face.

David finished thinking it through. He gave Susan a lopsided and unhappy grin. He said, "One of these days I'm going to stop underestimating you, I really am." He nodded several times, jutting out his lower lip, "You're right – about all of it. You're absolutely right."

She leaned over to squeeze his shoulder, beginning to smile uncertainly back at him. He lifted her hand from his arm, captured it in both of his, held it to his lips and kissed it. "I would have got there soon enough, you know," he said, half joking.

"Sure," she said, nodding slowly, her smile growing warmer, "sure."

He still held her hand between his. He asked, "So now we've agreed that we're totally buggered whatever we do, what's next?"

Gently disengaging from him, she put her pad down and swung her legs onto the floor. "Breakfast, of course," she said, "We've got work to do."

CHAPTER 31

LATER THAT MORNING
MONDAY 28TH APRIL

Susan turned off the radio, which had only been a murmur anyway.

"If the last hundred years have taught him anything about people," she said, "I guarantee it's that they're afraid of him."

David took this in. "It still won't hurt to sell it a little," he said. "The dissolving paper thing is a bit too creative. And then insisting on an airport, it's too much. We sound like we're planning, like we're in control." He considered for a second. "I think you're right that he won't expect anyone to stand up to him, but we can't afford to make him suspicious." He drummed his fingers on the steering wheel. "Maybe we can make it sound like we chose the airport because we want to get rid of him. Tell him we want him to get straight on a plane and not bother us any more. Psychologically that sounds more like something a victim would say – it sounds like fear is doing most of our thinking."

They were back in the car, retracing the path they'd taken across Wales the previous day. The mid-morning sun was well and truly hidden behind the low cloud which hung over the fields to either side of the motorway.

"I like it," Susan said. Then she smiled. "You're really getting the hang of thinking like a loser. First your little wounded Lassie thing on the boat, now this."

"The Lassie thing was a new low," he said, "but I was thinking about helping you as I did it. See the effect you're having on me?"

"You realised it would work though," she said, "they might have told us to make a booking like everyone else."

David nodded formally, in lieu of taking a bow, and said, "Office politics – the great teacher. Until fairly recently, I always seemed to be the most junior person in any meeting. I've found you have to create an environment in which someone can see themselves saying 'yes'. A lot of times they won't agree if it feels like you're getting the best of them. Letting someone play the hero or the bully is often the key."

Susan looked impressed but there was comical distaste in her expression too. "Swear to only use your powers for good," she said, seriously.

David gave her a suspicious look. "What? You don't manipulate people? At all?"

Susan made a face, "No, I mainly just hammer away at them, being all earnest. The manipulation only comes in afterwards when I try to patch up the damage I've done and keep them talking to me."

David puckered his lips, weighing her words and then announced, "That's sort of admirable, not trying to control people. It's a scruple I don't think I can afford, but it's sort of noble. Like tapping someone on the shoulder before you take a swing at them." He added, "You wouldn't catch me doing that."

Susan snorted, amused in a disapproving sort of way.

David looked troubled as something new occurred to him. He said, "I still think we've got a hole in our plan. I don't think we've cracked the bit where we get Dee safely away afterwards. If she arrives in that departure lounge with Jan it means she'll have checked in with him – and that means he'll know her destination. We could buy her a ticket and leave it at the airport for her to pick up, but he's just going to be standing next to her. Once he knows where she's going, he can just tag along if he wants." He glanced over at her, "I wonder how many flights have sold all their first class or business class seats by check-in time? Not that many, I reckon. He could just buy a last-minute seat on her flight and grab her again if he needed to. We wouldn't have achieved anything with all the cloak and dagger business."

Susan shoved him gently on the arm, "You're such a worrier; have a little faith," she said. She seemed amused.

"Susan," he said, "this is serious." As soon as he'd spoken, he knew he'd said the wrong thing.

Her face clouded over. "I know it's serious," she said, anger and irritation in her voice.

"Sorry, sorry," he said, "Of course you do. Of course."

She calmed herself and a few seconds later said, "I think the chances that Jan picked up Dee's passport are pretty slim. I mean why would he? So we buy three tickets for our flight. I get myself a black wig and make myself up to look like Dee. Then I check in as her, with all her luggage. Next, I ditch the wig, change my clothes, wait a half an hour and join a different check-in line, where I check-in as me. If anyone does recognise me the second time I can always say we're twins – the airline won't have Dee's date of birth, right? Given that we *are* sisters, I don't see how we're going to get caught out."

David was processing this. "But Jan also buys a ticket for

Dee?" he asked.

"Right," Susan said, "You leave her passport with information once I'm done with it – you tell them you found it – and then Dee picks it up when she gets there – she just says she dropped it. That way Dee can be simultaneously checked in on two flights, only one of which Jan knows about. Her boarding card for the first flight gets her into the departure lounge, but then we switch to the second ticket once we've got her away from him."

David's expression was still pensive. "I'm just thinking about that second ticket. You pretend to be Dee in order to check in, but then that ticket goes in your pocket until it's time to get on the plane. That ticket never gets seen by security or passport control or any of those guys. So that ticket is skipping several steps. Will they let her on the flight if they've no record of her coming through departures?"

Susan shrugged, "I don't think they check that stuff. But even if they do, what are they going to accuse her of? We've got the real Dee, with her passport and ticket, ready to get on a flight. They can suspect her of teleporting into the departure lounge, but I think they still have to let her on the plane. They'll assume security screwed up."

David was nodding, looking tentatively convinced. "It works, doesn't it? And what about the other ticket, the one Jan buys? Won't that cause problems when Dee doesn't show up for that flight?"

Susan said, "Well, since there's no luggage in the hold, they'll just take off without her eventually. Maybe it'll cause some trouble down the line if they investigate, but I don't think they'll ever figure out what happened. No smuggler or terrorist is going to pull this trick because it doesn't really achieve anything. We booked someone on two flights and only used one of them. It's hardly worth making a fuss over."

"Yeah," David said, looking like he was finally convinced, "Yeah. I get it." He gave her a quick smile, "So where do you want to fly to?"

Susan looked out of the side window at the damp clouds brushing the tops of the hills, the misty air heavy with drizzle, soaking every part of the green land. "Somewhere warm," she said, then added, "with regular flights to the US so we can get Dee safely away."

They drove in silence for several minutes before Susan said cautiously, "Listen David, I want to do a little more practice."

David looked curious. "You mean...?" He flicked his eyes towards her bag on the back seat, where the headband and bracelets were stored.

Susan nodded. "Yeah." She volunteered, "I figure we're going eighty miles an hour, there's plenty of other cars on the road, so we're anonymous. If some adept registers me, what can he do about it? We're travelling better than a mile a minute. We'll be out of his territory before he knows what's happening. Plus, who lives right by the motorway? Like I say, I don't picture these guys slumming it."

David wasn't really following her argument; he simply waited for her to stop talking so that he could speak. He said, "This makes me very uneasy. You were messing about with that stuff on the way out *and* on the way back. Why do you need to do it again so soon?"

Susan glanced up at his expression, "What, you think this is like a drug or something?"

David was slightly agitated, "I don't know what it's like. But I'll tell you this: I don't think it's good for you. I'd like to believe there are some adepts out there who fight on the side of the angels, but realistically I doubt it. According to the stuff you've read, they're a pack of power-mad psychopaths." He looked at her, "Aren't they?"

Susan conceded, "But it's not the magic that makes them like that." She looked defensive as she realised how weak that sounded. "I really don't think it's the magic, David, I think it's who they are. Any power is like that. How many big-shot politicians do you think are still good people doing good work? Any power can corrupt you if you love it enough. But I don't. I don't want that sort of power at all."

David sounded almost pleading as he said, "Then why do you want to use that thing again? Why not leave it alone? If it's not addictive?"

Susan took a deep breath and spoke in a calmer voice, "Because I don't have time. Jan's had a hundred years and I've got a few days." She twisted round to face him. "Magic is the only thing we've got that might possibly slow him down, push him off course, surprise him a little. When he's got that power there's nothing you've learnt in your martial arts classes that could make him even break his stride. He could literally kill you with a wave of his hand and keep going. It wouldn't make any difference if you had a knife or a gun or half a dozen friends with you. He'd go right through you. This is the only thing that might slow him down."

An unpleasant thought was dawning on David. "You mean you'd bring your gold bands to the airport with you? You'd take him on?"

Susan gave nothing away in her expression. "If needs be," she said carefully, "I don't plan to. But if things go wrong, I need something that I can throw at him to buy a little bit of time."

David said, "You mean so that Dee and I can get away while you fight him?"

Neutrally, Susan acknowledged, "Just in case. In case it goes wrong. We need something."

Susan's words hung in the air for a minute and then she tried to lighten the mood. "What's that cheesy line? If you don't have a back-up plan then you don't have a plan."

David made an effort to smile despite his grim expression. He said, "I'm not happy about this, Susan."

"No," Susan said patiently, "I don't suppose you are."

Instead of reaching for her bag, Susan sat still. Minutes passed.

When Susan spoke again, enough time had passed that the mood between them had distilled into something else. "Do you ever get a phrase stuck in your head?" she asked distantly. "I've got one that keeps playing over and over at the moment."

David didn't speak, wondering whether Susan would go on. She did. "My Dad had an older brother. He's dead now. He was in Europe during the war – in France I think. He'd visit us sometimes when we were little kids." Susan's voice was dreamy, reminiscing, "He had this thing he said that became like a catchphrase with Dee and me for a while. He'd tell us what he was up to or sometimes he'd even tell us about the war, usually some harmless little thing. Then he'd say, 'Out of my depth and still functioning'. I can picture him saying it with a grin. Dee and I would copy it because it sounded so grown-up, like a joke we didn't understand. Out of my depth and still functioning."

She shook herself, trying to shrug it off and said, "That was a creepy kind of a Hallmark moment, wasn't it?" She avoided David's gaze for a moment.

David had been watching her closely as she spoke, stealing as much time away from the road as he could. Some aspect of her story had clearly touched him. Now he wanted to reciprocate, to tell her something, but he was struggling. "You..." he said and tried again, "You're just…" He had another go, "When I think of you I…"

And then instead of being serious they were both laughing. Susan said, "Eloquently put. You know, a lot of guys have trouble articulating their feelings, but you're just able to tap into this amazing ability to express yourself; I suppose you'd call it a gift."

"Ha ha," David said, in a mocking voice. "It's not easy. There aren't any bloke words for what I was trying to say." He was still laughing and looking self-conscious at the same time. "Anyway, you've ruined it now with your mickey-taking. That was my one attempt to reach out. I'll probably be emotionally closed off for life now."

Susan undid her seat-belt and twisted round so that she could reach over onto the back seat. Her fingertips were extended towards the strap of her bag. As she stretched, she needed to lean against David's shoulder. It brought her close enough that she could murmur in his ear, "I think I know what you were trying to say." Then she nipped his earlobe with her teeth.

"Ow!" he said, more surprised than pained. "Behave!"

"Yeah, yeah," she said, retrieving her bag.

Susan clipped the bracelets on, settled the gold band on her head. Then she fluffed her hair around the band to hide it from anyone peering into the car.

"I meant to ask: that's just ordinary gold?" David asked.

"Yup," Susan replied. "Now, shush."

He glanced over occasionally to see what she was doing, but beyond a look of concentration on Susan's face and the half-closed set of her eyes, there was no sign that anything was going on.

As before, a sheen of perspiration appeared on Susan's skin after a few minutes of effort.

Suddenly there was a screech of tyres as the Saab skidded. The
rev counter plummeted and the car bucked as David twitched the
wheel, fighting the skid. A horn blared from behind them.

David looked instantly charged with adrenaline, peering around
at the other cars, looking for any clue to what had just happened.

"Shit," Susan said loudly, then, "Sorry. God, sorry. That was
me. I lost it for a minute."

"What?" David demanded, then blew his breath out angrily,
"Jesus. You did that?"

Susan looked awful, grimacing with embarrassment. "I'm so
sorry. I'll stop now. There's nothing to worry about. It's over."

David breathed deeply for a few seconds, waiting for the
adrenaline to dissipate, biting his tongue in the meantime.

Susan said meekly, "I'm making shields; I needed to practice
them. I've been playing with the rain."

Now that his attention had been called to it, David focussed on
the windscreen, noticing the lack of moisture on it, the dry screech
of the wipers, despite the fact that the day was as wet as ever.
Even as he noticed its absence, the rain started hissing onto the
windscreen again, droplets once more driving into the glass.

"I must have touched the engine with one of the shields," Susan
said. "I'm tired."

And sure enough she looked tired. She was breathing hard and
the perspiration on her cheeks looked cold. Her eyelids trembled
slightly.

"Don't worry about it," David said finally. "It just took me by
surprise. We're still in one piece." He didn't sound enthusiastic but
his anger was gone.

Susan took this opportunity to bring something up. Her voice
was very quiet. "When we call him," she paused to let David figure
out whom she was referring to, "can you do it?" she said, almost

whispering.

David was caught slightly off guard, "Er, I suppose. If you want me to."

Susan nodded, "I've been thinking about it and I'm just not sure I could keep it together." Her voice wobbled a little. "If I don't think about what she's going through, how frightened she must be, then I'm sort of…" She puffed air for a moment, emotion not exertion disrupting her words. "Then I'm sort of alright," she finished at last, her voice straying higher and higher as she tried to keep from crying.

Having got the words out, she sobbed a couple of times now.

"Of course," David said, "Of course, I'll do whatever you want, but…" he paused. "I'll do it if you want me to, but don't decide yet. It might be better, given how you sound now, it might be better if it was you." He added softly, "He wouldn't suspect anything."

She looked up at him, through her tears, a hurt look on her face. "That's so calculating," she said, gulping back her tears.

David said nothing, just left her to struggle with her anguish.

So quietly he almost didn't hear her, she said, "You're right. I'll do it."

CHAPTER 32

They were back in London by the afternoon. Both of them were looking drained, Susan terribly so. They were both determined, however, that rest could wait – they had a number of things to organise first.

First they needed somewhere to stay. Neither of them had any confidence that their usual addresses were unknown to Jan. If he knew where Dee was staying, worse still if he had questioned Dee, he might know anything by now.

They opted for a hotel and David suggested that they stay at the one he had driven Dee to, the one she had been staying at when she was taken.

It was amazingly expensive, but they were going to need to get to Dee's belongings somehow and it would be a lot easier if they were staying in the same building.

Besides, as David pointed out, he had to accept that his life was going to change now. He'd been saving up to go travelling, in fact he had more than he really needed stashed away, so they might as well draw on those savings now. Because now he really was going travelling, albeit not in the way he'd imagined.

David checked in for both of them, requesting a twin room – there hadn't even been a discussion about taking separate rooms this time. Susan sat in one of the armchairs in the hotel's foyer reading a newspaper as David completed the transaction. She sat some distance away and gave no sign that she was with him. Once he had moved away from the desk, she put the paper down and strode up to the reception.

"Excuse me, my name is Dee Milton. I'm afraid I've lost my room key," she said to the man on the desk, exaggerating her American accent.

"Which room are you in, Madam?" he asked.

Breezing past the question, Susan said, "I'm over from New York, you see, and I'm just terribly jet-lagged. I can't keep anything straight." She pointed down at his computer terminal, "It's M-I-L-T-O-N. Dorothy, but I go by 'Dee'."

He tapped away at his terminal for a moment and then asked, "Do you have any identification, Ms Milton."

"Well, I do of course, but it's all in my room," she said smiling sweetly. "I can give you my home address or telephone number, any of that sort of thing."

"Yes, that would do," the man said. Susan reeled off Dee's details.

"I think I just locked the key in my room," she said, "If someone could let me in there that's probably all I need."

The receptionist gave his cool smile and beckoned over a young valet. He whispered something in his ear. The younger man came out from behind the counter and said to Susan, "If you'll just follow me, we'll get you sorted out." He led the way to the lifts.

Susan chatted away, as the young valet smiled politely, "Of

course I wouldn't normally touch alcohol at lunchtime when I'm at home. I think it must be the jet-lag – so disorienting. Have you ever been jet-lagged?"

"No, Ma'am," he said. When they left the elevator, she blinked at her surroundings, making a show of being a little disoriented. She allowed him to lead the way to the room.

A minute later, Susan stood in the middle of room 319. The valet was hovering by the door. On one of the bedside tables she quickly located a paper packet containing a credit-card-style plastic key. It had obviously held two of them originally.

"There it is," she said, turning and holding up the key. "Thanks so much."

"Quite alright, Madam. Enjoy your stay," he said, retreating into the corridor and closing the door.

Susan had a quick glance round the room. There was little of interest to see; housekeeping had obviously tidied the room since it had last been used. It wasn't even clear which of the two standard-double beds Dee had used.

She picked up the phone, dialled zero and asked to be connected to David Braun's room. She spelled his name. A moment later it was ringing.

On the second ring, David answered.

Susan said, "I'm in room 319. Why don't you come down?"

"See you in a sec," he said, hanging up.

He was knocking at the door less than a minute later.

Between them they peered into drawers and slid back the doors to the hanging space. Susan snapped the light on in the bathroom and explored within.

"There's not much missing," she said. "Even her shoulder bag is here. It looks like she stepped out with just her phone and her pocketbook, and maybe a coat."

They spent a few minutes packing up Dee's things, returning her clothes to her suitcase and garment bags. On the writing desk Susan found a partly written postcard with the words 'Dear Mom and Dad' at the top, but nothing more. Reluctantly, Susan dropped the card into the wastebasket.

They carried her bags up two floors to their own room, which was almost identical to Dee's. Putting down the bags, David began to pace, obviously busy thinking.

Susan sat down on the far bed. She was rummaging through Dee's shoulder bag. "Well, at least we've got her passport," Susan said. "Unfortunately, mine's in Cambridge."

David looked like he wanted to groan at the news, but he didn't. He said, "Well, I suppose we've got quite a bit of travelling to do then. I need to pick up some stuff from my flat. It might be best to do all this tomorrow morning, before anyone's up. We can get a little bit of sleep and do our driving when there's no traffic."

Susan said, "Yeah. We still don't know if Jan's got any accomplices, whether he's got people watching the places we might visit."

David said, "Well, he's done his own dirty work up until now. If he was going to call in reinforcements, I think he'd have done it before this point. And he doesn't need to set traps for us any more; he's got Dee."

Susan said, "Even so…"

David finished for her, "Even so, we'll be careful. Early tomorrow morning is a good time for that. No one's alert at 4 a.m."

"Certainly not me," Susan agreed. "Oh and while we're at it, we need to drop into the Professor's place in the City too."

This time David did groan. "Of course," he said, "What about your parents' ranch in Idaho?"

"It's a house and it's in New Mexico and I think we can do without my prom dress and twelfth-grade yearbook for now," she said, mock-witheringly.

David nodded, "Oh, good," he said.

Despite the fact that they were joking with one another, there was a growing tension in the room. They had yet to contact Jan and the knowledge that the time for the call was approaching was beginning to affect them. Neither of them seemed ready to broach the subject yet.

David sat down at the writing desk. "I should call work," he said. "I need to tell them... something."

"Tell them you fell in love," Susan said, flopping down face first on the bed.

He pretended to consider this seriously, "I suppose it's not *that* far from the truth," he said.

Before Susan could make any sort of response he snatched up the phone and started dialling. He said to her, sounding business-like, "I think it's a good idea to sort of combine the truth in with what I tell them. It'll make it easier to keep the story straight later." He was holding the phone tucked under his chin listening to it ring. He added enigmatically, "I think you're about to get a promotion."

Just then the call was answered and David asked to speak to Reg Cottrell. When David was through to him, he started off by saying that he wasn't going to be coming in to the office for a while. Then he asked how things were going. From the way the conversation progressed, it was obvious that David's star had risen very high within the firm. He had rescued the business from ruin by retrieving Dass's property, despite the considerable risk to himself. He was also getting credit for urging the partners to dissolve Dass's account as swiftly as possible. David's prompting had resulted in a number of immediate changes being made – changes which would greatly reduce the firm's liability if Dass's estate found some basis for making a claim.

Reg assured him that a compassionate leave of absence would present no problem for someone of his good standing.

"It's my fiancée's family," David explained. On the bed, Susan twitched. "There's sort of a family crisis and I really want to help out. She's American and we may have to go over there."

David was silent while Reg responded. Susan was now sitting up on the bed watching him. David was saying, "Well, I haven't told that many people. We haven't set a date or anything."

Reg talked some more, then David said, "Well that's very kind of you Reg. Please express my thanks to the other partners too for being so understanding."

Another pause as Reg spoke. Then David said, "Well that certainly makes things easy for me. I'll call in a fortnight, then, let you know how it's all going. Thanks again."

He hung up. Turning to Susan, he said, "Wow. They're thinking of making me a partner. Reg practically insisted I take some leave. Sounds like we're *both* getting promotions."

Susan got up from the bed and came over to the writing desk. She slid down to sit on David's lap, hooking her arms around his neck. She put on her breathless Southern Belle accent. "And what about your poor little fi-an-cée?" She sang the three syllables.

David looked a little awkward, but put his arms around her too and said, "I thought if I told them I'd only just met you, then my running off round the world with you might sound strange. This way's easier if you end up having to talk to them for some reason."

She nuzzled his neck, "No proposal? No courtship? No *ring*?" she asked, teasingly.

"I'll tell you what," David said, "if we're still alive in a month's time, you can have anything you want – rings included."

Susan slid off his lap, pouting a little, "You're no fun any more," she sulked.

"I said you could have anything you wanted; what's not fun about that?" he asked.

"I liked it when I could tease you about stuff. You're supposed to wriggle more and blush. It's fun," she insisted.

He said, "Susan, I think maybe we're past that point. Compared with everything we've been through and all that's going on now, you can't expect a little teasing to even register."

"Oh well," she sighed, "I'll just have to think of a new game." She started to walk towards the bathroom. "We have been through a lot together," she conceded. Just before she disappeared through the doorway she said, thoughtfully, "Do you think we're ever going to have sex?"

Though she couldn't actually see David from the bathroom, her voice drifted back through the open door to reach him. "See? You can still squirm after all," she called.

* * *

They'd both laughed when Susan emerged from the bathroom, but it didn't last long. It was time to call Jan and any attempt at humour sounded false.

With the moment upon them, Susan's spirits plummeted. Her light-hearted, almost flippant façade only worked provided nothing reminded her of Dee and what she might be going through.

Unable to keep the thought from her mind any more, she tried to ask David what condition he thought they might get Dee back in – but she struggled to say the words. She wasn't able to frame the question in any way she could bear to utter.

From what she was able to get out, David guessed what she was driving at and gave her his opinion. He said that harming Dee at this point would get Jan nothing. In fact, from the point of view of being able to move freely with her, the less distressed she was the better. It only made sense for Jan to hurt her if he didn't feel he was getting full cooperation from them. Since their plan was to appear totally compliant, hurting Dee would only jeopardise that cooperation.

Susan wasn't wholly convinced, but his words obviously helped. She took a couple of minutes to compose herself and then picked up her mobile and dialled.

"Hello?" the cultured voice on the other end of the line said, "To whom do I have the pleasure of speaking?"

"It's Dee's sister," Susan said curtly.

His voice had an airy, theatrical quality as he said, "Ah, the elder Miss Milton. But look at the time. You really must have gone to ground if you've only just received my message. I wonder where you scurried off to. I was just beginning to think I'd have to raise the stakes."

"What have you done to Dee?" Susan said, "I want to talk to her."

Jan sounded less good humoured as he said, "Yes, well we'll get to that part in a minute. I'm sure you've watched enough television to have an inkling of the form here. We make our arrangements first, then you speak with your sister and we conclude with you making some empty threat about what you'll do to me if I put a scratch on her. Yes?"

Susan said nothing. Jan went on, "Silent agreement, I trust. Very good. Here's your first question: are you prepared to give me the documents I want?"

Susan hesitated a moment and said, "With some conditions."

"Ah, tut tut tut," Jan scolded, "We'll come on to the horse trading. Yes or no? I'm sure Dorothy here is hoping you'll say the right thing."

"Yes," Susan said, through tight lips.

"You're sure? Splendid. Dorothy is looking relieved. Now, have you got a pencil? I'll tell you what we're going to do."

"No," Susan said firmly.

"I beg your pardon? No, you haven't got a pencil?" Jan said.

"No, I don't want you to tell me your plan. I don't trust you," Susan said.

Jan sounded as though he was considering this, "I suppose trust is a rare commodity. Shall we ask Dorothy what she thinks you should do?"

Susan's breath caught in her throat and she bit her lip. "Just please listen to what I've got to say," she said.

There was a pause and then Jan said, "Alright. Tell me."

"You're not stupid," she said. "If I just bring you the collection, you have no reason to let me or Dee go. And you escaped when the police arrested you. We need to meet somewhere where you can't hurt us and then you have to agree to leave the country, straight afterwards."

"I see," Jan said. "But what choice do you have? Here is Dorothy, as frail a creature as I've ever seen. Think of what I can do to her if you don't cooperate. Just think." He sounded as though he were about to do something right that second.

Susan sounded frantic, "No, please don't. Don't hurt her. Just listen to me for a moment."

When Jan made no response, Susan said, "You want me to believe you'll let us go when you've got what you want, but now you're telling me how easy it would be to hurt my sister. You have to give me some reason to believe you won't just kill us both. If you don't, then you're not giving me a way to save her, you're offering me the chance to die with her." Susan was gasping as she talked, trying not to cry.

Again, Jan made no sound, but the line was still open. Susan said, "If you agree not to hurt her, if you agree to meet me somewhere where I might be safe, if you agree to leave the country as soon as you've got what you want, then I'll bring you the collection. But don't ask me to commit suicide when it won't even help Dee."

Jan said, "Tell me what you propose." He sounded angry and dangerous.

Susan said, patiently, "We meet at an airport – in the departure lounge. You come without any hand luggage and I'll watch you walk through the metal detectors. So no gadgets or weapons." This had been one of the things Susan and David had agreed. Susan would show no sign that she believed in magic. She would also make no mention of David. She went on, "I'll print a copy of the collection and have it ready for you. If you try to take it from me or you don't bring Dee, I'll destroy it. I'll use water-soluble paper, so you might want to be careful how you handle it."

"Go on," Jan said, sounding good humoured, almost amused, once again.

"Once we've made our exchange, I'll take Dee with me and we'll get on a plane. You get on yours and you don't come back; you let us get on with our lives," she paused a moment. "You'll need to buy Dee a ticket and you'll need her passport, which I'll leave at the information desk."

"Very good," Jan chuckled. "Am I allowed to make a suggestion? I take your point; if I want you to risk your neck then I need to offer you a little reassurance. I could give you my word that all I want is the collection, but I can see you might not be swayed."

Jan cleared his throat. "So why don't I make it easy for you. I'll stay away completely. I'll send someone harmless, my little friend Sati. She's about nineteen, skinny as a beanpole. She'd come up to Dorothy's shoulder. I'll tell her to wear something impractical for concealing weapons."

Susan was stuck for something to say. He continued, "I'll still leave the country. That fits very nicely with my plans, but little Sati I think, needs to remain behind. How about you and her take domestic flights? It's easier for you both to get home; you can get a train if you don't want to fly and it means we don't have to muck about with passports. She'll take a longer flight, let's say Aberdeen, and you can have your pick of the shorter trips. How does that suit you?"

"I…" Susan wasn't sure, "I suppose so," she said, sceptically.

"It's everything you were asking for and more besides. I have one or two things to do tomorrow," he coughed and cleared his throat again, "but Wednesday should give us time to arrange things."

Susan said, "And you won't even be there?"

Jan replied, "Nowhere near. I would expect you to destroy the collection if you come to believe otherwise, but I won't be nearby, I promise you. Good enough?"

Susan hesitated for a few seconds and then simply said, "Yes."

Jan said, "Well, shall we say 2pm at Gatwick North Terminal? And I expect you'll want a few words with your sister. Now don't be alarmed, but it's better all round if she remembers as little of this ordeal as possible. For that reason, you may detect the effects of Valium when you speak with her. I'm sure you wouldn't wish her to be frantic."

There was a pause and then Dee's voice said, "Hello?" She sounded groggy.

Susan's hand flew to her mouth. "Dee, it's Susan. Don't worry about anything, we're going to take care of everything."

"Susie? It's really you?" Dee said, slurring her words.

Susan said, "It's Susan, Dee. Dee, are you OK? Are you alright?"

Dee said, "Oh yeah." She sounded confused. "Maybe a little sleepy."

Then Jan came back on the line. "Let me know if there's anything else I can do for you." Then he hung up.

Susan set the phone down and turned to David, her eyes bright with tears. When she finally spoke, she said, "I think Dee's alright and I think he's going to let us have her back."

David came over and wrapped his arms around Susan and they sat that way, not moving, for a long time.

CHAPTER 33

TWO DAYS LATER
WEDNESDAY 30TH APRIL

"I think I can see her," Susan said.

A glass wall separated the shops and seating of the departure lounge from the security area. Susan and David were standing looking through the glass at the three lines of people who were shuffling towards them – each line making its way toward a metal-detector arch. Adjacent to each arch stood an x-ray machine.

The woman Susan had been staring at turned to talk to a friend, revealing her features for the first time. She was laughing as she turned. It wasn't Dee.

David said, "Do you know what I like about going to the dentist's?"

Susan turned to look at him momentarily, grateful for the distraction, but sceptical about this particular remark. "You like going to the dentist's?"

"How long have you been in Britain? It's sarcasm. I hate going to the dentist's." He shrugged his shoulders in a caricature of tough posturing and said, "As you can imagine, I don't care that much about the pain, but I'm not too enthusiastic about the feeling of powerlessness. Not appealing." He went on, "Anyway, the bit that always amuses me is when they take a dental x-ray and everyone runs out of the room to hide. I mean it's perfectly safe for me, but they still scatter like, er, rabbits," he said, looking unsure about his choice of simile.

Susan's eyes were flicking from person to person, scanning the crowds entering the security area. She paused for a brief moment, considering David's words, and said, "I think it's the fact that you get two zaps a year and they'd get twenty a day."

"I know," David said, lazily, "So how do you think these guys feel?" David indicated the nearest operator of the x-ray machine. "Spending all day sitting nine inches from a continuously operating x-ray source powerful enough to see the inside of a metal briefcase."

Susan snorted but didn't reply.

A moment later, she said, "It's her."

David had been checking a different queue. Now he followed Susan's gaze and picked out a tall, slim girl with dark hair just entering the security area: Dee. She was wearing a black mohair jumper and white jeans which Susan could see even from this distance were filthy. Dee seemed unsteady on her feet and her arm was looped through the arm of another girl several inches shorter than her.

The smaller girl had olive skin and black hair. Her features might have originated in India, though her attire certainly hadn't. She was wearing skin-tight purple trousers in tissue-thin rayon, silver boots and a stretchy pink t-shirt too small even for her slight frame. The t-shirt said 'Babe' across the front in silver glitter. It was a cheap and cheerful party outfit worn by a girl young enough and attractive enough to make it seem fun – except it looked uncomfortably out of place here – especially when contrasted with the girl's drawn expression. The dark smudges under her eyes suggested anything but a fun-loving existence. They gave her the appearance of someone almost sick with worry.

As they watched, the Asian girl jerked Dee forward, moving her several steps closer to the x-ray machine. Despite Dee's drugged and scruffy appearance, she still looked healthier than the girl holding her arm.

David said wonderingly, "She can't be an adept, can she?"

Susan also sounded surprised, "Less adept, more addict, I'd say. She reminds me of some of the girls I saw at the shelter when I was volunteering. She looks kind of like a hooker – and not a very successful one."

David was beginning to register disgust as he stared at the girl who was dragging Dee towards them. His voice was free of any humour as he said, "I see what he meant: she's not hiding any weapons."

"Well," Susan said, "we should probably still be on our guard. We'll wait until they're through the metal detectors and then drop back a bit."

Dee and then her minder passed through the arch of the metal detector without triggering the alarm. They had no hand luggage beyond their mobiles and Dee's small purse.

Susan said to David, "You probably shouldn't risk her seeing us together."

David nodded and moved away to stand by one of the public telephones. He picked up the receiver and began muttering indistinct nonsense as though in the middle of a call. His sidelong glance alternated between Susan and the two girls approaching her.

Susan had her carrier bag in one hand and an open bottle of mineral water in the other. Inside the bag, a sheaf of white, laser-printed paper was visible through the transparent sides. She stood stiffly in the centre of the departure lounge, more or less in the path of those emerging from the security area.

Dee spotted Susan and reacted with a bleary smile, but in slow motion, as though she was too drunk to know quite what was happening. Susan's face was a rigid mask.

"You're Sati," Susan said to the Asian girl.

The girl's tense face wrinkled in disgust at Susan's words. "No, I'm Priya. That's what he calls me, though. It's some sort of joke," she said, almost spitting the words out in her tired London whine.

Susan looked at Dee and then back to the girl. "You haven't hurt her?" Susan asked.

"I haven't hurt anybody," she said and sighed deeply – an involuntary sound she didn't appear to realise she was making.

"You don't work for Jan?" Susan asked, tentatively.

The girl gave a joyless laugh. "You've got some papers to give me," she said, "I'm not to come back without them."

Susan looked unsure. The beginnings of concern for the girl crept into her voice, "Is he threatening you?" she asked.

"What do you think?" the girl said angrily, as though the words were exhausting the last of her energy. She held out her hand.

Susan looked at her for a moment, confused, as though she were being asked to shake hands, and then she realised the meaning of the gesture and placed the plastic bag in the outstretched hand.

Grasping the bag, the girl gave Dee a little shove in Susan's direction. Dee tottered forward a couple of steps into Susan's arms.

Through clenched teeth, Priya said, "Hope your sister's alright." Then she turned and walked away before Susan could say anything more.

When Priya had disappeared, David came forwards and helped get Dee to one of the nearby seats. He said, "No one appeared to be watching you. It was just the girl."

They sat together, Susan stroking Dee's hair. Dee's head was resting on Susan's shoulder, her eyelids drooping. Susan said, "That girl seems like just as much of a victim as we are. God knows what he's holding over her."

David looked down at Dee, taking in her slack features and dirty clothes. "How is she?" he asked.

Susan lifted Dee's head and looked into her eyes. Dee smiled lopsidedly back at Susan. "Doped to the gills, but she doesn't seem to have a scratch on her. If it's just Valium, it should wear off in a few hours." Susan wrapped her arms around Dee, squeezing her gratefully, rocking them both slightly as she did so. Dee didn't resist.

After a few moments, Susan said, "Help me get her to the gate." Her face showed that she was holding back any sense of relief for the time being. Her features were set in the same slight frown she had worn for the last hour.

* * *

An hour and a half later, they were in the air. Dee was by the window, still drowsy and not quite up to speaking, but she was nowhere near as listless and groggy as she had been. Susan sat in the middle, with David taking the aisle seat.

Just as the seat belt signs went off, Susan turned to David and said, "What am I missing? Have we done it? Have we got away with it?"

David said, "You've been holding your breath for about two hours now, haven't you?"

She gave him a nervous smile. "Uhuh," she agreed.

"Well," David said, "You, me and Dee all seem to be in one piece. It's looking pretty hopeful, I think."

Susan said, "You think it's safe for me to let my breath out?"

He reached across and took her hand. He nodded.

"Thanks," she said. "I want you to know I realise it wasn't easy for you to let me plan all this and for you to just follow my lead, and I really appreciate the fact that you did it despite how difficult it was."

David took in her little speech. "You thought it all through, you came up with a great plan," David said by way of explanation, "at *least* as good as anything I would have thought of. I…" he hesitated.

"What?" she said, smiling, encouraging him to continue.

"It's just that I was hoping we could talk about this stuff," he said.

"About what? I can't think of anything to say except 'thank you'," she said.

David said carefully, "I mean about why it was… an issue in the first place. You know, the trust thing?" He paused, "I know it's not the best time, but it's as good a moment as we've had for a long while and I need to talk about this sooner rather than later."

Susan looked uncomfortable but she didn't try to stop him talking.

He drew in his breath and said, "Susan, I can see that you've got some feelings for me, whatever you say. And I, um, well I hope you know how I feel about you, how much I care about you." He smiled. "I just want to… to settle all this… whatever-it-is that's in the way – whatever it is that's not right between us." He came finally to the point, "I'm hoping you might have got to the point where you feel you can trust me."

Susan looked awkward, shifting in her seat and considering her words before saying, "It's not quite as simple as that," she said.

"Sure. OK," he accepted, "But that's why I want to talk about it."

Susan said, "You really want to do this?" She didn't sound angry; she sounded like she was hoping that he'd say 'no'.

David said softly, "Don't you think I've done enough, shown that I'm prepared to risk enough, that I deserve to know?" He said it gently, but the challenge in his words was still evident.

Susan said, "Alright. If you're sure you want to have this conversation." She was gathering herself to speak, obviously not relishing it, but pushing ahead before her resolve weakened. "It's not so much about whether I trust you or not; it's that you don't trust me – at least not in the one way that I need you to."

Her voice became tender. "I don't blame you for that; it's just how you're made. But ever since I met you it's been obvious to me how you think. It's just not part of your nature to let someone else tell you how to make your decisions – to let them know what's really going on in your head. You can do it if you try, but it's an effort and every time you're put under pressure, you go back to what you know: thinking and acting on your own – looking out for other people, but not consulting them first."

She laid a hand on his arm, "You can see I'm not criticising you, can't you? It's just who you are. Just like it's the way I'm made that I can't handle it. I bet there are a million girls who would love you to take care of them, to take over, but I'm not one of them. I can't be."

David tried to reply, "I don't... I haven't really..." But he couldn't finish the sentence.

Susan said, "That's why I got so angry every time you ran off by yourself without talking to me. I mean yes you were being irresponsible some of the time too, but it got to me because it was rubbing my nose in the fact that I had two choices and both of them were lousy: I could let you sweep me off my feet or I could push you away. What I couldn't have – and what I need – is a proper partnership. I don't need saving, not if it means surrendering, letting go of who I am. That's what my mother did – and it didn't work. She let my father take over and it made her miserable. It was the only way she could be with him, but it wasn't right. When I look at what it did to her, I realise that I'd rather be on my own." She was close to tears as she spoke those last words.

David was struggling to frame his reply. He wanted to dispel what she'd said, to disprove it. "That's not true," he said. "I mean it's true I've been like that in the past, but it's not set in stone. I have more respect for you than anyone else I know and I let you do your thing when it came to getting Dee back, didn't I? Not a word of complaint."

Susan nodded, "And it nearly killed you," she said, "I could see that. Which is why I'm so grateful you did it anyway."

David said, "You're wrong, Susan. OK, it ruffled my feathers a bit, and I suppose you're right, I have never placed myself in someone else's hands like that before. You've read me correctly: I don't like letting someone else into my thoughts. But it's different with you. I trust you. That first time might have been difficult, but I'd do it again. You don't need to give in to me. You don't need to change. I like you as you are." He stopped talking, suddenly looking vulnerable, uncomfortable and then he pushed on, his voice sounding strange as he said, "Or to be a bit more accurate, I love you as you are."

Now Susan was crying – gently, not hurt, but too moved not to cry. She sniffed and said, "I want to believe that. I want to believe it more than anything. I'm doing my best, but you have to understand who I am." She looked over at Dee who was stirring in her sleep, shifting about in her seat. Susan lowered her voice, "When we were growing up, all my parents did was push me. They were only happy when I was achieving something. Dee… God, Dee just had to be, to exist, that was enough. Wherever she went, she made friends. She didn't have to do anything, she was just herself and people responded. I've never been like that. Unless I'm pushing myself I'm not happy, I don't feel happy with myself, I don't feel… lovable. I'm not sure I *am* that lovable unless I'm busy doing something I do well. I'm not someone people just adore because of who I am. If I'm special in any way it's because of what I'm capable of. Which is why I can't follow in my mother's footsteps. I often wish I was like Dee, but I'm not."

Susan stopped speaking, letting her words sink in. After a moment she realised she could hear something from the seat beside her. She pivoted round to see that Dee was awake and she was laughing. It was quiet laughter, but nonetheless it was deep – slow belly-laughs which shook her whole body.

"Dee," Susan said, concerned, "are you OK?"

Dee continued to laugh for a minute and then said, "Four years and eighty-eight grand." She laughed some more, apparently helpless to stop herself.

David and Susan watched her, confused – relieved that she was awake and talking, but disconcerted by her behaviour.

Getting herself under control, Dee said, "I went to a therapist every week for four years to talk about exactly how charming and lovable I felt. How many hours is that? I don't know. But never once did it occur to me that I was the lucky one."

She sat up straight now and twisted to talk to Susan. "You're right, Mom and Dad never gave me a hard time; they didn't bitch at me about my grades, they didn't nag me if I wasn't learning new things, if I wasn't getting picked for school teams. In fact, they didn't really complain about anything, whatever I did, however late I stayed out or whoever I stayed out with. Towards the end, just before I left home, I was determined to get them to notice me, to get their attention away from you for just one second. And you know what? I couldn't. So I left. I left them with their one perfect daughter, the one they cared about."

Dee started laughing again and then said, "And guess what? You felt unloved too. The one who got every second of Mom's attention every day of every week; you felt unloved too."

Susan looked shocked, "I never knew," she said.

Dee shrugged, "Well I guess it's not everyday chit-chat. 'You feel unloved? Hey, me too Sis.'" She paused a moment and said, "I went to see Mom about it last year. My therapist thought it would be good for me. And maybe it was. It doesn't change how I feel about me, but it stopped me resenting Mom." She had Susan's total attention now. She went on, "You know what she told me? She sat me down, like I was a kid again, and said, 'But Dorothy, honey, your father and I decided not to treat you the same because you weren't the same.' Mom said, 'I grew up trying to be a good daughter just like your father tried to be a good son. It didn't matter who we wanted to be, we were expected to behave a certain way and we were treated a certain way. Your father and I promised ourselves we wouldn't put you and Susan through that. We'd acknowledge that you and your sister are individuals, with your own personalities and strengths and we'd encourage those strengths, not stifle them by trying to get you to conform. We never pushed you the way we pushed Susan because we could see that you already had all you needed to make it in the world. Susan we worried wouldn't get there without a push and if she didn't reach her potential we knew she'd be miserable.'"

Susan was sniffling again, "She said all that?"

Dee nodded, "I can't promise I've got every word right, but it's close. Even if I wasn't a journalist, I'd remember that conversation."

Susan said, "I always figured she was trying to live through me, do all the stuff she'd always regretted not doing."

Dee said, "Who knows? But I can tell you what she believes, because I could see in her eyes that she meant what she was telling me. She believes she pushed you because she knew how it felt not to be stretched, to fall short of what she could have been and she was determined to spare you that pain."

Susan was crying now and it was setting Dee off. Susan turned and wrapped her arms around Dee and Dee did the same.

"Jesus," David said, pretending to be disgusted. "We're in Britain now. You're not in the land of the spontaneous group-hug anymore."

"Shut up," Susan sniffed, separating her right arm from Dee and reaching over to grab David. She pulled him to her so that the three of them were pressed together.

They stayed that way for nearly a minute with Dee and Susan alternately sniffing and sobbing quietly, almost happily. After a moment, David stopped resisting. The clinch was only broken when a stewardess stopped at their aisle and asked if everything was alright.

David separated himself from the huddle and said, "Family celebration," indicating the two tearful girls, still hugging. "You wouldn't have any champagne, would you?"

"Certainly sir, I'll see what we've got," the stewardess said, bustling away.

"None for me," Dee said, letting go of Susan and clutching her head. "I feel worse than the morning after my twenty-first. You guys celebrate my safe return for me. And maybe when you're done, you can tell me what's been going on while I've been on my little pharmaceutical vacation. Nothing about the last few days makes any sense and oh my god," Susan and David both looked round to see what had alarmed Dee. She was looking down at her grubby white jeans, "What the hell am I wearing?" she said.

CHAPTER 34

Susan and Dee were hugging again as they stood to one side of the security gate at Manchester Airport. Passing them were a steady stream of people making their way through to international departures. David stood next to the two girls, one of his hands resting on Dee's shoulder, his foot on the edge of their luggage trolley.

Susan said, "I don't think it'll be for long, Dee. It's your choice, but Lincoln and Petey will take good care of you if you let them. They mainly work relocating women with abusive husbands, so this isn't too much of a stretch for their professional skills. Anyway, they're funny guys, tough as shoe-leather and they know how to make people feel safe." She gave Dee a final squeeze. "And I promise I'll let you know the instant we can all get back to normal."

Dee nodded, "How will I recognise them when I get to Newark?"

Susan laughed, "You'll recognise them. Big white guy, medium-sized black guy – they'll be arguing. Ask information to page the Zorro Brothers if you have any problems. That's what they called themselves when we used to work together."

Dee laughed, "Oh right, because you were…"

Susan finished the sentence for her, "Zorro's little sister. Exactly." She was laughing too.

Then Dee became serious and hugged Susan one last time, "You be careful." She looked over to David, "You both be careful. Whatever it is you're caught up in, I hope it gets sorted out soon. When the craziness is over, maybe you can both come visit. I'm betting you'll need a vacation before much longer. I know I will."

"Take care, Dee," David said, leaning over to kiss her on the cheek.

Dee picked up her carrier bag – it held magazines and various goodies for the flight – and walked away from them. She was wearing the clothes she'd bought in one of the airport's shops after they'd landed; her previous outfit had gone straight into the store's rubbish bin.

With much waving and blowing of kisses back at Susan, Dee presented her boarding card to the woman on the security desk and disappeared in the direction of the departure lounge.

Once Dee was out of sight, Susan said, "I hope there *is* a point where we can get back to normal. I just want to get her safe first, then I'll worry about what happens if we're still in this position a month from now."

David said, "I can't see it taking that long. Between you and me, we'll come up with a way out of this before then." As he spoke, he slipped an arm around her waist and she leaned in to him, relaxing.

David pointed to a row of seats nearby, "Can we sit down for a couple of minutes? I'm knackered." Then he added, "What was the

Zorro thing about? I didn't follow."

Susan said, "Come on, you must know Zorro? They got that show over here didn't they? Fighting for justice et cetera?" She made a sweep with her hand, whipping out the letter 'Z' in the air.

David said, "Yeah, yeah. I know who Zorro is. How does that link to you?"

She stopped dead, turning to face him, slightly puzzled. "Did we never get around to this conversation?" She frowned, "I guess we didn't," she shrugged. "Well, that's what I do when I'm not being a history nerd: I fence. In fact..." she said, adopting a swagger for a moment, "when I was a teenager I was told I might go all the way, might end up on the Olympic team." She made a face, "It didn't work out because of us moving around so much with Dad's work, but I was on track for a while. Anyway, when I was about twelve and I first got the fencing bug, I used to pester everyone, wanting to know if Zorro ever had a little sister. I think I was hoping for a role model I could identify with – ideally one who wore braces. I don't actually remember it, but it's one of those family stories that's now passed into legend." She gave him a silly sort of grin and shrugged.

Then she turned serious for a second, adding, "That's what pushed me into practicing with Jan's tribute. I figured if adepts fight with blades, it's only the magic side of things that would put me at a disadvantage. I mean, if I can learn to make a shield the way they do, I might actually stand a chance against one of them."

David was looking confused. "Blades? I'm not following."

Susan looked shocked, "Jesus. Didn't we talk about this either? I know the Professor and I had a really long chat about it. Shit. Sorry. It's been a hectic week," she said, looking embarrassed. She explained, "Adepts can't use magic to attack each other, right?"

"Yeah," David nodded, slightly impatient, "I got that bit."

Susan squeezed his arm, meaning 'sorry', and said, "So they have to find some other way to hurt each other. But the thing is, an adept can just wrap a shield right round himself and he's safe – so you can't force anyone to fight if they don't want to. The problem is that with a complete shield in place you can't move – it's a bit like being inside a block of ice – you're protected, but you're kind of trapped too. So if you want to remain mobile, or you want to be able to lash out at the other guy, you can only make a partial shield – one with gaps in it – gaps you can stick a sword through. That's how they fight." She acknowledged, "I mean I'm sure they prefer to kill their enemies while they're asleep in their beds, but if that fails they use swords."

David asked, "Not guns?"

Susan shook her head, "Think about it," she said, helping David push the trolley towards the nearby seating, "You want to fight someone and you've both got guns, so you both create big shields. Obviously you're only going to let your shield down at the instant you fire. But then the other guy's shield stops your bullet. So you both need to fire at the same time, like in a duel, because that's the only time both shields are down. If it works you're both dead, and if someone's timing is off you're both alive – and either way it sucks. But swords can be used defensively; even with quite small shields you're not totally exposed because you're using your blade to defend yourself. In those kind of fights, most of the damage gets done with ripostes. You let the other guy's sword through and then turn your defence into a counter-attack, because that's the moment you know where the gap in the other guy's shield is."

David asked, "If you can make a shield at will, how does anyone ever get hit?"

Susan, "Because it's not fast like moving your arm, it's slower, like moving something heavy. You can move or change a shield like this," she swept her arms around a little, like she was dancing, "But not like this," she executed a little lunge-parry-riposte at startling speed. A nearby child tugged its mother's arm, pointing at Susan, but by the time the mother looked round there was nothing to see.

They sat down, "That's…" David said, obviously wondering what it was, "pretty amazing," he concluded.

"Yeah," Susan said, "Isn't it? Even if I'm kind of amateurish when it comes to creating a shield, just wearing tribute and maintaining minimum concentration will stop another adept using magic on me. So I just need to trust to my mad fencing skills. I reckon a crappy adept who was good with a sword could take someone whose abilities were the other way round."

David volunteered, "Well, I've done a certain amount of kendo."

"Hmm," Susan said, unconvinced, "That's mainly a slicing weapon. It's gonna be tricky to slice, because the blade covers so much territory; you're likely to catch the other guy's shield wherever it is. You really want a thrusting weapon, like a rapier. You follow back along the other guy's line with your riposte." She thought for a moment, "I guess if the other guy had a slicing weapon too it might work, because he'd need to pretty much dispense with his shield in order to swing it. But unless you get to choose the other guy's weapon for him, I wouldn't try it."

David looked irritated, "Nearly fifteen years of martial arts and none of it is any use."

Susan said, "Well, it hasn't exactly been wasted. With your speed and strength and balance, you'd learn to fence in half the time it would take any normal mortal."

She gave him a twinkly smile and added, "So you'd only need eight years to get as good as me," she pointed to the people around her, "instead of twice that for everyone else."

David gave her a sarcastic smile.

Susan leaned on him, snuggling into his jacket and said, "I'm sorry I hadn't told you all that stuff. Especially after my big speech about you not including me when you're busy devising your grand schemes."

He enfolded her with his arms. "Well, I know now," he said, and then added more graciously, "And you intended to tell me; that's the difference. It's just that the world's been wall-to-wall mental lately."

She buried her face in his collar, pressing the tip of her nose against his neck. "You forgive me then?" she asked, indistinctly.

"Mmm," he agreed. "Not only are you forgiven, but I'm going to find a way to prove that you're officially part of the inner circle, when it comes to planning my life. That's a promise."

She sighed against his neck – happy and exhausted at the same time. "OK," she said sleepily.

A few moments later, David's mind had wandered sufficiently for him to say, "When they decided to make these seats from sheet steel, do you think they were worried that too much comfort would tempt people to sit here all day and they'd miss their flights?"

Susan shifted slightly and mumbled, "They are kind of brutal."

He said, "The design brief was obviously 'whatever else, make sure their arses want to leave the country'."

Susan gave a muffled giggle and then lifted her head, sitting upright in her seat. "I'm going to find a bathroom and then get us some coffee. Watch my bag will you?" she said.

"Yup," he replied. He glanced up at a digital display showing the time. "They'll probably let us check in soon."

She nodded. "Why don't you give the Professor a call, let him know how we're getting on. I'll have a word with him when I get back." She gave him a rapid peck on the cheek and then stood up. She glanced around, orienting herself and then set off.

David sat for a few minutes, lost in his own thoughts, before he pulled his mobile out of his jacket pocket and paged through the phone's memory looking for the Professor's number.

A few moments later it was ringing. "Cambridge 2616," the Professor said.

"Professor Shaw – Joseph – it's David."

The Professor sounded delighted, "David. What news from the front?"

David smiled, "So far, so good. Dee's boarding her plane about now, Susan's just off getting some coffee and I'm sitting around doing nothing. Things seem to be looking up."

"I'm delighted. I gathered from your tone that the news was good." The Professor's voice took on a note of concern as he said, "Susan's sister: how is she faring?"

"Better than I really dared hope," David said, gravely. "Physically she's fine, though a bit groggy. He kept her tranquillised, which probably made it a lot easier on her. I'm sure it wasn't his intention, but the whole thing seems like a dream to her. She knows she was kidnapped and taken somewhere, but by the time it had sunk in, she was chock-full of Valium. Could have been a lot worse."

"Still, the poor girl," the Professor said, "One can only imagine."

David went on to say, "You should have seen the girl escorting Dee; she's obviously being coerced into helping."

A moment later he picked up his original thread, "No, it all went perfectly. The only slight disappointment, if you can find fault in such a lucky escape, is that Dee can't tell us much about Jan. She doesn't know where she was taken even. The only thing she could say was that she overheard the tail-end of a phone-call as Jan was coming in to check on her. She heard him mention Section Five. It means nothing to us; we wondered if you'd heard of it. I assume it's some sort of... er, what's the male equivalent of coven?"

The Professor answered mechanically, as though his thoughts were elsewhere, "A coven is a collection of witches, who may be of either gender," he stated, but there was a note of alarm in his voice as he went on to say, "Section Five is not a coven, however. At least not the Section Five that I'm familiar with."

David asked, "Well, what is it then?"

The Professor said, rather gravely, "It's an old name for MI5. It's the domestic intelligence service."

David didn't know what to make of this news. "Why would he be talking to MI5?" David looked thoughtful, "Although it does make you wonder what they know. Do you suppose the government is aware of adepts?"

Instead of answering, the Professor asked, "Did Dorothy overhear the context in which the name was mentioned?"

David rubbed a hand across his forehead in a gesture of weariness. He said, "Sort of. She thought she heard him say, 'You're supposed to be Section Five, you tell me.' Though she wasn't too sure about it."

"David, this is a concern," the Professor said. "When I discussed recent events with Susan, we concluded that Jan operated alone, at least in terms of what you might call 'field operations'. We've seen no sign that he has willing foot soldiers he can call upon. But on the other hand, we thought it likely that he had contacts he *could* go to for information or perhaps equipment. We had tentatively ruled out contacts within the police force, because he seemed to be in the dark regarding the investigation into the Marker's theft. Yet somehow he was able to locate Dorothy. And his information on Dass's travel plans were spot on too. The latter could be explained by the existence of a secret ally within Dass's organisation. Dorothy's whereabouts, however, would have required a different sort of informant."

David asked, "Was he tracking her credit card? Might someone be passing him that sort of information?" Then he muttered to himself, "Though he didn't seem to be able to track Susan's or mine."

The Professor obviously had a different thought in mind. He asked, "Do you know if Dorothy had made recent travel plans? MI5 routinely keep an eye on who's entering or leaving the country."

David said, "I don't know how far she'd progressed with them, but she was making arrangements to return home just before she was snatched." He was beginning to sound very worried as he said, "You think he might have traced her through a plane ticket? Oh my god." David was on his feet now looking around him.

As David anxiously scanned the throng of people in the terminal, looking for Susan's face, the Professor was saying, "MI5 would certainly keep track of flight bookings. It wouldn't be uncommon for them to search for particular surnames. From what little my sister used to say on the subject, it seems that sort of information is freely available to the department. Advances in computerisation and the current paranoia over air travel will have made it even more common."

David was moving towards where he'd seen Susan last. He said, "Susan reckoned Jan came around to our plan quite suddenly. We assumed we'd manipulated him into it. Stupid! It was probably the mention of airports that got him interested." He glanced back at their luggage, sitting abandoned now.

Unsure what to do, he strode back towards the trolley, to where they'd been sitting, and stood up on the seat. His eyes urgently searched the crowd, flitting from one stranger to another, looking for that one familiar face.

The phone was still to his ear, "He suggested we take a domestic flight; he said it was easier for all of us because it was a shorter round trip. We agreed because we didn't want him to know we were planning to leave the country. He also volunteered to send someone harmless instead of coming himself, which sounded great." David's voice was tight with tension. "But that would have left him free to come up here ahead of us."

The Professor had already thought it through. Quietly, and without optimism in his voice, he asked, "You are trying to locate Susan, yes?"

David was still searching, "I can't see her anywhere," he said, sounding wretched. He looked up at the time on the digital display; she had been gone fifteen minutes. He was still thinking aloud as he spoke to the Professor, "He even volunteered to take the farthest location for his assistant. He wanted to make sure we chose somewhere nearby."

The Professor said, quietly, "I'm rather afraid that once he discovered your destination, he intended to drive there."

David's eyes had stopped roving across the crowd. They weren't focussed on anything now. David had arrived at the same conclusion. He said, "Because if he had someone with him for the return journey, someone travelling against their will, he couldn't take them on a plane."

"Quite so," the Professor gently concurred. He said calmly, "David? I'm going to be going on a trip shortly and I need to share a few of the details with you. Why don't I leave you to look for Susan now and perhaps you'd be kind enough to telephone me back once your search is completed."

"Right," David said and hung up.

He almost seemed to be in shock. He climbed down slowly

from the seat he'd been standing on, his movements tentative. Then he put the phone away, taking several attempts before he found his pocket. Then he shook his head sharply, focussing on his surroundings.

David turned to the middle-aged couple who had just sat down several seats along from him and said, "You couldn't keep an eye on my bags for a moment, could you?"

They looked uncomfortable and it was obvious that they were going to say 'no'. David said, pleadingly, "Just a couple of minutes. I'll be right back."

"You shouldn't really even ask me that," the woman said, "Don't you watch the news?"

David turned away from them. He looked at the luggage. Out of the corner of his eye, he could see the couple watching him. If he left now they'd alert the police.

Then something occurred to him. He grabbed Susan's bag from where she'd been sitting and sat down with it on his lap. He rooted through the contents. No phone.

Fishing out his own mobile, he brought up Susan's number and pushed the green button. Holding it to his ear he could hear it begin to ring. Four times it rang, then five.

Finally it was answered. Background noise: a car? A man's cultured voice said, "Interesting. So you're working together." He took a breath, "First things first: if you were very swift you might be able have the roads blocked, but I think we both know it wouldn't stop me and it wouldn't get you Ms Milton back in anything like one piece."

David couldn't seem to find his voice.

Jan continued speaking, "I don't hold a grudge," he paused to cough unpleasantly, "in fact I find your deception rather endearing. You must have been so proud of yourselves." His tone grew colder,

"On the other hand, of course, you must realise that your credit has run out. I won't be listening to any more ingenious suggestions you might wish to make. You will simply do as you're told this time."

David's mind was racing. He licked his lips and found himself holding his breath as he struggled to take in this horrifying development.

"Hello?" Jan said, "You know, it would help us get this all sorted out if you'd be so kind as to speak when you're spoken to."

"Sorry," David said, without thinking. He hesitated a moment longer, his expression one of frantic concentration. Then he said, "I'm ready to do whatever you want, no argument, but there's something you need to know: Susan's sick. She has," he cleared his throat to disguise a moment's hesitation, "she's got liver cancer. She can't handle you drugging her like you did Dee – it could kill her." He gave Jan a second to consider this and said, "I know she'd do anything to stop you getting those papers, but you must promise me you'll ignore her if she suggests you drug her. Whatever those papers are, they're not worth her life. All I care about is keeping Susan safe. Look after her and you can have whatever you want." He sounded desperate, as though he could hardly think straight for the worry.

"Well, that's all very heart-warming, particularly the touching faith you have in my promises." Jan's voice was muffled for a moment, suggesting he was moving around, "She certainly looks healthy enough to me," he said after a moment, "but I've learned that looks can be deceptive. At any rate, I like your attitude. Do just as you're told and you'll have her back in no time. Simple obedience, no conditions."

David said, "No conditions from me, just prove to me that she's fit and well before we meet and I'll turn over the papers." His voice was closer to the tone he used when talking with Banjo – less cultured, less the voice of someone used to being in charge.

Jan said sharply, "No conditions except that one, you mean." But then he softened, "Which I can live with. It is traditional, after all." His voice took on a business-like quality, he was instructing David, talking down to him, "This level of obedience is good. But don't do any more thinking; don't get sneaky. I don't want you wasting your time coming up with some ingenious…" he broke off for a second, coughing again, "some ingenious little scheme that will get you killed. We'll meet tomorrow, when I say we'll meet, at a place of my choosing. You'll bring the papers and I'll bring your girlfriend. When you get there, you wait outside and phone me to say that you've arrived. I let you speak to her. If we're both happy with how that goes, you come inside and we perform the exchange. It'll be somewhere in Central London, so make sure you're in the vicinity by then. Anything you want to add?"

David said nothing.

Jan concluded, "Good boy," and hung up.

CHAPTER 35

THAT SAME AFTERNOON
WEDNESDAY 30TH APRIL

David called the Professor back a few minutes after his call to Jan. It had taken him a little while to compose himself before he was ready to talk to anyone.

The Professor answered the call immediately, saying, "Has he taken her?" the question coming without preamble.

"He's got her," David confirmed, the weight of the world in his voice.

A leaden silence lay between them. David eventually broke the spell by telling the Professor about his conversation with Jan and what he thought Jan's responses implied. David had formulated the beginnings of a plan while he had been talking to Jan, but – as he confessed to the Professor – there were huge holes in it.

He shared the few details he had worked out. "I want him to think that I'm reasonably brave and reasonably stupid. And macho wouldn't hurt either."

"Good, good," the Professor said encouragingly, "It seems to me you've been using your head in some dreadfully unsettling circumstances." The Professor's voice was full of grave energy.

David gave a weak smile and said, "I appreciate the moral support, Joseph. In case you were wondering, I am coping. Unfortunately I'm going to need to do a lot more than just cope."

He added, "I think the way to stay sane is just to think about nothing else except getting Susan back." David paused for a few moments and said, "The thing that's really giving me trouble is what to do about the collection. I don't suppose Susan would want me to let Jan anywhere near it, but I can't see any chance of getting her away from him unless I let him have what he wants."

The Professor said cautiously, "It seems to me that you're in an almost impossible situation. And I won't presume to tell you the best way to resolve it. You know as well as I do that if Jan is able to rejuvenate himself he will continue to ruin lives for as long as he walks this earth." He paused for emphasis and said, "But there have always been wicked men like him in the world – and you surely didn't make them the way they are."

David said nothing and the Professor tentatively offered a few more words. "I don't know if philosophy is appropriate at such a moment, but it seems to me that your dilemma is not an entirely new one. Many doctors have been asked to extend the life of a murderer or a tyrant and many have done so without qualms – and without the unbearable ultimatum you are confronted with." He took a deep breath, "Whatever you choose, you may end up beset by guilt – I would simply suggest that you choose whichever burden you think you will be most able to carry. That is all you can do: think about what you are best able to live with." He concluded, "You will certainly be in my thoughts."

David didn't respond. It wasn't clear how many of the Professor's words he had taken in or whether they had helped. The Professor didn't attempt to say more.

So their talk moved on to other matters. Before the original plan came unglued, David and Susan had been planning to travel on from Manchester to Spain. That thought abandoned, David was now planning to return to Gatwick as soon as he was able. He arranged to drive up to Cambridge later that evening and drop in on the Professor, with the aim of collecting a few of the things he would need the next day – the collection included.

Next David asked, "Do you happen to know the whereabouts of a good, modern chandler?"

Once the inevitable question had been resolved of how David came to be interested in such a thing, the Professor suggested a firm he had once used, many years before, and who he believed were still trading – though he could offer no reassurance that they had moved with the times.

Another thought occurred to David, "I've got a lot of planning to do. You haven't discovered anything I should know about – no new powers? Jan's got no tricks up his sleeve so far as you know?"

The Professor replied, "There can be no absolute guarantees. But the collection is remarkably consistent on the matter. I have Susan's translation here. Just give me a moment…" The Professor could be heard rustling papers. Then he came back on the line, "Here we are. Let me summarise it for you."

David listened in silence. The Professor said after a moment, "Some form of clairvoyance. The ability to heat or to cool. The ability to make what Susan refers to as a shield. A pushing force and a shattering force. And a healing ability which they can learn to influence. That, and the fact that magic protects against magic.

It's a formidable list, I'll admit, but it hasn't stopped many of their kind meeting sticky ends at the hands of ordinary citizens over the years."

David didn't reply, he was biting his lip and considering the Professor's words. After a few seconds of silence he brought himself back to the present and asked, as heartily as he could, "So what's this about a trip; when are you setting off?"

The Professor replied, "I thought it might be a good idea to make myself scarce and to spend a few weeks down in Cornwall. I will probably set off first thing in the morning. If all goes well, you will still be able to contact me. When Susan was staying with me, she suggested I might like to enter the twenty-first century – or at least make use of its technology. She had some specific suggestions and I have taken her advice. I now have a brand new laptop computer and a mobile telephone."

The Professor continued, "One of my very capable students is travelling down with me; she believes that a fortnight of diligent effort on her part, though not sufficient to turn me into what she calls a 'hacker', may suffice to impart a few of the basics. When you retrieve Susan, you can tell her my student is also helping me with PGP; she'll know what I mean."

David took down the Professor's new mobile phone number and his e-mail address and agreed to call as soon as he'd had any more contact with Jan. Then they said goodbye.

David was back at Gatwick by early evening. The next leg of the journey, from the airport to where his car was parked near Banjo's house, took longer than the trip from Manchester. He loaded his and Susan's luggage into the car, for want of anywhere better to stow it, and set off for Cambridge.

When he eventually arrived, the Professor welcomed him warmly. The two of them talked late into the night and it was nearly three o'clock by the time David had made his way home and closed the front door of his flat behind him.

The Professor had wondered about the wisdom of David returning to his own home. But David felt, with an exchange planned for the next day, there was little point in Jan coming for him now. Whatever the validity of that reasoning, each time David woke up with a start in his own bed, he found himself alone and unharmed.

David had come away from the Professor's with the paper originals of the collection, while the Professor now had the encrypted disc – and a mental note of the password. The papers were still there when paranoia got the better of David and he checked their hiding place at eight o'clock the next morning.

By half eight, he was on a bus heading into town to visit the chandler the Professor had mentioned.

By one in the afternoon he had ticked off all the items on his rather exotic shopping list. It was as he was walking back to his flat from the bus stop that his mobile rang. It was Susan's number.

"Yes," David said, answering the call, his tone as neutral as he could make it.

"Got a pen?" Jan's voice said, sounding jaunty.

David grabbed a pen from his pocket and snatched a receipt from one of his shopping bags. "Go ahead," he said.

"The priory church of Saint Bartholomew the Great," Jan said. "It's between Bart's Hospital and Smithfield Market. Be there at two-thirty this coming morning. Don't arrive early and don't bring anything with you except your phone and the collection. Call me on this number before coming through the door. Got all that?" Jan said, "I don't want any mistakes."

"I've got it," David said, his voice tight.

"And make sure you bring the real collection," Jan said, "I'll be giving you a little test before you're allowed in."

"OK," David said, sounding resigned.

Robert Finn

"Chin up," Jan said, "It's nearly over." He hung up.

David grabbed his purchases and walked quickly back to his flat. Half an hour later, he was trotting back the other way again, a full-sized hiking rucksack slung over his shoulder.

Chapter 36

The next night
Early friday 1st May

The church lay just outside London's old City walls, wedged into a corner where the normal rules of archaeology had lapsed. The new hadn't covered the old here, it had simply crowded it to one side.

The ancient church seemed to be set almost in the garden of a block of post-War council flats. The path to the main door of the church cut across the grass, but in a channel – being several feet lower than the much newer lawn around it. The buildings on either side loomed so close and so high that the church – despite its solid, Norman bulk – was almost hidden away until one was upon it.

At this time of night, all the lights inside the council flats were extinguished – only those on the outside walkways were still lit. The nearby market was silent and David encountered no one else as he walked up from the bay where he'd parked his car.

As he made his way along the path, the ground rose steadily around him until he stood just outside the church. He was carrying his phone in his right hand, a heavy flight case in his left. He was wearing a lightweight sweater and no jacket: an outfit ostentatiously devoid of good hiding places, unlikely to antagonise Susan's captor.

Pausing a few metres from the darkened vestibule, David set the case down for a second and dialled Susan's number. "I'm here," he said, when it was answered.

"Read me something from the collection," Jan instructed him.

"What?" David replied.

"Take a piece of paper out of the collection," Jan said in his lecturing, schoolmaster voice, "and read something to me from it."

David opened the flight case, lifted out one of the clear wallets and began to read a passage in Latin.

"Enough," Jan said, as though David's pronunciation offended him, "We're ready for you." There was a pause, some muffled words, and then Susan was saying tentatively, "David, it's me." Her tone was uncertain, but her voice was clear and strong – and she still sounded like Susan. Whatever her physical condition, in some important, fundamental sense she was unharmed.

Hearing her voice, David found himself imploring her, "Don't worry, Susan, don't worry."

Then it was Jan's voice again, saying, "Yes, yes," impatiently, cutting into David's reassurances. "Alive and well, as promised. Now, please join us," he said.

David ended the call and slid the phone into the pocket of his jeans. He pulled open the heavy oak door of the vestibule, letting it bang closed behind him, and crossed the flagstone floor, passing through the inner door and into the space beyond.

Inside, the church was like a great geode: enclosed and encrusted, dark and glittering, full of jutting pillars and cramped geometric niches – the high, vaulted centre was like the hollow at its mineral core.

Above the entrance, spreading up the back wall, was an elaborate church-organ surrounding a pulpit. Its chambered wooden mass now plugged the blunt stone end of the ancient chapel like a wasps' nest.

At the heart of the church lay a stone font flanked on all sides by rows of low pews. At the edges of its mosaic floor, walls of stacked stone arches rose three tiers high to support the roof's shadowed spars. Beyond the pillars of the lowest tier, a cloistered path encircled the whole expanse, leading back to the entrance.

As David stepped out of the cloisters and entered the high-ceilinged space, he saw Jan and Susan standing at its centre. Susan was leaning heavily against the blocky, limestone font.

What light there was came from flickering clusters of votive tapers and from a dozen or more heavy candles, thick as artillery shells, held in tall metal standards.

As Jan turned to face him, David could see that his appearance was altered. An ink-like stain had spread across his neck and the bottom of one cheek, black like an unhealed bruise. And yet this was not the damage David had seen the last time the two met; this was some new corruption. One side of Jan's neck now bulged as though something were forming within.

Despite these signs of unchecked morbidity, his movements were agile and fluid, and a new gold circlet glinted on his forehead.

David's gaze shifted to Susan. She was still leaning on the font, but now he could see that this was not through weariness; she was tied to it. Two ropes were wrapped around its solid base. One extended a metre out from the stonework to loop around her ankles, binding them; the other was fastened to the central chain of a pair of chrome handcuffs which secured her wrists.

Physically, she seemed unharmed. She looked tired and tense at the same time and she returned David's gaze anxiously, searching his face as though she hoped to learn something important.

The font she was anchored to lay at the meeting point of two aisles, which ran at right angles to each other, cutting through the rows of pews. One path stretched the length of the central space, following the line of the roof, the other spanned its much narrower middle. Together they formed a slender cross with Susan at its heart.

David began the walk down the longer aisle towards the two figures. Jan waited for him, watching every step intently.

When he was still fifteen metres from Jan, he stopped and set the case down. Then, releasing its catches, he flipped the top open and stepped back. He moved to one side, retreating between the pews, leaving the case sitting by itself in the aisle.

"Where are you going?" Jan demanded, testily, as David withdrew.

"There's your papers," David announced, pointing to the case, as though it was an explanation. He lowered himself onto a pew. He was leaning back, drawing away from Jan as though he were cringing.

Jan sighed, as though exasperated from dealing with an imbecile. He strode down the long aisle towards the case, his footsteps sounding loud in the empty church. He warned, "If you've booby-trapped that case, I can still kill her from here."

Jan stopped just short of the case and beckoned. Obligingly, it tipped onto its side and a sheaf of plastic wallets slithered out onto the stone floor. He bent down and picked up a handful of the nearest ones. As he did so, his spine curved and the compact, guard-less sword strapped diagonally across his back stood out in silhouette. Gold flashed at his temple.

He flipped through a couple of folders, attempting to keep one eye on David and occasionally glancing back towards Susan, who remained tethered and immobile a dozen metres behind him.

Jan read for a moment, unmoving, intent upon a particular document, and when he glanced up, David was nowhere to be seen.

"You," he growled, "Come out." His right hand moved instinctively toward his sword, which lay snug across his back, the top of its grip just level with his shoulder.

Suddenly David leapt to his feet and began running. He had been momentarily concealed beneath one of the benches and now he'd broken cover, racing away from Jan, round towards the shorter, transverse aisle which would lead him to the font.

Before he disappeared from sight, his hands had been empty; now he was carrying weapons, a sword in each hand. Something else was different too; a double-loop of gold chain was wrapped around his temples.

Jan dropped the papers and turned, his inhuman senses suddenly revealing the presence of a second adept. For a moment, it didn't occur to him that it could be David. His eyes flicked instead towards the entrance (David temporarily forgotten) as he reacted to the new threat.

An instant later his gaze returned to David, registering at last the glint of gold.

Now Jan sprinted back the way he'd come, whipping his sword from its sheath and yelling something incoherent.

David reached the font first. In his left hand, he was also holding a black velvet bag. He opened his fist, throwing the bag and one of the swords at Susan's feet. Now that he had a hand free, he grabbed the scabbard of the other sword and pulled it loose. The blade he revealed was long, perfect and slightly curved: a Japanese sword, a katana. It had a single, exceptionally keen edge which ran the length of the blade's outer sweep.

A moment later, Jan reached the font, striking at David in a cutting attack which caused their swords to collide.

David was able to deflect the blow. He retaliated by bringing his blade slicing up towards Jan's exposed middle, the bright tip arcing towards the other man's stomach.

But the lethal edge never reached flesh; an invisible barrier turned the assault aside. Jan sprang back.

David now stood between Jan and the font. While his concentration held, Jan would not be able to attack him directly with magic. He shuffled backwards, making sure he was close enough to Susan that she too would be protected.

"The bag," David said urgently, twisting his head slightly to talk to Susan. All the while he kept the point of his sword aimed at Jan's face, his blade held out in front of him in a two-handed grip.

Jan faced him in a very different stance. He was standing sideways-on to David, his blade extended one-handed, reminiscent of a traditional fencer, except that his left hand was down by his hip, not held up in the air.

Jan's sword was a peculiar hybrid. It was narrow and straight, with a sharpened tip, a little like a fencing foil, though not so slender – but the blade was flatter and both edges had been ground to razor brightness. It could thrust as well as slice.

As David and Jan faced each other, eyes locked and swords ready, Susan did as instructed. Severely hampered by her bonds, she tipped the contents of the bag onto the floor. Jan's old headband and two more heavy gold bracelets, like the ones on David's wrists, tumbled out. She ignored the bracelets – she was still wearing her own – but she grabbed the headband and pressed it quickly onto her head.

Susan's eyelids flickered for a moment as she concentrated.

While Susan had been retrieving the headband, Jan had taken several steps to his left, circling around them both. Now he lunged, not aiming at David – instead intent upon Susan. David jumped forwards, bringing his blade down to deflect Jan's.

As Jan's blade was beaten down, his eyes flicked towards David, who had been his target all along. He allowed his blade to be carried downwards, and as he did so he let the tip drop, disengaging his sword from David's, but leaving David committed to the movement, a victim of his own momentum.

Once Jan's blade was free he swiftly reversed its direction, bringing it back across David's extended body, the tip scoring a channel in the meat of David's left shoulder, the point catching for a moment in his muscle before tearing free.

David gasped, and then recovered himself. He moved round to place himself once more between Jan and Susan.

Jan snapped, "Where is your shield, boy? Do you even know what you're doing?"

By way of an answer, David stepped forwards, cutting twice at Jan, once at his head, the second time at his waist. But as if to underline Jan's question, both blows were deflected by unseen barriers.

Susan whispered to David, "I can make a shield, you don't need to protect me, but I can't break these handcuffs; I don't know how." She sounded desperate.

Jan ignored, or failed to hear, the whispers. He said, "Also: interesting choice of weapon." His tone was mocking.

"Folded Japanese steel," David replied, through clenched teeth. "The finest swords ever made; they can cut right through an opponent's blade."

Jan looked contemptuous. He said, "Fascinating schoolboy hyperbole. But did no one ever tell you that they're useless when fighting the Awakened?"

David moved a little to one side of Susan, stepping slightly away from the font, giving himself room to fight.

"Funnily enough, it did come up," David said, trying to sound conversational. "Hopefully, Susan has a little more faith in my judgement than you do." He glanced meaningfully at her. She frowned, puzzled, searching for the meaning in his words.

They were now in a triangle, equally spaced from one another.

David and Jan maintained eye contact, the tips of their blades almost touching. Susan looked from one man to the other.

David said, "She advised me to get a sword like hers." Behind him Susan had picked up her weapon – a long, straight blade, elaborate guard, a needle-sharp point, but no edge. She had unsheathed it, but with her hands cuffed, her grip was awkward.

David continued, "Of course a weapon like that," he nodded towards Susan's sword, "also has its disadvantages." He explained, "You can't cut with it."

Jan looked disdainful for a moment, evidently convinced that David was rambling. A moment later he lunged at David's mid-section, beating David's blade aside, demonstrating the use of a thrusting weapon. David was unable to parry in time, but jumped back quickly enough that the thrust missed him.

David took a second to recover, adjusting his stance. Behind him, a look of comprehension blossomed on Susan's face. She switched her sword to her left hand, holding it out of the way, and leant on the font, her fists out in front of her.

David said, "Think what a fool I'd have felt if I'd put a knife in that bag and then discovered you'd used handcuffs." He raised his sword above his head and Jan instantly shifted his weight back, ready to retreat. Then David pivoted towards Susan.

Susan spread her hands, stretching the chain of the handcuffs taut across the flat stone top of the font. David's blade whipped down, aiming for the centre of the chain.

Jan, momentarily wrong-footed, realised what David was doing and braced his back foot, trying to turn his retreat into a lunge.

David's blade flashed down and buried itself in the top of the font, parting the chain at its left-most link, dangerously close to Susan's hand, the blow landing just as Jan leapt forwards.

David tugged the sword free and jumped back, but not quickly enough to stop Jan's blade reaching him. The tip pierced his side, sliding in below his rib cage, a hand's width of blade entering his flesh.

David sprawled, falling away from Jan. A gasp was pulled from him as he collapsed.

Susan, her wrists no longer joined, whipped her sword around in her left hand, the tip scoring a track across the side of Jan's head, which caused him to duck and scuttle to one side, taken by surprise.

Once again, they were spread out in a line. Now Jan was on one side of Susan, David on the other. But whereas Jan was tentatively smearing the blood from his head-wound around his cheek as he tried to inspect the damage, David was still on the ground.

Susan stood between them, sword held expertly in her right hand – but her legs were still tied, the rope wound tightly around her ankles, keeping her from adopting a fencer's stance or taking a full step.

David scrambled to his feet, his left arm clasped across his torso, immobilising his torn muscles as much as possible. His right hand held his sword, the tip waving unsteadily in Jan's direction, bobbing and dipping as David struggled to stand up straight.

Jan stood regarding him. He grunted, as if to say he didn't consider David much of a challenge. Then he began moving round towards his injured opponent, keeping well clear of Susan.

As he passed her she lunged at him, her sword pushed out to its furthest extent, but it wasn't enough to reach him. He gave her a sneering look as her sword-tip jabbed the empty space to his right.

"I should think you're regretting you didn't put a knife in that bag after all," Jan said, an unpleasant smile on his face.

David twitched a couple of times in what might have been pained laughter. "Yeah," he conceded, "cuffs *and* rope. You think of these things afterwards and you could kick yourself."

Jan approached him, moving to his right so that for a third time they were all in a line. This time Jan was in the middle, his back turned towards Susan, who was just too far away to reach him.

"Well, what now?" Jan said, "She can't get free. You seem unable to defend yourself. And your nonexistent grasp of the arts is stretched to its limit in simply preventing me crushing your heart from over here. Is there any more to your brilliant plan? Or does it end with you bleeding to death, leaving me with the collection, and your girlfriend tied to the spot ready for me to kill at my leisure?" When David didn't answer immediately, Jan prompted him with a mild, "Hmmm?"

David nodded. "I'd got one or two other ideas," he said, "but this isn't quite the right time."

Just audible over David's hoarse breathing was the drip-drip sound of droplets of blood falling from the fingers of his left hand and splashing to the hard stone floor.

"No," Jan said, sourly, "I don't suppose it is."

Looking down at David's wound, and the blood leaking from his side, he added helpfully, "If only you had a week, you could probably heal that. Let's see what you manage to accomplish in the five minutes before I kill you." He took a step forwards, beginning to crowd his adversary.

David staggered for a moment. He tried to say something but a sudden twinge of pain made him catch his breath.

He tried again. "I had this big dilemma," he said, trying to keep his sword from dipping. "Do I let a shit like you rampage around, screwing up people's lives for another hundred years or do I risk getting the woman I'd do anything for killed because I decide to get in your way?"

While the two of them had been circling, Susan had been picking at the knot that secured her to the font. It was pulled impossibly tight. There was no way she would be able to loosen it using just her nails and a sword with no edge. She stretched out towards the nearest of the hefty candlesticks but it was considerably beyond her reach. She closed her eyes and concentrated hard, but the weighty brass holder scarcely rocked on its broad base.

"It's a tricky one," David was saying.

He took a few steps to his right, focussing hard, beginning to look more purposeful. Jan responded, circling in counterpoint, his expression indulgent, as though he had all the time in the world and was prepared to delay killing David until he'd learned anything of interest his victim might have left to say. His diseased features registered confidence.

Circling, David almost tripped. He righted himself, ignoring the stumble and said, "A friend of mine told me I should choose whichever option I'd be best able to live with. So I thought about it last night. Which would be the biggest burden?" He twitched with painful laughter again and Jan looked at him quizzically.

Finally David said, "Then I realised something." He moved to his right a few steps and then to his left, pulling himself upright as he did so. Then he darted to the left pushing forwards, Jan's sword moving instantly to block him. He pulled back.

"I realised that I really don't need to worry about it," David said, his voice growing triumphant, "Because there's no way I'm going to get out of this alive."

As he said it, he dipped to the right, slashing at Jan, who raised his blade to parry and was forced, by the energy of the attack, to take a step back.

Susan hopped as far away from the font as the rope would allow, stretching it as taut as she could. David slashed a second time at Jan, his sword glancing off the shield Jan was projecting, then he extended his blade lunging at full stretch to hack at Susan's tether.

Jan had been pressed back for a moment, but he had recovered again before David had completed his manoeuvre. David had created an opening through which he could push forwards, but there was nothing to prevent a counter-attack. As David lunged, he left himself completely open to Jan's retaliation.

For a split-second Jan's face registered surprise that David would risk something so reckless. Then, as quickly as it had come, his surprise evaporated and his jaw tightened with anger. As David's sword swept down, severing all but a single strand of Susan's rope, Jan stepped forwards, switching to a two-handed grip and brought his blade flashing down, the edge catching David's wrist, cutting deep into his flesh, splitting the ulna and stopping just short of severing the hand.

For the second time, David fell sprawling to the ground. This time his sword tumbled from his ruined hand.

Susan jumped back, whipping the rope tight and snapping its last few intact fibres; the loops around her ankles came uncoiled. Freed, she launched a flurry of attacks at Jan, almost knocking his blade from his hand and causing him to flinch even as his shield deflected the more violent of her thrusts.

Jan was beaten back, forced to step away from David's body. He adjusted his stance a little, obviously withdrawing his shield slightly to give his blade more room, and engaged Susan, relying on his swordplay to blunt her assaults. Confident and capable as he was, he couldn't help being pushed backwards and their conflict edged down the long aisle of the church, moving further from the entrance.

"Maybe I was too hasty in what I said to the boy," Jan said, breathing hard. He dipped his head towards David's prone form, "I couldn't have done *that* without an edged weapon." Susan looked at him with disgust, her lip curling back from her teeth.

She said nothing. She was in a rage, all her furious concentration channelled into the overlapping barrage of attacks she hurled at him, her shield shifting neatly to ward off his counter-attacks.

On the ground, David was stirring. He was protected from Jan's invisible attacks only so long as his concentration endured. Susan and Jan would both be able to sense it if he faltered. Susan stole a glance in his direction. "Focus, David," she called.

David didn't reply, but he began to crawl away from the font and into the relative safety of the pews, dragging his sword in his left hand.

"He'll drop his guard soon enough and I'll put him out of his misery," Jan assured her.

She took advantage of his remark to press the attack. He snatched his hand back from her darting blade. He said, "It's lucky for you that you can fence."

Susan shrugged. Her tone extremely clipped, she said, "We'd have just found some other way to stop you."

"Of course, this is not exactly fencing," Jan said, ignoring Susan's remark. "That nonsense they teach these days with their springy toy-swords. And awarding points for a tap that would get you gutted a split-second later if you tried it in an alley fight."

"Oh, please," Susan said, sweeping her blade up for a second so that Jan could see it. Far from being a light, modern design, she showed him a heavy, traditional rapier with a rigid blade. She began to push him back even harder, saying, "Given what I do, did you think I'd only learn the modern stuff?"

As she said this, she was able to run the shaft of her blade along Jan's sword, pressing him slightly off target, so that the brutal lunge he unleashed passed harmlessly to her right, while her own point bit into the muscle across his rib-cage.

Though the thrust struck a rib and failed to penetrate, it gouged a furrow along his side, which instantly welled with blood. The dark, synthetic material of his long-sleeved top was now ripped, exposing the wound.

Jan yelled in pain and launched a counter-attack at Susan's head, slicing instead of thrusting with his blade in an attempt to catch her off guard. It was too slow; she easily withdrew ahead of the advancing weapon, her shield stopping the attack dead.

Jan jumped back and dipped around the other side of a wooden lectern, placing it between them.

Several metres back, behind Susan, David had crawled in amongst the rows of seats. He was beneath the same bench he had hidden under earlier. In his weakened state, he seemed to be struggling with something.

Jan dropped back a little further from the lectern, but each time Susan made a move to circle around the obstacle in order to close with him, he darted in the opposite direction, keeping it between them. Susan retreated slightly hoping to be able to make a dash to one side.

Though Jan's expression was pained, his voice was still steady as he said, "Whatever you've been taught, the rules are different here." He took another step backwards, as though he was about to run one way or the other. Susan dropped back too, opening the distance between them, so that the lectern wouldn't obstruct her if she had to sprint after Jan.

"For instance," Jan said, breathing hard, "defensive cover needs to be kept close to you," he nodded towards the lectern which sat in the open space between them, "or it becomes a target," he concluded and then his eyelids flickered. The wooden lectern exploded, breaking into several large pieces, one of which struck

Susan in the chest, hurling her backwards to sprawl amongst the pews.

Now, for the first time, Jan and Susan were more than a couple of metres apart. This was David's cue to haul himself, struggling, to his feet. He had something grasped in his left hand – his right hung uselessly at his side.

Jan caught the movement and stared defiantly at him. He opened his arms wide, inviting attack from David, the air almost seeming to stiffen as he adjusted his shield. "Whatever that is, boy, it won't be enough."

David was holding what looked like a whisky bottle. He banged its base on the pew beside him and then hurled it, as best as he could, towards Jan.

To the side of the whisky bottle had been taped an upside-down marine flare. With its cap twisted to arm it, the flare needed only the sharp rap on the bench that David had given it to ignite the chemicals within. A blinding red glare hissed into life, lighting up the bottle as it flew through the air, smoke pouring from the blazing tube.

The bottle struck Jan's shield and was repelled. It dropped to shatter on the flagstones, the angry, bass whump of ignited petrol suddenly illuminating the entire church. At the heart of the spreading flames, Jan's shield had created a little bubble of protection, through which the fire could not pass.

But a second later, the burning liquid had seeped under the lower rim of his defensive barrier and begun to burn within the bubble.

For a moment, the bubble remained – a smaller fire within, screened off from the greater conflagration – and then Jan screamed and the bubble disappeared. For several seconds, Jan was lost within the flames.

Susan lay beyond the reach of the fire. She pulled herself

431

painfully to her feet and retrieved her sword. Then she began to move closer to the burning fuel, attempting to get a look at Jan. At the same time David fell back, to lay helpless between two rows of seats, for the time being unable to move.

As Susan approached the blaze, the flames abruptly dipped. The fire was beginning to die down, despite the fact that unburned petrol still washed across the flagstones. Within the waning flames, Jan rose from the ground to stand, sword in hand, his scorched features a mask of concentration.

The temperature around him plummeted, the flames dying down further and the air taking on a curious crystalline quality as it chilled. A few seconds later, the last licks of flame sputtered out and the burning flare was suddenly extinguished. Above him a dust of ice crystals was spiralling down from the freezing air, glittering and catching the light as they fell, to lay amongst the hard frost at Jan's feet. The breath steamed from his mouth as he gasped air into his scorched lungs.

Jan's shirt was partly fused to his chest now and huge ragged gaps had been opened by the fire, beneath which his dusky skin was charred and tight. His hair had shrivelled exposing patches of soot-blackened scalp. The skin of his face was pulled back from his teeth, giving him a permanent snarl.

Susan took a step towards him, raising her sword. As she did so, she glanced across at David. A look of panic crossed her face. "I can't sense you, David," she yelled, "Concentrate!"

Jan attempted to speak, but no sound emerged except a dry wheeze. He coughed, curiously abrupt and rapid, like an animal, an unpleasant swallowing sound accompanying the effort. He tried again to speak, "Shouldn't be long before I can pick him off," he said, his voice a brittle whisper, his whistling breath distorting his words.

432

"David," Susan called again, urgently, "You need to stay awake or he can attack you."

There was no reply. She glanced rapidly over to where David lay. Looking up, she saw that Jan was directing a look of focussed intensity in David's direction.

Before Jan could muster any sort of attack, Susan launched herself at him. His sword rose unsteadily to divert her first thrust, but she slipped around his blade to inflict a long, shallow wound on his blackened forearm.

He hardly seemed to notice the damage. He withdrew a little, gathering his shield and attempting to keep Susan at bay. His eyes flicked once again towards David.

In desperation, Susan jumped back and turned to face David too. Her eyelids dipped, allowing her eyes to close completely for a second. With a crash, a split appeared in the row of pews behind David's position and a handful of splinters exploded into the air.

"David!" Susan screamed and turned back just in time to deflect Jan's lunge. She wasn't quite quick enough and the tip of his sword plunged into the muscle of her thigh. She sucked in her breath convulsively as the damage registered. It was a clean puncture and, though deep, had not badly torn the muscle. She could still stand, though her leg trembled a little as she did so.

"David," she called again, no longer shouting.

"I'm here," he said groggily. She shuffled rapidly backwards and risked a look in his direction. "I'm here," he repeated, even more weakly.

He attempted to pull himself up onto the nearest pew, succeeding on the second try. His useless right hand lay in his lap and his jeans were stained black with blood. His left hand loosely gripped his sword, though its tip rested on the pew in front. His eyelids drooped even as she watched.

Wrestling her attention back towards Jan, she began to circle him, batting the tip of his blade away repeatedly, but not closing sufficiently to give him an opening. She allowed him no respite and pressed him so hard that he had no chance to think of anything but his own defence.

Gradually she turned him around so that his back was to David. Now she began to attack in earnest. She tied up his blade and leapt past it, time and time again, nicking his flesh and twice missing him by millimetres with thrusts that would have skewered him. Steadily she forced him to retreat, approaching the pew where David had propped himself, sword in hand.

Jan was increasingly unsteady on his feet. His reactions were slowing and he was barely able to maintain an adequate defence. Against his will he was being inched backwards towards an armed enemy.

And at last, Jan's exposed back was within reach of David's sword. But David seemed to be in trouble. He struggled to lift the weapon and it nearly slipped from his grasp. Susan pushed Jan a step further back and still David couldn't attack.

At last, with a frantic flurry of attacks she sent Jan's blade twisting from his grip to whirl away into the darkened rows of seats.

"David," Susan hissed as she moved in for the kill. But David's face showed only an apologetic smile, drained of all energy. The sword dropped from his left hand and his eyes closed.

Jan sprang back, jumping over David's legs and snatched up his opponent's fallen sword. A moment later, he had its tip pressed into the flesh over David's heart, his hands gripping the hilt ready to drive it home.

Susan hesitated.

Jan made his strange gulping swallow and said, "You decide."

Susan was clearly gauging the distance she would have to cover to disable Jan. There was no way she could move quickly enough to stop him dropping his weight onto the blade.

Susan let the tip of her sword dip until eventually it rested on the floor. She stood there panting, looking at Jan as defeat crept at last into her expression.

"The sword," Jan said, jerking his head to one side.

She cast her weapon aside.

"And my band," he said, nodding towards the circle of gold around her temples.

She lifted the headband free and tossed it after the sword.

"If I were you," he said, "I'd have kept fighting." He lifted the gold chain from around David's lolling head and threw it to one side. "Surrendering won't save you," he said, patiently, his voice rattling as though something inside were trying to tear free, "Though I suppose it means you won't have to watch him die."

He lifted the sword from David's chest and brought it to his side. Then he took a breath and closed his eyes for a second. Susan was hurled backwards to tumble among the seats on the other side of the aisle. She lay where she fell – conscious, but stunned.

"If it's any consolation," Jan said, "I wouldn't have let you live however this had turned out."

He raised the sword and advanced on her.

A banging door distracted him.

From over by the entrance, a woman's voice said, "You'll give us a bad name, Jan."

Walking down the aisle was a very tall, blonde woman with pale Scandinavian skin. She was immaculately dressed in a tailored grey wool suit with a faint white pin-stripe. In her elegant hand she carried a rapier with an elaborate basket hilt. She gripped it carelessly as though she were holding it for a friend.

Jan's head whipped round to look at her. For a second, with his bared teeth and wild expression he seemed feral, cornered. "How did you find me, Karst?" he demanded.

"Some old man," she said pleasantly, "presumably a friend of whoever you're busy torturing at the moment."

Jan was backing away now. He seemed to have forgotten all about Susan. He was retreating towards where he'd last seen his own sword.

Karst was taking in the scorched stone floor, the splintered lectern, the bodies and the blood. She tutted.

She jumped up to walk gracefully along the seats rather than between them. She was making for the open flight case which lay abandoned at the end of that row of pews.

When she reached it, she glanced at the scattered papers and began to pick them up. "I think the old man lied. He threatened to share this collection with the world if we didn't help. It looks like that was never in his power."

Then she shrugged agreeably, "Oh well," she said, "I suppose I promised to come straight here instead of spending a pointless hour searching your lair." She dropped the collected papers into the case and fastened its lid.

She turned now to face Jan and began to advance upon him purposefully. He had found his sword and swapped it for David's, but he was still backing fearfully away from Karst, his recovered blade evidently giving him little comfort.

"Tell me where the Marker is," Karst said, icily, "and we'll come to an arrangement which doesn't involve me spitting you like the roast you now resemble."

Jan was shaking his head and retreating.

"You need all the friends you can get," Karst said, patronisingly. "This is a chance to get in my good books. Where's the Marker?"

"Nowhere you'll think to look, Karst," Jan said with all the defiance he could muster.

She held up her left hand and inspected its unblemished skin for a moment. "I should say I have another seventy years before I need it again." She was almost upon him now. "In that time I think I can find it without you."

Her sword flashed out towards him. He blocked it at the last possible moment only to find that she had already countered. He attempted to beat her thrust aside, but even as he began to move, she had flicked her blade a third time, so fast it was like watching a film from which frames were missing. She landed two quick blows, her sword leaping out to sting him as though of its own accord. And then with a final, effortless reverse she broke his sword just above the grip.

The silver blur whirled, to stop, tip first, pressing into his windpipe. "Those two," she said, indicating with her eyes Susan and David, "both victims or is one of them an accomplice?"

Jan said, "The girl is with me."

Karst said, "Hmm," as though she would think about it. Then she placed the point of her sword under Jan's chin and ran it diagonally up into his skull. As he crumpled, she slid the blade free and flicked its tip to remove the blood. Jan's body dropped like a sack of grain.

She left his corpse where it lay and walked across to stand over Susan, who was cradling her broken arm, still sitting where she had fallen. She looked up at the other woman with frightened eyes.

Karst reached out with the tip of her sword and ran it gently up the side of Susan's head as though probing for anything solid concealed within her hair. Then she peered behind Susan, glancing at her wrists which were now bare.

"Forget this happened," Karst said, with what might have been a smile. She wandered for a moment over to where David lay in a spreading pool of his own blood. She gave him only the briefest of glances before transferring her attention to a display table set against one wall of the church. The white tablecloth beneath the display was plastic, textured to look like cloth. With her left hand, she whipped it from the table, scattering leaflets and a bookstand.

Then she strode back to Jan, spread the tablecloth on the floor and rolled his body onto it with one neat suede boot-tip.

She wrapped him in the cloth and then, apparently without effort, she hoisted Jan's shrouded body onto her shoulder and walked back to collect the case. Dipping at the knee, she grabbed its handle in her left hand, her sword still in her right and strode back to the entrance. With a bang, the door closed behind her and she was gone.

Susan struggled to her feet and limped, as quickly as she was able, over to where David's body lay. She fumbled the phone from his pocket, one-handed, and dialled.

CHAPTER 37

To: Dee_Milton@AtlanticMagazines.com
From: Zorro_Lil_Sis@hotmail.com
Dee,

It's very sweet of you to say it, but I'm
sure any big sister would have done the same.
And of course I keep thinking that you'd have
never got mixed up in all this in the first
place except for me. But anyway, thanks. I'm
proud of you too.

First order of business is to get this
encryption thing set up. David's got it
working for his e-mails so we can't let him
show us up. There are definitely a few things
I don't want the guys in your IT department
reading. I'll send you a couple of links to
help you figure it out.

So anyway, I think Mom and Dad can stop
worrying about us. If we can survive this
sort of stuff, their parenting can't have
been too disastrous. I'm planning to give

them a call in a few days, so we'd better get our stories straight – I don't think they're ready for the R-rated version.

And oh my god, I can't believe you're seeing Petey. Not that I should be surprised. He's kind of a prince, when you get to know him – as I guess you've found out. Unfortunately for you, dating him will mean letting Lincoln crash at your place and raid your refrigerator. Which is a little like trying to keep a rhino as a pet. It's definitely going to put a dent in your grocery bill.

It's weird that you might not have met Petey if this whole thing had never happened. I know that doesn't make it OK – it must have been truly awful for you – but I look at David and I wonder whether we'd ever have got together under normal circumstances. After what we've been through, I can't imagine not trusting him – or wasting time worrying that he doesn't love me. I mean he was prepared to go down fighting if it meant I'd be alright. Beats flowers any day.

So I suppose I'm just saying there are one or two consolations in all this. Plus, Petey can really get you plugged into 'the street' (is that the term?) like you were in Chicago. He can get you into clubs whose existence you had never previously suspected. Just don't wear your good shoes.

Do you think Dad will say something stupid when he finds out you've got a black boyfriend? I really hope he's found his way out of the Fifties by now. I know it won't even register with Mom. And just in case you're wondering, I never had a thing with either him or Lincoln. In fact when I met them, I assumed they were going out with each other. Don't tell them I said that.

Anyway, we're staying out here for a while. Neither David or I are in any hurry to get home – wherever that is. We're going to get David's pal Banjo (must find out his real name – I assume he wasn't christened Banjo) and his girlfriend out here. Maybe you and the Pete-ster can come too. I'm afraid there's absolutely nothing to do here, but for once I'm guessing you might be able to cope with that. The flights are my treat, by the way – I'll explain more once we're using our secret decoder rings. Anyway, keep in touch.

Your lovable sister,

Susan   x

p.s. If you and Petey come you'd better invite Lincoln. He'll pine and wreck the furniture if you leave him on his own.

To: WorldOfBanjo@hotmail.com
From: SecretSquirrel@EuroMail.com
Encryption: PGP 8.0.2 Freeware for Macintosh

Banjo,

I'm glad to hear that Melissa is still under the delusion that you are somehow a catch (!). Long may it last.

I'm told you came to visit me while I was laid up, but I'm afraid I can't have been much company. I was still away with the fairies. By the time I knew what was going on, Susan had decided to kidnap me.

And, I finally worked out what you were on about with that little Zen riddle of yours about Susan wanting my help. It looks like I twigged it just in time - though I did cut it a bit fine.

I don't think Susan can really ask for more proof that I'm prepared to share the big decisions with her than the fact that I planned a rescue attempt for her where she had to take over halfway through. Some people might call it half-baked, but I thought: get her on her feet and give her a free hand and she'd find a way to sort the whole mess out. And sure enough, she kicked his arse.

If I hadn't fainted (and feel free to keep that fact under your hat) I think she'd have finished it right then. Though I'm sort of glad for her sake that she didn't have that on her conscience. Not that he didn't have it coming, but I suspect it would screw you up a bit anyway.

When it came down to it, it wasn't as difficult as I thought, trusting her. I think it helps if you find the right person. Or maybe I was ready. Who knows.

Anyway, after saddling her with half the rescue, Susan'll probably start complaining that I don't take responsibility next.

Nah, I'm only joking. She's been a saint, looking after me. She pulled me out of that hospital when I was still in a pretty bad way. They hadn't even finished explaining that my hand was buggered for good, though they'd told Susan. You could see that they thought she was mental, dragging me out of there while I was still at death's door - but with my agreement they couldn't stop her. And of course she had a slightly more effective remedy in mind.

The next problem was getting me on an aeroplane while I was half-dead. In fact, her broken arm wasn't sorted then either - she was adamant that she wanted to get us somewhere safe and quiet <u>before</u> we started any of that occult healing malarkey. The flight to Athens was actually pretty funny, in a macabre sort of way. My stitches started coming undone halfway through the flight and we were sure we were going to get stopped coming through customs for bleeding on their floor. Then they'd have wanted an explanation of what Susan was carrying around in her bag (more about that in a minute). We made it though.

Anyway, I have to say this island is paradise. There's about thirty people living here. There are two bars and two restaurants, both down by the jetty where visiting boats can tie up. Then there's a church - but no priest - and a few houses. We're up the top of the hill with the most amazing view of the sea.

Robert Finn

I can see Susan from the window as I'm typing this. She's got her olive tree to sit under and a book – no goat unfortunately – but I don't regard that as any great loss. And I'm actually typing this two-handed after only a fortnight. You should have seen the state of my wrist when we took the bandages off. It was enough to turn you vegetarian for life. What a mess! Now I've just got a few odd-shaped lumps around the wound and a lot of new pink skin. Still looks weird, but it works OK and it doesn't even hurt! The hole in my side is nearly fixed too.

It took a couple of days to work out how to do the healing trance thing. Just using the mojo makes you heal fast, but there's an accelerated healing thing you can do if you know what you're about and you're in a hurry.

In fact, according to Susan, that's what Jan was doing all evening before I went to meet him for the exchange. Apparently, he was having to spend hours healing himself everyday, but it was obviously a losing battle. Maybe he was a lot older than we thought. Or maybe it was genetic – perhaps if he'd led a normal life he'd have been dead by forty.

Anyway, if he hadn't told me well in advance where he wanted to meet, I would have been stuffed. I wouldn't have been able to hide anything there (though god knows, that was a job and a half persuading them it wasn't a bomb or drugs or something). But he needed to spend a few hours in his trance, getting ready for the meeting, so he made the call

444

early. It's amazing how the little details can make such a big difference. If he'd left the call to the last minute, I might not be here now. (Though I still wouldn't be without the Professor's intervention of course.) Or maybe it didn't all hinge on that call. Like Susan says, maybe we'd have just found another way.

Also, I've got to apologise for siccing/sicking (? that thing you do with attack dogs anyway) Hammond on you. I just needed a name and address in the UK that I could give him in case he wanted to contact us. I know he's a bit of a knob, but we'd still be sorting things out if he hadn't got involved. It helped that Dass was Italian because Hammond instantly thought Mafia (do they still exist?). And Susan was able to tell him a story that had a surprising number of real facts in it. We left out Dee's kidnapping because he hates DIY crime-fighting, but we told him about Susan being taken and the ransom being the collection. Plus she explained away the fact I didn't involve him by saying he'd warned me not to contact the police. Then when she got to the bit about someone from Jan's old firm turning up to bump him off, she said you could hear Hammond muttering, 'gangland-style killing' like he was almost excited. He seemed to consider the swords just a part of the ransom that the 'hit man' had missed, which helped. Don't worry though, you don't need to get all this straight. He knows you weren't a witness to any of it. I just thought you'd want to know. He even helped me get my car back from wherever they'd towed it to without me having to pay a button for it. Result. Susan says the keys are in the hall drawer, so help yourself if you want to.

Well, I think that's enough for today. Except I did threaten to tell you about Susan's bag. I don't know if Jan believed my little lie about Susan being sick or he just didn't feel the need to keep her drugged up - whatever it was, she was in much better condition to spy on him than Dee was. She still doesn't know where he stashed the Marker, but she did spot one of his hidey-holes - one that Karst missed. Susan, gutsy (insane?) woman that she is, went back there while I was having fun being operated on and she swiped the goodies. She found a quite staggering amount of cash, mainly in dollars, and a kind of notebook or diary. I can't read a word of it, but Susan's working her way through it and she thinks there might be all sorts of interesting info in there. She even found a bit where Jan was complaining that no one wears hats any more. But it's true: we don't seem to trust people who cover their heads. Makes sense.

The bottom-line there is that I'm probably a good bet if you need a sub. It certainly means Susan and I don't need to worry about working for a living for a little while. (You'll be pleased to know that my bosses are holding my job until I'm well - though I can't see myself going back.)

Anyway, I'm sure I don't have to say to be a bit cautious with this e-mail. As I understand it, the encryption is pretty unbreakable stuff, but don't let Melissa read it over your shoulder, she might start to worry about you.

Have one on me,

David

p.s. Hurry up and book some flights out here. I want to see what the fierce Greek sun does to your soft albino skin.

Robert Finn

To: SecretSquirrel@EuroMail.com
From: jhs1192@cam.ac.uk
Encryption: PGP 8.0 Freeware for Windows

Dear Susan and David,

Assuming you crack the code and I've done everything correctly, you'll be reading this sitting in the sunshine somewhere in the Aegean. Imagine that! It'll be talking pictures next.

But enough levity, I'll press straight on with the apologies and grovelling. I hope it's clear to both of you that I didn't intend to take away your right to choose your own destinies. I know you haven't accused me of such, but you may nonetheless be thinking it. I ask you to believe I wished only to help.

I gave David a certain piece of advice – having of course prefaced my remarks with an assurance that I would never presume to offer direction (but I suppose hypocrisy is the least of my crimes). No sooner had I spoken than irony struck; I succumbed to my own words. When I contemplated David's options it seemed to me that – whichever path he chose – he would soon carry a heavier burden of guilt than any young man should have to bear.

And really the decision was never in doubt. David would of course choose to save your life, Susan, if it were in his power to do so. I realised that if I were happy to transfer

the burden to my own shoulders, it opened
up the possibility of sending you a little
help. By communicating your predicament to
Dass's surviving associates I believed I
was sealing the fate of both the collection
and the Marker: they would once more be the
instruments of wickedness. But I decided to
press on anyway.

I am delighted beyond words that the Marker
has not been found. The collection is no
great loss, considering that we retain our
own copy and the knowledge it contained must
largely have been known to Dass's erstwhile
associates already.

At any rate, I determined that giving up the
Marker might well be the price that would
purchase your lives. And I felt I could live
with the thought of aiding the enemy for
whatever time I have left. It also seemed
clear to me that David would not be prepared
to grasp at that particular, desperate straw
for fear, Susan, that it would seem like he
was betraying you. You had after all made it
plain that you intended to deny these people
their precious treasure. I would rather you
lived, even if it ended our friendship to
arrange it - but surely David could not go
against your heartfelt wishes quite so easily.
It was a decision I felt only I could take.

I hope you'll forgive me a hopelessly
melodramatic image - perhaps my monstrous
vanity will even amuse you - but the situation
put me in mind of throwing myself on a
grenade, but in a karmic sense if you take my

meaning. Ridiculous, mawkish bravado, I know,
but irresistible nonetheless. I like to think
that whoever one day writes my obituary, they
will now have more material to work with than
just the phrase 'diligent scholar'.

I let those I contacted believe that you were,
both of you, held ransom pending delivery of
the collection. I promised them that I would
not make its contents public on condition
that they remove Jan from the picture and let
you two innocents go free. As I understand
it, they cleaved to their word with a lack
of integrity matched only by my own – an
occupational hazard, perhaps, when liars
treat with villains.

I wonder now if, despite all the many
dangers you both faced, the moment when
Karst deliberated over your fates was not as
perilous as any. Had she caught a glimpse of
gold upon either of your fallen forms it might
have sealed your fate. Yet, a little quick
thinking on your part, Susan, completed the
job Jan started when he disarmed you – and so,
despite himself, he helped to save you from
Karst. If between you (Susan) and Jan you had
failed to conceal all that gold jewellery,
might she not have dispatched you both simply
to err on the side of caution. Then again, it
occurs to me that she saw Susan as a protégé.
Consider: I have found no mention of women
adepts anywhere in the collection. Ah, but we
needn't dwell on these things. Not now that
the sun is shining (where you are at least)
and all is well.

So rather than ramble on all day, I'll save

the rest of my idle thoughts for the next
instalment. I'm going for a walk along the
head in a moment - the sea air agrees with
me, or at least I imagine it does, which is
nearly the same thing. Today I have the heart
of a lion.

Of course, perhaps my improving health has
nothing to do with the sea. It could be the
change of pace or some subtle but important
alteration in my diet. It could even be those
very interesting meditation techniques I've
been studying in the collection. (If my dear,
departed sister could see me decked out in
her jewellery I think she'd despair for me.)

Which leads me to my parting thought. When
you have both mended and taken some time for
yourselves - I am thinking in terms of months,
after all you have been through - once you
feel you have recovered, we'll have to give
some thought to what we want to do about all
this. There are things here that perhaps the
world at large should know.

At any rate, I think I can safely say I'll
still be in the land of the living when you
feel it's time, so don't hurry back on my
account. And I'm sure Susan will want to know
that I believe I've found another code in
the collection and the contents are rather
disturbing. Naturally, they are three hundred
years old, so disturbing or not, they can
wait until Autumn (though whether Susan's
curiosity, now doubtless piqued, can also
wait we'll have to see).

I'm going now to see if I can locate an ice

cube. Can you believe it; I have a new tooth
coming through!

Yours with all possible best wishes,

Joseph Shaw

The End

Ex Machina

CHAPTER 1

I've never actually been to prison, so this is a guess, but I bet when you get out you don't think *I know, I'll write my prison memoirs now, while it's all still lovely and fresh.* I should think the first thing you do is try to blot it all out (check your phone-book under BOOZE, HOOKERS, TATTOO REMOVAL, DISNEY WORLD®).

Like I say, I've never been to prison, but nevertheless these are my prison memoirs and I'm writing them now, before I forget, even though it's the last thing I want to do.

In case you're interested, what this has taught me is that a person really can change, but without doubt there's a price to pay. Starting over means you lose touch with who you were.

Your old memories begin to feel like someone else's, some person you don't know very well... which is a more than a little unsettling. It's like finding the aftermath of someone else's shopping spree on your credit card statement, someone else's low grades messing up your college transcript or someone else's hair clogging up your shower drain. (You'd probably got the message even before that last example.)

At any rate, the new-improved-you can still remember all of the bad decisions the old-you made. Your memory is full of all those stupid things, but the motives no longer make sense to you. What was I thinking? Why did *that* seem like the smart thing to do? How could my thoughts have been so small?

Because the truth is that you find you can't squeeze back inside your old way of viewing the world anymore; the new you won't fit. You can't unlearn the lessons that caused you to grow and you can't wriggle back into your old, cramped mindset. That's what I meant about prison. I feel like I was trapped inside that claustrophobic maze of wrong choices and bad instincts for so long that it's a blissful relief to be free – despite what I went through. And I wish I could part company with that old me forever. But instead I'm clinging on to it, doing my best to record those thoughts before understanding evaporates, the way a confusing dream begins to evaporate once you wake up. I'm going to relive it all so that I can explain it to you.

So welcome to the old, even-more-annoying me. You'll have to put up with my day-to-day trivia for a little while before we get to the real meat-and-potatoes, because it's all bound up together.

So let's get on with it.

My name is Jo, which (regrettably) is short for Josephine, and the story I need to tell you starts in Cornwall. That's in the windy south-west tip of some rainy islands just off the north coast of Europe, in case you don't know. I've spent about nine of my twenty-six years in those islands, but I still think of myself as American. I prefer the big city, but at this point I'm a long way from what I prefer: I'm in the middle of nowhere.

How did I get here? Well, I think you could say that finding a post-doc slot was always going to be a challenge for me. But that's fine; I didn't really want a conventional position, the mainstream kind most people compete for. I'm not into that straight-ahead, plain-vanilla academia. Besides, all the fertile dirt is in the gaps between the disciplines. If you can find yourself a niche that's new and still a little precarious, you tend to find that the rules are looser and the people are weird enough that they don't notice your foibles. In between the disciplines there's not much status quo to disturb and no traditional way of doing things, so my (ahem) unconventional résumé is less of a liability. Under the right circumstances, it might even be a fun talking point. Whoop!

My problems started – at least this current set of problems – around the time I submitted my thesis. Instead of seeing it for what it was, my doctoral supervisor couldn't seem to get beyond the fact that…

None of which you need to know, so forget it. What with all the arguments and acrimony, though, I needed to find a new place to hang my hat – all the better if it was a long way from New York. Which is how I came to be back in the British Isles, my occasional second home.

Taking this post was a pretty straightforward decision, mainly because there were no other offers on the table – despite my mostly stratospheric grades, despite my publication credits, despite my fund of delightfully colourful tales involving legal wrangles with the governing board of a major East Coast college. Imagine. This was the only offer.

Now Cornwall is about a hundred miles further out from civilisation than many people think the UK extends. And while I suppose I don't actually *hate* the countryside, I do wish there was something there other than bugs and wet sheep. Somewhere to buy books would be nice. In fact, why not a variety of stores selling a rounded selection of modern consumer goods? Oh, and a choice of international cuisine too. And if the local residents could be exposed to the outside world occasionally, just enough to let them understand accents from non-agricultural parts of the English-speaking world, well that would be ideal.

None of those things being the case, I'd developed something of an enthusiasm-deficiency with regard to my new surroundings. The ill will over my thesis made me feel like I'd been wrongfully convicted of something, so Cornwall seemed like the unjust sentence that went with it. For the first few weeks of my banishment here I don't know that I did much except simmer and fume at the double-plus ungood way things had turned out. There was pretty much nothing about this new situation that I liked, on top of which there was nothing to take my mind off it.

The field station where I was based was run by Professor Shaw; the whole thing was his show. He was an old friend of my mother's (emphasis on old) and I suppose I should be grateful to him for offering me a post-doc spot at all. But honestly, I can't imagine there were too many other takers. And anyone who survived the cultural desolation out here would soon be scared away by the prospect of what joining this project would likely to do to their career. (How fortunate that mine was pre-wrecked!)

We were based in a few buildings that I think must have been used for some fish-related activity until recently. There was a large dormitory block adjacent. A ten-minute walk away was the village of Swaffet: ten houses, a post-office/general store, a church hall and two pubs. An hour away by bus – assuming they were running – was the nearest major town: half a handful of well-worn chain stores, no bookstore, no decent library, and a scruffy Pizza Hut bringing up the rear. Unless you had the use of a plane, your options for a fun night out were limited.

The outlook for our project was similarly non-stellar. If I'd had a career warning-light, it would have started blinking before I'd unpacked my bags. I'm not a history buff, but this place had 'fringe' written all over it. If these people were doing solid, mainstream work, you can bet it would all have been taking place back at the Professor's college in Cambridge, at the centre of the universe, not out here in the sticks. There's only one reason you head out into the wilderness like this and it isn't to get away from the envious glances of colleagues or the feverish anticipation of the journals; it's so you can crawl away to die, academically speaking.

In fact it occurred to me that maybe Professor Shaw hadn't jumped; maybe he'd been pushed. Maybe this project and the field station were all about the college giving him enough rope to hang himself. Let him waste a bunch of taxpayer's money and they'd have a reason to show him the door. Otherwise they'd struggle to retire someone with his reputation and connections.

Insightful as that analysis might seem, the few times I tried to discuss our doomed mission with the other conscripts, I'd gotten a cold reception. They were obviously relishing their exile from the real world. And why not? No competition out here to show them up.

My part in the project started out with a disjointed list of responsibilities, some of which made sense to me, others not so much. I'd been told not to worry about publications yet or exactly what my final role would end up being; we'd deal with all that once I'd 'found my feet'. In the meantime, I was doing a little bit of everything – mainly rent-a-tech chores.

One of my first jobs was to set up a secure computer system. Not a problem for me, except that whoever had been working on it before I arrived had really messed it up. I'd hardly begun to get it unscrambled before I was getting flak about why it wasn't finished yet. And when I pushed everything else aside and made it my top priority, I got it in the neck for falling behind on my other assignments.

It wasn't the ideal way to recover from my doctoral fiasco. And to be honest, my spirits hadn't been that high when I arrived; a month on and they were falling fast.

Just for background, in case you care, I'd had a pretty tough time of it lately, and before that... well, more of the same really, with varying degrees of crappiness. So what would have been nice is if I had been cut a teensy little bit of slack. But was I? It turns out that I was not.

During the day, the nagging and the requests for 'updates' were really starting to make me stressed, which didn't help me work any faster, believe me. On top of which, what started out as polite enquiries about progress were getting bitchy and snide a lot quicker than I think was called for.

In fact, in record time I'd been made to feel totally unwelcome, out of step and unappreciated. Any chance I had of job satisfaction had vanished when the bitchiness started because I knew that when I *did* finally manage to get caught up, instead of 'Good job!' I'd be hearing an aggrieved chorus of 'About time!'.

The only part of the day I *almost* looked forward to was clocking off and trudging up the hill to The Red Hart (or The Retard as some of the team pointedly mispronounced it, in honour of its core clientele). There I could sit in ostracised silence and enjoy a couple of eye-watering glasses of *vin de sinus medicine*[1].

On my first couple of trips to The Retard I'd had some problems getting the alcohol dosage exactly right. Naturally, I wanted to suppress the newsreel that played in my brain, the one that looped endlessly through the day's little humiliations and setbacks. But on

---

[1]   Tourist tip: try not to ask for wine in a rural British pub. But if you do and the barmaid looks worried and says, "Ooh, I know we used to have some," then consider yourself forewarned.

the other hand, when dealing with hooch of this calibre, caution was indicated. More than once I'd accidentally over-medicated my brain's vertical hold. I'd weaved back to the dorm to lie on my bed, not daring to close my eyes, for fear of triggering that queaseful head-in-a-tumble-drier feeling.

A month in and I'd settled on an RDA somewhere between three-and-a-half and four glasses per night – a little more if I was off my meds (which topic I'll get to in good time). One lingering niggle was that however restrained I was in my drinking, the industrial run-off the vineyard used to melt the grapes always made for killer headaches the next morning.

After five weeks my reserves of perkiness had dried up, and now my problem-solving faculties were bypassing the question of how to get my assignments back on track and jumping right to exploring possible ways off the project.

And that's the way it was until – in amongst all that gloom and griping – I made a discovery. Out of the blue, I found something genuinely interesting.

In fact better than interesting: intriguing, fascinating, impossible.

It began to dawn on me that there was something going on at the field station besides the project I knew about.

The official line was that they were combing over some old documents, translating them and researching their backgrounds. This activity was being coordinated using some new project framework, which, when they were done, they were planning to publish. It included a certain amount of tricky IT and some clever process stuff – both of which I was going to play a big part in. But that was the extent of the project according to the outline I'd seen.

But I stumbled upon something else entirely.

My first clue involved the Procedures and Administration

Committee. The committee would meet once a week, sometimes more, supposedly to discuss all the dull what-have-yous that kept the field station running: liaison with the distant main campus, project finances, maintenance, personnel, etc;

There were only six researchers at the field station, plus some support people, so you wouldn't have thought there was a mountain of work for an admin committee to do, but nevertheless they seemed pretty hard at it whenever I caught a glimpse.

Knowing what I know now, I've got to hand it to them: 'The Procedures and Administration Committee' is a great name. It's about the least tantalising title you could imagine – a fine example of reverse branding. The only hint of undisciplined ego was allowing it to have a cool-ish acronym[1].

The secure e-mail facility and the encrypted file-store I was asked to set up were for the committee (or the PAC as I later discovered they couldn't resist calling themselves). The Professor described their requirements and then took me aside to let me in on their 'little secret'.

Conspiratorially, he told me that the government were thinking of shaking up the way universities were structured and funded, and the Professor was on one of the working parties looking at alternative approaches. The implications, he said, were 'enormous'. This Procedures and Administration Committee had a secret mission. Hidden from the world, they were discussing ways of 'literally revolutionising post-graduate teaching in this country'. But, epoch-making though these changes might be, they were still only possibilities, only suggestions. If details of these embryonic proposals were to leak out it could 'set some hares running', maybe stir up opposition and controversy, even outrage, about initiatives

---

[1]   Mind you, in the States, a PAC is something to do with politics. So not much shine on that particular apple.

that were still very much at the hypothetical stage. At this point, the committee's deliberations must remain *sub rosa*[1] – hence the need for a secure computer system. Better safe than sorry.

Wow. Imagine how excited I was to be let in on that scoop. The sense of awe and revelation I felt was comparable to the first time I realised that America used a political system that was both federated *and* bicameral. Amazing.

In other words: yawn.

But this was just another piece of hand-stitched, lovingly-crafted subterfuge. I'm sure the government does the same thing – and if they do, I'd like to think they call it 'drabbing': taking cool stuff they want to keep under wraps and making it sound so craptastically lame that you really can't be arsed[2] to pry into it. As in: "That's classified. I could tell you, but then I'd have to bore you." It was like finding out that by day Clark Kent was a mild-mannered reporter, but by night he... whittled ornaments.

So the big secret was nearly as boring as the cover story. Which might have been the end of it, except that I'm just a little bit nosey.

I created the e-mail accounts and the public/private encryption keys they wanted; I set up the secure file-store... and then I peeked.

It actually wasn't that easy to peek. My little buddy Daniel (more about him later) had obviously been asked to add a little security of his own on top of what I'd put in place. He'd set up some encryption that was independent of mine, the result being

---

[1] I've never known anyone like Professor Shaw for using a phrase like '*sub rosa*', when 'shush, it's a secret' would do.

[2] Excellent Brit expression: to not be arsed to do something. Unfortunately for Americans, you just can't say it right without an authentic British post-alveolar frictionless continuant.

that neither of us could decipher a committee member's locked documents without colluding. Except that I soon found a way to log in as Daniel – from which point I could unravel his devious little tricks and get at the contents of their secret files.

Ironically, if the PAC hadn't decided to set up two separate layers of security I would never have bothered to delve into any of it. First off, by locking me out of their files they more or less challenged me to get access to them, wouldn't you say? And secondly, I was just a little bit suspicious that they were overdoing the cloak-and-dagger stuff – *enormous* implications for post-grad teaching notwithstanding, there was just too much security in place.

And once I knew that something was going on – something more than a government working party, that is – I noticed lots of other suspicious details.

My favourite bit of weirdness concerned a PAC-member called David Braun, who plainly had a thing going with the senior researcher there, Susan Milton. He was sort of good-looking in an ugly kind of way, and though he talked like a suit, he walked like a soldier. Everything about him said he was in control and he got what he wanted. Which is why I just couldn't quite take him seriously as a Catering Supervisor.

An explorer? Yes. Maybe a mountain-climber. Equally, I could imagine him in dress uniform getting a medal for something *hush-hush*. I could even see him as a Wall Street type, worth $200 million at 30, having started with nothing. But if he was a catering supervisor then my butt is a pumpkin.

Of course he didn't really have anything to do with catering and I found out later that the title was just part of the overall 'drabbing' – combined with Susan Milton's sense of humour.

David wasn't part of our research project; he just showed up for the PAC meetings. He'd obviously been somewhere hot recently, and not just for a few days. While the rest of them had that late-in-the-year British pallor from months (possibly years) without sun, David was burned a toasty brown – all except one wrist, which was much paler and looked a different sort of burned – not as in sunburned, as in acid-burned. It could have been creepy, but actually it just looked sort of rugged. Plus it wasn't like he had a claw or anything; his hand was fine, it was just the pigment that seemed to be messed up. It seemed like a clue.

As well as David, Susan and the Professor, there were two other members of the PAC: Daniel, my old buddy, and a non-entity called Theresa. She was mousy and unremarkable, and I never really discovered why she was involved with the team. Daniel, though, was a useful sort of a guy. Not *me* smart, but not a dunce by a long way. And for a history whiz, he was a remarkably fair techie. He was also a) in a band, b) reasonably buff and c) devoted to me.

But before you decide that he's a scrumptious muffin and I've got it made, I should tell you that he's two full inches shorter than me, has frizzy red hair, bad skin and has – to the best of my extensive knowledge – never had a proper girlfriend.

Which doesn't stop him making furtive little attempts to ask me out every few weeks. He doesn't have the guts to actually come out with it, of course, but he's always inviting me to things or complimenting me on something – like a shirt I've had for ages, or my hair, when it's exactly the same as it was the last time I saw him. Why he can't get it together sufficiently to say, "Jo, will you go out with me?" I don't know. I mean, I'd slap him down, but at least he'd have the satisfaction of being a man about it.

Sure, I know I treat him like crap, but deep down I really like having him around. For the most part. In small doses.

So anyway, once I'd got past Danny Boy's security measures,

I took a quick look at what the PAC was saying to each other. I couldn't imagine any of it being very interesting, but I thought I'd see whether I was right about David and Susan having a *thang* going on.

I prised open one of Susan's archived e-mails dated a couple of weeks before I started on the project and hit the jackpot right away: Dear David, miss you, love you, blah-blah, snuggle-bunny, blah, murder, blah, hearts and kisses, yours Susan. So I was right. I patted myself on the back and thought no more of it.

Oh but wait. What was that about *murder*? I read that section carefully. Susan was responding to something David had said. He had concluded that a man named Teracus probably *had* been murdered by someone called Jan. David had been in mainland Greece apparently for the express purpose of investigating this guy Teracus's death.

The idea burst in my mind like a rammed SUV. My imagination lit up with the impact and all sorts of burning questions were thrown into the air. Who was David really? In what capacity was he investigating? Who could Teracus be (and what sort of name was that)? Who was this murderer, Jan? Why did Susan, a historian, need to know about any of this?

Then I got a foolish, sinking feeling. It dawned on me that the murder they were referring to could be some ancient event and Susan's interest was just part of her research. If I'd studied the liberal arts a little harder, would I have recognised the name Teracus as some historical figure, perhaps some Roman consul whose unexplained death was even now causing bunched underwear in common-room debates around the world? Was I following in the footsteps of the apocryphal New York citizen who, when asked what he knew of the murder of Julius Caesar, insisted that he hadn't seen a thing?

But that feeling of deflation and foolishness only lasted a moment. Reading on, it was clear that this wasn't some riddle from antiquity they were discussing. Susan's e-mail went on to say something about Teracus's hotel bill including a record of numbers he'd called. I cast my mind back to what little I knew of Ancient Rome. I was relatively sure that they didn't have phones in those days – or if they did, then I was quite sure that the technology to provide itemised billing by room hadn't been perfected until long after Rome fell to the Visigoths. My money was on this being a recent event.

So I knew that David and Susan were investigating a recent murder. Next I wondered whether they were working alone or if other members of the PAC were involved. It seemed most likely that it would be a personal thing between the two of them. Maybe Teracus was some weirdly-named uncle of Susan's and David had seen so many Chuck Norris movies that he was happy to play the vigilante and volunteer to investigate. Maybe sleuthing was his early Christmas gift to her.

That in mind, I forced open a few of the Professor's e-mails, glossing over a couple of duds before I found one that answered my question – and raised about a million new ones. The bulk of the message concerned arrangements for the next PAC meeting; it also touched on the agenda, and there it was: a reference to Jan.

Towards the end of the message there was also an aside about Jan's name. The Professor, it seemed, had found a reference in Jan's notebook to his real or former name being 'Janu', which he believed meant 'life force'. "Ironic," the Professor concluded, "because it seemed to be the one thing he lacked, besides a moral compass, that is. Of course it also means 'knee' in Sanskrit, but I consider that an irrelevance. Even if we imagine it as some manly pseudonym, akin to a mafia *soprannome* or a wrestler's *nom de lutte*, it's a little out of kilter as a nickname. Fighters might revel in titles such as 'The Hammer' or 'The Fist', but I would think that attracting the nickname 'The Knee' is something you would be eager to live down."

I tried to find alternative ways of interpreting that note, wondering again if he could be talking about something remote, hypothetical, scholarly. But I just couldn't make it come out that way. It all seemed immediate and personal. The e-mail seemed to say that Jan was a) a murderer, b) known to at least one member of the PAC and c) apparently now dead. And let's not forget, Jan was on the PAC's meeting agenda. This wasn't about PAC members going off on a tangent about their outside interests; it was something they held meetings to discuss.

The tiny cogs in my brain were spinning like pin-wheels as I considered what I might do about all this. I was still thinking it over when an opportunity presented itself.

Now if you know anything about reading other people's mail you'll know it's not a spectator sport, so I'd tucked myself away somewhere private for my little session of electronic B&E. I was sitting in front of our server-farm's main console. The console, along with all the rack-mounted processors and the comms paraphernalia, was tucked into a storage room on the ground floor of the field station's main building. Apart from me, only the Professor had a key to the server-room door – and he had no earthly reason to use it, barring emergencies. The white noise of so many cooling fans tended to drown out conversation, and the expelled heat turned the room into a sauna, but the server-room was a good place to go if I didn't want to be disturbed or interrupted. (Nerds among you may like to chuckle appreciatively over the fact that I called the room the Fortress of Servitude.)

That said, as I sat there, turning over the content of those peculiar e-mails in my mind, I became aware of distant thumping. Someone was at the door.

I cleared the screen of any incriminating evidence (even though the monitor faced the racking) and then I unlocked the door and peeked outside. Daniel was standing there. He was wearing a t-shirt depicting a caffeine molecule and he grinned his shy grin as I put my head out to see what he wanted. I didn't smile; it only encourages him.

"Hi Jo," he said, "Sorry to interrupt you. I need to borrow a cable if I can."

"Yeah?" I replied, noncommittally.

"Have you got that mini-USB one? We need it for the meeting," he asked.

That's right. It was Wednesday afternoon and the PAC would be getting together soon in the little conference room behind the Professor's office.

I was pretty sure they'd settled on that venue because it was so isolated. To reach it, you opened a fire door, went down three silly little steps and through a second door into the meeting room. The two doors were only five feet apart and they created a kind of airlock. You couldn't open the first one without someone in the room noticing, so that by the time you reached the second door everyone happened to be talking about the weather and most of the documents in the room were face down.

"What do you need it for?" I asked.

Daniel gave me one of his 'now don't be like that' looks – which always infuriate me – and said, "Well, I don't now that it really makes all that much difference *why*…"

He tailed off as he noticed the storm clouds gathering and my eyebrows getting closer together. There's something about his inoffensive, placid reasonableness that just makes me want to shake him.

Before I could pick a fight with him, he capitulated: "There are some photos we want to show. We need to hook the digital camera up to my laptop. It's not a big thing."

At that moment it really started to bug me that he was part of the PAC and I wasn't. Now that I knew it wasn't the ditchwater-dull snoozathon I'd imagined, it bothered me that they'd chosen Daniel and said nothing to me.

Irritated, I thought of asking him what a procedures and admin committee would need photos for, but now that I *knew* they were up to something I didn't want to seem too inquisitive. Plus, if I was honest, it was a dumb question. Even a *real* admin committee might find a reason to show pictures at its meetings. If I forced Daniel to tell me, he'd just lie and say it was holiday snaps.

I let the door bang shut and disappeared back inside leaving him standing there. A moment later I reappeared and held out the cable to him.

Then something occurred to me and without thinking I snatched the cable back as he reached for it.

"Oi," he complained, smiling, "No time for chase-the-cable. Work to do."

I suddenly realised that I wanted to listen in on this afternoon's meeting – and if I was going to eavesdrop then I would need a little time to prepare – not to mention get my nerve up.

To Daniel I said, "Sorry, I've just remembered this cable's iffy. If you can give me a couple of minutes I'll dig out the new one." I paused a moment and added, "You don't have to wait. I can leave it in the meeting room for you if you like." I gave him a big smile that I hoped looked authentic.

He looked almost suspicious for a moment – not about the cable, just about me volunteering to do him a favour. (It makes you wonder: if he's got such a low opinion of me, why does he want to go out with me?)

A moment later he smiled back, then glanced at his watch on its stupid, chunky wrist-protector strap and said, "Well I do want to find some grub. Can you drop it off before two? That's when the meeting starts." In other words, don't make me look bad. So he thinks I'm selfish *and* unreliable. That pretty much killed my fake smile.

Despite myself I snapped, "I *told* you I'd get it for you, OK?"

He made calming gestures with his hands and said, in his speaking-to-lunatics voice, "Alright, alright. That's great. Don't get your knickers in a twist."

So we left it at that and I ducked back into the server-room and locked the door behind me.

I already knew what I was going to do.

CHAPTER 2

At the far end of the server-room, the wall was covered with metal racking and shelving. The big spaces were filled with cardboard boxes stuffed to overflowing with all sorts of accreted techno-junk. I dragged one of the boxes off the shelf and began to rummage through it. Once I'd tipped most of the contents onto the floor I saw the old cell-phone I was looking for.

I turned it on. The battery was down to 50% and I wouldn't have time to recharge it, but a half charge would probably be enough.

Back at the server console I did a little searching and found the web-page of instructions I semi-remembered.

1) set the phone's ringer to mute.

2) short pins 2 and 6 on the phone's base.

I couldn't figure out an easy way to short the pins so I ended up kludging it by supergluing half a staple between them. Ugly but effective – and for a bonus point, I did it without permanently attaching the phone to my thumb.

The contacts on the phone's base were for connecting a head-set and the pins I'd shorted were for the head-set's answer button. In effect, this hack was like having the phone's answer button pushed in the whole time. Now, whenever I dialled the phone's number, the phone would auto-answer without ringing. I checked that it worked by dialling it from my regular cell-phone, and with the call in progress I adjusted the volume for optimum eavesdropping performance.

With the rigged phone in my pocket, I grabbed a mini-roll of duct tape and the cable Daniel wanted, then I made my way towards the meeting room.

The Professor's office was empty, so I wandered in and over to the door that led down to the meeting room. With my nose against the little wire-threaded window I could see down the steps to the second door and, through its tiny window, a little of the meeting room beyond.

I wanted to know that the room was empty before I went in. If I met someone, I could hand over the cable as my reason for being there but I couldn't very well plant the phone. That would require a second trip, this time without the cable and so with no excuse for being there. If I had to make a second trip and I bumped into anyone it would be obvious that I was loitering with some sort of intent.

As I craned to see into the meeting room, I was surprised to find that I was pretty keyed up. It wasn't like I was going to be tortured if I got caught, but I was actually getting sweaty palms contemplating my plan. I'd been in that room half a dozen times without giving it a second thought, but this time it felt like I was heading deep into enemy territory.

I reminded myself that I was just having a little harmless fun with people I saw everyday; I wasn't spying on trigger-happy Nazis. In fact, I was only paying the PAC back. They'd started the trickery by lying about what they were up to; I was just asserting my right not to be taken in by it[1].

I felt a little better with that thought in my head. In fact, I was a little bit pissed off with them now that I thought about it. They hadn't seen fit to trust me with their secret; I was just there to keep the computers running and to believe any old crap they made up about what was going on. I mean, was the project they'd recruited me for even real? Or was that just a cover story too?

No longer caring whether the room was empty or not I let my little surge of righteous annoyance carry me through the door and down the stairs. With only a hint of hesitation, I pushed open the meeting room door... to see the Professor sitting there chatting to Susan Milton.

They looked up together and I felt a surge of blood rush to my cheeks. Dammit; despite my recent self-directed pep talk, I still felt guilty – so guilty I was sure my face glowed with it.

But they seemed not to notice, so maybe the blush I could feel was only on the inside. The Professor finished his sentence – something about timescales – and said to me, "Just the fellow, as it were. Where are we with those subscriptions? Any news?"

I experienced that unpleasant feeling you get when you realise you've forgotten to do something – or when you eat something and then it moves. I'd promised the Professor that I'd set up subscriptions to several online archives so that members of the team could use them in their work. He'd reminded me three times to get on with it, the most recent of which was yesterday. I'd promised him emphatically and without fail to get it done by midday today. It was about one o'clock now and I hadn't even started it.

I searched for an excuse and remembered the cable in my hand. "It's Daniel," I announced without thinking. Realising my

---

[1] Damn, but I have wicked rationalising skills.

words made no sense I added, "I mean I'm just doing this thing for Daniel... well, for the meeting really; he said you really needed *this*." I showed them the cable – and then realised they wouldn't know what it was for. I was making a mess of this little performance.

Still waving the cable I explained, "He wanted to show some digital pictures at your meeting. Finding this cable sort of delayed me, but the subscription thing is nearly done."

Somehow it seemed fitting to blame Daniel for my failings. Fitting because in Ductile Logic World – where I spent much of my time – Daniel had been chosen by the PAC instead of me and thus he was the reason I was having to lie about what I was up to. See? It *all* makes sense.

The Professor eyed me for a moment and I thought he was going to get angry that I was making excuses. He never really has done, but I can't help it; he's just someone I'm afraid of disappointing – or losing. When he went through a bad cancer scare the previous year, and lost all his hair, it frightened the life out of me. It still hasn't grown back and it's a constant reminder of what could have been.

For a moment, as I stood there, I wasn't sure whether I'd pushed my luck too far with him. Then he clapped his hands as though this was just the sort of thing he wanted to hear and asked, "And you have the list of subscriptions?"

Arrggh. I realised I didn't. I knew he'd given it to me but I couldn't recall what I'd done with it. It was partly his fault, I thought, for dealing in scraps of paper in an era of electric e-mail and horseless communication. I made a sort of uncertain sound.

He glanced at Susan and then chuckled, saying to me, "No matter. There's a copy in your pigeonhole."

He didn't sound annoyed at all and I felt relief spread through me – which in turn reminded me how spazzful I was being at the moment. I was really going to have to acquire some metaphorical *cojones* before I'd take home any awards for spying[1].

The Professor turned to Susan. "We can discuss the rest of this later. Let's have some lunch." She smiled in agreement and they both got up, gathering their paperwork to take with them.

"I'll just…" I said, holding up the cable again as though I needed to do something with it beyond placing it on the table.

"Good, good," the Professor said and the two of them walked past me and out the door.

Once I was sure they were gone, I fished out the reel of duct-tape and the phone and scrambled under the conference table to lay on my back beneath its centre. I ripped off a long strip of tape and attached the phone to the table's underside. I added a second strip to make sure it couldn't come loose – being careful not to cover the microphone.

I was just wriggling out from under the table when I heard the outer door bang. Jumping to my feet I jammed the tape back in my pocket, realising at the last minute that my dark sweater was now covered in a million flecks of nylon from the carpet.

David Braun came through the door just as I was trying to brush the worst of it off. I kind of froze as soon as he noticed me and just sort of stood there. He said 'hi' and set his pile of papers on the table. He was picking out a seat when he became aware – at about the same time as I did – that I was *still* just standing there.

He looked puzzled and opened his mouth to say something – most likely "Are you mental?" – but I just mumbled "Thanks" (I'm not sure for what) and headed for the door. I paused long enough

---

[1] Hmmm. Do they have awards for spying? And if they do, do they announce the results or just lock the golden envelope away in a vault and let the winners figure out what's in it?

to pick up the cable I'd left on the floor and to place it on the table, and then I bolted.

My heart was thudding as I crossed the Professor's office and headed for the server-room. There was no one around and I tried to calm myself down as I walked. I went over my pep talk again in my head, reminding myself that these were not ruthless drug lords I was dealing with, they were career historians who had no reason to suspect me of anything – historians who'd lied to me.

I was feeling less freaked out by the time I reached the server-room door. I paused there for a moment and got my brain working again.

I decided I should get the Professor's subscription thing done before he really did flip out about it and that would take my mind off all the deception-related spazzing-out I seemed to be doing. Then, in a little under an hour, I'd listen in on the meeting and find out what the project I'd joined was *really* about.

Of course, to take care of the subscriptions I'd first need the Professor's list telling me what I was supposed to be doing. I turned around and headed back down the corridor and towards the main entrance.

Just inside the main door was a recess with slots for each person's mail. In mine was a piece of paper, folded in half. On it, written in fountain pen, were the words 'I think you forgot this'.

I unfolded the piece of paper. Double arrgghh. It wasn't a *copy* of the list of subscriptions; it was the *original* list the Professor had given me. No wonder he'd asked if I had it. I'd obviously left it behind after our last chat. So he knew I wasn't 'nearly done' with it. It seemed even luckier now that he hadn't blown up at me.

I kind of wondered whether maybe I *was* in trouble over this, but the Professor hadn't seemed too upset so I put it out of my mind. I grabbed the list and scuttled back to the server room.

And wouldn't you know it, the job turned out to be a real pain in the hind-section. Each library service had a different system for arranging group access and none of them were very well thought out. Infuriatingly, two of them required 48 hours to process new subscriptions – though they'd take your money instantly. I was not going to win any new friends when the team realised it would be another two days before they could use these sites. Just when I needed to get something done quickly I was hitting extra delays. Which was pretty much typical of my luck.

I got as far as I could with it and then checked the time. I'd more than used up my hour. The PAC meeting would already have started by now. I quickly put the whole subscription thing aside and snatched up my cell phone, hoping I hadn't missed too much. I pressed redial, with my thumb hovering over the 'End Call' button because some part of my brain was telling me that any second now I was going to lose my nerve.

I had to take the handset away from my ear and check the display to see if the call had gone through because there was no sound of ringing. Sure enough, a call was in progress. I bumped the speaker volume up as far as it would go and found I could hear distant voices. The conversation sounded like it was taking place inside a mattress, but I could just about follow what was being said.

Susan was speaking: "...more important to stay undetected than to learn something new. We're not especially on the clock; we don't have to rush into anything. On the other hand, if the Army learns about us... Well, the point is that being in the dark for a little longer is preferable to bringing the roof down on our heads. We should be patient."

The Army? WTF?

Now David spoke, "Oh absolutely. We need to do two things,

I'd say. First, make a really good plan for what to do if they find out about us. And second – and this is the important one – make absolutely sure they never find out about us."

Then I heard little Daniel clear his throat and speak. He was quieter and much more tentative than David. He sounded about twelve years old. "How do we compare... I mean to say, you and Doctor, erm, Susan, you've had experience with them, plus that was a while ago, so I should think you've progressed a little. I mean I'm sure you have, erm, progressed and I wondered whether there wouldn't be something you two might be able to do in the event of..."

Susan broke in politely. "Daniel, you're asking whether David and I could maybe handle these guys?"

Daniel found a little more confidence from somewhere and said clearly, "Well, respectfully, what I was wondering was how badly, um..."

"Right," Susan said, getting it, "how badly we'd lose. How badly they'd kick our asses."

I guessed that she glanced the Professor's way then, because I heard him mutter, "It's alright; I know about the existence of 'asses'; you needn't shelter me."

There was a pause, now that the question had been asked in a way that everyone (with the exception of me, of course) seemed able to understand.

A moment later, Susan said, "They'd kill us. They'd just plain kill us."

Again, I suspected she'd cast a look, this time at David, because he took up the explanation. He said, "Well, they'd probably have to work much harder at it than they'd like, but I don't think we'd stand much of a chance. We'd still be, um... Honey, what's the American for 'curtains'?"

Susan helped him out: "Toast. We would, in all probability, be toast."

I was struggling to make some sense of this. This didn't sound much like the *Army* Army. Daniel couldn't be asking if David and Susan could beat the *actual Army* in a fight, could he? Surely it hadn't slipped Daniel's mind about all the tanks and aircraft and men by their thousands with guns and how tricky it would be for one historian and a 'catering supervisor' to defeat the combined might of the military. So what Army could he be referring to? The Salvation Army? Even they weren't exactly a pushover – or so I'd heard.

With the phone still pressed to my ear, I turned in my chair and began typing at the console. As quick as I could, I created a little script that would fetch the documents in the PAC's secure store, one at a time, and run them through my decryption app. I was going to search their mail for answers while I listened to them talk.

The script was just a handful of lines long so I only missed a few seconds of conversation while I typed. As soon as a few plaintext documents were ready, I *grepped* them, looking for anything that contained the word 'Army'.

Straightaway I got hits. The first excerpt read: "The Army Who Witnessed Creation. Sometimes called The Witnesses. One of the groups known as the Awakened." So, not the Salvation Army; maybe not even the Jehovah's Witnesses. (Because clearly *that* would have made plenty of sense.) Plus, no mention of Jehovah. Obviously it was some other sect with a thing for the witnessing. I didn't have time to read any further because my attention was drawn back to the conversation I was supposed to be eavesdropping on.

Daniel was talking: "…I found some activity. I don't want to mislead anyone, but it looked like surveillance to me. But, you know, limited experience and all that."

Susan was obviously tuned into Daniel's wavelength as she said, "Which fits with one of the things I wanted to hear some discussion on today. Daniel thinks he found signs of electronic snooping; well, I'm pretty sure I saw signs of physical surveillance. I'm pretty much certain they're watching Jan's City Road place."

And, Dear Reader, just in case you wonder, this moment here was when it got *really* weird. Daniel once again found a little more self-possession than I thought he was capable of and said, "Well, I've been thinking about the statistics of this. We're estimating around a hundred years between regenerations, but what's the duration of the regeneration window? If we just pull some figures out of our, um, out of the air we could say that any time after about the ninety-year mark you might put your name on the list for use of the Marker. Let's also take a flying guess and say you drop dead at around a hundred and twenty-five years after your last regeneration, but that maybe most adepts wouldn't go past one-ten if they still had the Marker available to them…"

Susan interjected, "We only have one document that suggests timescales and…"

What the *hell* were they talking about?

David said, "Honey," obviously wanting her to let Daniel finish, but Daniel didn't seem fazed. He ploughed ahead, "Right, but what I'm saying is this: if the spread of physical ages within the army is random – which it might not be for reasons we can come back to – but if it *were* then you'd have around one in ten of them looking to regenerate sometime soon, but little in the way of panicking. Ten years from now you'd have a fifth of them on the waiting list with a few of them getting pretty nervous."

Susan wasn't quite sure. She said, "Not *that* nervous. Using your figures, if they *choose* to regenerate at a physical age of about a hundred, but they can live to one-twenty-five, then they've got more like two decades before they need to panic. Could be a lot longer."

Daniel was still on a roll. "Definitely, but the point is when they *choose* to regenerate. It must be based on something. There must be a feeling that adepts start to lose their edge, start to slow down a bit at that age unless they regenerate. Even if the *actual* effects are negligible it doesn't matter because the perception is the important thing."

Susan wasn't following: "The perception?"

David was ahead of her and said, "I get it. If everyone agrees you should regenerate at one hundred if you don't want to start losing your marbles, then anyone who goes much past one hundred will be under scrutiny. There could be nothing wrong with them, but there'll still be muttering in the ranks every time they forget someone's name or knock over the salt."

Daniel took over again: "Exactly. Because if everyone agreed there was absolutely no problem waiting until one-ten to regenerate, then one-ten would be the norm instead. It's really more about the accepted norms of the group than about their physiology."

Susan had caught up: "You're talking about organisational stresses; that's where you're going with this."

I'm guessing from the couple of 'ahhs' I heard that Daniel must have nodded. He elaborated, "Any leaders who go beyond the consensus age for regeneration will be seen as less capable, possibly ripe for challenge. Any of the worker ants who go beyond that age will feel let down by their leaders. They won't feel the leaders are taking good care of them. Either way you look at it, it puts pressure on those at the top."

The Professor spoke, "An appealing institutional analysis, Daniel. Losing the Marker could trigger a coup long before its loss has any quantifiable physical effects. In turn, the *prospect* of a coup will influence decisions made at the top."

The Professor was silent for a moment and then went on, "Of course the relevance of that analysis depends upon their tendency to topple their leaders. If a coup is unthinkable in their world then the current leaders need not concern themselves. But given what we know of their warrior-tribal mentality, I would say that any perceived weakness in the leadership, either physiological or managerial, is likely to provoke challenges to their authority. I'm inclined to agree that those who lead the Army can't afford to twiddle their thumbs for long."

For the first time Theresa spoke, "But what constitutes a long time for people who live for hundreds of years? Maybe their idea of a knee-jerk response still takes a decade."

The Professor said, "I'd be interested to hear all of your views, but I find myself swayed by Daniel's point. I can't help feeling that the rank and file will expect concrete results after two or three years. Those in charge have nothing, so far as we're aware, to show for Year One in terms of progress in finding the Marker. If their stance has been passive until now – and of course we don't know that for *certain* – but if it has, then I think we will see them go on the offensive within eighteen months or so."

I was still listening avidly, but my mind had ceased to even process their discussion. I was taking the whole thing in with the intention of replaying it in my head for, say, about the next six months as I tried to figure out what planet we were on and why I didn't seem to recognize it any more. I'd also need to just explore the possibility that my colleagues were a psychotic cult of delusional lunatics.

These thoughts coincided with a lull in the conversation. No one spoke for a few seconds and then David said, "Someone's coming."

There was much shuffling of paper and the Professor said, "Perhaps this is a good time to take a tea break, if no one objects? I have one or two errands to attend to, I'm afraid; could we break for an hour?"

There were mutters of assent and I could hear the sounds of chairs being moved. Then I heard the door being opened and someone said, "Professor, I'm very sorry to interrupt, but there's a delivery that needs your attention."

That was plainly all I was going to hear for a while and my focus began to turn away from the muffled sounds of the meeting room and towards the memory of the words I'd overheard. I considered hanging up the phone.

Then, over the open connection, I heard a beeping noise which for a moment I couldn't place.

"Did someone forget to turn their phone off?" asked Susan a little accusingly. There was obviously a 'no phones' rule.

I heard "Nope" and "Not me" and Susan saying, "Well somebody's phone…" She was interrupted by the phone beeping again. At which point I realized whose it was. It was mine: my bug-phone. It was receiving a back-log of text messages. I mean, what kind of phone beeps while a call is in progress? Maybe that's why it had been at the bottom of a box.

I'd turned off the ringer, but I hadn't thought about texts. No one should be sending messages to that phone. No one for weeks now – except of course goddamned spammers. As though they hadn't caused enough irritation in the world they were going to blow my first attempt at espionage. Immediately, sweat began to prickle my forehead.

I waited for someone to look under the table, to remember my earlier visit, to check the phone's call log and to come and find me.

CHAPTER 3

But, what do you know, the finding of my phone wasn't the disaster that lurked just around the corner.

I heard Susan say, "I won't shame whoever it is, but make sure it doesn't happen again please. Phones off."

Then I heard her mutter, "It better not be you, Mister cell-phones-are-a-blight-on-society." I assume she was talking to David.

And that seemed to be that.

I wasn't necessarily in the clear yet – who knew how many spam texts were floating around in the system for that phone – but I figured there was a good chance they'd all just been delivered in a big clump. There was no reason for the phone network to drag it out. I might just have gotten away with it.

One thing was for sure, though; I wasn't going to try listening to the second half of the meeting. I was *preeeetty* sure that phone had a low-battery alert too. I'd avoid running the battery down with any more calls, then I'd retrieve the phone later.

I was kind of annoyed with myself because it was such a silly slip and I should never have made it. But the annoyance couldn't really get a foothold; anxiety over nearly being caught and fascination with what I'd overheard were competing much harder for my attention.

Once the PAC seemed to lose interest in the subject of beeping phones, my fear of discovery halved – which allowed my upended sense of reality to grab the lion's share of my attention. What was this world the PAC thought they lived in? Was it some sort of game being played with straight faces? Were they just monumentally confused about... pretty much everything? Could any of what they were talking about be real?

I'd been doing some pacing while I thought about it all, but now I ended the phone call and sat back down at the console. I wanted more information.

I started opening the decrypted PAC documents and began reading. There was even more craziness contained in the first document I looked at than had been hinted about in the meeting. I read a note that discussed the powers of these 'adepts' and it seemed to be describing something akin to telekinesis.

If any of this was to be believed, the PAC had stumbled upon a whole world of strangeness, complete with super-villains, and the PAC-members themselves were trying to get their bearings while simultaneously working to thwart the forces of darkness.

I read on, mesmerised. It couldn't be real, but it was a mighty queer sort of hoax – and to what end? If it was all deception then it involved numerous conspirators and preposterous amounts of preparation – every member of the PAC had put on a show on the off-chance that someone was listening in. Unless this was all somehow for my benefit (and that way lay full-blown paranoid schizophrenia) it was clear that the PAC believed their own crazy version of reality. I didn't share their belief, but I was already sure that there must be *something* extraordinary going on here. They couldn't *all* be crazy, so they must either be right... or the hoax was being perpetrated on them. It was pretty fascinating, however you looked at it.

I paused to think for a moment and I happened to glance in the direction of my notes – the ones concerning the subscriptions I was supposed to be setting up – and I recalled my earlier fleeting thought about the Professor – the one where I was so relieved when he failed to freak out.

And it was at that exact moment that someone rapped sharply on the door. So much for the server-room being a good place to avoid interruptions.

What a tumble of paranoid thoughts that sound released. I wondered which possible source of trouble was waiting for me in the corridor.

I opened the door wide to see the Professor standing there. "Do you have a moment, Jo?" he asked. For a microsecond I wondered if I was becoming clairvoyant. I think of him and he appears. But this wasn't about seeing the future; it was about waking up to the inevitable.

The Professor stood there pursing and relaxing his lips in a strange way and it took me a second to read the meaning in his expression: he was furious.

A sense of dread settled on me. I'd never seen him this angry with anyone before. Did he somehow know I'd bugged the meeting?

I swallowed, not saying anything, and stepped back into the server room, holding the door so he could follow me. Whatever had pushed him over the edge, it was clear that he was about to really lose his temper with me.

I found I couldn't meet his eyes with mine. His voice was

threateningly cold and horribly deliberate as he said, "I've just been informed that there are seventeen packing crates blocking the corridor in the dormitories. I'm told you arranged for them to be placed there." Seventeen crates? Crap. I was expecting one, maybe two boxes. God, this was going to look like I didn't give a damn how much disruption I caused. What peachy timing.

His gaze was hard and unblinking as he continued, "And the subscriptions… I didn't like to say anything in front of Susan, but we both know you haven't done a *thing* about them." I glanced up to see his eyes drilling into mine. "This really isn't good enough, Jo." The words weren't especially harsh, but his tone was heavy with a verdict of disappointment – so heavy I could feel it pressing down on me. He had made some sort of awful decision; I could tell.

Even before today, I had secretly known we would reach this moment. It had been coming for a while now. He hadn't even discovered the bugging; he'd just reached the limit of his tolerance – even without knowing the full truth. It was almost funny. Maybe, in fifty years time, I'd actually laugh about this.

But right now I was terrified. He couldn't be giving up on me, could he? That wasn't how this worked. He was the rock, the stern but dependable uncle-figure who might tut and grumble but who stood by me nonetheless. His patience wasn't supposed to be exhaustible, to run out. That was an important part of the lousy deal the Universe had forced on me. Professor Shaw was part-compensation for the loss of my mother and the fact my father had 'moved on, emotionally' as one therapist put it. That's why Professor Shaw's patience had to be limitless. If his distant, hesitating affection for me was all I got in place of two functioning parents then that affection had *better* be inexhaustible.

And what? I couldn't even have that now?

Whatever painful announcement lurked at the end of this conversation, it was fast approaching. He launched into it, still stiff with irritation: "I have come to accept your inability to think of others, so the chaos in the dormitories isn't unexpected. It is your attitude to work that *baffles* me. I know you're more than capable of completing the tasks you're set and you seem willing enough when they're discussed. And yet you seem determined to let down anyone you make a commitment to."

Was he going to throw me off the project? Was that what he was leading up to?

I knew my failure to speak up, to defend myself, would only make his anger worse, but I found I was trapped inside the realisation that I'd finally pushed to breaking point the one person I believed would always support me.

Then, thankfully, I heard myself begin to say something, to stand up for myself. Only what came out was this: "But you *said* I didn't really need to rush…" I couldn't finish the sentence; I sounded pathetic, whining, childish. I looked at the Professor out of the corner of my eye and now he *really* looked angry. *Here it comes.*

And I was right. His temper boiled over and he began to speak with unrestrained emotion now. His chin jutted and his eyes were wide and fierce as he said, "I have always tried to do what's best for you, Jo. I have been patient and I have made allowances. I know, too, that life has been difficult for you." He pointed a finger straight at me and declared, "But believe me, young lady, it has been *just* as hard on others from whom I never hear excuses, in whom I can safely place my trust and upon whom I can always rely. We have passed the point at which my tolerance seems to serve any useful purpose. It seems only to encourage you in your faults and to give others reason to suspect favouritism on my part." He drew up a breath and said, "Tell me, is there any reason why I shouldn't ask you to look for a position elsewhere? Any reason I shouldn't do that this minute?"

But I was way ahead of him. In my mind, I was already out of work and unemployable. The fact was, I had no family to turn to and no close friends. I had used my work to create some sort of framework for my life, to provide me with a direction, and that prop was about to be taken from me.

I had money, but what I didn't have was anything else to cling to – and that's a dangerous combination. Once I was kicked off this project, I wouldn't be offered another post, I knew that. *Then* what would I do? I knew I wasn't strong enough to start again, to find something new – or even to resist the temptation to let everything slide. I was terrified that the few strands of my life on which I still had a good grip were about to slip through my fingers.

Though I would have given anything not to, I began to cry – silently at first and then out loud. Fat tears rolled down my face. I knew how wretched and unsympathetic I must look, but that just made me feel worse, just confirmed the hopelessness I felt.

Brought up short by my tears, the Professor said, with hesitation, "Jo, I…" His voice was neutral now, the anger back on its leash.

Through my abject tears I saw something in him change and I thought for a moment he was going to put his arms around me. And I realised that I very much wanted him to do that. But whatever new emotion he was feeling, it wasn't pity. "Pull yourself together," was all he said and then he turned around and left.

* * *

I sat on my own and cried for a while.

When the tears eventually began to subside, I reflected on

something a therapist once told me about personality problems. He said that whatever you have too much of – be it anger, sadness, paranoia or even confidence – all those excesses start with putting yourself too close to the centre of things, with believing that everything is about *you*.

So maybe the secret is not to take life too personally, not to get upset. Just let things wash over you.

But then what would be the point of living like that?

After the Professor left, I dropped into my chair and sat there, brim full of self-pity. My own feelings, my own predicament, filled the world and nothing else registered.

I might talk a pretty good game from time to time, but all the way back to the death of my mother I'd really just been papering over the cracks. I was beginning to think that by now I was *entirely* paper and cracks.

There was an irony as unavoidable as a migraine in the realisation that the arrival of my dead mother's belongings was what tipped Professor Shaw over the edge. It somehow seemed to close a vicious circle that had begun with her death.

My brain snagged on that thought and for maybe half an hour I dangled there, wretched and intermittently tearful.

Then, gradually, I became aware that my gaze had settled on my cell phone.

Pretty soon now, the meeting I'd been so keen to overhear would be back in session. Man, that all seemed like a long time ago.

The desire to know what was going on in that meeting seemed remote and sad for a moment, like reading a great review for a movie that was no longer showing. In another life, I would have loved the chance to follow it up, to discover what was going on, but there was no point now.

Of course, depression is like that: a familiar weight that settles on you so heavily that you can't move, you can't even *imagine* playing an active part in your own life. All you can think about is the weight and a feeling like falling.

Regardless, a single bright thought flitted to and fro in my gloomy mind, like a tiny, silvery fish darting through the silted hulk of a drowned ship. What if?

What if what? There wasn't much of my attention to spare for anything besides emotional wallowing, but mustering all the enthusiasm of a death-row inmate catching sight of the laundry instructions on his jumpsuit I gave this distraction a listless sliver of my concentration.

What if... I could prove myself?

It didn't cause much of a stir among my doom-laden thoughts. No more than a tag reading 'Wash strong colors separately' would distract you from thoughts of the gallows.

And anyway, who would I prove myself to? Why would it matter? Where would I even find the energy? And how would I feel when inevitably I failed?

Then again, this secret that the PAC was keeping was something big; what if I could help them with it? I was at my quirky best working in uncharted intellectual territory – in areas where the academic infrastructure wasn't built yet – and that was exactly the terrain confronting this project. Whereas most people couldn't work without a map, without some fixed points to steer by, I could. That was high on the list of reasons why I fitted in so badly wherever I went: I didn't like living inside someone else's framework; I'd kick at it, try to rearrange it, attempt to construct my own.

I suppose you could say I was kind of an intellectual off-roader. Plus, I didn't know a lot about any one thing; I just knew a little about almost everything and I could make connections. Boy, could

I make connections. Which meant that maybe *I* was what this team needed – not some neat-and-tidy, colour-inside-the-lines team-player used to being told how to think, but someone like me.

Impossible as it seemed, I felt a little reflexive twitch of enthusiasm at this idea. Maybe it was just the last shudder before my motivation gave out for good, but this thought had somehow attracted my full attention.

As everyone knows, people with big brains don't behave any better than the rest of the population, they just rationalise better after the fact. Well, the idea that the PAC and me might be a match made in heaven was making more and more sense to me as a plan for the future – but it was making equally good sense as a desperately-needed rationalisation of my failure-strewn past.

I mean, what if trail-breaking, pioneering research wasn't just my forte, it was my oxygen? Well then naturally I'd have felt stifled where I was, stuck in the airless academic suburbs all my life. Maybe it was just my worthless luck to be born too late, into an era where most of the academic wilderness had already been paved over? Maybe I'd struggled all these years to fit in because I needed the kind of mental challenge that just didn't exist any more.

The signs were all there. I knew I was something of an academic cowboy but I'd always tried to suppress that side of me. But maybe what I needed all along wasn't a bit more discipline, maybe what I needed was a frontier to tame[1].

This new revelation took hold so thoroughly that for a second I couldn't think why my eyes itched and my nose needed blowing. Allergies? Oh wait, that's right, I'd been crying my eyes out a little while ago. Well that mood had well and truly left me now; the depression had been shoved back into the iron box it slept in. My

---

[1]   OK, so cowboys didn't tame frontiers, they supervised cows, but we're talking 'in the popular imagination' here.

tears had dried up, leaving only the rebound lightness you feel after a really good sob.

Now all I needed was a way into the PAC.

CHAPTER 4

As my mood lightened, I felt fired up and full of purpose (and *maybe* a little manic too). Somehow I would patch things up with the Professor. I wasn't sure exactly what my current, post-ragged-upon status was, but I didn't think I was off the project yet. I reckoned I was in the penalty box but still hanging by a thread (to use a well-known sports & embroidery metaphor).

I needed the Professor to forgive me and I needed to be drafted into the PAC – after which I could make myself indispensable (which at that moment I was convinced I could do).

(I didn't want to think about whether my new plan would actually work; I wanted to act before the moment passed, before this wonderful sense of purpose could desert me.)

I would definitely need to apologise to the Professor. I had to persuade him to grant me a stay of execution. Which he would do, right? Sure, I'd been pushing my luck with him for years, but this was the first time he'd really called me on it. So *technically* this was only 'swipe one' (as they ought to say in baseball when you *don't* strike the ball). Baseballing types get three lives, cats get a preposterous nine lives for sitting around licking their butts all day; *I* should get at least *one* chance to redeem myself[1].

Anyway, once I was out of the penalty box there were two things I would need to work on: intelligence and leverage. Intel, because I had to learn more about the strange world the PAC had uncovered if I was going to make myself useful to them. And leverage because I'd need a way to persuade the group – or at the very least the Professor – to let me join the inner circle.

Step one was my speciality: soak up everything there is to know on a new subject, organise it, then start filling in the gaps. Step two was just the opposite: my Achilles heel. I didn't have any leverage, any favours to call in and (face it) I wasn't likely to win through on charm alone. In fact the only person I could think of who still cared about keeping on my good side was Daniel.

Well, so be it; I'd start with good old Daniel.

And there was no time like the present. The Professor would need to cool off a bit before he'd want to hear anything I said – even if it *was* an apology – but I could still get busy. I'd go and find Daniel right now.

I checked the console's clock and thought about Daniel's routine. Then I let myself out of the server room and detoured to the ladies' toilets. During the day I don't wear make-up, at least not in the usual course of things, but Hysterical Blotchy Female wasn't the look I needed right now.

When I'd tidied my face up a little, I hot-footed it out the main entrance and round the side of the building towards the back-door to the kitchens. The PAC's hour-long break was nearly up but there was a fair chance that most of them, probably including the Professor, would still be loitering in the refectory, drinking tea.

---

[1] Though on reflection I might not justify myself using *exactly* those words.

Clichéd though it sounds, it's what British academics do. But I knew Daniel liked to have a crafty cigarette with his cuppa, which meant he'd be out of doors somewhere, despite the intermittent rain.

Outside, the chronic drizzle was in temporary remission, but everything was still soaked. As I left the gravel drive, a certain reluctance around the lower pant-leg told me that the cuffs of my jeans were greedily drinking in the moisture from the grass. That was going to look glamorous.

I rounded the corner of the old stone kitchen buildings and, sure enough Daniel was there, talking to the scruffy cook in his stained white cook clothes, the both of them puffing on what the British still insist on calling fags. I wondered what these two had in common; were they discussing Charlemagne or casseroles? Or, knowing guys, perhaps they didn't bother with conversation. I'd heard that most male bonding is based on a primitive system of grunts.

The cook saw me approaching and said something to Daniel, then stubbed out his smoke and vanished inside. Daniel looked up as I got near. His hand dropped to his side and instinctively shielded his cigarette, like he'd caught sight of the principal – I think it was just a public-school[1] reflex. His expression, though, was relaxed and friendly. With his other hand, he raised a forefinger to tip the brim of his imaginary Stetson and said, "Howdy, Ma'am."

I collected myself and for the second time that year turned on a smile in his presence. I wasn't quite sure what I was going to say, but the best way to find out was to start speaking.

I said, "Can I have one?"

---

[1] You prolly know this already, but in the UK public means private. And private tends to mean special – as in 'he takes the *special* bus to school'. So public schools are the ones the public aren't allowed in to.

He looked surprised and said, "I thought you'd packed it in."

"I still weaken when things get stressful," I said – so that he'd ask me to explain; though the truth was that I never smoked any more. It kicked up my asthma, so the fun had gone out of it. If I smoked at a party I'd spend half the night wheezing. Cigarettes = cool, but struggling to breathe = extra not-cool.

"So what's causing you stress?" he asked as he held out first the pack and then his lighter. I took a Marlboro Light – all anyone ever offered me – wondering if they even make other brands of cigarettes any more. Ever the furtive smoker, Daniel made the pack and the lighter appear from thin air and then disappear again once I'd lit up. I remembered that he could also roll his own with insouciant skill – something that I found simultaneously downmarket and a little bit charming.

I puffed without inhaling and said, "Well... too much boredom, mainly." I took a mouthful of smoke and added, "But I also screwed up." His expression became appropriately concerned.

I sighed, trying not to overdo it, and blew a little smoke into the moist air.

I said, "I'm really struggling to concentrate, what with the brain-dead stuff they've got me doing. It's so unbelievably monotonous that I can't help zoning out sometimes. But then I miss some silly detail and get in trouble. I need a challenge, you know? Something to keep me awake." Again I smiled at him and he smiled back, nodding. See how devious I can be?

He offered: "Yeah, but we're still setting up. There's bound to be some donkey-work to begin with. Once it's all up and running I'm sure you'll get something meaty to work on."

I turned to look at him. "Well, *you* seem to have plenty to occupy your brain," I said. "That procedures and admin thing is obviously a lot more interesting than it sounds." I looked away again, out over the expanse of wet grass, wondering what he'd make of that remark.

Out of the corner of my eye I could see him cast a nervous glance at me. I did my best to be nonchalant and kept my eyes fixed on the downcast sheep that dotted the drenched hills. A second or two later I could tell he'd looked away. My focus stayed on the sheep, giving him plenty of time to speak.

But he said nothing so I decided to make him sweat a little, make him think he'd given something away. I faced him and asked, "You've gone quiet; did I say something?"

"No, no," he assured me.

I pressed him, looking worried, "You sure?"

He said, "No, it's nothing."

Which meant I could say: "Daniel, people only ever say 'it's nothing' when it's something. Is there something about the committee I'm not supposed to know?"

Corny? What are you talking about? The word you're looking for is *masterful*. No way was Daniel an experienced enough liar to be *sure* he hadn't let something slip, now or in the past. I mean how else could I know that something was going on? By spying on him? Don't be ridiculous.

Daniel took a sharp drag on his cigarette and looked awkward. "Erm, Jo…" was all he said.

I threw him a rope, in my new role as master manipulator. "It's OK. You're not the first person to hint that the committee are up to something. I was just hoping that whatever it is, you might put in a good word for me; maybe I could be a part of it too." Simper, simper.

Now he really was uncomfortable – probably thinking through what he was going to say when the PAC hauled him over the coals for blabbing. He tried standing his ground: "What do you mean? I didn't say anything."

Again, courtesy of day-time soaps, that was an easy one to twist. I said, "You didn't *say* it, but you made it pretty obvious, don't you think?"

I was still searching for a way to make him open up. I gave him big eyes and said, "Pleeease. It's driving me crazy doing the mindless stuff. I really need, you know, a challenge before I go out of my mind."

Clang. Bad choice of words. It would probably be best if I left out the references to being a crazy person. But it was too late. His expression shifted from discomfort to concern. Couldn't he see I was being metaphorical? He said, "Listen, you're not back on those patches of yours, are you?"

That was the wrong direction for this to go in and it was an argument we'd already had more than once. I said, "That's got nothing to do with it. I'm talking about finding something interesting to work on."

He didn't take the hint. He softened his voice even more and said, "I just think you'd find everything easier without that stuff. You don't need it."

That preachy, hand-holding tone of his really gets on my nerves. I tried not to let it rile me but, trust me, it's instantly infuriating. I couldn't think what to say next... but that didn't seem to stop me blundering on: "I'm asking you to do me a favour. Is that such a big deal? Do you have to make it so hard?" Listening to my own words, I sounded anything but calm now. I wasn't even doing a very good job of keeping my voice down.

And apparently I'd encouraged Daniel on his little social-worker trip. He'd switched to his most calm, most caring voice – the one I especially hate. He said, "Of *course* I want to help. You know that. But if something's bothering you, we should talk about it. Then we can think about what to do."

Well, that wasn't even him talking; it was obviously some article he'd read about handling People with Problems. Is your friend on DRUGS? If you suspect that someone you know may be ON DRUGS, first reassure them that you're there for them. Crazy druggies need *a lot* of reassurance. Then patronise them to within an inch of their lives while remembering to keep repeating their name – it builds trust. And remember, adopt the troubled but patient tones of a kindly uncle even if you happen to be a year younger than them.

It made me want to scream. Right on cue, he said, "Look, Jo, you know you can talk to me…"

I didn't let him finish. He obviously wasn't going to help me and I certainly didn't need him practicing any more of his Talking to Troubled Teens bullshit on me.

I held up a hand to cut him off. "Fine, fine," I said, "Thanks for the lecture; it was very helpful." I turned and walked briskly back towards the main entrance, leaving him struggling for words like a landed fish trying to breathe.

I was annoyed with myself for getting mad just as quickly as I always do. I couldn't seem to hit a compromise between fear of being found out and over-confident blundering.

Halfway back to the main entrance I realised I was still carrying a lit cigarette and dropped it into a puddle. It made an abbreviated fizzing noise that sounded a bit like the word 'snip' as it went out.

So much for Daniel.

It was a setback. I was bloodied, but unbowed though – not to mention hacked off, as they say in these parts.

I hadn't got anywhere with my first attempt to get some leverage on the PAC, but maybe I could focus on the intel for a while, until I'd regrouped.

I took some deep breaths of wet air, reminded myself I was on a mission, then I headed back to my lair. It was time to read the rest of the PAC's mail.

After all, when in doubt, research.

(Note: an even better maxim, learned some time later is: try not to let the research get you killed.)

CHAPTER 5

Once more I was back at the server room and now there was an envelope pushed under the door. It was the delivery note that came with the crates – the crates that were apparently blocking the corridor in the dorms.

This was hardly today's top story, but all the same I couldn't ignore it. If it didn't get sorted out pronto the Professor would never come down off the ceiling. And I needed him to get over his conniptions so that I could remain on the project. I also needed him to get over it so that he would consider asking me to join the PAC. And finally I needed him to get over it because I couldn't bear him being mad with me. It might be distant affection that I got from him, but I valued it all the same.

So the crates. And while I was thinking about that little chore and how I might quickly cross it off my to-do list, another chore came to mind. I needed to hassle the tenant of my house in London about rent and looking for lodgers and being less of a butt-pain. And I'd been putting that off because – surprise, surprise – I didn't want to do it.

Again, it didn't sound like a priority compared with researching the alleged fight against superpowered evil, but things would really come unglued if I didn't tackle it soon.

Just before I'd left England to start my PhD in the States I used the majority of my father's Gewissengelt[1] to buy a house. I've been criss-crossing the Atlantic all my life, so I knew one day I'd be back. And buying property seemed like a smart investment in the long term. Plus in the short-term, it promised to bring in some rent and give me a base when I visited London. I mean, it sounds plausible, right? But, upon further inspection, it turned out that life wasn't that simple.

Like all good Americans, I'd believed my own propaganda. Confident in my plan, when I moved back to the UK I'd foolishly set things up so that rent from my tenants was the only thing topping up my bank account (unless you counted the drip, drip, drip of my miniscule project wages) and lately there'd been no rent. Which was a problem because bottles of Ouzo Extra Collapso don't pay for themselves. With no rent coming in, I'd drained my current account with impressive speed and kept on going. My overdraft had inflated alarmingly, bursting through its credit limits and triggering a volley of penalty charges like buttons popping off a fat man's shirt. While the adage 'ignore it and it'll go away' might work a treat on medical problems there seemed to be a dogged inevitability about debt that no amount of neglect could dispel.

Maybe I needed to spend a weekend in London to see if I could get things back on track. I could try to sort out all the rent-related nonsense and at the same time have a few days R&R away from Yokel-World and this project. It would give me a chance to think

---

[1]   My advice is to just ignore words you don't understand. I mean I'd probably explain them if they were important, right? Hmmm, now you've got me wondering.

through the PAC revelations.

For a moment that all seemed tempting, but to my surprise I realised I actually didn't want to leave right now. I'd got work to do here, what with the ingratiating and the snooping and the unravelling of forbidden mysteries, etc. So I decided to put off the London trip – though I'd need to slap a band-aid on the problem in the meantime.

I know, I know, this doesn't sound very relevant. But, boy, will you feel stupid if some of this stuff comes up on the test and you skipped ahead.

So anyway, something had to be done about the rent. *Or* I had to find another source of income. Admittedly, I could probably raise some cash if I didn't mind asking my father for help. But I *did* mind asking my father for help. I'd save that option until I'd run out of kidneys to sell.

Tucked away in my Fortress of Servitude, pondering my options, I was still feeling a little of that post-weep rebound-high; it was making me feel unusually dynamic, and I figured I should fix as many problems as possible before I slumped back into my trademark malaise. So I would head over to the dorms to call my lodger, Noola[1] The Pain-in-the-Ass, from my room and while I was there I could take a look at the distressing crate situation.

Before I set off, I took all the PAC mail and documents I'd decrypted and copied them to a flash drive. Now I'd be able to read them on my laptop in the privacy and squalor of my own room.

* * *

---

[1] It even annoys me to write the word 'Noola'. I mean, why give your child a traditional Celtic name like 'Nualla' and then spell it phonetically? It just reeks of history absorbed from the backs of cereal boxes.

The drizzle had started up again (hooray!), but this time, as I tripped between the puddles, I managed to keep my jean cuffs from rehydrating. Sadly, now my hair was gulping moisture from the air and getting set to do its frizztastically adorable dandelion impersonation. Thankfully I made it to the dorm's outside door before my locks reached the point of no return. (In my case, water is to hair as heat is to popcorn.)

Up the stairs, through the fire door and sure enough: there were boxes running all the way down the dorm corridor. They weren't packing crates as I'd been picturing them, just reinforced cardboard boxes, and if they'd actually been blocking the passage when they were unloaded, they weren't now. Someone had spaced them out a little and it was no longer *impossible* to get past – providing you could walk with your knees pressed tightly together. I'd concede there still wasn't a lot of corridor left for foot traffic, though. Crap.

I really wasn't expecting so many boxes. What was in them all?

Last time I'd called up to check on my father (translation: to get some money) I'd spoken to Mrs Revilla, the housekeeper. She could hardly wait to tell me that Dad was getting rid of all Mom's things. Probably wife-number-two objected to all the mementoes of wife-number-one around the place. Or maybe it was current-girlfriend/potential-wife-three who was grumbling.

It occurred to me that as an added bonus maybe Dad had worked out that disposing of Mom's things would also erase any unpleasant reminders that he'd had a daughter by his first wife. Pretty soon, the only evidence that I'd once lived there would be a string of entries on his bank statements. Which is why I tried to make sure those little bookkeeping mementoes of me were as eye-wateringly memorable as possible.

Anyway, when Mrs Revilla had told me the plan, I did a little flipping out and a little ranting and I demanded that my mother's things be sent to me, rather than thrown in the trash. I wasn't going to allow her memory to be edited out of existence like that.

Let me stop there a second. Maybe I should be clear on something. Not that I think I should have to explain, but sometimes people act surprised when... What I mean is, Mom died a long time ago and sometimes people accuse me of acting like it was yesterday. I don't see that it matters, but yes I was very young and now I'm comfortably into my twenties, so perhaps a really well-adjusted person would view the whole thing as just some childhood setback or something. A hiccup best forgotten.

But that's just it, I *have* forgotten it. It's not something I've really talked about to anyone who isn't a registered therapist, but I have no real memories of my mother. I was five when she died and so, logically, I should recall all sorts of things about her. But everything I know is secondhand, learned from pictures and from talking to people who knew her. I'm sure if I was still seeing any of my former therapists they'd link that fact to my wig-out over the plan to ditch her things. My only connection to her is through the effects she left behind and I don't *care* that it's twenty years later; wanting a link to your mother is not a phase you grow out of.

Anyway, after the funeral, her clothes and a lot of her things were given away to charity. Someone had saved a few books for me, for when I was older, and the rest had been put into storage ever since. I imagined that by now we were down to maybe a photo album, some ornaments and a few bundles of letters. I was expecting a box or two like you'd get when you have a new stereo delivered; what I got was a *collection* of boxes like you'd get if you had a hockey team delivered. The thought that there was this unexpected mountain of her personal belongings still in existence, a whole consignment of clues to what she was like... well, it was a little daunting.

As I was unlocking my door I saw that the box nearest to me had a plump envelope securely taped to its top. The word 'Inventory' was block-lettered on the envelope's front. I fished out my little Juice pocket-knife and snapped open a blade. I used it to slit the envelope free and open it up. Inside were a half-dozen sheets of laser-printed paper, stapled top-left, which exhaustively listed the contents of all the boxes. Box 6 immediately caught my eye as it mainly contained 'personal correspondence'. I could fit one box into the free floor space in my room without trapping myself in there permanently, and the lucky winner was going to be box number six.

Now, what was I going to do with the rest of it?

More or less straightaway I got an idea. There were two little windows in my room, high up on the wall opposite the door. I couldn't see anything from them – unless you count a piece of sky – without standing on the bed. And it wasn't worth the effort; if I did climb up to take a look, the view consisted of a muddy lane running down to a barn. A rusty red gate of tubular-steel was the only bright spot in the sodden green-brown scene – unless someone parked a car down there. The apron of stone-chips in front of the barn door seemed to serve the project team as an overflow car park.

I'd never really thought of it before, but that sort of implied that the barn was part of the same parcel of land as the dorm and the office buildings. If we could park there, maybe we had the use of the barn. Maybe I could stash the remainder of the boxes in there.

That sounded more like a question for Susan Milton than the Professor (or was that just my cowardice talking?). I'd have to talk to her about it once the PAC meeting ended.

OK. Now (deep breath) for Noola. I brought up the number on my cell-phone and hit send.

She answered promptly with a drawn-out "Yeah?" and already

I was tempted to hang up. That accent.

I mean I'm hardly a xenophobe; I've spent nearly half my life outside the US. And I'm the first to admit that a lot of foreign accents sound delightful. I could listen to someone read bus schedules in French and find it charming. The story of Goldilocks told in Russian would stir my blood and leave me eager to join the epic struggle of bears versus tow-headed interlopers. But with some accents, a little goes a very long way. Noola's ultra-nasal vowel-wringing Australian was just plain wearying at the best of times. A compliment from her sounded like a complaint. So when she whined – which she did constantly – it was an adenoidal dirge that brought to mind stoned cats squabbling.

"Noola? It's Jo," I said.

"Jooooo. It's good you called; I wanted to taaaaalk to you."

"Really?" I said unenthusiastically, "what about?"

"Listen, this place is a dive. This neighbourhood I mean. Do you know what happened to me? I was mugged. Took my phone, my wallet. They even, can you belieeeeeve it, cut the ring my grandmother gave me for my eighteenth right off my goddamned finger. It was insane."

Gulp. "Are you OK?" I asked.

"Well, I'm still breathing, but believe me I'm not over the moon about it. Jerry and Katya moved out?" Wait, that wasn't a question, she was just doing that annoying thing where you twang up at the end of every sentence. "I've had to cancel my credit cards, buy a new phone and if I'm out late I have to get a taxi back. Someone should do something about this place."

For some reason, she was talking about all this as though it were my fault. I mean, I just wanted some rent; I wasn't planning to run for government on a law-and-order ticket. I said, "Erm, well, Noola. I'm sorry to hear all that and I'm glad you're OK… I mean not hurt. Listen, I was calling to ask about the rent situation you see I haven't…"

She didn't let me finish: "I can't belieeeve you're asking me that." She sounded outraged and offended, as though I'd demanded to know how anyone could stand the sound of her voice. She launched into it: "I took this place because it was cheap. I didn't know that was because I was signing up to get robbed on my way home. You know, I could have been killed… or worse." I didn't ask what she meant by that.

I suggested as tactfully as I could: "Well, I understand that. But the place was cheap because you agreed to help me find lodgers. That was the deal."

"Yeah," she said as though I'd made her point for her, "and how many people do you suppose want to live in a house where they get attacked on their way home? Not that many, Jo. Not that many. Right now my rent money is going to pay for replacing what was stolen and on taxis so I can get home at night without having to worry about…" She gulped air and fought to finish her sentence, "… what might happen."

Her righteous anger had morphed into self-pity at the end there. She sounded like she was fighting back the sobs.

I didn't see how I could push it. I mean, *I'd* be pretty freaked if someone cut a ring off my finger. Wouldn't you have to wonder, just for a moment, whether they might take the finger too? Shudder.

"OK, OK," I said, "I'm sorry to bring it up. You're obviously pretty upset…"

She butted in with: "You're bloody right I'm upset," but she was more sad than angry.

I pressed on, "…so I won't bother you any more. Maybe we can talk in a week or so. OK?"

I was already sorry I'd called, but she wasn't finished with me yet: "To be reaaaally honest with you, Jo, I'm not even sure how I feel about living here any more. I'm going to have to see what I think about the whoooole idea."

She said it like forcing her to think was adding insult to injury.

Time for me to bail: "Well, OK. Listen I have to go, but I'm glad you're sort of alright. OK, bye then," I said.

She just sniffed and muttered something sorrowful. I hung up.

Well, that was a bust. Weirdly, I felt *almost* good about it though, because I hated doing things like that, hassling people for money. It had been a disaster, but then I knew in advance it would be and I did it anyway. Go me.

I hadn't solved the problem, but I could, in good conscience, put it out of my mind for a few days.

I spent the rest of the afternoon and the first part of the evening alternating between the contents of the PAC's filestore and the contents of Box 6. I struck a strange sort of equilibrium: first I'd take a tiny, measured dose of emotional turmoil by lifting something out of the box containing my mom's things. When the nostalgic swells threatened to turn into a dark wave of melancholy I'd plunge back into the crystalline surrealism of the PAC's world. Their actions were impossible and absorbing and had the power to pull me out of the unpleasant headspace inhabited by thoughts of my mother's last days.

From time to time I also glanced nervously at the door, expecting the heart-stopping knock that would mean my spying had been discovered, or that some other crappy thing had happened. But no knock came.

All in all, I didn't know how I felt about going through my mom's things; it was too big a feeling to get an overall impression of. But on that other matter, the PAC, I felt my feelings shifting, changing. There was the beginning of acceptance, of the idea that it wasn't a hoax or a mass-hallucination, but something else. I wasn't ready to believe it was all true yet, but I was increasingly sure that there was something solid at its core. And that, I can tell you, was a strange sensation.

I'd discovered an account, almost like a diary, of what had happened to David, Susan and the Professor the previous year and how they had become involved with this guy Jan. It was interesting to speculate about why they'd written it. Did one or more of them worry that they might not be around to tell their replacements the tale?

I read it avidly and then read it again. The main points were these: someone called Dass was the head of a sort of superpowered mafia called the Army Who Witnessed Creation. Jan was an ex-member of this cult/crime family/coven who had now gone rogue. Jan stole something called the Marker from Dass. The Marker was supposedly some sort of passport to immortality for which Jan then needed the operating instructions. Jan killed the previous owner of those instructions, but the key documents, along with lots of others on the subject of supernatural powers, eluded him and ended up at the London School of Antiquities being studied by Susan Milton.

Meanwhile David Braun was hunting the Marker on behalf of Dass, initially unaware that he was working for a superhuman criminal mastermind and that the missing item was a magical artefact. When David learned there were documents describing the Marker, he teamed up with the expert studying them: Susan. The two of them ended up caught between Dass and Jan as old owner and new fought over the Marker. The Professor also became entangled as he tried to help his favourite student, Susan.

After Jan killed Dass and stole the Marker for the second time he came after David and Susan, who were by now on the run from him with the Marker's instructions tucked in their back pocket.

Jan's vicious efforts to retrieve the instructions from the pair culminated in a showdown in which he nearly killed them both. What saved them was intervention by the Professor. He contacted the business front for Dass's organisation, and anonymously tipped off another member of Dass's cabal, a woman called Karst, as to Jan's whereabouts. Karst intervened, killing Jan and retrieving the precious documents. Jan, however, had refused to divulge the secret of the Marker's current hiding place to Karst. The PAC had every reason to believe that The Army Who Witnessed Creation, perhaps now headed by Karst, were still hunting for the Marker.

The summary of the summary. Karst and her superpowered colleagues were still out there. The PAC were laying low while learning all they could.

Phew. Not exactly an everyday tale of ordinary folk, is it?

It was around nine when I finished reading that account and I felt I'd earned a drink. I gave in to temptation, slipping out of the dormitories and climbing the hill to the pub. No one I knew was there and I drank my wine in silence while failing to focus on a couple of back issues of Nature I'd brought along. I sipped gut-rot and thought about what I'd read.

Having failed to find the Marker, how long before the Army came for David and Susan? They'd hopefully be aware that Jan was acting alone and that David and Susan were his victims not his accomplices – just as Karst must have been when she let them live. But once they'd exhausted other avenues of investigation, wouldn't the Army decide to 'interview' David and Susan anyway, just to find out what their exact role had been and how they'd ended up at Jan's mercy?

Fortunately for our plucky heroes, it seemed as though all the bad guys who had encountered the pair were now dead: Jan, Dass and his two assistants. Only Karst lived, and she would have little enough info to go on. She knew both of them had been injured and that they'd been forced by Jan to hand over a cache of documents, including the instructions for the Marker. It was difficult to see how she could learn their names from that.

Could Karst trace the history of the documents back to the School of Antiquities and find Susan that way? For a start, despite the fact that Jan was an ex-member of the Army Who, he didn't know how to operate the Marker without instructions. That suggested that the Army kept the trick to operating the Marker a secret, maybe to prevent exactly what had happened: an insider stealing it. But Jan had found a copy of the instructions elsewhere. It stood to reason that the Army had no idea that such a copy existed or they'd have done something about it.

Even once the documents had reached the School of Antiquities, only a few academics would have known about them. There were very few people who could describe those papers well enough for someone to establish that they were the same ones that Karst took away with her. On the other hand, Karst had those documents in her possession, each piece of paper neatly labelled in its own little plastic wallet. According to what Susan had written, they weren't a dead giveaway – they didn't have the college seal and a phone number printed on them or anything - but maybe Karst would find a clue in the wallets or the labels that led her to the School.

If Karst discovered that the documents had once been at the School of Antiquities, would that enable her to find Susan? Susan had only spent a few weeks there on a secondment. But on the other hand there weren't that many women associated with the project. Could Karst tie a memory of a bloody and battered young woman lying on the floor of darkened church to an academic secondment from Professor Shaw's Cambridge college? Or was there some way she could discover that the half-dead body lying among the pews was a man called David Braun? You wanted to say 'no' on both counts, but on the other hand was it something you'd want to hang your life on? David and Susan – and perhaps the Professor – must be living with the constant threat of discovery. I wondered if I really wanted any part of that.

Assuming I believed a word of it, of course.

Closing time rolled around soon enough. Not *totally* drunk, I tottered back down the hill – deciding on a whim to make a detour before returning to the dorms. I made my way to the main project building and slipped inside.

Moving through the darkened corridors, I sneaked into the Professor's office with the semi-inebriated intention of retrieving my phone from the meeting room. I mean, what could possibly go wrong with that bright idea?

CHAPTER 6

The Professor was firm, but not angry, as he spoke. He was almost his usual self, although he wasn't quite turning gleeful cartwheels yet. He said, "I hope you can see: I need to take some sort of action. I can't allow this to be a repeat of the previous times you have neglected your responsibilities."

I reckoned I was winning him over but I still had some work to do.

I was standing in his office, having pleaded my case. Today had been a good day and a string of successes had given me the confidence I needed to seek him out. And even now my luck was holding. So far, this conversation had managed *not* to veer off the rails and plunge into the tall grass.

Success number one today had come when I woke up and realised that I'd survived last night's impressively stupid decision to recover my spy-phone while under the influence of toxic grape-products. The main building had been deserted and dark, and there'd been no one to witness my heavy-footed tiptoeing, my missteps and self-shushing – followed by my weaving escape. You could say that I'd shot myself in the foot and missed. Hooray!

Then, this morning, finding myself with miraculously little in the way of hangover, I'd set to work scaling my chore-mountain and trying to clear the backlog of project work. I hadn't quite got caught up – I was *waaaayyy* too behind for that – but I'd taken a huge bite out of the problem. There was plenty to show for half a dozen hours of intense application.

And top of the notable achievements list was the fact that I'd called the relevant companies about our pending subscriptions and arranged a string of day-passes to tide us over while they futzed about with the paperwork. Then I'd apologised to the team for the delay. I'd very nearly done that in person, but, you know, that would have been a miracle. Instead, I *personally* emailed them to say I was sorry about how long it had all taken and to update them on the good news about the temporary fix.

That didn't just scratch an item off the Damoclean To-Do list; it actually made me feel good too. I almost got a kick out of being a good little worker-bee.

And there was more. I'd tracked down Susan Milton and wheedled the use of part of the barn so's I could store my crate collection. She'd agreed, on the condition that it was just for a few days, until I could arrange an alternative – but it seemed a good bet she'd let me extend it for longer than that. She was a little vague about what the team was currently using the barn for, so once she'd given me a key, I went to check.

She'd got part of the ground floor set up as a basic gym and there was a cleared area in the centre. I know she was an avid fencer and was maybe into martial arts, so I figured this was where she practiced. I was pretty sure that team money was paying the rent on the barn – and her training was hardly team business – so I figured I had just as much (or little) right to use the space as she did.

Anyway, once she'd agreed to share the barn with me, I phoned a man-with-van number I found in the yellow pages and persuaded a couple of local yokels to shift the crates into the barn for the princely sum of twenty quid. Not bad, and they were available that morning, so the whole thing was sorted by lunchtime. I'm *all about* takin' care of bidness [insert high-five here][1].

Towards the end of the afternoon, feeling pretty good about everything, I decided to tackle the most dauntingest chore of them all: generating a little détente with the Professor. And call me emotionally crippled, but I actually made some notes about what I was going to say before I sought him out – a refreshing change from my usual policy of stampeding around until I fall into a hole, as I'm sure you'll agree.

I figured that some apologising was required, but at the same time I needed to seem less of a neurotic mess than I'd been recently. The best way to persuade him not to give up on me, I decided, was first to persuade him that I could look after myself, that I wasn't going to be a burden to him however things turned out. I needed to appear capable, stable, productive – and appropriately concerned about repairing any damage done. Easy, right? So I went in and I told him that he didn't have to trust me, he could just let my future actions speak for themselves. I was putting myself on probation with him and if he didn't think I was doing right by him, then *I'd* remove myself from the team.

It was all pretty sneaky, when you think about it. I mean, no one enjoys the burden of propping up an emotional basket-case; but on the other hand, pushing them overboard generates a lot of guilt. I'd reframed the problem for him by appearing to have whipped myself into shape already. *Now*, if he threw me off the team, he

---

[1]   Hmmm. That makes me seem whiter than ever, doesn't it?

wouldn't be jettisoning a neurotic wreck, he'd be creating one. In fact he'd be knocking someone down who was gamely trying to make a come-back. If he did that he'd be looking at a man-sized helping of guilt – so to seal the deal I offered to find my own replacement should he decide that I still wasn't up to scratch. I mean lightening his administrative burden on top of everything else, how could he refuse?

And refuse he didn't. But he didn't totally roll over either – though he seemed to be coming around. I guessed that his previous outburst had been a long time coming and that there'd been considerable momentum behind it. He wasn't about to rescind everything he'd said right away. That would be like admitting his big blow-up had been about nothing. On the other hand he was obviously looking for a reason to believe me. I couldn't tell yet which side of the fence he was going to come down on.

Worrying that I might be losing him, I mentioned the crates – hastily explaining that they were all taken care of and throwing myself on my sword a little more into the bargain. Then I told him what was in them.

I explained, "I knew they were coming, I just didn't know when they'd get here – or quite how much stuff there'd be." He was listening attentively so I went on, "But I suppose this has all been hanging over me ever since I called home. The PhD thing really knocked me back and then I found myself worrying about what was in the crates."

That all sounds very manipulative, but it was also true. I was levelling with him here.

"You were worried?" he asked, wanting to understand what I was telling him.

I explained, "Not worried exactly… but I knew I'd be finding out new things about Mom. I know that's what I've always wanted, but it's still a big deal. It's the unknown. I started thinking I might end up disappointed. Maybe she'd still be a mystery to me. Or worse still, I might find out something I didn't really want to know."

"I can see how you might find yourself thinking that way," he said guardedly.

Like I said, it was easy to say this stuff because it was pretty much true. But at the same time I didn't want it to edge over into some sort of charity appeal – you know, all 'pity me'; I knew what a turn-off that would be.

I said, "I know it's not an excuse. But I want you to believe I'm going to do all the things I've promised to do, and I figured if you knew what had been bothering me – and you knew that it was in the past now – you'd see that I meant it." This was scarily open and honest for me and I was glad I'd got it all out without becoming self-conscious.

He digested my words quietly and then asked, "When you say it's in the past... you've already made some headway looking through your mother's things, then?"

"Well, just the tip of the iceberg," I said, "but what I mean is, it was the *anticipation* that was stressing me out. Now that her things have arrived, you know... well, it's done; the die is cast, if you see what I mean. Whatever I find out, I find out. There's nothing I can do about it, so there's no point in freaking out."

I thought he might say something, show some sign of approval or agreement, but he was still looking thoughtful. Was he unconvinced? Or was he concerned about some other aspect of all this?

Delicately, as though wishing to inspect the contents of a can of worms without spilling any, he said, "This difficult business is still certain to upset you, I'm sure. Anything that brings you closer to your mother's memory is likely to rekindle your sense of loss, I would imagine. I would say to you, Jo, that there's no need to rush here. You can choose your own pace. This is not something that needs to be undertaken all at once."

When he said those words, he was obviously not thinking about my status on the project at the moment, he was thinking about *me*. I was relieved, both because it showed that he still cared about me and because it hinted that he was letting go of his previous anger. And yet he was obviously still hung up on something and I didn't quite see what it was.

I tried to sound self-assured and chock-full of resilience: "Right, but there's no sense in dragging things out. I can tackle this and then move on." I made a sound that was intended to be a brave little laugh, though it needed a bit more practice.

I continued, "Then I'll be able to focus properly on other things, like the project for instance." Was that too much? Too clumsy? It sounded a bit like toadying, but at the same time it was still mostly the truth.

Top of my wish list was still learning more about the PAC, but today's successes had also given me a tiny taste of how it might feel to be a good little chore-monkey, instead of a renegade – and it felt sort of… peaceful. I was wondering if it might *not* be the worst thing in the world to toil obediently in the salt mines for a while and to try a few tentative sips of that numbing brew known as (ugh) 'team spirit'. After all, I'd have my out-of-hours sleuthing to keep me from getting bored or feeling like a total sell-out.

The Professor, though, was still hinting at whatever it was he was hinting at. "Of course, of course. I'm just saying that you don't have to decide now. Keep on top of your work here and it's up to you how quickly you progress with your mother's… uh, with her things. If you find yourself a little overwhelmed, there's nothing to say you can't take a break for a while, now is there?"

Well, he certainly didn't seem to be angry with me any more. His tone was kind and full of concern. But I didn't quite see why he was labouring this particular point. I sort of wished he'd get past it and onto discussing my future. His words were a little confusing.

Then a possibility occurred to me. Perhaps he thought I'd discover something among my mother's things that would upset me. He was suggesting that I not jeopardise my attempt to get back on an even keel by rushing to learn more about her life. That suggested he knew something I didn't and he thought I wouldn't be able to handle whatever it was. That would fit with his words and his current demeanour.

I didn't quite know what to say... so I settled for blurting out the first thought that occurred to me: "Well, I know you and she went back a long way. Is there something I should know?"

He looked like he *really* didn't want to be asked that question. He prevaricated: "I'm just saying that you have been through a lot and you're obviously still coming to terms with..." He sort of trailed off, and made a gesture with his hands that I took to mean 'and so on'. Nice speech.

Suddenly we seemed to be past the part of the conversation where I pleaded for mercy and into some new phase where he hinted awkwardly and I became increasingly troubled.

"Professor," I said, "if there's something you want me to know, why don't you just tell me?"

He almost blushed – impossible though that sounds. What kind of secret could make him so awkward? In my experience there was a pretty short list of topics that could unsettle someone like that. He looked as ill at ease as if I'd asked him to explain to me where babies come from.

Of course that was a silly, stray thought but, just for a second, I wondered why it had popped into my head. He knew something about Mom; did it involve him too? And he was embarrassed about it. And now there was this thought in my head: sure I knew where *most* babies came from, but what about me? Did I know where I'd come from?

I'm not sure how old I'd been when I worked out that I was named after him. I've always been aware that 'Jo' is short for 'Josephine' and 'Professor' is short for 'Joseph', and I've sometimes wondered about it, in an absentminded sort of way. I figured that he'd been a really important person in Mom's life. But up until this instant I'd always assumed that his importance to her was entirely platonic. There was no way it could be anything else, was there? He must have been in his sixties when my mom was his grad student. At the very least he was in his late fifties and she'd only been twenty-something.

Though I knew they'd stayed in touch even after she met Dad and moved to the States.

"You're not telling me that…" I mumbled.

I knew Dad had been unfaithful, but it had never crossed my mind that Mom could have been. Plus, the Professor was a non-sexual being, surely everyone could see that – even my troubled and lonely mother.

Oh god, except that I'd always felt that she'd hooked up with Dad because he was strong and self-assured and someone she could respect. I figured she'd been looking for a little bit of a father figure and a little bit of a hero to worship. I'd felt that she didn't want someone to be close to, so much as someone impressive to look up to. And you couldn't deny that the Professor might fit that bill too.

I didn't know whether to be disgusted (which I definitely was anyway) or angry or upset or what. In fact I was sort of paralysed because in my mind I was conducting a high-speed review of the last twenty-six years, trying to examine every event I could recall, to see how it fit with this new possibility.

Everything was the same and yet I was seeing it all from a shocking new perspective. With each memory I could summon up, I asked the question 'how would this be different if Mom's old friend was really my father?' I mean, the more I thought about it, the more I realised that his presence in my life had always gone considerably beyond the call of duty if I was really just the daughter of a favourite student.

Without me thinking about it, my mouth sort of fired up of its own accord. "Are you trying to tell me that you and she were... that you were *involved*?"

He was a little taken aback. Maybe he was surprised that I'd figured it out without him having to say more. Unusually for him, he stumbled over his words as he said, "Not in the way... I mean to say, Helen and I had a bond, certainly, but if what I think you're saying or rather asking me..." He was really struggling with this now: "Your mother and I were, I suppose you could say thrown together by circumstances. I've never said anything to you because I really wasn't sure you were ready to hear..."

He had *that* right because I sure as hell wasn't ready to hear it *now*. His discomfort had obviously reached some sort of maximum. Short of outright fainting, there was no way he could look more awkward, seem more guilty. My mind was over-revving and I couldn't even tune in to what he was saying now, his attempts to back out of the situation he found himself in.

What was I going to find among my mother's things? Love letters from him? Did my dad realise he wasn't my dad? What had he thought when my mom wanted to name me 'Josephine'? Oh god, no wonder he always seemed to be competing for the title of World's Most Halfhearted Parent.

I cut the Professor off in his pained rambling and sniffed

back the first unwanted but pathetically inevitable tear. "Listen Professor," oh god, I could hardly call him *that* any more, "I can't handle a long explanation right now."

I wanted to get out of there immediately because I could feel more tears on their way and I'd had enough of weeping in front of an audience for the time being.

"Maybe we can talk about this later," I said, hurriedly. My voice was a starting to tremble as I spoke, but I kept going because I didn't want to give him a chance to start talking again. I didn't want him to start offering me details or telling me how he felt. I had plenty to consider before we got into any of the unbearable specifics.

"I appreciate…" I tried to keep my voice level as I sniffed back tears, "you keeping me on the project and I'll certainly bear in mind what you said about me staying on top of things, but if you don't mind, right now, I'm going back to my room."

I more or less ran out of the Professor's office and back to the dormitory block. And once I was in my room, I realised it wasn't far enough. I needed to get much further away from the Professor and this project.

So I called a taxi to meet me at The Retard, threw a bunch of my things into a big bag, and left the dorm building. The haste and busy-ness of my departure kept me from thinking. I made it onto the lane that headed up the hill without anyone spotting me or seeing where I was going, and frankly, that suited me fine.

CHAPTER 7

I know what you're thinking…

Well OK, I know what *I'm* thinking: I freaked out… again. And I didn't give the Professor any sort of chance to explain or clarify. But this wasn't about being fair to him or not; it was about not wanting to blow any more of my emotional fuses this week. He'd just finished advising me that I should take my nervous breakdowns slowly and in bite-sized chunks (always remembering to chew). And just because they're *my* breakdowns, that doesn't make them any more pleasant to be around, with all that wailing and distress. So I headed for the hills as soon as I realised that my emotional rollercoaster ride was picking up speed again. If it turned out I was going to make a scene, then I was going to do it in private like a grown-up for once.

In fact recent introspection had helped me come up with a theory. I was starting to think that emotions were like drugs – and not the good kind. If you can't 'just say no', then at least you should know when you've had enough.

I decided to handle this situation a little better than the last one

– and to try to get myself back under control. And for that, I would need some privacy.

So I bailed, figuring that we could have our heart to heart and get into the sordid what-have-yous some other time. I'd take this crisis on the instalment plan, just like the-academic-formally-known-as-the-Professor had suggested.

Which reminded me of how, earlier in the week, I'd thought about going to London – and I'd decided against it. Well, I still thought London was the wrong destination, but I really wanted to go *somewhere* – somewhere away from it all.

Fortunately, all the isolation I could ever need was available, free for the asking, right on my doorstep. It was the very isolation I was always complaining about and it offered solitude in abundance. I decided to head to a place called Dartmoor, not far from the field-station.

Dartmoor is where the British armed forces practice surviving the elements. They dump their trainees into its expansive wilderness without proper equipment in order to teach them the value of… erm, paying attention in school so you can get a cushy desk job when you graduate – or something like that.

Anyway, I figured they prolly wouldn't choose that location to practice their survival skills if it was too full of picnic spots and friendly hikers. Comfiness is a hated enemy when you're trying to instil military-grade gumption. Yes indeed. Which made it the perfect place for me right now.

The idea of Dartmoor had popped into my head just as I got back to my room, so I'd dragged my giant holdall out from under the bed and started throwing anything that looked warm and/or waterproof into its dust-lined interior. Then I carefully added my laptop and a handheld GPS unit. Mind you, I had a GPS card for my PDA so I debated taking that for a minute. Oh and I'd need some books to read.

Then, remembering that a good storm-out required both spontaneity *and* speed of execution, I settled for grabbing whatever came to hand. And I only came back and unlocked the door once to snag a mini printer for the laptop. I reckoned that the best way to have an emotion-free weekend would be to concentrate exclusively on the Secrets of the PAC, and to put everything else out of my mind until further notice. To that end, I might want hardcopies of some of those secret documents so I'd have something to ponder as I prepared myself for the melancholy loneliness of the bleak, wind-scoured moors[1].

I'm probably making all this sound kind of flippant, but it wasn't at the time. I was feeling sort of jumbled up inside – not sure if I was really hurt or not, but not willing to think about it either.

As I shoved the printer into the giant holdall, some impulse made me pause a moment before zipping it up. A crazy idea had occurred to me. Quickly I fished out the key for the padlock that held closed the cupboard doors above my bed. In there was where I kept my jewellery box – mainly things of my mother's that I'd inherited. I didn't wear them very often, but I kept them with me.

Anyway, I fetched the box down and laid it in the bag, pushing it into the folds of a sweater. Then I resealed the bag. It was almost too heavy to carry now. Fortunately, I only had to lift it while I was getting it down the stairs; after that, the road up to the pub was just about level enough to let me drag it along on its diminutive little wheels.

Out on the lane, the din the bag made as it clattered over the bumps in the road, its tiny nylon casters whirring like turbines, sounded like someone feeding gravel into a hairdryer and I almost

---

[1]   Such preparation quite possibly involving loitering in the nearest town, eating scones in warm tea-rooms.

expected a crowd to congregate and follow me up the hill, curious to see what all the noise was about. But the lane was deserted and I reached the pub without seeing another soul. Two minutes later the taxi arrived and I was off.

My first thought was to have the taxi take me to the nearest railway station. From there I'd get a train to one of the corners of Dartmoor. But once I was snug on the doughy back seat of the old Toyota, the tropical-pine smell of warm car-freshener in my nostrils, I wondered how much of a slog that trip would be. The driver confirmed that I'd need to change trains in Exeter. I could see a forty-mile rail trip turning into a whole evening of slow trains and waiting on damp platforms. Of course when I learned that the taxi driver could take a credit card payment for his fare, the problem melted away: it was going to be taxi all the way for me. It would bring the horrible day of reckoning with my bank a little closer, but at least this trip would be painless. And wasn't the point of this getaway to indulge in a little painlessness?

Once the driver had lobbed his entire stock of conversational-openers — and I'd listlessly batted them away — he turned his attention to the car stereo. He nudged up the volume to the point where it was just about audible in the back and nodded along to a selection of what the tranquilised-sounding announcer called 'classical mellow classics'.

I let the early evening hedge-rows and saturated meadows slip past the window and attempted to put questions of paternity far from my thoughts. Fortunately I had a once-in-a-lifetime distraction to occupy me. I'd reached the point in my reading of the PAC's secret files where things were starting to get not just interesting (I mean it was *all* interesting) but also revealing.

Susan Milton had concocted a sort of 'how to' manual on the special powers of the bad guys. I'd tried to read a little of it when

I got back from the pub the previous night but for some reason the blurry words wouldn't stay in their proper order. Digging out my laptop now, I picked up where I'd left off and was pleased to find that focussing on the text was no longer a struggle.

One thing that struck me straight away was the implication that Susan was writing from personal experience. The bizarre abilities she was talking about were being described first hand. She'd even begun the colonisation of this new field of knowledge in time-honoured style: by coining some jargon.

A footnote suggested that 'magic', despite being the obvious description for the activity in question, wasn't really 'a helpful or appropriate term'. I'm not sure I agreed with that statement – I thought it summarised things very succinctly – but I could totally see why she'd shy away from that particular word. It was much like the way I'd prefer to be called a 'recovering survivor of emotional trauma' instead of a more conventional term like 'crazy person'.

Isn't it funny how much the words matter? I remember watching some old low-budget docutainment on TV, where a scientist was explaining that what primitive people thought of as witches might simply be young women with psychic powers. I mean, like calling it 'psychic' instead of magical counted as an explanation. No suggestion was offered for how psychic powers might work, but everyone seemed to feel better now that they'd switched to a modern, sciencey-sounding word.

The TV-show people obviously felt that the Powers of the Brain were somehow allowed to be mystical and unknowable, because of all the alpha waves and complicated structures and unwieldy Greek names, whereas magic had only nature to draw upon for its power – and nature was just a bunch of plants and rocks, right? A cool word like 'neuron' could make you think of all sorts of potent possibilities, whereas the word 'stick' probably wouldn't.

No doubt Susan Milton had covered this all in one of her arid academic-style papers: speculating about why brains are more appealing these days as sources of mystery than nature.

Oh and here's a thought: maybe the answer was that – as people have been telling each other for decades – we only use 10% of our brains and who knows what we could achieve if we learned to tap into the rest? That's sarcasm, by the way. That 'statistic' makes me want to grind my teeth. I mean if I didn't know what 90% of something was for, I wouldn't shout about it, or get all superstitiously ignorant and label it 'Source of Mysterious Powers'. It was no better than writing Here Be Dragons on the bits of the map you hadn't visited yet.

Anyway, Susan's notes seemed to be turning the clock back on that neurons-versus-sticks question. Given a choice between explaining superpowers in terms of the outer world of nature or the inner world of neural physiology, she favoured nature. And I had to agree that it was a lot easier to hide an explanation of mystical abilities out there in the roomy expanse of the universe than it was to conceal it inside our rather cramped skulls.

In one passage, Susan had attempted to describe the knot you had to tie your mind in before you could command any of these powers; she had called that mental exercise 'Connecting' (with a capital 'C') – like there was a gap that had to be bridged before you could tap into some reservoir of magical power.

Just like with the Marker, expensive jewellery seemed to play a role. A gold band encircling each wrist and another around the forehead was apparently a pre-requisite for Connecting. Old hands at this sort of thing – those the PAC called 'adepts' – referred to it as 'tribute'.

I'd have been tempted to dismiss gold accessories as simply good showmanship, like an old-timey stage magician's silk top hat, but the PAC claimed that nothing would work without it.

I'd sat in on enough physics lectures to be totally intrigued at the role precious metals played in the PAC's weird world. The ability to work with purified metals underpinned the Industrial Revolution, and it seemed a strange coincidence that it should play such a big part in this occult branch of technology too.

The final piece of jargon Susan suggested was also intriguing. The list of magical powers was extensive but simple enough: Heat, Freeze, Shatter, Shield, Push, Presence and Heal (again, all with capitals). She called each of them 'Surfaces'. It was like each power had its own invisible membrane through which you could interact with the world. Reach out with your mind through, say, the Freezing Surface and you could lower the temperature of an object. Project your concentration through the Shatter Surface and an impact like a hammer blow would strike the point you were focussing on.

It seemed that Heal would work whether you concentrated on it or not, but it was most powerful if you focussed it. And Presence somehow warned you of the approach of other Connected adepts.

I just had to stop and wonder at this point: were they serious?

Even if they were, their words reminded me of the instructions that came with a blues harmonica I once owned. To bend a note, you simply had to "change the angle of airflow to put more pressure on the top of the reed" as you blew. Right. We were in explaining-colours-to-sightless-people territory here. This terminology might make sense to those who already had (or believed they had) experienced Connecting, but it left me confused.

Finally was something called Quell. It seemed that Connecting for the first time was hellish difficult, but the mind quickly adapted[1]

---

[1]   Even then I wondered whether 'the mind adapted' really meant 'the mind was altered'.

and soon it took a conscious effort *not* to Connect if you had your 'tribute' in place. A mental exercise called the Quell state was how you held off Connecting.

Hmmm. The phrase 'intricate delusional structure' flitted through my mind. But it sure was interesting stuff.

So, what else did the documents say? One of the e-mails I'd read made it clear that the PAC still retained a secret electronic copy of the document cache that Army bad-ass Karst had confiscated. The PAC were still mining that cache for information – but keeping very quiet about it. And they'd found other occult documents to add to it since.

I wondered briefly how much research into magic was being concealed inside the legitimate work of the project. From what I could gather, stories of magic had been at the centre of Susan's previous work. But that was before she began to *believe* in any of it. Her run-in with various members of the Army coven – both current and renegade – had changed her outlook.

And with the Army Who still out there – and possibly looking to tie up any loose ends as they searched for the Marker – Susan had good reason to leave myths, legends and tales of the occult well alone. The documents that members of the project claimed to be working on now were all mundane histories of early Britain, and its neighbours, written after the withdrawal of the Roman legions. No magic here. No sir. Perish the thought.

The tricky thing for them was that once you start to look for it *all* old documents talk about magic. Every one of them. You read Homer and Virgil and there, in amongst the deeds of warriors and kings, are superhuman deities performing impossible feats. To pick another random example, the otherwise reliable Roman history of the conquest of Britain talks about Druids using magic to frighten the legionaries. It's the same for all ancient histories – especially the religious ones. The church may frown on any talk of magic today, but in the old days they made it their mission to *fight* magic, not to disprove its existence.

Susan and the gang had obviously worked out that some of the old documents floating around weren't superstitious bunk; they were the real deal. How they separated the bona fide stuff from the crackpot ramblings, I had no idea, but suddenly the way the PAC was wrapped inside our project made a lot more sense. If a document was reasonably magic-free they studied in their day jobs and talked about it at seminars. But if it seemed like it might contain nuggets of occult gold they sneaked it back to the bat cave and worked on it in secret.

That way they could analyse old documents and make use of every scrap. If an insight was practical, it went into the secret PAC files; if it was historical, it went into the public record for the project and helped to keep Susan and the rest of them off the Army's radar. It was all very clever.

That and the drabbing made me think that someone in the PAC knew a lot about operational security. That person was either ex-intelligence or they read a lot of spy novels. Knowing who attended the meetings, I was guessing the latter. A good geek can probably match the NSA[1] for ingenuity, and instead of costing billions of dollars, your only outlay in hiring a geek is a few buck's worth of ramen[2] and a handful of Amazon book tokens.

I found I was utterly absorbed as my mind romped through the details of the PAC's secret activities. When I next looked up from my reading, and occasional head-scratching, we were driving up

---

[1] The vast and secretive US National Security Agency, whose acronym is sometimes translated as No Such Agency.

[2] The Brit translation would be 'Pot Noodles'.

the little high street of Meaves Edge on the borders of Dartmoor. This was where I planned to spend the weekend.

I had the driver drop me at the County Arms Hotel, the most impressive building in the town square, and twenty minutes later I was in a warm room, sprawled on an over-soft bed watching an undersized TV and thinking about dinner.

In spite of my hunger, I was suddenly tired and everything – evil, the PAC, and certain personal questions of which we will not speak – all seemed better left for the morning.

I made a quick trip downstairs, where the hotel's bar brought me scampi and chips before I could doze off into my sauvignon. And it was well before ten o'clock when I tumbled into bed and gave myself up to the sucking quicksand of fatigue. And, while the fifteen or twenty times that doors slammed or that drunks yelled in the night might have pulled me close to consciousness, none of them could keep me from sleep. The next thing I was truly aware of was the morning light perforating the badly drawn curtains. My first thought was of today's big experiment[1] – the experiment for which I had brought along my jewellery box.

At ten o'clock I was in the hotel lobby waiting for a minicab to arrive. It would take me to one of the quieter roads on the edge of the moors and leave me there. By five minutes after ten, I was settled in the back seat watching the hotel disappear behind me.

As we left Meaves Edge, the Welsh-sounding driver was assuring me that once I was done with my hike, returning to civilisation would be 'a doddle'. He explained, "See, I'll tell Kenny, the gaffer like, where I dropped you. And when you call in, just say it was Davey dropped you off and he'll know what's what. Any of the drivers'll know this spot. And if Kenny's not on,

---

[1]   That is to say, *breakfast* and today's big experiment: they were my first thoughts.

which he won't be at that time, just tell the new guy, whatsisname. Remember to tell him Davey G. 'cos there's a Dave Williams on afternoons. Not that I've met the new gaffer yet, but I've heard he's alright and any of the lads will tell him who I am, they all know me. Not so much on the afternoons of course, because I don't work then, but there's bound to be someone around unless there's a match on, like today. Actually, come to think of it, Saturday isn't really your best bet. You wouldn't rather come out here tomorrow, would you? Or Thursday?"

Annoying as it was to listen to someone who thought that reassuring me was somehow more important than actually being of assistance, I had a little bit of sympathy for him. Surprised? Well, it's not always about me, you know? Plus, he was doing something I do the whole time: telling people what they want to hear, filling the gaps in people's expectations with white lies and nonsense. It was like listening to myself as played by a confused Swansea-born cab driver. So in that sense, I suppose it *was* all about me. But as for what he was saying, I reckoned I'd take my chances: today I was feeling adventurous.

"How about this?" I suggested, "Drop me at a payphone and then when I call in, I'll give the address they print above the phone."

"Not too many phone boxes along this stretch, Miss," he warned, drawing in his breath. "One up at the point and the only other is outside the Wanderer's Ease and that's your lot."

Mustering some patience, I enquired, "Well, how about one of those two then?"

He considered it, and was prepared to concede: "I could drop you at the Wanderer's Ease, that way if the outside phone's not working you can go in the pub. Can't guarantee they'll be doing any food today, though. It's not really the season. Round here's deserted this time of year."

I didn't remind him that 'deserted' was what I'd asked for. I just told him I'd risk it.

He brightened: "Barry'll do you a toasty though, no problems. Just tell him Davey G. sent you. You might have to describe me, as Barry's a bit of dope with names and faces. Loves his football though so I don't suppose he'll be around today. Anyway, there's a path from the back of the pub leads up onto the moors. Council put in plenty of signs around there for walkers and so on, so you should be alright. Just don't let the beast get you."

He pivoted around for a moment to grin at me. "No, I'm only joking. There isn't any beast," he explained, very pleased with himself. Perhaps I was witnessing his first ever attempt at humour. What an honour.

When he let me out of the overheated taxi I stood for a moment in the cold October air, savouring the drop in temperature. I was bundled up like Bibendum[1] and that cab had been stifling. Now the snapping breeze snatched away all that excess heat, leaving a delicious, refreshing chill.

The sharp wind was delightful for all of twenty seconds... then I felt the first shiver start as a droplet of rain on a horizontal trajectory caught me in the eye. But pluck and gumption were in good supply today and I strode towards the hills before hypothermia could get so much as a toehold. It so happened that I had the, ahem, robust physique of a walker; it was time to find out if I had the constitution to go with it.

* * *

---

[1] The Michelin Man. Jeez, get an education.

Tired, bedraggled and frozen solid to the touch in a few places, I sat in the Wanderer's Ease an impressive four hours later. Impressive because I wasn't dead – although the moment didn't seem far off. In the meantime, blessed Jameson's Whisky was melting the ice crystals in my bloodstream and stuffing my pounding head with soothing cotton-wool.

I'd trudged for half an hour, trying to keep my bearings and looking for a sheltered spot where I could see but not be seen. Probably I needn't have bothered. I saw no living creature, except a crow, while I was out there. I began to imagine that the crow was circling after a while, maybe waiting for me to collapse, before he feasted on my carcass. But perhaps he was just curious to see what I was up to. I was after all, attempting to perform magic.

I'd sat and stood, paced and pondered, chanted and concentrated for two hours until I began to worry that my body temperature had dropped into single figures. A print-out of instructions from the PAC's secret library was in one numb hand, a pattern for me to concentrate on was gripped in the other. A doubled-over gold chain was doing a fine job of drawing the remaining heat out of my brain and dissipating it on the bitter wind. Likewise, an unfamiliar weight of gold chain dragged at each wrist. All very bling I'm sure, but it made me feel like an idiot. No, better yet, it made me feel like Mister T's dumpy white niece, and as the great man might have said himself, I was a 'fool'… and maybe an 'ugly mudsucker' too.

I'd got nowhere; nothing had happened. Not a tingle, not a twinge, not (as they say in these parts) a sausage.

The fact that there'd been no audience watching me didn't help much. I felt as foolish as if a crowd had gathered and tickets had been sold. Magic? Me, who had sat in more science classes than Albert Einstein had had hot dinners. Me, who could (after half a dozen vodka and Red Bulls) tell you the technical flaws in virtually every episode of The Next Generation, DS9 and Enterprise – and even come up with a few suggestions about how each one could have been corrected. Me, who knew more physics than any biologist, more biology than any computer scientist and more computer science than anyone who didn't have a y-chromosome and a listing on the Nasdaq. I'd somehow talked myself into believing that magic was worth an afternoon of frostbite and peri-terminal exposure tying my head in knots. What was next? Pyramid worship? Crystals? (shudder) *Astrology*?

Well, I'd learned my lesson. First, I was going to dose up on excellent, restorative Gaelic spirits. Then I was going to get a taxi back to the County Arms Hotel and soak in very hot water up to my nostrils until coldness was but a fading dream and damp clothing a distant memory. Then, tomorrow, I was going to read through every document I'd brought with me and figure out what was *really* going on with the PAC.

CHAPTER 8

By three in the afternoon on Sunday, the day after my unsuccessful hike'n'hex, I was starting to feel human again. I'd like to claim that when I woke up that morning, all my physical woes could be traced to the psychic after-effects of a near miss with the supernatural. Or just to an afternoon spent in the ice box of moorland a few miles from my hotel room. But in the interests of total accuracy I have to admit that the bar immediately *beneath* my hotel room was at least as much to blame.

I'd been feeling pleasantly fuddled and moderately thawed by the time the taxi took me away from the Wanderer's Ease. Back at the hotel, I found that the whisky had parched my throat and after a long soak in the tub I was getting a dehydration headache – and I was ravenous. Fortunately, downstairs, the hotel bar was once more ready to meet the challenge. A damn fine roast beef sandwich, a basket of chips and a family-sized helping of mulled wine served in something that looked a little like a beaker arrived in minutes. I settled in to munch and slurp and apply juice to as much of my face as possible. And when I was done, a minion emerged from behind the bar and, through the wonder of modern ingenuity, lit an instant fire in the grate. It was gas-powered, fake-logged bliss.

I had them refill my beaker on several occasions (although my recollection is not entirely clear regarding the exact number). And I vaguely recall trying out a toddy the barman recommended from his time in the navy[1]. Beyond that point, I have one or two snapshot memories of talking to (or at) strangers in the bar, a single impression of pressing my overheated forehead to the cool window back in my room and a final vague sense of searching for the bathroom at around 3 a.m. As usual, no dreams came. And so endethed that particular day.

Someone hammered on my door at about ten the next morning, calling out something unintelligible in the baffling glossolalia favoured by maids the world over. I managed to send them away and went to stand under the shower for a while, waiting for order to return to my magimixed wits.

I felt a lot better once I'd had some breakfast... and it had stayed down. I wasn't yet up to the challenge of reading or even thinking, but I could look at the people walking past the hotel's front window without feeling sea-sick.

After breakfast, I went for a slow totter around the village, bought a bulky Sunday newspaper (which later went into the bin still sealed in its taut polythene), and contemplated the merits of smoking a cigarette... but abandoned the idea as I usually do. Ibuprofen, vitamin C tablets and a cold yoghurt drink seemed like a better idea.

The middle of the day passed in slow motion, including the taxi ride home. I was back in my dorm room at the project field station by two o'clock.

---

[1] I think that should have been a warning, right there.

I'd had the cab drop me off a little way from the buildings and I'd managed to make my way inside without encountering anyone. I wasn't tired enough to sleep, but I wasn't alert enough to do much except brood a little. I laid on my bed, a soft pillow under my head, and let my mind wander.

I tried not to think about my last talk with the Professor, but that was one of those don't-think-about-pink-elephants deals where the harder you try the less you succeed. Our last disastrous encounter action-replayed in my head a couple of times and I discovered that somehow my feelings had shifted. Right after it happened I was full of emotion, feeling like I might burst with it. The Professor's words had seemed laden with significance and hidden meaning. But now that impression had evaporated and I couldn't muster a sense of panic as I recalled his awkward protestations and oblique hints.

In theory, he could be my (gulp) father – nothing impossible about that – but I found I didn't believe it. Shocking and uncomfortable as the thought had initially been, the truth was that it would be too *convenient*. A wrenching revelation like that would be a great excuse for me to obsess, act out and generally behave badly.

If my suspicions had turned out to be true, it would simply be the latest and largest in a line of crisis-of-the-week bombshells that I continually manufactured as a way to keep me firmly at the centre of my own little melodrama.

The tired reality was that I had a listless father who had been drawing away since before I was born. And that offered no fuel for my emotional burn-outs, no ongoing justifications for my graceless behaviour. A tectonic upheaval in the structure of my family, my background, would be just what my inner drama queen needed to keep the turmoil rolling, but it didn't have the weary weight of truth.

And I knew that once I overcame my horror, the Professor would have made a much better father than the one I'd been assigned at birth. Deep down this was more of a wish than a fear.

Nevertheless, the Professor had been trying to keep *something* from me with his butter-fingered dissimulating, something he was horribly ill at ease over – and I'd pretty much convinced myself that what he was hiding wasn't a shiny new parent for me.

When the conversation had got uncomfortable for him, his nervousness seemed to take precedence over his not-inconsiderable need to scold me. It seemed like he'd rather turn a deaf ear to my failings than risk revealing some agonising truth in my presence, so I was pretty sure I wasn't going to like it, whatever it was. 'What could be so bad?' I thought, unpleasantly aware that it was a phrase that would work well as famous last words.

* * *

Round about six-thirty the ebb and flow of queasiness seemed to recede for good and I was left washed-up on the far shore of Hangover Straits feeling weak but alive. Now that I was out from under the weight of all that alcohol, my curiosity was coming back to life. And it was beginning to pluck metaphorically at my sleeve.

The first time I'd pried into the PAC's secrets, my picture of the world had cracked right down the middle; either magic was real and everything else I've thought in the last twenty-six years needed reassessing, or it wasn't and the riddle of the PAC was an unexplained hole in the otherwise tidy fabric of the world. I was still in need of some answers.

I pulled on my boots with the sudden idea of taking a stroll down to the barn where my mother's things were now stored. But I wasn't after clues about my mother. Rather, I'd realised something about Susan Milton. She had an office in the project building and a 'set' (which was college-speak for a small suite) in the dorm building and yet she chose to keep some of her things in the barn. Intriguing, no? I was a good way through my reading of the PAC's electronic documents and I was as confused as ever; I wondered if it was time to have a glance at the *non*-electronic goodies they kept squirreled away at the bottom of the lane.

I stepped out through the front door of the dorm block. Somewhere, behind the smoky looking clouds, the sun was touching the horizon. The damp air nuzzled unpleasantly at my exposed neck and tickled my nostrils as I slipped and tripped my way along the mist-sheened cobbles of the lower lane.

Reaching the gate I glanced up at the barn's top windows: they were dark, which was good. In the most ungainly way imaginable, I hauled myself over the top bar of the gate and crunched – as quietly as I could – across the gravel drive towards the barn's side door. The main doors were wide enough to admit a tractor – or for that matter a brass band riding on llamas – but they were shackled closed. The side entrance was secured by an ancient mortice lock, to which I'd been given a long, iron-black key.

I undid the lock and paused, thinking I'd heard something – a gasp, perhaps. I held still, waiting for it to repeat itself, and wondered if it was some common rustic occurrence – anxious badgers perhaps – or something man-made from inside the barn.

A sharp sound, like a slap, came from the interior of the barn. Opening the door a fraction of an inch, I could see that a dim light glowed from the far side of the dark space, but my view was blocked by all the junk stacked near the entrance. Clearly there was someone in there.

I considered my position for a moment. I had a reason to be here: my mother's things. So if I encountered anyone, I was in the clear – providing they didn't catch me doing any pantomime-style skulking. So if anyone approached, I'd just clump about to make it clear I was here for entirely-non-clandestine above-board-style activities. But until I was discovered, I'd do my best to imitate a tiny church mouse.

Carefully, I pulled the door wider until I could fit my head through the gap, and took a proper look around. The sky behind me was fading into murky twilight and it was nearly as gloomy outside the barn as in, so there'd be no sudden burst of sunlight to announce my arrival.

There seemed to be no one at my end of the barn. But from behind the dark shapes of cupboards and racking I could see a faint, flickering light emanating from the far corner and hear indistinct sounds as if a struggle were taking place.

Seeing no one near me, I slipped in through the gap and allowed the door to swing softly shut behind me. Under its own weight, it would stay closed but wouldn't latch – which suited me fine.

I took several silent steps into the shadows and towards the light. And I heard what sounded like a man's voice say something I couldn't catch and then a woman laughed – almost a giggle. It began to dawn on me what I was sneaking up on. Ahead, some unidentified couple were enjoying a little private snuggle-time.

Which should have seemed like none of my business, but I found I was just as curious as if I'd walked in on a secret meeting of the PAC. Assuming one or both of them were on the project team, who were they? We each had our own rooms, and there were no anti-fraternising rules that I was aware of, so why would anyone sneak out here? I couldn't resist a puzzle.

I glanced up at the top window and noticed that it was covered, though I couldn't see with what. No lights would show to anyone outside; someone wanted to visit this place without broadcasting their presence.

I edged forwards, careful not to step on a rake or snap a twig – the two main hazards in any stealthy endeavour. With careful positioning, I found I could peer through the tangle of junk hanging from the beams and on into the open area beyond – and I could do so with very little chance of being seen.

Thirty feet away, a single bulb illuminated a tangle of sweaty limbs and shining steel.

David Braun and Susan Milton were in some sort of intimate clinch – albeit a fully clothed and heavily armed one. With a gasp they separated and I could see a little more of what they were up to. Both of them were smiling as they circled one another, and both of them were carrying swords. Clearly they were duelling, though their expressions suggested that they had no intention of actually hurting each other.

David was exploring Susan's defences. Watching the easy discipline with which she blocked his probing attacks and the unhurried precision of her ripostes caused a memory to surface. I remembered someone telling me that Susan was a fencer – and it looked like she was extremely skilful – not that David was exactly clumsy. He was fast, powerful and accurate, but his expression showed concentration, whereas Susan's was simply playful. She was the master here.

Suddenly Susan put up her sword with a move so quick that I could hear the whip of steel scoring the air that accompanied it.

"Let's use the blunts," she said, "I want to show you something." Bending to one side, she slid her sword into its vinyl case and picked up two others, which appeared to be made of wood. One of them she flipped towards David.

For a moment, I couldn't believe what happened next. The wooden sword snagged in mid-air, just outside David's reach. He set aside his rapier and a moment later the wooden sword was released from its frozen trajectory to drop into his empty hand.

"You're getting pretty nimble with those Shields," Susan said, appreciatively. "You don't have to stick your tongue out anymore."

"You're not too old to put across my knee, you know," David said, rotating his shoulder and settling the wooden sword in his hand.

A moment later, Susan attacked.

Impressive though their earlier engagement had been, I realised now that they had been holding back. Now I could hardly see tips of their practice swords, they moved so swiftly. Susan's smile had given way to a blank look of intensity while David was concentrating so hard his face was like a machine.

This time Susan was on the offensive and she hardly waited for David to parry each cut before switching to a new angle and driving in again.

"See," she said, through tight lips, "how I'm coming in high and to your right over and over. Gradually your elbow is coming out and you're opening up your left side."

As she said it, she struck low to David's right. Instinctively he dropped his arm to counter and she rotated her blade through a full three-hundred degrees, rolling her wrist, to bring the sword crashing in towards the left of David's head. Letting the power dissipate at the last minute, she angled down to tap him firmly on the shoulder.

"Nice," he said. "But I could Shield that side pretty easily, couldn't I?"

"Try it," she suggested.

David hesitated for a moment, like he was doing mental arithmetic, and then raised his blade. Once again, Susan began a rapid metronome beat of attacks, the majority of which were high and to David's right. Now that she'd pointed it out, I was fascinated to see his elbow moving away from his side as he struggled to block the onslaught.

And, just as before, once David was open enough on his left, she struck low and to the right. Just as before he dropped to block it and with ferocious speed Susan rolled her wrist to bring her weapon around and down again on David's exposed left side, aiming for his head.

With a woody thump, the weapon impacted – but instead of striking David's face, it slammed to a halt eighteen inches from his cheekbone, stopped short by the suddenly solid air. I was almost too stunned to follow when Susan reacted. The moment her blade struck the non-existent barrier, she recovered and lunged, cutting down towards David's feet.

Taken by surprise, he skipped to his right, anxious to get his shins out of the path of her sword even as Susan completed the move, slicing only emptiness. Then, as though she'd done it a hundred times before, Susan pushed her blade straight out ahead of her and into David's side.

"Ow," he yelped, though it didn't look as though she'd done him any real harm.

"The way you want to think of it," she explained, "is that as soon as I hit your Shield, I'm going to alter my attack so that the Shield is in your way and not mine. With your Shield covering that side, you can't parry on your left, which is fine. But for mobility you keep your Shield well clear of the floor, so I attacked under it. You had to jump back. You still didn't have room to parry on your left, but now you're not protected by your Shield either. And voila."

David patted his side thoughtfully and shifted the preposterous terry-cloth headband he was wearing (I noticed Susan had one as well) so as to mop the sweat from his forehead. "You make it sound like Shielding your vulnerable bits could be a bad idea."

Susan nodded. "I reckon it's smarter to place Shields a little to one side of the vulnerable spots. You can duck behind them quickly enough, but they don't limit you. And of course, if they stop an attack, you should move them immediately, because now your opponent knows where they are. It's probably best to have at least three different ways of arranging your Shields and to secretly switch between them to keep your opponent guessing."

"Sneaky," David said. "But let me have one more go at that attack. I want to try something else."

Susan gave David a moment to prepare himself and then began her attack again, just as he'd asked her to. Again, she pressured him so that his parries left him increasingly exposed on his left. Again, when he was suitably open, she cut low and then rotated to attack his left at head height. And again her weapon slammed into an invisible barrier, prompting her to lunge and cut towards his ankles. This time, however David hopped with his back foot, allowing the blade to whip beneath him, and then came down on his front foot... and kept dropping.

Susan had withdrawn and was beginning her strike along the centre-line, even as David allowed the leg supporting his weight to collapse. It looked like he was about to fall on his butt in order to get under her attack. But then, as Susan's blade came forwards, it became clear that David's little hop had allowed him to twist his body. It was like he was performing the world's lowest roundhouse kick: step, hop, kick – but performed while dropping into a crouch.

It was how a Cossack might kick, one leg folded under him, the other arcing out to the side. At full stretch, his head was too low and too far back to be in range of her thrust, while his sweeping, outstretched leg was still able to snare her feet and whip them out from under her.

She tumbled lightly onto the crash mats behind her. Before she could get her feet under her, David was on top of her, pinning her hands to the mat. He lowered himself so that she could hardly move at all.

I wasn't sure if this was still part of the fight.

"Yes?" she said, enquiringly, looking up at him.

"This is as far as I'd thought it through," he said, letting go of her wrists and bending his head down towards hers.

"I warn you, I smell bad," she muttered as he bent to kiss her.

A moment later, he broke the kiss, saying, "No you don't. You smell pretty." For the first time, I felt a flush of embarrassment about spying on them.

Plus I'd probably seen enough. I took a couple of silent steps backwards towards the door. If they'd finished with the swordplay they might be leaving soon – or they might decide to move on to the, ahem, close-quarters stuff. Either way, I reckoned it was time to retreat.

But this was obviously just a quick snog-break, because Susan laughed, saying, "Get off me, you big animal," and gave David a playful thump on the arm. He collapsed, as though she'd wounded him, allowing her to roll to her feet. A moment later he was standing too.

"Tired?" he asked.

She glanced at her watch – an incongruously dressy-looking thing – and said, "Ten more minutes?"

"Sure," he said. "What do you want to do? Tank training?"

Susan curled a lip in disgust but said, "Probly better. I'll be 'it' first, shall I?"

David nodded and retrieved his wooden sword. Susan went to stand at one edge of the open space. "I'll see if I can get to the towel over there," she said, indicating a splotch of white in the gloom, about thirty feet from where she stood. Her weapons lay abandoned on the crash mat.

"Ready?" David asked and when she nodded, he stepped forwards and began to swing his wooden sword quickly from side to side, striking alternately at Susan's unguarded sides. She, in turn, simply stood her ground, hands by her sides, with a look of deep concentration on her face, and let each hefty blow slam into the wall of air surrounding her.

Without letting up, David hammered away at her, striking high and low. And, while every blow landed hard, none of them came closer than a foot or so to Susan's body.

Stepping around Susan in order to attack from a fresh angle, David had to pause for a moment as he shifted his feet. In that second, Susan moved forwards, taking a step towards the towel.

In the next few minutes, Susan took advantage of four more hesitations, each time shuffling a step closer to her goal. When she finally said 'Stop' and checked her watch, she was still only halfway to the towel.

Now it was David's turn to be the piñata[1]. He managed perhaps three feet more than Susan before he raised his hand, but when Susan checked her watch it turned out he'd had a minute longer than she had.

While David caught his breath, Susan began zipping weapons into bags.

---

[1] A sort of mexican cocktail made from papier mache coconuts.

"Jog?" he asked.

"Went this morning," she said, sounding self-satisfied.

"I might skip for a bit then," he said, not sounding enthusiastic.

I was backing towards the door in earnest now, since they were obviously packing up.

"Sure," she said airily, gathering up her things. "It'll be nice to have the shower to myself for a change."

David looked up sharply. "Good point," he said. "Skipping can wait."

I was slipping out the door now and I could hear their voices getting closer. Trying not to make a sound, I latched the door and eased the giant key into the lock. I'd barely had a chance to re-lock the door and remove my key when I saw the doorknob twist.

A moment later, a muffled voice said, "Honey, have you got the key?"

I raced towards the back of the barn as silently as I could and ducked around the corner. Then I stopped, my heart thumping from my five-second sprint.

I could hear the door open, then close, followed by gravel crunching away into the distance as the pair moved off up the hill.

I waited for several minutes before peeking around the corner. The sun was long gone and it was pretty much pitch-black now. From what I could tell I was alone.

I figured I'd stay put for a few minutes longer anyway, just to be on the safe side.

Lowering myself to the ground, I leant my back against the side of the barn and stared up at the sky. A single gap in the clouds revealed a handful of stars directly above me.

I thought about what I'd seen in the barn and once again I felt my sense of the world shifting.

CHAPTER 9

So now I knew.

It should have made things simpler, but the simplicity didn't seem to have kicked in yet.

Was I sure of what I'd seen? Yes. Could it have been anything other than magic? Well, yes, I suppose it could, but I couldn't imagine what. If it wasn't magic then it was some other thing that you might just as well call magic.

OK. But then why hadn't it worked when I'd tried it? And why hadn't Susan and David needed gold like the PAC documents said?

The answer to the first question could be simply that I'm a klutz and a raging incompetent. The answer to the second one didn't take much deduction: there was gold in the ridiculous his-and-hers terry sweatbands they'd both been wearing: one at the forehead, two on the wrists. (Well, to be accurate Susan was wearing a fancy gold watch on her left wrist instead of a sweatband, but same deal.) It was an easy way to keep the gold hidden and comfortably in place – I just hoped it was worth the risk if the fashion police found out about it.

So, what did this all mean? Was everything in the PAC documents gospel?

I thought I should probably reserve a little bit of judgement, just in case. But there was no getting away from the heart of it. Magic. It was real and I'd seen it. (Or I was in my huggy-jacket in a padded room somewhere, hallucinating all this through a haze of Thorazine.)

Long after David and Susan had left the barn, I was still sitting on the damp ground ordering my thoughts… and then doing it all over again. The clouds cleared for a while and I stared upwards, unseeing, at the gallery of stars. The sense of vertigo from watching the heavens wheel above me matched how I felt. Then the cover closed in and a mist of rain began to fall, pattering against the trees. It was time to move.

I stood up, aware that more than two hours had passed and now my legs were achingly stiff from the cold and my butt was numb from sitting. The banged-up cartilage of my right knee was throbbing too; it never missed an opportunity to remind me of a long-ago moment of stupidity. And my jeans were soaked through. But at least while I'd been out here I'd managed to make some sort of peace with the events I'd witnessed in the barn.

I sneezed explosively into the quiet darkness, which served to break whatever rapture had held me in place. Twice now in one weekend I'd found myself half-frozen. I clumped along on my cramping, tingling legs, eager to get inside and into the warm.

Back in my room I put the convection heater on and angled it towards the bed. I snapped on the reading light and then, slipping out of my grass-slicked boots and clammy jeans, I turned out the main light and wriggled under the covers still wearing my thick sweater. With outstretched fingers I was able to pull my laptop towards me without getting up again.

Shivering, I hunkered down, waiting for the room to warm and began once again to read the PAC's secrets.

It was after two in the morning when I found I was dozing more than I was reading. Mostly I was going over things I'd read before, but this time I was thinking about what they implied, instead of wasting time wondering whether they could be true. What I'd seen in the barn had left me with no other option: I now believed the PAC's enemies were real.

But imagining danger when you're swaddled in duvet and warm as a biscuit is tricky. Instead of fear, I felt excitement and anticipation. Where I should have seen a nightmare ready to come to life, I saw an adventure.

I turned off the heater, the laptop and the reading light and laid down to sleep. For a moment, dreams rose up and I felt a Christmas-morning sense of promise and wonder, as though I were entering a new and brilliant world. But then the promise fell away and I dropped into my usual dreamless slumber.

* * *

The tiny gods of Random Play that live inside my music player chose Volcano Girls, by Veruca Salt, as my wake-up tune. Listening to the irresistible first verse it was a struggle to stay lazy and immobile, but somehow I managed it. As a concession to getting with the program, though, I opened my eyes and saw that it was light in my room.

Better get moving, I thought and then a colossal sneeze rattled my skull. *Sick*, I thought. *I'm sick*. In the night, creeping particles of *blah* had colonised my sinuses, my joints and the lining of my throat. Crap.

I rolled unsteadily out of bed, thankful that my room was warm, and grabbed sweatpants and a hockey shirt out of the pile on the back of my chair. Today would have been an ideal day to declare a 'sickie', but illness would just have to wait. I had Things To Do. Maybe I could get whoever was going in to town today to bring me back some cold remedies to help me soldier on.

I got myself ready and made it down to the refectory before the cook finished serving. I was happy with cereal, toast and tea, so he left me to it, scowling his usual scowl in my direction.

Theresa was talking softly with Blondy on the other side of the room, both of them holding mugs of coffee. Of course Blondy wasn't really her name, but I could never remember what it really was. Vanessa? Stephanie? Felicity? Who knew? I never knew what to say to them so I endeavoured to ignore them, hoping they would reciprocate.

They were still there when I finished eating so I slipped out unnoticed… except I was stopped in my tracks when the cook yelled 'Oi' in my direction and pointed to my dishes.

I was sure that the girls were laughing at me as I carried my breakfast things over to the counter, my chin reflexively tucked into my chest doing the Tall Girl Slouch, and added my crockery to the pile. Then I escaped without making eye contact. Just another day in Loserville.

A fresh sneezing fit overcame me as I neared the server room and I was scrabbling desperately and unsuccessfully to remove a Kleenex from my pocket when Daniel found me.

"Unclean, unclean," he intoned, as I finally clawed a tissue free and dabbed at my dripping nose. "You under the weather, then?" he asked.

I shrugged and made a face. "I'm alright," I said, unconvincingly.

"I'll tell you what you need," he chirped, not waiting for a response. "To do me a favour."

"Really?" I said, sceptically.

"I want to convince the landlord of The Retard to let Wounded Panther play a gig there," he said. "I need moral support. I'm going up there this evening."

"I dunno," I said, wondering what excuse I could give. And then I added, "I thought you were called Hammerhead."

I was trying not to sound interested.

"People weren't getting the irony," he explained. "Anyway, you're up there most... um, you know, a lot of nights. So it's not out of your way." He wheedled, "Go *on*."

I felt another sneeze coming on. "I'll see how I feel," I said, which seemed to satisfy him.

"Cool. Gotta dash," he said and skipped away. I rooted the key to the server room out of my pocket, accidentally dropped my Kleenex and felt an unpleasant wave of headrush as I bent over to retrieve it. Germtastic.

First things first: machine check. Everything looked good. Then I fired up my e-mail reader and was pleased to see that all our subscriptions were now set-up. I sent a group message to the research team letting them know the happy news.

OK. What next? Mindful of the unhappy role handwritten notes had recently played in my life, I let myself out of the Fortress of Servitude and went to check my mail slot. Bingo. Though not the good kind where you won things. There was a note from the Professor which glossed rapidly over our last exchange – he acknowledged that it was a difficult time for me – and then detailed a passel of scutwork that needed the Jo touch.

Automatically, my frustration levels began to surge. But then a thought struck me. This could be a test, to see if I'd meant what I'd said. The Professor might be looking for proof that my line about

Robert Finn

turning over a new leaf had some substance behind it. If I knuckled down and got this done without any wailing and eye-rolling I could maybe earn some useful Brownie points. *After a difficult start, Jo has learned to apply herself. She would make an ideal addition to any occult-crime-fighting organisation.*

With a quick tug of the forelock I got down to it. Despite frequent trips to the bathroom to steal more tissues – which I used to polish my nostrils a shiny red – I toiled away until lunchtime, at which point I quickly grabbed a sandwich and retreated once more to be with the machines. I even managed to avoid any human contact on my trip to the canteen.

After I'd eaten, I checked my e-mail again to find a note from Sebastian, Susan's doctoral student, asking for help with his laptop. I'd pretty much finished the Professor's trial-by-boredom assignment, so I headed upstairs to find Seb.

It turned out that everybody in the team had some techie problem or other that they needed help with. I felt a little put out to have this sprung on me, but the good news was that by the end of the afternoon I'd resolved every last niggle. In fact, if I hadn't drawn out the last couple of fixes I might have finished even sooner. But when we'd gone down for tea mid-afternoon, the Professor had come over and whispered discreetly that he'd like to see me in his office once I was done for the day. Hence the foot-dragging. I reckoned I was currently in the clear on the work front – in fact I was doing a bang-up job – so I wasn't expecting complaints there, but undoubtedly what he really wanted to talk to me about was our previous heart-to-heart – and I wasn't looking forward to picking up where we left off with that.

Nevertheless, five-thirty rolled around and I realised I couldn't put it off any longer. Like a condemned man being led to the bellows[1], I shuffled downstairs and tapped on the Professor's door.

"Come in," he called and I entered to find him fussing over the contents of one of his bookcases.

"Jo. Sit down. I've just made a pot of tea; would you like some?" he asked, all smiles. I nodded. It would postpone the inevitable for at least thirty seconds.

He had a tray of tea-things on his desk and he poured us both a cup, even remembering to add sugar to mine. I sat in the visitor's chair in front of his desk, leaning forward to take the cup and saucer when he offered them.

He settled himself behind his desk and after a moment he said, "I'm sorry about how things went last time. I don't know quite what impression I gave but I'm sure it wasn't the right one." Perhaps he'd rehearsed this speech because his voice was calm and confident, very different from Friday's awkwardness.

He took a sip of his tea – what you might call a little English courage – and pressed on. "The last thing we discussed... Well I want to be clear: your mother and I were never involved romantically. I think I may have inadvertently left you with the idea that we were." He looked up to gauge my reaction. To the best of my knowledge, I gave no evidence of one. I was holding myself in, waiting to see where this went.

He continued, "Helen and I were certainly friends, though. Good friends, but no more than that. She came to me for help and..." here he faltered slightly, "...and support. And I did whatever I could."

He went on, "Your mother had many obstacles to contend with and I happened to be near for some of her most trying times. I hope I was some comfort to her; I certainly tried to be a steady friend."

---

[1] Or whatever it is they're led to.

I said nothing and after a while he added, "So I hope that clears things up."

He sipped his tea in silence and I sat with mine on my lap, untouched.

I wasn't sure what I thought. Was I happy or sad? Surprised or relieved?

And then, out of nowhere, a swell of anger was suddenly upon me. He still hadn't told me the truth and he was hoping he wouldn't have to. I said, "There's something you're not telling me."

I could almost see him considering his options: deny it, play dumb, feign a heart attack. He took too long making up his mind. Whatever he said now, it would sound like a line, a tactic.

I gave him a little encouragement. "There's something in my mother's things you're worried about me finding. But I *will* find it, so you might as well tell me."

"I…" was all he could say. He set down his tea and we both waited for a moment.

Long seconds passed before he was ready. I held very, very still – almost like I wasn't there. I wasn't sure that I was any more eager than he was to hear what was coming.

He asked, "I imagine you know that your mother was often unhappy. Depressed, in fact."

Yes, I knew that. I nodded.

"Sometimes it would get very bad," he said, "*very* bad and she'd stop coming in to the department." He gave a sad smile. "She told me that some days she couldn't even get out of bed."

I knew she'd had problems. Maybe I hadn't appreciated how serious they were.

He gave another sad smile and continued, "I was used to her absences and I knew the reason for them. I always made light of them because I knew it would be difficult enough for her to return to work without worrying that a court martial awaited her. I made sure she always knew she was welcome."

Someone thumped along the corridor outside and he paused until they'd gone past. When he spoke again, his voice was no longer steady: "One day she didn't come in and I got a call from the hospital. She had tried to kill herself."

I felt the pit of my stomach drop and I thought I might be sick. He'd enunciated the words so carefully. There was no mistaking them.

He went on, expressionless now, sounding like a recording: "I sat with her until she woke up. By chance, she had been found almost immediately and the hospital had pumped her stomach. They found sedatives and rather a lot of gin."

I noticed a tear on his cheek as he caught my eye and explained, "Your mother detested gin. She told me later that she'd chosen it deliberately. A comforting taste wouldn't have been right, she said. And if she survived she'd have a colourful excuse never to touch it again." Again, the sad smile.

Numbly I asked, "So she expected to survive?"

He shook his head. "I don't see how. It was a winter morning, still dark. It just so happened that there was an accident in her building, one of the undergraduates cooking food in her room, lots of smoke. The fire brigade were called and the building was evacuated. No one could find Helen. A girlfriend said her bicycle was in its usual spot and someone else noticed that there was a light in her window. A fireman forced her door open. An ambulance was called. She couldn't have known any of that would happen."

I knew my mother suffered with mental problems; I'd always known it. I figured I'd inherited my hang-ups from her. I'd heard lots of muttering about her problems from my dad's domestic staff, and from relatives, when I was younger. I even knew that some of them believed her death was no accident. But that was just cruel gossip. They had their facts wrong. That's what I'd always believed.

That's what I'd always *known*. But the Professor's words told a different story.

He turned away for a few moments and blew his nose. When he turned back he was more composed. And he had more to say: "When your mother moved to America, she stayed in touch. I never allowed a letter of hers to go unanswered for more than a day or two, especially when she moved into the new house after you were born. I know she found it difficult to make new friends and with your father so busy... well, I think our correspondence helped a little. She told me that she saved my letters; they reassured her that sometimes life could be normal. She claimed she meant that as a compliment. Unless they were lost in all the upheaval I would imagine those letters are somewhere inside one of those wretched boxes.

"Towards the end..." he struggled.

And then tried again. "Before she died, we discussed her depression, the black moods that wouldn't leave her. How her medication wasn't helping. I didn't want you to read those letters not knowing what to expect, to have it come as a complete surprise." He leaned forwards. "But the truth is that I hoped I could persuade you not to read them at all." He was getting choked up again as he said, "You have had a lot of sadness of your own, Jo, a lot to deal with, and for the *life* of me I can't see how you could benefit from sharing in your mother's misery. Goodness knows it was more than *she* could bear. I didn't want you to read those letters because I didn't want you reliving your mother's pain. She wouldn't have wanted that either."

I realised I was crying, but I didn't say anything. I just sat there.

I was afraid I would spill my tea with my trembling so I set it down on the desk and then let my hands cover my eyes. I was sobbing quietly now.

That last day, Mom went for a drive, something she normally didn't do. She didn't like driving but she travelled right over to the other side of town; we never found any reason for it. It was an industrial park; just factories and warehouses. Then she stopped the car and got out, leaving the engine running. A truck hit her as she stepped out into the street. It had never made much sense. But now I knew why it had happened. It had happened because the first time she'd tried it, back in England, she'd been rescued.

I felt a hand on my shoulder and I realised that the Professor was standing by me. His face was so sad as he looked down at me. "Dear girl," he said, patting my shoulder. "Dear girl."

I reached up and he took my hands in his, and held them while I cried. "I'm so sorry," was all he said, repeating it softly.

CHAPTER 10

You're probably used to me being upset by now. Boo-hoo, twenty-four seven. Then the jokes, the flippancy before the next big drama. You're probably pretty tired of it. I know I am. Well, take comfort: we're nearly past that point now. I'll just say that this last slump was a big one. I mean even a stable, reasonably-together person would be hit hard by something like that, right?

I'm sure I don't need to explain why the discovery of my mother's suicide knocked my legs out from under me. You're human, you have empathy, you get it. But there were sides to the whole thing that deepened the hurt. Like for instance what it meant for my future. She was past caring, but what sort of legacy had she left me? How much of her self-destruct mechanism had I inherited? Was its timer counting down towards zero in *my* head now?

I knew enough to understand that traumas run in families. And since I don't suppose anyone *chooses* to lose their grip on the world I have to imagine it happens to you whether you want it to or not.

And besides the question of what she might have passed on to me, there was the question of what had been lost with her death. I didn't have any close family. My dad had long since decided to re-cast himself in the role of distant uncle. My mother had always been the one I had yearned to be closer to, to know more about. The fact that I couldn't remember her, even though she had died just before I was sent away to start school, had left me desperate to learn more. First she'd left and then I'd had to – Dad said it had already been agreed before she died – and it opened up such a chasm between us that I desperately wanted to fill it with something.

It had made me search for evidence of her in my personality, my mannerisms. I wanted to bring her closer, to soak up whatever I could about her past, her character, and to absorb it into me so that I would have some link to her, the one person I really thought of as family. Now, with this sundering, this axe-blow, I was suddenly horrified by the idea of being linked to her, of finding echoes of her within me. It was the last thing I wanted. Her influence suddenly seemed like the touch of a disease that I had to wash off.

And above all I felt betrayed by her. She'd left me alone in the world with only her example to guide me. And what an example it had turned out to be. My father hadn't known what to do with a daughter and it turned out neither had my mother. So whose idea was I? I mean, what was the point of me?

I'd been sent off to boarding school as soon as I was old enough, but I'd always wanted to believe that if my mother had lived she'd have kept me near her. And I had to let that hope go now. Neither of them knew what to do with me.

Ridiculous though it sounds, it made me think about Frankenstein – not the movies, but the book. In the original, the creature is having such a lousy time of it, he seeks out his maker to find out why he was created. He only becomes a monster when he learns that there is no good reason for his existence. He was a whim, an intellectual experiment – and ultimately a mistake. It makes you think; if the one who gives you life doesn't want you, has no purpose for you, doesn't care for you, then why should anyone else[1]?

Ironically – if irony is the right word for it – discovering that my mother had been seriously mentally unbalanced was threatening to push me over the edge too. Maybe this was what the Professor had been worried about when he learned that his old letters were in my possession: that I couldn't handle the shock of the truth.

I don't remember how I eventually came to leave the Professor's study. I remember being glad that he was there trying to comfort me – glad and pathetically grateful that someone still loved me – but I was still inconsolable. I think perhaps he brought me outside to get some fresh air after everyone else had left the office for the day.

Anyway, once outside, an instinctive desire to be alone came upon me. When that black weight presses down on you, some reflex makes you want to get away from other people. Other people interfere, they hold off the worst of it and that's not what you need. You have to be by yourself, and let it rage through you, unrestrained, so that you can find out how bad it is, whether there's hope, whether there's any point in fighting.

But I knew the Professor wouldn't let me go unless he believed I was coping. I had to persuade him that I wouldn't do anything stupid so that I could get away from him. I found that if I concentrated on the fact that I would be alone soon then I could stop the tears for a little while. Knowing that in a few minutes' time I could let it all out helped me get myself under control for a while. I dried my eyes, lifted my head up and squared my shoulders.

We were standing near the back door of the main building,

---

[1]   And it makes you wonder whether Mary Shelley's parents were freaks like mine.

outside the dark windows of the empty refectory. The sun had set some time ago. "I'll be alright," I lied, "I think I just need to walk it off."

He took some convincing, but by now I was breathing normally and meeting his eye. I even tried to smile. I think it came out more as a grimace but nevertheless he relaxed a little.

"I understand," he said, "Just don't stay out here and make yourself ill. I think you might be coming down with something." He gave my shoulder a last squeeze and let me go. Hands jammed into my pockets, I walked up the path towards the dorm building and the lane beyond.

I didn't know where I was going but it didn't really matter.

In the end, my feet carried me past the entrance to the dorms and on up the hill. I didn't think about it; I just kept going. If I was going to really lose my grip on sanity, this would be my chance, the moment when the full force of it would hit me and I'd snap. I waited for the storm inside me to reach its peak.

And as I walked up the lane, passing between dark fields, there was so little light that I was barely able to make out the hedgerows on either side of me. My feet knew this path – I walked it most nights – I was headed towards the pub. And though the last thing I needed was company, the lane didn't end at the pub; it wound on. I could turn off onto a quiet track, if I wanted – walk for miles and not see a soul, or be passed by a car.

The lights of the pub came into view and I could hear muted conversation and the music of the stereo. I hugged the opposite side of the road, keeping as far from the light and sound as possible. The cheeriness of the place was repellent to me.

And yet, I found I wasn't crying any more. The churning emotions had made me sick to my stomach but they hadn't overwhelmed me yet. I felt alone but not quite lost. Maybe it still hadn't hit me fully. Or maybe it had and I would survive.

"Jo," someone called out. Despite myself I turned. It was Daniel. He stood beneath the pub sign, his back against the pole. He had a scarf wrapped multiple times around his neck and his hands too were plunged deep in the pockets of his denim jacket. He looked frozen. Had he been waiting for me out here? I'd forgotten all about him.

I didn't say anything but I stopped walking. He ran over to me.

When he saw my face, the red eyes, all the signs, he knew I'd been doing some serious crying. I wanted to be irritated with him for breaking in on my solitude like this… but I found I wasn't. He looked at me with so much concern, and yet he wasn't crowding me. I could see that he wanted to help me, to comfort me, but he also wanted to give me space, to let me choose.

Into the quiet, I blurted, "Daniel, I found out something about my mother." I said it before I even thought about it, before I even knew I was going to speak. Hearing the words out loud stirred things up inside me again, and I knew I couldn't say anything else for a minute or I'd break down. Even my breath was catching in my throat.

Carefully, respectfully, he put one arm around my shoulder and led me towards the pub, explaining, "There's a table right at the back of the garden behind the wall. Everyone's inside. No one will know you're here." Somehow he knew that I wanted to be invisible.

Steering clear of the main building, he led me around to the back of the pub, through the darkened garden, with its empty tables, and into the deep shadows beyond. An ancient wall screened off the furthest corner from those inside and one battered table lay behind it. The upper storey windows in the main building let out just enough stray light for us to find our way.

Daniel sat me down and headed back towards the pub. He said nothing before he went, just lifted a strand of hair out of my eyes and departed. Two minutes later he was back. He put a drink of something down in front of me and then fiddled with the gas heater, one of those tall metal mushrooms that radiate heat from the glowing mesh beneath their hoods.

"They said I could put the heater on if I promised not to pester them anymore about playing a gig here," he said, smiling. The heater soon began to glow, its mesh rippling with heat. I found I could see my glass now.

I picked it up and sipped. Southern Comfort, no ice. I hadn't thought I liked it, but it tasted strong and sweet and it spread warmth through my chest when I swallowed. The heater, too, was starting to work and the feel of my cold skin thawing made me feel a little better.

For a moment I felt like laughing with relief. I felt crappy, but the drink, the warmth, Daniel's patient silence all helped. I was hurting but I wasn't dying. On an impulse I grabbed his hand and squeezed it. He nodded, as though he understood, but said nothing.

We sat there without speaking for a little longer and I continued to warm, both inside and out. I finished my drink and asked Daniel if he'd get us some more. I held out some money. He carried away the empties and was soon back with a couple of fresh drinks in each hand and some packs of crisps clamped between his teeth. He opened his mouth, dropping the packets on the table, and passed me another Southern Comfort.

Very softly, he said, "So. I think you must have had a horrible day." His voice was a whisper.

I pressed my lips tightly together and nodded, tearing up a little. I sniffed the tears back, aware of just how ladylike that must look.

I suddenly wanted to tell him, to explain everything, but I worried that I wouldn't be able to get the words out without triggering a meltdown.

In the end, when I started to speak I couldn't help crying, but it was a different kind than before. It felt healthier, like I was releasing something that had been trapped. The words came through in spite of the tears.

Daniel listened quietly. At one point, I faltered as I was telling him what the Professor had told me; he reached up and brushed my face, gently resting his fingers against the hot skin of my cheek for a moment before pulling back. Other than that, he just let me speak. And best of all, he didn't try to make this about *us* or to rush me and I realised for the first time how much he cared about me.

When I'd run down, exhausted all the words in me, and come to the end of the tears, he asked me, "What can I do? Is there anything you want?"

I considered it for a moment, then sniffed and smiled, saying, "Get drunk with me."

He looked a little unsure, just for a second, and then he nodded and said, "You're the boss." After that he looked around him as though he'd lost something. A moment later his gaze settled on the lights of the main building as though he'd only just noticed it. "Blimey," he said, "a pub. That's handy. I'll be back in a jiffy."

"Moron," I said, politely, as he gathered up the empties, and the scattered crisp packets, and walked back up the garden. He was gone for a few minutes, but I didn't mind the wait. I was warm, the alcohol had lit a crackling log fire inside me and I felt peaceful... in a slightly fuzzy way. I nearly giggled with the feeling of it. The world hadn't ended. I was talking with a friend who adored me and the pain, for the time being, had slid away.

When Daniel eventually returned he was carrying a tray. On it were more drinks and a couple of toasted sandwiches. As soon as I saw them I realised I was ravenous. I could have kissed him.

He held up a hand as if to halt me. "Now don't worry about this, but Tammy might join us," he said. "She works here and you might think you won't like her but you will. The sandwiches are on her."

For a moment I felt a bit put out that some stranger was going to intrude on our little haven of calm. I wondered if I was annoyed. But then I realised I really didn't mind. I trusted Daniel. At that moment I found I trusted him completely.

We'd had *several* more drinks and we were getting a little bit giddy by the time Tammy finally appeared. I was feeling happy enough to start teasing Daniel about his band. He was laughing and calling me unflattering names.

Tammy appeared out of the darkness and came over to the table, setting her drink down. In the dim light, I could see that she was beautiful – dark-haired, dark-eyed, with perfect skin. I realised I'd seen her in the bar plenty of times but I hadn't thought she was staff. She was wearing a giant, formless biking jacket that hid her shape and I remembered the regulars in the bar sneaking hungry glances at her whenever she moved. I prepared to hate her.

"Hi Jo," she said, like we were old friends, "I'm making some more food; are you interested?"

"Well I..." I said, a little uncertain. The sandwich had been delicious but it wasn't really enough.

"It's only chips; is that alright?" she asked "I'll make something else if we're still hungry."

"Great," I said, finding myself smiling. She went back inside for a minute and returned with a basket of chips in each hand. She had a chip clenched between her front teeth and was trying to blow on it. She looked ridiculous and she obviously didn't care. So perhaps I wouldn't hate her. Right now, I didn't think I hated anyone.

I soon discovered that Tammy was the new singer in the ever-changing line-up of Daniel's band. She told me the story of the disastrous gig they'd played that Saturday, making it all seem like her own fault. Loosened up from laughing at her exaggerations, I found I was happy to talk, so I told her a related story about a disastrous gig that the *previous* incarnation of the band had played back in London – and I made it all seem like *Daniel's* fault. Daniel wriggled good-naturedly with embarrassment.

At one point, I felt a stab of jealousy as Tammy suddenly snuggled up to Daniel, squeezing her slim hips close to his on the bench. But a moment later she pushed hard and slid him onto the ground. He lay there looking hurt but also laughing.

"What was that for?" he asked, looking up at her.

"It was Jo's idea," she explained, "She says you never get a round in."

Daniel attempted to say something in his defence but she sternly hissed him into silence with a zipping motion across her mouth. "Go," she commanded and then turned back to me, smiling. "So do you know any secrets about Daniel? Tell me something *really* bad that he's done. No, something *embarrassing*. Ooh, better still, something *evil*."

Reluctantly Daniel trailed back up the garden leaving us to gang up on him. He seemed to be gone a while, but it was getting difficult to tell because by this time I was starting to feel pretty drunk. Tammy was easy to talk to and I was feeling chatty. I realised that Daniel had been right to include her; it opened things up, stopped me from obsessing. At least that's what I *hoped* Daniel had been thinking.

Made brave by drink, I suddenly asked her, "Do you have a *thing* for Daniel?"

She looked surprised and a bit uncomfortable. "Well," she said, drawing the word out, "he's great and everything, but he's a bit old for me."

"What do you mean?" I asked, my mind not at its quickest. "You're…?"

"Nineteen," she said, sounding embarrassed. For some reason, that news made me very sad. What was the point of being twenty-six if you could be funny and confident and likable at nineteen. I felt old and crushed and useless. For a moment I forgot to speak.

"Besides," Tammy said, "he won't shut up about you. It's a bit of a turn-off." She laughed and I joined in. It's not easy staying grumpy with that much booze inside you.

Daniel came back then, with more drinks. "Did you know it's nearly closing time?" he asked me, "Can you believe it?"

I shook my head. "I thought it was about nine o'clock."

"Me too," he said. Then he turned to Tammy. "Dom might join us in a bit, once he's locked up. He says he wants to talk to you about where all the Southern Comfort went."

"Well he's a big old soft sod, then" she said, her accent sounding local for the first time that evening.

By the time Dom joined us, I was feeling I'd probably had enough to drink. I might even have passed that point a while back. It was getting very difficult to think and the minutes were starting to skip past in sudden jumps. Everything was getting hard to follow.

Dom, it turned out, was a kind-looking man the size of a mountain gorilla with a big gut and lots of white hair. He came out carrying a pint of ale, perched on the end of the table, and told us stories for a while. At one point he stood and picked Tammy up, twirling her around to illustrate some point or other. She yelled to be put down but could do nothing about it. She was only about half my size, but even so… I was amazed at how easily he did it and I wondered, like a child, what it must be like to be so strong, for things to be so effortless. Moments later she was back on solid ground with no harm done.

Time skipped ahead again and I realised that I'd tuned out for a while. Daniel was whispering to me, "I think we should go home." I'd rested my head on his shoulder for a minute and I think I must have fallen asleep.

Dom helped me to my wobbly feet and I gave him a big hug, which was wholly out of character for me, until you factor in my level of consumption that evening. I hugged Tammy too – she seemed to be mainly jacket – and she hugged me back, saying, "I hope you feel better. It was really nice talking to you." She sounded like she meant it.

And then Daniel held out his hands to lead me away and I hugged him too. "I'm going with you," he said, laughing.

"Still get a hug," I insisted, tripping on my words.

Everyone laughed and I focused for a moment on Tammy; she was staring at Daniel and the look on her face was hard to read – but not impossible. *She does like Daniel*, I thought, decoding the softness in her eyes. And then I looked at Daniel and saw that he was staring in my direction. *And Daniel likes me,* I thought, feeling smug.

We said some goodbyes and then Daniel and I went weaving down the lane. I'd had a great evening and I kept telling him so. "Good. I'm glad," he said each time.

At one point I'm pretty sure I kissed him and he said 'Thank you', very formally, and then we carried on walking.

I was fairly unsteady on my feet by the time we reached the dorm building and Daniel had to help me get up the stairs. He rummaged about in my jacket pocket for the key to my room, which tickled me like mad. "Hold still," he whispered as I wriggled and giggled.

"*You* hold still," I told him.

Eventually he found the key and helped me in. I flopped back on the bed and just lay there. When I realised I couldn't hear him anymore I sat up. He was gone and the door was open.

He returned a minute later with an empty waste bin and a pint mug of water. "Ooh, is it a magic trick," I asked, excited. "Do you need a roll of newspaper? I've got one somewhere."

He put the bin by the side of my bed and handed me the glass. I realised I was thirsty for something other than alcohol and glugged a quarter of it straight down.

"Will you be alright?" he asked. "Do you feel sick?"

"I'm fine," I said. "I had a lovely evening."

"Excellent. Well, goodnight then," he said. He turned on my reading light and put out the main one. He was backing towards the door.

"Was I a big embarrassment?" I asked.

He lent forwards and gave me a tiny peck on the nose. "You were lovely," he assured me. And then he left, pulling the door quietly closed behind him.

I flopped back on the bed again and thought about taking off my clothes. It seemed like a lot of effort. My eyes fluttered closed... and then snapped open again as my stomach lurched. I sat up quickly and the nausea subsided. *Better not lie down for a while*, I thought.

I swept some clothes onto the floor so that I could sit in my one armchair. Doubled over and grunting from the exertion I finally managed to unlace my boots and get them off my feet. That was much better.

I drank a little more water and thought about putting some music on. Provided I didn't close my eyes, I felt fine. Three sheets to the wind, but fine. I knew in the morning, I'd probably be all upset again, I could sense it lurking just over the horizon, but at that moment I could think about my mother and not feel bad. Maybe my thoughts were too jumbled to feel anything, but I was safe from the pain for now.

That feeling of safety led to an idea. I located my keys and used them to open the bottom drawer of my desk. Inside was a little plastic case containing anti-depressants. They were patches, like the ones to help you give up smoking, and they would feed a steady dose of medication to my bloodstream. I thought it was pretty likely that I'd be needing some extra help in the coming weeks. It was just a shame they took a while to kick in. But maybe there was still some in my system from the last time.

Need some skin to apply it to. I pulled off my coat and my thick sweater, then wriggled out of the thermal camisole I had underneath. There was already a patch on my right shoulder and it was due to come off. This one was something else; something called oxymethylphenidate. A doctor had prescribed it for me once when I had difficulty studying. The idea had been to take it for the few weeks of exam season, but it turned out it helped with more than just the studying. I ordered it over the Internet now whenever my supplies ran low.

I peeled off the old patch and applied two new ones: an anti-depressant and one full of OMP. Then I shivered and pulled a hockey shirt on. The alcohol had suppressed most of my cold symptoms this evening, but now my nose was beginning to run. I pulled the last of the tissues out of the box, nearly falling on my ass in the process, and wondered blearily what to do with myself until it was safe to lay down to sleep.

My eyes wandered round the dimly lit room before coming to rest on my unpacked weekend bag. *Yes,* I thought, *that would do nicely.*

CHAPTER 11

Something was different.

I opened my eyes and looked around my room. It was in disarray: clothes, boxes and bags everywhere. But that wasn't it. My room is often like that. I'd obviously made it worse before I settled down to sleep was all.

So what was different?

Like the bursting of one of those giant fireworks they have at expensive displays (black sky suddenly blossoming into rich colour) I remembered the dream. I never dream, but last night, when I finally settled down to sleep, I had – and it was still with me, vivid and powerful, almost more real than the room in front of me.

But that wasn't it either. I sat up in bed. I suddenly wondered what the hell I was wearing? The top half of me had clothes on but like I'd been playing dress-up.

I swung my feet out of bed and stood on an empty patch of floor still trying to put my finger on what was different. Then I got it. It was me. I felt fantastic. No cold, no hangover; my head felt like a winter morning in the mountains, everything crisp and clear.

I remembered the trip to the pub last night and before it my talk with the Professor. I touched that memory carefully, like it was a bone that might be broken, but there was no sudden splinter of pain. Last night's catharsis seemed to have worked a miracle.

After the pub I'd come back to my room. I remembered sitting in the armchair, careful not to let my eyes close in case the nausea enveloped me. What had happened next? I sat back down on the edge of the bed and tried to run the videotape of my memory past that point, but it kept skipping ahead to the dream, the amazing colour of it and the endless sound of the ice.

Before the dream, I'd apparently scrambled the contents of my room and tried on some clothes; I'd been more than a little drunk. Maybe if I'd been sober enough to form memories I wouldn't have been fooling around like that. Perhaps there was nothing worth remembering. Except the dream; that would be difficult to forget.

I remembered that I'd been inside the dream for a while before I realised it. First of all everything was white – or at least colourless – like low cloud on a dull day. There was nothing to see and I had no sense of being anywhere. The light was weak, filtered, so attenuated that there were no shapes, no colours, just the impression of distance. There was sound, though – a whole geography of sound.

Imagine floating on your back in calm water, your eyes half-focused on the featureless grey cloudbanks above. Then imagine that you could hear every ripple and swell of moving water all around you. Ten thousand individual sounds spread out like flowers in a meadow, like trees in a forest, on every side of you.

For a while, that's where I thought I was: floating. Then, in a synesthetic moment the sounds became flickering points of light against blackness and I was a speck at the centre of a twinkling, rippling aurora as wide as a thunderstorm. And then the sounds were sounds again and I realised that they didn't ripple, they creaked. And I didn't float, I was simply suspended.

The landscape around me, indistinct as it was, began to make more sense to me – not clouds but ice. Miles of ice. It had drained the light of its power, its definition, its ability to render shapes. I was at sea but it was a sea that had frozen, back before anyone could remember, before there were even people *to* remember. And I realised that the light which I'd thought was colourless was the most amazing pale blue – the colour of a billion tons of frozen ocean. Every photon of light in that vast plane was the same colour, which was why it hadn't registered as colour at all.

I listened to the creaking and cracking, like a heavy sailing ship flying before a strong wind. The ice creaked like rigging and cracked like the snapping of sails and shifted over itself in a million tight spaces with a sound like the roaring wind. It was like the ice itself was dreaming of the ship, yearning for it, and the sense of its motion was exhilarating.

My whole awareness of the world was through these sounds, but gradually I became aware that I could also see something. As one part of my mind rushed endlessly forwards, drawn along by the dream-ship as it raced ahead of the surging waves, another part of me puzzled over a shape that was forming before me.

In a minute I had it. A figure, distorted and compressed, caught like an insect in that weird, blue *azul* amber.

I stared at the slumped figure for a good long while before I realised that it must be me.

But there was more to the scene. Another shape was there, but this one was empty, insubstantial. It was the husk of a person and it lay there in front of the me-figure, almost at its feet. And there was one more element, one more presence that I struggled to resolve.

Finally I understood: it was the source of light. Right by that first figure, that twisted representation of me, was a pool of radiance. Something that glowed, but not like a lamp – more like an open window on a sunny day. It didn't create light, it merely admitted it to the scene, allowed it to flow out in all directions.

What was I to make of this? A human shell, long dead, and standing over it two shapes: one a dark figure, distorted, the other a perfect light, unblemished. Were they all aspects of me? Had the light been present all along or had it just now come into existence? I couldn't tell, but perhaps the being of light, devoid as it was of detail or features, was simply the possibility of something now awakened within me. The dark shape was a grotesque distortion of my image, hardly recognisable. How long had it lain trapped in the ice, collapsing, decaying? And the empty shell: if I peered closer would I recognise it? Would I see the vanished face of my mother, echoed in the dust of its ruined form?

Since my own mind was the source of these images it seemed I had only to open myself up fully to understand their meaning. Some part of me already knew the truth and I willed everything else into silence so that its message could be heard.

With a growing sense of certainty, I realised that the two versions of me, the twisted-dark and the glowing-light, would be with me for some time to come – they were both aspects of my nature. I couldn't expel the flaws of a lifetime in an instant, but I could begin the process right now. I could work to erase that dark, twisted version of myself and allow the other, brilliant me to come more fully to life.

But the vacant shell nearby – which I took to be my mother's lingering, haunting presence – I realised I could be rid of that influence right now. There was only one role left for her in my life; she could help me by serving as a warning. She would be a beacon to keep me off the rocks. By renouncing her in everything I did, maybe I could avoid her fate.

All this came back to me as I sat on the bed. The immediacy of it was intense, like the grip of a nightmare, but I wasn't frightened; I was filled with calm resolve. Immersing myself in the vibrant recollection of that dream seemed to have unlocked my memory. I now recalled the final events of the previous night and I shuddered at my stupidity.

There were still gaps and omissions but I could remember the heart of it. After a few minutes of sitting in the armchair, I had risen unsteadily and tipped out my weekend bag, trying to find the rain-crumpled pages I had studied on the moors. From a zippered pouch I had removed the gold jewellery that proved so useless two days before when I stood in the grassy lee of that windswept ridge. And once again I forced myself to focus on the rhymes and rhythms of a nonsense mantra, the interlocking geometry of a labyrinthine design, and I strove for that moment of clarity and control that had escaped me on the freezing heath.

Then, full of weary confusion, stifled pain, alcohol and the mingling drugs of my pharmaceutical support system, I achieved what had escaped me when I'd had a clear head and a hundred acres of solitude. The feeling that Susan Milton described as 'Connection' came over me.

Did I feel or just imagine the crackle as my throat and lungs were swept clear of cold-viruses, each one spitting out of existence like water droplets on a griddle? Was I imagining the twist of realigning cartilage as my right knee-joint slid free from its decade-old injury and lost its ache? I *knew* I wasn't imagining the sudden expansion of my senses. It was like watching the world through a bank of cameras and when I turned my head, they all panned at different speeds. It should have been disorienting, but it was just the opposite; the cascade of images complemented each other. My awareness of my surroundings was so much more rich than before, and each new sensation seemed to find some previously unused part of my brain ready to process it.

And I knew that if I'd wanted to, I could have ripped the door to my room off its hinges simply by thinking it, then roasted the wood to cinders just by wishing it so.

At that moment I realised that alcohol was what you chose to get drunk on if you couldn't get your hands on power.

I was sitting on my bed remembering all this and I didn't know what to think. Even once I felt that I'd recovered all the previous night's events I realised that there was still something missing. I could remember Connecting and the initial impressions of what that felt like, but what had happened next? *That* memory was gone.

Glancing down I could see that my wrists were still wrapped in gold. I checked my bed and, sure enough, between my pillow and the wall was wedged the heavy gold necklace I'd wrapped around my head. It seems that I'd actually gone to sleep wearing what the documents called 'tribute'. I just couldn't imagine what I'd been thinking, keeping all that on in bed. Had I simply passed out before I remembered to take it off?

The final surprise came when I stripped off my remaining clothes ready to take a shower. I was wearing even more jewellery – a necklace in fact – and I didn't recognise it. I fumbled at the back of my neck looking for the catch, while trying to see the necklace in the mirror. It didn't look familiar but I'd turned out so many boxes last night, including a bunch of my mother's newly arrived possessions – perhaps I'd discovered it amongst them. Try as I might, I couldn't retrieve the last of the missing memories.

I gave up trying to remove the necklace and instead studied it in the mirror for a moment. I could see that it was beautifully made and as I inspected its reflection a distant memory began to surface. I recalled my mother's interest in handmade jewellery. I vaguely remembered someone telling me that she'd created a number of pieces herself. Gazing at the wonderful design of it I had a growing sense that I'd seen it before. Somehow, last night, pretty much smashed out my mind, I'd managed to find this beautiful thing among her other possessions.

Lovely though it was, I wasn't about to celebrate her memory by wearing it. I was feeling so calm today that I found I was able to think about her with no more emotion than if I were pondering a shopping list. My dream-revelation seemed as right now as when it first struck me: her example should serve as a warning. I no longer felt any need to be close to her; her presence in my world was reduced to the role of a haz-mat sticker applied to a section of my life, something I could glance at to remind me of danger.

That said, maybe that was exactly why I *should* wear her necklace. I never go in for low necklines so no one would even be aware of it. Only *I* would know it was there and only *I* would understand what it symbolised.

The idea appealed to me so much that I resolved not to remove the necklace until the transformation I'd glimpsed in my dream was complete and the danger had passed. The necklace would come off when I no longer needed reminding of the terrible consequences of weakness.

And this new sense of determination felt good. It was a strange feeling to be so positive about the future and I wondered for a moment whether Susan and David experienced this whenever they Connected. They had certainly seemed happy enough when I spied on them. Maybe Healing worked on the mind as well as the body – though I hadn't seen any mention of it in the PAC's documents. Perhaps I was just feeling a buzz like the one you get from your first couple of cigarettes, a buzz that disappears when the novelty becomes a habit.

Hmm. Thoughts of smoking took me back to the night before and the feeling I'd had in my lungs and throat as my cold left me. And I remembered my knee injury, the excuse I'd been using since high school to get out of exercising, and how last night I'd felt it heal. Had it really, though? An unfamiliar thought occurred to me – a way to test my health that no one who knew me would ever expect me to try.

Like a lot of people I owned a pair of running shoes that had never been party to anything faster than an amble. Now I dug them out from under my bed, nearly choking on the dust, and then searched around for some clothes to run in. Half of modern fashion is sportswear, so even *I* had something suitable. Finding the right bra was more of a challenge; if this was to be more than an isolated occurrence I'd need to do some shopping.

When I stepped outside a few minutes later I was surprised at how early it still was. The sun was up, but only just, and no one from the project was around. It was pretty cold out, even with a fleece over my t-shirt, but my newly repaired lungs were able to cope. Maybe my asthma was history too.

Watching my breath steam in front of me, I trotted slowly up the hill.

I didn't set any records, but for someone with my lifestyle it wasn't a bad start. I ran for about two miles, starting really slow and speeding up a little, once I was warmed through. The damp air tasted great, and the shallow Autumn light glittering off the frosted meadows was remarkably beautiful. Best of all, my knee was giving me no trouble at all.

When I got back, I lingered outside for a couple of minutes, doing my best to remember the stretching exercises I'd seen runners perform. My muscles felt warm and full of blood; my breathing was deep and easy, and I suspected I was having my first proper hit of endorphins. Why wouldn't anyone in their right mind want to start their day like this?

Except that tomorrow, I might make it a little bit earlier. That way I could see the sunrise and it would give me a little more time before starting work. My room desperately needed a spring-clean and I doubted I was going to finish it this evening.

For a moment I was almost giddy with the rush of well-being. I was going to have to be careful that my head didn't fly off. This feeling was a little disorienting. I calmed myself down and concentrated on my stretches.

I *would* get up early tomorrow, though. Nothing had changed in my desire to learn more about the PAC and to find a way onto the team and it wouldn't happen if I was lying in bed sleeping. There was work to be done and I wasn't going to waste another minute.

I headed back inside to change and get ready. When I was finished showering and dressing I walked over to the main building to look for some breakfast. The cook was just setting everything up and no one else, as yet, had arrived.

"Morning," I said, adding, "I'm Jo," in response to his rather blank look. I realised I'd never really spoken to the cook before.

I said, "Can I ask you something?"

He nodded, without enthusiasm, and I said, "Listen, I want to try being a little bit healthier. I want to stay off the fried food for a while. What do you think I should be eating for breakfast?"

He scratched his chin and looked a bit surprised. Maybe he didn't get asked for his advice very often. But I figured he'd probably had to sit through a bunch of catering college lectures on this stuff and it was probably easier to get him to fix me something if it was his suggestion in the first place.

"Well, we've got the muesli," he said, "Some of the girls go for that. Did you want to do a bit of, what do you call it, de-tox then?"

"I don't know," I said, "I don't know much about those things."

"Well, for a de-tox I think you'd want to eat a lot of fruit, specially for breakfast," he explained, warming to his role as teacher. "Maybe drink some green tea. I've definitely got some somewhere because Doctor Milton likes it. And lots of water, which I always put out anyway." He pointed over to the big metal jug on the end of the counter which I'd never seen anyone touch.

I'd always found him kind of surly and aggressive, but it seemed like he could be pretty helpful if you asked nicely. I gave him an encouraging look because it seemed like he might have more to say. He thought for a moment and said, "I could get in a bit of fruit if you like, kiwis, citrus, a bit of colour. I've got an order to place this afternoon."

"You'd do that?" I asked appreciatively.

"Oh yeah, that wouldn't be a problem. Probably won't be in before Thursday though. Maybe try the muesli in the meantime. There's skimmed milk to go with it in the jug at the back," he indicated the table with the cereals on it.

"That's really kind of you," I said and then looked awkward. "I'm sorry but I can't remember your name."

"I'm Ray," he said, jutting his chin like it was a source of pride. "And you're Jo, then" he said, and for the first time since I'd joined the project I saw him smile.

Interesting.

"Thanks Ray," I said and headed over to get myself some muesli – though I wasn't feeling much enthusiasm at the prospect. I'd had it in the past and found it boring, but really it wasn't too bad, it just took a bit of eating. I was still chewing away when Daniel came in. His hair was all angles and he hadn't shaved yet. He didn't look all that well.

He seemed surprised to see me and came straight over to join me. "Hey. I was going to come and look for you once I'd had some tea – check you hadn't slipped into a coma. We guzzled a *boatload* of booze last night."

The cook wandered over and put a white mug of tea down in front of Daniel and said, "Wasn't sure you could fetch it yourself. You on the pop last night?"

Daniel just laughed and put his head down in his hands, pushing his fingers through his hair. "Yeah. It all went horribly wrong. Cheers for the tea, Ray."

The cook wandered away to finish laying out breakfast. Daniel took a couple of sips of hot tea, sighed with relief and said, "You look fresh as a daisy. I thought you might be feeling the effects a bit this morning."

I couldn't very well tell him the secret of my rapid recovery, so I made something up. "To be honest," I said, "most of what I drank came back up before it had a chance to do much damage."

He swallowed, queasily, and I added, "Sorry to be gross."

He cleared his throat and carefully avoided my eye. "The main thing," he said, "is that you seem like you're not letting it get to you." He wasn't talking about the booze, of course. "Probably a night out wasn't a bad idea. And, you know, if I have to, I'm prepared to risk my liver and do it all over again. If it would help." Then, sounding exhausted, he added, "But not tonight."

I caught his eye – to make sure he knew I meant it – and said seriously, "You've helped a lot already, thanks."

He was maybe a little surprised by my easy directness – it wasn't something I often achieved – but I could tell he was glad to hear the sentiment. He met my gaze for a moment and then he looked thoughtful, confused even. He said, "You know, you look *incredible* this morning. And your cold is gone. You should write to the Southern Comfort people. Offer to sell them your story."

"I do feel pretty good," I admitted. I wasn't planning to tell him about the magic, but I couldn't see the harm in sharing part of what I'd experienced – maybe enough to stop him becoming suspicious. "I had the most amazing dream last night and it really made me think. Made me realise some things."

"Yeah?" he said, meaning *go on*.

I hadn't actually intended to go into details, but he seemed so interested. "Well, you know dreams are always weird, right?" I said. "But I saw myself stuck in the middle of all this ice and I was just looking awful, falling to bits in front of my own eyes, if you see what I mean." And suddenly I didn't want to tell him the rest of the dream. I don't know why; it just suddenly seemed too personal – plus it sounded pretty dumb.

He saw my reluctance and said, "I won't make fun. I promise."

It would seem weird to just clam up, so I compromised a little and said, "It just made me think. I could stay stuck in the same rut for the rest of my life or I could change my approach, try something new. Be like this ball of light instead of staying trapped inside the sad, old me until I fall apart completely." I realised I'd been waving my hands a lot and I put them down now. "OK, I didn't explain that very well, but do you know what I mean?"

He shrugged agreeably and said, "Well, I understand the idea, definitely. I suppose the imagery is whatever makes sense to you. If I had that dream it would probably be about being on stage or something. Anyway, it obviously got your attention." He looked nervous for a second and said, "I was worried that maybe you'd, um, opted for a little bit of *chemical* assistance this morning."

Curiously, this suggestion didn't annoy me. Daniel knew about my patches and had never approved, so this wasn't anything new. I found the only question his words raised in my mind was about what sort of impression I wanted to leave him with. Was it better if he thought I was propping myself up with medication or if he thought I was fine without it? I figured it was easier not to have him fussing over me. "No drugs," I said, holding up my hands. "We had a really good evening last night and when you consider what I'd been through yesterday, that's a miracle. My weird dream just made me realise that if I could do it once, then I could probably do it everyday. It's about time for a change, is all. And you were a big part of helping me see that."

I was laying it on a bit thick, but why not? He was a good guy and if I wanted to keep counting on him I should probably give him some recognition occasionally. Plus, if I were being cynical, I could say that his ego would now keep him from doubting me because he couldn't take the credit for my improvement while simultaneously being suspicious of it. So whatever.

He gave me an appraising look. "You're not going to become a Buddhist or anything are you? This is just about remembering to look on the bright side a bit more, right?"

I nodded reassuringly, and he seemed satisfied. He looked over to the counter where the cook had finished laying things out. "OK," he said, "Well I need bacon or I think I'm going to croak."

"Right. See you at lunch. If you live," I said, and headed for the door. I gave Ray a wave on my way out and he nodded back. Not even nine o'clock and I'd made a friend.

And the day just kept getting better. I felt good, I was feeling really strong for once and people seemed to respond to that right away. Of course there was a part of me that didn't trust this transformation. God knows I've turned over a new leaf or two in my time – quite recently in fact – but this was a little bit different. This wasn't the usual ten-minute makeover. I had, after all, undergone a major physical tune-up last night, so there was every reason to think that it might have fixed up my mental machinery too.

I mean it had always seemed weird to me that anti-depressants could work, because it was absurd to think that the root cause of depression was a lack of *pills*. But on the other hand, what those drugs did was boost your serotonin levels in a few key areas. If 'Connecting' could cure the common cold and straighten mangled cartilage, it could probably blow the cobwebs out of your brain too.

When I started the day, this new leaf was just a good idea; by the end of the day it had become a reality. I'd managed one full day without screwing up, giving in, curling up, lashing out or blaming anyone for anything, myself included. I mean, hallelujah. And if I could manage one day then maybe I *could* manage another, particularly now I'd had a taste of how good it could feel.

With this frighteningly stable version of myself working on the problem, could it be long before I'd won over the PAC and earned a seat at their table? More than ever that was what I wanted and I'd never felt more capable of getting what I wanted in my life. I fairly hummed with purpose and drive. Even at the end of the evening, it almost took an act of will to stop bustling, to lie down and sleep – despite the fact that I'd had the busiest day I could remember. My final thought as I began to drift off was the realisation that I actually wasn't afraid – of the future, of other people, of what I might say or do. I had stopped being afraid.

I slept that night in total peace, and although I dreamed – endless visions of colour and movement – in the morning the details had all slipped away. I woke rested and ready to begin again.

CHAPTER 12

So it's true that *ideally* I wouldn't still be spying on anyone. But I couldn't really afford to wait outside until the PAC invited me in. I needed to know what was going on right now. I couldn't afford to be excluded.

Now, for anyone who doesn't know, there's a place in London called Tottenham Court Road. Nerds call it TCR and it is one of their holy places. You can pretty much buy any gadget you want there – including off-the-shelf surveillance equipment. You'd think you'd need some sort of licence or official permission to buy hidden cameras, bugs and sound-recorders that look like pens, but you don't. You don't even need to make a trip: a web browser and a credit-card is all it takes.

In fact, my needs were positively pedestrian compared with what else was on offer. I just wanted an audio bug with a short-range transmitter in it and then I needed something to pick up the signal. Right away I found a bug that was made to look like a mains adaptor – one of those dealy-bobs you use when you've got two plugs and only one wall outlet. It was voice-activated and drew its power from the mains current – and it was available for next-day shipping. I mean they were making it difficult for anyone with a healthy level of curiosity *not* to bug people, if you ask me.

So a week had gone by since I'd first Connected and I hadn't wasted a moment of that time. I was still feeling terrific, but my mood had settled down a little. I wasn't having those moments where I had to fight the urge to grin like a fool any more. I'd just fairly *torn* through every task assigned to me (while remembering not to make it look *too* easy); I'd built or repaired bridges with several members of the team and I'd continued to study the PAC's documents in detail.

A couple of times, when I headed out for my dawn jog, I'd taken my bag of gold knick-knacks with me so's I could do a little practice with the magic. I needed to get a minimum of a few hundred yards from the project buildings and the barn on the off-chance that one of the other members of the team was doing the same thing. The Presence Surface was like sonar for other adepts; when I Connected I'd become visible to them – and if I were detected the PAC would think the enemy was upon them and there would be a lot of running around and yelling and other stuff I didn't want.

But I had no problems with that or anything else. In fact just the opposite. Call it luck or call it natural talent, but I just took to the use of magic like I was born to it. From my reading I knew it had taken days before Susan had even basic control of a Shield. And it took her weeks of diligent effort before she could manipulate any of the other Surfaces worth a damn. Not so for me. I found I almost didn't have to try; my first instinct was unfailingly the right one. And in what amounted to my spare time, I had mastered what others had taken months, even years, to learn. I didn't kid myself that I was on a par with the Witnesses, many of whom had centuries of experience behind them, but I was certainly on the fast track.

My control was good enough that I was able to turn my two-twists-of-necklace headband into something a little more professional. I wound a filament of steel wire through the loose links so that the necklace would hold a shape, then I got it settled properly on my head, adjusting and twisting it until it was both comfortable and planted firmly in place. Then, for the next step, I'd borrowed a gold necklace from a non-PAC researcher called Nicola. I needed it so I could Connect in order to work on my own headband. I used the Heat Surface to raise the temperature of the gold links until they began to fuse together. It took half an hour, and persistence was definitely required, but the result was pretty impressive. I pulled out the steel wire when I was done and admired the result: a custom-made gold headband that wouldn't fall off.

So my accelerated progress with magic was certainly good news. Things were moving a little more slowly with my ingratiation into the PAC – but that was a people thing and they always take time. A week is an eye-blink when it comes to changing people's attitudes and I had a lot of fences to mend (along with building those bridges I mentioned). And while we're extending metaphors, as part of my overall self-promotion I'd also been planting a few seeds – a comment here, some gentle pressure there – which I hoped would bear fruit soon enough.

For instance, I knew Daniel was impressed with how well I'd got my act together, but I could tell he was worried it was temporary. With a few carefully chosen remarks I helped him conclude that what his pal Jo really needed was a purpose – ideally one she could share with those around her. Without it she might grow disillusioned, isolated and turn inwards again, but with it she might continue to improve and be gradually drawn out of her shell. In other words, I made sure he'd want the PAC to offer me membership because it was the right thing for *me*.

The Professor, on the other hand, was from an earlier era. He understood about purpose, but his generation were largely motivated by duty. I suspected that when he was growing up, young people weren't encouraged to keep their options for the future open or obsess about whether they were happy; they were told it was better to keep busy and get on with something useful. I made it clear to the Professor that shouldering some responsibility was really helping me to steady myself. It was an impression I tried to create with my behaviour rather than my words, whenever possible.

Like Daniel, he was sure to wonder how permanent my new diligence was too. I figured he'd feel most comfortable if he could keep an eye on me to see how I was bearing up, so I made sure we often found ourselves with a few minutes to chat, just the two of us. Sure, I'd go a little quiet from time to time, just to show I wasn't manic or a machine, but in all my dealings with him my watchword was 'steadiness'.

Susan Milton was a tougher nut to crack, partly because I knew very little about what made her tick. I knew she was a hard worker and very bright. And I knew she had a soft side, as evidenced by her closeness with David Braun. Beyond that, she was still largely opaque to me.

My best guess was that her main concern would probably be with my flaky personality. I had an idea that being a team-player didn't come naturally to her. I suspected that her instinct was usually to tackle everything on her own. If she found teams naturally uncomfortable then she'd want to keep things simple by making sure that no volatile personalities were added to the mix. She'd want to avoid any situation which might require too much complex diplomacy.

She also struck me as a 'good girl', someone who'd never

really rebelled; she was therefore less forgiving of others who had. This was guesswork but the course it suggested wasn't a high-risk one. I decided that my priority with Susan would be to seem calm, reasonable, even a little unimaginative – in short, less of a highly-strung liability than my background suggested. Her priority would be the good of the team, rather than my welfare, so I did my best to seem like an asset.

So that was how I behaved; I was also making some changes to how I looked. That Saturday I got the bus into town and did a little shopping. It was basic psychology really: one way to change the impression that I was flaky was to get rid of as many of the outward signs of flakiness as possible – anything a person might conceivably associate with a troubled personality. So gradually I started to take better care of myself. Nothing over-the-top, because drastic change is also a sign of problems, but I made sure my nails were neat and unbitten, my hair was tidy and presentable and I put a little more effort into keeping my chin high and making eye contact. I gave up slouching and I stopped being so jumpy around people. From time to time, in a restrained way, I even smiled pleasantly, to show that I wouldn't bite.

On my shopping trip I picked up a few clothes in lighter colours than I usually went for. Again, nothing jarringly out of character, but I had a habit of wearing old jeans and patterned sweaters in muddy tones and the overall impression it gave was that I wanted to be inconspicuous, that I wanted people to not look at me.

Now I wanted my appearance to say 'look or don't – I'm comfortable either way'. I wasn't trying to grab attention but I wasn't actively deflecting it either. So I found some lighter-weight sweaters in solid colours, no patterns, and a couple of pairs of jeans in shades other than denim-blue. My plan was to still revert to the bulky, dowdy, blah outfits occasionally but to balance them by doing something more imaginative with my hair or maybe (gasp) applying a suspicion of eye-liner and popping a pair of colourful studs[1] in my ears. (In fact I hardly needed cosmetics; my skin tone and circulation were so much improved that make-up would have been overdoing the transformation.)

My room, too, I kept neat and tidy. Not Marines-Corps neat, but orderly – like I cared about the space I spent time in. Two decades of on-and-off therapy and psychiatry might not have helped me *achieve* a healthy mental balance but it was just the thing for helping me *fake* it.

* * *

Towards the end of my second week as a member of the occult fraternity, I found out that the PAC were planning to have a meeting. I thought it would be a good opportunity for them to start the process of including me in the group, so I laid some groundwork to that end.

I came up with a few technical tricks to help with the project work. I thought it my impress the PAC members and help them to see how useful someone like me could be to them.

Also, on my own initiative, I tracked down an ancient book that was coming up for auction in Edinburgh the following week. I had chosen it carefully because it was an occult title that I was sure would pique the curiosity of the researchers. Then I approached Susan and asked if she thought it might be of interest. She was very keen to know more and I apologised for not having any more

---

[1]   OK. Studs rapidly gave way to clips. One problem with occult regenerative powers is that they interfere with a gal's piercings. Would anyone spot that I no longer had pierced ears? Unlikely. But I made a mental note to check the ear-lobes of anyone new I met.

details, explaining that I'd discovered it while looking for other items on the project's behalf, but that I wasn't sure *this* was quite their thing. (I didn't want to let on that I knew about their interest in the occult.)

She assured me that it was just what they were looking for, so the next day I sought out Susan again and told her what else I'd been able to discover. Not only had I researched the title that was up for sale – and written her a little gloss – I'd also researched the seller, discovered what else he might have in his private collection and made suggestions on how he might be persuaded to sell some of it. The point I wanted to make was that I could trace things and people, and pull together background information on them, in a way the PAC could surely use. I was careful not to give any hint that I was making that particular point, or that I suspected more was going on with them than met the eye.

But I knew the PAC were still delving into the loss of the Marker and were trying to track it down without alerting the Army's spies. They were going to need skills like mine.

I'd given the whole thing a lot of thought and with growing certainty I'd decided that the Marker was the key. If I could help them find it, my credibility problems would be a thing of the past. Now I was looking for a way to get started on that.

The final piece of groundwork I laid for the meeting was the most important – and it involved Daniel. The evening before the PAC meeting, I invited him out to the pub. The plan was to enlist his help and get him to sponsor me for membership of the inner circle. But I had to do it without letting on that I knew what they were up to. Effectively, I had to apply for the job while appearing not to know it existed.

Unexpectedly, the first hurdle came when we arrived at the bar and he offered me a drink. The phrase 'no thanks' was on my lips almost before I realised it was a little out of character. For this stage in my rehabilitation, I should be coy and say *Well, I shouldn't*, or I should make it clear that two was my limit, something like that. I shouldn't turn down the offer without a little internal struggle, or a slight suggestion of regret. I'd turned over a new leaf, not become a Puritan.

Truth be told, I don't suppose Daniel would have noticed either way; it was just a reminder to me to watch what I said. It had also taken me a little by surprise that I actually *didn't* feel like a glass of wine. It reminded me of those tests they give you when you go to the opticians. You know the ones, where they flip a little monocle of glass backwards and forwards in front of one eye and then ask, "Better with or without? Now look again. Better with or without?" In the past, my view of the world had always been 'better with' a little alcohol. But now that I wasn't feeling any pain and I had good reasons to want a totally clear head, alcohol seemed like a distraction. I was becoming 'better without'. Fine and all, but it had crept up on me.

"Listen, before I forget," Daniel said when we'd got our drinks, "Tammy's having a party on Saturday and she wondered if you wanted to come. A few people from the project will be there, Seb, Felicity... moi."

Even the new me felt a hint of jealousy when I thought of Daniel and Tammy and the implied chumminess of him doing her inviting for her.

I snuffed out that feeling immediately. Jealousy I could do without; it was corrosive and pointless – especially now that I had enough guts to go after what I wanted. The new me was (I was pretty sure) quite capable of grabbing Daniel by the lapels and saying, 'Forget Tammy, concentrate on me' if that seemed like the thing to do. So why seethe inside when you can just seize what you want? The only question was: what *did* I want?

Cold though it might sound, I didn't need Daniel as anything more than a friend. I'll admit, until recently I've occasionally thought about us becoming more than that – if only I had the guts to do something about it. It was something I'd daydream about from time to time. But that was then; I had other considerations now; I had work to do.

On the other hand I needed Daniel's help and keeping his friendship probably meant keeping his interest. Which meant not letting distractions – like pretty part-time barmaids – absorb too much of his attention. I needed to perform a little adjustment of his attitude here.

"Oh that's such a shame," I said, "I'm probably going to be in London this weekend. I need to take care of some things at the house." It wasn't just an excuse; I was really considering it.

"But you *might* be around?" he asked.

"Well, it's *possible*," I said. Then I looked downcast, put my hand on his arm, and said shyly, "Anyway, you'll have more fun if I'm not there. You know I'm not big on parties. It'll give you a chance to spend some time with Tammy."

He looked a little awkward and had to hunt for his words. After a moment he said, "But I'd much rather you were there. I wouldn't have asked you otherwise."

I made a little bit of eye contact and teased him: "I thought the invitation was from Tammy?" He said nothing and I added, "Well don't have too much fun without me, will you?"

I figured that was enough – a bit of flirting, a bit of guilt-tripping – I doubted anything too irrevocable would be happening this Saturday even if I wasn't around to keep an eye on him. On to other matters.

"Listen," I said, "I wanted to ask you about something."

"Sure," he said, agreeably, sipping his pint.

"So… it's about the project," I said. "I mean, you can see I'm making an effort to do my bit and make up for the, um, horrors of the past. Right?"

He gave a firm nod, which seemed to mean 'absolutely'.

I went on, "I'm not asking for a favour; I don't want to put you in an awkward position. I'm just hoping that if you think I'm doing a good job on the project and that I'm ready to take on a bit more, that you could let the team know. I totally understand that I've got some way to go before I'm considered anyone's first choice, but I'm really trying to do my best not to let anyone down. I just want to make sure someone notices."

"I can tell you," Daniel said, "everyone's noticed."

"Really?" I said, "Well, that makes me feel better. The thing is, though, because I've screwed up in the past, everyone's pretty careful not to give me anything too important to do. And I don't see how I'm going to prove to anyone that I can be reliable until someone trusts me with a challenge."

"Well, I'm sure no one wants to overload you, particularly when you've been through the wars lately," he said.

"No, no, I get that. I do. I'm just saying that when you get to the point where you *personally* think I could handle something more challenging – *if* you get to that point – will you make sure the others know it? That's all I'm asking."

He shook his head, as if to say it wasn't even a question I needed to ask. "Of *course* I will," he said. "In fact I was planning to say something at the meeting tomorrow."

Which was just what I wanted to hear. I thought about driving the point home, but I'd got what I wanted; I should quit while I was ahead.

So with that out of the way and dealt with, we chatted for a little bit longer, mainly about Daniel's work. I was attentive for as long as I could manage, but my attention started to wander after a while. As soon as a decent interval had passed I made the excuse that I was tired and headed back to field station.

In truth, I was trimming back on my sleep at the moment because I had so much to do. It was so easy to do that I was a little appalled with the amount of time I must have wasted in the past, snoozing when I could have been doing something useful. But, since I'd wasted most of the hours I'd spent awake too, I didn't the see the benefit in dwelling on it.

Before I returned to my room, I dropped into the main building. Almost everyone had gone home – which suited me, because I needed to plant my bug. But first, I ducked into the server room and rummaged around in my box'o'bits for a cable. The receiver for the bug was a black metal box about the size of a pack of cards out of which protruded eighteen inches of aerial. I taped it behind a tower server in the corner of the computer room, letting the aerial run up the wall. Then I plugged the audio output of the receiver into the sound card of the computer. Finally, I logged onto that server and downloaded a copy of Wavepad from the net so that I could record, clean up and edit whatever I overheard. Once it was ready I let myself out, locking the door behind me, and went to plant the bug.

I tapped on the Professor's door and got no answer, so I went in. The room was in partial darkness, only a desk lamp was still on and the man himself wasn't around. Quickly I slipped through the far door, down the steps and entered the pitch-black meeting room. I had to feel around for a moment to locate the light switch before I could see anything.

Placement of the bug was going to be tricky. There were two wall sockets, neither of them in great positions if acoustics were your main concern. I selected the far one because it was out of sight unless you were tucked right in that corner. There was a recessed slider on the back of the adaptor/bug and I used a fingernail to drag it to its 'on' position. Once it was plugged in, the bug would be live.

It was an awkward stretch, the table was in the way, and I had to contort a little to reach it. As I stood up again, Susan Milton was coming through the door. "Oh it's you, Jo," she said, obviously expecting the Professor.

What a difference a couple of weeks had made. There was no crescendo of panic inside me, no rabbit-in-the-headlights expression on my face. I was as cool as a bushel of Icelandic cucumbers.

Big smile, to show I was happy to see her (not guilty or surprised – happy). I said, "Oh hi. I'm glad there's someone else around; this place is a bit creepy at night."

She nodded, but didn't depart. She was obviously going to want an explanation for my presence. *Keep it simple*, I thought. "I borrowed the mains adaptor from in here," I said. "Figured I'd better put it back in case Daniel needed to plug his laptop in for another slide show."

"Right," was all she said, not giving much away.

"Anyway, all done," I said cheerfully and breezed past, adding, "G'night."

I headed back to the Fortress of Servitude and hit stop on the recorder's toolbar. I could see from the squiggles on the waveform display that something had been captured. I converted the file to

MP3, named it 'Neil Sedaka Live pt1'[1] and plugged my severely-hacked-and-modified iPod into the server in the corner. Then I copied the recording to the player and took a listen. Not bad at all. I could hear myself a lot more clearly than I could hear Susan (and boy, did I sound weird) but everything was intelligible.

With this set-up I could leave the recorder running and transfer it to my iPod later to see what I'd captured. I could even log in remotely, re-direct the audio stream over the network, and eavesdrop live from my dorm room if I wanted.

If I'd done my preparation properly then during tomorrow's meeting, the PAC would consider admitting me to their hallowed circle – and I'd be listening in.

---

[1] You remember when you learned Venn diagrams in school? Well, in one circle put all the people who are tech-savvy enough to poke around the directories of someone else's iPod. In the other circle put all the people who like Easy Listening music from the Seventies. The overlap of the two circles is called the 'intersection' of the sets. Notice how it's empty.

CHAPTER 13

It was a couple of hours before dawn on the day of the PAC meeting and I found I'd had enough sleep already. I boiled my little mini kettle and made some of that weird tea that Ray, the cook, had recommended. It was sort of addictive in a bitter kind of way. But from what I could gather, of all the things in the world with addictive properties, green tea is about the healthiest of them.

I wrapped my quilt around my shoulders, folded my legs underneath me and settled into my armchair to read the final instalment of the PAC documents. Actually it was the final instalment of documents actually *written* by members of the PAC – their collection also included a lot of PDF[1]'s of more ancient documents – most of them in languages I didn't speak).

These last few were speculative essays discussing the origins of magic. I have to admit that when I first found out what the PAC

---

[1] Just ignore any jargon words I use that you don't understand. If it matters that you know exactly what I'm talking about then I'll explain it. That said, if you don't know what a PDF is I hope you've got a good reason, like you're Amish or you were born in 1850.

were into, the thought that most intrigued me was: if magic *did* work, then *how* did it work? Since then, the question had been rather edged out by other considerations and I found that my interest had waned. But I remembered turning the possibilities over in my mind and wondering who else had tackled this question, and whether they'd come up with any possible answers.

And now, for the sake of completeness, I was reading the PAC's thoughts on the subject. I *had* wondered whether the preponderance of history majors in the team would result in a lack of scientific curiosity about the underlying mechanisms of magic. Not so. David Braun, it seemed, had studied engineering, and unsurprisingly that mindset led him to wonder about the rules and origins of magic. Little Daniel too had taken all manner of science-side courses in his time, including some philosophy of science classes. His main interest seemed to be the implications of magic for a universe that ran on science – or vice versa. In other words, either magic was a sort of science or science was a sort of magic – or the universe operated according to two separate sets of rules. That last possibility threatened to blow my mind – and I was pretty sure it was a nonsense scenario. It seemed to me that whatever the rules were that governed our reality, they must be consistent with both magic and technology, because both of those things existed. Medieval peasants might have thought magic was supernatural – beyond nature – but I didn't. Discovering magic had to be the same kind of thing as finding a novel sub-atomic particle, only more so: it was all part of the same puzzle.

So I felt sure that magic must also be good physics at some level. What I couldn't quite get my head around was the question of whether magic could function using just the physics we currently knew about – the four forces, the ever-growing menagerie of particles, the hotly-debated complement of dimensions – or would we find that to explain magic we'd have to discover a whole new field of physics?

Naturally, I couldn't answer that question, but it made me think of Arthur C. Clarke's often-quoted third law of prediction: "Any sufficiently advanced technology is indistinguishable from magic."[1] Turn it around and what it says is that anything that looks like magic must really just be technology that's very advanced. Deep.

Actually I fudged the syllogism there, didn't I? Clarke's law really only says that something that looks like magic *could* just be advanced technology – in other words, it could be science that someone has harnessed to serve a purpose. Logically, the other possibility is that magic is science that doesn't need harnessing; it's just built into the world. Again, deep. Did magic work because human brains had somehow evolved to be remote controls for the hidden forces of nature?

I decided to stop thinking about this stuff and just read. Because my purpose in going over these essays wasn't to unravel the secrets of the universe; I was more interested in any clues they might contain about the PAC, the Army or the all-important Marker.

By the time the sun's first rays were lightening the gloom outside my window I had satisfied myself that there was very little of immediate use to me in any of those papers. So I shucked off the quilt and changed into my running gear.

Two weeks of running, a bit of healthy eating and a complete

---

[1]   Do you care what the other two are? Do I? Here they are anyway:

i. When a distinguished but elderly scientist states that something is possible, he is almost certainly right. When he states that something is impossible, he is very probably wrong.

ii. The only way of discovering the limits of the possible is to venture a little way past them into the impossible.

magical overhaul of my physiology had done wonders… although I was still a slightly pudgy twenty-something with chunky thighs and no upper-body strength. But I was in no rush. After a year of this I was sure I'd be in great shape. And who knew how buff I'd be after a couple of hundred years. (Yup, increasingly, everything led back to finding the Marker.)

* * *

Meeting time rolled around soon enough. I hit record on my monitoring software and checked that I was picking up good audio. At this stage of the meeting the noise came mainly from the motion of chairs, papers and mugs of hot caffeine, but I also detected the odd 'hi' and 'excuse me' so I knew the bug was going to do its job.

As the meeting began I listened in for a while, but the first order of business was a yawn. The Procedures and Admin Committee might be a front for a group of occult White Hats, but from time to time they still used it as a forum to discuss actual procedures and admin. I double-checked that my recording set-up was capturing everything and then I set off to put this time to better use.

I wonder if the PAC realised that the one weak point, from an operational-security point of view, about gathering themselves together in a (supposedly) private room, was that it left them exposed elsewhere. Any evil mastermind will tell you that you need henchmen: full-time big, dumb, totally obedient minions who stand around and guard your stuff and keep an eye on the prisoners.

The PAC, on the other hand, were all officers. They didn't have a flunky class who could patrol the perimeter in ill-fitting black jumpsuits while the higher-ups strategised. They probably thought it would be impolite to treat someone like a second-class citizen and exclude them from meetings by having them do the gruntwork. Man, evil gets all the breaks.

So, blessed as I was these days with bucketloads of icy sang-froid, I dropped into Susan Milton's office and poked around among her things for a while. In my hot little mitt I clutched an anti-virus install disk – my excuse for sitting at her desk in front of her computer should anyone come in. And it was a bust. Of course I didn't really need to be in the room to work on (or spy on) her computer – I could do that from afar – this visit was about physical items of interest: PAC-related paperwork, maps with Xs on them, glowing amulets, etc; None of which I found.

I retreated. Then I screwed my courage to the next highest sticking point and ventured into the Professor's office. For a moment I considered having a proper nose around. But in the corridor outside I could hear other people in the team passing the door. Plus, you never knew when someone in the PAC meeting might nip out for a comfort break. The chances of detection were a little too high. Undoubtedly I could bluff my way out of any awkward encounters but it didn't seem worth the risk. I'd be better off coming back at night.

So I withdrew, opting to bide my time. Maybe I hadn't learned anything from my physical snooping, but in the meantime my bug would have recorded around three-quarters of an hour of the PAC's cloak-and-dagger conspiring. (At least I hoped it was cloak-and-dagger; I didn't have much use for a recording of the fierce debate over personal use of the photocopier.)

About then a growl from my stomach interrupted me, so I made a detour via the refectory, on my way back to the server room. I grabbed a plastic carton of what I hoped was a tuna salad, plus a bottle of water, and waited for Ray to finish what he was doing so he could take my money.

Then a strange thing happened.

Blondy, who I think I decided was really called Felicity, was in there reading a dry-looking book and sipping from a steaming plastic cup of what appeared to be hot water. Did thin girls really drink hot water? No wonder they were so grumpy.

Anyway, I paid and started to walk out. Felicity looked up as I passed her, caught my eye and beamed me a smile. And what a smile it was. I vaguely remembered hearing that she was into girls – or was that Theresa? – anyway, the look she gave me definitely registered, even on my low-powered, straight-person's gaydar. Not that I cared what she did to amuse herself, but what unnerved me was the smokingly coy look I'd given her in response. Oh. My. God. I hurried out of there.

I'd as soon not talk about this, but the fact is that what with my bouts of depression, the anti-depressants to tackle the depression, a head full of neuroses and the black hole where my self-esteem should be, I pretty much had the libido of a bonsai tree. If a nice-looking guy smiled at me, I'd freeze. Or so I always imagined. I couldn't remember it happening in reality. Anyway, Felicity had checked me out and I'd fired back a smouldering look of barely disguised interest. WTF.

Was it possible that as my libido thawed after years in suspended animation I'd discover that I was gay? What was I, living in a soap opera?

I realised that for the first time since the dream, and my big decision not to follow in my mother's footsteps, I was freaking out. For a moment I was in danger of dropping my salad[1]. I took a deep breath and shut down this cacophony of thoughts. A momentary echo of the ice dream flashed into my mind and I focussed on the

---

[1]   That sounds like a euphemism for something but it isn't

untroubled cool of that scene. Calm. I was calm again.

I'd think about this some other time, but I couldn't help considering what would surely be the *ultimate* talk-show question: did magic make you gay? Or maybe just into girls, whatever biological equipment you happened to be fitted with. Was that why adepts were 99% men? Was that why the church got such a kick out of burning witches – they were really burning ungodly lesbians? There was obviously more going on here than I'd prepared myself for and it made me wonder if I was the only one who'd experienced this, ahem, side-effect.

I mean I'd been there in that barn, and if Susan Milton had come over all SSO[1], she was hiding it magnificently well. Which meant there was a pretty good chance that this had nothing to do with magic-use. Gulp.

Anyway, I put all that out of my mind. Since I wasn't actually having any sex, what did it matter what kind I wasn't having? The Catholic church and I would have to agree to differ on that point.

Thankfully, I'd put my little panic behind me by the time I sat down behind the main console in the server room. My spring-cleaned psyche seemed to find its way back to equilibrium so much quicker than in the old days. And when I put something out of my mind, it actually worked. My focus was now on the record of the PAC meeting. I had fifty minutes of audio to listen to and I began hopping through it in one-minute increments, searching for the end of the admin chatter and the beginning of the secret-squirrel stuff.

I had to jump forwards nearly half an hour before I heard Susan say, "OK. I think we can move onto the next section. Daniel, there was something you wanted to say before we get on to Theresa's update?"

---

[1]   Same-sex oriented.

That sounded good. Chances are it would be about me. I hadn't been certain that Daniel would be direct in his methods, but I was pretty confident that he'd find *some* way to champion my cause. He wasn't exactly a bulldog, so I thought he might opt to have one or more quiet one-to-ones with other members of the team, but here he was having requested a slot on the meeting's agenda.

He cleared his throat and said, "Thanks. If it's alright with everyone, I want to say something about Jo Hallett. And I want to make a suggestion, even though I reckon there'll be some fairly strong reactions."

He went on, "You all know that Jo and I are friends, which maybe means I'm prejudiced. But it also means I know her pretty well. If you've worked with her then you know that she's one of the most intelligent people around. You also know that she lost her mother when she was younger and she's not had a very stable upbringing. That doesn't sound great, I know, but I don't think it should put us off either. What I've got in mind is that we should think about bringing her into this group.

"I reckon if it was just a question of her abilities, there'd be no problem. She's just unbelievably clever and she has a ton of knowledge on all sorts of useful subjects. And a lot of what she knows is in areas where this group isn't especially strong. Not only that, but they're areas we *ought* to be strong in." He paused a moment. "The downside is that in the past Jo's been... well... unreliable, difficult and touchy. To be honest, she can be a real pain to work with, but lately she's put in a huge effort to improve. Personally I think right now she's as sorted out and together as she's ever been. I'd say she's at least as together as I am," he laughed, but no one else joined him.

He went on, "I know some of you might need a bit of persuading, but I think Jo would help a lot more than she'd hinder. And if we don't choose *her* then we need to look for someone else with the same skills... and I'd rather take someone I know and that the Professor knows – even though she has problems. With a stranger we'd have no idea what we were getting."

There was a lengthy pause, and I guessed that eyes had turned towards the Professor because he started to speak. "It's *true*..." he said hesitantly, "Jo has put in an absolutely heroic effort of late. And bear in mind that she's not tackling the most rewarding of assignments currently. I've withheld from her some of the more fulfilling tasks, largely to see how she fared when she had only her own work ethic to sustain her. And I have to say that she has distinguished herself. But I also have to say, her improvement comes hot on the heels of some very conspicuous low points."

Daniel, bless him, jumped in: "But Professor, you know she always struggles around the anniversary of her mother's death."

I hadn't realised that Daniel knew the date my mother had died. And if I was worse around that time then *I* hadn't spotted it. Nice job Daniel. That, and the unexpectedly strong case he was making on my behalf had really surprised me – you know, in a good way.

Daniel went on, "Now that that's passed, she's really settled down." He cleared his throat. "I understand she recently found out a few things she hadn't known about her mother and they knocked the wind out of her for a bit, but I think overall she's better for it. I think it's helped her get over some of her bad experiences. I mean, you all must have seen how hard she's trying now."

There were a few seconds of quiet and then Susan spoke.

"Daniel," she said, and just from the way she said his name I knew this wasn't going to be good news. "I know she's your friend and I don't mean to insult her, but to be frank, Jo's a disaster area when it comes to responsibilities. It might not be her *fault*, but that doesn't change the fact. And from what I can tell, she's always been a disaster area. I'd have serious misgivings about taking her on even in her *current* capacity, now that I've had a chance to be around her. I'm certainly not about to trust my life to her – and that's what membership of this group means. We all trust each other with our lives and I think you all know that's not an exaggeration. Jo might have some skills the team needs, but she'd also be its biggest liability – right from day one. I'm sorry to be harsh, Daniel, but she spends most of her free time so drunk she wouldn't know what she was saying or to whom. And the things this group knows aren't just about trust; they're also about how well you can carry a burden. We can't place the weight of the world on the shoulders of a girl whose idea of an impossible challenge is starting work on time."

Well that was that. I couldn't see anyone supporting Daniel's suggestion now that Susan had taken a wrecking ball to the idea. The Professor had clearly had his reservations even before she spoke. And I didn't expect Daniel to be able to mount a defence against someone as forceful and sure of herself as Ms. Milton.

But once again Daniel surprised me. "Hold on, though," he said. "I'm not disputing what you're saying, although I don't think Jo's problems are as bad as you make out. But maybe there's a way to compromise. I agree with you that being in this group is about trust, and handling the responsibility, as well as having the right skills. But that's also true of anyone else we bring in instead of Jo. They'll need to somehow prove themselves because to start with we won't be sure of them. We won't know how they'll cope or whether they're going to let us down. So if we want to get someone with Jo's skills we're going to have to put that person through a probation period before we make a final decision on them. Well, why not give the same chance to Jo?

He pressed on before anyone could cut in: "On the down-side, we know she's been flakey in the past, but on the up-side, in a sense she's already one of us. The Professor, if you'll excuse me pointing this out, has done more for Jo than her own father ever has. If she's loyal to anyone, it's to the Professor – and to me. With an outsider we'd have to figure out their loyalties and we'd have to hope they didn't blab about us to whoever they share their secrets with. Well, in Jo's case, I'm pretty sure the two people she's closest to in the world are already in the group. I think if a total stranger can have a trial period, a probation, then Jo deserves one too."

Damn. Nice recovery. Daniel was on tip-top form today. I'd been hoping things would go a lot more smoothly than they had, but Daniel appeared to have hauled my figurative ass out of the fire.

I listened to the debate for a few minutes more. David Braun spoke up and said that he didn't know me, but he trusted Daniel's judgement and that a probation sounded pretty reasonable to him – if they could figure out how to test me without trusting me with the whole enchilada (or kit and caboodle as he put it).

Then Theresa chimed in and said, "I'm sorry Daniel; I know you like her and you think she's a good egg underneath it all, and I know you're close to her Professor, but for my money Jo Hallett is poison. She might not mean to be but she can't help it. I agree she's a genius, but as a human being she's a nightmare. She'll be trouble from the word go."

Several people tried to respond to that, including a slightly shrill-sounding Daniel, but the Professor won out. "Dear boy," he said, and I understood that he meant Daniel, "don't concern yourself; you'll have a chance to speak. But let me see if I can save you the trouble."

In his best may-it-please-the-court voice the Professor said, "Theresa, can I ask, is it your opinion that Jo would let us down at the earliest opportunity, or thereabouts?"

Sounding awkward, Theresa said, "I'm not being mean about her. If anything I feel sorry for her, but that doesn't mean I want to trust her with my life."

The Professer persisted, "But you don't think she'd be able to acquit herself satisfactorily for any extended period of time?"

"No," Theresa said.

I could now see where the Professor was going with this. He went on, "So if we *did* allow her a trial period to prove herself, provided that it was of reasonable duration, you'd be confident that she'd make a hash of it?"

"I suppose," Theresa agreed.

"So, although you'd be averse to her joining the group, you wouldn't actually be averse to allowing her a trial period," he asked, his voice calm and intelligent, like a trial lawyer lining up a key witness.

If Theresa disagreed, I couldn't hear any evidence of it. The Professor was almost at his summing up now. "And do you feel the same, Susan?"

She replied, "I can't say that I'm delighted at the idea, but I can't think of a good reason to deny her a shot – provided we're careful about what information we share. However, I wouldn't want her to join the group *automatically* even if she somehow survives the probation period without screwing up."

"Fair enough, I should say," the Professor agreed. "Does *anyone* object to the idea of a probationary period?"

After a pause, which I took to contain both silent agreement and unvoiced resignation, he said, "Very well. And how long should it run for?"

There was some horse-trading and some unhappiness on both sides of the matter, but the discussion remained remarkably grown-up. And from Daniel's continued silence I concluded that the Professor had guessed his thoughts correctly – and probably handled the matter with a little more deftness than Daniel could have brought to bear.

When everyone had been heard from, the probation period had been talked down from six months to two. Whether that decrease was a triumph for the Professor's and Daniel's confidence in me, or Susan's and Theresa's certainty that I'd screw up quickly, I couldn't say.

Unfortunately, two months was still a hell of a long time to twiddle my thumbs for. I could do it if I had to – behaving myself wasn't much of a challenge any more – but that time could be put to much better use. Jumping through training hoops for the PAC was certainly not the most productive thing I could be doing.

I decided I'd take no action of my own until I heard the exact terms of the probation and discovered what kinds of tasks they were going to test me with, but in the meantime I'd cover my bases by coming up with a plan of my own – a plan for recovering the Marker without their help or their permission.

If I was able to secure the Marker and the group still excluded me, they'd be sabotaging their own plans. And possession of the Marker would make my probation period irrelevant.

In fact, if I had the Marker, I had to wonder whether the PAC didn't become a little bit irrelevant too.

CHAPTER 14

It was two days after the PAC meeting and I was finally due to have a proper meeting with the Professor late that afternoon. The previous day he'd come over to talk to me as I sat in the refectory during the afternoon tea break. I was in nerd-heaven reading a book on wifi security written by three wily Russian dudes. Not exactly Anna Karenina, I'll grant you, but likely to do me more good in the short-term.

When the Professor said he wanted to see me, he hinted that he had something important to talk over besides the usual chit-chat about current and future chores. Three guesses what that was about. We set a time and then he went on to say something about the team's plans for the Christmas holidays. As I sat looking up at him, my mind wandered away from what he was saying and a random detail that had been tickling at my subconscious for some time finally clicked into place. I realised I should have worked it out at least two weeks ago.

See, I was thinking about the health problems the Professor had had. I'd known for a number of years that he had some sort of illness, but when I met up with him about eighteen months ago, I remember being shocked at his deterioration. I had dropped in to see him at his home in Cambridge – this was before the field station project had even been mooted – and when he came to the door he looked like a ghost. His skin was nearly translucent and his cheek bones bulged like hip joints beneath his thin flesh. In a weird way, he looked more alive than he had for a while and there was a superficial improvement in his appearance: the lines were less visible and his complexion was unblemished, glowing almost. But it was an unnatural sort of vigour. The disease was thriving, not him. The changes resembled good health about as well as a bruise resembles a tan.

He was reluctant to talk about it, but I suppose there wasn't much to say. I could tell it was bad – but I didn't feel I could push him to say more than he wanted to. So we talked about me.

Gradually, though, his mood lightened and I began to suspect that I'd dropped in at a particularly low moment, because over the course of half an hour, the sense of weary resignation had completely left him and he became as perky as ever. By the time I left, I wondered if things could really be as bad as I'd initially thought.

He'd been busy for the next couple of months – and I knew part of that time was spent receiving treatment for his condition. And then he decided to get away for a while, to recuperate down in Cornwall. (I knew now that he'd gone down there during the business with Jan and the Marker.) When I was next in the UK, he happened to be on a flying visit to Cambridge, tying up loose ends, having decided to relocate to Cornwall permanently, and we met up for lunch.

He was transformed – a new man – and almost giddy with his new lease of life. He announced that despite ominously long odds, his treatment had been a great success and he was free of cancer for the first time in years.

That was the only time he put a name to his condition, but I'd guessed anyway. Looking back on it now I can imagine what lay behind his miracle recovery. He had obviously discovered the same wellspring of health that I had.

Try as I might, I couldn't picture the Professor using any of the other magical abilities besides Healing. But my imagination conjured an image of him sitting in the back parlour of his Cambridge cottage. Having bolted the door, I could see him settling into an armchair, his eyes closed and gold twinkling at his temples. In my imagination, his head was still covered in fine, slightly unruly white hair. The man who stood in front of me now, though, had not a single hair on his head.

He'd told me that his treatment had caused his hair to fall out and that his doctor wasn't surprised when it declined to grow back. And that was the detail which now resolved itself in my mind. His hair *hadn't* fallen out, I realised. He had shaved it off and continued to do so – his eyebrows too, though I hadn't noticed before. Why? Well, I was pretty sure I knew the answer to that: because his hair wasn't grey any longer.

In fact, I reckoned he was probably rationing his use of Healing in order to keep his appearance broadly consistent with a man of his supposed years. (I realised I never *had* known his exact age). He looked a vigorous seventy, just as he had when I'd been growing up.

Thinking about it, moving to Cornwall had made sense for Susan Milton, and to a lesser extent David Braun. The assassin Karst had seen Susan's face and perhaps David's when she had arrived to dispatch her ex-colleague Jan. But the Professor too had a reason to get away. He looked like a man barely out of his sixties when I was reasonably sure he was actually well into his eighties – and that disparity would only get more noticeable. Coming to magic so late in life, he'd never possess that vastly extended youthfulness of the lifelong adept, but I suspected the Professor would still look a year or two off retirement age on his hundredth birthday – assuming no calamities befell him before then.

How weird must this last year have been for the Professor? From what I could gather, magic use hadn't changed David or Susan very much – at least physically. Even if they'd been twenty years older the change would have simply been a matter of degree; but a dying man in his eighties who suddenly found the years rolling back towards his youth would have a great deal more to adjust to.

A few weeks back, at the height of my floundering and flailing, I'd been shocked when the Professor had lost his temper with me over my various failings. Sure, he'd had ample reason, but it was out of character for him, not just in our relationship, but for his behaviour in general. But then he was a man coming back to life. It was no surprise that his temper flared more suddenly and burned hotter than it had for years and that it sometimes got the better of him. Everything would seem more real, more immediate. I wondered if he chafed at having to act older than he felt.

I caught myself envying him, but for the life of me I couldn't think why. I had every advantage, every opportunity that he had – and more besides – so it was a strange thing to think.

I tuned back in again, just in time to catch the gist of what he was saying. They were closing the field station for ten days over the Christmas period, so wherever I was going to be then, it wasn't here. Perhaps I should surprise my father on whichever resort island – and with whichever woman – he was spending the holidays? Hmmm, I think not.

After tea break was over, I got back to work. These days I was spending more time in among the researchers and less time in the server room. Partly that was because I was taking an interest in what they were up to, partly that since I wasn't dodging work I didn't need to hide away so much – and partly it turns out that not being afraid of people had suddenly made total solitude less appealing. Besides, a person could log into any computer from any other computer, so being cooped up with the servers was more of an excuse than a necessity for most tasks.

When I was done for the day, I headed back to my room. Shipshape as it now was, there was still some residual clutter that needed lobbing overboard. I'd finally managed to get all my correspondence and financial paperwork sorted out. I couldn't pretend that my finances themselves were in very good shape, but at least I had a picture of what was going on. High on my list of non-magic-related chores was to schedule in a butt-kicking trip to London to put my deadbeat lodger, Noola, firmly in her place. Most of my net worth was tied up in that house and it needed to start generating an income for me. Immediately.

Here too, I reckoned that not being afraid of people was going to make a difference. Noola wouldn't really stand a chance. And if she gave me a hard time I could always break every bone in her body with the force of my mind. You know, not that I would of course. But there was nothing quite like knowing you could snuff a person out like a gnat to put you at your ease with them.

Anyway, on the clutter-removal front, I finished separating out all the odds and ends I wanted to get rid of into a big cardboard box. Then I began the hassle of dragging it out to the dumpsters behind the dorm block. Fortunately for me, I encountered Daniel as I was half way down the stairs and he offered to help.

The box wasn't that heavy, but it was bigger than you could get your arms around, so two pairs of hands made the task a lot more manageable.

"Any news on your plans for the weekend?" he asked, walking carefully, one step at a time, backwards down the stairs.

"I think I really need to spend a weekend in London," I said. And since the truth wasn't a problem here, I added, "I haven't had any rent for a few months now and I'm pretty much broke. I need to get something sorted out."

He looked disappointed, but he nodded. "So what's in the box?" he asked.

"Oh, just junk. The landfill needs this stuff a lot more than I do," I said.

"Right," he nodded. "This is one of the boxes that your…" I knew the next word he was going to say was 'Mother's' but he made a last second substitution. "…delivery came in."

"Like I say, the landfill needs it more."

"Sure, sure," he said, anxious not to ruffle my feathers even though I could see he was working up to attempt just that. "You're not going to throw all your mother's things away though, are you?" He was trying to sound reasonable, conversational, lighthearted.

Wow, it was so nice not being crazy any more. Instead of flying into a hissy fit, I shrugged (as best I could while carrying something heavy) and said, "Some of this is my junk, not hers. But, you know, I don't need this stuff and she won't be coming back for it." Hmmm, that came out a little darker than I'd intended. Maybe I wasn't *totally* cured. On the other hand, I wouldn't have *attempted* this conversation three weeks ago; we'd have been knee deep in wailing and used Kleenexes by now.

"I guess not," he said, sounding like there was still some doubt about it. "But, you know, we could just as easily take this down to the barn and stick it with the rest of the boxes. If you suddenly remember you dropped your passport in here, you won't have to mount an archaeological dig to get it back. Plenty of time to throw things away later."

"Thanks, Daniel, but this isn't really a spur of the moment thing. I'm not doing this because I'm all worked up; I'm just clearing some space in my room," I said.

"Not emotionally distraught. Got it," he confirmed.

"You could even see this as healthy," I said, as we reversed through the fire door and out into the late autumn chill. The sun had set and a dim light the colour of hot coals was all that remained. Whether Daniel was convinced or not, he let it go, silently carrying his end of the box all the way round to the little dumpster corral.

We manhandled the box into the maw of the nearest giant bin and then walked back towards the dorm-room entrance. "I'm actually heading back to the project building," Daniel said as we turned the corner. "I'll see you later."

Going off to brood, by the looks of things, I thought. Still, not really my problem.

I scooted back inside, happy to get out of the cold. Originally my plan for this evening was going to involve putting in a little preparation for tomorrow's meeting with the Professor. He was going to ask me to do something related to the PAC, but something sufficiently tangential that it didn't let too many cats out of their bags regarding the PAC's true mission. I'd intended to get a head start on whatever it was tonight, before being asked, but I found that my espionage skills hadn't been quite up to the job of discovering my assignment ahead of time.

When I'd reviewed the recording of the PAC meeting, I was expecting to hear them decide what my first, probationary penance should be. What I'd heard instead was an agreement between

Susan and the Professor to discuss it after the meeting... in the Professor's office. Which was a pain because I hadn't bugged his office. I hadn't even purchased a second bug just in case I needed it. Very poor.

Anyway, since I couldn't prepare for tomorrow, I had an evening free. I spent it writing an anonymizer: a chunk of software that an Internet sleuth (like myself) could hide behind. When I was online, searching for clues to the Marker's whereabouts, I didn't want the Army tracing my location – assuming they were out there.

I was going to set up the anonymizer on some free webspace I had my eye on, hosted out of Taiwan. From what I could gather it was run by asylum-seeking Chinese anarchists, who I was pretty sure wouldn't be sharing their records with anyone. So that's where my Internet trail would dead-end.

But just in case someone got through that, I had another trick in mind. Lots of people connect to the Internet over wireless links these days and most apartment buildings are full of these wi-fi signals. What you might not know is that there are people who cruise around mapping all these signals and logging their findings online. Thanks to them, I'd found two Internet connections in the same building – an apartment block in Capetown, as it happened – and neither of them had changed any of the security settings from their defaults. I was going to hijack one wireless base station and use it to connect to the other. Anyone who traced my activities back to South Africa would find a wireless point in someone's apartment and assume I was somewhere nearby, using my laptop to log in.

By midnight it was all ready. All I needed now was a target. But that was a job for another time. I called it a night, cleared my mind and was asleep in minutes.

Faded azure sea-ice filled my dreams and some time in the night the unending icescape gave way to flickering images and whispers of conversation that when I awoke I couldn't recall properly. But neither could I get them out of my head for some hours.

CHAPTER 15

The Professor was talking. "I'm sure you have many questions and I'll answer them all… eventually. For now there are some explanations that I would rather postpone." He gave me a moment to digest that and went on, "If that's not acceptable to you, or you're uncomfortable with a request of this nature then you should say so. I'll drop the matter and we'll say no more about it."

Necessarily, I was playing the fool, not letting on what I knew. Mind you, I only had the half the picture, so it was only partly play-acting. I asked, "Isn't this a matter for the police? I don't want to get in their way."

He explained, "They are no longer actively pursuing the matter. You have to understand that while the stolen documents were of enormous interest to us, they were not especially valuable in monetary terms. Quite simply, the police have better things to do than hunt for our missing paperwork. Their main interest in this case was resolved when the criminal behind the robbery met his end. The evidence relating to the crime led to him and so the enquiry died with him. They have no leads on finding his associates and I suspect they place criminals killing their own quite low down on their list of crimes which must be stamped out."

"Yes, but why would a gang of criminals steal documents that only academics put any value on?" I was almost enjoying asking questions that I knew the Professor couldn't give truthful answers to.

"Ahem, well, um…" he said, clearly collecting his thoughts. "They might have stolen the collection in error. Those documents were housed in the same building as various objects of quite considerable value. And they couldn't be expected to hand the collection back once they realised their mistake."

"No," I agreed, "they'd most likely just destroy them all. Wouldn't they? Do we have a reason to think they didn't?"

Again he took a moment to construct a reply. "Quite. But we aren't searching based on the probability that they *did* destroy the collection; we're searching on the *possibility* that they didn't." He went on, "And anyone interested enough to steal items of historical interest might show some reluctance in destroying them. Flawed though the theft might have been, an expert was certainly involved, and it's difficult to imagine an expert who doesn't have some attachment to his subject matter."

Not a bad piece of yarn-spinning, really, for someone thinking on their feet. The Professor was a halfway reasonable liar when he wanted to be, though his delivery could use some polish.

"OK, Professor. It certainly sounds like a challenge; I'll find out what I can," I said.

He held up his hand and looked positively grave as he said, "The most important point I must impress upon you is the need to avoid attracting unwanted attention. I know you are exceedingly knowledgeable in these matters, so I'll leave it to your judgement. But before you begin I would like you to estimate the risks of

627

inadvertently alerting any remaining members of the gang to our presence. If you don't think you can do this *in silenzio*, I would ask you not to undertake it at all. A determination from you that it is unsafe to proceed would be even more useful to the team than the successful recovery of the collection. I say that because ensuring the safety of everyone concerned is our highest priority here."

He went on, "We must assume that the criminals have computer experts of their own who may very well be lying in wait, so to speak. I previously asked Daniel to explore our options in this matter and his conclusion was that we should leave well alone. He believed that someone *out there...*" he waved his hands vaguely, presumably to indicate the Internet, "was keeping electronic watch. He felt it would be exceedingly difficult to uncover any useful information without coming under scrutiny. He said that it was best abandoned completely... unless we could enlist *you* to handle the matter. He has an opinion of your skills that borders on the reverential, and I'm prepared to take his word for it."

I nodded slowly, to show that I appreciated the gravity of what I was getting into. "I understand, Professor. I'll be extremely careful. I have a couple of ideas for concealing myself that, to the best of my knowledge, have never been penetrated by anyone."

The Professor obviously wanted to spread it on thick. He added, "The initial loss of the collection and the events surrounding it were notable for the sheer number of violent attacks, and even deaths, that occurred. These are tenacious and ruthless people whose attention we must not attract. I would rather not spend my twilight years hiding in the Falkland Islands disguised as a sheep farmer. Discretion, caution, stealth – please let these be your watchwords."

"Hey, it'll be me on that island too, if I screw things up," I said. "Just me and the sheep. And some annoying old farmer constantly muttering 'I told you so'."

"Well, it sounds like we have a meeting of minds, then," the Professor said, with the flicker of a smile.

"Yup. I would like a little time to work on this, though. The better I prepare, the more invisible I can make myself. I'd like two weeks to get ready, if that's OK. There are programs I need to write," I said, adding, "I'll still be able to get some of my regular project work done, but this thing will need a reasonable chunk of time if I'm going to do it properly."

He pursed his lips thoughtfully. "A fortnight sounds acceptable. Are there any other resources you will need? Any assistance?"

Thank you for asking. "Well, there are some bits and pieces back in London that would make the job easier. Plus they have computer stores there…" I spread my hands to indicate the lack of such things here in Cow Country.

He was considering it. I went on, "It makes the job easier, plus it's one more level of security. It's harder to trace anyone in a big city and it gets the focus away from the project. If anonymity is our big thing, we don't really want to attempt this using the only high-speed Internet connection for miles around."

"And you'll give me updates on how it's going?" he asked. He was clearly leaning towards saying 'yes'.

"Why don't I phone you at six pm each day? Just to check in," I suggested. "You can keep me up to date with all the gossip."

"Well, it *would* give us a chance to discuss the latest celebrity indiscretions," he said thoughtfully. He'd obviously made up his mind and had moved on to the sarcastic part of the conversation.

"Ex*actly*," I enthused. "If it's alright with you, I'll head to London on Saturday morning and use the weekend to take care of some personal things. I'll get to work on Monday and call you that evening."

He nodded agreeably. Which, I reckoned, concluded our discussion. I said 'Adios' and left him to it. My next stop was my dorm room to get my coat. It was still a few minutes before sunset and I wanted to get out and go for a walk. I had some thinking to do... among other things.

I wandered up the lane, flexing my fingers to keep them warm and stamping my feet. I was thinking about the assignment I'd been set and how it tied into the overall situation with the Marker. The Professor and Susan had made an interesting choice for my first probationary task. They had asked me to track down the collection of documents that Jan had stolen from Susan's old workplace – which had subsequently been swiped by Karst, once she'd dealt with Jan. The documents were presumably in the possession of whoever had taken over from Alessandro Dass as local big cheese of the Army – quite possibly Karst herself, if Susan's recollection of her tailoring was any indication of her status.

But this wasn't really about the collection. After all, I knew that the PAC had an electronic copy of the entire collection. No, this was about spying on Dass's organisation: the Army Who Witnessed Creation. The Professor needed a way to make an investigation like that seem psuedo-legitimate, so he'd invented an academic angle to all this. He'd admitted that the Procedures and Admin Committee were up to something – Daniel must have told him that I suspected as much – but he hadn't admitted what it was yet. Instead, he'd asked me to do something very unorthodox which nevertheless maintained the fiction that this all related, however indirectly, to an academic project.

In his version of what had happened to the collection, the Professor had allowed the lines to blur between Dass's organisation and their rogue alumni, Jan. In his version, a gang had stolen the collection, and in an internal squabble a couple of gang members had been killed, including the mastermind behind the robbery. This implied that someone else was in charge now. He was letting me think that I was investigating the people behind the robbery, when the truth was that the thief, Jan, and those who killed him were working against each other.

And naturally there'd been no mention of magic or the Marker in his version of events.

From reading the PAC's secrets, I knew what had really happened – that Jan had stolen the Marker from Dass and then taken the instructions for its use from the museum Susan was working in; he'd also killed Dass in the process. Then Dass's agent, Karst, had killed Jan and taken the collection away with her. The Marker remained wherever Jan had hidden it. Or so we assumed.

It was possible that the Army had already discovered its hiding place and retrieved it. We wouldn't necessarily know if they had. But we knew they'd looked pretty hard for it in the months after Jan's death. Daniel thought they were still looking.

Of course, maybe they were just being tidy-minded, but it seemed more likely that they were still hunting for it in earnest. The PAC believed the Army were also lying in wait, in case someone else made a grab for the Marker. If some third party found it, the Army could swoop in and take it from them. If they failed, the Army could still swoop in – to interrogate them and find out what they knew. And I *really* didn't want to be someone the Army tried to prise information out of.

I wondered, did the Army think some accomplice of Jan's might try to retrieve the Marker? We were fairly sure that Jan had acted alone.

Or maybe the Army were specifically looking for the man and woman Karst had glimpsed that night in the church. She'd seen two injured people who weren't Connected, who weren't wearing gold, and she'd ignored them. They were just civilians who'd got in Jan's way. But if she hadn't given them much thought at the time, you can bet that her attitude had changed once the Army's other lines of enquiry had dried up. By now I was fairly sure that Karst wished she'd asked to see some IDs before leaving that night.

But the Professor mentioned none of that. He was hiding one search inside another and so would I. Hunting for the collection was his way of having me spy on the Army – but I'd use the investigation as cover to look for the Marker itself – though I wouldn't neglect the Professor's assignment completely. If I got anywhere *near* the Marker, I'd certainly want to know what its previous owners were up to and whether they were right behind me. So I'd spy on the Army *and* look for the Marker – and, fortunately, I could use the same technology for both.

Relocating to London was an added bonus. I wouldn't have to hide what I was up to from those around me, plus I could sort out the lodger situation while I was at it. And there was one more advantage: I wasn't planning to limit myself to Internet sleuthing when it came to finding the Marker. If I unearthed any clues as to its whereabouts, I was going to follow them up. In person.

If the Professor thought it was dangerous trying to track Dass's people online, he'd be horrified at the thought of me risking their wrath face to face. Three weeks ago, I couldn't tell a lie about a late subscription without panicking; now I was planning to get between a society of ancient killers and their most precious possession. I supposed it was as good a way as any to find out how much progress I'd really made since then.

CHAPTER 16

London. They say when a man is tired of London, he's also tired of quotations about London.

I got the "fast" train back to Paddington station, caught the languorously torpid Bakerloo line down to Waterloo and changed onto the Northern Line. My house was near Stockwell tube station in an area I'd selected as being up-and-coming. Unfortunately that was four years ago and it still had just as far to up-and-come. Stockwell needed to pull its finger out.

There was a big cheery sign just outside the exit of the tube station informing travellers that they were now in a high-crime area where muggings were routine. Which was nice. If I remembered correctly, this was also the place where the Met had first implemented its shoot-to-kill policy concerning Brazilian electricians[1]. Clearly I wasn't about to sell up and make a profit any time soon.

My route took me away from the main road and into the warren

---

[1]   If you're reading this in, like, the year 2255, ask your talking computron to find the relevant Old Earth news story.

of side streets and cul-de-sacs beyond. The quickest way to cover the last few hundred yards to the house was to cut through an alleyway linking two streets. It ran behind a disused warehouse and it was dingy, and frequently smelled appalling – but sticking to the sun-lit streets added five minutes to the walk. I was dragging my huge roller suitcase and I didn't want to haul it one foot further than I had to.

The bag's wheels sounded especially loud as they rumbled and crackled over the grit of the path as I turned into the secluded alleyway. I was struck by how isolated you could feel in the middle of the city if you found the right (or maybe the wrong) spot.

Halfway down its length, where you couldn't see what was up ahead because the path detoured around the metal fence-stakes of an electricity sub-station, I heard something: a human sound I couldn't identify. I looked around and saw no one.

To the left, ahead of me, a set of iron stairs ran up to the warehouse's boarded-over rear firedoor. Beneath the open treads of the heavy steps, the gloom was all but impenetrable... until I suddenly realised that a man was hiding in the shadows there. Despite my newfound steeliness, my heart gave a little thump of alarm. (I suppose it's possible that even the steeliest of folk benefit from a little shot of adrenaline from time to time.)

I kept walking, my gaze flicking between the path ahead and the half-seen figure in the shadows. As I drew level I got a better look at him in the feeble, slatted light penetrating the ironwork of the stairs. He was sitting on the ground, legs out in front, his back propped against brickwork that was furry with mould and grime. He had on greasy black jeans and a filthy, punk-style angora sweater hitched up at the waist exposing a triangle of pallid abdomen. He looked like the day-old corpse of a homeless Ramones fan. He had slipped one ghostly pale arm completely out of the sweater and stretched it out by his side – a syringe hung by its needle from the flesh.

For a moment, I wondered if he was even alive – whether a good Samaritan should maybe call an ambulance for him. But then a feeling of disgust welled up in me and I was neither afraid of him nor concerned for his wellbeing. I'd seen human refuse like him all my life and they never changed. They were parasites and that was how they deserved to be treated. If he was still there the next time I came this way I might put him out of his misery myself.

I kept moving, and just before he was lost to sight I saw him move and a sound like a hiss came from his lips. I realised his eyes were open and he was staring at me. The look was unwavering, predatory, malevolent. I had to admit that if I was going to encounter him like this, with my 'tribute' buried in my bag, it was probably a good thing that he was incapacitated: laid out by the heroin, and unable to pursue me.

A moment later I laughed quietly at my own cowardice. I didn't need magic to handle a hundred and ten pounds of busted veins and opium-addiction.

She hadn't been specific, but my shrewd deductive mind reckoned it was a fair bet that *this* was where Noola had been robbed. She'd been coming home from a night out, probably late in the evening. And in my experience, junkie-predators like this one tended to keep vampire hours, so pub closing time fell squarely within their working day.

They also tended to find themselves at least one partner in crime, it being difficult to mug healthy members of the public when your body has to extract most of its usable calories from poppy juice.

In summary, this would be a good spot to avoid once the sun went down.

Robert Finn

I was glad of the fresh air and the light when I emerged into daylight on the other side of the alleyway.

Moments later I reached the house and let myself in. All was quiet and the living room was empty (though I noted three ashtrays that were full – not bad going if only one person was living here). I dragged my case up three flights of stairs and unlocked the door that led to the top floor, which was my private part of the house. Nothing seemed to have been disturbed, though the place was a little musty. I pushed up one of the elderly sash windows, letting in the distant traffic sounds of South London, and a hint of a breeze. Then I changed into old clothes and got busy.

By five in the afternoon, when I heard the front door open and close, I had done the unthinkable: I'd cleaned, vacuumed and tidied. The place hadn't been in a *really* horrible condition, but neither was it very well looked after. In fact, if I hadn't lived most of my life with the domestic instincts of a dung beetle, I'd have probably been more disgusted with Noola's housekeeping than I was. What was weird was that even in the old days I'd never liked living in squalor, but for some reason it hadn't seemed like my job to do anything about it.

I was downstairs in the kitchen when I heard Noola's shopping bags rustling in the hallway. I was interested to know how she'd play this confrontation; I suspected she'd go on the offensive with her usual mixture of bullying combined with playing the aggrieved victim. It was not only a potent combination for getting one's own way, but it tended to frighten the life out of me with its sudden emotional tangents.

What was different on this occasion was that I could hear Noola's heavy tread approaching and I didn't feel anxious. I wasn't dreading her complaints, her demands and her sheer volume as I usually did. When I thought of her now, I no longer felt like a child about to be told off by an angry and unpredictable grown-up. If anything, she was the child now. I even found myself smiling and looking forward to her opening salvo, fascinated to see what preposterous complaint she'd use to put me on the defensive.

"Oh my *god*, Jo," she screeched, "You frightened the *crap* out of me. I thought someone had broken in. You know what a bundle of nerves I am since the robbery. Why didn't you call to *warn* me you'd be here?"

I noted that her hair was now my least favourite style in the world: bleached-blonde dreadlocks. The skin around her nose-ring looked angry and red. Much like the rest of her.

The smile on my face grew broader as I turned to face her. I was smiling because I was immune to her. I could feel myself wanting to apologise, to explain – or at least to answer her question – but I held myself in check.

She was irrationally angry and blaming it on me: every instinct I had told me to placate her. Deep down, I'd always suspected that people got angry with me not just for the reasons they gave, but because I irritated them with my poor social skills and my thoughtlessness. They were *right* to be angry with me and I knew it. I deserved it.

Except now, that all seemed like nonsense. I kept the impulse to give in to her under firm control. It was amusing, really, to see how she set about pulling my strings – and to feel myself wanting to respond. But this conversation wasn't going to be directed by her.

She had put down her bags in the doorway, blocking any exit I might wish to make, and now she was glowering at me, one hand on her hip, the other tapping the air in front of her in time with her words, like it was the eject button for my self-esteem.

My turn to speak. "*I'm* wondering whether to throw you out," I said, conversationally, "Or maybe I should give you another chance."

She drew herself up. "Well, of all the *gall*," she replied, sounding especially incensed. "I could have been *killed*. If I knew what was good for me I would have walked out and never come back. But I stayed, I took care of this place and I tried not to let what happened rule my life. I thought it might be too much to expect some concern, to expect that you'd ask me if I was feeling any better, to maybe say '*thanks*, Noola, for not leaving me in the lurch'. Because you see, where I'm from, Jo, people don't burst in and threaten someone who's been through what I have. I really expected better from you."

Her anger had crescendoed and then given way to outraged pain. The old me, which I could still sense lurking somewhere in the back of my brain, begged to be allowed to make excuses, to whine. It was a small voice, though, and it no longer had any power to make me do anything.

"Let me explain something," I said, in a calm, almost regretful tone which Noola initially misinterpreted as defeat. "You don't pay rent, you don't find anyone else to pay rent and you don't do a good job looking after this place. That's all I'm interested in. I couldn't care less if you were chopped into kebab meat the next time you stepped out of that door. It's not my problem. You're my lodger, not my girlfriend; you understand that, don't you?"

I could almost see the grinding of mental cogs as she failed to process my amiably offensive tone, my coldness, my ridiculous question. She just simply had no response. It was all I could do not to laugh out loud.

But I was feeling generous – and a little curious – so I didn't hassle her. I gave her a few seconds to recover her wits. I wanted to see what she'd come back with.

Her eyelids flickered for a moment with impotent anger and at last she spluttered, "I could *sue* you. I could take you to court and make your life a misery. Anyone who would take advantage of a person like this, when they were at their most vulnerable, deserves what comes to them. If you're not careful I'll end up *owning* this place with the damages I could get. You'd better *really* be sure you want to mess with me." Her defiance seemed to have once again energised her and obliterated her earlier hesitation.

Now let me stop there for a moment. I'm going to tell you what happened next in just a minute – but first let me tell you a scenario that didn't happen. It didn't happen, but it appeared in my head, fully-formed – including details of how Noola would react. This is what I imagined:

I imagined holding up my hand to cut her off.

"When you were 'attacked', Noola," I saw myself asking, "was it in the alleyway over there?" I would point in the direction of the cut-through I'd used.

"What's that got to do with anything," she would demand.

"Was it in the alleyway?" I'd snap loudly, taking a sudden step towards her.

She'd flinch with alarm, as though she was worried I was going to lunge at her, but she wouldn't reply.

"Let's assume it was," I'd say more calmly. "What do you suppose would happen if I took this key," I'd hold up my front door key, "and gave it to one of the junkies back there? Just handed it over."

She'd look shocked now, and uncertain. "What are you *saying*?" she'd demand, as though I'd switched to a foreign language.

"What if I told them to just let themselves in?" I'd ask, savouring the words.

Then a thought would occur to me: "What time do you usually go to sleep?" I'd ask – and then wave the question aside. "It doesn't matter. I'd just tell them to make sure it was really late, two or three in the morning maybe." I'd be genuinely interested as I asked, "What do you think your *lawyer* could do about that? Do you think he could come round and make sure that you were alright, that nothing *unpleasant* happened to you?"

She'd be staring at me now as though I was poisonous, her eyes bugging with fear. "What are you *saying*?" she'd ask, repeating the question – only her voice would get quieter with each repetition. She'd be gone by the morning, I knew that.

But I didn't say any of those things. I simply possessed the sudden and clear knowledge of how it would play out if I did. Whole and complete. And to tell you the truth I was a little shocked at myself. I mean, creepy much? I've invented little revenge fantasies before, but this was so efficient, so ruthless, so professional. It wasn't a fantasy of terrifying Noola; it was a *technique*. Not that the words I *actually* said were all that warm and fuzzy. In fact they made me sound like an evil, scheming bitch, but they had a little less of the decompensating serial killer about them.

What *really* happened was this:

"Well, the thing is, Noola," I explained, "I've been going through my paperwork and there's a problem. I forgot to renew your tenancy agreement when it expired and you forgot to remind me. You add that to the fact that you decided not to pay rent a while back and on paper at least, it doesn't even look like you live here any more."

"Of course I live here," she insisted, testily, "all of my *things* are here."

"Are they?" I said pleasantly, giving her a moment to think about that question. "See I decided that you should be in the small room, so I boxed your things up and locked them in there."

Before she could explode at me, I pressed on: "So you can get lawyers involved if you want, but it puts me in an awkward spot. I mean I could *cover* for you: tell the authorities that you really live here, that I believe you *intended* to pay your rent. Tell them that even though your tenancy agreement appears to be entirely verbal I consider it binding. In other words I could *help* you to sue me..."

Again I gave her a moment to think her situation through. "Or I could gather up your stuff and take it to the dump," I concluded brightly. Then I set about applying some salt to the wound: "Then I could ask the police what I should do about an ex-tenant who's made a copy of her door key and lets herself in when I go out." I played out the hypothetical phone call I'd make, for her benefit: "Yeah, I think she's in the UK on some sort of *visa*. What? Yes, she's used threatening language to me, but I don't *think* she's stolen anything. Maybe I should check?"

Enough play acting. By the look on her face I suspected that if I looked hard enough I might just find that she'd liberated one or two little trinkets from around the place. But more importantly, she was realising that I could certainly tell some convincing *lies* on the subject. I summarised the situation for her: "If it's that, or lose this house, well frankly I'd rather it was *you* on the street instead of me."

She was thankfully speechless – and rather deflated looking. I stepped over her shopping bags and headed for the stairs. "I've got some work to do," I said over my shoulder. "Have a cup of tea and think about it. Either you're gone in the next twenty-four hours or we get back to normal. You pay your rent – including what you owe – and you start looking for some housemates."

From halfway up the stairs I added, "If you write me a cheque this evening, I'll even let you sleep in a real bed tonight."

I reckoned even if she decided to go, I'd probably get at least *some* back rent from her, out of fear. She knew I could make a lot of trouble for her and she probably knew now that I'd really do it. She'd either go quietly or she'd stay and behave. I didn't think she'd try to fight me. But I did have one nasty surprise in mind in case she wanted to cause trouble. I'd swiped an out-of-date credit card of hers when I moved her stuff, lifting it from her dresser using a Kleenex, being careful not to smudge any fingerprints. If she provoked me, I'd change the locks and then snap off her credit card in the front door, making it look like she'd tried to jimmy it. I particularly liked the fact it would make her look incompetent as well as criminal. Which of course she was.

It was all a matter of resolve, of how far I'd go. I could scratch my own face and tell the police she attacked me. I could break some crockery and claim she went berserk. I could daub some paint around and call her a vandal. Sure, she was a cunning and ruthless manipulator, but her range was limited: it was all verbal sparring and amateur theatricals. I could take it to the next level where she'd be hopelessly out of her depth and she knew it.

In the grand scheme of things she was such a minor annoyance that she really wasn't worth the effort, but that's how you keep things minor: you make sure that you're prepared to go further than they are and that they know it.

Once I was back upstairs, in my attic room, I got to work setting up a couple of workstations that I'd need later in the week. I tended to keep all the valuable computer stuff locked away, so it all needed hauling out now and cabling up. It kept me busy for quite a while and I only thought of Noola again when it started to get dark. I went downstairs to see what she'd decided.

She was still there – sitting on the sofa, a mug of cold tea in her hand. She looked sad.

Time to throw her a bone. I'd rather she stayed and got the place organised instead of me having to go out and look for a new tenant. I'd shown her what I was made of, I'd given her good reason to be afraid of me; now it was time to have her forgive me.

"Noola?" I asked gently, "What does your mother do?"

She glanced up at me, a little nervously, and gave me a forlorn look. "She's a school teacher," she said, without a hint of defiance.

I sat down on the other end of the sofa, keeping to myself "A little while ago, I found out that my mother killed herself," I said. Noola looked surprised, though it was difficult to guess exactly what she was thinking. She looked at me properly now, giving me her full attention.

I went on, "My dad remarried. He never wanted kids in the first place. I've moved around too much to have a lot of friends. It's just me. Me and this house."

Noola put her mug on the table and studied me, but there was a hint of softness about her look.

"My mother never fought for things," I said. "She made excuses and went with the flow and eventually it dragged her down. She wasn't able to handle anything. Not even being alive."

I turned to face Noola now. "I'm sorry about before," I said, sounding humble yet sincere. "I was very hard on you."

My hands were clasped together and I squeezed my fingers tightly now, to show how much emotion I was holding in.

"But I'm not going to end up like my mother. I can't let that happen. It might make me a bitch…" I said. And I let out the breath I'd been holding and gave a weak smile. Noola smiled a little too. "…but that's better than giving up."

"Listen…" she said. She sounded respectful now, even concerned.

But I pressed on, "You see, I don't trust anyone right now. I wish I *could*, but I can't." I gave her a brave smile. "I want us to get along. I *like* having you here. But I have to look out for myself because no one else is going to."

Then I made eye contact and said, "You *will* stay, won't you?"
I sounded anxious.

Earlier, I'd knocked the stuffing out of her. Now I'd humbled
myself. Her pride would no longer be telling her to leave. If she
stayed, she could tell herself that she was being gracious: accepting
my apology, taking pity on me. And I'd made it her choice. All in
all, it would be a lot easier for her to stick around... and we all want
an easy life.

Sure, in a week or two, her confidence would return and she'd
try to reassert herself, but all it would take would be a sharp look,
an edge in my voice and she'd remember our little showdown this
afternoon.

"I had no idea," Noola said, referring to my mother. "I don't
know what you must think of me going on about my problems all
this time, after what you've been through. Of course I can stay."

I'd never seen Noola like this but I'd been sure she must have
other scripts she could follow, other roles she could play besides
just the pushy whiner.

I'd shut down the whiner and, lo and behold, here was a whole
other side to her opening up. Probably this was how she was with
kids or people she was looking after: this was her in the role of
'protector'.

And often that's all there is to controlling people. They have a
handful of roles they're comfortable playing – or at least familiar
with – and if you want to bump them out of one then you have
to make it easy for them to drop into a different one. You can't
deny them all the roles they're familiar with or they become
unpredictable. They get hysterical or they close themselves off
completely.

I was fortunate that Noola possessed a compassionate side; I hadn't been sure. Now I knew that she had a protective role she was comfortable in, I could feed that: I could ask for her help, lean on her for her support.

On a hunch, I gave her a hug and made sure it was a little bit pathetic on my side. She didn't reject me. "It'll be alright," she said. "We can look out for each other. After all, I'm eleven thousand miles from home," she laughed. "We're in the same boat really."

Excellent.

Well, that was more than enough female bonding. As soon as I could do so without appearing to hurry, I got to my feet. Looking sheepish but reassured I made to head back upstairs.

Oops, I thought. I'd probably better head off a confrontation over her room.

"Listen," I said, "I want to get your old room redecorated, really make it nice – do something special. Will you be OK in the spare room for a bit?" I handed over the key.

She nodded. Good. And who knows, I might even make good on that promise to redecorate. Either way, it would buy me some time.

"I, um," I said awkwardly, "I have some work to do," by way of excusing myself.

"Right," she said, "Maybe later we could go out for a curry or something. What do you say?"

It would probably be a good idea, just to cement this new version of our relationship, but I didn't really have the time. I had to be careful about rejecting her, though.

"I have to sort through some of my mother's things," I said, sounding a little choked. "Maybe another time."

That should do it.

Then I put Noola out of my mind and climbed back up to the top of the house thinking about my next task: to learn what I could about the life and times of a man called Jan.

CHAPTER 17

It was Monday morning: day one of my investigation. I'd spent Saturday night and Sunday morning finishing off the cracker's toolkit I'd need if I wanted to explore other people's systems with anonymity. The only problem was that I didn't have a target.

For me, the idea of tracking someone online was a strange hybrid of the familiar and the unknown. I knew about IP addresses and cookies, digest access authentication and traceroute, http and email headers – all that gobbledy-gook. On the other hand, I knew nothing about land registry records, credit checking, voter rolls, tax records, Companies House and community charge payments. If you broke down the act of tracing a missing person into individual tasks, half of them I'd fly through and the other half would mystify me.

I had many of the skills I'd need but no idea where to apply them. It was like searching for your car keys with a microscope. I really needed pointing in the right direction.

But, in the absence of a guide, I decided to let my starting point be the information I already possessed. Thanks to the PAC, I had

Robert Finn

three former addresses for Jan and the aliases that he'd owned or rented them under. In addition I knew the name under which he'd bought and insured a car. And I had scans of a US passport in a fifth name that Susan had found among his things.

The residences were what drew my attention. It wasn't just that Jan might have left clues behind; they were also mailing addresses: destinations for revealing correspondence of all sorts to pile up in – especially now that he wasn't around to tidy it away. Ideally I'd poke around and find an invoice for a safety-deposit box, but I'd settle for something less obvious.

But would his old properties still be empty? Wouldn't his death have triggered some process of resale and liquidation? I didn't really know happened when a person died[1]. But with all those aliases in play, and no corpse to examine, it seemed unlikely that news of his death had reached all the relevant officials. If the bills were still being paid then one or more of those addresses might be just as he'd left them.

Unless, that is, the Army had got involved. They would be used to slipping in and out of identities just as Jan was. It would be easy for them to provide a wife or son or daughter ready to inherit from each of his aliases. It would give them fuss-free access to everything. Which meant those addresses were either treasure troves of information or traps – maybe both.

I wondered how far I dared go to find out.

I wanted to look around Jan's house and maybe read some of his posthumous mail, but I wanted to do it without being captured, tortured or killed. I'd have to take things one cautious step at a time.

To start with I'd limit myself strictly to surveillance – just

---

[1] One of mankind's oldest questions. But I'm thinking more in terms of bureaucracy than theology here.

looking for signs of the Army's presence. Actually getting inside would be stage two and it would only go ahead if I saw nothing – absolutely nothing – to indicate there was a trap waiting for me.

I quickly settled on the Notting Hill address as my first target. It was undoubtedly the coolest of the three properties. All other things being equal, if you owned a really nice place you'd want to spend the biggest chunk of your time there. Or so I reckoned.

It would be an easy trip too – under an hour door-to-door. And I was only planning to look around the neighbourhood, so there wasn't much need for preparation. That morning I made the decision to go there and by early afternoon I was on my way.

I wore regular street clothes; the only bit of spycraft I indulged in was a detail I'd picked up from Susan's diary: I took a carrier bag of Tesco groceries with me. Weird I know, but it's pretty much built into the human psyche that you can't be suspicious of a woman lugging a bag full of toilet rolls, pots of yoghurt and oven cleaner. Plus it was a handy place to hide my tribute, along with a pair of dusty Victorian opera glasses – which was the closest I could come to binoculars at short notice.

On my way there, I ran through a few scenarios. There was a limit to how much I could learn by peeking at the house from the end of the road – and even doing that was a risk. On the other hand, if I got up close there was a better chance of being seen – seen and followed – followed and investigated – and from there it all might unravel.

So I settled on a third option – what you might call an occult fly-by. I'd find myself somewhere to hide that was close (but not *too* close) to Jan's house, I'd Connect, and I'd check the Presence Surface for other adepts active in the vicinity. If I detected nothing I wouldn't really be any the wiser, but if there *were* contacts, that would tell me all I needed to know. I'd break the Connection, hide my tribute and bug out, never to return.

Or that was the plan. It seemed easy enough, although when I got near to the house I hit my first snag. This was an expensive neighbourhood: the houses were huge, the gardens were wide and the walls were high. It wasn't the sort of street that had bus shelters, alleyways and corner shops for people to skulk in. Each residence had that subtly fortified look that nervous millionaires tend to prefer: the kind where the architect's priorities seem to have been space and light, closely followed by good fields of fire and defendable access points, just in case the revolution came a little sooner than expected.

In the end I found a pedestrian path that led through to a pocket-sized park one street over. The path ran between a couple of houses and it was close enough to Jan's old residence to just be within range of the Presence Surface while still being out of direct line of sight.

Before I tucked myself away there, I took a good look at the house in question – but there was nothing especially revealing to see. It was a corner property, it looked well-maintained, the curtains were open and there were no obvious signs of life. To learn more, I'd need to make use of more than just the usual five senses.

About twenty feet down the path, I found a handy tree to stand behind. Then I waited until I was sure there was no one approaching from either direction and I put on my tribute.

Instantly I felt a jolt of adrenaline. My attention was fixed on the Presence Surface as it unfurled around me and spread out to touch the world. And immediately, pushing up through the Surface, were a string of contacts the colour of desert sunlight – bushy blossoms of light, each one a Connected adept. I counted seven before my scrabbling hand managed to snatch the headband from around my temples. Jan's old house was crawling with enemies.

I was momentarily shaken and did nothing. But a second later a thought pushed its way into my head: *Run*.

I felt foolish. I was out of sight of the house. I'd arouse more suspicion if I broke into a sprint than if I simply put my weary head down and carried on walking, groceries in hand.

Run, the voice in my head insisted. And despite myself I got moving, setting off down the path, moving as quickly as I could without breaking stride.

Run, the voice thundered and just then I became aware of the nearby squawk of a walkie-talkie; it was coming from just over the wall I was standing behind and it was moving. Just up ahead, was the gate for that garden. I would need to pass it in order to get away. I ran.

At the same time, I snatched the headband out of the shopping bag, stuffed it into my jacket and let the bag fall to the ground as I sprinted along the path and towards the gate.

As I reached it, the gate rattled violently but didn't open. Whoever was on the other side shook it frantically and I heard a voice, so close that the speaker might have been by my side, yelling for the key.

I pounded down the path hoping to reach the far end before the gate opened. I was running flat out now, thankful beyond words for the morning jogs I'd been taking, and all I heard behind me was rattling and swearing.

At the far end, I dashed around the corner, sprinting for the patch of greenery beyond. As I left the path behind me I heard a shattering crash and the sound of splitting wood. I guessed that whoever was back there had got impatient. Who knows how many months they'd been staking that place out and at the critical moment, someone had mislaid the key. My good fortune was almost certainly someone else's extended beating.

Fifteen seconds later I was through the little park, out the other side and onto a main road. There were cars, shops, lots of people and plenty of places to conceal myself.

I slowed to a walk and ducked swiftly into a charity shop – figuring that it was the last place any sane person would expect me to hide. Any self-respecting enemy of the Army would have had a black Range Rover with tinted windows idling at the kerb ready to roar off with a squeal of smoking tyres. Instead I peered out from behind a rack of second-hand wedding dresses and tried to keep an eye on the street.

A slim man with the build of a dancer and the dress sense of an Italian film star flew out onto the street and stopped dead, turning one of the fastest sprints I'd ever seen into a nonchalant saunter in the blink of an eye.

He looked first one way and then the other along the street, his eyes apparently taking in every detail. I was sure it was impossible for him to see me through the shop window, behind my barricade of voile and taffeta, but nevertheless I pulled back even farther and watched him through a gap in the shelves of children's books.

A moment later my view was blocked as a bus pulled up at the stop in front of the charity store and two old ladies got out. I seized the moment and moved quickly out of the shop, jumping onto the bus just as the last passenger boarded.

I flashed my travelcard and rushed past the driver to stand halfway up the bus's stairs, where I would be hidden from view from almost every angle. The bus doors closed and the vehicle moved away from the stop.

Again, I took it for granted that no adversary the Army had ever faced would flee on public transport, and once the bus was a few hundred yards down the road and round a corner I set about coaxing my heart-rate back down into double figures, reasonably sure that I hadn't been seen and wasn't being pursued.

It happened more quickly than I'd expected – my breathing returned to normal and a sense of calm purpose pushed aside my anxiety. I was back in control.

I'd learned a couple of lessons here. Firstly, I'd reminded myself not to underestimate the Army: they were real, they were active and they were following the same trail that I was. And secondly, I'd learned that in future I really should listen when that inner voice tells me to run.

CHAPTER 18

Tuesday, day two of sleuthing and today I thought I'd try a new approach. I'd maintain at least a minimum quarter of a mile distance between me and anyone trying to kill me. Today would be all about coffee and the Internet.

So what did I know now that I hadn't known yesterday? Well, I knew that the Marker wasn't in any of Jan's houses. How come? Well because the Army had been there and they would have crawled over every brick, plank and tile of each address. If they hadn't found it in a year, then it wasn't there.

The obvious, no-brainer conclusion was that Jan hid the Marker somewhere other than his known residences – and he didn't leave behind any obvious record of it, because either the Army or the PAC (who had a notebook of Jan's) would have noticed.

He had put it somewhere we hadn't looked – and yet it would also need to be somewhere that Jan could have quickly retrieved it from if he'd needed to. He would have wanted to be ready to make a run for it at any moment and I wondered what sort of hiding places were convenient, discreet and always accessible – and whether any of them would leave a data trail.

The classic I'd already mentioned, the safety deposit box, would imply bank records, a key, account details. In these days of cross-selling and direct marketing, wouldn't any commercial deposit service be writing to him every five minutes? Naturally, he could redirect correspondence to another residence or a post office box but they too would generate paperwork. At the very least a locked box needed a key. If the Army had found any mysterious keys, they'd had a year to figure out what they opened. So a commercial hiding place, like a lock-box, wasn't the likeliest answer in my view.

What about public property? A loose stone under a monument, a crypt, a hole in the ground in the woods somewhere? That could work, I suppose, but this needed to be somewhere Jan could reach easily, so it was probably in Central London. He just didn't have time to head off to the countryside. And how much public property was there in the middle of London that wasn't scrutinised, frequented, patrolled or covered by security camera? Jan would want 24 hour access, but he wouldn't want to be observed or risk anyone else discovering his hidey-hole. What was public, but secluded and open night and day? A church? A station? A park? A hotel? There were dozens or even hundreds of each of those.

Again I seemed to have reached a dead-end, but my plan was to keep at this until I came up with something I could act upon, so I tried coming at this from a different direction.

What if Jan couldn't reach the Marker for some reason and didn't want anyone else to find it? After all, if he got captured he couldn't very well spring into action at *that* point and conceal it. What he'd need was a system like a dead man's switch, something he had to keep resetting while he was around. Then, if he was somehow removed from the picture, the mechanism would be triggered and automatically hide the Marker.

Something like that might allow him to hide the Marker in his home, right where he'd want it, while still allowing him to keep it out of reach of his enemies if anything went wrong.

Now, *that* was a promising line of enquiry.

So what might fit the bill? Refuse collection was the first thing to spring to mind. But unless he actually kept the Marker in the dustbin by his back door, the scheme wouldn't work. Plus, would you really want to trust the miracle of the ages to foxes, unreliable collection schedules and one's ability to separate platinum filigree from eggshells and bacon rind once a week?

I wondered what else might work in a similar way.

I tried to think laterally. What about buying something on hire purchase? If you failed to keep up the payments – because you were dead or captured – then it would be repossessed. Hmmm, except that repossession would probably take months and require getting a warrant to break into the house. I discarded the repossession idea.

But the idea of payments led onto another avenue of thought. If Jan *had* constructed a dead man's switch, he'd need to use some sort of scheduled collection. Something like that would probably cost him money and that might leave a trace. If the collection itself was something innocuous, something that no one would suspect because it made sense for reasons that had nothing to do with the Marker, then the relevant payments might be overlooked by the Army.

I pictured Jan hiding the Marker among his shirts and then removing it before the laundry service collected it each week. No, that wasn't it either.

It was a farfetched scheme, but that was what I liked about it. All the easy options would have been explored; I could take that as read. I mean, stash the Marker under the mattress? The Army would have checked. On top of the wardrobe? The Army would have checked. I needed to look somewhere they wouldn't have thought to look and this idea fit the bill. If it got me nowhere, I could always go back to the more conventional possibilities.

So what was my next step? Well, ideally I wanted to get into Jan's bank records to see if he'd been paying for any sort of collection service, but that was easier said than done. Why couldn't he have done the decent thing and left a laptop lying around with the details of an online banking service still in its web cache?

I wondered if a man like Jan would even use something like Internet banking. Wouldn't a person who relied on magic be kind of a luddite? But then I remembered seeing a news cutting in the PAC's private store which mentioned that Dass's killer had used a radio transmitter to track his victim's car. So Jan obviously had a little experience when it came to technology.

And thinking about online banking triggered another memory. Susan had scanned Jan's notebook into a file and then made some annotations. One of them concerned a couple of numbers and a word that Jan had written on the back page of the book. They were:

```
10183461
1555635971
Punarbhava
```

Susan's annotation read "Password? It's the Sankrit word for 're-birth'. But what do the numbers mean?"

You probably think I should have checked that notation out as my first priority, right? But, really, what do two numbers and a word mean? They could be anything. I mean even if you knew they pertained to something on the Internet, there's still a lifetime of possibilities to check – and we *didn't* know it was an Internet thing. They could be details of Jan's tailor for all we could tell or maybe the location of a hidden stash of weapons in Patagonia: a map reference and a phone number in some far off land, plus somebody's surname.

Except they weren't.

I'd tried logging in to nine other UK banks or building societies before I found one that required two numbers of the right length and a password – and of course I did this all from behind my anonymizer[1] via my wireless cut-out in Capetown. I keyed in the digits, provided part of the password…

…and I was in.

Sweet.

First of all, I noticed that Jan had just over nineteen thousand pounds in his current account and a hundred and six thousand in his savings account. The second thing I noticed was a line in the top right-hand corner of the window that read 'Last log in:' and then gave a date and time from last year.

Well, it couldn't be helped. The next time someone logged into this account, that last login info would be displaying *today's* date and it would be obvious that I'd been here. That's to say, I hoped it wouldn't actually be obvious that me, Jo Hallett, had been here, but it would be obvious that *someone* had logged in.

Hmmm. The last log-in date was around the time of Jan's death. Did that mean no one else knew about this account? It was definitely possible. I checked the preference screen and saw that he'd ticked the boxes instructing the bank to make any correspondence electronic rather than paper-based.

Then I clicked on another link and found a facility to view old statements going back two years. When I pulled up the first page of a statement, there was an option to download a copy in a choice of

---

[1]   And for all you techno-pedants out there, I first spent a considerable amount of time rewriting it to handle HTTPS. Happy now?

formats. Handy. I chose Microsoft Excel format... and then realised that I was using an anonymizer; it would ruin my concealment if those files came directly to my home machine. I wasn't going to be able to download files unless I rewrote my damn software for a third time. So I settled for viewing them in a web-browser and taking screen prints of each statement. I consoled myself that it was probably a lot more secure this way. I wasn't sure if the Army themselves had the techno-chops to trace me once they became aware of this account, but if they'd successfully impersonated Jan's next of kin, they could always get the police to work on the case for them.

Even if they involved the police, I was pretty sure that no one in a nylon shirt and clip-on tie was going to unravel *my* security.

When I'd copied all the current account statements, I did the same for his online savings account and his Visa card. And then I copied a lot of very boring 'messages' offering him mortgages and insurance, just in case one of them pertained to something other than selling more financial services. With the brutal latency introduced by the various cut-outs, all this took forever.

Finally, there were only two more items to copy: a list of standing orders and direct debits, and an e-mail address that was listed under the account-holder's contact details. Interestingly, the name on the bank account was Mr N Harrington and the e-mail address was `Niall.Harrington@onlineuk.com`. It wasn't an alias that I'd seen anywhere else, which meant I might be in possession of some information that the Army didn't have yet.

When I was finally done, I had just under ninety pages of print-outs. I wiped the logs of the wireless access points I'd used in Capetown and told the anonymizer to destroy itself and then run a program that would lunch its way through the hosting server's records. I wouldn't be using either of those systems again. If I

Robert Finn

needed to do any more online sleuthing I'd load the anonymizer onto a new server somewhere, and see if I could locate a fresh wireless link elsewhere in the world – perhaps in Johannesburg this time, just in case anyone bought the idea that a South African was behind this.

Tomorrow I'd start the job of going through the screen-prints line by line looking for something that matched my dead-man's switch theory: a gardening company that cleared bags of leaves, a charity that collected bric-a-brac... or failing that, a payment to 'Acme Safety Deposit Boxes Inc'.

CHAPTER 19

Monday had been brush-with-death day[1]. Tuesday had been taken up preparing for, logging onto and copying Jan's bank records. And Wednesday was mainly eaten up going through each entry, trying to figure out what it might pertain to and making some sort of guesstimate on whether it was a red herring or a golden goose.

Fortunately, I could put a lot of those payments to one side for now because I was only looking at recurring entries. If some service was making regular collections then I'd imagine they'd want regular payments, so I made a separate list of all repeating monthly outgoings. Quite a few were utilities or services that obviously didn't involve any sort of collection. I worked through the rest and by the end of the day, I'd crossed *all* the entries off my list and had nothing to show for it.

Then I tried adjusting my definition of 'recurring'. After all, Jan only came by the Marker shortly before his death. To arouse

---

[1] Part of Flossing-with-Danger Week

the least possible suspicion, he'd have weaved his concealment mechanism in with a service he'd been using for a long time. But maybe he hadn't thought that far ahead. I started looking for regular payments which only started up six months or more before he died.

There was only one new entry and it was an insurance company. So far as I know, the only thing they collect is money, so that one was out as well.

Even when I just looked in the last three months before his death, I found only a single additional payee: The Clipping Service. I knew what a clipping service was; they collected press cuttings on whatever topics you set them. Was this a firm that collected news stories on Jan's behalf or was it just a cutesy name for a gardening firm? The latter would suit me better, although the former would still be intriguing.

I did a little digging, no pun intended, and learned that The Clipping Service was in fact a hairdressers[1]. A lesser woman might be getting frustrated by now. My patience, fortunately, was limitless these days.

It had also occurred to me that my dead man's switch theory could be correct without there actually being a regular payment or collection. Like, maybe he made a telephone call each week that said, 'nothing to collect this week'.

Then again, the more I thought about that idea the more it seemed to suck.

Maybe he'd had an accomplice after all. An accomplice would just notice that Jan was dead, grab the Marker and scarper (as they say in these parts). Sure, a commercial service, like a gardening firm who cleared away garden refuse, was a very clever way of

---

[1] What's the link between hairdressing and puns? Do they all have to have names like Curl Up And Dye, or From Hair To Eternity?

making it seem as though the Marker had just vanished, but on the other hand, there was such a thing as over-thinking things. An accomplice could just flat-out sprint for South America as soon as he'd snatched the Marker. Maybe there was accomplice and he'd simply managed not to leave a trail, and that's why the Marker was still unaccounted for.

Plus the dead man's switch idea didn't make sense with just any old service. A gardening firm wouldn't file the leaves and grass they collected; it would probably burn them. And even if they mulched them instead, you wouldn't really want a piece of priceless platinum to be lost among tons of rotting grass.

I couldn't tell if I was making progress in puzzling out Jan's scheme or gradually demonstrating to myself all the reasons it couldn't work.

At the end of each day, the Professor was there to receive my call and we would have a pleasant little chat. I tried to exude the kind of older-and-wiser, weary strength that you expect from felons who were going straight or Country singers who'd kicked their forty-year bourbon habit. I didn't have much to tell him about progress on the search, but then I reckoned I had at least a week before he could realistically expect any revelations.

After I put the phone down following our Wednesday call, I thought back on the conversation. Then I thought about the fact that the Professor had offered to call me tomorrow instead of the other way round... which led me on to thinking about Jan *getting* a phone call each week rather than making one. Why this train of thought was worth mentioning, I couldn't say. But there was something there; I just didn't know what yet.

I also found a few minutes on Wednesday to dash out and deposit the rent cheque I'd received from Noola. She appeared to be planning to stay and to pay her way. With minimal 'handling' from me she was behaving herself and even tidying up around the place. Assuming the cheque actually cleared, I could consider the Noola situation dealt with, for now.

On Thursday, having checked all the repeat outgoings from Jan's account, I started looking at all the one-off expenditures. Dead end followed dead end, and by the end of the day I had nothing worthwhile to show for my efforts.

Friday dawned and before settling down to work I went out for a run. I wasn't sure the net effect was actually beneficial when you factored in the carbon monoxide, the volatile organics and the unpleasant nitrogen compounds in the London air, but exercise was good for my brain chemistry. Endorphins and a healthy blood-sugar level made it easier not to be depressed. Plus, I just found I liked starting my day that way.

While I was out jogging, the answer to that earlier puzzle came to me. I could call the Professor or the Professor could call me. Jan could pay a collection service or a collection service could pay him.

Suddenly I wanted another look at those statements. I wanted to check whether there were any regular *incoming* payments in Jan's bank records. I picked up the pace a little and then took a chance. I cut back through Mugger's Alley in order to save a little time. I figured it was waaay too early for junkies to be up and about. At this hour of the day they were probably still fast asleep dreaming of bugs under their skin.

I needn't have worried; the alley was deserted and I was home a minute later. Eager though I was, I waited until I'd taken a shower before re-examining Jan's bank statements. Wrapped in a thick terry robe, with a pink towel twined around my head like fondant topping, I sat down with the print-outs and a highlighter pen.

I couldn't find a recurring amount, but I *could* find a recurring name: Achtung Antiques. The payments had only been running for two and a half months, and the amounts varied greatly, but they were weekly, which immediately caught my eye. Granted, there were a couple of weeks with no payments at all, but there was still enough of a pattern to make it seem worth investigating. I put another shovel full of coal on the Internet connection and went in search of Achtung Antiques.

There wasn't that much to find. Google Local showed a store by that name less than a mile from Jan's Notting Hill address. They didn't appear to have a web-site.

The good news was that I had something promising to investigate; the bad news was that I would have to do so in person. This needed to go better than my outing on Monday had.

I'd need a cover story to use when I visited the shop and started asking questions – and it had to work whether I was talking to a real shopkeeper or an Army stooge on the look-out for suspicious visitors.

I needed to ask the payments that had been made to Jan's... I mean Niall Harrington's account. I could pretend to be a relative, or a cop, or someone from the lawyer's office handling his will. I could even tell the truth, sort of, and say Mr. Harrrington was a bad, bad man and I wanted to retrieve some property he'd taken, which the police had given up on finding. But that sounded idiotic and the other suggestions I'd come up with were all straight out of TV Clichéland.

In the end, I figured that it was about 90% certain that all those payments from the antique store would turn out to be exactly what they appeared to be: Jan selling off some antiques. Which meant I could use the least suspicious line you could use in a store: "Hi, I'm interested in buying something."

Unfortunately for me, I didn't know exactly what Jan had been selling so I couldn't go in and ask for it specifically. But if I said I'd been to his house, then I could just ask if they'd handled the sale of *any* of his things – and that I liked everything of his that I'd seen. And if it turned out that those payments *weren't* for antiques, it still didn't look totally suspicious. Who had a big house in Notting Hill without at least a few antiques? It would just suggest that someone else had handled the sale.

Next I really needed a reason to have visited Jan's house that would hold up under the scrutiny of a genuine shopkeeper (easy enough) and also a spy for the Army (much trickier).

I decided to keep it vague. I'd be a neighbour who had been to Mr Harrington's house on a couple of occasions, for reasons left unspecified, and who was interested in buying anything he'd parted with. I figured it would sound ghoulish if I said I knew he was dead, so I'd claim that when I asked after him, I was told he'd sold up and moved away.

So now I needed to look the part. What do women my age wear if they're rich and privileged? I did a little research courtesy of Hello magazine and some other, less deferential publications. It was scary what you could find out. It was easy enough to pull up a list of the brand names favoured by Prince William's current girlfriend, complete with pictures of when she'd worn each item and marks out of ten for how she looked. Sadly, most of those clothes would make me look like a moose in fancy dress, but then she *was* nearly ten years younger than me. Fortunately there were other, shall we say sturdier members of the British nobility, who still wanted to look their everyday best when they weren't on a horse or at a ball.

I suspected that women who ran antique shops in expensive parts of London had a keen nose for class, income and pedigree, so just to be on the safe side I made an appointment to get my hair styled and my eyebrows plucked. Despite many years of living in England, on and off, my American accent hadn't diminished much – which probably worked in my favour. The relationship between class, accent and wealth was much less obvious on the other side of the pond. Plus, my daddy didn't spend all that money on private tutors just so that I could sound like the downstairs maid.

Maybe all this preparation sounds like overkill; I'd probably only be in that shop for ten minutes. But the Army don't kid around. If I was going to cross the Afghan border at night carrying false papers you'd expect me to get my story straight and not to muddle my chadri with my kameez. This might not be a war zone, but it was still enemy territory. Dass had nearly killed David Braun at his smart home in Belgravia just because he was a loose end. If it could happen to him in Belgravia, it could happen to me in Notting Hill.

In the end, it was Saturday morning before I was finally at the door of a very exclusive looking store round the corner from Portobello Road. The windows had far too little stock compared with the few antique stores I was familiar with. I suspected the less in the window, the more it cost.

I'd spied the place out quickly the day before, but hadn't approached. The name Achtung Antiques had been bothering me and I wanted to check it was selling actual old antiques and not Modernist salad tongs in red and yellow plastic. My outfit said 'old money' not new bohemian. I needn't have worried, though.

As I pushed open the door, I could see my reflection in the glass. I looked virtually unrecognisable. A month ago, I would rather have been dipped in barbeque sauce and fed to the dingoes than wear a Chanel rainbow-tweed suit and a silk blouse. My hair alone would have had me reaching for the hemlock. Man, but you needed some chutzpah to dress like this and not feel self-conscious. No wonder nobility inherit their titles; unless you're raised to this sort of thing from birth you don't stand a chance.

But that was hardly a helpful way to think. I was smarter and far deadlier than the women who customarily dressed like this. One day soon I might even have in my possession the means to live forever. Didn't I have reason enough to act aloof?

A little bell tinkled as I entered the store. I let my gaze wander, ignoring the welcoming smile and head-tilt of the proprietoress. She fluttered over a couple of minutes later and said, "Celine Dubois. *Do* let me know if there's anything I can help with."

"Hmmm, I don't see it here," I said.

"What were you looking for, Madame? Perhaps I can help you find it," she asked brightly. Her accent was hard to place. It seemed like it wanted to be French but was keeping its options open.

"A friend of mine, I think you bought a number of pieces from him; I was hoping that you still had some of them," I said. Antique-lovers call old chairs and things 'pieces', right?

"Oh really," she said, sounding delighted that I was telling her things, "and what is your friend's name?"

"Niall Harrington. He was a neighbour of mine and I always admired his taste. I remember once he recommended I drop in here and look around. I was hoping if I did that I might find some of his charming pieces," I said.

She looked sad. "Ah, Mr Harrington had so many lovely things. I was very sad when our business was concluded," she sighed. I noticed that she dropped the 'h' in 'had' but not 'Harrington'. It really made you wonder which part of France the Dubois family called home.

"Yes," I said, "when I enquired after him, I was told he'd moved away. It was a surprise."

"Oh no," she corrected me, "he'd been planning to go for a couple of months. He was unable to take his collection with him and so he'd decided to let it go." I assumed by 'let it go' she meant sell it. From her phrasing you'd think he had simply allowed it to evaporate into the air instead of doing something pedestrian, like swapping it for cash.

So he had told her he was leaving, but she didn't appear to know that he was dead now.

"*Do* you still have any of his things?" I enquired. I think I'd worn out the word 'piece' in the first few seconds of my visit.

She glanced at the table I was leaning against and said, "Well, of course you'll remember this lovely 18th century card table. Although I think this particular item has at last found itself a new home."

I was definitely getting the impression that when operating in this price range, one didn't actually refer to money changing hands. Instead all parties had to pretend that antiques simply moved on of their own accord from time to time – a little like wild birds visiting your garden; you could try to coax them, and they might linger with you for a while, but you could never be sure when they'd flit away again.

"Really?" I said, attempting to admire the table, "This was his too?"

Then I decided to take a chance. I needed to find something bulky enough that it might hide a secret compartment. This card table was positively anorexic. I was looking for something with a little more meat on its bones. I said, "He had a desk I rather liked. I only caught a glimpse of it, but I wondered if that had made its way to you."

"The Davenport or the Secretaire?" she asked.

Having no idea what those words meant, I went with the one that sounded weightier. "The Davenport."

"Ohhh," she said, sounding as though I'd given her bad news.

"No longer with us."

Well, we could play this game all day. I needed to get to the heart of the matter. If Jan had hidden the Marker, it would presumably be in the last consignment of furniture they collected from him.

"Niall said that you had rather an unusual arrangement. You would send someone to pick up a few items from him each week. Did I get that right?" I said. If I was wrong, she might give me a strange look, but probably wouldn't rush out into the street yelling for the police. Even if she was an Army spy, it didn't really give grounds to be suspicious. From the Army's point of view, just saying I knew Mr Harrington was the interesting part.

She looked embarrassed for a moment and then said, "Well, he asked me not to talk about it." I gave her a friendly smile and plenty of silence – which she could choose to fill if she wished.

After a few seconds, she appeared to take some sort of decision and said, "But since you're telling not asking, I can't see the harm. And anyway," she said, glancing pointedly towards the back of the shop, "since when is it unprofessional to have an actual conversation with a customer?"

I nodded and smiled some more, full of encouragement. "Exactly," I said.

She added quietly, "My name's really Cheryl, by the way. Doesn't mean I don't know antiques, does it?" Her French accent obviously knew when it was beaten. It had withdrawn and her underlying London vowels had burst through.

With a look I attempted to convey my shock that anyone would think otherwise. "Well obviously," I agreed. "And Niall *has* left the country. I can't see him minding now," I pointed out, hoping I sounded conspiratorial and chummy.

"We still have most of his *final* few pieces, but I have to say I always wondered why the rigmarole," she said. "You don't happen to know, do you? Why the business with the weekly collections?"

So there *were* weekly collections. I was feeling heartily gruntled that I'd been right. I said, "I imagine he held on to his favourite things until the last moment. He didn't want to part with them until he was just about to leave. In fact, maybe he was already gone when you collected them."

She nodded, as though I was very wise. "He said they'd been in his family a long while. I suppose one forms attachments. He didn't seem like a sentimental man, but it just shows you can miss the signs."

"I'm fascinated," I said, hoping I wasn't laying it on too thick. "How did it work? He left a few items out for you each week, then?"

"That would have been a *trifle* unusual. This was *much* more peculiar," she said. "He had that giant workshop space all cleared out and filled with some fabulous things, mainly Victorian, a lot of furnishings. Each piece had a card on it and each week he'd redo all the cards."

I nodded, wanting her to go on.

"Well, the only things the cards had on them was a date and a price. And the prices were always bargains. You were supposed to compare today's date with the date on the card. If it was still in the future you'd leave the piece; if the date had passed, you'd take it. That was the arrangement," she explained.

It was very clever, I thought. For whatever reason, he had some antiques to sell off, but instead of disposing of them in one go, he'd parcelled them out to last several months. And then each week that he *didn't* include the Marker was another week when he got to check that the collection system was working properly. At the most superficial level, there was nothing suspicious to find. A man about to go on the run had gradually sold off his furniture. Only the collection scheme was peculiar and you'd have to suspect it existed to go looking for it.

She concluded, "And one day we turned up to find all the dates were in the previous week. So we took away everything. I had to have the men make a second trip. When he first created our arrangement, he said when that happened, when we'd taken everything, then that was it, our business was at an end and he'd prefer me not to discuss it with anyone."

She nodded her head gravely, as if to say: *yes, it was all very strange*. And then she seemed to realise that she hadn't exactly kept her word to him. She looked doubtful for a minute.

"I won't tell a soul," I reassured her. "And I'm sure he wouldn't have mentioned the arrangement to me at all if he hadn't wanted me to know about it."

That seemed to satisfy her and she began to lead me round the showroom, pointing out the three other items – two chairs and a sideboard – that had belonged to Mr. Harrington. She told me there were three more pieces in their store room at the back: an armchair, a bureau and a credenza (whatever that was).

"So how many of the pieces in that last collection are still here? What have I missed out on?" I asked.

"Well, we've already parted with a lovely Queen Anne escritoire and a Regency pedestal desk," she admitted.

Hmmm. The desk and the escritoire (which I had in mind was a thing with drawers and a flap for writing letters on) were both losses. You could hide a thing like the Marker in either one.

Clearly, I was going to have to come back here when no one else was around and check over all the items from Jan's last consignment. And if I didn't find anything, I'd have to track down the two items she'd already sold. But at least it looked like I'd only be breaking in to the premises of ordinary mortals. Now that

I'd had my theory about weekly collections confirmed, I was sure that Jan had concealed the Marker this way. Which meant that the Army didn't know about this place, otherwise they'd surely have recovered it by now.

"I know it's an imposition," I said, "But could you show me the items from your store room? Once I've seen everything I can go home and think about what I might have room for."

"Of course," she said and led me through a doorway and into the large dusty area beyond. It was a great expanse of cloth-draped shapes. I made a mental note of the layout and where Jan's pieces sat in the overall scheme.

When I'd spent a suitable amount of time appreciating what I hoped were the salient features of each, Cheryl escorted me back to the sales floor.

"I'm afraid I forgot to ask your name," she said, as we neared the front door.

"Anne Wexham," I said. 'Wexham', because it was one of the surnames Jan had used elsewhere. I figured if anyone asked questions later about my visit, that surname would send them on a wild goose chase: they'd think they were looking for an accomplice of Jan's. And I chose 'Anne' because I figured if it was good enough for a princess it would work for me.

Just before I left, something occurred to me. I said, "Do you mind if I ask you something? Where did the company name come from?"

Cheryl looked around before answering and even then she kept her voice low. "Well, they're terrible snobs here. The owner maintains it was a condition of one of the firm's investors, a wealthy German gentleman. But the truth is that when they moved to Notting Hill, they changed the name to sound more up-market and European. It used to be Acton Antiques."

She chuckled and I joined in. I knew my London suburbs just well enough to see why she was laughing.

As I let myself out, I made sure to take careful note of the alarm sensors on the front door, the transducer in the corner for the ultrasonics and the closed-circuit TV cameras.

I had some breaking and entering to plan.

CHAPTER 20

I hadn't seen any mention of it in the PAC's notes, but a person who was Connected could see pretty well in the dark. I didn't need the sun to be up for me to get a good look at the back of the Antique store.

Of course, it wasn't exactly 'seeing'. It was more like an extended sense of touch. I could feel things close by, though anything more than forty or fifty feet away was just a mushy blur. Distant buildings were bulky and indistinct, like trying to read a Braille headline with your shoulder. The cinder block by my cheek, on the other hand, was pocked and coral-edged: almost crystalline in its sharpness.

It had seemed obvious to me: if you could Shatter something on the other side of a wall, it stood to reason you needed a way to see it was there, didn't you? But the PAC still seemed to be in the metaphorical dark on that point. Which, irony fans, was probably because they didn't spend enough time in the literal dark. I'd guess they did pretty much all of their training in well-lit rooms. And even if you did dim the lights, you tended not to really notice these extra sense impressions if your eyes were open and you were straining to see. You had to really concentrate on the Surfaces – and to start with, it helped if you kept your eyes closed.

It was easiest if you used the Push Surface, the one for applying pressure to the objects around you. It really was like a sense of touch, because if you focused too hard on the texture of something, you could find that object sliding away from you. It reminded me of an electron microscope I'd once seen demonstrated, where the target was a dried housefly. As the operator zoomed in, to show the delicate hairs around one of its compound eyes, the hairs drooped. The act of viewing them applied enough power to cook them.

Seeing with the Shatter Surface was similar to using Push, but there was more of a sense of tunnel vision. The Freeze and Heat Surfaces had their uses too. You could tell the difference between a mannequin and a live human even in zero light, just by sensing their temperature. Of course learning to use each Surface in this way could take years – and decades more to really master.

I was in my element, though, unperturbed by the lack of light. It was like that venerable adage about night being a dear friend to the old and a cloak to the young – which, take my word for it, sounds better in Latin because of the amiculus/amiculum friend/ cloak wordplay.

Which was… nothing to do with anything. What was I going to say? Oh yes. When I'd left the antique store the previous morning, I'd lingered in the street talking into a silent mobile phone, while using it to snap pictures of the front of the building.

Later that day I'd returned on a scouting mission. It was just before sunset when I found myself spying on the goods entrance at the back of the store. By then my perfect hair had been jammed into a woolly hat and I'd undergone a sort of reverse makeover – part of which involved issuing a last minute reprieve to an old fisherman's jumper and a pair of scruffy jeans that otherwise would have gone into the garbage. I'd dowdied myself up and removed every trace of make-up. You'd have had to really have a thing for staring at frumpy women to recognise me as the fancy-pants shopper from earlier that day.

So, cunningly disguised as myself from a month ago, I'd found my way to the road that ran behind the antique store. You could reach the back of the shop from there by turning off the street, which was mainly residential[1], passing through a pair of high chain-link gates and walking fifty feet down an asphalt driveway.

The first section of the driveway was shared with another business, which made it sort of communal ground. I'd reckoned I could loiter there for a little while without attracting attention. Remember, it didn't look like the Army, with all their wary paranoid deadliness, was involved here. So I just had to make sure I didn't look too much like a furniture thief and I should be fine.

From where I'd stood, I'd been able to see there was a large yard leading to the store's rear loading bay, and a ramp to one side, for wheeling things up to the level of the store room entrance. The entrance itself consisted of a reinforced door adjacent to an enormous heavy-duty metal roller-shutter, which was wide enough and high enough that you could carry a grand piano through it... on its end, if you felt the need.

The setting sun still provided enough light to get a good look at the rear of the premises, but from that distance there wasn't much to see. So once I'd committed a few details to memory I headed off to pick up a few pre-heist essentials and then I went home.

Now I was back for the third time, in the early hours of the

---

[1]   Britain has only the haziest grasp of zoning. A country that can put a nuclear power station next door to a nature reserve can't get worked up about commercial premises adjacent to family homes.

next morning, standing thirty foot away from the rear loading bay, crouched behind an old storage bin full of de-icing grit. I'd hopped over the chained-up security gate easily enough and I was tucked behind the last piece of cover before reaching the back of the building. Before I got any closer I was checking that I hadn't missed any security cameras on my earlier visit.

It was just after 3am on an overcast night and the neighbourhood on all sides of me was asleep. There was very little sound and nothing to suggest trouble ahead.

I peered into the dark corners of the building's recesses as best I could using my eyes, and then I pulled my hood down and used the Surfaces to explore in more detail. Still no sign of a camera.

A CCTV camera with a good lens can register an image when it's so dark that owls are stepping on each other's feet, but you still need *some* light for them to work. For that reason, security cameras that are intended for night-use are normally sensitive to infra-red and have a special light-source built in, or maybe slung underneath. Of course, being infra-red, you can't actually see the beam the light-source puts out with your eyes, but it would show up fine if I used the Heat Surface to look around. And I wasn't detecting any such IR illumination.

On the other hand, cameras with Passive IR sensors might only switch themselves on when a warm body came near. With that in mind, I removed a chemical hand-warmer from my pocket and activated it. When it was toasty warm, I hurled it towards the building. A little nudge using Push and it struck the rear door right by the lock. The packet dropped onto the concrete and lay there, clearly visible to me through the Heat Surface, blazing away in the infra-red. Hand-warmers run a little cooler than human flesh so I gave it a little encouragement with Heat, just to make sure it would trigger any sensors. Still no sign of any IR light-sources, so

I reckoned it was safe to approach.

From what I could tell from my previous two trips, all the doors and windows had magnetic switches to register when they were opened. Any windows that weren't made to open had conductive-film strip-sensors fitted, which could tell if the glass was broken. From outside, I could sever the connection to any of the sensors using magic, but that would only trigger the alarm. I needed another way in.

When I reached the rear of the building, I climbed up the drainpipe near the bottom of the ramp and swung myself onto a flat section of roof. While skilful use of Push made it easier to haul myself around, I still had to remind myself that my muscles weren't very strong. Even when they only had to carry half my weight, my fingers sometimes struggled to maintain their grip.

I could only marvel at the person I'd been. I'd known for most of the last twenty-six years that my body, being female, had only a fraction of the testosterone of a man's, so I was always going to find it difficult to maintain muscle mass. But had I compensated by doing plenty of strength training? I'm surprised you even have to ask.

Now that I was up high, I could see over the security fence into the next property. It looked like a good direction to head in if things went, as the English would have it, pear-shaped. Fortunately, with the lack of a moon, I wouldn't be all that easy to see up here. The black clothing would help too – and not just because it made my thighs look slimmer.

I didn't have to worry about being seen from the street at the front of the shop because the building itself hid me. The front of the building had a high, pitched roof, with the ridge running parallel to the road. The lower rear section, where I stood now, was flat, punctuated by a couple of vents and a new looking heat exchanger for the building's climate control. I shuffled over and examined one of the vents to see if I could remove the metal louvres of the cowling. The dimensions where the vent passed through the roof were a little small for a grown-up to get through. Even if I could remove the whole cowling unit, it would be a tight squeeze.

(Probably) no harm in trying though. It would be a lot of metal to burn through, and trying to Shatter it free would make a noise like a grenade going off. I ran my hands over the metal and used the Surfaces to probe the joints inside, trying to find a weak point. I could sense two bolts which held the main part of the assembly fixed to the frame it sat in. With a little science and a heaped helping of concentration, I reckoned I could break the bolts without waking the neighbours.

First I Heated the bolts, dividing my concentration equally between them to make sure they were both properly roasted. After a couple of minutes, I could feel the temperature really start to climb. Through the Heat Surface I could sense the metal glowing yellow, then orange – ripples of hot colour pulsing against the washed-out ambience of the background. I kept Heating, all the way up to a cherry red. That was hotter than many adepts could manage, but I needed the high temperature to make the steel brittle. One final burst of Heat and then, with all the speed I could muster, I Froze them, pushing hard, dragging them down from red-heat, to room temperature, and quickly on down below zero. Moments later I could sense flakes of frost piling up on the bolts' glassy threads.

Then, gathering my focus, I Shattered the bolts at their mid-points, first one, then the other. They fractured loudly in the dead air. But it wasn't a troubling sound like glass shattering or a dog's bark starting up. It sounded like deep ice cracking and for a moment I saw the pale-blue light from my dream.

No time for that now, though. With a bit of jostling and twisting,

I pulled the vent-cowling free of the roof. From immediately below I heard the thump and tinkle of a sheared bolt dropping onto some priceless heirloom and then bouncing away into the gloom. Between their AC and the damp climate, these vents probably didn't get much use and this one was filthy. I set it down on the roof next to me and peered into the hole.

The floor was about twenty-five feet below me: a long way to jump for someone with the muscle tone of a boiled Muppet – even with occult assistance to cushion the fall. I'd need to hang, *then* drop – while attempting to miss the chest of drawers immediately beneath.

I lowered my legs through the hole and, as gracefully as possible, wiggled my hips through the gap. Careful not to snag my backpack, I slid down until I was hanging by my hands. The metal edge of the vent's frame dug sharply into my palms, cutting through the fabric of my gloves, but I held on long enough to rock my centre of gravity a little to one side. Then I let go and was falling through empty space. (Without meaning to, I found myself imagining the sound a person might make if they dropped twenty feet to land on a glass display case.)

Again, I needed to use a little Push to avoid impacting coccyx-first, but my trajectory allowed me to reach a strip of empty floor and avoid the many looming, cloth-shrouded mounds of slumbering Victoriana. Then I hit the ground and an electric crackle of pain shot through my ankle.

My eyes watered, involuntarily, and I sat down with a bump.

Pulling off my gloves, I sat there for a moment massaging the fire in my tendons with my bleeding hands. I still had many of my old, self-pitying instincts from all those years as a willing victim of life's unfairness and it took me a couple of seconds to suppress the swirl of pain and tearfulness I felt. I touched the necklace at my throat to remind me to be strong and that did the trick. The door slammed shut on all that neurotic nonsense and I was once again all business.

I took a few minutes to focus on my hands and my ankle, working the Healing surface over the damage. My palms had only superficial cuts; I would have ignored them completely except that I didn't want to leave pools of my blood at the scene of a crime. My ankle required a little more work – and, plus, it wasn't optional: I needed to be able to put my weight on both feet, maybe even run if it came to that.

Ten minutes later my ankle felt fine. It wasn't back to full mobility but it was pretty close.

Next, I directed my concentration to the lip of the frame far above me. I worked my way around the sharp edge, scorching the metal with Heat, until I was sure I'd barbequed any blood I'd left up there: a precaution in case the London bobbies watched CSI.

Then I pulled on my gloves and stood up to look around, picturing the layout from when Cheryl brought me back here. The dust-covers draped over so many boxy shapes made the room look like a miniature town after a massive snowfall, all banked sides and softened outlines – particularly so, as the Surfaces couldn't discern normal colours, rendering the scene as pale as a ghost's breath on a winter morning.

I found the bureau first and pulled the cloth from it. It looked very promising as a hiding place, with drawers all up the base and a hinged front that opened flat to reveal more recesses. Of course, I was looking for a *hidden* drawer or a secret compartment, but still, there was enough wood here, and enough structure, to offer plenty of opportunities for concealment. Carefully, I slipped my focus in through the joints of the frame, along the smooth timbers of the carcass, behind the backs of the drawers and under the surface of the inner compartments. It was tricky, delicate work, and I found nothing except wood, glue, handmade screws and some tufts of cotton rag entombed since the bureau was made.

On to the next item, which was an armchair. It was even trickier than probing the inside of the bureau. The metal springs in the stuffing and the taut threads of the webbing confused my senses. I was tempted to tear the thing apart, but in the end I ran through the internal space of the chair using Freeze and after that I found I could distinguish the chilled metal from the warmer organics. Now I could focus on the multitude of metallic loops and twists and it became obvious that they were all springs and pins, not platinum filigree.

The credenza was a bust too, and because of its size it took a lot of checking. I'd already eaten up an hour since I jumped over the gate, which made it 4:00am now – and I still had the three items out on the sales floor to check. I'd wanted to be out of there by 4:30, because I knew there were people who actually get up at five on a Sunday. Granted they were mostly golfers and fishermen, but just because they were crazy didn't mean the police would necessarily ignore a call from them.

On the other hand, I hadn't wanted to get here any earlier. London is such a boozy, good-time gal of a city that half the population is still busying throwing up their kebabs at 3am – and the police are out in force keeping an eye on them. It's a real challenge finding a good time for bad deeds.

So I'd checked out the furniture in the stock room and found nothing. Now I approached the door that led out to the sales floor. I stopped in front of it to look for alarm sensors.

There was a magnetic switch fastened to the frame that would set off the alarm if the door was opened without taking some sort of preventive action first. Fortunately for me it was on my side of the frame. Evidently burglars were supposed to force their way in at the front of the shop and work backwards from there. Silly me for breaking in all wrong.

In the pocket of my jacket I had a double-syringe of rapid-setting epoxy. I took it out now, uncapped it and applied huge globs of resin around both halves of the sensor. Then I warmed it a little to speed the reaction along. Time was ticking and I could sense some part of me growing restless over how long this was taking, but it wasn't a good idea to rush these things. By now I'd had some practice at ignoring the little voice in my head that wanted me to panic or lose my cool or give up.

I probed the room behind the door as I waited for the glue to set.

I gave it ten minutes, keeping the glue at about body temperature to aid the curing. Once it was hard to the touch, I went back to the storage area and over to the workbench on the side wall. When I'd been shown around by Cheryl, I'd noticed a tool chest there and now I started pulling open drawers looking for suitable tools. I found a razor-sharp wood-chisel and a large screwdriver with a taped handle. I brought them back with me to the door and began using them to gently pry the magnetic sensor out of the wood. Naturally I had to help the process along with a little magic, warming the wood fibres and pushing the screws out from the back.

Gradually, the sensor was coming loose but it was taking an age.

I checked my watch and decided to take a risk in order to save some time. I packed the sensor in a tight Shield and applied a little Shatter to the frame of the door, directing it along the grain in the areas around the sensor. The hundred-year-old wood split neatly and the sensor came free, complete with a patch of gloss-painted woodwork, forever joined to the two halves of the sensor in one resinous lump. I was sure that no one outside the building would have heard a thing.

I collapsed the Shield and let the sensor assembly dangle from its wires. Then I reached in and pushed the tumblers of the lock mechanism aside, unlocking the door. But I didn't turn the handle yet.

First I directed Freeze at the two PIR sensors in the corner of the room beyond, until I could sense ice building up on the front of the detectors. Then I frosted up the lenses of the security cameras. Only then did I open the door and step out onto the shop floor.

I felt very exposed, being able to see out through the tops of the shop windows, over the furniture on display, and into the deserted street beyond. There were lights on in the display windows, but painted backdrops screened off most of the store from anyone looking in. I could see spits of rain hitting the glass of the window which was a good sign: bad weather made it even less likely that someone from the Neighbourhood Watch would be taking a stroll at this hour. But if someone did pass by, all they'd see beyond the top edge of the window display was blackness. It was dark as a starless night in the back half of the sales floor, except for the lone constellation of twinkling LEDs that belonged to the phone, the cash register and the thermostat.

Moving swiftly now, I made my way to the card table. It took only moments to check and then I was on to the first of the chairs. I was beginning to get a sinking feeling as I finished it and started probing the second chair. Now there was only the sideboard to check. It took me nearly ten minutes to be sure, but when I was done, I'd satisfied myself that the Marker wasn't in the store.

Damn it.

Which meant it was in one of the pieces they'd already sold.

Now I would have to find the store's records of its sales.

While the storage area at the back was a single storey construction with twenty-foot ceilings, the front of the building, which was clearly much older, had an upstairs – in fact, the outside windows in my photographs suggested an attic space above the first floor[1].

How many doors with how many sensors would I have to get past? How many cameras? I didn't know, but it wasn't like I could pack up and go home. I paused a moment just to think through my options.

OK, I suppose I *could* go home and come back another night, but the owners would know they'd been burgled, and like most people once the horse has bolted, they'd probably fit newer, stronger stable doors. Alternatively, I could say to myself, *hang the sneaking around*, and just rampage through the place, gambling that I could find what I wanted and get out before anyone reacted to a triggered alarm. The third option was just to carry on, let the clock keep ticking, and trust either that I wouldn't be discovered, or if I was, that one or two standard-issue policemen wouldn't pose much of a problem for me.

Actually, even half a dozen *armed* police weren't going to slow me down much; it was just a question of much of a ruckus I was prepared to raise if I found myself cornered. All in all, it seemed best to keep going, keep quiet and trust in the universal instinct to laziness that keeps most nosey people in bed on Sunday mornings.

The decision made, I was maybe five minutes into this plan, when I decided to change tack. Why? Well, I was still working

---

[1]   That's the British use of 'first floor'. Confusingly, if I were back in the US, I'd *already be* on the first floor. Which would have saved me some time. Huh?

on the door that led to the next floor when an urgent peep-peep-peep noise started up; it was coming from the direction of the store room.

I dashed out to investigate and found the main panel for the climate-control system lit up like a radioactive Christmas tree on the fourth of July. Above the sound of the alarm, I could also hear the sound of rainwater pattering onto the dust-covers from the hole in the ceiling. Crap. The weather was getting in and it had set off the temperature/humidity sensors.

I ran back to the sales floor, placed one hand on the door to the stairs and blew the lock out through the other side of the frame. Then I threw the door open and ran upstairs, feeling ahead of me with my mind, looking for the heavy, resonating bulk of a filing cabinet. Doubtless, everything was electronic these days, but I was sure they'd still store their signed delivery notes for a while.

I had to shatter another lock before I found the right office and then I had to calm my heartbeat so that I could concentrate on the tumblers on the first of three filing cabinets. Not even *I* could read ink on paper without using my eyes, so I turned on the overhead light and quickly ascertained that all the paperwork in front of me pertained to wages and employee records. I was just Pushing open the lock on the second cabinet when I heard the heavy metal shutter of the loading bay downstairs being opened. I glanced out of the nearest window, which overlooked the street in front of the shop, but saw nobody down there yet.

Now something cold shifted inside of me and I really began to move quickly. Checking the second filing cabinet, I could see the files I was looking for. I clawed my backpack off, grabbed a wedge of delivery notes six inches thick and thrust them into the pack. Then I grasped an equally thick sandwich of goods receipts and shoved them in next to the delivery notes. I zipped up the pack, strapped it back on and ran from the room.

I turned, and with something icy squeezing my heart, I ignited the remaining contents of first one and then the other filing cabinet. Then I burst through the door of the room opposite, figuring it must lead to the back windows of the building.

Into the room – and in the corner I spied a safe. Perfect. I lashed out at it through the violence of the Shatter Surface, cratering the door with a single heavy blow.

Good enough.

Turning back, I blew out the rear windows as the fire began to roar and to light up the hallway behind me. This was just like the old days: no time to hesitate. I leapt out onto the flat roof and sprinted to the back edge of the building. Without pausing to see who was below, I jumped, Pushing into a high arc over the security fence and dropping down into next door's parking area. It was a thirty foot fall from the highest point, but for this manoeuvre I had plenty of room to land. I rolled as I hit the concrete and this time my ankle held.

I tore through the next fence as quietly as I could, aware of the gathering orange glow immediately behind me, and then scrambled up, over the roof of the next building and down onto a footpath beyond. From there I could thread my way through back streets, moving rapidly on quiet feet, until I was half a mile from the shop. I took a deep breath then and found the cold weight in my chest loosening its hold.

I smartened myself up, tucked the hood, gloves and gold into my backpack and stepped out onto the main road to look for a cab. I got lucky and I was just settling into the black leather of the back seat when the first of the fire engines blew past.

CHAPTER 21

This was a strange feeling. All the elements for panic were present, but I was calm. It was like watching someone stick a scalpel into an anaesthetised arm – my arm. I should feel something: react, scream and shout, but I didn't. My calmness was unbreakable.

But somewhere, beneath the calm, I *was* reacting. Like a madman in a cramped cage, in some deep dungeon, one part of me was silently, impotently freaking out about the previous night's events. Torching the store, the destruction, and the memory of a frigid feeling like flying as I crashed through doors, tearing up anything in my way. In a carefully sealed off part of my mind I was half hysterical because for twenty years, whenever I'd lost control of a situation, I had always turned inwards and imploded. I was always the first and only casualty of my meltdowns. But last night had been different, uncontained, explosive. I'd radiated an angry, surging wildness that felt unpleasantly familiar. My brain had pulsed with destructive impulses, they'd multiplied like bacteria, until they burst out of me, assaulting my surroundings like a shockwave. I knew I would have cut down people with the same savage efficiency that I used to demolish inanimate obstacles in my path.

But the dominant part of me maintained an arctic composure, gliding across an emotionless surface beneath which my tiny, weaker self was trapped. After all, there was no problem. I wasn't seen last night, I didn't fail. No harm was done to my plans. I came away with everything the situation had offered me. The Marker wasn't there, so the next best thing was information about its whereabouts, which I now possessed. There was nothing to berate myself over. The mess was someone else's to clear up and nothing linked me to it.

The only uncertainty was over the police follow-up. There was no sign that I'd tried to steal any antiques, so the investigation was unlikely to view this as a conventional burglary. I didn't especially want the owners of the store to notice the gaps in their paperwork, put two and two together, and warn their clients that someone might be coming to rob them. So I'd had to improvise a false motive for the break-in. On the spur of the moment, the best I could do was to hint at an employee theft gone wrong. The botched safe-cracking would point the police towards a different kind of robbery and the torched employee records would hint that a former member of staff was involved; why else set light to the files unless it was to cover your tracks?

I thought there was a fair chance that the false clues would send the police down the wrong path. And if it didn't work, if the police somehow concluded that the break-in was about stealing client invoices, and the recent customers of the store were warned to be on their guard, well so be it.

It had been noisy – showy even – the way I'd handled things, but there was nothing to be ashamed of. And yet this other noise in my head wouldn't stop its bleating. It was extremely distracting. So

I clamped down my emotions – squeezing as hard as I could – until that twittering voice was throttled into silence.

The effort set off a headache that came from nowhere and seemed to bury its sharp sting just behind my right eye. For a horrible moment, I thought my struggle for composure was going to rupture a blood vessel. But then the headache passed and my control returned. I was feeling fine again – and there would be no more whining and flailing. I just would not stand for it.

I'd taken a shower when I got in and then laid out on my bed for a while, hands behind my head. I couldn't sleep, but then I never had slept much. It was enough that I was able to breathe, to feel my chest rising and falling, to be free.

I wondered how swiftly I would need to act now, to follow-up on last night's captured intelligence. It seemed more important to be thorough than to be quick. The only other task with a conceivable claim on my time was the job of investigating the Army on the Professor's behalf, and really, that didn't seem all that important any more. I told myself, my whining other self, that I would take care of it sooner or later, but privately I was rapidly realising something: I was finished with the PAC. All I cared about now was the Marker.

* * *

Around 7 am, I put on some coffee and found bread and fruit to eat. Noola, if she was in, was still sleeping; her door was closed. I took the coffee back up with me to the top room, pushed the bolt across and spread out the papers from last night's raid.

First, I turned to the receipts. They listed each purchase the shop had made, and somewhere in the pile would be one detailing the last collection from Mr. Niall Harrington. When I found it, I compared the items it listed with my stack of invoices. When I found a match, I could see from the invoice the name and addresses of the customer who bought the item.

Cheryl/Celine had said that only two items from the last Harrington collection had been sold and I hoped she was right. Two was a manageable number when you were planning break-ins.

My money was on the desk being the Marker's hiding place. I had it in mind that a 'Regency pedestal desk' would be about half a ton of intricately worked, endangered hardwood – a perfect blank from which to whittle out a secret compartment. To an anxious adept with something to conceal, it would feel like a safe hiding place.

By 10 am, I'd double-checked the paperwork and confirmed Cheryl's version of things: only two items. I had the contact details for the owners of both the desk and the escritoire, neither of which were in London. So I'd soon be making a couple of road trips. Well, *one*, if I got lucky first time. I decided to get the train out to where the owner of the desk lived that afternoon. Depending on what I found, I might even stay over and attempt my raid on the place that very evening.

The house was near Penshurst, a village in Kent, that according to the sheaves of entries Google retrieved for me was plenty picturesque and mucho historico (I'm paraphrasing). It certainly looked that way from the pictures. I pulled up some maps and saw that I had quite a trek from the station to the house in question – not a problem when I was reconnoitring the place in daylight, but not ideal for a fast getaway after I broke in. Train travel for something like this was a joke. I was really going to have to find myself some adequate personal transport.

I brooded on that for a while, eventually deciding that it was important enough to be worth delaying my retrieval of the desk. I'd still take the train down that afternoon and 'case the joint', as they (used to) say; I'd maybe hike a little through the nearby countryside too, to get a feel for the surroundings, but I wouldn't break into the house until I could come up with something better than a brisk jog as my getaway strategy.

And I already had an idea for how to solve the transport problem, so I did a little research – memorising what I read and picturing the instructions in my mind. A bite of lunch and then it was time to make my way to London Bridge to catch a train to the Kent countryside.

* * *

The trip to the manicured wilds of Kent was uneventful but a success. I returned with photos and sketches of the house where the pedestal desk now resided; I knew what the occupants looked like and I could make some sort of estimate of how best to raid the place.

The owners seemed to be a couple in their sixties, plus a cat; none of them seemed likely to pose much of a problem.

I came back to London in the early evening and headed home for a little nap. I was finally feeling tired enough to need a couple of hours of sleep. In the end I slept until 10pm, which was fine; I only had one more task to perform that day and there was no point in starting it too early.

Before going out, I found some dark clothing, a black wool cap and a heavy leather jacket, and then I left the house heading for the West End. I'd printed out a list of central London multi-storey car parks and now I made my chilly way, on foot, from one to the next. I finally found what I was looking for just round the corner from Leicester Square: half a dozen motorcycles parked on the deserted roof of the car park. And most importantly, there were two of the same high-end make and model: Yamaha YZF-R1's, both in dark blue, both a few years old.

I loitered in the shadows for a couple of minutes, waiting to see if anyone else was around, and simultaneously checking out the closed-circuit cameras. Under my cap I was wearing tribute and now I Connected in order to burn out the sensors in both of the nearby security cameras.

As well as the two R1s I was interested in, there was another bike at the end of the line-up, a ratty old BMW tourer, which had a new-looking helmet padlocked to its seat. I cracked the lock, pulled off my woolly hat, and put the helmet on my head – being careful not to dislodge my headband.

Then I went over to the R1s and got to work removing their number plates and swapping them over. The one on the left looked a little more dinged up, so I decided that would be the one I'd leave behind.

Next I cracked the two shackle-locks securing the bike I planned to take. I hopped on, placing my hand over the slot for the ignition key and concentrated.

It was a fiddly lock, but after thirty seconds or so, I had lined up the tumblers and twisted the cylinder. The bike's instrument panel lit up.

Now for the moment of truth. Sitting astride the R1 I started the engine.

It was a very different thing *reading* about riding a bike to actually doing it. But then again, the only two bikers I knew were a little lower down the intellectual pecking order than the average drummer. If they could do it, so could I.

Kick-stand up, clutch in, put it into gear, little gas, let out the clutch. Not bad. I actually got the thing rolling. No stall and no rubber-scorching wheelie. I ran the bike forty feet across the roof, moving slowly, heading for the edge of the down ramp – and then I brought it to a halt. Turning my head I closed my eyes and reached out, finding the back of the R1 I'd left behind. I Heated the rear licence plate until it was just a lump of charred and smoking plastic. Then I did the same for the front plate.

When the police identified the bikes I was about to wreck, I wanted to make sure they relied on chassis numbers for the R1. When they figured out that one of the bikes was missing and started looking for it, they'd be searching for the plate numbers I'd just incinerated.

And if anyone ran a check on the plate number I was using, they'd find a description that matched this bike, and probably think no more of it. One day soon, those records might list the bike as 'destroyed', but that was better than recording it as 'stolen': the police don't go looking for destroyed vehicles.

Next, I sought out the gas tanks of each bike in the row, lining them up in my mind and *squeezing* Heat into them. I tried to cook them all up together, but it was tricky doing it evenly. At any rate, when one finally ignited, the others blew immediately.

The explosion was a little more than I'd been expecting; it blended into a single, colossal crash which actually sent a couple of pieces of debris hurtling my way. Something hard pinged off my visor, and a piece of metal thumped into my upper arm, causing me some pain even through the leather. I reckoned next time I'd put a Shield in place first.

Filthy black smoke poured out of the fire and flowed along the concrete ceiling, occasionally revealing heat-rippled glimpses of the roasting and broken machines inside the flames. It looked like a scrapheap in hell.

I turned away from the fire and gave the bike a little throttle, letting out the clutch and pulling slowly away from the scene of my second count of pyromania that weekend. I managed not to tip the heavy bike over in the corners as I spiralled carefully down the car park's ramps. I had to Shatter one more camera that might otherwise have captured a clear image of the bike, then I forced up the exit barrier and gave the throttle a little blip as I pulled out onto the dark street.

Belatedly, I remembered to turn on the bike's lights, but even with them on, at slow speeds I found it much easier to ride with my head down, my eyes closed, *feeling* the road, concentrating on my balance and the revving of the engine.

I kept my speed down, heading away from the West End, and drove around the quieter back roads near the edge of the City for most of an hour, getting the hang of the bike. Then I turned south, crossed the Thames and threaded my way back to Stockwell. A couple of times I opened up the throttle, just to see what it was like, whether I could handle it – and it felt fantastic. I managed not to fluff any gear changes or have the thing topple on me as I sat at the lights – though on one occasion I only managed that with a little occult shove at the last minute.

I reckoned I'd give myself a couple of days more practice before I officially declared this bike my getaway vehicle. I'd also rig something with the ignition switch. I couldn't afford to spend best part of a minute concentrating on fiddly tumblers every time I wanted to start the thing. I figured I'd disconnect the multi-position key-switch Yamaha had fitted and instead route the wires to a regular switch and a push button. Flip the switch, push the button and anyone could start the bike in seconds. Just to make sure that anyone didn't, though, I'd wrap the new controls in polythene, smother them in Epoxy and glue them under the tank cover. The bike would be adepts-only then. Only someone Connected would be able to reach under the seat, *through* the glue, and flip the controls. Regular humans would find it a distinct challenge to steal.

I left the bike a couple of streets away and walked the last two hundred yards home. I wasn't tired – in fact I was a little bit psyched from riding around town – but I was happy to lie on the bed, letting my thoughts drift. Instead of sleeping, I spent a couple of hours in a Healing trance, letting it do the job of sleep – and a little more besides. It was an old trick and a good way to always be at your best. Then, around four-thirty, I went for a walk. And as my feet wandered the empty, dayless streets, my mind wandered among the many branching paths of the plans I was making.

CHAPTER 22

Jeez. I saw why they made those bikes so fast; with that engine noise you're not going to be able to *sneak* away. Fortunately, if I kept the revs down to little more than an idle I could almost convince myself that I was being stealthy as I drove through the back roads of the Kent countryside. If asked whether they remembered anything, I didn't want half the county to say, "Well I did look out of my window when I heard a sound like a fighter jet taking off, and I saw this girl going by on a blue motorbike."

A week had passed since the weekend of the antiques fire and the car park fire. I'd swiped the bike in the early hours of Monday morning, initially thinking that I might take it down to Kent the next day. But I'd gone for a long walk after my hog-heist, and I'd done a lot of thinking. I'd worked through each step of my plan to recover the Marker, and I'd visualised as many contingencies and branch-points as I could. Different scenarios might come to the fore depending on how the previous step turned out (i.e. what went wrong) and I wanted to pre-think all of it.

I reckoned my chances of finding myself surrounded by a

contingent of Army assassins rose dramatically the closer I got to the Marker. If they were on to me, I'd need to have my escape route planned before I made that last dash to grab the Marker.

On Monday I checked in with the Professor, even though I really wasn't planning to go back – but I figured there was no sense rushing to burn any bridges yet. If I failed to find the Marker, the PAC might still be useful to me.

The Professor was eager to hear if I'd learned anything new, so I threw him a bone. I told him that I'd discovered Dass was part of some secret society called The Army Who Witnessed Creation. It wasn't news to him, of course, but it proved I was making real progress on the sleuthing.

Then, a few days later, I shared a couple of titbits on the non-magical history of the sect that I happened to recall – nothing terribly useful, some famous names from the past, a few details on the evolution of their territory. It was old news really, but it captured the Professor's imagination. He was very impressed and wanted to know where I'd found that information. For a moment I couldn't recall, so I made up a lie about managing to hack into Interfinanzio's computer system and finding some of Dass's personal files.

He sounded me out on that, clearly wondering if I'd stumbled upon any references to magic, but he didn't want to come right out and ask. So I played dumb: as far as I was concerned, this was still Harriet the Spy, and not the X-Files.

Checking in every day was starting to become a pain, so I also told him that I was coming down with something and I probably wouldn't phone for a little while, until my poor throat was feeling better and I was ready to get back to work. And we left it at that.

So it was the middle of my second week in London before I was ready to head down to Kent. I'd taken the bike out a half a dozen times, and driven round for an hour or so. While I wasn't ready for [insert the famous bike race of your choice] yet, I was feeling pretty comfortable getting around on the thing. The one hiccup had come when I ran low on gas and pulled into a petrol station. I'd stopped at the pump before I remembered that filler caps have locks on them – and without tribute, I wasn't going to be able to be able to open this one without a hammer or a cutting torch. So I headed home, grabbed my tribute, sprang the lock, and made it to the nearest petrol station without running out of gas completely. I left the filler cap unlocked after that and hang the risk of petrol theft.

* * *

On Wednesday evening, I made my final preparations and then drove down to Penshurst. I got there about 7pm – comfortably after dark – and parked the bike outside a nearby pub where it wouldn't attract attention. Then I walked the couple of hundred yards to the house. It was red-brick with a tile roof, but it was old – I'd guess at least two hundred years. The windows were mullioned or bastioned or whatever the word was. They were made from coaster-sized diamond-shapes of glass set in a lead lattice. They'd be child's play to get through.

I found a way to get off the road and circle round to the back of the property. The land behind the back garden was open and beyond their fence there were lots of trees for cover, and after that farmland. I've never been much for climbing trees, but it seemed the sensible thing to do here. So I hauled myself up and found a good perch from which to observe the back of the house.

Downstairs, the curtains were drawn – though I could see the lights were on – but upstairs the curtains were open and I had a view right through into the master bedroom. Several times I caught glimpses of the lady of the house as she passed the window. She was getting ready to go out. She had on a floor-length gown in grey satin and she was fixing her hair and trying on jewellery. After twenty minutes or so she went away for a minute and came back carrying a mug of something that steamed. She went somewhere with the mug in her hands and a minute later the upstairs lights went out. Soon after that I glimpsed her downstairs, checking that the kitchen door was locked.

They were definitely going somewhere, which was perfect.

In the still night air, I heard a car door slam and the distant echoing ring of a doorbell. I was fairly sure I could hear an engine idling too. Intrigued, I sprang down from the tree and trotted back round until I reached the road. I didn't emerge out onto the lane but loitered in the bushes – from where I could see a taxi on the sweep of gravel in front of the house. A moment later, the couple came out, the man in a tuxedo and the woman with a fur wrap over her grey gown. The man dallied for a moment, just inside the door, kind of hunched into the wall with one hand up by his nose. It took a second for me to figure out what he was doing: he was pushing numbers on a keypad to set the alarm. Then he closed the door behind him, they both got into the taxi and it pulled away.

So the house was going to be empty. And an alarm wasn't any trouble. This was looking like child's play – assuming children burgled houses – which I'm sure they do these days; the little tykes.

I went back to my tree at the rear of the property and waited, giving the owners twenty minutes to come back for their tickets or to remember that they'd left the bath running, but they didn't return.

From my perch I could tell that the road at the front of the house was fairly quiet – maybe one car per minute – but you'd still have to be ODing on testosterone to break in the front way. The back garden, on the other hand was very private. The house had only one near neighbour, whose curtains were all closed. If I went in that way, there was no one to see me.

I shuffled along my branch, leaned out and then jumped. With a little Push I was able to clear the back fence and roll lightly onto the grass of the lawn. Very nice. It was a strange feeling: one bit of me calmly controlling my tuck and roll, the other part of my brain jabbering that I'd never had a gym class in my life that didn't end badly. Fortunately the capable side of my personality seemed to have settled into the driving seat on a permanent basis.

I loped up the lawn and stood to one side of the back door, in the deep shadows there. There was a window just next to me, which appeared to be for an old-fashioned pantry. There was a ventilated mesh thing that I associated with the larders of old houses.

Reaching out with my mind, I probed around the edge of the pantry window. I could feel a smooth plastic lump on the other side of the frame: undoubtedly a sensor. Concentrating on the fine detail I could tell it was in two parts, just like the sensors on the doors back at the antique store. It was just a simple magnetic switch – separate the halves to trigger the alarm.

Now, as you'll undoubtedly recall, lead melts at 327°C. A little hot for a sauna, but still an achievable temperature to aim for when you're planning to do a little occult metalwork. Working my way all around the lattice of the window, I applied Heat to the lead beading until it began to wilt, and the lattice of the window started to come apart. With a gentle application of Push I made sure that it slumped out towards me, rather than inwards.

I slipped out of my leather jacket, held it like the net firemen hold for jumpers, and caught the drooping nougat of soft lead and chunks of window glass as it sagged free from its frame. I should say I caught *most* of it; a couple of diamonds of glass dropped a foot or so onto the flagstones. They clattered a little, but didn't break.

It didn't sound like much: no louder than someone dropping a metal fork onto a hard kitchen floor. Even so, I set the glass down, put my jacket back on and stayed where I was, ready to move, waiting for any sign that I'd been discovered.

I gave it three or four minutes, which felt like thirty, and when nothing happened, I climbed in through the empty window frame – being careful not to kick the magnetic sensor with my boot. In the darkness, I could sense the jars and bottles on the shelves around me and I managed to move past them without knocking anything over. I had to use Push to release the catch on the pantry door before I could open it and step out into the shadow-filled kitchen. The house was silent around me.

I left the lights turned out and stood in the centre of the kitchen, reaching out beyond the walls to investigate the nearby rooms. Beyond the kitchen I could sense the cavity of a hallway just inside the front door. From there, doors led off to other ground floor rooms and a staircase doubled back on itself to connect with the upstairs landing.

The largest pocket of empty space I could discern lay the other side of the staircase. Leaving the kitchen, I quietly crossed the hall and opened the door into a large sitting room. The space felt cool and dusty, compared with the kitchen – unlived in – and various pieces of old furniture were arranged around the room, including a baby grand piano by the window.

No pedestal desk though. Neither was it in the other main room on this floor: a warmer space that contained a TV and a gas fire – both recently turned off but still leaking heat into the room.

So I made my way slowly upstairs trying to minimise the creak and chirp of the old timbers as I shifted my weight on the treads. The time-warped wood amplified every movement and my footsteps seemed like they might bring the staircase to life, causing it to start up like a steam organ at a fairground. Sure, I wasn't making a fraction of the noise needed for the neighbours to hear, but I couldn't help feeling that a professional would move a little more stealthily.

As it turned out, there was a better reason than just professionalism for keeping the noise down. As I reached the upstairs landing, the tread of the top step croaked like a frog as my weight lifted. A moment later, a bleary voice called out, "Mum?"

I froze, ready to run or fight. The door ahead of me opened and a woman in her early thirties shuffled out, her hair a snarl of bed-pressed curls. She was wearing thick, fleecy pyjamas and holding a Kleenex to her stuffy, red nose.

"Did you guys…" she asked and then saw me, a stranger, clad in heavy black clothes, my head hooded, standing at the top of her stairs, illuminated by the light spilling out of her room. She started as she caught sight of me, and then a moment later jumped back with a yelp and tried to slam the door to her room.

Chances were that she had a phone in there. I leapt forwards, getting my shoulder to the door before she could close it. For a second we struggled and then I added some Push from my side and she was rammed backwards, stumbling over her own feet. She back-pedalled, colliding with a dainty-looking table and went down.

I took one step into the room and had to duck as something heavy and made of marble smacked into the wall beside my head, its weighty corner punching through the wallpaper and kicking out chips of plaster. She'd heaved one of the ornaments from the toppled table at me. I took another step and looked around for a phone; maybe she had a mobile. A moment later she grabbed the other ornament, a tall, thin African statue of a face. It was made of some dense-looking black wood and she leapt at me swinging it like a club.

I reacted without thinking, punching her out of the air with a pulse of Shatter. I saw her head slam sideways off the door of the wardrobe hard enough to splinter the wood and then she went down like a marionette with its strings cut.

For a moment I stood panting, unsure of myself. I'd nearly hit her a lot harder, except I'd messed up the attack. Even as I was lashing out through the Shatter surface, pouring force into the blow, I was simultaneously pulling back, draining the power of the assault. A part of me had tried to stop the blow even as I had summoned the energy to attack her.

But despite my inner conflict, she'd been thrown pretty hard into that door.

I just stood there, wandering what to do next.

A moment later I heard an unpleasant sound. Blood was bubbling as the woman breathed. She was alive, but her head was arched back, her arm under her. It was painful to look at her in that contorted position.

I took a step forwards, determined to help her, before my self-control kicked in. We were here for one reason alone: the Marker.

As a concession to my clamouring conscience, I decided that when I was done here I would take the phone off the hook and dial the emergency services – just before I left – but not until I'd found that desk and got what I came for.

The desk wasn't in the woman's bedroom – which I imagined her parents used as a guest room when she wasn't visiting – and I doubted it was in the back bedroom I'd spied on earlier from the tree. (I remembered the hot drink the mother had been carrying now and realised who it had been intended for.)

I extended my senses and tried the next room along. I could feel, even before I pushed the door open, that it was a study.

The desk I was looking for sat under the window. I crossed the room to place my hands on the leather inlay of its top surface. I spread my fingers and set about infiltrating my senses into the structure of the wood, feeling out the mechanism of the drawers, testing the spliced joints of the frame.

There was something here. Something.

I could sense a space inside the desk, barely an inch under the tooled leather top. I explored around the edges of the cavity, trying to see how the parts of the desk fitted together. A few moments later, I found the hidden lock. The maker of the desk had added a strip of wood that ran in a groove along the underside of the desktop. If a person opened the top drawer, stuck their hand in about ten inches and felt upwards with their fingers, they would find a depression just deep enough to get some purchase on. Placing two fingers in the depression and pulling forwards would slide the strip in its groove and unlock a hidden catch.

Except that someone had severed the strip. Pulling on it did nothing now. There was no way to undo the lock anymore… unless you could reach inside the desk with your mind and manipulate the locking mechanism through an inch of solid mahogany. Like my bike, this hiding place was adepts-only now.

Probing carefully, I found the break and moved my focus past it until I reached the internal lever it used to be attached to. Then, I applied Push to activate the mechanism. An unseen catch beneath the front of the desktop released, allowing it to angle up like the hood of a car, pivoting on secret hinges.

I lifted the lid, sending a lamp, some stationery and various knick-knacks sliding onto the floor. Inside, under the lid, was a shallow tray, lined with velvet. In the tray were papers. I lifted them out, looking for something beneath them, looking for the Marker. Surely this was the hiding place: somewhere that only Jan could reach.

But there was nothing except papers.

I crouched over the opened desk and probed the velvet lining: was there another layer? Did the tray itself lift out to reveal something beneath? I focussed so hard that I could feel each indentation in the cloth. With a surge of adrenaline I found a depression in the nap that matched the shape of the Marker. It had been here once, pressed into the velvet. But now it was gone.

I felt rage mounting inside me. Not the meek, whining, emotional part of me. Now, for the first time, the ruthless, calculating part of my brain was feeling rage and it *refused* to be thwarted like this.

I sat down on the floor next to where the lamp lay and turned it on. Despite its fall it still worked, and by its light I examined the papers, hoping that they would give me the information I needed. For a while I couldn't make them out, but as I hurriedly scanned them, hope rekindled itself and the rage drained away. There were details here of another place that Jan owned and a sketch of something. It was another hiding place – a *final* hiding place; I felt sure of it.

I took a moment to shut the desktop, clicking the catch closed. Then I put on a show for the police: ripping open a couple of drawers until I found a wallet containing banknotes in several currencies and a number of savings books. I grabbed them, bundled them together with the papers from the secret compartment, and zipped them into my backpack.

Back out on the landing, I headed for the stairs... but found I was desperate to look in on the injured woman. I couldn't help myself; I wanted to see if she was still breathing. I was imagining a spreading pool of blood, her ragged breathing catching and slowing until it ceased.

I shook my head, pushing those thoughts out of my mind, and headed downstairs. On the hall table I passed a telephone and I stopped in front of it. With my gloved hand, I laid the receiver to one side, punched the digits for the emergency operator and made to move towards the back door. For a second I couldn't force myself to leave; I was frozen in place, and then I heard the voice of the operator repeating her question: "Which service do you require? Hello?"

"I need an ambulance," I yelled towards the receiver and that seemed to free me to move my feet again. I ran into the kitchen and turned towards the pantry intending to leave the way I'd come in.

But another rebellious thought stopped me. I'd give the injured woman one more chance at getting some help. I remembered her father configuring the alarm before he left, which meant it was on.

Instead of heading for the pantry window, I ducked down behind the kitchen countertop, focussed on the back door, and blew the lock inwards. Still attached to a chunk of door, it bounced past me across the tile floor and slammed into something out in the hall. The backdoor was flung inwards and now, from the front of the house, I could hear an alarm bell starting to ring. I ran out through the open door and down the garden.

When I reached the rear of the property I jumped, Pushing myself up and over the fence, tucking into a ball as I crashed through some tree branches, and landing on all fours among the leaf litter. I stood and dusted myself down, then I trotted through the woods, and across the corner of a ploughed field, until I could see the roof of the pub. I hopped a fence, finding myself on a footpath that led along the side of the pub's car park.

I Froze out the single light that illuminated the path and stood in the darkness, feeling with my extended senses across the expanse of asphalt beyond, hunting for the bike.

I found it, and spread out my focus looking for observers. At that moment, the car park seemed to be empty of people. Narrowing my concentration once more, I felt my way along the bike's frame until I located the epoxied controls and I started the engine.

Once it was running, I sprinted to the end of the lane, stepped over into the pub garden and walked briskly back to my idling bike. I pulled on my helmet, jumped on and shoved the bike forward on its kickstand, dropping it into gear and moving quickly out onto the road. I flicked on the lights but kept the revs low and the throttle barely open until I'd covered a half mile and I dared to make a little noise.

Throughout all of this – right from the moment I'd slammed that woman's skull into a wardrobe door – I'd been in shock. The ruthless, practical part of me was in sole charge, while whichever remnant of my old self it was that possessed a conscience looked on in stunned horror. Only twice in the following ten minutes had my humanity surfaced: once to make that phone call, the other time to trigger the alarm.

I roared back up the A21, staying under the speed limit, and tried to keep my mind from fracturing into two separate halves – with whatever consequent loss of sanity that might entail.

The impact of skull hitting wood played over and over, and I knew that something had changed.

CHAPTER 23

Do you ever have dreams where you watch yourself from the outside? I've heard that sometimes people who've come close to death say they saw themselves from above, as though their spirits had left their bodies and were looking down on them.

I felt like that now, except my spirit was trapped inside me – no longer wholly connected to my body but still imprisoned within it. I could monitor myself, see what I was doing, but I wasn't in control.

The sense of paralysis and dread that crept over me as I realised what was happening brought to mind something disturbing I'd once read in a medical journal, about the recipient of a limb transplant who was gradually driven to the edge of madness by the feeling that his pale new flesh, though a part of him now, still wasn't his own. He had finally insisted that the hospital cut off his new hand so that he could get some peace. With a feeling that grew like an itch beneath my skin, I thought I knew how he'd felt.

When I'd first used magic, when I had the ice dream, I had thought that magic was freeing me, fixing me. I thought it had cured me of whatever it was that had always held me back, that had screwed things up for me. I'd welcomed this improved, stronger me – unfamiliar though it was. That new strength was disorienting but wonderful and everything had suddenly seemed so easy, so effortless. But now I'd come to realise it was effortless because it wasn't me doing it. I found everything easy because all I was doing was watching, while someone (some thing?) pulled the levers, took the strain and made my decisions for me.

What ever was happening to me, I was no longer in charge of my life.

The feeling that things were badly wrong in some new and horrible way had been growing inside me for days. I had watched myself with an increasing sense of isolation, even disapproval. I found myself acting even before I'd considered what I wanted to do. And if I did reach some sort of decision ahead of time it seemed to have no effect: I'd see myself follow some totally different course of action.

So why didn't I fight? Why didn't I even realise what was happening? Well for a time I thought I knew what it was: it was simply the old, neurotic me reacting with spite and resentment to my new, capable attitude to life. The old me *liked* being miserable, was comfortable in its familiar pit of despair, so *of course* that part of me felt unsettled, hijacked even.

Long ago sessions with half-forgotten therapists had even warned me this would happen. The old and bad would feel familiar, the new and good would feel strange. I had to embrace the new. But I'd never managed it, partly because the bad voices were the ones that seemed most like *me*. So initially, when I'd noticed this growing sense of split personality, that's what I thought was causing it.

And even then I'd felt like something bad was happening, but somehow I hadn't been able to dwell on my concerns; my mind refused to lock on to the problem. As soon as I started to focus on the *wrongness* I was feeling, everything slowed, it became difficult to concentrate, and my mind wandered. But if I abandoned that train of thought I felt better, more purposeful. My head only stayed clear if I concentrated on the task in hand: the search for the Marker. Nothing else mattered.

I now realised that some internal censor in my head had been pulling the plug on more than just my sense of wrongness. There were questions that I should have been asking, riddles that had fascinated me just a few weeks before, that I couldn't seem to find time for now. Like, where did magic come from? How did it work? Given who I was, I should have been obsessed, *relentless* in fact, when it came to those questions. But I'd hardly given them a thought – hardly *been able* to give them a thought.

I'd caught myself thinking over past events and remembering things that had never happened; I recalled facts that I'd never learned, like the information about the Army that had just popped into my head when I was talking to the Professor.

I mean, *I* didn't know Latin; I certainly didn't have a pet Latin maxim about the dark, even though I'd chuckled to myself about it. *I* hadn't watched opium devour old friends, yet I felt the residue of that anger as I walked through the junkie's alleyway. *I* shouldn't have known how to manipulate the Surfaces like a master of two centuries' standing but it came to me like I was born to it. None of this was me.

Then this evening something had shifted; something had torn. I had been too horrified by my own actions to carry on as before. And with my conscious awareness of the rift, came a change, a divergence. Now that I knew – absolutely *knew* – that some other agency was at work here, I found my true thoughts starting to separate themselves from their impostors. Someone was still steering the motorbike, watching the road, mulling over the contents of the documents from the desk, but it *distinctly* wasn't me. *I* was mentally huddled in a corner gibbering to myself and panicking.

It now seemed obvious to me that magic was something more than the PAC had realised; it was more than just a way to affect the world. It *did* something to you. It implanted itself in you.

But it didn't just alter what it touched; it added to it. So where did those extra memories come from? Someone's agenda had overridden my own – where did it originate? Was there an actual personality at work here? Could there be some sort of intelligence behind magic, a being at the heart of it all who could influence adepts, who could subvert them while letting them think they were in control?

Yet I didn't think Susan or David had experienced this, or the Professor. Had Jan? Had Dass? Why hadn't I heard of this phenomenon? If other adepts had felt what I was feeling, sooner or later they'd for-damn-sure notice – or those around them would. Not only had I read dozens of the PAC's documents on the nature, tradition and application of magic without seeing a mention of such a thing, I had also glimpsed the layers of knowledge and memory that had coalesced in my mind from elsewhere – knowledge that allowed me to manipulate magic like a master – and it didn't include the memory of being influenced, of having to guard against being controlled.

And yet there was something…

I 'remembered' (though it couldn't be *my* memory I was drawing on) a facet of the training embarked upon by new adepts (in the days when there *had* been new adepts – that was another fact that appeared from nowhere). I recalled an exercise to ward off distracting influences and fey moods which might otherwise settle upon the novice. The more I thought about it, the more it seemed to hint at an outside agency invading the vulnerable minds of those new to magic. But it was a fleeting, tenuous thing they were guarding against – like an unwanted daydream or a gloomy mood that was difficult to shake – all in all about as much of a problem as an annoying song stuck in your head. Was that some mild strain of the full-blown affliction I was suffering from? Was I the only one to get the virulent form of this malady? What was so special about me?

But wait. Hadn't there been something else? I vaguely remembered pressing 'delete' in exasperation, shortly after I began to read one of the PAC's scanned, ancient manuscripts. Which document? Why had I deleted it? I struggled to recall the moment, and that effort detached a scrap of sequestered memory and allowed it to float up to the surface. The outside influence in my head had forced me to erase a document in which someone began to recount a dream they'd had and I wondered what I would have found if I'd read on. A clue perhaps, an echo of my own predicament?

It was tantalising, but whatever else that document contained, I was sure it wasn't the sole surviving mention of a legion of possessed adepts, their minds all slaved to some controlling entity. There was no getting around it: if others had had their heads invaded by something with the same implacable strength as the force that was controlling me, then the PAC's collection of manuscripts should be full of warnings.

As far as I could see, these were the only possibilities: 1) Those possessed aroused no suspicions in others and were unable to tell anyone that they were possessed – which didn't fit, because lots of people had noticed a profound change in *me*. 2) Every adept was possessed so there was no one left unaffected to raise the alarm

– but I didn't believe that David, Susan, the Professor and the Army Who were under the same influence as me – for a start wouldn't we all be one big happy family? 3) I was pretty much the only victim of this force.

I couldn't think of any other options. Either I was the only one, or few enough others had been affected that the PAC documents held no mention of them. I'd somehow fallen victim to a side-effect of magic use that everyone else was immune to.

It figures, I suppose.

And there was another, perhaps more disturbing way of looking at this[1]. I mean, if it was just me, how did I know that magic was to blame? How did I know this wasn't a problem more psychiatric than occult, if you see what I mean? Instead of fixing me, could repeated exposure to the Healing surface have scrambled some important circuit in my brain? Had magic taken a mind weak from two decades of neurosis and created a fracture – a full-on psychotic break? Maybe this whole crisis was bubbling up out of a crack in my subconscious. Perhaps I was inventing these foreign memories and concocting a mission for myself the way a paranoid schizophrenic invents voices and weaves them into some urgent, but ultimately deranged objective.

At least I hadn't killed anyone. Yet.

This was not a happy line of thought.

If it was my own mind that was disintegrating then how could I hope to battle that? I would be fighting against my self. But then the alternative – some sort of demonic possession – didn't appeal much either. All you could say in its favour was that at least if my oppressor was real (whatever I meant by that) then maybe they could be beaten.

---

[1] Or, given that we were talking about possession here, maybe it *wasn't* more disturbing.

Then something obvious and duh-worthy struck me. If this was all part of some psychosis then that meant I was inventing everything, that I was conjuring up my false memories and my impossible knowledge out of thin air. So how come I was doing such a good job of it? A schizophrenic might imagine himself to be Jesus Christ, but that didn't mean he could walk on water. Thinking you were Napoleon didn't make you a military genius. If I'd *fantasised* all these insights into the use of magic, how come they all worked? I might still be crazy, but that didn't mean I was imagining things.

Someone else was in my head.

* * *

So, like I say, I was in shock. After I left the house in Penshurst and the injured woman, I had withdrawn inside myself; I had let the other me run everything while I tried to come to terms with what I'd seen and felt. I've given you the gist of it, but getting to the point where I knew this other personality was real, that someone – or something – external was influencing me had taken several hours of fevered introspection – with revelation alternating with disbelief – in which time my body drove itself home, courtesy of its eerie new master. When I started paying attention again, I found myself looking at the papers I'd (we'd?) removed from that antique desk. They were spread out on my bed and I was stretched out next to them examining them minutely. My tribute lay on the bedside table next to me.

There were official-looking bills, handwritten notes, confusing scribbles. Since my eyes were looking in that direction, I decided to give them my attention for a little while. Whatever else happened, I needed to understand the mission I found myself on.

I joined my puppet master in looking over Jan's secret papers. From what I could make out, Jan had another address, a place we hadn't known about. But there was something strange about it. Among the papers was an invoice for all sorts of charges relating to this new property and many of them made no sense to me. I couldn't figure out what most of the abbreviations meant. In fact the address itself was strange. It clearly wasn't a conventional house, but I couldn't work out whether it was a flat in an apartment block, a room in some commercial building, or just a plot of sub-divided land. The address was in East London, in somewhere called New Charlton, along from Greenwich, south of the river.

Yes, I would go there tomorrow to spy out the location.

But that wasn't me talking. *I* hadn't just decided to go there. It was so easy to mistake the thoughts of this other presence for my own.

I was going to have to examine every notion, every impulse that passed through my mind, in order to decide where it had come from. How else could I begin to trust – and perhaps to reclaim – my own mind?

But I realised I had an advantage. Ever since my new owner had arrived, he had been doing the same thing – separating my thoughts from his and pushing his to the front. (Wait, did I say 'he'? I realised that I thought of this other personality as male; somehow I knew that.)

OK, well *he* had been using something a lot like 'cognitive therapy' on me. From my own experience I knew it worked by teaching someone to recognise their negative, destructive thoughts and to shut them down – or at least interrupt them. That's what he'd been doing to me, except he'd been derailing any thought process of mine that didn't fit his plans. My brain already had several weeks' practice at this internal censoring process. Now all I had to do was flip things around and apply that same process to cutting off *his* thoughts instead of mine.

And this interloper hadn't had it all his own way. He hadn't met with total success. The real me, the old me, had got past him on a number of occasions. It was the old me who stopped him killing that woman tonight. (A wave of guilt rose up as I thought of her. I'd attacked her with such violence that it horrified me.)

But then it wasn't *me* who'd done it; at least I knew that now. *I* was the one sabotaging the attack, metaphorically grabbing his arm. Even so, I felt horrible. I should have fought harder, realised sooner what was going on. For a while I couldn't stop thinking about that woman, wondering if she was alive, whether she was still lying there, drifting closer and closer to death.

But then I caught myself. I'd done what I could and obsessing wasn't going to help. I would think about this guilt later; right now I needed to focus on things that would help – like figuring out how I was going to extricate myself from this mess.

A moment later it dawned on me that I'd just successfully tested my new weapon: I'd cut off an unproductive train of thought about the injured woman. In the old days, I'd have disappeared into my own head for hours when faced with that much guilt, but this time I'd seen that line of thinking for what it was: a distracting mental loop that would prevent me from fixing the situation. I had recognised a bad impulse and shut it down – and *he* was next. I had no idea whether I could beat him, but I could sure as hell fight him.

There was even a chance that I could *force* him out if I just concentrated hard enough. Maybe I could stand up to him and take back control by exerting my will powerfully enough and refusing to let him manipulate me. After all, it was my body; I'd grown up in it; it was used to taking orders from me. Surely I had what followers of golf, or was it hockey, called 'the home court advantage'... if I could only use it.

I stood up, right that moment, scattering papers onto the floor. I could sense him trying to stop me but I forced my body to obey me. I willed myself to step over to the table and then I grabbed my mobile phone, calling up Daniel's number. I didn't even need to think about it; he was the one person I could trust to believe me and to help. I pushed the button to dial.

It began to ring.

And ring. Then it went through to his answerphone.

Damn it.

"Daniel Maclay has left the building... for the time being. Please leave him a message." Then there was a beep.

What the hell should I say? I just started talking: "Daniel, there's something I need to tell you. Actually it's something the whole PAC needs to hear. It's about me, about how I've been behaving. I... it hasn't really been me, not the *real* me. I need to see you all as soon as possible. Call me when you get this. It's important, Daniel." I hung up.

It was a ramble, I knew, but I hadn't wanted to spell out the details any more explicitly, because then I'd have come off as crazy. You just couldn't blurt out something like this in ten words or less. You really, at the least, needed to set the scene.

Throughout the call I had feel the presence fighting me, but I had got my way. I put down the phone and sat back down on the bed. It had been an immense effort – taking back full control for thirty seconds had exhausted me as though I'd just run a marathon – but I'd done it. The strain hung heavily on me now, though underneath I was feeling elated. This seemed like the first taste of victory.

And then the fatigue got worse, ratcheting up and up in sudden jumps as though someone was pulling out the fuses, one-by-one, that fed power to my body. Suddenly I was struggling to even keep my eyes open.

I let myself flop back on the bed, worried that I'd fall if I didn't lie down. I was still in control, able to direct my limbs, decide what I wanted my body to do, but it was a body drained of energy.

I felt darkness starting to close in, as though I was being lowered into the ground. I was still looking out at the world, but it was from the bottom of a hole that kept getting deeper, and which took me down with it.

Was I dying?

Now the world was a diminishing circle far above me and I knew that soon it would disappear completely.

Just before I passed out, something came to me. The clash with my invader was twisting and buckling the seams of our shared consciousness and the vats of memory were beginning to spill over. I realised this: that my mother had never made jewellery. The necklace I was wearing was nothing to do with her. Why had I thought otherwise?

It was from him.

That seemed important somehow, but now my eyes were closed and my arms and legs weighed so many tons that I couldn't think how I could move them. The bed underneath me pressed into my back and it felt wonderfully, sinfully soft. And then the light was gone and blackness was everywhere, and all around me I could hear the ice cracking and shifting as it had done for uncounted centuries. In the faraway dark I began to make out the threads of pale-blue sunlight, filtered through miles of frozen seawater. And then, once more, I was gliding across the ice sheet, imagining I was on the deck of a ship racing ahead of the wind. There was nothing to think about except the driving arctic gale hammering and snapping at the sails, and the naked exhilaration of speed.

It was just as I'd experienced before, just as that long-ago writer had detailed in his journal… the journal I'd glimpsed momentarily on my laptop screen, just before a sudden, forceful impulse had brought my fingertip down on the delete button. The document had disappeared, just as the world was doing now.

CHAPTER 24 – TOLD BY SUSAN MILTON

The barn was quiet; I was on my own. David would still be in the air – moving further away from me with every second. He wouldn't be landing for seven more hours. For the first time in what seemed a long while I had no training partner.

I wondered how he was doing. He wasn't crazy about planes although he refused to admit it. And I worried that when he got to Hong Kong he'd get himself into trouble somehow. It was like a gift with him. But, bless him, he was also tenaciously good at getting himself out of trouble too. Maybe it was all the practice he got.

I wish I could have gone instead – not least because there was a reasonable chance that he'd buy the wrong manuscript and pay over the odds for it – but everyone else had been unanimous: I should keep a low profile. As they pointed out, Karst barely got a look at him back in that church.

Add to that the fake information I'd given the hospital when they tried to treat his injuries and it was clear: there was far less chance of the Army Who tracking him down compared with me. If only I'd done a better job of covering my own tracks then I could be sitting next to him now, annoying him and biting his earlobe when he tried to sleep.

But I hadn't *entirely* forgotten how to train solo. I limbered up and worked through a few fencing drills with the sabre. It made just the right ripping noise as it cut the air and I could feel my balance, centred and responsive, shifting properly through the steps.

A year of Healing trances had done good things for my range of motion. It had been fine before, excellent even, but now it was back to that double-jointed springiness I vaguely remembered from competitions in my freshman year of high-school.

David had been teaching me some Kendo katas, so I worked on one of those next. But I fudged the changes and messed up the footwork, so I abandoned that idea. He'd have to show me it again.

Without my training buddy, I couldn't practice combat properly, but I decided it might be a good chance to work on something less athletic. There were some concentration and control exercises I wanted to spend more time on. Dexterity through the Push surface had been a big thing with me for a while now – really, ever since I'd first Connected.

And in my pocket I always kept one of those little plastic mazes with the ball-bearing inside to help me work on my fine control. David bought me a new one whenever he travelled – or I should say whenever he passed a really cheap-looking novelty store – and I had some horribly garish treasures in my collection. I realised after a while that he was buying the ugly ones on purpose. That tricky sense of humour of his playing up again, no doubt.

Anyway, I had a new exercise of extreme, fiendish difficulty to work on; though it sounded easy enough. I dropped a tennis ball and then bounced it, just using Push. The closer to the floor one kept the ball, the more accurate one's timing had to be: lots of small, quick, regular taps. And even if you made things easier and bounced it high, to give yourself more reaction time, that just made directional control trickier. The concentration required was intense. It just wore you down the longer you worked at it.

Today seemed like a day to really test myself. I thought maybe I'd been letting myself off too easy lately. I'd make this a real fiery test of stamina. And it was less of a problem to really push myself if David wasn't around; I'd been on at him not to over-train so I was always careful to follow my own advice in front of him. Today, though, I felt like going for it.

The worst thing with this exercise was that I tended to bunch my shoulder muscles and give myself a stiff neck and a headache. I'd tighten up my shoulders even though this was supposed to be a purely mental exercise. I'd *really* be missing David when I had no tame masseur to rub my neck later.

Anyway, I threw the ball out into the middle of our sparring circle and gave it a slap with Push. It spun off at some crazy angle and I had to start again. Pretty soon, though, I found a good rhythm.

After a while I really got into it, trying variations, walking the ball around the circle, bouncing it from side to side. It would get away from me and I'd have to start over, but I kept the drill going. I was totally absorbed and I quickly lost track of the passing time. I finally had to stop because the sweat was running into my eyes and I couldn't reach my towel without taking my eyes off the ball.

I mentally called break time and stopped to catch my breath. This was hard work. I rooted out my water bottle from my bag and sat on the edge of the old couch. I swallowed half the water without pausing; I reckoned I'd sweated away easily that much already.

The tiredness I was feeling wasn't just from the exercise; I was fairly sleep-deprived too. I hadn't slept all that well the night before and it seemed to be catching up with me now. I was used to David being around and I'd kept waking, thinking that he'd got up and wondering what was wrong, if there was a problem. And each time I had to remind myself he was in London, because he needed to be at the airport in the morning.

Sitting there, I was tempted to call it a day, but I found I was just a little annoyed with myself. The plan had been to make this a marathon session and I knew I had a little more in me. I found David's jump-rope and tried some skipping. I really went at it, getting my heart pounding and my blood flowing.

When my legs started to cramp and I couldn't stop the trembling in my calves I switched to the punch-bag, pounding the cracked leather until my shoulders and lats were screaming.

A moment of dizziness brought me back to reality and I decided to stop and sit down for a minute. I've got a lot of stamina but I was coming to the end of it now. This work-out had become kind of brutal.

It was exactly what I told David not to do. I liked to think that I'd helped him get a little better at spotting the difference between discipline and masochism, and since I'd stopped him over-training, he was actually in better shape than when I'd met him. So I really should have known better than to torture myself like that.

I found a spare bottle of water and perched on the arm of the couch to drain it. I was actually feeling sick from the training; I couldn't remember the last time that had happened. Sitting there, panting, I realised that the lack of sleep, and the strain of pushing myself so hard, were really starting to gang up on me.

I let myself slide off the arm and down onto the couch itself. It felt so comfortable that it was actually a little bit tempting just to take a nap here. But I'm used to that temptation. I'd never get any training done if I gave into it. I made to get up...

But I didn't; I stopped. There was some stray thought wriggling in my mind and it seemed important. But it had flitted away for now. I wanted to capture it before I got up and maybe drove it away for good.

Nope, it was gone. Even so, I decided to give myself a couple more minutes rest. My heart was still thumping and I wasn't feeling great. And this ratty old couch felt like a feather bed at the moment. I leant back, stretching and then relaxing, and allowed my eyes to close just for a little while, as I tried to find that important thought again.

My mind wandered and for a few minutes I think I must have drifted off entirely. For a while, probably less than five minutes, I was dead to the world – and I had the most extraordinary dream – a dream that for a while I couldn't quite recall. Only my reaction stayed with me, the sense of something strange and vivid, but the detail itself had passed behind a cloud and I couldn't make it out.

I wondered why the experience seemed so sharp, so unusual... but then I *was* sitting upright with my neck stretched back over a dusty sofa – it wasn't exactly conducive to normal sleep patterns. I was a little surprised that I didn't dream of being folded in half backwards.

I woke from my doze with a start, and rescued my neck from its painful stretch. For just a second I didn't know where I was. *Man*, I must really have been out of it.

I got another little jolt of surprise when I noticed I was still wearing tribute. Whenever I wore it I thought of myself as being ready to fight, it was like strapping on my mental armour or something. And I didn't like the idea that I'd fallen asleep like that; it sort of mocked the whole idea of being in steely-eyed combat mode.

I must be getting old, I thought to myself. Dozing off during the day wasn't something I ever did. But growing up I remembered how my grandfather could fall asleep in a chair practically in mid-sentence. But he had been ancient when Adam was a lad, as David would say. I rarely found sleep that easy.

As I mulled over the residue of my dream, I found that my thoughts had drifted to the subject of Jo Hallett. I still didn't know how I felt about her as a person, even though she'd won over the Professor and maybe David. Daniel Maclay, of course, could see no wrong in her. But for my part, I didn't totally trust her recent transformation; it seemed too good to be true.

If she'd changed for the better and put her troubled past behind her then I'd have liked to know the reason for it. I certainly believe people *can* change, but I don't know how often they do so without a little nudge. I wanted to know what had nudged her.

Somehow I couldn't see Jo just waking up one day and deciding to sort herself out. And I knew she could be a manipulative brat when she wanted to be; I'd feel happier if there was a reason to think this wasn't all just play-acting on her part.

I thought back over her behaviour in the last few weeks – before she headed off to London. I tried to recall my impressions. One moment in particular jumped out at me for some reason. I'd been working late one evening and I'd bumped into Jo in the meeting room. I hadn't thought much about it before, but now, for some reason I couldn't get it out of my mind. There was something about it...

She was such a sneaky little bitch; I bet she was up to something.

That thought sort of hit me out of nowhere. I was a little shocked at myself. I must be *really* tired – and maybe a bit cranky. David always fussed about his blood sugar, making sure to snack if he trained – claimed he was as brusque as a doctor's receptionist if he forgot to eat. Maybe I'd contracted his tendency to hypoglycaemia. I should get up and find some food.

I pulled the sweatband off my head, breaking the Connection. It wasn't until that moment that I realised I'd even been holding a Connection all this time. I shook my head to clear my muddled thoughts. I knew my own mind and I didn't like this feeling of mushy, moody daydreaming – losing my train of thought, dozing, forgetting I was Connected – it made me feel uncomfortable. I clapped my hands loudly, once, and jumped up. *Enough*, I thought.

I wrapped a towel around my damp neck and packed everything away. Then I locked up the barn and trotted up the hill towards the dormitory block, my bag banging against my back. My sweat-drenched clothes felt unpleasantly clammy in the chilly night air and I hurried to get inside.

I was showering, letting my mind wander, when my thoughts drifted back to what I'd been thinking in the barn: about Jo and our encounter in the meeting room. That memory seemed brighter than the others; it glinted like a broken bottle on a sandy beach, and I wondered why it was bothering me so much.

Jo had been running a little errand, she'd said. That thought, that she was up to something, my sudden vehement distrust of her, it had seemed so out of character for me that I was inclined to follow it up, to see if my subconscious was trying to tell me something.

Once I'd changed, I went back out into the cold and walked over to the main building. I looked up at the windows as I punched in the door code: everything was in darkness. I had to turn on lights everywhere I went: the entrance, the back corridor, the office. The place was deserted. I walked through the Professor's office, down the steps and into the meeting room. Turning on the light, I looked around, momentarily not seeing the thing I was looking for.

I ducked down and there it was, behind the table. I leaned over the table, reaching my arm out and pulled the mains adaptor out of the wall socket, holding it up to the light. Straightaway I knew my suspicions were correct. This wasn't what it appeared to be: the weight was wrong, even the kind of plastic seemed wrong, and there was no maker's name.

I went back out, through the Professor's office, and into the hallway. There was a maintenance cupboard with a few tools in it just past the main entrance. I headed there now, unlocked the door and rummaged around until I'd found a small enough screwdriver. I undid the screws holding the adaptor together and pulled off the top.

It was full of circuitry. This thing was a bug and I'd seen Jo planting it.

I didn't bother to lock up; I headed straight for the Professor's room, the two halves of the bug in my cupped hands, to tell him what I'd discovered. I was fairly sure he had a key to Jo's sanctuary, where all the computer equipment was kept. I wondered what we'd find in there if we looked.

I thought about knocking on Daniel's door too, asking him to join us. He'd know more about bugs and radio waves than I would; he might know what else to look for... but he was also devoted to Jo. I'd involve him once I was sure what was going on. Theresa would be a better bet. I was certain I'd seen a couple of semesters of Physics classes on her college records; she might know how bugs worked. And she'd have no problem investigating Jo.

Theresa was on the phone when I knocked on her door, but she hung up and said she'd join me in the Professor's room in five minutes. I didn't explain why I needed to see her.

Then I knocked on the Professor's door and he answered a

moment later, a book in one hand and a pair of spectacles in the other that I knew he still liked to hold while he read even though he didn't need them any more.

"Susan?" he enquired, puzzled but friendly.

"We have a problem," I said, "and I think Jo Hallett is behind it."

The three of us – the Professor, Theresa and me – stayed up pretty late that night. The Professor found his spare key to the server room and we filed over there. It only took Theresa a couple of minutes to point to a little black box, with an antenna sticking out of it, and identify it as a receiver. Its audio lead was connected to the computer it sat on, which was how Jo would record whatever the bug overheard, Theresa said.

We couldn't get past the computer's security, and we didn't spend a long time trying. We left everything where it was and trooped back again, to the Professor's room, and he made tea. Then the three of us tried to work out what was going on and what we should do about it.

The look of deep, banked anger on the Professor's face was one I had never seen before and for the first time since I'd met him, I found myself thinking that you wouldn't want to get on the wrong side of him. Whatever Jo was up to, it seemed like a safe bet that she'd come to regret it.

CHAPTER 25 – TOLD BY JO

This is how the loss of a loved one feels. You start to wake, rising up out of nothingness, feeling light, cleansed by sleep. The world comes closer and you start to smile waiting for your day to start. And then it drops on you, all the weight of your problems, your pain. You remember what happened and you feel sick. You'd hoped it was a dream but wishing it away was the dream and now that you're awake it's back.

With me it wasn't loss, but it came to me in the same way. One moment I was waking, untroubled, unafraid – the next moment it all fell back into place and I found myself locked at the centre of a life gone wrong.

And with awareness came the instant weariness of knowing that today would be another fight.

And yet, on the heels of the weariness was a sort of strength. I pushed away the tired thoughts, the feeling that it was all too much for me to cope with. And that determination felt familiar. I knew that as long as I lived, I would start every day like this: shutting down the bad thoughts and choosing to be strong. And right now, I thought I could probably handle that.

For a moment after waking, I didn't move. I took stock. I was still lying on the bed, still dressed in last night's clothes – only now it was light outside. That meant it was at least half seven in the morning, probably later. I'd been out for over nine hours.

At least I was still in the spot where I'd passed out. For a second I'd worried that once I was unconscious *he* would have taken control. I'd have got up from the bed like some zombie rising from its grave. My body would have been sent out on some errand, doing god knows what. But here I was. I didn't appear to have moved. Maybe he'd been asleep all this time too.

But surely he wasn't asleep any more. With a sense of climbing dread, I waited for something to happen – for my body to jerk, to start moving of its own accord, to stand up without me willing it to.

It didn't happen.

I tried to detect his presence, to get some sense of what he was thinking, whether he was still there. But there was nothing. No sign that he was still in my head.

Then a final thought from last night slotted back into place: the necklace. It came back to me now. When I first saw that thing around my neck, I hadn't recognised it. But gradually it had started to look familiar. After a little while I could recall seeing it before, remember hearing about how my mother loved to make things like that; I thought I'd even seen it around her neck once or twice. But now those memories no longer seemed like mine. When I tried to recall seeing the necklace around my mother's neck, her expression came out wrong. I realised now it was just a fragment of an old photograph; her features frozen in the camera's flash. The memory of her wearing the necklace was a fake, a composite designed to fool me.

He had created that recollection – and others – layered them up from fragments of other things. I'd only been fooled because he'd never let me dwell on the inconsistencies; he would cut me off, distract me, redirect my attention.

Whatever the necklace was, it was something from his world, not mine. I remembered my decision to wear it at all times and now that felt fake too. The necklace must be his trap-door into my head, his tunnel under my defences. Somehow he'd found a way to put this noose, this yoke around my neck.

So perhaps he *was* out there in the ether, subtly influencing other adepts, whispering softly to them – but he had managed to go far beyond that with me; he'd established a permanent presence in my brain. I was convinced that as long as I wore this necklace, he would be in a position to control me. Without it, he might diminish to just a nagging thought or a persistent daydream. He'd be the frail influence I'd read about.

If breaking the necklace would break his hold then in a few seconds it would be done, and I was confident I could fight him for that long. I reached up and under the neck of my shirt. I grasped the fine gold wire. It was delicate, eminently breakable. If I just pulled hard enough it would stretch and snap and I would be free.

I pulled. I felt the wire digging into my neck. I pulled harder. I could picture a purple groove forming in my flesh as capillaries under the skin burst. I pulled harder still, wincing at the pain.

Stop. I heard the voice in my head, ringing clear like struck metal. For a second I froze, releasing the pressure on the necklace. Fear flushed cold water into my veins. My hand trembled at the sense of violation, the shocking closeness of his voice. But I wrapped my fingers around the gold wire and started to pull again.

Stop or your friends will die.

I will prove it to you. Call them. Speak to them. Even now

they are in danger. Call the Professor and you will see. Speak to him and then decide if you want to do this.

I stopped pulling. What should I do? Was this a trick? But what would it achieve except to buy him a couple of minutes? Why would he bother with that?

Perhaps he had sent someone to intercept me and they just needed a few more seconds to reach me. Was he stalling?

Gird yourself and wait. Once you see that no one is coming, call your friend. Then you will know what I can do.

Gird myself? I supposed he meant I should Connect, ready myself to fight off an attack. Did that mean he'd read my thoughts? Could he hear everything I was thinking? And what about his suggestion; was that a trick too? If I Connected, would that give him some extra power, enable him to better control me?

Your thoughts are like worms writhing; you must learn to compose yourself. You believe you are making a decision but all you do is tally your fears. Well, sit and tally and writhe as long as you wish. But if you remove my sign your friends will be killed, and then you will be killed, and I will find someone else to share my power with.

Now he was telling me to do nothing; did that mean I should act? I could feel his disgust at my panic, my paralysis and second-guessing. I calmed myself as best I could.

Help me for a short time and I will make no further requests of you. You know what I am looking for. I want the Marker and nothing more.

You have already profited from my presence. I have taught you so well that no one can stand against you. Soon you will be free and you will be invincible. What I ask is quickly done and easily so. You have everything to gain by helping me.

But if you fight me than you will have nothing and be left

with nothing and no one living will remember you.

Then, once again, he commanded me **Call your Professor**.

I was shaking so badly that I could hardly pick up my mobile, but I gripped it in both hands and scrolled through the numbers until I found the Professor's. I dialled and waited for him to answer…

"Hello?" It was him.

"Professor, it's me, Jo. I need to talk to you," I said.

"Oh, is that what you need?" he said, anger quivering in every word. "Well I also need to talk to you, so we are in agreement. I want you to get on the first train from London, get yourself down here, and do it now," he said and then I heard him slam down the receiver.

I was stunned. I'd never heard the Professor talk like that. What had my tormenter done to make him act like that?

After the Professor hung up on me I just stood there. I didn't move.

I was upset, thrown off balance by his rejection. And I also knew that my situation had altered, that something important had happened at the field-station in my absence. Maybe it should have been obvious, but I couldn't work out what it was or what it meant.

Do you understand?

That voice, it sounded so loud and deep, and yet it made no sound; it was only in my head. But my mental acoustics must have been impressive because his words rang like trumpets at a coronation. But I *didn't* understand yet.

Why was he like that? What did you do? I thought, and I realised my words were reaching him.

I visited your friends. I caused them to realise what you had done, how you had spied on them. I put the knowledge of your betrayal in their minds.

Oh.

Despite the fact that I could feel my confidence shrivelling, I dug deep for some reserves of bravado. *Well you'll have to do more than get me fired from the project to scare me. I've survived a lot worse than that,* I said weakly.

Ahhh. You still don't see. I have proved that I can pass information to your friends. If you refuse to help me, I will pass information to your *enemies*. I will tell the Army of Witnesses about your companions and where to find them.

You know what they are capable of? Imagine how it will be for your friends if the Army's wolves find them. Can you picture what their assassins would leave behind? Then you would be completely alone, waiting for the butchers to come for *you*.

He allowed me a moment to consider.

I want a few days' more of your cooperation. It costs you nothing. And then I will be gone. You will be free to waste your long and pointless life however you see fit. Your friends will still be alive. And you will be safe.

I am patient. If you disappoint me, I can find someone else and start again. You will not have the same opportunity. And we are so close to finishing. You can almost taste your freedom; why would you doom your friends and yourself now?

Think on it, he said. Unnecessarily. I couldn't do anything else *but* think on it.

I didn't know if *he* was providing it or my own imagination was conjuring it up, but I could almost see the twisted bodies strewn through the project buildings. I could picture myself returning to find them like that, all dead. Daniel cut down, the Professor ripped apart. He could make it happen.

And however I turned it, whatever angle I looked at it from, it seemed like my tormentor had found a way to beat me. I tried to find some hope that he was only lying to me or telling half truths. What if… yes, what if he hadn't influenced anyone? Maybe he'd only *witnessed* events at the field-station and was now claiming the credit for them. That was a straw I could clutch at: maybe the truth was he didn't have the power to influence anyone but me.

How do I know you didn't <u>discover</u> my friends were angry with me and pretend that you made it happen?

Ask them when they learned of your deceit. It happened while you slept, after you decided to defy me. After you decided to tell them about me. It happened while I kept you here, insensible. Or do you doubt it was me who made you sleep? Does it all seem like a coincidence?

If it *was* all a coincidence, it had arrived right on cue. No way I fell asleep all by myself last night. It was like being anaesthetised. So I would concede that my unconsciousness was his doing. And why knock me out unless he had an errand to run elsewhere?

Would he put me to sleep in order to spy on the PAC for a few hours? He couldn't be sure he'd see anything. A few hours, randomly chosen, weren't much good for spying; but they might be perfect if you had a specific task in mind, like passing on information. So if I accepted that he could put me to sleep, how much did I want to bet that he couldn't also reach into other people's minds if he wanted to? Would I bet my life and the Professor's on it? Daniel's? The rest of the team's? That final straw had been snatched from my grip.

Unable to maintain my doubt, I felt resignation setting in like nightfall. For a moment I'd felt strong and defiant. I thought that discovering my enemy's presence would allow me to fight him. I'd had hope. But now, that hope was dimming. It would be so easy for him to execute his threat; all he would need to do was hint to the Army, just give them a *glimpse* of our location, our identities, and they would find us. I was certain that they were already straining at the leash, sniffing for our scent.

So what else could I do? I couldn't run, just tear off the necklace and make a break for it, leaving my friends to die. You needed a level of professional ruthlessness that I didn't pretend to possess if you wanted to pull off a really colossal act of cowardice like that. You needed real discipline. Guilt of that magnitude would skewer someone like me, and if I fled, I'd spend every waking hour squirming on its hook.

Could I make him let me go? Fake my own death, make it seem like an accident? He was in my head so I didn't see how. I mean, he was probably listening in on this very thought, so how could I deceive him? Unless he actually *witnessed* my death, I couldn't see how he'd buy it. And even then, if he thought I'd planned it, spite might still motivate him to hurt my friends.

I had no more straws to clutch. There was only one choice left open to me and he knew it. Now he was waiting until *I* realised it too.

Of course if you still doubt me, we could try another approach. I'll lay your reservations to rest by bringing the Witnesses down upon your friends and then you can beg me to help you escape when the wolves come for *you*. If the *prospect* of your friends' deaths won't motivate you, perhaps the *memory* of those deaths will do a better job.

OK, OK, I thought, *I get it*.

But then I realised something. My tormentor couldn't follow *all* of my thoughts. I had admitted to myself that he had won and yet he had given me a final sales pitch to close the deal. *I* knew I was beaten, but he hadn't picked up on it. Was there some way that I could use that? Could I learn to control which thoughts he saw and which ones he missed?

Hope twitched a little on its death bed.

I would have to be *so* careful. I couldn't even begin to make a plan against him until I could be sure I could conceal it and I couldn't even imagine what that plan might involve considering he could look out through my eyes and hear with my ears. I mean how could I even *begin* a task like that?

In fact, until I gained some measure of control over my privacy, I shouldn't even be thinking this thought (OK. So I had to distract myself.)

I should think about… about the fact that my situation seemed so overwhelming that it was making me nostalgic for my old problems. (Yes.) I remembered grumbling that the work at the field-station was boring and that some of the people were unfriendly. I latched onto that memory and soaked up the irony of it. I mean, boo hoo. How did my earlier situation even register as a problem? That recollection seemed as remote as playground name-calling now. (Good. Let go of any resistance. For the time being.)

I felt a new emotion now – neither happy nor sad. Maybe it was acceptance. It was time to acknowledge my defeat.

What do you want me to do?

Ahh. Those words will save your life.

Good. Your first task is easy. I find myself concerned for your health. I think you need to take some more of your medicine.

I knew what he meant; the image slid into my mind along with his words. He wanted me to apply the patches I had worn before – the anti-depressants and the oxymethylphenidate. They must make his task easier, I guessed. Somehow they must make me more compliant, or maybe easier to monitor.

I'd last applied the patches right before that disastrous night, the night I'd dreamed of the ice, the night when he must have come to me for the first time. Those patches would both have run out a week later, but somehow it hadn't occurred to me to take them off before then, even though I'd been feeling fantastic and would no longer have felt a need for them. More of his twisted cognitive therapy no doubt: interrupting any thoughts he didn't approve of. So effective was his distraction that I hadn't thought to peel off the old patches until I'd returned to London, by which time they would long since have been depleted. And of course I hadn't applied any more; I mean, why would I? I was feeling unstoppable. Trying to influence me to reapply them at that point might have made me suspicious and it probably hadn't seemed worth the effort; I was being an obedient puppet.

I hesitated now, though. Howlingly ironic though it was, I really didn't like the idea of medicating myself at this moment. When it was just me in my head things were very different. The patches had seemed like a harmless piece of cheating, a way of cutting a few corners in my day – but now the rules had changed. The drugs didn't feel like my slippery little friends any more; they'd switched sides and were working for him – and that made me feel queasy and vulnerable. It was like the difference between ending a heavy night's drinking passed out on your own sofa or down at the bus station. One was immature, the other was Russian roulette. Applying the patches now might mean more than giving up the fight; it might mean giving up the *ability* to fight.

Maybe I could say I'd left the patches in Cornwall.

You keep some in your ditty bag; I've seen them. Go and get them now.

Was he responding to my delay in acquiescing or had he read my mind that time? And what the hell was a 'ditty bag'? Wherever it came from, he didn't get *that* bit of vocabulary from out of *my* head, though I knew what he meant. I kept a couple of transdermal patches in my wash bag.

My instinct was to stall, but from what I could see, there was no compelling reason for him to be patient with me. He could have the Army kill the people I cared about and still get what he wanted. To him it would just be a gesture, a useful lesson. It would put only the smallest crimp in his plans. He'd just have to send me into hiding as soon as he tipped the Army off, and then keep me below their radar until I'd grabbed the Marker for him. He might even have a hiding place in mind.

Weighing it up, it seemed like he had a nice, big stick he could use on me and very little reason to hold back. If I stalled or refused to obey, he could obliterate the PAC just to see if my attitude improved. And he'd still retain one king-sized threat to hold over me: the prospect of my own violent death. I reckoned I was going to have to do as I was told.

So without any further delay I went into my bathroom, slipped out of my top and applied a patch to each of my upper arms: a metered dose of SSRI anti-depressant and another of OMP.

The anti-depressants would take weeks before they affected my mood, but I had no idea how soon they might influence his control over me. The drugs would begin to hit my bloodstream in minutes and then I guess we'd see.

I stared into the bathroom mirror looking for any clue that someone else was looking out through my eyes. I wondered how he felt looking at my reflection in the bathroom mirror and seeing my freckly chest, my second-best bra.

I remembered my little lesbian moment of a few weeks back and suddenly it made sense to me. I had a male consciousness lurking in my head, colouring my thoughts and supplementing my memories. So I wasn't turning gay; I was simply being controlled by a male presence.

You'd have to be quite the homophobe to see that revelation as a cause for celebration.

Listen, what do I call you?

For some time now, I have been called the Sleeper.

And when I get the Marker, how am I going to hand it over to you?

When the time comes I will show you. No more questions. We have work to do.

He'll show me? Not tell me? Interesting choice of language. *You're the boss. What's my next task?*

There was a pause.

Tell me, what will happen if you do not return to your friends today, as instructed?

I guess they'll call. A lot. And then they'll send someone. (No point in trying to lie about this.) *And I suppose if I duck whoever they send, they'll get worried and make me a priority, maybe come here en masse.*

So you need to find a way to stop them pestering us. You may determine how best to achieve that.

And remember, I have my own way to stop them interfering... but it is permanent. Invent something just as effective if you want me to spare them.

I didn't like how this was shaping up. *Wait, wait; I'm doing what you want; I'm not fighting you. You threatened my friends' lives to get me to behave and I'm behaving. You can't say you'll kill them anyway unless I do some other thing. There have to be rules. If you don't give me any reason to believe you'll spare them, then I might as well not help you.*

I see you are confused. Perhaps I should clarify your position.

Your friends will be no trouble to me if they're dead. But you want me to keep them alive. So you must make sure I never

have a pressing reason to eradicate them. If they interfere, I will kill them; if you need to be taught a lesson, I will kill them. Make sure I *don't* have a reason to kill them and I will let them live.

Is that clearer now?

So psychopaths like sarcasm too. *OK, but how should I persuade them to leave me alone?*

You know *my* way; I'm giving you an opportunity to come up with a less bloody alternative.

Well, at least tell me what you did, exactly. What did you tell them about me?

I let them know you placed a device in their meeting room allowing you to make a record of their conversations. I would imagine they also suspect you of reading their correspondence, their secret papers.

Right. Great. So they knew I was spying on them; what would they make of that revelation? Would they think I was working for the enemy, planning to betray them? I hoped not. Surely they wouldn't jump to that conclusion without evidence to the fact – say, some clue that I was being blackmailed by the Army. And there was no such evidence. Plus if the Army knew about the field station, wouldn't they simply have sent their people in to torture the truth out of everyone? Why screw around with bugging them? The PAC would see that, wouldn't they? I *couldn't* be an Army agent.

So they must have thought I was spying on them for my own personal amusement, rummaging through their secrets for kicks – like some teenage hacker – and now I'd blundered upon a secret they'd already decided I couldn't be trusted with.

And you know, for a moment, I honestly couldn't recall if that was how this had all started. Had I been doing this just for kicks, in the days before the Sleeper had arrived? What had motivated me back then? It all seemed like such a long time ago. I couldn't remember being that person, thinking like that. I might be up to my neck in trouble now, but at least my behaviour made some sort of sense to me; these days it was the *world* that was insane.

With the stakes so high, it seemed that the lives of my friends now depended upon my ability to find an alternative explanation for why I'd spied on the PAC – a reason that said 'leave me alone' instead of 'come and get me' – something that would keep them out of the Sleeper's way and therefore safe.

I'm going to call Daniel. He'll be sympathetic enough to at least let me speak.

There was a pause.

Acceptable. But I will consider any slips of the tongue to be deliberate, so select your words with exquisite caution.

With all my heart, I wanted my call to Daniel to be a coded cry for help. I wanted to use some odd phrase only he would catch, introduce some subtle tone into my voice that only he would recognise. But for that to work I needed to exploit the fact that Daniel knew me well and the Sleeper didn't. The problem? Daniel might know me well, but the Sleeper was inside my head, and he held Daniel's life in his hands. Anything Daniel might spot would come through loud and clear to the Sleeper. Without a way to hide my true thoughts, secret messages were out of the question.

And I had only the haziest idea of how to conceal my thoughts. My only clue was a growing suspicion that strong emotion played a role, making it easier for him to read me. And I'd be most keyed up when I had the most to hide, which would tend to give me away – which meant for now, no tricks.

I dialled Daniel's mobile and he answered without delay. I could hear music playing and I guessed he was still in his room.

"Hey Josephine, what's up? I saw you'd left me a message; I

was just about to play it," he said. Obviously he didn't know yet what the others had found out. The PAC would probably tell him last.

"Hey Daniel," I said wearily, taking a moment to organise my thoughts. "Well, no surprise I suppose, but I have a problem. You'll hear about it soon enough."

He sounded concerned. "Oh? Well, why not tell me now?"

Time to put on a show.

I allowed a good helping of the (very genuine) panic I was feeling to show through in my voice. Then I took a deep breath and launched into it: "You want to know what the problem is? I'm a little bit *freaked out* Daniel. Oh, I knew something was going on with the PAC; I knew you all were hiding some nasty secret – and I wasn't happy about it. I wondered what you could be doing that was *so* bad, but no one would talk to me. I was a part of it and no one would tell me what *it* was. So I decided to find out anyway."

"Ahh," was all he said. Thinking this through as I spoke, I realised, if I was going to be angry I'd have to claim I'd only just discovered the truth. Otherwise exploding now would seem peculiar.

There was outrage in my voice: "I knew it was bad, but... but last night I played a recording of a PAC meeting I'd made. I'd wanted to know what the hell I'd been dragged into so I bugged the meeting room. Maybe I shouldn't have done it, but everyone was lying to me and I wanted the truth. And given what I heard, I'm hardly the criminal here. You were talking about people being *killed*, about the PAC hiding from the killers, spying on people, plotting against them. I didn't listen to all of it. I'd heard enough. I still don't know what to make of most of it." I pushed the emotion a few notches higher. "I mean, are you people *insane*? What on earth do you imagine you're doing? I thought I was joining an academic team, I thought you had some groundbreaking project I could be part of, and I discover you're... I don't know what, part of some sort of cult – a cult that seems involved in more than a few *murders*."

"Jo," he said, trying to reassure me, "we haven't *killed* anyone."

"Are you sure?" I shot back. "Didn't you have a pretty good go with someone called Jan?"

"*He* was trying to kill Susan and David," he explained.

"He wanted to kill *them*, they wanted to kill *him*. In the end someone else murdered him first. I mean *listen* to yourself."

Now I spoke slowly and firmly, "I don't want any part of this. I want out. Please tell the Professor from me that I want him and his team to leave me alone. If *any* member of the PAC comes *near* me, if anyone tries to get in *touch* with me, I'll call the police. I swear. You freaks need to stay *away* from me."

I was out of breath with emotion now.

"Jo, listen. Don't do anything hasty, alright?" Daniel said, "We're really *not* the villains here. I mean, for goodness sake, it's *me*; you know *me*." He took a breath, almost a gulp. I could picture him pushing his hair back. "Look, take a bit of time. This all seems very weird, but if you think about it I'm sure you'll realise I wouldn't be a part of something unless I thought it was the right thing to do. Just please promise me you won't do anything until you've given yourself some thinking time?"

"I don't know, Daniel," I said, calming down a little, softening, "I don't know what to make of this. Maybe I *do* need some time."

Then I abandoned the calm: "But so help me, if I see a familiar face, if I get the impression that you've sent someone to shut me up I really will go straight to the police, and anyone else who'll listen, and I'll tell them everything I know about what you're up to. You and the Professor can explain the whole thing to the cops."

"You won't have to do that," he assured me, "I'll make sure you're left in peace to think things through. Take a bit of time, let the shock of this settle down for a while and then give me a ring. We can talk about it. When it's all sunk in a bit more we'll talk the whole thing over. OK? That's fair, right?"

I said nothing for a moment. Then I let myself sound small and weak and said, "OK, Daniel. Alright."

"OK then," he said, with warmth in his voice.

Hesitantly he added, "I wanted to ask you about something else, but it can wait. Maybe next time. Until then, take care."

"Sure," I said glumly and hung up. I hadn't needed to make him hate me, thank god, but he wouldn't be galloping to my rescue any time soon either. It was a painful thing to do, but I thought it had probably worked.

The Sleeper had turned the PAC against me and now I'd finished the job. Daniel would convince the others that I wasn't spying on them for kicks. He'd paint a very different story: that I'd just wanted the truth and now I was freaked out and threatening to turn them all over to the police. They weren't going to like me any better as a snitch than as a sneak, but it should keep them away from me for a little while. Unless I was mistaken, I'd just done a damn good job of cutting myself off from my only source of help.

Masterful. I believe the boy will do as you asked. He sounded pleased.

And this can form the pattern for our future enterprise, if you wish. I will name the destination and you may plot our course and take the trick. If you can achieve my aims without inflicting great injury upon your own then so be it. I can be fair if fairness serves me. The choice is yours.

I found his turn of phrase a little hard to follow but I was guessing this was the carrot to go with the big stick he'd been waving. He was saying if I followed his orders, he'd let me organise the details myself. I supposed it was a good offer: easier for him if he simply watched me do all the work – but good for me too, just in case I needed a little wiggle room to put my brilliant plan for personal and general salvation into effect. If only I *had* a brilliant plan.

What do you say?

Depends on how much a person likes guilt, I suppose. I've got a feeling I might regret coming up with ways for you to get what you want.

Anyway, what's next?

Next we investigate the address mentioned in Jan's papers. Find out what you can in advance and then we'll pay a visit in person.

I was happy enough with that request, at least the first part. I could trawl around the Internet looking for info, during which time I could a) surreptitiously think about other things and b) avoid placing myself or others in immediate jeopardy.

By now, I was so paranoid about the Army that when I Googled the address, I only put in the general location. I didn't really expect the Army could check Google's records to see who searched for what, but who knew how much data-traffic the intelligence agencies monitored as it made its way between private citizens and their favourite web-sites. And if the intelligence community knew something then maybe the Army knew it too. That didn't stop it being sheer paranoia, but I felt better for rationalising a little.

Even keeping things general, the mystery of this address quickly revealed itself. Was it a flat, a room in a commercial building or a plot of land? None of the above. It was a berth. And I assumed there was something anchored in that berth. Presumably Jan had a boat, either a barge or a house-boat I would imagine, and it was on the river a little ways east of the Millennium Dome.

I had no idea how many house-boats there were dotted around the Capital, but I knew it was easy to forget that London still had miles of canal running through it. You'd turn a corner and happen upon a section of ancient waterway threading between loft-converted warehouses. Jan's berth was in a dock which let out directly to the Thames itself, but I wasn't able to find out much about it. Most mentions of that stretch of water dated back more than a century. The land around it seemed to be given over to a cement works now – and that was about all I could learn.

So much for spinning out the research; the next step was to go there. Time to consult my demonic master.

Do we sneak in or break in? Or make up some excuse to be there?

Suggestions? Remember, time is precious.

Well, it's the middle of the day. If we want to go now, it'll have to be in plain sight, I reckon. So we'd better come up with a reason to look around.

Which would be?

I don't know, maybe an estate agent. I've got the name Jan used to rent it and a few other details. I can fake up a letter from him that says I'm allowed to inspect the property, maybe with a view to finding a purchaser. I can also make up a couple of business cards that identify me as a property agent. That would make it easy for me to take pictures and ask a lot of questions.

That sounds promising. Get to it.

Great, I thought, without enthusiasm. First, though, I needed to take a shower and have some breakfast. I insisted upon it.

With that out of the way, I forged a letter and a couple of business cards. Jan had used the name James Jenkins on correspondence relating to the berth and I didn't have a sample of his signature for that name. On the other hand, I thought it was a fairly good bet that neither would anyone else – at least not on site. And anyway, who checks signatures except a bank? I found a good fountain pen and signed the letter with a flourish *somewhat* inspired by the way Jan signed his other pseudonyms.

In my wardrobe, I found a navy blue suit in some manmade material and a pale lilac blouse with some kind of ruched thing happening at the front. It looked sort of estate-agenty to me. Then I remembered that Noola had a wig. Before she'd had extensions and turned them into dreadlocks she'd had a nuked-blonde-with-dark-red-roots look. Frankly it made her look as though her hair had been irradiated and now her follicles were bleeding, but she seemed happy with it. She'd also bought a neat, redheaded wig to wear to job interviews and for dealing with those of a more conservative disposition when it came to coiffure. I went downstairs and swiped it. It wasn't an impenetrable disguise, but it was better than nothing.

In this get-up, I'd be taking the tube, not the bike, and doing some walking, so I dug out a long coat. I also found a big purse that looked businessy and inside it I put all the bits and pieces I planned to take with me: digital camera, notepad, tape measure – which raised a question.

Do I wear tribute? I think I can get the headband under this wig without it looking like my head's bulging oddly.

There was a longish pause and I wondered if there was anyone there. I hadn't had any luck yet detecting the Sleeper's presence. Did he disappear on who-knows-what errand from time to time and I didn't notice?

Then he answered. **You can maintain the Quell state without my help? Otherwise I will have to take control.**

I guess he didn't want us to make our way to the Marker's

secret hiding place while broadcasting our presence to every nearby adept.

It's easy enough. And I can slip out of the bracelets in a second if I have a problem.

Very well.

I hadn't found the Quell state difficult and it meant I wouldn't have to fumble around looking for tribute if something bad happened.

I had one more idea for what to take with me: a metal detector. It might reveal something the Surfaces didn't. I wasn't intending to lug one of those long-handled beachcombing things with me, but I might be able to pick up a stud detector. Ingeniously enough it was a device that had nothing to do with the male physique and everything to do with locating pipes and wires inside walls, and you could get one from most hardware stores.

The only question was, how much should I be helping? If the Sleeper simply wanted me to hand over the Marker, and then he'd keep his word and let me go, then anything I could do to speed this quest along was a grand idea. If he pretty much planned to wipe me and the PAC out, then all I was doing was digging my own grave. Unfortunately I didn't have a lot of evidence to help me decide which it was. It would help if I knew why he didn't fetch the Marker himself. Was he incapacitated and that's why he needed it? I pictured a body wrapped from head to foot in bandages, like the soldier in white in *Catch 22* – but in this case masterminding his own cure through some as-yet-unexplained exercise of magical mind-control.

I knew that most physical wounds could be cured with the Healing surface – in fact most would cure themselves sooner or later without you even concentrating; you just had to Connect. So far as I knew, only extreme old age required the Marker – as the Healing surface didn't offer immortality, only a healthy and very long life. So maybe he was some dusty fossil in a wheelchair somewhere, his dry hands clutching his cane as he concentrated on making me run round London looking for his holy grail.

Either way, I couldn't quite figure out why he didn't have minions. How was he even alive if he was helpless and had no one to obey him? It seemed strange to picture an adept with superb control of his powers who, for some reason, had no followers and no fortune. With his powers, he should certainly be rich. It made sense that he was old – very old – so what had he been doing with his life up until disaster struck and he needed to be rejuvenated by the Marker? I couldn't see how a powerful adept could end up a bed-ridden pauper immobilised by old age. With money, servants or even a little mobility he could be searching for the Marker without my help. And without those things, how was he keeping himself alive?

As I was thinking all this, I was looking up the address of a hardware store where I could buy a stud detector. I was doing my best to guard my thoughts – though it was pure guesswork whether I was doing it right – but even if he could read me, I figured the Sleeper couldn't begrudge me my curiosity. He could *command* me not to think about who he was and where he came from, but he couldn't expect me to obey; nobody could really control their own curiosity.

I found a suitable store and called up a map to show me where it was. Then I hit print. I got out of my chair to grab the print-out and a sudden surge of disorientation hit me. I grabbed the edge of my desk to steady myself. The feeling was familiar, though the overwhelming intensity of it wasn't: it was the patches kicking in – and it was something more. For a second I stood there, not daring to move, clutching the desk for support. I thought I was going to throw up.

I could feel my mind getting softer, mushier, my thoughts losing definition. I could almost picture the barriers around my mind getting more porous as the chemicals reached my brain. I imagined I could feel the Sleeper pushing forward, wriggling further into my mind, worming his tendrils into my thoughts. And with that feeling came another sensation, an awareness of something in motion. A dizzy, spinning shape rose into my mind. It twirled and turned in on itself, like some abstract, geometric animation.

What was this thing? Had it spilled across the connection between our minds? I didn't know, but somehow its shape reminded me of Connecting.

I'd never really thought about it, but the sensation of Connecting was really about configuring your thoughts in a certain way – into a pattern, in fact. When I Connected I was bringing this pattern to the forefront of my mind. In its shape, the Connection pattern resembled the drawing I'd first seen when I'd tried to use magic that time on the moors. Those mental exercises I'd performed involved staring at elaborate patterns of ink on paper – someone's attempts to capture in a line-drawing the rich, moving shapes an adept must hold in her head.

The Quell state used a pattern too, though it was a very simple one. And this new writhing shape that was forming in my mind reminded me of both of those others. Was it related to them somehow? And yet it seemed incomplete. I had the feeling that it would be a powerful thing indeed if it was whole.

A moment or two later and the shape began to fade. My disorientation lessened.

I didn't know what this experience meant or what had just occurred, but it seemed to be over now. I couldn't be sure, but my suspicion was that the Sleeper had pushed a little too hard as he tried to take advantage of the drugs' growing effect on me – and in his haste he had caused us both a few moments of disorientation and nausea. But who knew for sure?

I snatched up the map, grabbed my bag and headed downstairs and out into the cold. I was grateful for the jolting chill of the icy air and the feel of my heels hitting the hard, frost-lichened pavement. Walking the winter streets was simple, physical and sharply real – a few moments of normality to distract me from the war being fought inside my skull.

CHAPTER 26

A whiff of stagnant-pond-smell told me I was getting close to a reservoir of sluggish water. Of course I knew the river was just the other side of the wall, but despite all the junk that was pumped into it, the river itself seemed to be odourless. It was the musty water of a wet-dock I could smell.

The path I'd been walking along reached a flight of concrete steps that would take me up and over the wall. On the other side was the broad enclosure of a private dock and beyond it the river.

There were half a dozen house-boats lined up along a wooden jetty, packed side-by-side like piglets on a sow as my Pappy might have said, had he been a redneck instead of a banker. The jetty was on the land-most side of the dock. The dock itself was a square basin, maybe fifty yards on a side, which jutted squarely off from the broad and sinuous main channel of the Thames. I could just make out another inlet on the far river-bank, five hundred yards away. From a high enough altitude I imagined this section of the river would resemble a python that had swallowed a roll of quarters, sideways on. Kind of.

Beyond the boats, a thick wall separated the dock from the river, except for a ten-yard gap in the middle that was sealed by two low lock-gates that looked a little like paddles from a giant pinball game. I could see the exposed and gleaming steel pistons which attached the gates to the opening mechanism hidden under the dockside. My guess was that the gates were more or less watertight because the level of the river on the other side looked to be a few feet lower than in the basin. You obviously had to pick your moment to activate the buried hydraulics and swing the lock-gates apart; opening them now would flush the dock like it was a cistern.

There were six boats tied up to the wooden jetty, plus two derelict-looking barges along the side walls. A couple of the house-boats must have been nudging sixty feet in length, but none were much more than six feet wide – something to do with the width of the canals they evolved in, I supposed.

The wooden jetty began a few feet out into the water and you reached it by walking down a short ramp from the stone dock-side. The only way onto the ramp, though, was through a gate, which was guarded by a little sentry box.

On either side of that gate, a high chain-link fence screened off the jetty from anyone who might fancy their chances at jumping across from dry land.

I strode up to the gate, ready to present my pseudo-credentials and found the little guard-hut empty. A sign on the hut's door stated that it was manned 24 hours a day by PerimeterForce as part of their Instant Response Guarantee. The gate was unlocked, not even latched (nice work, PerimeterForce) so I strolled through and clattered down the ramp on my daring inch-and-a-half heels.

Down on the jetty, the berth-numbering system looked to be a little arbitrary, but after a little to-ing and fro-ing I found 4-14J, the address I'd seen on Jan's papers. It was the farthest berth from the ramp, and the boat it contained was set apart from the others. It looked quiet – deserted even.

Only one of the other boats showed any activity at all, and it was at the opposite end of the jetty. Its engine covers were up and a man in baggy overalls was leaning into the housing, tools spread out on a purple towel to one side of him. If he noticed me, he gave no sign of it and seemed unconcerned by my presence.

I took a good look at the boat in 4-14J. It was a little shabbier than the average, but not the shabbiest. Tiny, scruffy curtains were drawn on the dusty windows and the deck needed sweeping. Sun-faded red paint was blistering near the prow. Or was the prow at the other end? Let's just say the front. The rudder was clearly at the far end, the end that stuck out into the basin and towards the river.

All the other boats were snug up against the jetty, noses touching dry land, but 4-14J was standing off by several feet. There was a stretch of dusty black-green water between the wooden platform I stood on and the deck of the boat. The gap wasn't an insurmountable obstacle, but it made this boat the least likely to receive casual visitors.

I could see that the back of every boat was roped to the next and on 4-14J that rope had been shortened. That was what kept it from drifting in to the jetty. It also kept it close to its neighbour, and right now the two were as close as stink on a weasel as my non-existent Uncle Billy-Bob would say.

I broke the background litany of the Quell state and Connected, immediately stretching out with my senses to touch the boat, alert for the sparkle of recognition that would occur if another adept was operating nearby. My best bet, if I did detect someone, was probably to turn around and run – to thunder up the ramp and just keep going. I didn't have a sword with me and I wasn't sure I could use one anyway, so running like hell would be the better part of valour.

I did not tell you to Connect. He sounded furious. Oops.

Sorry. Well, no harm done. There's no one here.

I knew from the Sleeper's own shared knowledge that the best way to avoid a trap is to Connect early, while you can still get away. So why was he snippy? Didn't he want me to stay safe? Maybe he just liked to be consulted.

Trying to look like I knew what I was doing, I jumped onto the boat one berth to the left of Jan's, which also had its curtains drawn. I ran along its running board for a few feet and leapt onto the foredeck of 4-14J (if 'foredeck' is nautical for 'front porch'). No one peeked out from the boat I'd used as a stepping stone. The boat I'd landed on likewise failed to disgorge Army assassins, river police or angry pirates (in descending order of likelihood).

I was at the front and the door to the boat's interior appeared to be at the far end, so I needed to get back there somehow. There was probably a trick to it, but moving along the boat from stem to stern (or anyways from snout to tail) was extremely difficult. There was a flat lip of black-painted wood, maybe six inches wide, that jutted out from the steep side of the boat a foot or so above the water line. If I leant forwards, and grabbed hold of the roof of the boat, I could shuffle sideways along the lip, balancing myself with my hands. My shiny leather gloves were particularly unsuited to marine gymnastics, but I kept them on anyway.

Perhaps the right way to do this was to clamber up and walk along the roof itself, but that somehow seemed too conspicuous, like dancing on the table when you're supposed to be keeping a low profile. I attempted a shuffling sideways-hop, while trying to tuck my bag under my arm, and I managed not to jump right off the boat and into the cloudy depths below. Fortunately my ugly, black shoes were sombre enough – and thus unused enough – to still have some tread left on their plastic soles. I crabbed my way to the back porch of the boat, managing not to trip on the anchor chain or the rope that stretched across to the boat next door. Then I climbed down into a foot-well kind of a space that contained the rudder handle, the seat the driver would occupy, a couple of items of nautical paraphernalia and a pair of locked wooden doors leading to the interior.

I ducked down out of sight and gathered my focus. With my Surface senses spread out, sweeping across and into the boat, I panned quickly through the vessel without encountering any sign of an enemy. So no one was *currently* Connecting in there.

I altered my focus to scan for other possible dangers which might await me in there. It was difficult to get a clear picture of the cluttered and complex interior in any detail, but I didn't detect anything moving or register the signature of body heat. I did the same for the boats nearest me, and a quick pass found no heat signatures there either.

I suppose someone could be hiding in the water, but I doubted it. You couldn't create a decent Shield in water and you couldn't penetrate it properly using the Surface senses. Most adepts found immersion in water undesirable to the point of phobia. If no one was in the boat, they weren't likely to be under it; it should be safe to venture inside.

I took one last look up at the dockside above me and the flood-wall beyond. This was an ideal place to ambush someone, unless they were part dolphin. Only one (dry) way out, high ground on three sides and a river at your victim's back. I hoped there was no one up there on the wall right now, thinking those exact thoughts.

I turned my attention back to the boat. The low doors sealing off the interior were held closed by a padlock which was hooked through a chunky iron hasp. I squatted down, sitting on the backs of my heels to take a closer look, steadying myself by placing a hand on the overhang of the roof. Putting my other hand on the padlock, I closed my eyes and felt inside the metal for the mechanism and the tumblers. One, two, three, four. Once they were all lined up, I rotated the barrel and the bolt popped open. I set the lock to one side and opened the doors.

A breath of nasty, fungal air puffed up at me and I held my breath, turning my head for a moment to give it a chance to dissipate. Then I stepped down into the gloom.

Naturally the dim light didn't bother me. I closed my eyes and allowed the shapes of the things around me to register through the Push surface. It felt a little like pulling plastic-wrap over a tray of sandwiches, the wrap taking up the shape of what was beneath it as you tucked it into place. I could sense that the inner spaces of the boat were intricate and multi-chambered and it was immediately clear it was going to take me a while to examine them all.

The interior of the boat was dry and dusty, inhabited by some secretive species of nook-loving mould. The table and shelves immediately in front of me were empty and a discarded running shoe lay on the far bunk. I walked over to the bunk and sat down next to the sneaker, placing my bag on the rucked-up blanket by my side. Sitting still would make it easier to sweep through the hidden spaces of the boat, to search its recesses for hiding places. It was a lot of volume to cover in detail, but I got straight to work, beginning with the floor beneath my feet and combing the space below the deck in strips, working backwards in the direction of the jetty. The muddy blank of the water outside was like the frame around a picture I was studying.

Many times I sensed something within the structure or fabric of the boat, and had to pause to identify it. The engine compartment particularly was a nightmare. And I spent several minutes checking whether there was anything besides gasoline inside a gas-can that sat on the tiny foredeck. In that particular case, it would have been quicker just to go up there and tip out the contents.

None of these curiosities turned out to be the Marker sitting snug in some hidey-hole. At times during the search I was aware of the Sleeper's presence pressing in on my consciousness, scrutinising – and perhaps assisting – and I filed away the sensation, hoping it would help me to spot those moments when he was *least* aware of my thoughts and actions.

When I'd finished exploring the cavities nearest the hull, I leaned back against the bulkhead and let my focus infuse the timbers above my head, scanning within the woodwork of the top half of the boat – until once again I had traversed the full length of the vessel.

No luck.

Time to try something else, I thought, and dug the stud detector out of my bag. Like a geriatric house-painter, I ran the tip of the instrument in painfully slow strokes up and down the panelled walls, pausing each time the machine registered something. Most of what it told me I already knew – though on one occasion it found a metal spar running behind the back of a cupboard which I hadn't noticed before. It did me no good, though: a careful mental probe of the space around the spar failed to find anything of interest, like, say, the release mechanism for a hidden compartment. There didn't seem to be anything to find, which I guessed the Sleeper wouldn't be happy about.

It was now coming up on two hours since I'd arrived and I had completed my third exhausting scan of the boat – two occult and one electronic-with-occult-follow-ups – with nothing to show for it.

Robert Finn

What now?

We keep looking. He was emphatic and I could sense his displeasure. **This time instead of looking for the Marker itself, we look for clues: papers, hiding places where the Marker might once have been kept, any personal effects.**

Ohh-kaaay. I was starting to feel drained. This was like trying to read fine print in bad light while balancing on one leg. It was enough to give you a migraine after a while.

On the other hand, it was better than being dead, so I set to work again, inching my way along the craft, no longer looking for the bright hardness of filigreed metal, instead alert to the presence of anything soft and out-of-place. For variety, I worked in a spiral this time, corkscrewing my way along the boat from muzzle to fetlock, imagining that I was peeling it like an apple skin.

Twenty minutes of that and I was really starting to flag. A headache was swelling behind my eyes and I was beginning to feel dizzy and a little nauseous. My concentration kept slipping and at one point I even broke the Connection for a second, without meaning to – which brought a wordless rebuke from the Sleeper that reverberated through my mind like a slap in the face.

But then something changed and after that I sensed that he was taking a lot more of the strain, directing my focus with less input from me, like a pilot taking over the controls from an exhausted co-pilot... which was a much more innocent analogy than the reality of our relationship.

Even with his help, the muzziness in my head grew as the minutes rolled by and I realised that the pattern I'd glimpsed earlier was once again rising from the floor of my mind, contorting and folding in on itself like before. A metronomic chant went with it. It began to sound in my head, faintly at first, but soon quite discernible. The pattern was even more distinct this time, but I knew it was still incomplete. I still had no idea what it meant.

I sensed that the Sleeper was nearly as weary as I was, which I'd guess was why this pattern was leaking across the link between our minds. As he kept us both focussed on the search, and as we both grew more and more drained, I found myself catching glimpses of foreign images from the overspill of his memories – random snippets that I could tell came from him – slopping over the link and into my brain.

None of it was very clear or easy to interpret, it was all edges and out-of-focus corners of things, but I filed every impression away as best I could. I desperately wanted to know more about my tormentor; any clue about his origin or his real intentions might reveal something I could use. Above all I needed to know whether he really planned to let me go – me and the PAC – once he was done with me.

With the pattern in my head continually devouring itself and the influx of foreign thoughts tumbling along behind, it was getting a little hard to think straight. The Sleeper was putting all his attention into maintaining the search and, consequently, everything else was starting to slip. I found myself wondering how long he could keep at this, and a split-second later I felt the echo of that thought coming back to me. The barrier between our minds had become so weakened as he poured his focus into the unrelenting examination of the boat, that I was hearing my own thoughts as they made contact with his consciousness. I was experiencing them from his perspective as well as my own, creating a kind of mental echo. If I tried, I was fairly sure I could see through the barriers around his mind.

I tried not to allow my exhilaration to register for fear it would attract his attention. I disowned the feeling, refusing to react emotionally despite what this could mean. Gently, subliminally almost, I attempted to draw more of his thoughts towards me. It was the most peculiar sensation I can ever recall feeling. The dominant impression was of cold, but behind that was structure: rank upon rank of memory – just out of reach.

Afraid to disturb those dense-packed strata of memory, I turned my attention to the inward-folding pattern, attempting to bring it into better focus, to summon a little more detail from his side of our mental link. I hardly dared put any force or urgency behind my attempt; I didn't know what little thing might alert him to what I was up to. I tried to think calming thoughts and gently *drew* the images to me.

As I watched, my perspective on the swirling pattern tilted and I realised that it was one of a series of patterns, lined up in his mind like rifles on an armoury wall. It was difficult to count them, but I thought there were seven. Maybe more. Each was different and yet they were all related somehow. At the far end, I recognised the basic shape I had copied and taken out to the moors with me. It was the pattern for teaching novices to Connect. In fact (the knowledge crystallised within me all by itself) it was *called* 'Connect'. And next to it, was the simple, ghost-like inversion of Quell. Their geometry was straightforward compared with the tendrilled, multi-layered complexity of the other patterns, but I sensed they were all aspects of a common purpose – like keys on a keyboard.

Given that I knew the name and function of those first two shapes, I couldn't help wonder: what was the significance of the others? I focussed on the shape that lately had begun to invade my mind… and all by itself, a word dropped into my mind: 'Home'. Behind it I glimpsed another shape and another word, almost like the legend beneath an illustration in a book. Part of it coalesced in my mind: 'Pattern…'.

Whatever 'Pattern…' meant, it seemed more familiar than the

rest. I didn't see how that could be but it was definitely reminiscent of something. For a moment I couldn't think what. Then it came to me: it reminded me of the necklace I was wearing. And as I thought it, the full legend revealed itself to me: 'Pattern Link'.

And the knowledge flowed in with the name. This was how the Sleeper had constructed my necklace. That first time, while I was unconscious but still Connected, he had established a temporary link to my mind, but it was too weak to last for long or to let him accomplish much. So he had worked fast and done his best to seize control of my drugged and boozy brain. He had used this symbol, Pattern Link, forcing it into my mind and directing its focus onto the few scraps and oddments of gold remaining in my jewellery box. The symbol's power had fused the metal, compressing and extruding it into a two-dimensional likeness of itself. As it neared completion, the Sleeper had caused me to place it around my neck. The cold metal had somehow softened and flowed until it reformed into an unbroken tracery around my neck and the Sleeper at last had a subject he could properly control. From that point on, he had a path straight into my psyche. He'd been able to influence, coax and manipulate me without me realising it. And I'd taken credit for every change he'd made, never suspecting I was sharing my head with a stowaway.

It was such a relief to unravel even a corner of this mystery and for a moment I was heady with the revelation.

Immediately I tried to calm myself.

Once I was a little more composed, I gently focussed in on the shape called 'Home' and painstakingly attempted to tease out the memories that went with it. I knew, somehow, that this pattern was the key to the Sleeper's plans for me and I had to discover what it meant.

Slowly I gathered the threads of his memory to me and

knowledge began to weave itself together in my consciousness. His recollections were siphoning in a thin stream across the link between our minds, slowly and quietly.

Then I felt the Sleeper's thoughts shifting and I willed him not to notice what I was up to. I was nearly there. I almost knew its purpose. The Home pattern was for...

Then I had it, just as the Sleeper took control once again, his attention no longer on the search but turned back to rest upon me.

Well?

For a moment I thought he knew what I'd been doing. But then I realised that some part of my brain had been keeping track of his search, and if I thought about it for a second, I knew that he'd stopped because he'd found something on the boat. He had located a pouch – through the Push Surface it felt like a thin plastic wallet – taped underneath one of the boards of the deck in the next compartment along. He wanted us to go and investigate.

I got off the bunk, now, stretching my lower back and rotating my head to relieve the stiffness I felt from sitting so long immobile.

I opened the bulkhead-door to the next compartment and stepped through into the compact space beyond. I'd stood here before when I ran the stud detector over the walls – and I'd found nothing then. In front of me was another door six feet ahead and there were cupboards to both sides. I knew they were empty except for a few tins of food. On my second mental sweep of the boat, I'd even searched inside the cans, in case they contained something other than baked beans, sweet corn and chicken soup.

On the floor ahead of me stretched a piece of fraying dark-blue carpet. It covered the middle strip of the painted decking along the centre-line of the boat. I bent down and ripped up the carpet, tearing it free from its tacks. Now I could see the wood beneath.

I needed to lift out part of the middle plank – a section about two feet long. But the piece I needed to remove was dogged into place by a couple of wooden pegs on the plank's underside. The pegs pivoted on dowels and locked under the boards on each side. The problem was that the pegs were inaccessible from above, so you couldn't tuck them out of the way until you'd lifted the plank – but you couldn't lift the plank free until you'd folded the pegs out of the way. It was another lock that only an adept could open – unless one was prepared to rip the floor up – or maybe fiddle around on your hands and knees for half an hour, sliding a steel rule between deck joints. I was pleased I didn't have to take either of those approaches.

I reached in and Pushed the pegs round on their pivots until they were flush with the sides of the plank. Then I got my fingernails under the sides of the board and pried it out of the floor. Sure enough, on the underneath was a clear vinyl wallet, the A4 kind that stationers sell for keeping paperwork in, and it was fastened to the bottom of the plank by two long strips of duct tape.

The wallet closed with a sort of toothless zip like they have on resealable food bags. I pulled the zipper open and lifted out the papers, walking back to the bunk with them and putting them in my bag. Then I went back and resealed the wallet, put the plank back in its place, and Pushed the pegs round until the board was locked down again. When that was done, I laid the carpet back in place and trod it down with my shoes.

I inspected my handiwork to see whether there was any sign that I'd been here. As I tipped my head down to squint at the carpet in the dim light, I suddenly felt like my brains were sloshing forwards in my head. It was a horrible feeling, brought on by my extreme

Robert Finn

tiredness. In fact I was pretty much dead on my feet by now. Just looking down at my feet had made me sway with exhaustion. I figured it was time that my all-powerful master called it a day and I got out of there before I actually fell down.

If the Marker was here, I think we'd have found it. So can we go through the papers back at the flat? I'm completely exhausted. We can figure out what they mean once we're somewhere safe.

Yes. We can return home now.

That was a relief; he was in a sensible mood. Most likely he was knackered[1] too. His mention of home made me wonder which Home the Sleeper's pattern referred to; I was fairly sure I managed to keep my interest to myself, though. Having felt the echo of my own thoughts in the Sleeper's mind I had the beginnings of an understanding for the way our link worked – just a beginning, mind you, but I had a sense for what carried: what he might overhear and what he might miss. It was like learning to whisper all over again: every adult could do it (if they chose to), but little kids sometimes struggled with the concept. You had to learn to speak and be quiet at the same time – and I thought I could see how it might be done.

Did that count as a victory? The possibility that I could think without being overheard? If it *was* a victory, it was a small one. My overall position was definitely not strong. He could see through my eyes and hear through my ears and I had no way to stop that.

And, although I knew I could fight him for short periods of time, the medication would make it so much harder. With the drugs now flowing through my veins I doubted I would be able to seize control of my actions for more than a few seconds. And even then, the Sleeper still had a couple of threats he could use to command my total obedience. So it wasn't a victory, but it was an

---

[1]   A posh British word meaning enervated or greatly fatigued

768

opportunity.

I needed a plan.

Damping my thoughts to a stealthy murmur, I thought back on the collection of patterns I'd seen ranked in the Sleeper's head. Besides Connect (which seeped into every adept's brain until you were hardly aware it was there) I knew pretty much what Pattern Link did – it made a necklace that could link two minds together – and at the last second, I'd grabbed a general idea of what Home was for.

I believed Home would take me somewhere – somewhere *central*. Central to what, I wasn't sure. But from the halo of meaning around it, I could tell what use the Sleeper had in mind for it. He would use it to bring me to him. But of course he would wait until I was holding the Marker before he activated it.

On its own, that was a frightening thought – the idea that he had a way to instantly abduct me – but what *really* troubled me was the knowledge that the Sleeper had at least three more patterns, maybe more. I knew with the certainty of stolen memory that each one commanded a power outside of what any sane person had ever achieved.

I should explain what I mean by that. As he infused my mind with his own skill at magic, I'd acquired lots of other information too. And besides what the Sleeper had shared with me, I'd also pored over the PAC's collection of old manuscripts, and the notes they'd written detailed their speculations. The overall picture I'd assembled told me that the patterns the Sleeper possessed were what was known as Greater Powers. These were powers beyond what you could achieve through the standard seven Surfaces. In the PAC's notes they were sometimes flippantly referred to as 'guru level' powers. Adepts had known about them forever, though they were exceedingly rare, and there was one thing everyone agreed upon: they were out of reach to normal people – normal adepts, that is.

Only a few unworldly elders had ever mastered a Greater Power and to do so they'd had to spend the majority of their long lives ridding themselves of ambition and every other material and physical desire.

It was believed that only the enlightened could even *discover the existence* of a Greater Power. It took decades, at least half a dozen of them, to reach a state of affectless and transcendent emptiness within which one of the deep secrets of magic might be revealed. Most who tried never met with success and no one – not one person in the recorded history of the world – had ever mastered a power and then resuscitated enough of their ego to put it to worldly use.

If you came by a Greater Power it was because you had obliterated your desires, your ego even. You couldn't master that power and then use it to take over the world. At least no one ever had, even though it was every power-mad adept's dream. The PAC's papers included just a flavour of the eternal and avid interest in the subject and those papers all agreed: no exceptions had ever been found. Greater Powers would not come to the ambitious or the worldly.

And when you catalogued the few enlightened souls who had manifested some Greater Power there were perhaps half a dozen gurus in all – depending on who you believed – maybe a couple more and maybe fewer. And in each case they had mastered only a single Greater Power.

From what I'd seen inside the Sleeper's mind – that plus a little arithmetic – I knew that he had mastered at least five Powers. *Five*. I'd seen the common or garden patterns – Connect and its simple inversion Quell – and then at least five others. It was unprecedented;

even the knowledge that had spilled over from the Sleeper's mind itself told me that. He had done something no else had been able to do. That no one *should* be able to do.

I also recalled from the PAC papers that described the Marker that its creation was credited to a Greater Power so rare that it had only manifested itself once, in ancient China, at least a century before Julius Caesar was a twinkle in his father's eye.

Given what I now knew, I could guess that there was a pattern for making Markers too, presumably called Pattern Marker – just as Pattern Link had made my necklace, my mental shackle – and I could tentatively assume that the Sleeper didn't possess it. If he could make Markers, I couldn't see why he'd have me crawling around on my hands and knees looking for one.

I knew his control of the Surfaces was formidable because that skill had flowed into me, had been deliberately pressed into my head. And with that skill had come sufficient knowledge to place his abilities in context, to know that these were the skills of a great master. But it now seemed that he was something even more fearsome, something unheard of – a master of *multiple* Greater Powers who had *not* shed his ego, and who had very definitely not renounced his claim on this world. Somehow he had accomplished what a hundred generations of adepts had declared impossible (however much they'd wished the opposite was true).

Not for the first time I began to wonder what the Sleeper would do once he had the Marker in his grasp and had used it to regenerate himself. I had struggled with the question before, but now I knew two new things. First: he might very probably be the most powerful adept who had ever lived. And second: the pattern he carried in his head, the one called Home, would take me to him, wherever he was. Somewhere he had a body in need of repair and when the writhing shape that increasingly haunted my mind was finally activated, I knew I would find myself standing next to that broken-down body. I wondered, with a sick nervousness, what would happen after that.

And I knew that I'd find out soon.

With all those insights and fears swirling around in my head as I left the boat, I experienced a moment of total desperation. At my feet was a boat hook and for a split second I thought about picking it up from the deck and just whacking myself over the head with it. In my many layers of clothing, I'd flop over the side and sink down into the ooze without leaving a trace. I was sure I could do it before he could stop me and then it would all be over.

Maybe it would be better for everyone if I did it – better than unleashing the Sleeper on the world. It might even be the best death I could hope for now.

But I didn't do it. Not only was I afraid – we shouldn't underestimate the importance of that – but it would leave the Sleeper furious and vengeful. I'd be giving Daniel, the Professor and the others maybe a fifty-fifty chance of waking in the night to find an Army assassin at the foot of their beds. Even if I gave no thought to my own wellbeing, bringing my life to a sudden, violent end would do nothing to help my friends.

And from my friends, my thoughts turned towards my mother. Here I was, contemplating taking my own life and I'd been led to this point by my revulsion for her suicide. What was the word for that?

For a moment, my mind drifted back to a college English class I'd taken years before. The Professor who took the class was so picky that she interviewed every applicant individually, putting them on the spot with her fierce questions. She had commanded me, "Define irony." I forget what I replied at the time, something about it being a kind of higher justice invisible to most of those it affected. I think she'd been favourably impressed. She'd let me on the course at any rate.

But I think if I was asked what irony was now, I'd give a different definition. I'd say it was the piercing pain you felt when you realised what fate had done to the shape of your life.

As I made my way back to my flat I struggled to find some way to untwist the knot my life had been tied in.

CHAPTER 27

Nuclear weapons. That was the closest analogy I could find in the non-magical world. I'd seen inside the Sleeper's mind and there, lined up in his mental armoury, were five suitcases, each containing an atomic bomb.

Or maybe that wasn't a good analogy, because I had no idea what those symbols in his head might do. They were in the same league as the symbol which created the Marker, but what did that tell me? What was comparable to immortality? 'Pattern Link' had allowed him to pull me on like a glove and effectively possess me for weeks before I became aware of his influence and began to oppose him. What was comparable to demonic possession? And 'Home' hinted at something even greater: the source of magic, maybe: its central point. What might await me once he triggered that symbol? Was there some master control room for magic which the Sleeper had chosen for his lair? Was his proximity to the endpoint of Home what had given him access to this incredible arsenal of powers?

I didn't know what those remaining powers might be, the

ones I hadn't been able to see, but that didn't stop my imagination generating bizarre or terrifying possibilities on a minute-by-minute basis. Adepts couldn't use magic directly on each another when both parties were Connected, but I pictured the newly rejuvenated Sleeper reaching through an opponent's Shield and dropping him in his tracks. Then I imagined some awful battlefield weapon, seeing a dozen soldiers turned to drifting ashes by a single, vengeful thought. A moment later I imagined a super-Shield, vast and thick, protecting a building and capable of turning aside a missile or absorbing its destructive force.

They were all just comic-book daydreams, recycled pieces of B-movie nightmares: my imagination could churn them out all day long – but that didn't mean they were impossible, untrue. Even if the truth was more subtle and low-key, more insidious than the flashy superpowers I was dreaming up, surely one of the five symbols would cause a shift in the balance of power in the world. Even the symbol I knew best, Pattern Link, could do that.

Once he was out in the world again, fit and young, the Sleeper could dig his claws into many more brains. There was no reason to think my necklace was for adepts only; it worked whether I wanted it to or not, regardless of whether I concentrated or not. What might he achieve with a few dozen of his zombies in the world? I didn't like to ascribe too much self-awareness to myself, but it had been my own vanity that had stopped me recognising that he was the reason for my newfound success. And I wasn't the only person in the world who suffered from vanity.

Might he not find vain and powerful people whose self-importance would never allow them to suspect that he was the power behind their throne? When I thought of egos so great they took credit for everything around them, was I not describing the leaders of the world? They were ripe for the picking.

Six months ago, all I had to worry about was a flaky temperament and my own genius for self-pity. By this time a week ago I had the vicious assassins of the Army to avoid. By this morning I had every reason to fear for my life and the lives of my friends at the hands of an enemy who had invaded my thoughts. And now, as much as I wanted to ignore it, I found myself fretting over what the Sleeper might do to the rest of the world once he was able to bring his power to bear on it.

In any sensible, believable version of reality this would not be my problem. A responsibility like this should not and could not fall onto shoulders like mine. It was so wrong as to seem almost like a global joke at my expense; I was being mocked by the hidden engine of fate itself[1].

Even as I acknowledged how ridiculous that last thought was – that it was just my old, neurotic impulses contributing their two-cents-worth – I was forced to admit that therapy couldn't cure *this* problem. There's nothing like discovering the fate of the world is now your responsibility to make you re-examine your feelings of being put upon.

The Sleeper was a problem bigger than the PAC and bigger than me. In fact it was a problem so serious, so huge, that it was almost a relief that I could think of no way to derail his plans; it lifted the responsibility off of my shoulders and demoted me to the status of helpless victim. If I couldn't stop him then I wasn't to blame for what he did.

And although that realisation was crushing, at the same time it was a comfort; it let me off the hook and allowed me to reconcile myself to the inevitable.

---

[1]   Isn't it weird how feeling insignificant and possessing minuscule self-esteem doesn't stop a person also developing a sense of victimisation the size of a city block or allowing their paranoia to grow beyond all limits?

And then, of all the accursed luck, the beginnings of a plan began to occur to me.

* * *

It was raining as I walked back from the tube station – spiteful Winter-in-London rain – and my wig was starting to look like the pelt of a drowned fox. I glanced around me and, seeing no one about, I pulled the wig off and stuck it in my bag. I tucked the gold headband in after it. Now at least it was my own hair that would frizz up and glue itself to my face.

I put as much urgency into my stride as I could, hoping I'd get to my front door before the icy raindrops worked their way any further down the neck of my coat. But I was so weary from the search of the boat that I didn't have a lot of speed on tap.

I knew I could save myself several minutes of exposure to the elements if I cut through Junkies' Alley so I left the pavement and crossed onto the gravel of the path, turning in under the shoulder-height branch of a fading plane tree. Fat, frigid droplets were brushed loose from the tips of its boney twigs and they pattered all around me and onto my skin.

I suppose I should have been concerned about the human reptiles who lurked in the grimy shadows here, but really, they were so thoroughly outclassed by the other menaces in my life I couldn't muster much of a sense of threat. I wondered if I should put my headband back on my head just in case they wanted to challenge that assessment, but I didn't bother. Any sense of peril I had after the tiredness had taken its cut was fully employed worrying about the Sleeper. And my emergency reserves of panic I was saving for the Army. Sorry, nothing to spare for the junkies, maybe next time.

I passed the iron stairs under which I'd seen a pair of predatory eyes tracking me that first time through here, but this time when I peered in, no one looked back. I reached the twist in the path by the big transformer and found I could see the road on the far side just up ahead of me.

And then I heard something.

"'Scuse me, wait a minute," a voice behind me slurred. Someone had been standing in the tall, shadowed bushes next to the grey enclosure of the transformer and now he crashed out on to the path, holding up a trembling hand that looked a little like a dying crab. He wasn't the one I'd seen before, but he just had to be a junkie. His eyes were mounted too deep in the black wells of their sockets and his cheek bones had risen to pallid prominence through the thin flesh of his face; he didn't get that way just by skimping on the wheat-grass and cutting a few yoga classes.

"Hold on, wanna ask you a question," he breathed, stumbling after me, sounding just as tired as I was. It would be almost funny, in a gallows-humour sort of way, if he chased me: me too tired to run, him too messed-up to catch me.

For some reason I said 'Sorry' to him – maybe it was some latent piece of middle-class programming reflexively triggered by his begging tone – and then I scuttled out onto the pavement at the far end of the path.

There was still an hour or two of daylight left, so I doubted he would actually chase me. But I slid my hand into my bag and explored with my fingertips until they encountered the cold smooth edge of my headband. I wasn't planning to stop, but I decided that if I looked round and saw him following me, I'd go back and deal with him: break a couple of bones, maybe. It would probably be doing him a favour – get him some medical attention. Otherwise I just didn't have time to be threatened by amateurs. I nudged those thoughts in the direction of our link, knowing how the Sleeper felt about junkies; he'd approve.

For some reason, that particular thought flaked loose another layer of false memory and I remembered something.

I'd already learned that my earlier, visceral hatred of junkies had come from him and now I discovered something else – and it didn't seem like he'd planted it deliberately. It was an intact fragment of knowledge that had somehow slipped across the link and embedded itself in my head. I drank in the flavour and scent of it, priming myself to recognise his signature from this scrap, to be alert for a similar imprint in my thoughts. But beyond this memory told me of him, it also told me something useful about the world – something that I might be able to use.

I looked back over my shoulder and saw that my would-be attacker hadn't even made it out into the daylight. My fingers withdrew from my bag.

Five minutes later I was home, the locks were on the door and I was upstairs, in the top bathroom, underneath a hot shower. The wig had made my scalp itch and now my skin was getting a good scrub. And the shower was a pretty good place to wrestle with the inadequate scraps of my plan. My mental autopilot could handle the soap-and-water side of things while the rest of my brain struggled with the life-and-death stuff.

If I could have strung the shower out for a couple of hours I would have done. This plan I had – that I was *beginning* to have – was a little insane – insane and complicated and it didn't work. I kept finding gaps in it. It was like taking a handful of pieces from three different jigsaw puzzles and hoping they'd make a picture – in my current predicament I'd have even settled for something abstract and modernist – but the more I looked the more holes I found.

779

And I wasn't putting this together sitting at one of those General's tables, crowded with model battalions arranged in rows, using a croupier's squeegee to fine-tune their deployment. I was struggling to find the one right combination of choices that would trigger all the events I needed to happen and I was doing it while putting a third application of conditioner on my distressed hair under water that had gone cold.

And the whole thing might even be possible, I might even be able to work it out, if I wasn't so goddamned tired. This was the most important piece of decision-making I'd ever had to do (or, I supposed, ever would do) and I could hardly stay on my feet for the fatigue that pulled down on my arms and eyelids and ladled tar onto my mental cogs.

The solution eluded me, despite the fact that I now had one huge and luminous ace up my sleeve. Despite my inability to assemble a coherent plan, I believed I had resolved one of the biggest intangibles in my situation. I reckoned I might have actually figured out the hiding place of the Marker, but I was so dizzy from exertion that I couldn't clarify my own thinking enough to feel sure. I didn't even think I could keep the Sleeper out of my thoughts for much longer. Fears pressed in upon me and I found myself worrying: what if my defences come down? What if he catches a glimpse of what I'm up to *and drags the whole thing out of me? Then I've lost whatever advantage I might have had.*

What advantage will you have lost?

Damn, damn, damn. He can hear me.

Yes, I can hear you. I'm inside your head, you unbelievable fool. What are you attempting to keep from me? It's something relating to the Marker isn't it? I can sense that much.

I got out of the shower, busying myself for a second or two by fussing with the towel. I struggled to blank my mind, to think only of nothingness. But it was impossible. It would have been impossible even if I were pin-sharp instead of dead on my feet. You just can't *not* think of something.

I am not inclined to give another lecture. I will simply prise that knowledge out of your head and that is not something you will enjoy. Once that is taken care of we can consider how you might benefit from an illustration of the price of disobedience; I am thinking particularly of the demonstration we discussed earlier, the scheme involving the abundant loss of life.

He was certainly getting a taste for the snarky speeches. I wasn't sure whether he *could* actually tear the knowledge out of my mind, but even if I'd been tempted to find out what *that* felt like, I had to be careful. I didn't want him rampaging through my brain, bursting through every barrier. I reckoned I could give up the location of the Marker without giving *everything* else away. And moreover, the jolt of adrenaline that came with being discovered had given me a temporary burst of strength which I was able to put to good use: I reckoned I now had a working idea of how to screen the bulk of my thoughts from his gaze – for as long as my concentration held. And I was becoming sensitive enough to his presence now that I was sure he wasn't overhearing this particular soliloquy.

But I could feel myself beginning to fade again almost immediately. I decided to tell him what he wanted to know before my mental defences collapsed completely. There was a time for resistance and this wasn't it. Wrapped in a bath-robe, I left the bathroom and flopped down on my bed, resigned to what was coming.

OK, here it is.

You were a nautical man once, right?

For a second, I could actually feel the shock radiating from his side of our link and into my mind. I'd caught him by surprise. And he was plenty tired too; he wasn't guarding his thoughts any better than I was. He hadn't expected my question, despite the many clues he'd allowed to slip through his fingers.

It's not a trick question. I just wanted to ask you something: that long-handled boat-hook thing we found on the house-boat; what do you think it's for?

There was a slight delay before he responded.

It is not a boat hook, as you call it. It is... unusual. Not a design I am familiar with. But then I do not consider a floating dog kennel to be a legitimate vessel. I have no knowledge of those waterborne dormitories. The owners might use such a pole for anything.

OK, next question. Why would a house-boat need an anchor chain?

And I'd done it again. I'd stopped him dead in his mental tracks.

He was thinking it through, trying to get ahead of me, I could sense it. The delay before he replied was even longer this time.

Perhaps... these 'craft' must stand off from shore from time to time. His words came slowly. He was unsure of himself. I could tell he didn't much like that feeling.

So why would the anchor be down when the boat is tied up in dock?

Yes. Yes, I see. Something has been attached to the anchor. You have impressed me. We will return to that place at once and raise the anchor.

Wait a minute. Just hold on.

Across the link, I could feel him bristling at being told what to do.

You refuse?

Not exactly. But first, don't you want me to tell you what the boat-hook thing is for?

He was fairly squirming with impatience now. He hadn't been able to contain his excitement when he realised where the Marker must be, and now he wanted to charge out there with all guns blazing. And yet he didn't want to miss something important. He was struggling to solve the puzzle that he knew *I* had already solved and he couldn't do it.

Tell me. *Now*.

Inwardly I sighed, and I realised that he wasn't the only one feeling a little irritation. I was running out of patience too.

You know, to be honest I've had more or less enough of you ordering me around. If you're so smart, work it out for yourself. And if you're so powerful, then you can <u>make</u> me tell you.

It was a reckless thing to do, but the microscopic fragments that were all that remained of my god-given self-esteem could still prickle me like splinters. I felt, before I was done, I really had to take at least one stand against him. There would be plenty of opportunities for me to get myself killed before this was all played out and it just didn't seem right to allow that to happen without looking him straight in the metaphorical eye at least once and defying him. I'd been right a moment ago. There *was* a time for resistance and *this* was it.

For a second I couldn't tell how he was going to respond. And then a mass of ill-will struck the edge of my mind like an iceberg, peeling back the thin steel of my defences and bursting in towards the core of me. Its brutal bulk seemed ready to crumple me flat me like a Coke can.

I screwed up what little determination I had left and resisted him. It was like trying to lift a car off your chest. The weight just kept piling down on me. I could feel his strength, how much of it

there was, and I could gauge it against my own. With a flicker of
surprise I realised how powerful I actually was, but at the same
time, I could see that it wasn't enough. He was going to win.

I struggled and fought for what seemed like an age, and
gradually, inevitably, the weight descended on me. I must have
looked like I was having a fit as I lay on the bedcovers twitching
and straining at nothing. If I had been tired before, I was beyond that
now, dropping down into a whole new realm of surreal weariness.
If I kept this up much longer I really thought I would pass out. I
held on until we were both woozy with fatigue and then, with a
final, defiant thrust, I shoved him back momentarily and called a
halt, acknowledging my defeat.

OK. Stop, stop, stop. You win. You win. I'll tell you.

He was masking it, but I knew he was just as drained as me.
He'd just had a little more practice at pushing himself than I had
– centuries of hard discipline will do that for you. He was also
boiling mad at my defiance; our earlier exchange had really rubbed
his nose in my smartness. Funny how that never seemed to bring
out the best in people, going back as far as I could remember.

The pressure on me dissipated and I awaited his response.

Now. Was all he said and it was deafening, like the blast of a
fog horn experienced from close range. He didn't need to explain
further.

*Let me show you. I'll explain it all; I'll lay it out so you can see
everything.*

My arms and legs felt boneless with fatigue, but I rolled into an
upright position and stood up. Then I went to my desk and fetched
the papers we'd retrieved from the secret compartment in Jan's old
desk. I selected one of the papers and laid it on the bed. It was a
print-out of scheduled flight times between London and Rome and
it was a couple of years out of date. Nothing very exciting there, it

being information available to anyone with an Internet connection, but scribbled in the margins were a number of complex doodles.

I left them there and went to hunt through my bag, at last pulling out the papers we'd collected today from beneath the decking of the house-boat. I selected a single piece of paper, this time a receipt from a pharmacy, and placed it face down on the bed next to the list of flight times. On the back of the receipt was another of Jan's doodles, something long and thin, with a boxy outline at one end, lying next to a big shape like the side of a whale.

Then I fished out my laptop, fired it up and opened Illustrator – a drawing program. I'd had a lot of practice with it and was kind of a whiz at putting together complex diagrams – in fact I could draw faster with it than anyone I knew – and now I took Jan's doodles and re-drew them on the computer so that they became clear and neat. I could have roughed something out quickly enough, but instead I laid it on thick. I refined and added details until I could feel the Sleeper's patience fraying. I hit print and fetched the following hard copy:

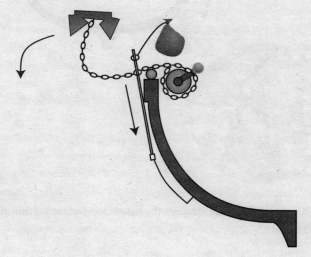

You get it?

What is that? Explain it.

Look, just let me draw the second part. It'll make sense then.

I began a second drawing, working rapidly but still putting in more detail than strictly necessary. I knew it would annoy the Sleeper but I reckoned I could live with that, all in all. Maybe he'd get so angry with me he'd have a stroke and I could go back to my regular life – whatever form *that* might take.

Even though I'm normally wicked fast and accurate, exhaustion was relentlessly joggling my elbow as I drew. A couple of times I had to close my eyes and pause because I was actually finding it difficult to focus. I felt like I'd been up for days, maybe a week, but I pressed on. At last I hit print and fetched this:

It even had a little through-the-magnifying-glass section for extra detail.

Let me take you through it. On the first picture, you can see that there's a spike that sticks up from the side of the boat, under the waterline, right? You slide the hollow end of the boat-hook onto the prong and that lets you drop things down and thread them onto the spike, OK?

I tapped the first of Jan's doodles. If you squinted at it right you could see it as a muddled drawing of just that. The detail was much clearer in my version.

First you take a link of the anchor chain and drop it over the boat-hook and down onto the prong. Then you put the thing you want to hide in a bag and attach a cord to it. Put a loop in the end of the cord. Now you pass the loop over the pole and drop the bag over the side. The bag dangles from the spike and its cord sits on top of a link of the anchor chain. Now you can remove the stick. And that's the first picture.

I pointed to the second of Jan's doodles and then switched to my version of it.

If anyone hauls up the anchor chain without putting the stick in place, the rising chain lifts the loop of the bag free of the spike and the bag just drops into the sludge on the bottom. If you bring up the anchor like that you find nothing. But if put the boat-hook back in place first, you can haul the bag up. It's fiendish; I'm not surprised you took so long to get it.

Ouch. Maybe that last comment was a little too much. I could feel rage radiating across the link like desert sun through a windowpane.

Get up. We're going there now.

It's too late in the day. Get real. I can hardly stand.

Almost before I knew what had hit me, he had seized control of my motor functions. I was on my feet and hauling dry clothes out of the wardrobe with absolutely no conscious involvement on my behalf. Maybe I could have fought him but I hardly had the strength.

I'm sorry, I said, and tried to mean it. I didn't like being a puppet. Sure, being a willing accomplice was morally painful and guilt-inducing, but watching him pull my strings and march me round the room like his toy was hideous. It reduced me to an instrument of his will, which made me feel less than human. I resolved that I would at least retain control of my own limbs even if I had to relinquish everything else.

I'll do it. I won't fight you. I'll get ready and we'll go. You've won.

Cautiously I took back control and he didn't oppose me. I pulled on my clothes. Moving at all was an effort, but I didn't feel like baiting the Sleeper any more. It had already been an exhausting day and now we'd both used up what little energy had remained. If we clashed again, I didn't think there'd be enough left of my will-power to stop him reading my thoughts with as much as ease as leafing through a confiscated diary.

This time I didn't bother with a disguise. I chose jeans, solid boots and a heavy sweater for warmth. The only embellishment was a dark wool cap that I found on the floor of my wardrobe; I used it to cover the headband. The cap itched like crazy, which come to think of it was probably why it was on the floor, and I immediately regretted not picking out something different. But I didn't want to stretch the Sleeper's tolerance any further by dithering over my choice of outfits.

I was about to set off when I caught sight of all the papers lying on my bed. *Should probably tuck these away* I thought and gathered them up. I grabbed a folder from the bookcase and slid the papers in amongst some college paperwork, then I returned the folder to its shelf.

I pulled on a coat and clumped down the stairs. When I stepped out of the front door I found that the drizzle had let up. I judged that there was maybe an hour more daylight, although the street was already quiet. I'd only gone a few steps when I had to scratch my head furiously through the cap. I didn't stop, but a moment later I had to pull the cap off completely so I could get my fingernails into my itchy scalp.

Relax, I'll put it back on if we see anyone.

I neared the entrance to the cut-through, the Junkie's hang-out, and my feet slowed.

Why do you hesitate?

Um, don't you think we should go around? There might be someone in there and I'm asleep on my feet. It just seems safer to go round.

With both of us so tired, he wasn't having much more luck hiding his thoughts from me than I was from him. His weary anger was a constant presence. I think he was finding living in my head was a bit like sharing a dorm room with me; he'd had enough of my whining long since.

When he didn't respond, but just simmered to himself, I added: *Sorry, but just to be on the safe side.* There was a noticeable whimper to my mental tone and I could sense how irritating the Sleeper found it.

I do not cower from those parasites and I am getting tired of reminding you to obey me. The next time I even suspect you are defying me I will punish you. If I sense you are delaying me, I will kill your friends and then perhaps you will learn how to take orders instead of kicking at every instruction like a child in need of correction.

Wow. Someone was getting pretty pouty. But I didn't have the necessary grit to argue with him. I turned obediently into the alley and made my way once more through the dank semi-darkness.

In theory, I had nothing to worry about: the most powerful adept in the world was ready to assist me if I had to fight off a couple of over-medicated, ninety-pound purse-snatchers. Though, maybe in hindsight it would have made more sense to cover the enticing gleam of gold at my temples.

Even when I took a false step on the wet ground and in my numbed exhaustion nearly tumbled onto my ass it didn't seem like a big deal.

I'll admit that when I felt a clammy arm snake around my throat a cold draft of fear blew through me, but even then I didn't doubt myself. Even though I was feeling a little high on exhaustion, I knew that in a second I'd lash out and there'd be shrieks and moans and unpleasant snapping sounds and a couple of addicts would finally have a good reason to dose up on morphine. All I had to do was focus…

And yet I couldn't. A second junkie kicked my legs out from under me and I went down, my collision with the ground knocking some of the wind out of me. The hard edge of a fore-arm (so skinny it felt like greasy cloth over naked bone) was still pressing hard into my windpipe and the acid stink of unwashed flesh was in my nostrils. I tried again to Connect and if my brain had been a gun, instead of a bang there would just have been a dry click. I was so weary that Connection wouldn't come. That's the moment when panic finally reared up, bellowing, and began to stampede through my brain. This was not good.

And then I felt the headband being torn from my temples and at that point it occurred to me that I might be in truly serious trouble. Despite the pain, despite the panic, my first fear was for how the Sleeper might react, what awful revenge he might take for allowing this to happen. Since he'd revealed himself, I'd been desperate to remove the necklace, but I knew that as soon as I did, I would be dooming my friends. In my mind it had become their lifeline, something I had to keep safe whatever else might happen – and even now I could feel grimy hands reaching for it.

I started to kick and scream (though no sound made it past the choke-hold on my throat). I struggled furiously even as I felt someone dropping their weight onto my legs. The pressure on my throat was making it difficult to keep breathing and I couldn't tell if the black clouds swarming across my vision were from lack of oxygen or some retribution the Sleeper had unleashed.

Just before my head hit the gravel, I felt hard fingers plucking at the clothing around my neck. Someone, somewhere said, "She's got a necklace on." And then I felt a new sort of pain as the gold wire at the back of my neck dug deep into my flesh. "Gimme the pliers," the other voice said and somewhere around that point I slid down into a nightmare where angry zombies with icy hands used a selection of tools to pull out my fingernails one by one and all I could think about was what would happen to my friends now that the link to the Sleeper had been severed.

CHAPTER 28

I knew an old guy once who told me about how, when he was younger, his worn-out Ford had been stolen. He was kind of surprised when the police called him, saying it had turned up, still drivable, some miles away. The police reckoned a couple of hippies stole it to get to a festival. This guy, who was kind of a hippy himself, got the bus to the police impound yard. "They ran off, but they left behind your things," the policemen said, handing over the car keys. *Hmm*, thought my friend, who always kept the car empty of belongings because the door locks didn't work properly. So he drove around the corner, pulled in, and performed a little inventory. The thieves had bolted, leaving behind a long afghan coat in his size, a handful of really cool bootleg cassettes, a full tank of gas and – when he popped off the plastic cover in the middle of the steering wheel – a brimming bag of grass, right where he always kept his own stash. What a nice story. I thought of it as I was coming round.

When I was about 90% conscious I realised that my face hurt, just on one side – the side resting on the gravel. I lifted my head and a boom of pain detonated in my head. Being choked unconscious had left me with a headache so large it seemed to cram my skull to bursting point. Broken bones, blood, severed limbs? I sat up, aware that I was lying in a puddle of oily rainwater and I began patting myself, figuring it was the easiest way to find out what was attached and what was broken.

I could hardly believe it when I failed to find any injuries. Well, any major injuries. I touched a tender spot on my scalp and my fingers came away bloody. The flesh of my scalp was already puffing up around the cut, but even in my most hypochondriacal moment I couldn't convince myself it was much of a wound.

Even though I was sitting up, I was aware that I wasn't thinking clearly yet.

Above me stretched the dark coral of bare plane tree limbs outlined against a dimming cloud-locked sky; around me was the alleyway. As I took stock, I pictured a miniature maintenance crew reconnecting downed circuits in my nervous system. The gravel on my cheek, the water-melon-sized headache, the cut on my scalp – each one made its presence felt in turn as the lights came back on in my brain. Next to arrive was a bone-deep ache in the muscles of my back and legs. I couldn't tell if I'd been kicked, fallen down, or just laid awkwardly in my stupor. Whatever the reason, I was stiff as a lacquered board.

Once the circuitry to my nerve endings was restored, my body's repair crew evidently set to work hooking up my higher mental functions. With a jolt of nausea reminiscent of sudden deceleration I remembered my situation. The feeling was like sleepily glancing at the bedside clock and having it occur to you that right now you're supposed to be in an exam. It was like that, except in a world where they kill your friends if your grades drop.

How long had I been disconnected from the sleeper? Phone

gone, watch gone, no way to tell. OK, well… it was still light. In fact it didn't seem any closer to sunset than when I left the house. So I hadn't been unconscious very long. There'd only been an hour of daylight left when I closed my front door, so I couldn't possibly have been out for more than 45 minutes. My best guess, based on nothing more than intuition, was that I'd hardly missed any time at all – maybe five minutes. But even if I was right, that five minutes might seem like five hours to the Sleeper, who was suddenly disconnected from the world, unable to oversee his slave, and doubtless fretting that all his plans were going south. Cut off like that, his mind might be bubbling away, brewing up venomous schemes for reprisal. What might he have done already? And what if I was wrong and I'd been out for a lot longer than five minutes?

Losing consciousness had never been part of my admittedly sketchy plan. Everything else, though – believe it or not – was going better than expected.

You see, I'd figured out a way forward during a moment of surpassing despair. Hitting that low had made me realise something – something that finally allowed me to gather up the unruly strands of my planning and plait them neatly together. The secret had been to remove a single disruptive thread from the bundle. With that one gone, everything else came together tidily.

My mistake, it turned out, had been to expect too much, and that had prevented me from making any progress. Like those aspiring gurus I'd been thinking about, I'd been holding on to too many of my earthly needs; I could only achieve more by striving for less. Poetic sounding, isn't it? The practicalities, though, were grim.

My moment of clarity had struck when I tried to imagine the Sleeper releasing me. He would have his Marker, I would no longer be of use to him, and he'd simply send me away with a pat on the back and a heart-felt thank you. "Stay in touch," he'd call after me, waving.

Look a little closer and you'll see that there's something wrong with that picture. It just wasn't going to happen. He was never going to let me go. It was obvious.

So where did that leave me? I already knew that I couldn't run from him.

Put those two facts together and you arrived at this conclusion: it was no longer about me – simple as that. The Sleeper was going to kill me. And that realisation freed me to see things as they really were. If I withdrew just one requirement of my plan – the need for me to survive it – then everything else gelled. I could see a way to save my friends, even to hand them the Marker. And I could thwart the Sleeper for the foreseeable future – or until he could find another slave. And that could be a very long time if you factored in the memory that had surfaced as I was walking home. Just before I'd let the Sleeper overhear my thoughts about the Marker, it had come to me: there were no new adepts.

The old guard, virtually immortal as they were, took every opportunity to eliminate the up-and-coming competition. It was spelled out in the PAC manuscripts if you knew how to interpret them: a stranger was just a mortal enemy you hadn't met yet. There were no tender, impressionable young adepts for the Sleeper to prey upon, because if any arose, they'd be swiftly despatched by those currently in power. The PAC lived in camouflaged obscurity in a damp field in the middle of Cornwall mainly for that reason, and the four of us – the Professor, David, Susan and me – might well be the only candidates for mind control that the Sleeper had seen for a century – at least in this part of the world. The Sleeper had been very lucky to find someone as vulnerable as me.

But like I say, this wasn't about me. With that liberating thought in my mind, I realised that if I was able to remove myself from the picture in just the right way I could keep the Sleeper bottled up indefinitely. All I had to do was make my death look like an accident. Before, when I'd decided against trying to fool the Sleeper, it was because I couldn't see him buying any scheme I might have for *faking* my own death – but what if it wasn't faked? What if it was for real and the only fake part was making it seem accidental?

But how to pull that off? Step out in front of a bus? Total the bike at high speed? Sneeze while cleaning my service revolver? I'd keep those as my back-up options. Right away I figured the junkies would be my best hope. See, I didn't actually need them to kill me outright, just to mug me and steal the necklace. That would give me a little time out from under the Sleeper's gaze in which to set up the finale.

Of course, I couldn't be certain they'd jump me, but I could certainly push my luck. And I'd hit the Street Crime Jackpot on my first attempt.

By way of preparation, I'd completed what the Sleeper had started: the process of utterly exhausting the both of us. The junkies could only overpower me if I was defenceless, so I needed the Sleeper to believe that I was too tired to Connect. Not much play-acting required there. I'd sparred with him and struggled against his efforts to control me until both of us were weary almost to the point of collapse.

Then I'd goaded him until I could be sure he'd react angrily when I meekly suggested avoiding the alleyway and playing it safe. It was important that he remembered the decision had been his and not mine. And I thought I could rely on his expansive ego to dismiss any suspicions that I'd cleverly manipulated him.

It also hadn't required much acting skill to panic just before I blacked out. I really was frightened for the lives of my friends and the thought of what I had to do next had leant a real quality of desperation to the performance. With the exception of me passing out, things had pretty much gone according to plan. But what I couldn't predict in advance was whether I would survive the mugging.

If I didn't, then the drawings showing the location of the Marker, together with the papers giving the boat's location, were right there, in amongst my college paperwork, for the PAC to find. Earlier, I'd put my college ID in a different pocket from my wallet so that it wouldn't be stolen when the muggers swiped my cash and credit cards. So when the authorities found my body, they would pretty quickly link me to the Professor. My college employment records and my passport both listed the Professor as my next of kin, so there'd be a good chance that he would be the first to go through my things. I'd set things up so that the PAC could pick up the trail of the Marker.

But that was just a backup. I thought it was pretty unlikely that the junkies would kill me.

I was expecting to have to do that myself.

If I woke up after the mugging, my plan was to run a couple of quick errands and then retrieve the necklace. Just before I put it back on I'd have a simple task to perform – one brutal act before I could rest. I'd need to find something sharp and slice open an artery. Then I could restore the link to the Sleeper just in time for him to catch the final act. If I died while he was inside my head, monitoring my every move and sensation, there'd be no doubt in his mind.

I'd make it clear to him that in reclaiming the necklace from the muggers I'd been severely wounded. He'd have to take that part on faith, but he'd have seen through my own eyes the most important parts: the mugging itself, and then, a little later, me gasping my authentic last. It would be like he'd ducked out of the room to grab a soda during the last few minutes of my televised life story: when he left the heroine was being attacked, when he got back she was dying. He could fill in the missing part for himself.

What I wasn't sure of – what I wouldn't know until the moment came – was whether I could do it. Kill myself, I mean. My plan was to inflict a good, deep wound in the thigh – make sure I found that femoral artery. I could bleed out from that in just a couple of minutes and in the meantime it would incapacitate me, preventing me from reaching help.

It wasn't instantaneous, though; I should have long enough to settle the necklace back in place and bring the Sleeper up to speed before I lost consciousness.

I was praying that I wouldn't lose my nerve when the time came, but there was a sick feeling in my guts like my internal organs had been scooped out and replaced with a couple of bags of iced water. I'd found myself hoping that the junkies would finish the job for me, so I didn't have to.

But, wouldn't you just know it, here I was still alive, sitting in a puddle of filthy rainwater and struggling not to throw up at the thought of what I had to do next. *Screw it*, I thought, and twisting onto my side, heaved the contents of my stomach into the weeds.

With that out of the way, it was time to get busy. According to my plan, if I was still alive after the mugging, I'd need to Connect in order to overpower my attackers and retrieve the necklace. For that I'd need tribute, and I'd already noticed some suitable jewellery in Noola's room when I'd moved her things. Of course I'd ditch the tribute before I put the necklace back on, so there was no danger of the Sleeper Healing my injuries. But first I had to get back to the house.

I staggered to my feet and tried to run. I took three wobbly steps and nearly lurched straight into a wall. I corrected my direction and set off, in a limping jog. I'd have laughed if I thought I'd be able to stop again: my agonising trot reminded me of a wounded pantomime horse.

I was desperate to get out of that alley and back to my house before any more time passed. I tottered along as quickly as I could and was soon outside my front-door. My house-keys were gone, but there was a spare set hidden beneath the straggly branches of the front garden's lone shrub. God knows what sort of spectacle I presented, but I managed to retrieve the key and get inside the house before any passers-by could spot me and shriek at the sight of a filthy, blood-spattered crazy-woman wrestling with a buddleia davidii.

If I was quick, I would have time to make one phone call before I had to return to the alleyway and conclude this awful, grim business. I'd gone over it a dozen times and in my plan, it was always the Professor I was going to call: the man in charge and the one who I most wanted a final chance to explain myself to. But as I ran up the stairs, slipping and stumbling, heading for the top room, it just came to me that I would call Daniel instead. It was like a parting gift to myself: the idea of hearing his voice brought a flicker of warmth to the nuclear winter that had taken hold inside my head.

I would call Daniel.

It's strange how the mountainous, unstoppable weight of destiny can turn on such delicate moments.

I searched out his number. My mobile was gone, so I called him on the house phone. It rang and rang, and for a moment I thought I wasn't going to reach him. While I waited, in agony for him to answer, I checked the time. Now I could see that it hadn't been more than ten minutes since the necklace had been cut from around my throat. Even so, ten minutes…

Daniel answered. "Hello?" he said, uncertainly. Maybe he had this number in his phone's memory and knew it was me. He wouldn't know what to expect; he was wary. But it was still mighty good to hear his voice.

"Daniel, it's Jo," I said, emotion threatening to catch in my throat. The old me would have cried at a moment like this. The new me came pretty close too.

He used that slow-paced, kind of hushed, talking-to-a-lunatic voice as he said, "Jo. How's it going? You feeling OK?"

Even that tone couldn't annoy me. I saw it for what it was: a sign that he was trying to reach out to me as carefully as he could. I let myself bask for a moment in the concern I could hear in his voice. I *knew* that calling him had been the right to do. I'd needed to hear how much he cared, before I… well, you know.

I said, "Daniel, I have some things to tell you. Now don't interrupt. You just have to listen and please, please trust me. Can you do that?"

Was that a lot to ask? "But Jo," he said, "wait a minute, there's something I need to tell you." He was suddenly all full of pep about whatever-it-was. Now that he'd realised I wasn't going to spaz out on him he was bursting to speak.

"Sorry Daniel, but that's interrupting," I said firmly. "Unless what you've got to say involves all of us getting killed very soon, then my speech takes precedence. Fair enough?"

"Killed?" he said, momentarily shut down. But only momentarily: "Well, OK. But believe me, you'll want to want to hear this."

By the way, that story earlier – the one about the hippy and his car – there was a point to it. The Sleeper was gone from my head right now, but he'd spent the last few weeks fixing up the place the way he liked it. He wanted his quest to succeed and all he'd had to work with was a whiney white girl with bad muscle tone. So he'd rammed as much of his guile and his gift for manipulation across the link as he could. Even though I'd pretty much learned to tell the difference between what was his and what was my own, that didn't mean I couldn't make use of what he'd left in my head.

With several big chunks of the Sleeper's Machiavellian play-book grafted into my head, I knew I could wrap Daniel around my little finger if I wanted to. I could push his buttons, get him to listen attentively, make him hear what I had to say.

It would be so easy, but something stopped me. I knew I could reel off some script the Sleeper had left me and have Daniel snapping to attention. But this was my last chance to talk to him and I wanted it to be *me*, and not some clone of the Sleeper, who spoke the words. I grew up not knowing how to control people – not having the confidence or the skill – and now I had both. It raised the question: in the past, was it only lack of opportunity that had stopped me from treating those around me as playthings or servants? Well, I had the opportunity now and I decided that for my last human act, I'd show a little restraint. I would let Daniel talk.

I said, "Daniel, I *beg* you, make every second count. You've got one minute to tell me whatever it is."

Bless him, he said nothing for a moment, realising I really meant what I said and figuring he needed to get his words out right. Then he launched into it: "OK. Remember when I helped you carry a load of your mum's things down to the bins? Well afterwards, I came back again and retrieved it all. You can shout at me later, but I was sure that one day you'd regret chucking that stuff out. I was planning to keep it until you were a bit less upset about it all. But I didn't want to make things worse, so I went through it all, in case there was anything bad in there – anything you didn't need to see. Shout at me later for that too. Anyway, I found something."

He continued, "It was a big Fedex envelope addressed to your mum and it was still sealed up. There was a receipt with the envelope. It was signed by Maria Revilla." He said the name slowly, unsure of the pronunciation.

Without thinking, I said, "My dad's housekeeper. Since I was little."

"OK," said Daniel, "well the date on it started me thinking. The receipt told me where Mrs. Revilla collected your mum's package from, so I Googled a newspaper story about your mother's death and compared addresses." Now he sounded each word out carefully, so there'd be no misunderstanding: "Your mum died outside that same Fedex office."

"What?" I said, finally beginning to understand. "Are you saying she was collecting a package when... when she died?" His minute was now up, but I was no longer watching the clock.

He said, "Your mum never got there so the company probably called again. Your housekeeper had to collect the envelope and for some reason she didn't put two and two together and link the address with your mum's death."

No surprise there. Mrs Revilla wouldn't have driven herself; she'd have just called a cab and probably handed the while-you-were-out card straight to the driver. Plus... the memories were coming back now. "When I was little, Mrs Revilla, she had kind of a drink problem for a while, I think. As a kid I'd figured she was just sad about my mom's death, but..." I was putting this together as I was talking, re-evaluating the judgements I'd made as a little girl: "but I when I think back, her loyalty was always to my dad. I don't think she even liked Mom, so... maybe she was drinking all along. Might explain why no one opened the door to the Fedex guy first time around, and how come the package needed collecting. No surprise she didn't recognise the address."

"Right, right" Daniel said, barely able to contain himself. "So your mum drove all the way across the city because that's where the parcel office was. And why would anyone kill themselves on the way to collect a package?" he said. "Jo, it *must* have been an accident."

I felt tears coming now. The Sleeper's instincts, still in place even without their owner present, rose up to push the emotion aside and I let them, was grateful for them. They allowed me to clamp down on the surging swell of roiled-up feelings.

Even so, I was pretty choked as I said, "Daniel?" It really wasn't much more than a throaty whisper. "I don't know what I'd do without you. I don't deserve you, but I do appreciate you. You know that, don't you?"

I felt a sudden urge to tell him everything and to apologise for every wrong thing I'd ever done. But again, those ruthless Sleeper reflexes blocked the impulse – and again I let them. There were other priorities than my guilty conscience here.

"Well, I…" he said and tapered off. Finally, something had taken the wind out of his sails. And thinking about wind and sails made me think of the Sleeper, the ice dream, the house-boat. I glanced at the clock, seeing that we were a whole minute over Daniel's allotted sixty seconds.

"But you… you should hear what else," Daniel was saying, his voice picking up speed again. "You'll never guess what was inside the envelope. Oh and you can shout at me later for opening it."

Two minutes fifteen since I'd said 'go'. Even having this conversation with Daniel was risking his life. I had to snap out of this and get moving.

"This is plenty for now, Daniel. Maybe, um, maybe another time," I said, choking up, knowing there wouldn't be any more times. Then I gathered up the emotion and put it away, getting it good and locked down this time. I cleared my throat and tried again. "There's no time right now, Daniel."

I needed to bring Daniel up to speed, maybe mumble a slightly coded goodbye, and then get going, before sentimentality wrecked everything. Except that I couldn't speak. Something was happening inside me. That makes it sound ominous, but it wasn't. It wasn't magical either. I think it was just the effect of Daniel's words, the meaning of them propagating through me. It was something to do with him and something to do with my mother and maybe something to do with me too: a ripple of hope fluttering through my chilly heart, simple and human. Maybe it was my mother's last gift to me. And I couldn't move while it unfolded inside me.

"Jo?" Daniel said, puzzled at my silence. "Jo?"

"I…" was all I said. What if? What if? It was all I could think for a moment.

And then I was suddenly free again. The change was completed. What if I didn't die? What if I fought to live? I could even see a kind of way that it might happen.

It would be risky – much riskier than going obediently to my death – I'd be gambling with everyone else's lives – but I wanted to fight – I needed to fight. If there was a chance of defeating the Sleeper then I should seize it. And with a rush of brilliant energy that burst through me like Summer returning to the frozen world, I knew that it was the right thing to do.

In a flash my plan rewrote itself and I realised that I would need an insurance policy, some way to protect my friends if my first attempt failed. And no sooner had I thought it than I realised Daniel could help me make it happen.

As if on cue, he said, "You wanted to tell me something?"

The words rushed out of me: "Daniel, something big is happening and we're all in a lot of trouble. You need to forget everything I told you last time we spoke. I was being forced to say those things. The truth is that I know everything the PAC has been doing, I know all about the Army Who Witnessed Creation, and I know about the Marker. I think I even know where the Marker is. And if you don't want it to end up in the hands of someone far worse than Jan then you'll do something for me." I debated telling him all about the Sleeper but that would just slow everything down at a moment when speed was vital. Possession took a bit of explaining.

Daniel didn't speak, just gave a surprised little sigh when he heard my words. So I started to tell him exactly what he needed to do.

And all the time I was speaking I was also thinking about what *he'd* told *me*. I mean, in a way it didn't make any difference. Without even meaning to, I'd made a sort of peace with my mother and this didn't change it. For a little while now, instead of looking up to her as a parent, our roles had somehow become reversed, and I'd been able to think about her almost as though *she* had been *my* daughter. Maybe it was something to do with having a centuries-old adept living in my head. And when I thought of her like that, I no longer saw her failings as grievances for me to resent; they were simply the burdens she'd had to carry and they were heavy indeed. They made her seem frail, in need of looking after, and all I felt for her now was pity.

And now Daniel had told me that she *hadn't* given up. Maybe her demons would have beaten her in the end, but somehow, knowing that she'd had more strength in her than I'd realised, that she'd still been fighting to live on the day when she died, well it made a difference. It made me wonder if there wasn't more strength in me too.

And as Daniel listened carefully, I told him, "I need you to come to London tonight and to bring something with you. This will sound strange, but you need to trust me about it." And I gave him the details. He wasn't crazy about fetching what I wanted – never mind that the details of where I wanted it brought were positively bizarre – but reluctantly he agreed.

I couldn't ask any more of Daniel, put him in any more danger, but the thought of reinforcements did cross my mind. "I don't suppose Susan Milton has come down off the ceiling yet. I imagine she's still pretty annoyed with me."

Daniel said, "I don't know. She took off suddenly. I think she's picking David up from the airport." I could almost hear him shrug. "I won't pretend she was a supporter of yours. She was the one who found out what you'd been up to. The last time we talked about you, she went off in a huff, but I think she's coming back tomorrow if you want to try talking to her."

Tomorrow? That wouldn't do me any good, and David Braun wasn't even in the country right now. For a moment I thought of trying to reach Susan on her mobile and explaining it all to her. Both she and David were pretty useful adepts – for novices – and with their help my plan might run a lot smoother, but I was down to my last couple of minutes here. Persuading Susan to cut me a break because I was possessed, well that was not a conversation you could rush. I would have to go it alone – as I'd always known I would.

"No problem," I said, trying to mean it. "So you'll do what I asked?"

"Yes," he said, quietly. "And you really won't tell me what this is all about?"

I hated keeping him in the dark, but I couldn't see any alternative.

"I'm sorry Daniel. I would tell you if I could." I just couldn't have him jumping in to save me and getting himself needlessly killed.

It was time for me to go – past time really – so if I wanted to say some sort of goodbye, just in case, it had to be now. What to say?

I swallowed. "I just want you to know that I'm doing my best, Daniel. I'm doing what I think is right."

I think he really sensed, then, that this was serious. He'd heard the finality hiding behind my words, my need to sum things up.

"If it helps you with any of this," he said, with considerable pain in his voice, "I love you."

"Thanks," I sniffed, tearful despite the self-control I'd inherited from the Sleeper, "That helps a lot. Take care, Daniel," I added, and then I hung up.

I was sitting on the edge of the bed, the dead phone in my hands, and I felt like I could have stayed there without moving forever. But time was slipping dangerously fast through my fingers – time that would burn us all if I wasn't careful. I was beyond tired and the glimpse I'd caught of my reflection in the mirror made me look like I'd been hit by a garbage truck, but I had work to do. And there were still a couple of things to take care of before I left the house. I dashed into the bathroom, upended the little trash-can in there, and hunted around for what I needed. At the same time, I twisted one arm out of my sweater and wrestled with my t-shirt.

When I was done, I scooped the trash back into the bin and pulled my clothes straight again.

Then from my desk I fetched the spare key to Noola's room. I rushed downstairs, let myself in and rummaged through her things until I found her hidden jewellery box. I'd noticed a suitable replacement headband when I'd gone through her stuff, but now I needed bracelets too. She had a couple, but they were trashy looking things, and one of them seemed suspiciously like gold-plated crap.

I had no idea how economical you could be with the gold and still be able to Connect. I hoped that Noola's cheap taste in jewellery wouldn't be the hairline fracture that caused everything else to fall apart.

With the gold in place, I summoned the Connect pattern and immediately felt the blossoming of my senses, as invisible membranes rose around me and displayed the essence of the world. I felt relief loosening the tension in my chest. I was tired, but not *too* tired. The Sleeper had believed my display of weakness earlier, in the alleyway, but the truth was, I still had a little left in reserve.

But I couldn't appear too chipper. Howling with the sting of it, I dug my fingernails into my scalp wound and dragged blood across my forehead: the worse I looked, the less suspicious the Sleeper would be. Then I deliberately collapsed the Healing field so that it wouldn't repair the damage I'd sustained. Now I just needed something to cover my head before I went out where people could see me.

The cap I'd worn before, the one I'd chosen because I knew it made my head itch, well that was wherever my bag was: gone. Instead I grabbed a baseball cap, jammed it down over my headband (ignoring the pain from my head-cut), and pulled the peak down to cover the blood streaked across my forehead. Then I rushed down the stairs, exactly like my life depended on it.

Out the front door, down the road and into the alleyway. By my reckoning it was now twenty minutes since they'd choked me unconscious on this spot; where were my muggers now? They must have some place where they holed up while their latest victim was recovering and staggering away, and I didn't think they were home-owners. I extended my awareness via the Surfaces, looking for body warmth and peering in through the walls and high windows on either side of the alleyway, probing into the corners and the crawl-spaces.

I sensed movement.

Then, sliding out from under the iron stairs came the junkie with the killer's eyes. He recognised me, I could see that. Languorously, he looked past my shoulder, checking for signs that I'd brought the cavalry with me. And then he glanced the other way, alert for someone approaching from behind him. Seeing no one around, he advanced on me.

I must have looked like I'd fallen out of a tree and into a dumpster. I was smeared with blood, and moss from the ground; I was dirty and bruised, and I still wore the same stained and filthy clothes I'd woken up in when I'd last stood here. I must have looked like an easy target.

As he stepped forwards, he dipped, picking up a length of wood with the bright edge of a broken hinge glinting from one end of it. Then he straightened, continuing to advance on me.

"I need my things back," I said, resting my hands on my thighs for support as a squall of tiredness blew through me and rocked me onto my heels. *Hmmm, mustn't fall down yet*, I thought to myself.

Seeing that I could hardly stand, he ignored my question and stepped close enough to swing at me. With surprising speed for someone with a medicated nervous system he whipped the lump of wood at me, aiming to catch me across the head. Instead, the weapon struck a barrier: a layer of air with the consistency of tank armour that prevented his blow from reaching me.

Then I Shattered the wooden club to splinters, leaving him suddenly speckled with cuts and clamping his stung hand between his legs as though I'd laid his palm open with a whip. I stepped forwards quickly and kicked him in the kneecap. Not hard enough to destroy it, but enough to send him pitching backwards. The brick wall behind him broke his fall.

Then I rearranged my Shield, and drew it inwards to clamp him around the throat, trapping him against the wall, unable to fall down. He writhed, his heels digging chunks from a section of scabbed asphalt, but his neck stayed trapped.

"Where are my things?" I asked, squeezing the Shield a little tighter and making his eyes stand out as though his brains were inflating.

He didn't speak but his gaze flicked over to the bulk of the heavy transformer. I left him hanging and explored in that direction with my extended senses. On the other side of the fenced-off electricity sub-station, through a narrow gap crowded with climbing weeds, there was a square of cement and a door, not visible from the alleyway. Behind the door was body heat.

I turned towards that heat, before remembering something. And then, pivoting back, I drove the second joint of my right thumb, backed by a tight fist, into his left temple. It was my first time hitting someone and I had only a fragment of the Sleeper's memory to guide me. I caught him square in the temple and released the Shield, allowing him to collapse on the ground, where he remained. But I damn near broke my thumb doing it. If the Sleeper had a real, physical body somewhere, he obviously had hands like elk hooves.

Leaving the downed junkie behind me I stepped over to the transformer. I laid the bushes flat ahead of me and scrambled through the gap between the enclosure's metal fence-posts and the wall, narrowly avoiding an abandoned syringe that would have driven itself up through the sole of my boot.

The muggers had found a way into some sort of utility building: a one-room brick structure with a few water company meters and pipes inside. I could feel movement and warmth on the far side of the door, beneath the pipework.

The door in front of me was closed. Reaching out with my hands I grabbed the door handle and pulled. It moved a little but wouldn't open. I felt behind the wood and detected a bar, dropped into place to hold the door shut. Something prevented me from moving it.

Well, no time for finesse. I flattened myself along the building's wall, to one side of the entrance, rotated a Shield into place, and then blew the door off its hinges and into the weeds. A spike of ejected doorframe whined towards me like a bullet and clipped my Shield, spinning off into the bushes like a severed airplane propeller.

I rolled my Shield around and stepped in through the doorway.

Inside I could detect two pairs of legs that disappeared beneath some dripping steel plumbing. And in the snug space behind the pipes I could feel a candle flame fluttering like a leaf against the Heat Surface. I Froze out the flame, leaving the two figures cowering back there in the little light that reached them from the doorway. They scrambled to their feet and edged to one side, beginning to emerge from behind the pipework. I heard a metallic snap that I took to be the catch of a knife opening.

A body rushed at me, just a shadow in front of my eyes, but clear as a Mondrian sunrise through the Heat Surface. He lunged head-first into my Shield, losing his footing in the impact. I felt rather than saw him stick himself with his own knife as he slipped. I wrapped the Shield tighter around me and reached out across the floor, probing for my belongings.

On cue, the other junkie, the one I hadn't seen before, rushed me. I caught him as he slammed his head on my Shield and I morphed the barrier as quickly as I could to catch him and enfold him. Then, as mindful as I could be of my injured thumb, I hit him in the nose with the heel of my hand. He moaned loudly, making a noise that reminded me of an angry seal, and I released him and let him topple into the corner.

By now the other one was back on his feet, one hand clamped across his self-inflicted wound and the other one once again holding the knife. He didn't charge, just stood warily, holding the weapon between us. Did that make it my move?

I began to Heat the knife. It took a few seconds for him to notice and he shifted it in his grasp, unsure of what was happening. A moment later, he gasped and dropped it on the dusty floor. He back-pedalled and I stepped forwards, wrapped my hand in the loose sleeve of my sweater and picked up the knife by its handle.

I applied a little Freeze to the grip to stop it burning through my sleeve and then I roared out at the blade with Heat until it began to ripple with a crimson glow. The metal clicked and pinged from the heat. I gathered the cowering junkie into a wraparound Shield and advanced on him as he struggled, finding himself suddenly unable to move.

I held the glowing knife level with his eyes and asked, "Where is my necklace, the rest of my things?"

"Do I know you?" he stuttered helplessly, staring not at me but at the knife's glowing point.

I growled irritably and he flinched. "You don't remember me? You choked me unconscious about fifteen minutes ago if that helps," I explained.

"Sorry, sorry," he pleaded, as though an apology might be all I was after. And then he added: "It's over there." He nodded his head to towards the pipework and the space beyond. "Few things in a bag on the roof. Maybe yours too."

I ignored him for a moment and felt across the floor once more. I could sense a cardboard box and within it, bracelets and what I took to be my phone. Transferring my attention to the roof above me, I was able to sense a pressed-metal housing with slatted sides – something to do with the machinery here, maybe – and within the housing, a bag (canvas perhaps) full of hard shapes and something worked into filigree. That had to be the necklace. Focussing hard, I flipped the loose metal side off of the housing and gave the bag a good jolt with Push. It slid across the roof and dropped into the bushes just outside the door.

I can't imagine which member of the gang was steady enough on his feet to climb up there and conceal things, but it would have taken me a while to find that hiding place without help. Aware that I was still standing, holding a blisteringly hot blade close to his face, my captive asked tentatively, "Ahh, what are you going to do with that knife?"

I smiled at him.

"Stab someone," I said, shutting off the Heat and beginning to Freeze the whole blade. "It's important to put on a good show."

He was staring at me horrified, and I explained: "God knows what diseases a person might get from a knife like this, but it should be safe now." And, gritting my teeth, I rammed the blade deep into the flesh of my shoulder.

Even though the metal was cool, it felt like it was still at a thousand degrees. The knife went in about an inch and a half and stayed there when I removed my hand. For a moment, I was hopelessly dizzy with the pain.

I tried to steady myself and I wondered whether it had been easier to bury a knife in my shoulder knowing that my original plan had called for the wound to be a death sentence. Horrible though this had been, it was still easier than the sacrifice I'd been preparing myself for. Now that I'd decided to live, this wound only had to demonstrate how desperately hard I'd fought to regain my link to the Sleeper.

Again, a tumble of dizziness spun my brain, and then hysteria threatened to take me for a second as I giggled, thinking what would happen if I passed out now, what these two would do to me, and how events would unravel for the PAC without my help. Thankfully, a moment later, the dizziness faded.

"Sorry about this," I said, my teeth gritted against the pain. I squeezed the Shield around the trapped junkie's throat until he couldn't breathe. I'd recognised his sleeve from when that skeletal arm had slipped itself around my neck, and I knew he was the one who'd half throttled me. It made this easier to do.

Less than a minute later his expression had gone from desperate to peaceful and I let him drop. His chest still rose and fell and I turned away from him. I gave the box in the far corner a Push and it slid out from under the pipework. I tipped it up with the toe of my boot and turned out the contents. Then I grabbed anything that looked familiar. Gathering those things up, I went outside and dropped it all on the ground next to where the bag had landed. Then I emptied out the bag onto the ground.

There, on top of the pile, lay the mangled lattice of my necklace. It was stretched and distorted and the sight of it devastated me. I hadn't expected it to be ruined and I didn't see how I was going to mend it. I'd pictured repairing a broken link or two with a few dabs of Heat, but I could see the filigree was pulled completely out of shape. Dozens of the hair-fine strands had elongated or snapped completely.

Still, I wrapped it around my throat, holding it in place using the arm that didn't have a knife stuck in it.

And felt nothing: no sense of the Sleeper's presence.

Hello?

I knew my thoughts weren't reaching beyond the confines of my own skull. Some subtle psychic ambience was missing, the micro-echoes I'd learned to associate with a functioning mental link. When you knew what to listen for, it was the difference between speaking from a stage and talking into a pillow.

With no way to contact the Sleeper, my plan was starting to disintegrate. A curl of panic, like a rising wave sweeping towards shore, was rearing up inside of me. I pushed it down, refusing to lose control now. I *had* to re-establish the link to the Sleeper, there *had* to be a way – and I *had* to find it now.

I was always telling people how smart I was; it was time to prove it. I had to think: to put the nausea and weariness and hurt to one side, and concentrate on working this problem through. There had to be something I could do.

And at last, a possibility occurred to me.

I remembered the glimpse I'd caught of the Sleeper's thoughts, the layered bulk of his memories and the neat array of Patterns, like live butterflies pinned in a row, their wings still beating in slow-motion, each shape cycling through its own sequence of convolutions. I could see those shapes clearly if I closed my eyes. I picked out the shape of Pattern Link and tried to bring its exact form into focus. And to my shock, as I concentrated, it flared and expanded in my mind, blossoming into fullness and suffusing me with its distinctive power.

Hardly knowing what I was doing – what *it* was doing – I felt the breaks in the necklace merging together and the tortured strands healing themselves, tightening back into their proper arrangement. The metal tensed and gathered like tendons pulled tight and the necklace settled itself over the torn skin of my neck from where it had recently been ripped.

Its work completed, the Pattern began to drain and collapse, its petals turning to ash, just as I felt the breaking storm of the Sleeper's presence rolling back in on me like my own personal typhoon. I snuffed out the remnants of the Pattern as swiftly as I could, hiding it from his awareness.

Then I could do what I'd been yearning to do for most of today: I could rest. I let my knees buckle, closed my eyes and collapsed like a human accordion. Only desperation had kept me from passing out before now and I no longer kept up that fight.

Let this all be *his* problem for a while.

CHAPTER 29

I stopped battling the exhaustion, the pain, the symptoms of growing blood-loss, and let myself drift away. My physical body still existed somewhere, off in the distance, but it was miles from where my disconnected mind tumbled gently through space, rolling over and over towards nothingness.

As though I was watching it happen through the foggy lens of a cheap telescope I could see my distant body crumpling, my limbs losing tension like noodles in hot water. I felt a sense of relief as the world receded. I guessed that I would catch a last glimpse of my body at about the moment my good shoulder hit the dirt. Finally, I could rest.

And then, with a jolt, the Sleeper snatched control. I'd dropped to my knees, but before I could topple sideways to lie in the soot-specked weeds, he reanimated my limbs, pulling tension back into my muscles and halting my collapse.

Let me sleep, I pleaded, a little deliriously. *I can't do any more.*

Far from being sympathetic, the Sleeper exuded prickly

suspicion. Plainly, he couldn't tell whether he'd been conned and my stuporous wilting wasn't helping him discover the truth.

His mind bellowed at me: **If you have deceived me here, you will *pay*.** And he did that thing with his words where they rang like angry trumpets.

Well if that's your attitude, I thought, and once again dropped backwards into the waiting arms of fatigue, which carried me away, not just from my body but from the Sleeper as well. I left him in sole and unopposed control of my body. I allowed my mind to simply loll. Psychic dead weight.

Far away, I was vaguely aware of him orienting himself, looking out through my eyes, forcing my body to stand. He stuffed a few things into the bag that lay at my feet and hefted it in a way that would hide from casual observers the hilt of the knife protruding from my shoulder. Then he pushed his way through the bushes, squeezing past the buzzing grey bulk of the transformer.

Back on the gravel path, he stepped over the inert junkie I'd discarded there. Then he retraced my earlier route, along the alleyway, out onto the street and back towards the house.

How many did you kill? he asked as we left the alleyway behind us. His tone suggested he was almost impressed. The question drifted up to my untethered mind from far below. I answered like in a dream, words appearing without my involvement. *Don't think anyone's dead. Just settled them down a bit.*

My voice slurred in my head like I was drunk. I was really only half conscious, and thinking at all was an effort I couldn't be bothered to make.

I caught distant glimpses of what he was doing, but it was intercut with moments of delirium where I floated, blissfully lost among imagined fragments of June sky.

The Sleeper had got us home and all the way upstairs. I barely registered our progress – though I was absent-mindedly aware of taking a spill on the final set of stairs before my room. Diluted and vague, the pain of a banged elbow came through as though it had happened a long time ago. Everything had such a dreamy quality to it, as I continued to let my consciousness drift like an inflatable lounger in a forgotten Summer swimming pool, leaving it to the Sleeper to pick my body off of the carpet and get me up those last few stairs. Once in my room, he steered us towards the bathroom.

The change of scenery did nothing to revive me; all that white tile was the perfect blank canvas for my imagination, which projected swatches and snapshots of dream colour against the out-of-focus, bare ceramic.

But reality came whistling back into razor-edged focus when the Sleeper leant over the sink, grasped the handle of the knife, and pulled. The pain centres of my brain lit up like a lightning strike. He might as well have connected the hilt of the knife to the mains.

With the blade removed, he kept the heel of my hand pressed into the nova of the wound and drew down the Healing Surface so that it was folded and concentrated around the hole in my flesh. My other hand braced us against the edge of the sink as I felt my knees suddenly dip, unstrung by sudden light-headedness.

But gradually the crackles of high-voltage pain that raked my nerves began to dissipate and the blood that I could feel welling, and then running hotly down my side, slowed from a trickle to a drip, and then stopped completely.

He took me back into the bedroom, dropping me into a chair, and allowed the Healing focus to dilate, spreading it out like a blanket across my other injuries. The scratchy throb from my scalp-wound grew steadily duller and the hard straps of pain in the muscles across my back began to loosen their aching grip.

After thirty minutes wrapped in the Healing field, the only

injury remaining was the clotted hole in my shoulder – within which I could feel new fibres of skin and muscle itching as they sought each other out, twitching like insect antenna, then brushing together and knitting tight. The process began to slow once the worst of the damage had been undone.

Bathe, put on clean clothes and then we will set off. I want to retrieve the Marker tonight.

I just laughed. Out loud. I didn't mean to; this wasn't like earlier when I *wanted* to bait him, but I just couldn't help it. I'd figured the best way to allay his suspicion that he'd been conned was to share with him my total helplessness and physical disarray. Before the mugging I'd been running on fumes. Now I had the healthy skin tone and alert expression of an organ donor, post-donation. My clothes looked like I'd found them when I was unclogging a drain. And my brain was badly-made Jell-O.

The final touch, driving a knife into my shoulder, had been about buying me a little time. I wasn't sure it was necessary, but I didn't want the Sleeper thinking we were good for any more active duty today. I needed to give Daniel a chance to run that errand for me just in case I needed it. It hadn't occurred to me that the Sleeper would assess the perforated bag-lady he saw in the mirror and declare her ready for action.

For some reason, he seemed to think he could wring a bit more useful work out of me today before I dropped dead in my tracks like some Victorian pit-pony. Exhaustion had my heart thumping painfully in my chest as though something in its mechanism had been thrown out of alignment by the abuse I'd racked up recently. This was madness and I roused myself to tell him so. A few, final drops of adrenaline leant me some eloquence.

You're welcome to try, but personally, I haven't got it in me. If the Marker is there, then it's <u>been</u> there for a year. It will <u>still</u>

be there in twelve hours. Can I remind you that I'd put in a pretty full day even before I got choked unconscious and stabbed. I know it must be frustrating having to tolerate my frailty, but I think it's pretty clear that I've reached my limit for today. Can't we interpret the fact that I got the snot beaten out of me by a couple of emaciated dopeheads as a clear sign that I've been overdoing it? In case we run into trouble when we go to fetch the Marker, I wouldn't mind being able to put up a bit of a fight. Right now I can neither see straight nor use both of my arms. I mean come <u>on</u>.

The shoulder will be healed by tomorrow. And in the morning we won't need to break into the dock; we can just walk in. There'll be less risk of trouble and we'll be in infinitely better shape to handle any problems.

I reckoned he was probably convinced, but I needed to give him a way to save face if he wanted to concede the point. I figured I'd give his ego a pat and let him blame this all on me. *I don't know how you're managing to keep going, but I just don't have anything like your stamina.*

No, you don't, he snapped. **Understand that this is the last allowance I will make for your weakness. If you have to ask me to take pity on you again I will take that opportunity to put you permanently out of your misery.**

I took that huffing and puffing to mean that he was reluctantly agreeing with me.

Understood. I tried to sound meek but sincere.

That really was a relief. Now I was free to get out of my filthy clothes. I didn't even want to think about the long-term health risks of rolling around in that alleyway. I suppose it was the least of my worries, but it made my skin crawl. I found a black garbage sack and put my sweater and jeans straight in there. They weren't worth saving. If I wanted something suitable for getting mugged in again,

I'd just start fresh with a new outfit.

Then I stripped off the rest of my things – including Noola's jewellery – and took my third shower of the day. Thank god for hot water, is all I can say. It was no substitute for a couple of weeks drowsing in the sun on a quiet beach somewhere, but it was still bliss to my battered body. I tied a hand towel over my shoulder to keep the direct force of the shower from hitting the partly healed wound and that seemed to work OK. After I'd scrubbed and scoured for a few minutes I began to feel less contaminated, like I'd erased the filth from the alleyway.

Tempting though my soft bed was, I made a heroic stand and ignored its beguiling call for another half an hour while I returned Noola's jewellery to her room and made myself a huge sandwich, which I ate accompanied by an enormous glass of milk. I don't normally drink milk, but somehow it seemed like the thing to do, like I was giving the Healing field a few more nutrients to work with than if I'd just drunk water. Or maybe it just reminded me of being a kid.

Finally I crawled into bed. It must have been all of 8pm but I felt like I'd been anticipating this moment for weeks. The ridiculous excess of pain, adrenaline and exertion I'd experienced today had dramatically narrowed my sense of perspective. I couldn't think in terms of the big picture right now. I had food in my belly and clean cotton sheets beneath me. As far as I was concerned, tomorrow was another lifetime for a different me to handle.

I set my alarm for 6am and let the lapping waves of sleep work their way up my body. I felt them lift me free of the Earth and pull me down with them into that ancient, dark ocean where I lay drowned in dreamless black for a small eternity.

Sometime in the night I thought I heard something, but sleep had trapped me under its colossal weight, as though it owned me now, and I couldn't have stirred to investigate the sound if my life depended on it. Which, naturally, it did.

* * *

Eventually I awoke to the sound of my clock radio. Its buzzer sounded exactly like the collision warning of a passenger plane from a disaster movie I'd once seen, which might explain why my first thoughts on that morning were 'Pull up, pull up.'

I cut off the alarm with an unsteady swat of my palm, and then I just lay there for a moment, letting my waking mind re-integrate itself after the elemental disorder of sleep. Any residue of drowsiness was driven out of me by the cavalry charge of problems galloping back into position.

This was the day. Despite my resolve to fight, there was an excellent chance that this was the end of the line for me. Somehow I knew that at the bottom of that anchor chain there really was a watertight bag – I could picture it – and it really did contain the Marker. I believed Jan's scribbles proved it.

The Sleeper had been driving me towards this day ever since he had first chanced upon the marinaded wreck of my boozed-up, drug-dilated brain, lying prone and inviting, still Connected to the magical ether. It took me back to the moment when I'd seen that opium-sprawled junkie with the needle dangling from his arm. That was how I must have looked to the Sleeper. He was like a car-thief finding a drunk passed out at the wheel, the engine still running. Who knew how many decades he'd scrabbled uselessly at the iron-hard minds of resolute, disciplined adepts, unable to get any purchase. Even David and Susan, novices though they were, each had more willpower than any three other people I knew. While the Professor, despite his genial manner, had a core of granite.

If finding a slave hadn't been a big enough prize for the Sleeper, there, in my recent memory, were references to the Marker. It was like stealing the keys to the entire candy store from a baby.

And while I'd slept last night, another of his plans had reached culmination. Without needing to analyse it, I could sense that the Home Pattern was there in my mind – whole and ready now. Unless I stopped him, the Sleeper would activate it as soon as my fingers touched the Marker.

Somehow our link had deepened and expanded, and when I thought about it, I found I could even catch blinks of detail, shutter-quick glimpses through the Sleeper's own eyes: millisecond flashes looking down at his ruined body in its mineral prison.

I couldn't properly interpret those tightly compressed images, couldn't really say what I was looking at, but I knew approximately what they meant. Somewhere, the Sleeper lay crippled and physically powerless, unable to move – but possessed of an intact mind. That mind had curled like a lurking spider underneath the surface of the magical world, watchful, alert – ready to dart out and snatch up a suitable victim.

Then I had come along and he had ensnared me.

In a fair fight, I didn't kid myself that I could beat him. And now that he'd weakened my mental defences with the drug-patches, I knew I stood even less of a chance. But since that talk with Daniel, I'd realised that if I could just hold my nerve, I might be able to deal the Sleeper a blow that would leave him drowning in doubt and despair.

With that thought hidden in my mind, like a gun tucked into the back of my jeans, I readied myself to return to the boat. Another hour basking in the invisible warmth of the Healing Surface had reduced my shoulder wound to an ugly knot of reddened skin: an ache and an eyesore, but not a liability any longer.

I didn't bother with the idea of dressing up and impersonating an estate agent. Neither the Sleeper nor I had the stomach for charades. We both knew that this was the finale, what I think they call the endgame. If along the way I had to assert myself a little and deal with a security guard then so be it; as soon as my fingers touched the cold metal of the Marker, all mundane concerns would be behind me.

I trudged down the last flight of stairs and approached my front door. I hoped that the Sleeper would interpret my leaden reluctance as a sign of weakness or fear. I could hear winter rain intermittently pattering against the front-room windows and I paused for a moment to look at the heap of coats piled over the coat rack and to find something warm and dry to wear. The decision was made easy when I noticed that my favourite fleecy jacket had slipped off its peg and lay on the floor by the front door. I picked it up, dusted off a grubby sleeve and zipped it around me. With a hand that felt as heavy as regret itself, I opened the door and stepped out into the spit and squall of the raw and chilly morning.

CHAPTER 30

Out on the street, some of the inevitable grimness of my mood lifted and a little gallows humour started to work its way in. Probably just the early stages of hysteria, but I'd much rather laugh at something serious than face it with humourless maturity. Why multiply the unpleasantness of the situation by refusing to joke about it?

Under my Chicago Bears cap, I was wearing gold. My wrists too were gilded. In my mind, the quiet, refrigerator hum of the Quell state kept me from Connecting.

I was walking to the station. By unspoken agreement with the Sleeper I was leaving the bike where it was. If he had his way, then I'd have no need of a quick getaway. Or rather, I'd be performing one of the quickest getaways in history, courtesy of the Home pattern. That wasn't exactly how *I* intended for things to turn out, but I didn't want to make the Sleeper suspicious by advertising the fact. I don't know what I was *supposed* to think was going to happen once the Marker was in my possession, but I wasn't about to bring the subject up. So there was no discussion, I just headed for Stockwell tube.

Once I reached the station, I queued for a ticket. My mind was on other things, when a fit-looking, twenty-something white guy struggling with a heavy backpack lurched away from the machine in front of me and struck me with the trailing edge of his pack. The gnarled metal pull of a zipper caught me across the cheek, scoring the skin. I drew my breath in sharply at the unexpected pain, dabbing instinctively at my face. My finger came away with a smudge of red on it.

The man turned angrily to see who had obstructed him and snarled at me, "Why don't you watch where you're going?" Then he pushed his way towards the ticket barriers.

Hmmm, I thought to myself. I was waiting for the anger to come, but there wasn't any. I'd expected, now that I could mentally separate the Sleeper's feelings from my own, that I'd sense more of the old me – and the old me would never have been able to let something like this pass.

But it seemed like such a small thing compared with what else was going on; I just couldn't get very worked up.

Thinking about my calmness, I decided that it probably came down to how you see other people. When I used to feel like a failure, I kind of looked up to everyone else and that made the way they treated me seem like a judgement; rudeness like I'd just experienced would make me feel sorry for myself for ages.

On a good day, I might have managed to view other people as equals: being snarled at by a stranger would feel like a challenge; it'd make me punchy.

But now all I saw was some young idiot putting his own problems on public display. He was obviously late, he couldn't manoeuvre his bag without bumping into people and in his tiny reality that was a major deal; it had stretched his patience to breaking point. That wasn't annoying; it was just a bit embarrassing. If you couldn't handle outsized luggage without losing your self-control, how would you handle the big things? How would you face your own death? I found myself hoping he lived a long enough life to get a little perspective.

Or he could maybe share mine; I seemed to have a little too much perspective right now.

The man with the rucksack had only taken a couple of steps when a short, black guy standing behind me sucked a little air through his teeth to make a tutting sound and muttered, "That's just rude." Then he called out, "*You* watch where *you're* going. You hit this lady, you know."

Out of the corner of my eye, I could see that the guy behind me was about half the size of the man with the rucksack. I smiled. He didn't know I could kill the man who bumped me without losing my place in the queue. He didn't know whether the guy with the rucksack would decide to make an issue out of this. He just knew he was standing up for me, and I liked that.

Sure enough, the rucksack guy turned, anger twisting his lip, and took a step towards the man who'd scolded him. His face had a look that suggested he viewed this as the final straw.

I supposed that now there'd be shouting and maybe a fight. I wasn't in the mood.

I stepped forwards and placed my palm on the rucksack guy's chest, halting him. "Remember how late you are," I said, looking into his eyes, "You don't have time for this." It wasn't some Jedi mind-trick; it was just the truth. He was only acting like a baby – a very tall, muscular baby – because he was under pressure.

The rucksack guy pulled the focus of his scowl away from the defiant man behind me and angrily met my gaze. Then he glanced at my cheek. I caught the microscopic drop in his self-esteem as he registered the cut, noticed the beads of fresh blood, realised he was to blame. Then he turned huffily away, nearly bumping into a truly enormous man who looked like he might break rocks for a living – perhaps with his hands.

The guy behind me gave a wheezy chuckle: "He'll be lucky he don't have some sort of *accident* this morning."

He amused himself for a moment, laughing at that, then asked me quietly, "How's your face?"

I turned a little and smiled warmly at him. "I'm fine, thanks," I said, and in a strange way I realised it was true.

He appraised the damage. "That's a bad scratch," he said, pretending to look worried. Then he laughed and said, "Luckily, you still pretty." The way he said 'pretty', it didn't have any 't's in it. *Pri-eee.*

I giggled. Nerves, I suppose. I mean it wasn't really funny and I don't think I've ever made a sound that you could describe as a giggle before. I'd be flirting next.

It was a shame dear Daniel wasn't around to help me with that. He'd waited a long time for some flirting from me.

I bought my ticket and made my way down onto the platform. Jammed in with a few hundred hassled-looking commuters, I found myself smiling again. What a psychiatrist might make of that, what with the swirling currents of death and self-sacrifice all around, I didn't know, but it felt quite natural. Who knew why? Not me.

A few stations along, I changed trains, and this time I was heading against the crush. When I emerged into the wintry grey of the wind-bitten morning, the rain had stopped. That was an improvement, though feral gusts still snapped at my ears and the back of my neck. I tugged my collar a little higher and wondered why the Sleeper was so quiet. We'd had a brief discussion about tactics a few minutes back, but that was it.

You still there?

It was probably safe to tweak him a little now. He couldn't afford to disappear off and rat out the PAC's location to the Army; he had to keep a constant eye on me. His holy grail was due to make an appearance in a little while.

Attend to your surroundings, not me, he grumbled, clearly not in the mood for banter.

His words seemed damped, muffled somehow. And I realised why, as soon as I thought about it. I'd been blocking him out of my head. Not completely, but I'd subconsciously narrowed our link to restrict his access to my thoughts. I hadn't even had to concentrate; the simple act of wanting to be alone with my own musings had restricted the flow of communication between us. It was moderately impressive. Another month or so and I'd really be able to give him a run for his money.

There, you see? Gallows humour.

On the last section of the walk to the dock, I took things pretty slowly, keeping an eye out for anyone nearby. When at last I reached the concrete steps that would take me over the wall and down into the basin of the dock, I stopped and had a proper look around. There was some activity far-off: the machinery of the cement works rumbled and boomed distantly like a spent thunderstorm, but there was nobody close by.

For some reason, I was much more keyed-up than the last time I was here. I had a sense of danger that wouldn't leave me.

I climbed the first few steps slowly, glancing over the crest of the wall and then pulling back. Beyond lay the guard-hut, the high fence and the wooden walkway that led down onto the pontoon decking where the boats were tied up. The tethered vessels looked just as they had before, with Jan's set off to one side and back from the others. Having seen nothing to alarm me, I raised my head again and took another, longer look.

I worked my gaze across the dock like it was a painting I was restoring: careful to bring out every detail and not to miss a spot. I couldn't see any signs of life. The boat with the engine trouble was quiet now, no evidence of the mechanic or his tools. The guard-hut seemed deserted too. I'd anticipated needing to do something about the guard and now I wondered if he *ever* showed up.

Cautiously, I worked my way up the steps, over, and down onto the dockside beyond. It felt a little like walking through a minefield: the surroundings looked innocuous enough but there was a finite chance that if I put a foot wrong something would blow up in my face.

Ordinarily, I might Connect now. If there was a trap, I should trip it and run. But last time we'd been here, the Sleeper had been angry with me over that. And just now, on the train, he'd made his wishes clear. I wouldn't Connect without his permission.

It seemed that my survival wasn't the first priority; recovery of the Marker was. I just had to get it in my possession – whatever the cost – and then he would bring me Home. So despite the fact that I'd be a lamb to the slaughter if the Army were lying in wait, he didn't want me to run. No, my job was to get onto that boat and to reach the Marker first.

I walked cautiously past the guard hut.

No sign of anyone within, though a dark-blue uniform jacket hung from a peg in the tiny interior. Did that mean the guard was nearby? If he was patrolling, he'd be pretty cold without that heavy wool serge between him and the elements.

I moved slowly down the gangplank which led to the floating pontoon deck and the boats beyond. I wanted to be alert to anything out of the ordinary, but it was obvious that the buffeting wind would drown out anything less than a shout, and my gaze was blurry with

Robert Finn

tears as the winter chill stung my eyes.

I reached the wooden decking and walked to the far end: the closest point to Jan's boat. With a last scan of the surroundings, I jumped onto the boat adjacent to Jan's, ran down the full length of its running board and leapt across to 4-14J, to land with moderate grace next to the rudder, in the recessed well at the back of the vessel.

Nothing happened: no sirens or yelling.

I picked up the pole that lay by my feet. Its hollowed square end was just as I remembered it, obviously intended to attach to something. I lowered it over the side of the boat, wondering how one located the up-tilted spike that it fitted onto. It wasn't possible to see more than an inch through the mud and algae in the water.

Leaning out a little, I noticed a groove notched into the handrail. It was one of many dents and pocks along the outer edge of the boat, but it looked a little bit more deliberate than the rest.

I laid the shaft of the pole into that groove and, using it as a guide, slid it down into the water. After a little poking around, the tip of the pole encountered something near the hull. I rotated the pole, trying to settle it onto the metal spike there. After a little trial-and-error I got it, and the pole slipped down into place. If I'd wanted to I could have let go now and the pole would have stayed put.

Next I had to raise the anchor chain. It was a simple mechanism: a little drum-winch with a hand-crank at one end like the starting-handle for an old-timey car. With one hand steadying the pole (because I didn't relish diving in to retrieve it if it fell) I gave the handle a turn and the anchor chain began to rise.

And then it stuck.

For a moment I couldn't see why, but by leaning out and peering back at the winch, I discovered a padlock with an elongated loop

832

that went through one of the links of the anchor chain and fastened to a metal eyelet bolted to the handrail. I tried to reach below the padlock and pull the chain up by hand.

Yeah. That wasn't going to happen. It weighed a ton, the angle was impossible and the chain was slippery. Problem.

Should I Connect? I need to break that lock.

There was a pause as the Sleeper considered his reply.

Yes. But remember to move quickly once you do.

I stilled the gentle, rhythmic oscillation of the Quell state that was looping in my mind. It ceased, and straightaway I felt the Surfaces rise and expand around me, filling like sails catching the breeze, and opening like the petals of an enormous, unseen flower. Without waiting for the sense of Connection to complete, I immediately reached out with the Shatter surface and cracked the mechanism of the padlock. I hooked my hand beneath the winch and pulled the fractured lock free.

It took only a second and even as my hands reached for the padlock, impressions began to flow in from the Surfaces. I grabbed the handle of the winch and began to wind up the chain at the same instant that fear solidified into reality.

One by one, three citrus-yellow stars flared: three clusters of gaseous light, like soft miniature suns, silently rising out of the featureless sea of the Presence Surface. Three adepts.

It was curious how the Presence Surface presented its threats so comfortingly: cool, graceful radiance to indicate the location of a killer. One was near me, on one of the other boats; the other two, no doubt ready to block my retreat, were beyond the dock wall, at the extreme limit of detection.

From the Sleeper's point of view, I only had to touch the Marker, to get it within my grasp, and the battle was over. I could feel him wordlessly pressuring me to work even faster as I frantically hauled on the handle of the winch. I obeyed as best I could, but I was desperately trying to think how this affected *my* plan – because *my* plan required me to destroy the Marker. And that was going to be suicidally difficult in the middle of a one-sided fight with a trio of assassins.

I know, my plan doesn't sound very impressive or sophisticated. And I suppose it wasn't, but I'd realised something. I'd realised that hate is over-hyped as a motivator; what keeps people going for the long haul is hope. The Marker was the object on which all the Sleeper's hopes rested and I planned to obliterate it in front of his eyes.

And if that wasn't enough to crush him, I had a final trick up my sleeve. I had a gift for him, something he had been after for a while now. Irony had finally taught me a useful lesson, and the lesson was that sometimes giving people what they want is the best way to hurt them.

And all I would have needed to put my plan into effect was about a minute or so of peace and quiet. Which wasn't going to happen.

Even as I struggled to invent a way out of this situation, at the same time as I was furiously working the winch handle, I saw a man step out onto the roof of a boat several vessels down from me. He was young, slim and dark-haired and he appeared to be wearing a suit, beautifully tailored from some silky charcoal-and-green cloth. He was the man who had chased me when I'd visited Jan's house in Notting Hill.

He yelled something melodious but insistent that I couldn't understand. Panicked, I yanked the winch handle even harder, figuring that I still had a couple of seconds before he crossed the intervening distance and reached me. I wanted to put a Shield in his way, but I was draped half over the side of the boat, dragging on the winch lever with one hand and steadying the pole with the other: there was no way to raise a Shield without getting in my own way.

Now the man stepped lightly from one boat to the next, and then the next, covering the six or seven foot gap with no more exertion than if he was stepping off a kerb. As he closed the distance, the dreary sunlight glinted from the gold stripe across his temples.

Glancing down, I saw that one skewered link of the anchor-chain was now working its way up the pole. And resting on top of the threaded link was a loop of braided steel cable. I reached down and grabbed the cable, pulling on it and hauling against the suction of the water.

I heard the man's heels thump down on the next boat along just as a tan-coloured sack on the end of the wire broke the surface, pouring water from its folds, and rising into the air. I straightened up and reeled in the wire, simultaneously placing a slab of Shield between the boats so that the young man's approach was blocked.

What I'd do next I didn't know. I could feel the Sleeper focussing on the Home pattern, bringing it to the forefront of our joined minds, ready to activate it. I was careful not to grab the bag itself – only the wire – so that he wouldn't be tempted to activate the pattern yet. Besides which, he'd be a fool not to have me check the contents first.

Pick up the bag, he commanded me, but I ignored him. I had only moments to act. Could I destroy the Marker before the man in the suit reached me? Perhaps I should relinquish it to the Army in exchange for letting my friends and I live. Then the Sleeper's revenge would mean nothing. But I couldn't trust them any more than I could trust him.

A clatter of thumping wood gave me a split-second's warning that something else was going on, but not enough time to react.

Then it all happened at once. The Sleeper poured his will across the link, trying to activate the Home pattern in my mind. I blocked him, amazed he would take even the smallest risk that the Marker wasn't in the bag.

Simultaneously, the young man pressed forwards, frowning as he found his path blocked by my invisible Shield.

And a new sun rose, blindingly close, bursting through the Presence Surface right behind me.

And as all these things were taking place, the woman who'd crashed out of the cabin doors behind me stepped forwards and cracked me firmly across the back of the skull with the cold iron pommel of a drawn sword.

The ringing blow whited out my senses for a second and shot numbness through my nerves, slackening my grip, so that the bag slithered free of my fingers and plopped back over the side of the boat like an escaping octopus.

Momentarily unable to balance, I staggered and fell backwards, banging my head on the way down, to lie blinking and dazed at the feet of a tall, fair-haired woman who held a sword, now turned point downwards, just above my sternum. In a single, quick motion she flipped the circle of gold from around my head with a twitch of her sword tip. The move incidentally sliced an inch-long cut into my scalp and shut down my Connection to the Surfaces with the finality of an axe-blow through a power cable.

I was still dazed from the impact, but despite the excruciating sensation that my skull had just been rung like a bell, I recognised her. She looked exactly like a sketch Susan had made of the assassin Karst. Well not *exactly* like: her perfect, pale features were distorted by a partly-healed scar which ran down one cheek and tugged the corner of her beautiful mouth into a lopsided smirk.

That had to hurt, I thought.

"Danik. The bag," she called, in unaccented, but somehow foreign English. As she spoke, she kept her eyes on me. She was staring intently at me, but not quite into my eyes. It was as though she was trying to see through my flesh.

"You're *young*," she said incredulously. "You have never been old, have you? Who has sent a child here?"

She moved, placing the point of her sword just below my ribcage and leaned forwards a little. I gasped for breath as the blade exerted painful pressure and threatened to rip through my clothing.

"You can tell me," she said, confidentially, "Who sent you?"

Meanwhile, the man Danik took a final light step across the five foot expanse of water and came to rest, apparently quite steadily, on the narrow handrail of the boat, the soles of his immaculate leather shoes somehow gripping the wood. The gusting wind fluttered the hem of his jacket but had no apparent effect on his balance.

He bent his knees, placed a gloved hand on the winch and dipped his other hand down to scoop up the metal loop where it lay, threaded over the pole, resting on the anchor chain. Straightening, he began to reel in the wire, careful not to splash any water onto his clothes.

"We've been here so long," he observed, his voice higher and softer than I'd expected. "that I was beginning to doubt you." His words were directed to Karst.

Karst ignored him and whispered once more to me, "Who sent you?"

From where I lay, I could see the stitching on his shoes, the ox-blood leather so dark it was almost black. I stared at his feet while Karst waited for me to answer her. I wondered what kind of person dressed like that.

"I really think she's no more than thirty," Karst said to Danik. "A strange choice. Perhaps she's a decoy, so be alert."

"We could torture her a little," Danik said, his quiet voice sounding playful and a little shy.

Karst shook her head. "I'm not in the mood. If it's in the bag then we're finished here. And so is she." She glanced over the side of the boat into the opaque midnight-teal of the water. "Maybe put her down there when we're done," she gestured with a nod over the side and shivered slightly as if to say rather-her-than-me. It seemed like it was the water itself and not the dying that made her shudder.

Danik flipped the bag up over the rail and down onto the seat by my head. "Do the honours," he said, and Karst lifted her sword off my sternum and pushed its point through the bag and into the wood of the deck-planks beneath. Then Danik grabbed a corner of the bag and pulled, the material parting around the blade as though it were a scalpel cutting through... through something innocuous and unrelated to my current situation.

Inside the bag was a sealed plastic envelope, like the one we'd found beneath the floor of the cabin inside, but this one contained a complex, intertwining filigree in some pearlescent silver metal.

Grab it. The thought boomed into my mind.

Karst had removed my headband, but not the necklace. The Sleeper could still retrieve me if he chose to. But even if I was tempted to obey him, I'd seen how fast that sword could move and I had no illusions about beating Karst's reflexes. Still, I thought, it was splendid to see that even in this predicament, the Sleeper could still find a way to dramatically shorten my life, even when I was down to my last couple of minutes.

I wondered if making a grab for my headband would be any easier. I might as well try, I thought. It couldn't make matters any worse. Careful not to betray my intention by tensing up, I prepared to make my move, at the same time attempting to ready myself for the bite of Karst's sword.

CHAPTER 31 – TOLD BY SUSAN MILTON

The Professor was even angrier than *I* was when he heard – and saw – what Jo had been up to. I think a big part of that was probably disappointment. I blamed Jo for what she'd done, but I think the Professor blamed himself as well. None of us like that particular sensation.

Even so, Jo's… well you had to call it betrayal, didn't you? It seemed like a pretty solid reason to get worked up. Theresa showed us how the technical side of it worked. Apparently Jo could just log in from elsewhere and pick up recordings of our meetings. It just seemed so *organised*. It took Jo's maverick streak to a new level, beyond what you could blame on petulance, and made it seem positively calculating.

The morning after it all came out, Jo had called the Professor. He came and found me afterwards; told me what had happened. He was embarrassed about how he'd acted. He'd let her have both barrels and then he'd hung up.

I gently suggested that she deserved it, but that didn't really mollify him.

He explained, "It's about what's *best*. She might have deserved another dressing down but that's an excuse, not a reason. If my behaviour makes things worse instead of better, then it was the wrong thing to do – provocation notwithstanding."

He added, "And when I scold others for their lack of self-control, it sits better with me if I'm not red in the face and bellowing at the time. Hypocrisy rather undercuts my point, don't you think?"

We were having this chat at my desk and at about that point, Daniel showed up. I motioned subtly for him to give us a minute. But I suppose Daniel was a little preoccupied because he didn't notice my gesture and instead came right over.

"Hey Daniel. This isn't the best time. Can you give us five minutes?" I asked.

He seemed pretty dejected and ignored my question. "I just spoke to Jo," he said.

That was the first of two calls she would make to Daniel that day. Later on, she would phone a second time and retract everything – but of course I didn't know that then. At the time I just wanted to know what she'd said. I changed my mind about making Daniel wait. The Professor would want to hear this too.

I said, "I'm guessing it wasn't good news." It sounded a little more flippant than I'd intended but no one seemed to notice.

Daniel relayed the conversation he and Jo had had, about how she wanted to be left alone. When he'd finished, the Professor and I were silent for a moment, considering.

"Where does that leave us?" I asked, wanting to hear what the others thought.

We kicked that question around for a little while. The Professor and I also filled in some blanks for Daniel. He knew the highlights of what Jo had been up to and we added a few of the specifics. We'd been planning to tell him later in the day anyway.

Daniel didn't try to defend her. I suspected he was doing a little of what the Professor had been doing: blaming himself. All he said was, "I think she knew she was being shut out of something and she didn't like it. Mind you, this wasn't how I expected her to act. She must have been..." He didn't finish that thought. He was obviously going over old conversations the two of them had had; you could almost see his lips moving.

Knowing that both of them were supporters of Jo in their own ways, I decided that it fell to me to kind of state the case for the prosecution – or at least push the conversation in that direction. I said, "Jo doesn't make it easy to be on her side, does she?"

No one touched that remark. The Professor asked Daniel, "Do you think she's serious? Would she go to the authorities?"

"I don't know," Daniel admitted with a gloomy sigh. "I wouldn't have thought so, but she seemed really worked up over what she'd discovered. She was almost frantic about us keeping out of her way. I think we have to do what she wanted: give her a few days to calm down."

"You don't think," the Professor asked gravely, "that's she's somehow being coerced?" He looked like he hadn't wanted to ask that question.

Daniel ran his fingers through his hair and looked even more frustrated. "I don't know what to think. I'm sure she's not betraying us, but there must be something going on. What I can't work out, though, is why she wouldn't want help if she'd got herself into some sort of trouble. She knows she can trust me. And she knows I wouldn't have made her beg; she could have just dropped a hint or two. But there was nothing."

I said, "So she didn't ask you to do her some favour... and not tell us? She just called to say we should all stay away?"

What I didn't know when I asked that question was that I was a little early. The call asking Daniel to do her a very unusual favour was still some hours away.

I scrutinised Daniel pretty closely as he replied. He was self-conscious but earnest: "She didn't ask me to do *anything* for her, except convey the message. And you know I'd only help her if I believed it was the right thing to do for all of us."

He obviously knew what I was hinting at. "Sure, sure," I said, "I just felt I had to ask. I'm not criticising your loyalty to Jo, I was just asking whether it was a factor here." I summed up, "So we just leave her alone for a while? You agree with that, Professor?"

"I am *far* from happy over this," he said, and there was that angry edge in his voice again, the one that hadn't existed when I'd first met him – the edge I knew belonged to his youth, until the Healing Surface had brought it back to life.

I could see that Daniel noticed it too, was maybe a little taken aback. The Professor concluded, "There will be words to be said, but this is not the right time. For now, I think we allow Jo time to reflect, and to accustom herself to the alarming world she has insisted upon entering."

"OK. Well I guess that's settled then," I said and there were nods all round.

The Professor took his leave and Daniel looked about ready to head off too, but I stopped him. "Have you got time for a tea break, Daniel? I want to ask you something," I said.

He looked mildly intrigued and perked up a little. He said, "Always a pleasure, never a chore. Will there be Kit-Kats?"

I smiled, reflecting on Jo and him, and thinking that he probably deserved someone better. Why couldn't he take an interest in someone a bit more stable, like Theresa for instance?

"There may be," I said, noncommittally. I logged off from my computer, got up, and grabbed my purse.

We walked downstairs together, heading for the refectory. As we walked, I said, "I just wanted to know a bit more about what's been going on with Jo. I've never really got to know her. In fact, I think I've missed out that part and gone straight to thinking she's kind of a pest." Then I added, "Sorry," because it wasn't my intention to offend him.

He shrugged, looking unhappy again – like he wanted to argue with me but was having a few doubts himself.

I said, "I mean, honestly, she *is* kind of a pest, but for all I know she might have her reasons. I remember that she got a sudden new lease of life – really started making an effort. I was even beginning to think I'd been wrong about her. Then all this happened. I realised I have no idea what goes on in her head."

"Yeah, well I'm not as much of an expert on that as I thought I was," he said. "You know, the day Jo turned over her new leaf was the day after she had some bad news about her mother."

Delicately I asked, "I thought her mother had died when she was little?"

He said, "When Jo was five. The thing is that she doesn't remember anything from then so it's all a bit of a minefield. Almost anything she finds out is likely to be a shock." He paused. "Anyway, I don't want to talk too much about her private business."

He was obviously debating with himself about how much more to say. "The day before, Jo and the Professor had a few words. I think the Professor said more than he'd meant to about Jo's mother, and Jo took it badly. I mean it was very depressing stuff. Then the next day she was a changed person. Totally over it, apparently."

I suggested: "Sometimes bad news is like that. It can make you consider where your life is going – maybe push you to make some changes."

"I'm sure there was some of that," Daniel said. "She definitely didn't want to follow in her mother's footsteps, but it still seemed very sudden and very... *complete*."

"How do you mean?" I asked.

"I don't know," he shrugged. "There was no transition, I suppose. She was just different." He paused a moment, snorted, and then said, "I thought maybe she'd finally realised what a fabulous person I was." Then he rolled his eyes a little to make it clear that no one could *really* be so foolish.

"So you and she..." I didn't say more. I wasn't even quite sure what I was asking. I was just looking for more information. I suppose I wanted to understand exactly what had tipped me off to Jo's deception. Something about it bothered me. I was half expecting Daniel to reveal something that would solve the mystery for me and then I could say: "Yes, that was it. I *knew* I'd noticed something peculiar." But it didn't happen.

He said, "We had a really nice evening in the pub. Jo got completely plastered. But in a good way. Not depressed drinking. It was actually the happiest I'd seen her for a long time. I made sure she got back to her room without falling down a well. I, er... I thought maybe we'd reached some sort of understanding. Like maybe we were a bit closer now." He was obviously finding this embarrassing to talk about. "But when I saw her the next day it was like a month had gone by. No hangover and she was a new person."

"And so far as you know," I said, "nothing happened between her getting home and you seeing her the next day?"

"I think she threw up," he said. "And she had a trippy sounding dream about being frozen."

"Frozen?" I asked.

"Stuck in the middle of a load of ice. She said it made her see that she'd been stuck solid in the middle of her life and it was time to thaw things out – or something like that. But what got her to the point that she was dreaming about making this big change, I don't know. Maybe they're putting Prozac in Southern Comfort now. Not that Prozac was what she needed."

I'd gone quiet for a moment, not paying attention to the last couple of sentences. I was fixated on what he'd said about her dream. "She dreamed about being surrounded by ice? So, exactly how did the dream go?"

"I don't know. If Jo said any more about it I can't remember it. You think it's important?" he asked.

I said, "I'm starting to wonder if Jo's mixed up in something a lot worse than we thought."

I didn't like this, not at all. How many people dream about being stuck in ice? I never had – at least not before the previous evening.

Maybe it was a favourite if you lived in Alaska or something, but not in Southern England in the fall. And yet Jo and I both dreamed of being trapped in ice – her, right before she changed, and me, just before I became suspicious of her.

I *knew* I'd read something about shared dreams, but I couldn't remember what. It was in one of the manuscripts we'd acquired earlier in the year, I was sure of it – one of the manuscripts we kept hidden away and didn't talk about outside the group, because the authors had been adepts.

Daniel, meanwhile, seemed to think I was accusing Jo of something, some conspiracy. He said, "Come on. She's done something stupid but she's still our friend. She hasn't risked anyone's life, for goodness sake."

"I wouldn't be so sure about that," I said. There was tension in my voice now. I didn't have the answer to this puzzle, but I knew where to look for it – and I knew I wasn't going to like what I found. "I'll talk to you later, Daniel. I've got something to do."

"If it's about Jo, then so do I," he said, and there was a certain amount of defiance in his voice. But I was already miles away, trying to remember which document in the PAC library dealt with dreams.

In retrospect, it might have been better to share what I was thinking with Daniel. I certainly would have done if I'd known he was going to get a second call from Jo later that day. But as it was, when she called, all he could tell her was that she had no allies any more among the PAC.

If I'd still been around I might have been able to set him straight on that point, but I was miles away by then, working on a plan of my own.

CHAPTER 32 – TOLD BY JO

I knew this was going to hurt.

I couldn't see a way to avoid Karst's sword completely, but maybe I could still reach my headband in spite of whatever she did to me. I'd psyched myself up to the point where I didn't think I was going to hesitate when my opportunity came, and now I was just waiting for the right moment – ideally when Karst was in the middle of saying something.

Determined to act soon, I gave myself a mental countdown from ten. But I'd only reached seven when Karst and the one she called Danik both reacted – to what, I couldn't tell, but it was like a subtle shiver had passed through both of them.

Karst's sword was still hovering near my sternum, but her eyes flicked up to scan the barrier wall that ran around the outside of the dock.

"Ideas?" she said. *How about not killing me?* I thought, but it seemed she was addressing Danik.

"Our Asian friends getting greedy? One Marker not enough for them?" he suggested. Then his eyes closed for a moment and he said, "I see two of them, moving."

"Yes," she agreed, "heading for the steps." I gathered from this that they'd only now become aware of the adepts beyond the wall. When I'd detected them earlier, I'd assumed that everyone but me was part of the same team – but obviously I was wrong.

The two behind the dock wall must have withdrawn after I became aware of them, because they obviously hadn't registered with Danik or Karst until this moment.

If they weren't working with my current aggressors, I had to wonder who they were. Regardless, they might be a useful distraction. Maybe I had a little longer to live after all. Possibly several minutes. I decided to hold off on making my suicidal grab for either the headband or the bag until I saw what happened next.

"If we have to fight, let's not stay on this *jävel* boat, eh?" Danik said. He sounded annoyed, but not worried.

I couldn't tell if either of them was genuinely concerned about the two newcomers. Their manner was as blasé and unruffled as before, but I thought I could still discern a slight shift in their postures, a tightness around their eyes. There was obviously some ethic of stratospheric cool they were both determined to adhere to, but it didn't extend to *total* nonchalance in the face of an advancing enemy.

Danik made as if to step across to the next vessel along with one of his dainty leaps, but the crunch of breaking wood and a distant cracking noise a split-second later stopped him. Someone had shot a piece of the handrail to splinters. With a bullet.

For a second, both of them blinked. Ordinary humans would have flinched; experienced soldiers might have ducked for cover; but these two – with a century or more of conditioning under their belts – their instincts were to wrap themselves in Shields. Eyesight was a distraction.

Which was my cue. For a moment, Karst was pouring her focus into folding the Shield Surface around her – it was automatic, reflexive. I doubted she had left a gap through which to stab at me if she noticed I'd begun to move.

By the time her eyes opened a half-second later, I was no longer directly under her blade. She saw me, but just too late to skewer me. Instead the tip of her sword plunged into the deck about an inch from my receding shoulder. And her Shield prevented her from trying again. It would take a moment for her to shift that invisible barrier and in that time I was able to grab my headband and set it back on my head.

Once again the universe blossomed, its hidden dimensions opening like gargantuan petals, and I was Connected. Karst's sword could still cut me if I let it, but at least she wouldn't be able to crack my skull like an Easter egg with just a sharp thought and a twitch of her nose.

I pulled in my Shield Surface, wrapping myself in its protective cloak, putting some solid air between my skin and the tip of Karst's rapier.

It was getting a little crowded here, to say the least. But for our Shields, Karst could probably have reached out and touched me if she'd stretched her arm a little.

I glanced up at the concrete steps and saw something that surprised me. A tall order you might think, given all that was taking place at the moment, but nevertheless it was true. Susan Milton was running towards me, a long canvas bag clutched in her hand. She had reached the bottom of the concrete steps and was now moving towards the guard hut. Behind her, I could see the black stick of a rifle muzzle protruding over the top of the wall. I couldn't see whose shoulder the weapon was clamped to, but I had my suspicions.

Danik chose that moment to test his luck. He was in an absurd position, still balancing on the handrail, a foot and a half away from the fist-sized hole the bullet had made. He undoubtedly had a Shield in place between him and the sniper, but he couldn't stay put. And I suspected that in him an adept's dislike of water was particularly strong. He sprang from his perch, his motion no longer dainty, but powerful and rapid like some sort of hunting animal. There was no preamble, he was simply in the air. And then a second later he was on the deck of the adjacent boat just in time to stop a bullet – or at least to slow it down a little.

The impact punched an exit-hole from the sleeve of his suit, instantly outlining it with red, in the general area where his left elbow would have been. Squeamishly I snatched my eyes away before they could lock onto the rent in his sleeve and focus on the excavated flesh beneath.

Danik had jumped out past the limit of his Shield, as he'd had to in order to reach the other boat, and evidently the sniper had been expecting that. The rifle had been aimed at the spot where Danik would land. All the sniper had needed to do was squeeze the trigger.

Danik handled having a chunk of his arm torn out through a hole in his sleeve a little better than I would have – which is to say he remained conscious. Nevertheless, screeching like a broken steam pipe, he toppled backwards into the water and into silence.

Karst swore. In German. One of the few words I knew in that language. But she still didn't register genuine distress. If I'd had to decode her expression I would say it read: 'Great! Another crappy day at work'.

Susan had passed the guard-hut now and was at the start of the gangplank that led down to the floating jetty. The sniper, meantime, had apparently decided that the time for gunfire was past because he'd leapt up from his rifle and was now on the concrete steps heading our way, his gun abandoned. As I'd suspected, the figure was David Braun.

Karst, muttering something under her breath, leaned over the side of the boat, allowing herself to fall outwards so that I thought she was about to belly-flop into the water. At the last moment she grabbed the handle of the winch to stop her fall, and steadied herself. Then, with the point of her sword held up towards the sky, she reached down and snagged Danik's collar. With extraordinary strength, she pulled herself upright and at the same time wrenched Danik's body half out of the water, flopping him onto the handrail on his stomach, where he remained. A hard line across the arch of his back was brought into definition now and I recognised it as the outline of a sheathed blade concealed beneath his jacket.

Then Karst twisted round and stroked the edge of her sword along the rope that joined the rear of this boat to the next. The motion was like a bow on a violin string and the strands separated at once.

While she'd been doing this, I'd tried to reach the Marker, but it was on her side of our back-to-back Shields.

I was getting nowhere with that, so I began searching my environment using the Surfaces, looking for some feature of our surroundings that I could use to my advantage.

I found two.

Meanwhile Karst flipped herself back onto the boat at about the same time that Susan reached the bottom of the ramp. Karst snatched the plastic wallet holding the Marker off the deck, where it lay just out of my reach, and slid it into the cross-over wrap of her stylish jacket. Then she ran towards the front of the boat, as though she and Susan had agreed to meet there and she didn't want to be late.

I took the opportunity to kick Danik in the head, but despite looking like a drowned rat, he still had a partial Shield in place. My boot was deflected away from his temple, but it still slammed into his shoulder, so it wasn't a complete loss.

He grunted and raised his head, staring venomously at me. I suspected all I'd done was rouse him from his daze. A second kick from me struck a much expanded Shield and did no damage at all. I desisted.

Susan was now standing on the deck in front of the boat. As I watched she finished pulling a sword from the bag she carried. She rolled her wrist a couple of times, causing the tip of the blade to tear through the air with a sound like a bedsheet ripping. Her face was blank but set. I felt a surge of pride and respect and gratitude, all mingled together, seeing her standing there ready to take on my tormentors. I also felt a heave of fear, knowing how formidable Karst would be, how unequal this fight would be.

Karst, for her part, had grabbed the rope that ran from the boat's nose to the deck and was pulling on it, one-handed. Infinitesimally at first, the boat gradually moved towards the jetty.

Karst had transferred her sword to her left hand while she held the rope, and it seemed equally at home there. Perhaps after a century or two of practice, everyone is ambidextrous. It was not a comforting thought.

The boat slid in towards the deck and in a moment Karst and Susan would be in range of each other's swords. But David wasn't far behind Susan. He was carrying a black nylon bag similar to the one Susan had just discarded.

With a moment to spare before the bladework commenced, Susan darted her eyes towards me and called out: "How are you doing? Is the Sleeper still in there with you?"

So she'd worked it out somehow. I suspected she'd dug out

the document I hadn't been allowed to read, the one the Sleeper had forced me to delete my copy of – the one that undoubtedly mentioned a vivid dream common among novice adepts, a tendency towards strange moods, and the nickname given to the force responsible: the Sleeper.

And it was a good question: was the Sleeper still in here with me? He was awfully quiet.

What is there to say? he ventured.

"I think he's waiting to see how this all turns out," I said. I felt I should offer some words of explanation: "When I found out he was in my head and I tried to get rid of him, he threatened to tell Karst about all of us unless I obeyed him."

That got Karst's attention. "You let *the Sleeper* control you?" she interjected, her tone mocking. "He's a ghost; he's nothing. And you've been doing his bidding." She tutted and announced to no one in particular: "This is the result when children play with magic. This should never have happened."

She sounded disgusted. Then, without warning, Karst was in motion, lunging towards Susan and unloading a staccato sequence of overlapping cuts at her head and torso.

Susan parried furiously, but Karst moved so rapidly it was difficult to even *see* the path of her sword, never mind defend against it.

Thankfully none of the attacks reached their target but the final reverse clipped a two inch section from the end of Susan's heavy blade; it bounced away across the jetty, ringing each time it struck the decking.

Susan gasped, clearly startled by the machine-like speed of the assault. She stepped back a little just as David arrived. For his part, he didn't stop, but turned a little to his left and leapt onto the next boat over, running along its roof – which quickly brought him level with Danik, who was hauling himself to his feet. The two boats were very close now and the two men were separated by just a couple of feet of water.

Time for me to make a contribution.

"Su... uh, Serena" I said calmly, realising at the last moment that I probably didn't want to use her real first name, "can you practice your tank training for a moment? You be 'it'."

I used the name that she and David had used when I'd spied on them in the barn. I now understood the term referred to wrapping yourself in a Shield, like a tank in a war movie; you trundled along slowly and relied on your impenetrable armour to protect you from close-quarters attack.

Susan glanced towards me, unsure. "Now," I said urgently. Karst looked over at me, unable to decode my message or discern the threat. She shifted her blade a little, unsure of which direction an attack might come from.

I gave Susan a second to comply and then pushed as hard as I could through the Heat Surface.

The first time I'd been here, I'd found a gas-can tucked into a corner in the nose of the boat. I'd searched it as a possible hiding place for the Marker. When my senses encountered it this time around, I already knew what it was. I'd been driving heat into for thirty seconds now and, when I judged that Susan was ready, I focussed hard and heaved the temperature of the petrol up towards its flash point.

A moment later, the can ruptured.

A lot of times when a bomb goes off on TV, they don't use dynamite or plastic explosive, or whatever the script claims is in the bomb; they use what I was using: gasoline and air. So when the gas-can exploded, there was a moment of unreality, of familiarity, like I was just watching this on television, like it was staged. But

855

the thunder of sound was shockingly real, as was the bucking of the deck and the blaze of heat that spilled over the top of my Shield and stung the skin of my face.

For Karst, who was standing two feet from the centre of the explosion, it must have seemed like the whole world had turned to flame. Her Shield caught some of the blast, but there were plenty of gaps: she'd wanted to give herself freedom of movement to use her sword and it had cost her dearly.

The explosion spun her into her own Shield and splashed fire up along her side and across her face. The force of the blast itself was modest, definitely subsonic, but the heat was ferocious. In a moment her jacket was ablaze and her hair burned along with it. I expected her to jump over the side, into the water, but instead she curled into a ball. The flames around her compressed, tightened… and then went out.

The boat itself was still burning and rocking, fire was running across the deck, spilling out onto the water. A black umbrella of smoke was roiling above us and climbing into the sky. Beneath the spreading black cloud Karst herself was sealed in a spherical Shield, cut off from any oxygen. I suspected someone with her extraordinary strength and athleticism wouldn't need to breathe for a minute or two if she didn't want to. Incredibly, throughout it all, she'd maintained her grip on her sword.

Susan's Shield protected her completely, though she looked plenty surprised. Danik too sustained no fresh injuries. David had a burning sleeve to contend with, but he simply stepped away from Danik and calmly lowered his arm into the water. No fuss or panic.

Karst, on the other hand, finally registered some emotion. She uncoiled from her foetal ball and yelled something. I assume it was some German swear word, but it was way beyond my limited grasp of Teutonic vulgarity.

Danik was on his feet now, trying to draw his sword from its sheath across his back, but he was struggling. It was slung in such a way that it was easiest to reach with his left hand, but too much of his left arm had been removed when the bullet had struck him to make that practical, so he was clawing beneath the collar of his jacket with his right.

As he fumbled he spoke. "Plan?" he enquired of Karst, and his tone sounded strained but far from hysterical. But despite his composure, blood was running freely from the cuff of his sleeve, splashing onto the boards and pooling on the deck by his feet. It was spreading in my direction and I tried not to stand in it.

Karst didn't answer immediately. She was pawing at the fused and charred remains of her jacket, trying to find the Marker amid the layers of charred cloth. Her skin had bubbled red on her hands and face but the muscles and tendons beneath seemed to still be working.

She pulled a strip of burnt cloth free and the Marker tumbled to the deck, dropping into a patch of burning gasoline. She bent slightly, obviously about to reach into the flames and seize it, when Susan jumped forwards and jabbed with the jagged tip of her blade towards the Marker. Karst snatched her hand back just in time. She straightened and gave Susan her attention.

Over her shoulder she called, "Danik. Get the Marker. If you get a chance, kill those two," she tipped her head towards David and me. "I'll clear us a path." So saying, she took a step towards Susan.

A wrinkle formed between Karst's pale blue eyes and she said, "I know you, don't I?" And a moment later: "You burned *Jan* like this, didn't you?"

Susan didn't answer. She clearly sensed that Karst was about to

Robert Finn

attack again and she was doing her best to be ready. Flames were burning in pools and puddles all around her, the fire on the boat was really starting to take hold, but Susan appeared undistracted; her focus remained on Karst.

I was looking around me, trying to size up the situation. I had no sword and no skill with one, so I couldn't fight. David was about to engage Danik – who had finally managed to draw his blade – and I was hoping the latter's horrible wound would hamper him, or at least throw him off mentally, otherwise things would go badly for David, I felt was sure. And Susan was about to face a second attack from a scorched and shaken-up Karst. But Karst – despite the awful transformation the fire had brought to her skin, her hair and her clothing – seemed undaunted. I wasn't sure Susan could survive for more than a few seconds against her.

Whether they'd meant to or not, David and Susan had cornered two superior opponents, neither of whom would want to swim for it. In the water, the two assassins wouldn't be able to create Shields and they risked being skewered as they tried to get back on dry land. Worse still, with a rifle added to the equation, they weren't even safe if they stayed in the water. And remaining on board a burning boat wasn't likely to appeal to them either, so their only hope would be to go *through* Susan and make it back to the dock.

As far as I was concerned, I needed to destroy the Marker and I needed either to neutralise the two assassins or at least get David and Susan out of their path. With seconds leaking away and my mind racing, I could see no way to make it happen. No way, except through sacrifice. My sacrifice. The 'Plan B' I'd been hoping to avoid.

I slipped my hands into my pockets and my fingers encountered the familiar shapes within. Daniel hadn't let me down. He had fetched my favourite fleece from my room in the project's

858

dormitory, all the way up to London. He had pushed it through my letterbox to lie at the foot of the coat rack. And before he had done so, he had put the drug-patches in my pockets.

"Hey!" I yelled, loud enough to get everyone's attention. "Before the killing starts I have a favour to ask." As I spoke, my mind was pushing, prodding, feeling its way, wriggling under damp stone looking for a particular spot.

For a second I appeared to have everyone's attention. "Erm, Serena?" I said. "Give everyone my apologies and say something nice to, erm, that guy I like, please."

She nodded, but with a questioning look. She was wondering what I was going to do. Last time I'd spoken cryptically there'd been an explosion; this time, everyone tensed.

Then there was a distant cracking sound, followed by a prolonged creak and a bass grinding noise. It was deep and low, like the sound of an avalanche beginning.

"Danik," Karst snapped, "*do* something about her."

Danik turned obediently and tried two or three times to get the tip of his sword through my Shield, but without any luck.

A second later, as the grinding sound continued, I caused one of the many spots of flame around us to flare. It was hardly noticeable with so much fire around us, just a six-inch stretch of rope burning a little more brightly as I Heated it. But it was a section of the rope that joined the front of the boat to the jetty.

The low groaning grew in volume and then, suddenly, the boat lurched and the water shivered. Several of the boats around us pitched; a couple knocked hulls. No one was fighting; everyone was trying to figure out what was happening.

"What is she doing?" Danik demanded, glancing at Karst. He had finally reached the limit of his sang-froid and sounded distinctly rattled. Karst had no reply for him.

Now a gurgling noise grew until it matched the grinding sound for volume. The barge on which we stood drifted back from the jetty, apparently under its own volition, and as the tether rope pulled tight, it severed with a pop at the point I'd been super-heating.

Now it became obvious what I'd done. I'd found the mechanism that opened the dock gates and I'd activated it. Water was rushing out of the dock into the river, where the level was currently about two feet lower. Boats were being pulled taut on their lines and ours – no longer tied to the jetty – was being swept towards the opening jaws of the gates.

Even though this was my idea, there was one thing I hadn't predicted. As water poured out of the dock and swirled around the boats, the dead security guard rose to the surface and I got my first look at him. He was about sixty, dark-skinned and a little paunchy around the middle. His features, though slack now, were gentle looking – though I suppose looks prove nothing. Nevertheless, it hurt me to see his discarded body floating there. I felt my reticence over what I planned to do to the two assassins melting away.

I hopped up onto the roof of the boat and walked towards Karst, who eyed me warily and tracked my approach with her sword-tip.

"Stop the gates opening," Danik called to her. I glanced back to see him looking around most unhappily now. His eyes shifted from the gates, to the water, to the receding dock, and back again.

"I can't find the controls. I'm not an engineer," she snarled.

"Well, break it then," he yelled.

"You've got worse problems than that," I said. "Check out the fuel tank. It's right beneath your feet – over this way a little." This last was addressed to Karst, who involuntarily glanced downwards, though there was nothing to see.

She would be reaching out with her mind, encountering the fluid volume of the brim-full tank, sensing the bubbling focus of

Heat at its centre. Even as she was learning about the threat from beneath her, the stern of the barge was gaining speed as it slid towards the opening gates.

"Cool it down," she shouted. But at that moment I Shattered the top of the fuel tank, letting in air to mix with the hot vapour. It was only a matter of time, now, before the expanding fumes encountered the dozen or so fires scattered across the surface of the boat.

Karst was struggling to cool the overheated fuel below, but my control was better. And as she fought to undo what I'd done she stared at me, real concern in her eyes. I said, "It's worth it to take you two with me." And then I smiled and stepped a little closer.

Now I was directly above the tank and part of it lay in the zone of protection around me, the personal space which another adept couldn't attack with magic. Now there was nothing she could do to stop me bringing a large fraction of the petroleum to a raging boil, Heating it until the volatile vapour poured out of the ruptured tank like steam from a kettle, expanding until it encountered a naked flame.

"Five." I said slowly and deliberately. And a moment later: "Four."

I locked eyes with Karst. "Three."

A muscle twitched in her blistered face as the boat slid out into the river.

"Two."

"The Marker?" called Danik.

"It'll survive a fire," said Karst.

"One," I said.

"Zero."

As I said it, Karst snatched at the Marker – coming away empty-handed because my Shield was in the way – and then, without stopping, she kicked off and dived into the water.

Danik stood, staring at the water, a horrified look on his face. And then he tucked himself into a ball in the stern.

Swiftly I grabbed the Marker, stepped down into the prow and curled up small, following Danik's example at the other end of the boat.

This time the explosion was much more forceful because half the interior of the boat had filled with gasoline vapour – the evaporated fuel mixing with the air and needing only a spark to unleash it. My Shield was slammed so hard by the expanding fireball that it cracked the planks I was anchoring it to. The centre of the boat was ripped open and flame swarmed around me, the heat held at bay by my Shield, but the irresistible brilliance of the fire almost blinding me. The deck beneath me pitched up as the vessel came apart and I was just able to catch a last glimpse of the dockside before fire blotted out everything. For a moment, I had seen David, back on the lip of the dock wall, the rifle once again in his hand, settling the weapon on its stand and putting his eye to the scope.

At least they would get Karst. Danik I suspected was in no better shape than me: surrounded by fire and about to be tangled in wreckage at the bottom of river.

And then I heard the Sleeper's voice. **Got you**, he said, as the Home pattern bloomed into life and a wall of black iron seemed to spring up between me and the flame, sealing it off and plunging me in an instant into total, icy darkness.

I felt my body cease to exist and with it went my consciousness.

CHAPTER 33

I was inside my dream – the dream of ice – and once again I felt the piercing sting of irony. It was fast becoming my most hated sensation and yet again it had caught me by surprise. Maybe that's in the nature of irony, but I hadn't expected to be humiliated so close to the end of everything.

I mean you know how it is: enlightened people look beyond the little things, they try to see the bigger picture, the hidden themes in their lives. And thanks to Freud, every little thing means something, or can tell you something about who you really are, what you secretly want. With the years of therapy I've had, when I dream, of course I analyse it and try to find the meaning beneath the surface – especially when it's the first dream I've had in years. It goes without saying that I know better than to take it at face value.

And yet here I was, standing inside that dream. It wasn't symbolic of anything; it was real and just as I'd pictured it – and I felt stupid for ever thinking it was anything else.

When the Sleeper had first come to me, my mind had been

filled with images of ice – a thousand miles of it on every side, shot through with old, slow, clear-blue light. I had seen myself trapped, twisted and calcified by my old life and in front of me lay two possible destinies: the cracked and settled husk of a dead future, if I followed in my mother's footsteps, or the glowing, glorious opalescence of the alternative: the possibility of true freedom.

And I stood now, within that plane of ice, looking at the calcified figure of the present, the dead husk of a failed future, the liberating glow of a better alternative – the three symbols from my dream – and I saw that they were real.

The walls around me truly were solid ice, cracked and fissured and ancient. At my feet was the rag-bound skeleton I'd believed symbolised my mother's fate. Whatever process of decay it had undergone was long since completed.

To one side of me was that soft compression of illuminated air that I'd mistaken for my salvation. What it really was I could only imagine. Gentle light, like down feathers, welled up within it and floated away into the space around me.

And finally, on the far side of the frozen bubble in which I stood, was the Sleeper, the living, mineralised corpse I'd imagined was a kind of ghost of Christmas Present.

I'd dreamed it all, and then, just as I'd done all my life, I'd made it about *me*. Always afraid that I was irrelevant, that I didn't matter, I'd twisted everything until I was somehow at the centre of things, the reason it was all happening. And when I'd finished rearranging and reinventing the world so that it revolved around me alone, I'd found that I couldn't bear it. The weight of it was crushing me.

In my version of reality, every random setback was personal, and every personal misfortune was malicious. If everything happened for a reason, then failure was a judgement, a verdict on me, and I couldn't stand it. Life with no meaning might be unbearable, but so was the opposite.

And then the Sleeper had saved me. He had pushed me aside and run my life at a reckless gallop searching for his own immortality. I was superfluous, irrelevant, subsumed. Not only was I not at the centre of the world, I wasn't even at the centre of my own life. And being connected to him was like being electrocuted, clamped to the current which burned through him like a torrent of lightning. It had paralysed me, then convulsed me and finally incinerated me, leaving nothing but a fine ash of my former self. My old view of the world was gone.

And now I faced the Sleeper at last. His sunken corpse was partly fused with the icy wall at his back and yet it pulsed with mineral life. The fat of his flesh had flowed with time and reduced, and the skin had hardened into milky glass which revealed the dark, glittering blood beneath, shot like verdigris threads through a marble mortuary slab.

His face was simply a wrapped skull, the skin pulled as tight as stretched paper by starvation. The glinting band of gold across his brow was now mortared to his cranium by accretions of lime and silted ice, built up steadily by years of dripping moisture. The remains of his moss-furred clothes hid the wreck of limbs beneath and whatever time had done to his torso.

He plainly had not moved for a century or more, and yet he wasn't dead. His eyes were sealed – the delicate, dried leather of their lids pulled drum-tight across the sockets which must themselves have dried up decades back – and yet I had the sense of being watched by him. He had lain where he fell and the wall had begun to grow up around him, the ice to swallow him, and yet he hadn't died.

Was I witnessing a stalemate between the action of the Healing surface and the forces of starvation and thirst? Or maybe here, at the source of magic, the rules were different.

I looked away from him and down at the bundled corpse by my feet and noticed for the first time the handle of a knife jutting from the rags, the blade caught in the crevice between two gristly vertebrae. Looking beyond, I saw of one of the long bones from its arm lying on the far-side of the corpse, separate from his body. The shaft of the bone was pitted and nicked as though it had been gnawed.

And what was this light that fell like blossoms carried on a summer breeze through a gap between the worlds? It could be only one thing. It must be Home – the point at which magic entered the world.

I began to see what had happened here.

The Sleeper had wanted power – more power than any adept had ever possessed. He wanted control of a Greater Power and at the same time he wanted to hold on to his ruthless ambition – then he could turn that Power upon the world like a weapon. And he had a plan for how to make it happen.

He had searched the world until he found himself a guru, some solitary, half-mad devotee so bereft of human greed and drive that he might actually penetrate the veil and embrace one of the great secrets. And the Sleeper would have looked for a particular kind of holy man – someone obsessed with the source of magic. Then, the Sleeper would have sheltered him, protected him and watched over him. And when the wise man had finally received his answers, the Sleeper would have been there too.

And I now knew the form that answer would have taken. The guru's mind would have received a pattern, the key to a Greater Power, and that pattern would have been Home.

However he had done it, the Sleeper had persuaded his holy

man to activate the pattern he had received and to bring it to life. He had found someone capable of travelling to the source of magic and he had somehow hitched a ride.

Plainly his first act once the journey was complete was to run his victim through. The Sleeper would not want to share the seat of power; he would want to keep the throne for himself. But I wonder if this is what he'd been expecting. Wouldn't he have imagined halls of gold, a palace in the clouds, the imagery of whatever romantic tales he'd grown up listening to?

The reality was a bubble in the bleak vastness of an ice sheet, which contained a glowing ball of energy – no way out and only a fresh corpse for company.

There was nothing to live on and yet he had not died. He had been trapped here, his body failing even as the Healing Surface kept his mind alive, maintaining the vestiges of a metabolism, moving a trickle of thickened blood through his arteries. With nothing to do, not even the capacity to move, he had turned inward. Whereas his holy-man had voluntarily cut himself off from the concerns of the world and the clamouring of the flesh, the Sleeper had it forced upon him: he was walled away from the world he'd known and his body was turning to ice. He had nothing to occupy him but the pursuit of Greater Powers and the search for a way out of his prison.

Nothing would have happened for the longest time, until the Sleeper thought he was going mad. But then, eventually, the Sleeper had begun to learn things. As the silent decades stacked up, he had unearthed first one, then another pattern and still he didn't find what he needed. Perhaps, eventually he would have discovered the one he needed: Pattern Marker. But would he have been able to construct his own Marker to resurrect his derelict flesh? He couldn't move any more. And the one I held in my hand now was made of platinum. I doubted whether there was any more of that particular metal hidden in this bubble. No, he was trapped here until he could summon another to help him. And in the meantime, he dreamed he was back on his ship, far out to sea, and he waited.

All these thoughts had run through me in a few seconds. Much of it was the Sleeper's own memory that had seeped into mine and I was remembering it as I gazed down on him. Across the link I sensed his mind stirring.

Place it upon me.

Now I was staring at the body from which that detached voice emanated. I was standing in the same prison that had confined him until thirst began to kill him and hunger drove him to gnaw the flesh of his dead companion.

I am going to suffer the same fate. I shared the thought with him.

No. We have a little water here and before the hunger becomes unbearable I will be reborn. Then, while you sleep, I will end your suffering and you will feel no pain. Your burden will be lifted – it is your deepest and most secret wish, to feel no pain, and I can grant it for you.

So were we both getting what we wanted? He would have a new life and I would be rid of mine.

You know there's a difference between calling something a burden and wanting to be rid of it. Burdens are often things we're so attached to that we won't let them go no matter how heavy they become.

I sensed a ripple of irritation in him. He had waited a long time for this moment. **There will be time enough for poetic thoughts. You have something that I need. It is of no value to you. Please be good enough to hand it over.**

It's true, I suppose, that you have the power to give me the most important gift I could wish for – but it isn't death. In fact you've already given it to me. You let me catch a glimpse of the world through your eyes.

It's also true that my life has been wasted on me and I can see why you might think the solution was to take it away from me completely, but I think all I needed was for you to <u>try</u>.

You've shown me death and I realise I don't like it. You've shown me what happens when people don't find a way to take some pleasure in what they have and I don't like that either. And you've shown me the suffering of others and I definitely don't care for that either.

Which brings me to you...

What are you talking about?

I'm talking about a question that's been bothering me. From your point of you, you've won. You've got everything you wanted: a means to build yourself a new body and a slave to fetch it to you. It's right here – right where you want it. So tell me, what happens next?

You want to know my plans for the future?

No. I want to know how you intend to put them into practice. This place killed you once. With a new body, all you've bought yourself is another painful death. I want to know how you plan to escape.

Give me the Marker and I will show you.

If you have truly had a change of heart then you do not have to die; I can take you with me.

Then you do have a way out?

I have a plan, if that's what you are asking, but first I need to be whole again. Neither of us can leave until I am reborn.

Right, right. Of course. Because only you can get us out of here and there's not much point in you leaving until you have some meat on those bones.

Exactly. I am prepared to reward you for your assistance. You need never work a day in your life or want for anything again.

And all I have to do is bring you this? I brandished the Marker.

Indeed. His impatience was palpable now. **So bring it here.**

You've promised me death, then you've pardoned my life, now you're offering me a future of luxury and idleness. And all you want is the Marker.

I'd better not keep you waiting.

I stepped over the corpse at my feet and approached the Sleeper's slumped form. His head was turned and I was so close now that I could see the pulpy flesh at the back of his neck, see the trembling of the skin as a livid blood-vessel throbbed beneath. The Healing Surface had preserved the tissue around his spine so well here that it could still pulse and flex, in contrast with what I could see of the rigid mineral carapace of his lifeless chest – only the flesh needed for brain function seemed to have been sustained.

I took a chilly hand from my pocket and made ready to lay the Marker across his partly covered rib-cage. My own heart was pounding in my chest with the tension of the moment. After this, there'd be no turning back.

Then I reached over, spread the patches on the skin of his neck and squeezed them firmly into place. Unlike the patches on my own arms, these were fresh and full of drugs, and there was a whole string of them. Mine, on the other hand, were spent. When my link to the Sleeper had been broken and I'd rushed back to the house, I'd hauled these discarded patches out of the trash and swapped them for the live ones the Sleeper had made me wear. The drugs in my system had dissipated by now – which was probably why the

Sleeper had said so little since we'd left the house this morning: I'd been shutting him out. Only when I addressed a remark directly to him had he been able to speak with me. And I hoped that meant I had enough strength for what came next.

With a row of patches in place on the Sleeper's neck I jumped back so that I wouldn't be entangled as he brought a Shield to bear. Then I tucked the Marker into my fleece and zipped it closed.

The Sleeper howled wordlessly at me and the pressure of his fury began to pile down on my mind like the weight of time itself. He threw against me the lonely centuries of madness, the burning resolve that had kept him alive. He raged and threatened me, he insulted and maligned me, and then he simply beat against my defences with the strength of a hundred thousand days of determination and need.

I staggered backwards, dropping to sit on the ice, alongside the last victim he had claimed.

He was stronger than me. Despite the gifts he'd given me, the wiles he'd shared with me, the portion of his own strength he'd leant me – he was stronger.

And I was weaker. Much weaker. Horribly, corrosively weak.

There was no way to resist him, no way to defend against his onslaught.

So I gave him the gift he had wanted since he had found me: the freedom to completely enter my mind.

I pulled aside my defences and opened up the shameful, piteous recesses of my worst doubts and bleakest fears to him. I let him into my sulking bitterness, my sullen rages, my self-loathing fits of spite and the uncounted endless nights where I lay sleepless and inconsolable, feeling sorry for every bad thing that had ever happened to me and every good thing that never would.

He had never known such weakness, never let it touch him, and now it was inside of him and he was choking on it.

I pulled down the walls that kept my demons at bay and let his driving, battering presence flood in and wash over the lot. He could have it. I was sick of it. Like him I wanted to live. But unlike him I had a life to return to. Everything he'd known and every friend and enemy he'd ever made were no more, gone down to dust and long passed out of memory.

He had anger and desire and ambition – enough to overcome me – but I had a home and a world I wanted to return to. I had friends I needed to make up with, relationships to build, real, honest sights and tastes and colours to experience. He had the black-and-white of willpower, but he had no anchor, no connection to the vivid, living warp and weft of the world and that fact was killing him.

The truth was that I could do for him what he had wanted to do for me. I could lift his burden.

It was the least I could do for him.

So as we struggled and fought, twisted and heaved, I reached out to him and I took from his mind the secret he had piled his hopes upon.

The Home symbol had a mirror-image, a reverse, and it was his way out. I grabbed that whole chunk of his mind and pulled it away – visualising as I did all the things I wanted to live for and releasing to him all the bad history I needed to leave behind.

I spread out my hands – one to touch the Sleeper and the other to reach his victim, so that his body too could be back in the real world and not rotting away to nothing here.

Then I made it happen: the Inverse Home pattern flared and opened, and the black iron walls dropped down as they had before, and I knew I was on my way back.

And with his last ounce of spite, before the long delayed moment of his death finally caught up with him, the Sleeper gave me another of his patterns – turned one loose upon me that I hadn't seen before. Its name was Revoke and it was the worst curse he could think to hurl at me. So, even as I struck the water of the dock, returning to the spot from where I'd been snatched, I felt the Surfaces fold in on me and the sense of Connection come undone and seal itself off from me with a finality it was impossible to doubt.

The water closed over my head in a world shrunk down to what my five original senses could detect – and the metal band around my head was now nothing more than jewellery.

CHAPTER 34 – TOLD BY DANIEL MACLAY

I looked after Jo until whatever had been in that river water was finally killed by the antibiotics.

I won't lie to you; I enjoyed it. Not so much her helplessness – though there was a little bit of guilty pleasure from knowing she couldn't answer back – but really because I'd wanted to help her for so long, to make her struggle easier and finally here was something I could do.

And I got back a very different Jo. It was still her, but it was as though we'd known each other as teenagers and then she'd gone away to war or spent years exploring the Amazon and now she was back, older, wiser and stronger. I felt like we were meeting up again after many years apart and the fact that it had really only been a few weeks didn't make the changes seem any less real.

The ordeal she'd been through sounded so traumatic that I couldn't see how she'd survived it, but somehow it had forced her to overcome the problems that had troubled her for years.

It was a painful story to listen to, as she spared us no detail, no matter how ashamed it made her – and the telling of it took several hours, with David, Susan, the Professor and me gathered around her bed.

She cried a lot in the beginning. I couldn't tell if it was relief or the memory of what she'd been through, but it seemed natural, cathartic. It wasn't the strangled weeping that had sometimes gripped her in the past: when the sobs seemed like they were tearing something inside her and I couldn't bear to see it and know I couldn't help.

Now she cried as though it was helping her to heal. The first time was when she told the Professor how it had all started out. And then again when she apologised to everyone for what she'd put them through. Susan cried too, which is something I didn't expect to ever see – especially as she'd been no big fan of Jo in the weeks gone by. I also saw a tear in the Professor's eyes at one point, but he was smiling at the time, so I wasn't sure how to read it.

And she cried a third time when she talked about injuring the women whose home she'd broken into – and then she swore to do something to help her.

When she'd finished telling her side of things, she was desperate to know what had happened after she had disappeared, whether David had been able to eliminate Karst and Danik once and for all.

So Susan told her about how Danik apparently went down with his ship – which Jo had apparently been expecting, but she was on tenterhooks to know what had happened to Karst. Had she escaped or had a shot from David's rifle finished her off? She sounded as though both possibilities terrified her equally.

David told her it was neither. Karst was found floating near the boat. In the explosion, some piece of flying debris had cracked her skull. And unconscious, she had drowned. David had screwed up his determination, ready to pull the trigger – and his relief at not having to do it was nothing short of jubilant.

He'd watched Karst's and Danik's bodies floating out beyond the dock-gates – face down in the water – until he'd been sure they weren't about to move. And then he'd tucked his rifle back into its bag, and he and Susan had concealed their swords and moved away from the dock.

Susan had been on the point of diving in and swimming to the wreck, determined to see what had become of Jo and whether she could be helped... until David had told her what he'd seen through the scope of his rifle. He had to tell her twice, assuring her it was true. He had seen Jo vanish just before the flames hid her from view. The bubble of her Shield was empty for a split-second before it collapsed, drawing the fire in with it. Jo was gone.

So the two of them had withdrawn, wondering what to do, puzzling over what Jo's disappearance might mean. The emergency services were arriving and they'd had to hide for a while. David had found a vantage point – an old, abandoned crane – which he climbed, carrying the scope from the rifle so he could spy on the clean-up operation. The security guard's body was recovered first, and then the lifeless remains of the two Army assassins were retrieved some distance downstream. Soon afterwards, a fire-boat arrived to extinguish the last remaining chunks of burning debris.

Then, just as he was about to climb down, David heard the faint echo of a cry, and saw two policemen hauling a struggling figure from the water. Maybe an hour after she had disappeared, Jo was back and she was alive.

The two stashed their weapons and approached, telling the police that their friend had insisted on going to investigate the first explosion while they themselves had searched for a phone box without success.

Apparently, the second explosion had destroyed any evidence

of gunfire and seemed to provide an explanation for the three floating bodies. Jo was credited with trying to rescue the others and she didn't dispute the suggestion – in fact she was too exhausted and waterlogged to say much of anything.

David and Susan brought her back and I took over the job of looking after her once it became apparent that she was sick, as well as battered and utterly exhausted.

On the third day of her convalescence, she was sitting up in bed and I was stroking her hair. I had done it once while she slept, because she seemed to be having a particularly unpleasant dream. She'd woken with a start and I apologised, was worried she'd think it was creepy rather than reassuring.

"Keep doing it. It's nice," she'd said and I'd kind of got into the habit if I was sitting close by, talking to her.

On this occasion, though, I had brought her something. It was the book I'd found inside the package her mother had been going to collect when she had been killed. It was a book on home-schooling. Jo was leafing through it, a tear rolling down her cheek, and every now and then she'd smile.

She said, "I can picture her reading to me, you know? When I was little. I could never do that before. She had a lovely voice. I think she would have made a good teacher."

I said, "She'd be proud of how much you've learned without her, I think."

"I hope so," was all she said and we left it at that. I'd wanted to tell her about the book when we'd talked before, but it had turned out better this way.

She put the book down and looked at me. "You got me through this," she said.

I shook my head. "I was hardly involved at all," I said.

"You were a friend when I didn't have any friends," she said.

"You found out the truth about my mother when I needed a reason to be hopeful. You trusted me even when I asked you to bring me the drugs, even though you despised them. And you gave me something to come back to when I was fighting for my life."

I butted in, "And I wrote a song about you, but since we don't have a singer right now, you'll have to wait to hear it."

"A song," she said, as though she wasn't sure she believed it. "What happened to Tammy?"

"She's travelling. I persuaded her to go," I said.

"And did she take a lot of persuading?" she said, teasingly.

"Not really. Asking her to sing the song I'd written about you seemed to do the trick. Anyway, it's better for both of us this way."

"I won't argue with that," she said, moving across so that she could rest her head on my arm.

We didn't speak for a few minutes and I wondered if she was asleep. Then she stirred a little and spoke drowsily: "I hope *you* get sick soon. Then I could look after you." She turned over and snuggled down into the pillow. So quietly it was almost a whisper she said, "I'd like that." And then she slept.

This omnibus first published in 2006

1

Proudly published by

Snowbooks Ltd.

120 Pentonville Road

London

N1 9JN

Tel: 0207 837 6482

Fax: 0207 837 6348

email: info@snowbooks.com

www.snowbooks.com

British Library Cataloguing in Publication Data

A catalogue record for this book is available from the British Library.

ISBN 1-905005-30-X

ISBN13: 978-1905005-307

Printed and bound in Great Britain

Typesetting errors? Email corrections@snowbooks.com